DYNASTY 21

The Outcast

Also in the *Dynasty* series:

DYNASTY

21

The Outcast

Cynthia Harrod-Eagles

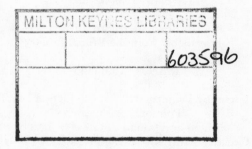

LITTLE, BROWN AND COMPANY

A *Little, Brown* Book

First published in Great Britain in 1998
by Little, Brown and Company

Copyright © Cynthia Harrod-Eagles 1998

The moral right of the author has been asserted.

A CIP catalogue record for this book
is available from the British Library.

ISBN 0 316 64445 5

Typeset by Palimpsest Book Production Limited,
Polmont, Stirlingshire
Printed and bound in Great Britain by
Creative Print and Design Wales, Ebbw Vale

Little, Brown and Company (UK)
Brettenham House
Lancaster Place
London WC2E 7EN

B12 398 866 X

Forth, pilgrim, forth! Forth, beste, out of thy stal!
Know thy contree, look up, thank God of al!
Hold the hye wey, and lat thy gost thee lede;
And trouthe shal delivere, hit is no drede.

Geoffrey Chaucer:
Balade de Bon Conseyl

SELECT BIBLIOGRAPHY

Adams, E.D.	*Great Britain and the American Civil War*
Best, Geoffrey	*Mid-Victorian Britain 1851–1875*
Burton, Anthony	*The Rise and Fall of King Cotton*
Burton, Elizabeth	*The Early Victorians at Home*
Catton, Bruce	*The Civil War*
Crow, Duncan	*The Victorian Woman*
Hansen, Harry	*The Civil War – A History*
Harwell, Richard B.	*The Civil War Reader*
Hopkins, Eric	*A Social History of the English Working Classes*
Reader, W.J.	*Life in Victorian England*
Robertson, James I.	*Jackson and Lee, Legends in Gray*
Rosen, Robert	*A History of Charleston*
Rostow, W.W.	*British Economy of the Nineteenth Century*
Scott, Anne Firor	*The Southern Lady 1830–1930*
Stone, Lawrence	*Road to Divorce 1530–1987*
Sullivan, Walter	*The War the Women Lived*
Time-Life Books	*The Battle Atlas of the Civil War*
Vansteamburg, Ary	*Rural Women at the Time of the Civil War*
Wilcox, Arthur M.	*The Civil War at Charleston*
Wood, Anthony	*Nineteenth-Century Britain*
Woodward, Sir Llewellyn	*The Age of Reform 1815–1870*

THE MORLANDS OF MORLAND PLACE

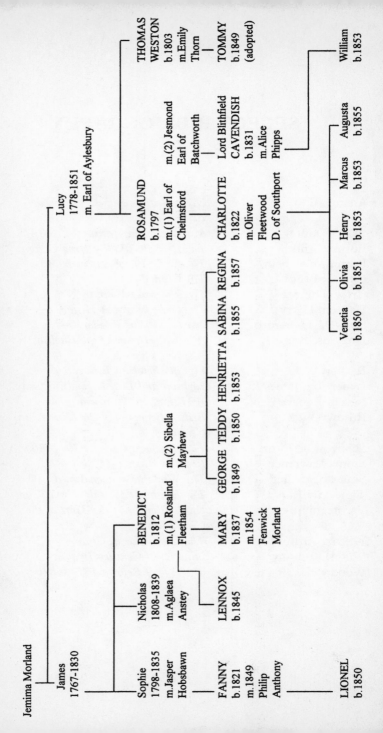

THE AMERICAN MORLANDS

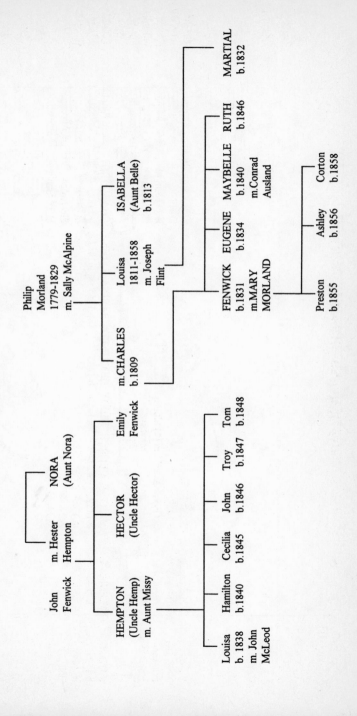

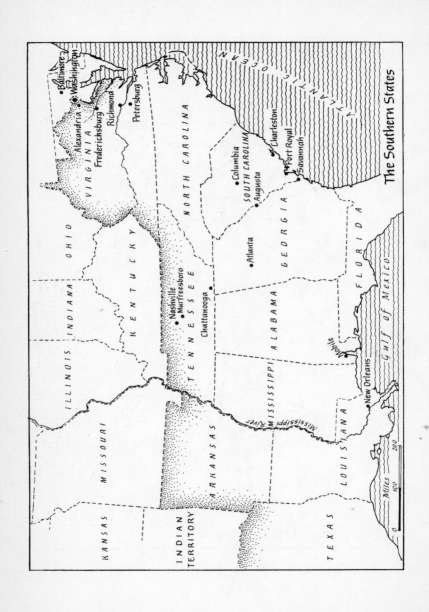

The Southern States

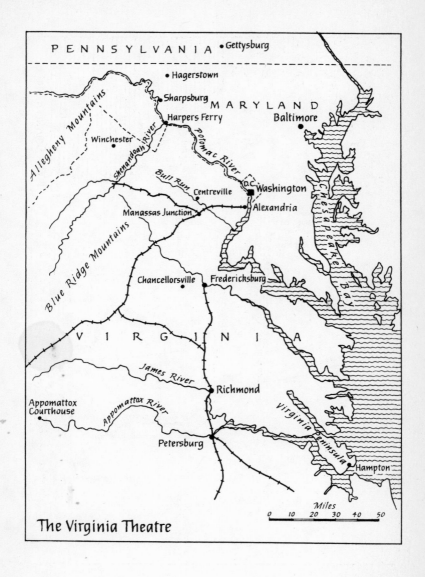

The Virginia Theatre

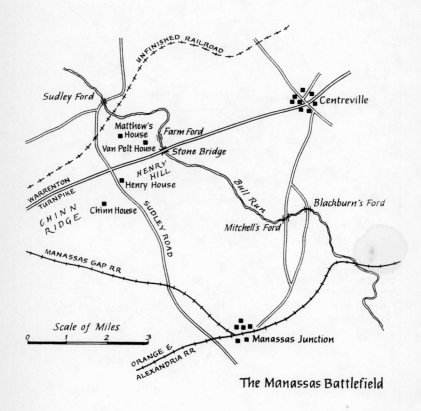

Sudley Ford

UNFINISHED RAILROAD

Centreville

Matthew's House
Van Pelt House
Farm Ford
Stone Bridge

HENRY HILL
Henry House

Bull Run

Blackburn's Ford

WARRENTON TURNPIKE

CHINN RIDGE
Chinn House

SUDLEY ROAD

Mitchell's Ford

MANASSAS GAP R.R.

Scale of Miles
0   1   2   3

Manassas Junction

ORANGE & ALEXANDRIA R.R.

The Manassas Battlefield

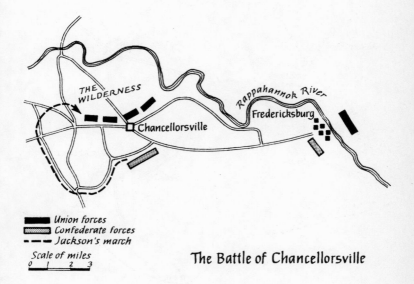

THE WILDERNESS

Rappahannok River

Chancellorsville

Fredericksburg

Union forces
Confederate forces
Jackson's march

Scale of miles
0   1   2   3

The Battle of Chancellorsville

BOOK ONE

Injustice

I do not love thee! – no! I do not love thee!
And yet when thou art absent I am sad;
And envy even the bright blue sky above thee,
Whose quiet stars may see thee and be glad.

I do not love thee! – yet, I know not why,
Whate'er thou dost seems still well done, to me;
And often in my solitude I sigh
That those I do love are not more like thee.

Caroline Elizabeth Sarah Norton:
I do not Love Thee

CHAPTER ONE

April 1857

As they walked down the steps and out into the sunshine, Harry Anstey looked at Benedict Morland and chuckled. 'Your face speaks volumes!'

Benedict stopped on the last step, his beaver in his hand. The sun pressed on the crown of his head like a warm hand; he lifted his face to it, and allowed his scowl to melt. The air was full of the delicious odour of hot chocolate from Terry's manufactory in St Helen's Square: it was hard to smell that and go on feeling cross.

Harry paused too, and taking out a cigar, spoke in phrases punctuated by the process of biting off the end and lighting it. 'I don't know – what you expect – from a committee. Even when – they do see the benefit—' A lengthy pause here while he applied the flame and got the cigar drawing satisfactorily. 'Twelve men,' he concluded, blowing a cloud of fragrant smoke towards the hot blue sky, 'can never act as one.'

Now Benedict smiled. 'Tell that to the Archbishop!'

'You must keep pegging away at it, that's all,' Harry said. 'The Corporation will come round in time.'

'Time,' Benedict repeated, as though it were an exotic ingredient unlikely to come to hand. But he was in no hurry to move. Standing on the steps, they were elevated slightly out of the flow of pedestrians who filled the flagway from side to side. Substantial people strolled, young men in a hurry dodged between, clutching their hats and leaning well out of the perpendicular. Beyond the flagway the press of traffic jammed the road almost solid: carts laden with vegetables, chickens, flour, baskets, furniture, dung; coal wagons, brewers' drays, gigs, flies and floats; private coaches with fidgety high-steppers and hired cabriolets with lean and stoical hacks.

'Look at that,' Benedict said, waving his hand. 'What do you see?'

Harry scanned the scene, drawing contentedly on his smoke like

3

a sucking-calf. 'I see that every vehicle has at least one horse between the shafts, which means excellent business for horse-breeders like my old friend Bendy Morland,' he said at last.

'Ha! But don't you see that the traffic is hardly moving?'

'I've lived in York nearly fifty years, and in all that time the traffic has never moved at more than two miles an hour.'

Benedict turned to him eagerly. 'All this press of vehicles proves that the city is thriving—'

'Doesn't it just!' Harry interrupted. 'I was talking to Smith in the club the other day – you know, the registrar – and he said the population has practically doubled since the railway came.' He smacked Benedict affectionately on the shoulder. 'You can take a lot of the credit for that, old man.'

'Oh, stuff! You did just as much yourself to bring the railway here. But that supports my point, Harry! Look how all the old fuss-pots were against the railway, and we had to coax and bully them into supporting it. But the railway's brought trade and wealth to York, and now the roads are so congested that it can take half an hour to move a wagon-load of goods half a mile from the station. And what can you expect, with a city built on a river which only has *one* bridge?'

'Me?' Harry said, stuffing his hands in his pocket and jutting his cigar towards the sky. 'I don't expect anything.'

'Everything that moves has to squeeze over Ouse Bridge, like sand through an hour-glass. When I ask for a new bridge direct to the railway station, you'd think plain common sense would say yes, wouldn't you? But what response do I get? "We'll think about it. Come back next year."'

'"Where's the brass coming from, young man?"' Anstey parodied one of the Corporation members. And he laughed, 'I don't think you should have called Fothergill a benighted old fossil, though! I don't think he liked it.'

Benedict barely smiled, reluctant to give up his complaint. 'If we replaced the Lendal ferry with a bridge, all this,' he waved his hand at the traffic again, 'wouldn't have to go through the centre of the city. Haven't they got eyes?'

'Eh, tha's nowt but an impetuous youth! When you get to my age,' Harry said comfortably, 'you'll have more patience. Give it another five years and I predict we'll have our bridge.' He changed the subject; living in the city, he noticed the traffic less than Benedict, who came in from the quiet of the fields. 'Where are you off to now? Are you going home?'

'Not at once. I was going to have a look at the building work down at Bishophill. How about you? Back to the office?'

Harry squinted up at the sky, and then down at the length of his cigar. 'I don't feel like going back just yet. Shall I stroll along with you? And, who knows, somewhere along the way we may be taken with the desire for a spot of something agreeable.'

'I thought you men of business never took luncheon? That's what you told me last week.'

'One has to keep a sense of proportion,' Anstey said wisely. 'Besides, I've got my boy working for me now. Arthur can take care of the office. What do we breed up sons for, if not to give us an easier life in old age?'

They assumed their hats and inserted themselves carefully into the river of pedestrians. They strolled with their hands permanently at their hat-brims, for the Ansteys and Morlands were among York's leading families, and they were returning greetings every few steps. Benedict was head of the Morland family of Morland Place, whose large estate lay just outside the city; Harry, a cadet of the large Anstey clan, was a respected lawyer. The Ansteys and Morlands had always been connected, and Harry and Benedict had gone to school together.

Benedict was forty-five, Harry forty-nine; both now had a sufficiency of grey hairs and a dignified amount of curvature under their waistcoats. They were, in fact, two sober, middle-aged gentlemen of substance; yet when they reached the three-way corner of St Helen's Square with Lendal and Coney Street they stopped of one accord and almost gawped like messenger boys.

Within a small compass were the post office, Hargrove's Library and Mrs Pomfret's millinery shop; and today the warm weather was causing the largely female customers to linger and chatter out of doors, like pigeons basking on the slope of a sunny roof. They were stepping on and off the kerb, climbing in and out of carriages, squeezing past each other in doorways, turning to greet each other and waving to acquaintances across the road; and every gesture, every movement, provided the gentlemen with a moment of palpitating interest.

'I wonder if we'll ever get used to it?' Harry said.

'Oh, I hope not,' Benedict murmured devoutly.

The wide skirts demanded by fashion had always been supported by a multitude of stiffened petticoats, but last year there had been a revolution. The cage-crinoline had arrived: a frame made of a series of thin steel hoops held together by tapes, and either sewn into a petticoat or tied with tapes around the waist. The difference to the wearer could hardly have been greater. Instead of heavy, cumbersome layers of linen, padded calico or horsehair, there was a light and airy cage within whose hollow shell a lady could move her legs with a freedom before undreamed-of.

But for the observer, particularly when he was a solid, middle-aged gentleman, the difference was even more profound. Before, a female had looked as though from the waist down she was carved out of a solid block of wood. But the cage-crinoline was a beast of a very different nature: the slightest movement set it swinging, so that ladies seemed to bob and sway and ripple like so many silken marquees in an unseen breeze. And any pressure on the hoops caused an opposite reaction on the other side, swinging the cage up like the mouth of a bell to give a tantalising glimpse of feet and ankles.

Measures had been adopted against such accidental exposure, but the measures proved more provocative than the problem: long linen drawers decorated with lace and frills and bows, and instead of the universal flat slippers of heretofore, delicious little high-heeled lace-up boots. A lady's least action had become fraught with fascination to the opposite sex. It was disconcerting. It was tantalising. It made standing on the corner of a fashionable street an extremely rewarding pastime.

'I saw a pair of boots in Peckitt's window the other day,' Harry mentioned. 'Green glacé morocco, laced all the way up to the calf.'

They paused for a moment in reverent thought, then sighed and roused themselves, and went on their way.

Halfway down Coney Street was Booker's, one of York's gentlemen's clubs. It was rather old-fashioned and stuffy, and in the past Harry and Benedict had both preferred more lively establishments like the Maccabbees; but now they were approaching the age of discretion they could see the value of a quiet place dedicated to comfortable chairs, solid meals and well-ironed newspapers. They slowed and turned towards the door, and at the same moment a lanky young man came bursting out and almost collided with them. He made a grab for his very tall grey hat, almost dropped his cane, and said, 'Dad! I was looking for you! And Uncle Ben too!'

The courtesy-uncle smiled at Arthur Anstey, who had once sworn undying love for Benedict's daughter Mary, but was now courting Maria Bayliss, the newspaper proprietor's daughter, with equal single-mindedness. 'No need to knock us down,' he said. 'A how-d'e-do would suffice to get our attention.'

Harry said sternly, 'You're always scampering about, Arthur. It's time you learned some dignity.' Arthur blushed, something his fair skin was prone to (and something, had he known it, which greatly endeared him to his Maria). 'What is it?' Harry went on. 'Something wrong?'

'Um, rather,' Arthur said, looking from one to the other. 'Would you please come back to the office, both of you? Something queer's come up.'

'Something queer' was a woman accompanied by a child, who had come asking for the Mr Anstey as was Mr Benedict Morland's attorney; she would not tell her business to anyone else. Harry, Benedict and Arthur all refrained from discussion on their brisk walk back to the office, but the haste with which Arthur had sought them out and the interested glances he kept snatching at Benedict's face, as they dodged through the crowds, told clearly enough what he thought. Harry, keeping his eyes to himself, was thinking the same. Benedict had had an adventurous youth, including some years as a railway engineer leading the irregular life of the workings; and he had always been attractive to women.

Benedict, his face inscrutable, was racking his brain to think who it might be, and coming to no conclusions. He didn't think he'd left any unfinished business behind him; but then, a rich man with a colourful past would always be a target for the unscrupulous. He was only glad that this female had made the first approach to Harry, rather than turning up on the doorstep at Morland Place: he was happily married and a father of five.

The woman was in the outer office of Anstey, Greaves and Russell, sitting on one of the small, hard chairs which were designed to test the resolve of less favoured supplicants. She was a plump female of respectable appearance, in her fifties perhaps, wearing an old-fashioned bonnet and heavy shawl, clutching a large, shabby reticule on her lap, and with two carpet bags at her feet. Benedict didn't know her; and as they entered, she looked at him and Harry equally without sign of recognition.

The boy, who was sitting on the chair beyond her, stood when she stood. He seemed to shiver, not with cold – it was warm, almost stuffy, in the office – but as an overbred horse shivers simply at the touch of the air. He was about twelve; a tall lad, pale-faced and golden-haired. He looked up briefly at the three men and down again at his boots, his mouth bowed in an expression of misery. His clothes were in the style of a gentleman's son's, but cheaply made and ill fitting. He wore mourning-bands, which presumably accounted for his unhappy expression. In the brief glimpse Harry had caught of his face, there seemed to be something faintly familiar about him which he couldn't quite place. Harry gave Benedict an enquiring look, and Benedict shook his head minutely. He had not particularly looked at the boy: it was the woman who interested him, and the woman, he was sure, was a stranger.

Reassured, Harry said briskly, 'Now then, my good woman, what's all this about?'

She made a civil bob, but returned his look with determination. 'Beg pardon, sir, but are you Mr Anstey, the man o' law I'm a-seekin' for?'

'Yes, yes, I am he, Mrs—?'

'Tomlinson, sir.'

'Very well, Mrs Tomlinson, and what was it that was so important you could not tell it to my clerk or my son? I'm a very busy man, you know.'

She was not to be intimidated. 'My business is for your ears only, sir,' she said firmly, with a significant glance at the outer-office clerk, Naylor. He was listening blatantly, his eyes on stalks. A strange woman with a child demanding to see a gentleman without delay could only mean one thing, as far as Naylor could see, and it was a welcome bit of excitement in his monotonous round of conveyances and wills.

Harry glanced too, and said, 'Very well, Mrs Tomlinson, you had better come through into my office. You can leave your bags here. They'll be quite safe.'

He gestured with his head to Arthur to return to his own desk, which Arthur did, hiding his disappointment. Mrs Tomlinson shoved the boy ungently back onto his chair, bid him stay, and prepared to follow Harry. Then she paused, looking at Benedict, to say, 'Beg pardon, sir, but who might this gentleman be?'

Harry said impatiently, 'This is the Mr Morland you were enquiring for.'

'Oh, indeed,' she said, looking at Benedict with round interest, and then passed before him into the inner office, leaving Naylor with a new puzzle to seethe over.

In his office, Harry took his seat behind his desk and gestured the woman to the penitent's hard chair on the other side. Benedict walked over to the window and lounged against it, seeming to give only half his attention to the woman, and the other half to the pigeons burbling on the roof-tiles. If this woman was after money, Harry would see her off. Her story would be full of holes a coach-and-four could drive through.

'Well, now, Mrs Tomlinson, let's hear what you have to say,' Harry said. 'And make it quick, please, because I'm a very busy man.'

She answered with spirit. 'Indeed, sir, busy you may be, but I shouldn't be here, I assure *you*, if there was any other way. I'm a respectable woman, and I have never had to do with lawyers, and nor has anyone in my family, so don't you think it!'

Harry blinked at this assault on his profession, and Benedict hid a smile.

Mrs Tomlinson went on, 'But trouble you I must, for the money is all run out, and I spent the last of it getting here, so I haven't a penny for lodgings or such. I can't go back and I can't go forrard, as you might say. I didn't rightly know what to do, and a rare pucker I was in, until I came upon a letter a-mentioning of you, and Mr Morland.'

'A letter?' Harry Anstey said. He glanced at Benedict. Here comes blackmail, his look said. Benedict raised an eyebrow and shook his head again. His conscience was clear.

Mrs Tomlinson was rummaging in her reticule. 'I have it here, sir, if you'd be so kind as to look at it. It was in a omberlope with your name on the outside, but not sealed nor directed, so I made bold to read it, in case it could help, which I was glad I did, as you will see. It's from Mr Mynott all right, for I know his hand, though he signs himself a bit different at the bottom – there, sir, Miniott he spells it there. Carlton Miniott.'

'Good God,' Harry said under his breath. Now he knew why the boy had looked oddly familiar.

By the window, Benedict had grown very still. His stomach knotted and his heart was beating a horrid tattoo. Of all the chickens to come home to roost! But it was not his business, he thought savagely. He didn't want to know!

'It was always by the name of Mynott I knew him,' Mrs Tomlinson went on, unaware of the palpitations she had caused. 'Which I was employed by Mr Mynott to housekeep and take care of the boy these five years – six come Michaelmas – and a more proper gentleman I couldn't have wished to work for, God rest his soul.'

Harry cocked an eyebrow. 'He's dead?'

'This fortnight last Tuesday – quite sudden, else I'm sure he would have left his affairs as a gentleman should. Always very considerate, he was. But as it stood, sir, I had no-one to turn to, Mr Mynott having no friends nor no relatives that I ever heard of, and me having nothing in my purse but the last of the housekeeping he gave me, which once it was gone – well, sir, I was at my wits' end! I could have taken myself off to my sister's in Pickering, but what was I to do with the boy? And then I found this letter in a drawer, addressed to Mr Henry Anstey, Attorney-at-Law, saying he hoped as how Mr Morland would find it in his heart to look after young Lennox. That's the boy, sir. So I asked around a bit until I found out who Mr Anstey was, sir, begging your pardon, and so I came to York on the train and pretty soon found out your direction. So here I am.'

'The deuce you are,' Harry muttered.

She shot him a suspicious look. 'And now, sir,' she continued firmly, making a preliminary getting-up-to-go movement, 'if you would very kindly take charge of the boy, I should like to be on my way. And if you could see your way to paying my wages for this last fortnight, I should count it Christian, for otherwise I shall have to walk all the way to Pickering, which for a woman of my age is a cruel thing to contemplate.'

She gave a quick and curious glance towards Benedict, evidently wondering how he came into all this, and then fixed Harry with a hopeful eye.

Harry read and re-read the letter she had given him, his mind working furiously. The envelope had written on it *Henry Anstey, Esq., Attorney-at-Law*, but nothing else, and it showed no sign of ever having been sealed. Presumably Miniott had been interrupted before he had added the direction, and had never returned to the task. The letter bore at the top Miniott's direction in Scarborough, and the date was three weeks back.

Mr Anstey,
Sir,
I would not now be troubling you, knowing in what little esteem you hold me, were it not that I bear a responsibility I am unable properly to discharge. It is not on my own behalf that I implore you to do what you can for Lennox, but for his sake, who is innocent of any crime but being my son. I am an old man, and my health is indifferent, and I fear I will not long survive to protect him. Indeed, I can barely do so now, being almost penniless. I have no-one to turn to, no family, no friends. What will happen to him when I die? I ask you, in the name of mercy, to intercede for me with Mr Benedict Morland, beg him for *her* sake, for the love he once bore her, to take care of her son. But a little expenditure would place him in a school where he could learn to be useful and support himself in a gentlemanly way: that is all I ask. I beg you, sir, I beg you. Benedict Morland is a good man, with some greatness of heart, as I have cause to know. Let him show his mercy to this innocent child, who will otherwise be destitute and friendless. Intercede for me, I entreat you.
Your servant, sir,
    Carlton Miniott.

The *she* of the letter was, of course, Benedict's first wife, Rosalind. It was an odd story, Harry reflected, and one which only he, apart from the present Mrs Morland, knew. Rosalind had been in love with Sir Carlton Miniott – a friend of her father's and twenty years her senior – since her childhood, but he had not been rich enough to suit her ambition. When Benedict came into his fortune she had accepted him with alacrity, declaring herself in love with him; yet all the time, both before and after her marriage to Benedict, she and Miniott had been lovers. Benedict's adored daughter Mary was in reality Miniott's child, a discovery which had broken his heart. Meanwhile Miniott, from being not rich enough to tempt Rosalind, had sunk through reversals to being only just able to support himself, having lost his fortune and his handsome estate at Ledston through bad business. Yet still Rosalind loved him. Again and again she had cuckolded Benedict, again and again he had forgiven her, until eventually she had conceived another child by her lover; and Benedict had finally declared enough, and sent her away. Miniott had taken her to Scarborough, where the couple lived on a pension from Benedict – that was presumably what Miniott had meant by the greatness of Benedict's heart. Benedict had meant eventually to divorce Rosalind, but she had died in childbed before he could make any decision about it, and that was that.

That was twelve years ago, of course, Harry reflected. Since that day Benedict had cut off all connection with Miniott, and had never spoken of him or the boy; whether he had thought of them, God only knew. But now here was the problem rearing its head again. There was a kind of insane logic about Miniott's appealing, *in extremis*, to Benedict. Their lives were connected in this peculiar way, tangled together with the thread of Rosalind's beauty and frailty. And who else was there?

The human side of Harry Anstey saw the logic, acknowledged the bond, but the attorney in him revolted. Benedict should have nothing to do with this. To touch it would be to mire himself deeper in something that had already cost him dear. Yet there was Exhibit A, so to speak, in the outer office – the boy Lennox. Clearly something had to be done about him.

He roused himself and addressed himself to Exhibit B. 'Very well, Mrs Tomlinson. Would you please wait outside with the boy while I discuss the matter with Mr Morland.'

She stood obediently, but looked doubtful, fearing she was to be fobbed off. 'Very good, sir, but you won't keep me long? I've done my duty bringing the boy here, and I've a long way to go if I'm to get to my sister's house tonight, which I must do if I'm not to starve to death, for I haven't had a bite to eat since yesterday and not a penny to buy myself anything until I get there.'

Benedict over by the window made a movement of impatience, and Harry rang the bell for the clerk. 'Naylor, Mrs Tomlinson will wait in the outer office with the boy until I call for them again. They are both hungry, so send someone out to the Swan for some bread and meat for them. Take it out of petty cash.'

'I could go myself, sir,' Naylor offered, longing for the chance to spread the news of the visitation.

'No, you're to stay and take care of them,' Harry said firmly, with a significant look that Naylor read correctly as meaning, 'and if they skip, you're for it, my lad!'

'Very good, sir.'

When the door had closed behind them, Harry came out from behind his desk and walked across to Benedict with the letter. He put a hand on Benedict's shoulder. 'Do you want to read this?'

Benedict still had his back turned, facing the window. His body was rigid, his voice strange as he said, 'You can tell me what it says.'

Harry was not prepared to read out those words, afraid of their power. He shrugged. 'It says he's penniless and dying, and begs you to take care of the boy for her sake.'

'For her sake? He says that? Does he use her name?'

'No. Would it matter?'

'To me, it would.' He turned with a desperate look. 'God, Harry, I've tried to forget. All these years I've tried. I thought I'd succeeded. And now this! I never thought it could still hurt so much.'

Harry said, 'You need pay no attention to his request. In fact, as your lawyer I must recommend you not to become involved.'

'You don't understand. *He* knew the power he had over me. That boy out there—'

'That boy is not your son! He's not your responsibility.'

'I didn't see his face. Harry, you saw his face, didn't you? He looks like her, doesn't he?'

'He has a faint look of her, perhaps,' Harry said reluctantly, 'but why should that make any difference? After what she did—'

Benedict shook his head, thoughts and words not connecting, trying to shake the blockage free. 'It's not what Rosalind did that matters, not now. It still hurts me, but it's over. She's dead. It's not her, and it's not me – it's the boy.'

'Yes, but—'

Benedict gripped his arm. 'He's Mary's brother, don't you see? And now he's her only relative in the world. I can't just ignore it and walk away. I owe it to Mary to do something.'

Harry frowned at this tortured reasoning, sensing trouble ahead. 'Well, at all events, I must advise you not to do anything precipitate. Take time, think about it, don't commit yourself to any course of action until you've considered the consequences fully.'

Benedict released Harry's arm in order to gesture helplessly towards the closed door. 'That's all very well, but there he is, you know. What's to be done about him – now, this minute?'

'Exhibit A,' Harry sighed in agreement.

'What?'

Harry waved the question away. 'We'll find lodgings for them for the time being. Enquiries will have to be made to see if Miniott had a man of business, whether he left a Will, whether he in fact had any other relatives. All that will take time. That female can take care of him for a bit longer. Do you want to pay her the wages she says she's owed?'

'Yes, I suppose so. She seems to have done her best, and we can't leave her penniless.'

Harry gave him a look of lawyerly cynicism. 'I doubt whether she's as destitute as she says she is. If Miniott died suddenly, I dare say she went through the house before calling anyone, and tucked away anything of value.'

'You think so?' Benedict said, startled.

'I wouldn't wager a groat on the contents of her luggage. But it's up to you.'

'Oh, well, I hate to be paltry. Pay her a month's wages and have done with it.'

'As you please,' said Harry. 'Now why don't you go home and talk things over with Sibella? She'll be able to bring a rational mind to the problem.'

'You think I'm not rational?'

'Not in this case. Go on, Bendy, take yourself off. Here, let me show you out the back way, so that you don't have to see them again. Come, don't argue, old fellow – much better not to torture yourself.'

He showed Benedict out through the rear lobby onto the outside staircase, which led down into a tiny back yard. A narrow arched tunnel running under the upper storey of the house next door led out to High Ousegate. The old part of York was a jumble of such hidden yards, alleys, tunnels, wynds and staircases, interlinked in a hinterland of secret routes – useful to the criminal element, but also, on more than one occasion, to clients with delicate business to conduct.

Returning to his office, Harry rang the bell for Naylor, asked him if the visitors had been fed, and explained in detail what arrangements he wanted made for their accommodation. Naylor noted them, and went out, to return almost immediately, red of face and apprehensive of eye.

'Mr Anstey, sir, I'm afraid – I'm sorry to say—' In the face of Harry's awful look, the confession burst forth unvarnished. 'The fact of it is, sir, the old dame's skipped!'

Harry made a gesture of exasperation. 'The boy, too?'

'No, sir, she's left the boy. Just skipped with her own stuff.'

It was all bad. Now he was stuck with the boy on his hands and no nursemaid. Why had she decided to go without the money? he wondered. Had she overheard something? Perhaps she didn't want the job of governess for nothing more than a month's wages. Or perhaps she did have things worth having in her bag, and had decided to make sure of them.

Harry gave Naylor a piece of his mind – more for relief of his own feelings than for justice, since he had called Naylor in himself – and then went to the door of his room and looked out, wondering what the dickens he was going to do with the child now. The boy was sitting obediently where he had been put, a platter of bread and meat untouched on the chair beside him. His head was bowed in misery, and when Harry appeared at the door he looked up briefly with such an absence of hope in his eyes that even Harry's law-toughened heart was touched. Lennox had so recently lost his father, and now he had been abandoned by the only other familiar face in his world, left like luggage on a hard chair in a solicitor's office.

Harry cleared his throat. 'Well, now, my lad,' he began. The boy gazed at him with wide blue eyes the colour of June sky; his hair was pale gold, almost primrose-coloured, his skin delicate ivory, barely flushed with rose. The ghost of his mother looked out for an instant at Harry, and completely unnerved him. He heard himself say, 'No need to look so blue. You'll be taken care of all right. How would you like to come home with me for a few days? My wife would be glad to have your company.'

Out of the corner of his eye he saw Naylor's jaw drop. He felt pretty astonished himself. Celia was a gentle soul, and always hospitable, but what would she make of this situation? And would she really welcome the child of a woman she had always disliked – a child of sin, moreover? But it was said now, and he would not unsay it; in Lennox Mynott's eyes there was, not precisely a gleam of hope, but at least a lessening of despair.

★ ★ ★

When he got back to Morland Place, Benedict took Sibella out for a walk. It was the only way to secure the privacy in which to tell her,

14

for wherever she was in the house, she seemed to have a magnetic attraction for servants, children and animals. So he invited her to take the air, communicating with eyebrows and nods that he had something particular to say, and, scraping off the limpet-like household with difficulty, almost hustled her out of the door. Her shawl slipped as she fumbled with her bonnet strings and, trying to catch it, she dropped her parasol. Benedict grabbed it before the young dog pounced on it, took her elbow and whipped her across the threshold, shutting the door on a last glimpse of the housekeeper's baffled face as she popped out of her room with yet another question on her lips.

'Anyone would think I was taking you away for seven years,' he grumbled. 'Is it always like this?'

'You have no idea, have you?' Sibella said. 'You think the house runs itself.'

'If you haven't enough servants, you have only to say so.'

'Servants don't run themselves, either. When I was a girl, I thought that married ladies had nothing to do but order the dinner. If I'd known what I was letting myself in for!' She sighed. 'Not halfway through the year, and already I'm behind. And if I don't start looking over the linens and the store-cupboards soon, it will be June and the harvests will start, and I won't get them done at all.'

'You shouldn't be doing so much. You've just had a baby.'

'Simpleton! What do you think *put* me behind?'

They stepped out onto the moat walk and she looked around with pleasure, drawing in a deep breath. The sky was an arc of perfect blue, the air was brilliant, the grass sparkled, and the walls of the old house were reflected in the still water, gently distorted as if they were made of soft bullion. A pair of swans, accompanied by last year's juvenile, drifted towards them casually, eyeing them for any evidence of a picnic. They seemed to float on fallen sky, their movement barely rippling the surface.

'Oh, this is heaven!' Sibella said. 'I don't remember the last time I was out of doors, except to go to the fowl-yard.'

Benedict looked at her anxiously. The new baby, Regina, was not yet six weeks old, and he rather doubted Sibella should have been out of bed at all, let alone doing all the things she did. 'Perhaps we ought to sit down, rather than walk,' he said.

'Perhaps not,' Sibella replied firmly, putting her hand through his arm and setting a moderate pace along the path.

'But you ought to rest more. Mrs Hoddle is always saying she can manage.'

'Is all very well her saying, but she can't,' Sibella said. 'And besides, I hate to be idle. That's the worst thing about having babies, the months of do-nothing. Do you know, I've calculated that altogether I've spent four whole years either pregnant or recovering from childbirth. And we've only been married eight years this autumn!'

'I'm sorry,' he said, not knowing what else to say.

'Are you? Don't be – I'm not,' she said, pressing his arm. 'But I do miss riding. And walking and all the other things we used to do. I'd be glad,' she said carefully, 'not to have another for a while.'

'We didn't precisely *mean* to have Regina,' he said, and then caught up with her meaning, and looked embarrassed. 'Oh! I see. Well, well. Yes, of course. It must be as you please, my love.'

She was charmed that he was so shy and diffident about it. He almost blushed; and she almost made a comment on that, and then wisely held her tongue. It was a sensitive subject, and it would be easy to hurt his feelings. Instead she said, 'I think a fine day in spring is the best of all. In June or July a day like this would be too hot for walking. Shall we go up to the fish-ponds?'

'Anywhere you like,' he said. He lapsed into silence, but Sibella was happy enough just to enjoy the air and his company. The dogs had slipped out with them, of course. Her pointers, Bell and Dancer, ran ahead smoothly, keeping step like horses, noses down, tracking smells back and forth across the turf. Benedict's old bitch, Brach, walked at his side as if her head were joined by a cord to his knee; his young dog, Artos, frisked about playing the fool, snapping at bumble-bees and rolling in the grass with his legs in the air.

They crossed by the top sluice and headed by common consent for the bench that overlooked the largest pond. A frog sprang with a loud plop into the water as they sat down, and Artos bounced down to the pond's edge to investigate, shoving his nose incautiously into the water and making himself sneeze.

'Doesn't he realise he's not a puppy any more?' Sibella said. 'The dog's a fool!' It was a judgement concurred with by Brach, his mother, who sat by Benedict's feet and watched him in silent wonder; and by the pointers, who ignored his invitations to play and flopped down in the shade under the bench, unfurling yards of frilled and dripping tongue.

Benedict made no response, and Sibella looked at him. His brow was furrowed and his eyes absent. 'What is it?' she asked, and a shadow of foreboding touched the back of her neck like a cold finger. Benedict rested his elbows on his knees, his hands loosely clasped between them, and staring unseeingly at the water, he told her about Lennox Mynott.

As his narrative progressed, her heart grew colder. Was there to be no end to the trouble that woman caused? Sibella had struggled for twenty years with her jealousy. Even after her marriage to Benedict, she could not escape the memory, reminded as she was every day by the presence of Rosalind's daughter Mary. That Sibella loved Mary, and Mary loved her, only made it harder. There had been occasions when she had come near to hating Benedict for ever having married such a woman; and then she hated Rosalind all the more for making her feel anything but love for her husband.

In October 1854 Mary had married and gone away with her husband to America, and at last a kind of hard-won equilibrium had been established. Though they missed Mary very much, her departure had removed a source of continuous friction, not so much in their daily lives as in their souls. The old chaplain, Father Moineau, had gone too, severing the last link with the painful past. Now there was just Benedict, Sibella, and their children. Sibella's jealousy had finally subsided; she had thought it had died.

But now this! Into the silence at the end of Benedict's narration she said, as Harry Anstey had said before her, 'It's not your business!'

He didn't immediately answer. His eyes were blank as he struggled to find the right words. Sibella thought that he looked suddenly older. There was tiredness in the lines of his face and the pouches under his eyes, as though this new burden were more than he could cope with.

'All my life,' he said at last, 'I've been letting people down. I've never told you this, but sometimes I dream that they're all standing round the bed, looking at me reproachfully. My mother. Liza and her boy. Serena Makepeace. Even Miniott, in a way. I can never forget that last terrible look he gave me after I knocked him down, when I told him I never wanted to see him or hear of him again.'

She protested. 'You can't believe that Carlton Miniott was your responsibility!'

'But Rosalind was. I shouldn't have sent her away. Once I knew what she was, I ought to have protected her from herself, taken steps to control her. I thought I was being kind to her, but really it was weakness. If I hadn't sent her away, she might not have died.'

Sibella felt sick. She turned her face away. He wished Rosalind hadn't died. Knowing everything he knew, still he hankered after her. Sibella's love was no compensation: she would always be second best.

Perhaps feeling something of his wife's pain, he said quickly, 'I don't mean I want her back; it's just that—' he paused, seeking for the words, 'I feel so guilty! I wish she hadn't had to die so that I could have you. I wish it could have been some other way.'

Wish, wish, Sibella thought. Always wanting the impossible,

never facing up to reality and dealing with it. The best thing Rosalind had ever done was to die, but she couldn't say that to him. Instead she said, 'So you feel guilty about Rosalind's death. What then? She's dead. You can't change that.'

He sighed. 'You're not making it easy for me.'

'Do you think it's easy for me, always to live in her shadow?'

Her spurt of anger roused him. He looked at her, distressed. 'Oh, no, don't think that! Never that. You're everything to me! That's why I want you to understand. All my life I've been failing people – not meaning to, but seeing them suffer because I did something or didn't do something—'

'You can't help that. No-one can help that,' she said impatiently. 'That's part of life. You have to do your best, and face the consequences.' She didn't have the right words. She wished now that Father Moineau were here, after all. He was the only one Benedict ever listened to. There was a stubbornness at the bottom of Benedict's lazy good humour, and the two things were bound up in each other in a way Sibella recognised but did not understand.

He went on as if she hadn't spoken. 'I was harsh with Mary, I think because I was afraid of being too soft. I couldn't trust my feelings. So I failed her, too. Well, that's the heart of it, really. She's the only one who matters in all this.'

'Do you think you should have made her heir to the estate, after all?'

'No,' he said with reluctant sureness. 'No, I was right about that. But there were things I could have given her that might have made her want to stay. She married Fenwick and went to America because I gave her nothing to stay for.'

'Bendy, she loved him,' Sibella said patiently. 'That's why she married him.'

'Perhaps, but why did she fall in love with him in the first place? There were plenty of local boys she could have had. And I didn't even give her a proper dowry, just that mean settlement. It should have been much more.'

'You had to keep the estate together for your own children,' she reminded him.

But he wanted to punish himself; to believe that Mary would have stayed in England if he had handled things differently. 'Well, now this has come up, this business of the boy. He's Mary's brother. I owe it to her to take care of him, Sib, you do see that?'

'No, I don't see.' She looked away at the horizon, her eyes grey as rain. 'But I see you mean to make yourself responsible for him, no matter what I say.'

'But I *am* responsible. She was still my wife – that's just a matter of fact. And, in law, any child born to her in wedlock is my child, no matter who fathered it.'

She could not argue on that point. She did not know the law, but if it were true, it seemed to her that it was monstrous. 'So what do you mean to do? You'll place him in a school, I suppose?'

'No, I can't do that. You know what happens to boys like that at school. I'm going to have him here, and bring him up with our boys.' Sibella could not speak. It was worse than she thought. Benedict smiled a watery, inappropriate smile. 'Don't look so grim! You haven't seen him. He's not a monster, just a little boy all alone in the world. A waif, really. You wouldn't turn a poor penniless orphan away from the door, would you?'

'Yes, I would!' she cried fiercely. 'If it was that woman's child, I would!'

'You know you don't mean that.'

'Don't bring that child into my nursery,' she said. 'There are other ways to help.'

'It's the way I've chosen,' he said awkwardly.

He was looking at her anxiously, but the truth was that he was the master and could do as he pleased. His anxiety was not that he might not have her agreement, which he did not need, but that she might make difficulties, and disrupt the calm atmosphere of his life. And still Sibella didn't understand. She knew what it was about: Mary, mostly, and behind that, his mother; yes, she knew *what*, but she didn't understand *why*.

'You have decided,' she said at last. 'You'll do what you want, no matter what I feel.'

He took that for consent, and the shadow passed from his face as though she had agreed wholeheartedly. He took her hand and kissed it gratefully. 'I knew you'd see it my way,' he said. 'You're the best of creatures.'

'It will make trouble,' she said. 'I warn you now.'

But he wasn't listening. 'It's the right thing to do, I'm sure of it. If I sent him away, I'd always feel there was yet another person I'd let down, and I don't think I could bear to carry any more guilt.'

CHAPTER TWO

Harry managed to persuade Benedict not to take the boy until the proper enquiries had been made. It would be pointless to settle him at Morland Place and then uproot him again because he had an uncle somewhere who would give him a home. 'He can stay with us for now,' Harry said. 'Celia's taken a fancy to him, and it's company for her.'

Lennox had arrived on Celia's doorstep the most miserable scrap of humanity in existence, bereaved, bewildered, lonely and afraid. Celia had been unable to have any more children after Arthur, and it had left a hunger unsatisfied. Lennox was no baby, but if ever a creature needed nurturing, it was he. So when Harry told her that Lennox would be staying for a while, she took pains to draw him out and find out something about his life. It had been an odd one. His father, though poor and an outcast, had never been able to abandon his former tastes and habits, and Lennox had been brought up as a gentleman's son. They had not always had a great deal to eat, but it had been eaten fastidiously, at a dining-table, with the last retained items of fine china and silverware. Their clothes were old and shabby, but Lennox never wore the heavy boots and moleskins of a labourer's child. Their single servant may well have eaten better than them, but she ate in the kitchen.

Sir Carlton Miniott had used up his time and energies by teaching Lennox, and since he was an exceptionally able man and Lennox a bright child, the education had been extensive: Latin and Greek, history, philosophy, mathematics, astronomy, French and a little Italian. Lennox was familiar with the great names of English literature, could criticise them intelligently, write a neat monograph, and debate a given topic from any perspective.

Outside lessons, they had had to be company and entertainment to each other. They had no instrument, but Miniott had taught Lennox to sing, and he knew a great many songs and poems by heart. They would recite to each other and read plays aloud, taking the parts between them. They went for long walks, and Lennox learned the names of birds, trees and flowers, and could sketch very nicely besides. He could play whist, piquet and cribbage, chess, tables, and draughts, a large number of lighthearted card games and parlour games, and twenty different sorts of solitaire. It had been an isolated life, but it had not been a gloomy one; there had been laughter, and there had been affection – a great deal of it, but all from one source.

That, Celia thought, was Miniott's real crime against his son, though perhaps there was little he could have done about it. Lennox had no friends of his own age, had never even played with another boy. He knew nothing outside the small, tight routine of his home. In their daily round, on their walks about the town, Papa spoke to no-one, and no-one visited them. Lennox did not even know that they were poor, for he had nothing to compare his circumstances with. At twelve, he was as learned as most grown men, a shy, unworldly, rather solemn boy. The most touching thing, Celia thought, was that he had no child's vocabulary. To Harry she described him as a 'queer little scholarly thing, quite like an old man'.

About his mother, Celia discovered, he knew only that she had died when he was born. He had never even seen a likeness of her, though Papa said that she was very beautiful, and that he, Lennox, was very like her in looks. 'But not in character,' Celia concluded. 'He's as good as gold – but very unhappy, poor mite.'

Sympathetic as she was, Celia could not guess at the depths of Lennox's unhappiness, and he had not the means to describe it to her. He had woken one morning to find the centre of his universe, the sun around which he orbited, was gone.

Mrs Tomlinson had woken him with a hard hand shaking his shoulder. 'Hurry up and get dressed, and then come down to the kitchen,' she said, her mouth set in a disapproving line.

Lennox stumbled awake, and sat up, puzzled. 'Am I not to wash first?' Papa said a gentleman must sponge himself all over every morning.

Mrs Tomlinson clicked with exasperation. 'Wash! Wash, the boy says! Never mind all that nonsense now! Get dressed and come straight down to the kitchen.'

At some animal level he perceived that the house was too quiet, and a fear was born. Something bad was happening. 'Is my father gone out?' he asked, and he heard his voice tremble.

'Thy father is dead,' Mrs Tomlinson said with a kind of grim relish, 'and we are in enough trouble. So do as you're told and don't go adding to mine with your questions.'

That was the beginning of it, the nightmare he couldn't seem to wake up from. First a doctor came, and then an old woman with no teeth who smelled of gin; each in turn was escorted into Papa's bedroom by Mrs Tomlinson and the door closed sharply. Then came a very stout and disapproving man 'from the Parish', who looked down his nose at Mrs Tomlinson and tutted over Lennox; and then a very thin and melancholy man with black crape hanging from his hat, who sniffed. Each of them had an urgent conversation in the parlour with Mrs Tomlinson, in which the words *pauper's funeral* and *the boy* were the only ones he could catch from his lonely lookout post on the stairs.

In between the visitations, Lennox wandered about the house in a daze: Mrs Tomlinson had forbidden him to step outside. Comfort had fled. Nothing was cleaned, no fires were lit, food appeared irregularly, and then it was only bread and cheese and no table laid, like a series of picnics without the jollity. Mrs Tomlinson had a number of callers at the kitchen door with whom she conducted sotto voce conversations. Lennox's dreamlike bewilderment was increased by the fact that things seemed to be disappearing from the house, though he never saw them go, and Mrs Tomlinson, when humbly questioned, had always 'no notion what you're talking about – what picture? – what chess set? – I've no time to be worrying about such trifles at a time like this!'

The time came when he was taken into his father's room to 'pay his last respects'. The dead body lay on the bed, horribly waxen and unnatural-looking, the lips drawn back from the yellowed teeth, and dark copper pennies on the eyes. Lennox shrank from it in horror. It was not his father. Mrs Tomlinson tutted and urged him to kiss the thing, and called him a heathen boy when he cried and said he could not. Later two men came with a cart, and Mrs Tomlinson took Lennox's hand and walked with him behind it to the graveyard, grumbling all the time under her breath. It was a day without sun, a grey blank sky, and a thin, gritty wind. A very tired-looking priest mumbled a few words, shivered, and went away, and Mrs Tomlinson grasped Lennox's hand and hurried him back home.

Shortly after that – Lennox never in after years could remember how long, for from the moment Mrs Tomlinson said, 'Thy father is dead,' he lived in a horrid dream where the hands of the clock moved without advancing time at all – they left the mysteriously emptying house for ever. For the first time in his life Lennox rode in a train, though he could take no pleasure in the experience. York was a further nightmare of glaring heat, crowded streets, noise. There were too many people; the world, he thought, was suddenly packed full of people who were not his father. Then the lawyer's office, curious stares from the clerk and the closed door of the conference. And then Mrs Tomlinson slipping quietly out, turning to wink at him, laying her finger against her lips with a roguish smile as if inviting him to play a game. But fear and misery made him perceptive. He knew she was not coming back, that she had removed herself from his life as permanently as Papa, and cast him upon the mercy of strangers.

The lawyer, Mr Anstey, had spoken kindly to him and taken him to his house, a place of extraordinary newness and luxury where his wife, a small lady with a worn face, had tried not to look surprised to see him. He had been sent to the kitchen to be given a bowl of bread and milk and stared at by the cook, and then to be stared at and put to bed by a reluctant maid-servant. Alone in the dark, he had lain awake for hours, listening to the murmuring rise and fall of voices which he heard, or perhaps imagined he heard, from the drawing-room where Mr Anstey and his wife were discussing what to do with 'the boy'. He supposed he would always be 'the boy' from now on: an object that something had to be done with. Suddenly he remembered his father's face, his father's voice, his smile; the comfort of his father's hand resting on his shoulder as they read Virgil together. Never again! Love and approval and belonging had gone out of the world. Lennox began to cry, and once beginning, could not stop. He cried all night, pulling the blankets over his head so that no-one should hear him.

Harry's enquiries were not long to make. The house where Miniott had lived in Scarborough had been rented, and contained little but its furniture: no books, ornaments, comforts of any sort. Miniott must have been very close to destitution, Harry thought, or else Mrs Tomlinson was the rogue he had taken her for. When the bills were settled, there would not be ten pounds left for Lennox. Harry learned that Miniott had been buried in a pauper's grave, so nothing marked his resting-place. One day Lennox might care about that, but as far as Harry was concerned, it was all to the good.

He could not discover that Miniott had ever instructed a solicitor in Scarborough, so he decided to go to Ledsham to consult with Miniott's former man of business, Kellington. He left Scarborough gladly. He could not feel easy in that pleasant seaside town since his youngest sister had drowned there the year before in mysterious circumstances.

Kellington told Harry that he had not had any contact with Sir Carlton since he sold the last of his land more than ten years before. On the other hand, Kellington had never been instructed to forward his papers to any other man of business, so here they were still, in a deed-box in the vault. 'So I suppose you might say I am still his solicitor. But as to there being any estate—' He shrugged eloquently.

'And is there a Will?' Harry asked.

'There is, but it was drawn up twenty years ago, and the sole legatee it names is now dead.' He eyed Harry keenly. 'There is a child, you say?'

'A son. But Sir Carlton did not marry the mother.'

'Ah! Then there is no question of his inheriting the title,' Kellington said, disappointed.

'None. But Sir Carlton acknowledged the boy and brought him up himself, and now there is no-one to take care of him. Do you know who is the next of kin?'

Kellington shook his head. 'A difficult question. It will be a distant cousin, my dear sir; a very remote connection. Sir Carlton had no brothers or sisters, and nor did his mother; his father's only brother is now dead, and *his* son, Sir Carlton's first cousin, died without issue six or seven years ago. One would have to go back to his grandfather's brother – a very tiresome search, and who would pay for all the work involved? There is no money with the title. I believe it will have to lie dormant until someone claims it. I shall inform the Herald in Waiting, and leave it to the College to decide. I really cannot see that I am obliged to do more than that.'

'Just so,' Harry said sympathetically.

'And your interest in the matter goes no further than this unfortunate child?' Kellington asked with well-reined curiosity.

'If there had been a near relative, he might have been persuaded to give the child a home,' Harry said. 'As it is—'

'Yes, as it is,' Kellington agreed tactfully.

Harry did not long debate whether it would be better to undertake a lengthy and expensive search for the next of kin in the faint hope that he could be persuaded to undertake the care and maintenance of Sir Carlton's penniless bastard, or to let Benedict have his way. Life was too short, he felt, to spend it knocking one's head against a brick wall. He could only advise his clients against folly, not keep them from it if they were determined. The sooner his involvement in the affair was ended, the better – though he admitted to himself privately that he would miss the little chap. Lennox hadn't been with them long, but already Celia looked ten years younger, and Harry hadn't enjoyed such challenging games of chess in years.

'I must protest, madam,' Mr Wheldrake said sternly, making it clear that from him a protest was a rebuke. 'I cannot believe that you have properly considered the full ramifications of this precipitous course of action, the likely consequences to your own tender offspring of introducing into the domestic locus an interloper of such indeterminate antecedents. Far be it from me—'

Sibella stopped listening for a bit. Mr Wheldrake always talked like that. She supposed it was Education, but it made her long for the old days when Father Moineau was the chaplain-tutor. The spherical Frenchman spoke a direct and practical language, and he had a dark, soft voice. Mr Wheldrake's voice was high and grating, and when Sibella didn't understand what he was saying – which was often – she rarely felt driven to find out.

Father Moineau had left a few months after Mary went to America. Sibella had been expecting his departure, for only his love of Mary had curbed his congenital restlessness. One morning he had come to her and said, 'Dear child, I have been comfortable here too long. I am called once again into the wilderness.'

'Which wilderness?' she asked, though she had guessed already.

'There are a thousand poor souls ignorant of God waiting for me in the workings,' he said. He had always had a weakness for railways. She had tried to dissuade him – Benedict had begged him – but it was no use. Gently and firmly he said goodbye to them, and set out on his own two small feet, with nothing but a pack on his back. Benedict had been desolated – Father Moineau had been his own tutor, and was more than a father to him.

'Don't cry, my son. We'll meet again,' said the old man as he left. But Benedict was not comforted. He didn't know Moineau's age, but it must have been seventy or more. If they met again it would probably not be in this world.

Moineau's departure left them with difficulties, especially as the governess, Miss Titchell, gave her notice only a few weeks later. She could not cope with the boys, missed Mary, and wanted a home of her own. 'My sister wants to start up a little school, and she's asked me to go and help her,' she said. Sibella noted the increasingly grey hair and careworn face and could only sympathise.

There followed a period of disruption, during which the boys ran wild. Advertisement failed to produce a suitable tutor. The best of the young clerics had livings waiting for them, or found preferment within the diocesan establishments; the second rank went into the universities and the better schools. Morland Place received plenty of applicants, but they were either old and seedy and pathetic, or young and needy and pathetic.

But eventually Harry Anstey's nephew John came up with a recommendation. He had just inherited the Anstey title and fortune and taken his seat in the House of Lords, where he came to hear of a man newly graduated from Cambridge who was looking for a position. Harry Anstey came to tell Benedict about it. 'I don't know anything about him, but John says he comes with good references. His patron in the House of Lords speaks highly of him.'

'Why doesn't this patron give him a position, then?' Benedict asked suspiciously, but Harry only shrugged. At the time he was in deep double mourning for his elder brother and younger sister, and had little energy to spare for such objective curiosity. Benedict and Sibella were both very busy people and the boys were disrupting everyone's routines. So Mr Wheldrake had been hired with the barest of interviews. His appearance impressed – tall and well-dressed, with an air and manner to make up for his lack of personal beauty – and his lofty way of talking, peppered with classical tags and references to acquaintances of high birth, had convinced them that they were lucky to get him.

The boys were rarely in trouble since Wheldrake's arrival, and Georgie had even begun to adopt something of his manner of loftiness and fashion. But a Morland Place tutor had other duties which the newcomer was less anxious to perform. The chapel horrified him, and the custom of daily mass he condemned as 'near Popery'. He had insisted that all the trappings be removed, and in the newly stark surroundings he consented to conduct rather brief daily prayers, and a single service on Sunday. Benedict was saddened, but Mr Wheldrake threatened to leave if he did not have his way. Benedict would not allow the ancient statue of the Lady to be removed from the Lady Chapel – he felt it might bring bad luck, a pagan notion he did not explain to the tutor – but the altar was now never decorated nor the lamp lit.

The Morland Place tutor was also expected to keep the household accounts, and to act as secretary to the master. Sibella had been struggling with the accounts since Father Moineau left, and somehow or other Mr Wheldrake never took them over from her. Paradoxically, she was too busy just keeping up with them to take the time to teach him how to do them.

Benedict was a little less retiring, and when Mr Wheldrake had been with them a month he asked him when he would be taking over his secretarial duties. Mr Wheldrake looked stern. 'Would you have me neglect the education of your sons, sir? For that is what I must do if you require me to undertake additional, secular duties. My time is finite. But if writing letters seems to you more important than educating my dear boys in their Christian and gentlemanly duties, or attending to the spiritual needs of those God has placed in your trust—'

Put like that, Benedict could only apologise, and go on managing without a secretary. There was something paralysing to the will about Wheldrake's grand manner, and doing the jobs the chaplain-tutor should have done made the master and mistress too busy to argue. The boys were well behaved when their parents saw them, and there were no complaints about them from the servants or the tenants, and that was the important thing.

It was Benedict who told Wheldrake that his charges were to be increased by one. He detained the tutor as he was leaving the breakfast table and with a rather defiant air delivered his prepared speech. 'I am taking into my household a young boy, Lennox Mynott. He is twelve years old, an orphan, and quite without family. You will educate him alongside my boys. Of course, there will be a difference between him and my sons – he has no expectations, and will have to be trained to be useful. You must equip him with suitable humility, but without giving my boys too much conceit of themselves. I leave it to your delicacy how to accommodate that difference. I wish him to be kindly treated, you understand.'

Benedict picked up the newspaper to indicate that the interview was over, but Wheldrake could not leave quite without comment. 'May I ask, sir, *why* you are taking in this child?'

'He was left to my charge. His father was – an acquaintance of mine.' Benedict rattled the paper. 'That is all. You may go now,' he said with unusual determination, and Wheldrake, for a wonder, went. It was to Sibella he made his protest.

She let him talk until she had had enough long words, and then she said briskly and a little impatiently, 'Really, it's no manner of use saying all this to me. If you have a complaint, you must make it to Mr Morland. The decision is his. I have nothing to do with it.'

'Nothing to do with the welfare of your own sons?' he asked sternly.

'Why do you think this boy poses a threat to their welfare?' she asked unguardedly, and let loose another diatribe. All she could gather was that he objected to the boy's obscurity and poverty. It hurt his pupils' standing to be educated alongside a penniless nobody, and he hinted darkly that pennilessness inevitably ran hand in hand with viciousness. She wondered whether perhaps he was worried about a reduction in his own standing, but rather than risk another half-hour's harangue, she told him again that he must argue with Mr Morland, not her, and hurried away before he could re-open his case.

Lennox arrived at Morland Place on a day of steady rain. When the carriage rolled in under the barbican he thought he was going into a prison but, as he climbed down, the glimpse he had of the façade through the darkness of the day was reassuring. Though it was large, there was nothing grim about it: it was a homely house, and over the great door was a white stone panel on which was carved a large, friendly-looking rabbit. This pleased him: he thought that perhaps they would be kind to him in a house with a rabbit over the door. He saw also, very worn but still legible, the word *Fidelitas*. Mr Anstey had impressed upon him that he was being given a home and security out of the kindness of Mr Morland's heart, and that he ought to be very grateful and humble and good in return. He looked at the rabbit, and the rabbit looked at him and seemed to wink in a friendly way, and he thought, yes, very well, I understand. I will show *fidelitas* towards Mr Morland, and his family, and the house. I will make them glad they were kind to me.

The resolve he made as he stood there in the rain waiting to be let in comforted and strengthened him, as the taking of a vow always must. But he discovered in the days to come that he needed all his courage, for apart from Mr Morland, no-one wanted him there. Mrs Morland was reserved and cold, and the servants were offhand and brusque, regarding him as nothing but extra work. But his worst trials were endured in the nursery and schoolroom. The nursery he shared with the little boys, who were eight and seven years old, and with three-year-old Henrietta and the two baby girls. He had a narrow bed at the far end, screened off from the others as though he were not fit to consort with them – and that was evidently the view of Georgie, who from the beginning treated him with startling arrogance, while good-natured Teddy followed his brother's lead in everything. Lennox was not to play with them, touch their toys or read their books, was never to draw near the fire or take a comfortable chair without their permission, was not to partake of nursery meals until they had eaten their fill and vacated the table – by which time there was not much left, for George had a large appetite. And the nursery maids supported George in this, for they adored him and saw nothing wrong with the establishing of a hierarchy.

In addition there were continuous snubs and insults to bear, being spoken to like a servant and expected to fetch and carry for a boy four years his junior – and sly pinches and kicks into the bargain, to which he must not retaliate. Despite the fact that George was stout and well fed and Lennox thin and hungry, the older boy could easily have physically subdued the younger; but he was constrained by his vow to be humble and grateful and good even more than by the fact that Georgie would report any behaviour he did not like, real or imagined, to Mr Wheldrake, who did not hesitate to administer physical punishment on Lennox's skinny frame.

Mr Wheldrake was the hardest cross to bear. The tutor hated

him with a passion Lennox could not account for and, no matter how hard he tried, Lennox could never please him, or avoid the dreaded ferrule. Lennox had been raised by a loving father whose mere frown was punishment enough for any sin: he had never been struck in his life, and worse, far worse than the pain, was the humiliation, and the bitter sense of injustice. Even in his lessons Lennox could not win approval. He was well in advance of the little boys, as he would have expected, given his age; but he soon suspected that he was well in advance of Mr Wheldrake, too. Early in their acquaintance he made the mistake of correcting the tutor when he mis-translated something in the day's portion of Virgil, and though he did it politely and humbly, Mr Wheldrake never forgave him. After that, if he made no mistakes in his work, Mr Wheldrake would manufacture some error for which to beat him; and if all else failed, he would beat him for the sin of pride, or for 'looking at me in that impudent way'.

Every night Lennox cried himself to sleep but learned to do it quietly, for if Georgie heard him, he would complain to Mr Wheldrake the next day that he had been kept awake and would not therefore be able to concentrate on his work. And Mr Wheldrake would discover in this another example of Lennox's sinful pride and selfishness which would have to be beaten out of him, for his own good.

Having settled Lennox in his nursery, Benedict felt able to forget him and return to his own concerns. Apart from the normal running of the estate, his restless spirit was always seeking to change and improve things. He was involved in several civic schemes in York, such as trying to get the new bridge built, and pressing to clear the notorious rookery of filthy courts and rotting tenements that were the Water Lanes. It was there that the outbreak of cholera had begun in 1832, the epidemic that had claimed his mother's life.

In addition to these embryonic schemes, he was building a row of model cottages for railway workers at Bishophill. This was in partnership with Lord Anstey, Harry's nephew John, who through his marriage to Benedict's ward Jemima owned a building company. It was a pet scheme with Benedict. In the 1830s and 1840s a lot of cheap housing had been quickly run up to accommodate the rapid influx of workers to the towns – Benedict himself owned a share in some in Manchester, known as the Morland Rents. Having been made with low-quality materials, much of this housing was now virtually derelict, but speculators were notoriously unwilling to involve themselves in building anything for the poor. Benedict and John Anstey wanted to prove that solid, decent, comfortable dwellings for the working classes could be built at a price that would still show a decent return to the investor.

The Bishophill cottages were being built to his own design, and would incorporate a number of ingenious improvements, including the same patent cooking-stove he was installing in all his own estate cottages. This last was precisely the sort of thing that alienated investors, who reasoned that the poor had always cooked over open fires, and that if you gave them luxuries you would spoil them for hard work. Benedict pointed out with vigour that a sick man was the worst worker in the world, and that dirt, hunger, damp and cold were the progenitors of sickness. His patent stove warmed the house, cooked the family meals and provided hot water for washing. Moreover, it worked so efficiently that the worker would actually require *less* coal, leaving more of his wages free to buy prayer-books for his children, something the prosperous classes always seemed terribly keen on, he had found.

And when he had a spare moment, Benedict liked to put his head together with the estate blacksmith and carpenter and fiddle about with ideas for machinery for farming. He had introduced a horse-powered thresher some years earlier – against the farm-workers' will at first, since threshing provided them with valuable if tiring winter work – but now that there was work in plenty for all, he wanted to design a steam thresher, a steam cider-press and a steam-powered hoe. The two former would need only a compact and efficient stationary engine, but the latter was more of a challenge, for any conventional locomotive engine was too heavy to use in the fields.

All in all, he had plenty to do, and Sibella could not understand why he must take himself off to London, as he was planning to do. She knew *why* he was going, but she rather suspected the official reason was not the real reason, and that there was something in Benedict that would never be content to stay still in one place for long. Father Moineau was his spiritual father in more ways than one, she thought to herself with a sigh.

On the eve of his departure, they received a surprise visit from Lord Batchworth. The earl's arrival at York station caused a stir, for even though York often received titled people, Lord Batchworth was an important man in the affairs of the nation, besides owning a large estate in Lancashire and a pretty slice of Manchester, including several mills. York station liked to receive persons of his lordship's mark with due ceremony, and show them that it knew how the thing should be done. When they arrived unannounced and accompanied only by a manservant, a secretary and an extremely modest amount of luggage, York station felt that it was not being given the chance to show itself to its best advantage. It felt, in fact, not a little put out, and escorted the earl's party to two common hack chaises with wounded dignity.

At Morland Place the surprise was more than equalled by the pleasure. Lord Batchworth was married to Benedict's first cousin, Rosamund, and relations had always been cordial between the two branches, though in their different spheres of life they did not often meet.

'I hope I don't put you out by arriving unannounced?' Batchworth said as he stood in the hall having his coat removed by Malton, the butler, and his trouser legs sniffed interestedly by a moving carpet of dogs.

'On the contrary,' Benedict said, 'this is treating us like real friends! I hope you have come to stay?' he added, looking at the luggage the footman was bringing in, and trying to guess from the amount how long the stay would be.

Sibella, who had been trying to remember what she had ordered for dinner, roused herself to add her urgings, and Batchworth said, 'You're very kind. I will be very glad to stay tonight. I must be in London tomorrow.'

'I'm going up to London tomorrow,' Benedict said. 'Perhaps we can travel together.'

Sibella excused herself to go and see about making the dinner more suitable for an earl, and Benedict led the way to the drawing-room.

'I hope I am really not an inconvenience?' Batchworth said. 'I can easily go to the Station Hotel.'

'No, no, I assure you, we're delighted to have you,' Benedict said.

'But at least let me send my servant and secretary to the hotel. You should not be burdened with them, too.'

'Don't think of it for a moment! The servants' hall is longing to entertain your man. I should be a twelvemonth in disgrace if I deprived them of his company.'

So Batchworth protested no more. When Malton had brought refreshments, and family news had been exchanged, he asked, 'What takes you to London tomorrow? Business or pleasure?'

'Business which *is* pleasure,' Benedict answered. 'It's the underground railway. Charles Pearson has arranged a meeting of the City Corporation; and then there's the usual round of investors to visit, and Parliament still to win over.'

'You've been trying for five years to get this particular balloon into the air, to my knowledge,' Batchworth said. 'Isn't it time to stop?'

'Nonsense!' Benedict said. 'I shan't give up until I've got my way! It's obvious that now so many railways have their termini in London, we must have a line to link them all.'

'Obvious to you, perhaps. To the rest of us, a hackney-cab seems quite sufficient to the case.'

'Yes, and look at the roads as a consequence! They were never intended to carry that volume of traffic. More often than not it's quicker to pay off the cab and walk, than to sit there and hope for movement!'

'Then what is your difficulty?' Batchworth said. 'Legs are free, aren't they?'

Benedict saw he was being teased, and laughed. 'Very well, but all the same, you can't stand in the way of progress. Our grandfathers were content to stay put, but now we've tasted the sweets of rapid movement, we will always want more. This is the age of travel! Look at the benefits the railways have brought: you wouldn't want to go back to the old days now, would you? And when the Metropolitan line is built, you will wonder how you ever did without it.'

'*If* it is built.'

'It will be. It must be. My dream is a complete circular route, linking all the termini, north and south of the river – but that's for the future. For now, I'll settle for a line from the new station at Paddington to Farringdon Street, taking in King's Cross and Euston. Imagine being able to come in to London from Bristol and depart again for Manchester without ever leaving the railway system.'

'Useful, I suppose,' Batchworth said guardedly.

'And, you know, one of the problems in clearing in the slums is that if you move the working classes out to the suburbs, they can't get in to work. With this link we can provide cheap workers' trains to bring them in and take them home. The Metropolitan Railway will change London: the slums cleared, the roads cleared, no more labour difficulties – just smooth, easy, rapid, reliable transport!'

'You make it sound idyllic,' Batchworth said when he could get a word in. 'But still, you know, an *underground* railway—'

'We can't afford to use up any more land. And to build a railway under the existing road, making double use of the route – you see the beauty of it?'

'But who in their right senses is going to choose to go down into a damp, dark, rat-infested tunnel? Even if you could build your railway, it would perish for lack of passengers. The investors would never see a penny of their money back.'

Benedict shook his head pityingly. 'They said exactly the same thing when we were building the Kilsby Tunnel. It's the purest nonsense. People just have to get used to it, like any new idea. Once the Metropolitan Railway is built, the passengers will flock to it. You only have to use your imagination.'

'Your task is to persuade Parliament,' Batchworth pointed out, 'and it's no use asking the Members of the Lower House to use their imagination. They haven't any. It's a condition of standing for election.'

Benedict's good humour was unquenchable. 'Oh well, I like a challenge. But that's enough of my concerns. I'm sure you had some special reason for calling on us.'

'Yes,' said Batchworth. 'I have some business to discuss with you, and a proposition to make – concerning the Hobsbawn Mills.'

Benedict made a polite sound of enquiry. The Hobsbawn Mills in Manchester had once belonged to his father, but they had been given to his sister Sophie as her dowry. On Sophie's death the mills had passed to her daughter Fanny, and on Fanny's marriage to her husband Philip Anthony. From the beginning, however, Benedict's father had kept a 25 per cent interest in the mills, and this now of course was controlled by Benedict, as head of the family.

'This has come up rather suddenly,' Batchworth said, 'and it's still unofficial, but Philip Anthony wants to sell his share of the mills – and indeed the whole Hobsbawn estate. He intends never to go back to Manchester, and he wants to use the money to extend his estate in Norfolk. He sees himself now as a country gentleman rather than an industrialist and he wants to improve the Norfolk estate for his son's sake.'

'This is the first I've heard of it,' Benedict said.

'I only heard of it myself this morning. Anthony's agent, John Scawton, came privately to tell me that Anthony has asked him to make discreet enquiries about a possible purchaser. That was when I had my idea, and I came straight to Morland Place.'

Benedict frowned. 'I don't understand. Why would Scawton come first to you? Does Anthony want to sell the mills to you?'

'Quite the reverse. Anthony still blames me and Rosamund for Fanny's leaving him. I'm the last person he would inform, and the very last he would sell to. Fortunately I know Scawton very well. He used to be a foreman of mine, and I've been in the way of doing him a service or two in the past. So he feels, I fancy, more loyalty to me than to his employer. In fact, it was I who got him the job as Anthony's agent – though Anthony doesn't know that, of course, or he'd never have taken him. But my influences run deep and wide in Manchester.'

'No wonder the Government values your services,' Benedict

said. 'I never knew you were such a Machiavelli! But what was the proposition you wanted to put to me?'

'I want to buy Anthony's interest in the mills, and I know he won't sell it to me. But he will have to approach you sooner or later – through Scawton, I can make sure it is sooner – because he will need your consent to the sale. When he does, I want you to buy him out. Then I will buy from you whatever proportion you please. I suppose you will want to hold on to your interest – you may even want to increase it. I would be happy to enter into a 50 per cent partnership with you, if that suited your ideas. Or I will take over the whole enterprise, just as you please. Oh, and I would like you to buy Hobsbawn House too, if he is selling it. But of course he must not know that I am involved in any way, or it will all come to nothing.'

'But what's to stop Anthony's finding another buyer, and coming to me with a *fait accompli*?'

'Leave all that to Scawton. He will convince Anthony that no-one else wants the mills, but that he thinks you will buy. You look disapproving?'

Benedict hesitated. 'I have no particular liking for the man, but I should not want to be a party to cheating anyone.'

Batchworth looked pained. 'You mistake me. I don't mean to cozen the man out of his property. I will offer him a good price, of course. The deception lies only in your not telling him that you are buying on my behalf.'

'Well, then, I suppose it's all right,' Benedict said slowly. 'But if you want to increase your property in Manchester, why must it be the Hobsbawn Mills? I'm sure there must be others, which wouldn't need an elaborate conspiracy to purchase. Or wouldn't it be better to buy some empty land and start afresh?'

The tired lines around the earl's mouth settled into grimness. 'No, it must be that estate and none other, because that's the estate he took from Fanny. And Hobsbawn House was her home. I must have them back.'

'Ah, I see,' Benedict said, though he wasn't entirely sure he did. 'It's revenge, then, is it? Once you have them, you'll make sure he knows?'

'No, not revenge. I shan't be crowing over him, if that's what you think.'

'Oh – no, I'm sorry – I didn't mean—'

'I don't want them for myself, I want them for Fanny. Once I have them, I shall put them into a trust for her, in such a way that he can never get his hands on them. And then, if I can ever find where she has gone, or if she ever comes back to us, she shall have her own again.'

Benedict had no more objections. Fanny Anthony had run away from her husband and child three years earlier and had not been heard of since. Benedict doubted that she could still be alive, for how could she support herself without the help of her friends, a girl who had been brought up in sheltered luxury and never even had to dress her own hair? But Batchworth's faith – or at least his determination to hope – was touching, and Benedict would not do anything to undermine what gave him comfort. Fanny had been like a daughter to him, and Benedict knew how much he had grieved for her.

'Certainly I'll do as you wish,' he said. They went on to discuss the plan in more detail. There was some land over towards Healaugh that Benedict had been planning to buy, but as he talked with Batchworth, he thought it might be better to put the money into taking up another quarter interest in the mills instead, and going into the 50 per cent partnership Batchworth had suggested. It never hurt to diversify one's business interests; and besides, cotton mills were full of machinery, and he loved anything to do with machinery. He had never taken much interest in the mills before, but he was sure there would be improvements to be made, especially to the steam engines. Three mills – three steam engines – and they were all pretty old. Mentally he was rubbing his hands at the thought of them.

CHAPTER THREE

When Lord Batchworth arrived in London he went first of all to see his step-daughter Charlotte, Duchess of Southport. He found her alone in the house. Oliver, the duke, was dining at his club that night; Batchworth's son Cavendish, who was still living with the Southports, was out as usual, God knew where, and his wife Alice was paying a visit with her mother to relatives in Somerset; Lady Turnhouse, Oliver's mother, was dining with the Tonbridges.

Charlotte, tired from a long day of committee meetings, had looked forward to a rare quiet evening at home and had ordered supper on a tray in her private sitting-room, but a visit from her step-father was always a pleasure. When she discovered he had not dined, she sent word to the kitchen for a second tray, but Laidler, the cook, had his pride. In a remarkably short time they found themselves sitting down to a table spread with a neat little omelet *aux herbes* for each, a dish of buttered asparagus, chicken cutlets flanked with ruffled peas, a piece of salmon under a cold sauce decorated with shrimps, a galantine of veal, a dish of mashed potatoes, a glazed lemon tart and a *blancmanger*.

Batchworth, always a good trencherman, did it all justice. He was a tall man, growing a little gaunt with age. His hair was very thick, brushed back from his face in a leonine way; it had been so very fair that its gradual change from gold to grey to white had gone unnoticed by Charlotte, but now she thought how nice a contrast it was to his brown complexion and bright blue eyes. He was a very attractive man, and warm, witty and kind to boot. She could see why her mother had fallen in love with him. It had been very hard for her at first to know that they had deceived her father together, and however badly her father had behaved later, she still felt what they had done was wrong. But she had long forgiven them, understanding at last that human relations are never simple, and impossible to judge from the outside. Hate the sin but love the sinner: that's what they had been taught, wasn't it?

They chatted at first of family matters and Charlotte's various activities. Now, as the dishes were emptying, Lord Batchworth dropped his bombshell: after this summer, he would be giving up the London house, and he and her mother would not be coming up to Town any more.

Charlotte jumped immediately to conclusions. 'Mother's ill! I knew there must be something wrong when you came up alone!'

'You are too sharp for your own good, missy! Your mother is not ill, beyond the normal trials of age. But she doesn't really enjoy London any more. Going into Society is a burden to her with her hands so bad.'

Charlotte eyed him carefully. 'You're sure that's the real reason?'

'Your mother's a proud woman. Going into Society involves eating and drinking, and she's always afraid she'll drop or spill something. She kept coming up for my sake, because I don't like to be in London without her, but she'd much sooner be at home with her horses and her moors – somewhere she can have her food cut up for her without causing comment.'

Charlotte resisted the little joke. 'You're sure you're not keeping anything from me?'

'I promise you.'

'But then why are you giving up Town as well?'

'My love, I'm nearly sixty-seven. Don't you think it's time I was put out to grass?'

'You're not a horse.'

'But I long for my green pastures as much as any weary nag. Your mother and I want to spend a few years pottering gently about the estate together while we still have health and strength.'

This at least made sense to Charlotte, who knew how much they loved each other. After a moment she said, 'It will be very strange not to see you in London. And what about Parliament? What about your committees and your good works?'

'I've done my part. It's time the younger ones took over. But I do mean to clean the rust from my lance for one last crusade before I go.'

'Oh, bravo! And what will your cause be?'

'The Divorce Bill.'

Charlotte saw he had come to the purpose of his visit. 'Begin at the beginning,' she invited.

'Very well. You know, to begin with, that the Lord Chancellor is to present a Divorce Bill to Parliament?'

'Yes, Lord Palmerston mentioned it at dinner last week. Mr Fitzalan was twitting him that he meant to bring divorce within reach of the working classes, and there was an uproar around the table. Mrs Wentworth grew quite purple. She said marriage was the only thing that kept the lower classes in tolerable order.'

'And what did Pam say to that?'

Charlotte lounged back in her chair in imitation of the Prime Minister's usual pose, and drawled, 'Divorce for the working classes? Good Gad, no! Mr Gladstone would never allow it!'

Batchworth laughed. 'You have him to a tee, my love! No, the sole purpose of the Bill is to tidy up the present muddle, with legal separations through the ecclesiastical courts and divorce through Acts of Parliament and so on. The Government wants to put the whole business into secular hands, a single law court in London to deal with all divorce and separation cases. It should make things much clearer, but certainly not easier for the working classes.'

'I should think not! How could they afford to leave their jobs and come to London?'

'To say nothing of paying for an advocate. But of course the last thing anyone wants is to see divorce becoming commonplace. That would be the greatest social curse this country was ever visited with.'

'So, what's your interest in the matter?'

'It's the perfect opportunity to try to bring in some amendments concerning the treatment of women – much easier than trying to bring them in cold in a separate Bill. I feel I have to do it, for our poor Fanny's sake. I think about her all the time.'

Charlotte had never told Batchworth that she knew what had become of Fanny. She was living at the Wellands' house in Lamb's Conduit Street; Charlotte had seen her there, in the arms of Peter Welland, and it had been obvious that she was heavily pregnant. It had been a great shock to Charlotte, and she had hurried away without letting them see her. Since then, long and painful consideration had convinced her that there was no purpose in interfering, or in telling anyone what she knew. With another man's baby, it was too late for Fanny to retrace her steps. Let her have a little peace at last, Charlotte thought, if she could find it that way.

'I think about her, too,' she said. 'But, forgive me, I don't quite see how a Divorce Bill has any relevance to her. Dr Anthony isn't proposing to divorce her, is he?'

'Why should he?' Batchworth said bitterly. 'As things stand, he has all he wanted – her fortune and her child – without having the expense of maintaining her. I want to do something for all those women the laws of matrimony treat so harshly.'

'In what way?'

He leaned forward in his animation. 'A woman with a bad

husband is helpless! He can divorce her for adultery and turn her out to live in penury and disgrace, keep her property and forbid her to see her children. But however badly *he* behaves, *she* cannot divorce *him* unless he commits bigamy or incest. He can lock her up, beat her, abuse her in any way he pleases; give away her money, keep fourteen mistresses under the same roof, frolic about decked in all the wreaths of Sodom and Gomorrah if he wishes – and she has no redress in the law at all.'

Charlotte nodded. These were hard truths. 'But that doesn't apply to Fanny. It was she who ran away and—' She stopped herself in time from adding *and committed adultery*; only she knew about that. 'There was never any suspicion that Dr Anthony committed adultery, was there?'

'No,' Batchworth said unwillingly, loath to allow Philip Anthony any stain of virtue on his character. 'But he treated her with cruelty all the same. And Fanny could not have divorced him, whatever he did to her. I want to see women have access to divorce on equal terms with men.'

'You'll have a hard job getting Parliament to accept that. Or the country at large.'

'I know, but I mean to try, at all events. And then there's the question of women's property.'

Fanny had spoken bitterly to Charlotte of the fact that as soon as she married Anthony, her entire fortune passed into his ownership for ever, leaving her dependent on him for her very pin-money. 'But do you really think Parliament would allow women to keep their fortunes on marriage? Would any man agree to marry on those terms?'

'Probably not,' he said, 'but at least we can try to alter the law with respect to the abandoned or separated wife. The husband keeps her money, and, for the rest of her life, any property she acquires or money she earns he is entitled to take from her, even if it leaves her destitute. I could tell you some harrowing stories, Charlotte, my dear. There was a woman, for instance, whose husband abandoned her and ran off to Australia with another female. The wife, to support herself, set up a school, which was eventually very successful. Then the husband, having failed in Australia, came back to England and seized all her property, including the school, and threw her out to starve.'

'Yes, I see how that could affect Fanny,' Charlotte said.

'Suppose she has begun a new life. She might even make herself a comfortable living but, at any time, Philip Anthony could seize it all.'

He reached for the decanter and refilled their glasses. Charlotte watched the stream of wine catch the candlelight as it fell into her glass, and said, 'Well, he'd have to find her first.'

Batchworth looked up, setting down the decanter. 'There's something else.' He told her about his plan to buy the Hobsbawn estate and put it in trust for Fanny. 'If ever we do find her again, I want her to have resources of her own, so that she can be independent, and choose for herself where and how to live.'

'You are very good,' Charlotte said, 'but—'

'Not good!' he said vehemently. 'I loved Fanny like my own child, and I let her down so badly. Why didn't she come to me when she left him? *Why?* She didn't trust me to protect her, and now God only knows where she is or how she's living! Anything I can do for her now must fall short of enough.'

Charlotte was silent, wondering painfully whether she should tell him what she knew. But Fanny was disgraced and ruined, whatever happened. There was no way back for her, now. And wouldn't it be worse for him to know that? Charlotte suspected that her step-father hoped rather than believed that Fanny was still alive. Better for them all that Fanny should be dead to them. And yet she hated him to suffer so. It was a terrible dilemma.

While she pondered, he had gone on, talking about his chance of success with the amendments. 'I won't be alone. There's a lot of support in the House – Lyndhurst, Thurlow, Eldon, Brougham – and we have a champion in the Commons in Gladstone.'

'Mr Gladstone? But surely he's violently against divorce?'

'Yes, he is; but as a Christian he believes that men and women must be treated equally. If there *must* be divorce, which he deplores, it ought to be on equal terms.'

'Well, I wish you luck,' Charlotte said, lifting her glass to him.

'I'll give them a bonny fight of it. One last crusade for a very elderly knight errant!' He smiled, and drank the toast. 'But I'd like more than your good wishes, love: I'd like your help.'

'Mine?' she said, startled.

'There is a group of respectable women, led by a Miss Bodichon, preparing to put pressure on Parliament. They'll attack the Commons; I'd like you to recruit support amongst the grandes dames of Society, to sway the Upper House. Will you do it, Charlotte my dear? For Fanny's sake – or, at least, in her name.'

The thing was right in itself; and Charlotte would do much for her step-father. 'Very well,' she said, 'I will do what I can.'

Batchworth reached across the table for her hand. 'That's my good girl! I knew how it would be. If Southport gives you permission – and I hope he may, because he is very liberal in his ideas about women – you can both be very useful to us. Palmerston listens to Southport. And he has a soft spot for you, you know.'

'Oliver?' she said, startled.

'No, Palmerston, you goose!'

'Oh, yes! But I don't know why you think I need Oliver's permission. He never minds what I do.'

'He may mind this, if it starts up old gossip,' Batchworth said meaningfully.

She frowned. 'You mean, about you and Mama? But nobody thinks of that now. You're accepted everywhere.'

'Not quite everywhere.'

'In any case, Oliver never heeds gossip. He doesn't care what people say.'

'I have to defer to your more intimate knowledge,' Batchworth said doubtfully, 'but I would have thought he *did* care, though he may hide it. And he may care a great deal more in the future. He is already being earmarked as the coming man, and may well be asked to form a government one day—'

'Oliver, prime minister?' Charlotte exclaimed.

'It wouldn't surprise me,' Batchworth said. 'Palmerston certainly thinks so. But of course it would depend ultimately on the Queen, and we all know that she is guided by the Prince, who has very strict notions of propriety.'

'Good heavens! It never occurred to me—' Charlotte was silent, pursuing these new and not wholly welcome thoughts. 'But I refuse to be governed by the prejudice of ignorant people. I shall help your campaign in every way I can.'

'Thank you, darling. But do ask Southport first, won't you?'

'It will be all right, I assure you.'

Charlotte found her canvassing hard going. In most drawing-rooms she was met with puzzlement or indifference, in a few with definite *froideur*. Lady Leuknor went so far as to say, 'I'm surprised at you, Duchess! Such an un-Christian notion. What God has ordained it does not behove mere mortals to tamper with.'

'The laws of divorce are made by man, not by God, ma'am,' Charlotte pointed out, which she thought must be a point to her, but Lady Leuknor merely replied, 'Precisely: by man, not by woman. It is nothing to do with us, my dear. You had much better not meddle.' And then she changed the subject so firmly that it would have been rude for Charlotte to resist.

The exercise made her realise that she did not have any friends among the ladies of the *ton*. She had a large acquaintance, of course, but mostly they tolerated her for her rank rather than liked her as a person. Outside her family her only friends were her waiting-woman, Norton, with whom she had gone through so much; and perhaps the people at the hospital, like the chief surgeon Sir Frederick Friedman. But they were not friends in the sense that she could talk to them about her inmost thoughts and feelings. It occurred to her, though without self-pity, that she had never had a friend apart from Fanny. In her childhood she had lived completely isolated, and in adulthood she lived in a stratum of society in which she would always be an outsider. Some in her position could have charmed their way in, but she had never broken the habit formed early of self-reliance.

Except, of course, that there was Oliver. Marrying him had been doubly joyful because she had not only loved him as a man, she had liked him as a friend, and to him she had always been able to unburden her heart. But lately the joy seemed to have faded. When Augusta was born the doctors said she must not have any more children, and since then she and Oliver had slept in separate rooms, which, she felt, put an unhappy distance between them. Though they had their different activities during the day, they had always come together in bed to lie embraced and talk in the safe darkness about what mattered most to them. How she missed those precious hours! She would have been glad just to share a bed with him, but Augusta had been conceived out of a moment of uncontrolled passion, and Oliver had said he would not put her at risk again in that way, and removed himself entirely from her bedchamber.

Without that regular intimate contact, it seemed that their busy lives were pulling them apart. It occurred to her suddenly that she could not remember the last time she had seen him to speak to – more than three weeks, at least. It was not an unusual thing for people of their rank: many couples, once the nursery was stocked with sufficient children, separated into discrete households, meeting only on formal occasions. It suited many people – perhaps most people, for all she knew – but not her. Having known the joy of real intimacy, she missed him dreadfully.

Oliver, of course, had always known he would be a duke one day, and had been raised in a solemn household of servants and protocol, of vast distances between rooms and between people. Oliver, perhaps, might always have expected his marriage to come to this; might even prefer it. It was hard for someone born in a cottage to know. Perhaps, she thought sadly, it was always a mistake for people to marry out of their station in life.

A few days later she was riding in the Park in the company of her secretary, Mr Temple. She liked to go out early in the morning, as her grandmother always had, before the world of fashion stirred, so that she could have her fresh air in peace and quiet. She had first asked Temple out of kindness, because he loved to ride and could not afford to keep a horse; but he was good, quiet company too, and since Oliver was never available to come with her these days, Temple made an agreeable escort.

She was surprised, but not displeased, to see Lord Palmerston approach her, riding a raking chestnut. He drew rein, doffed his hat, and said, 'Well, well. Here you are! Takin' the air? Good, good. The Park's best at this time of day, before the fools come out. Goin' to be a hot one, again.'

'Too hot, later, to be comfortable,' Charlotte concurred. 'And Wildey makes my life miserable if I get his horses in a sweat.'

'Tyrant, eh?' Palmerston glanced beyond her to her phlegmatic, nut-faced groom in his cockaded hat patiently sitting his horse at the requisite distance behind. 'Looks a positive fiend,' he said solemnly. He noticed Mr Temple now, and gave him a pleasant nod. 'How now, Jack?' Temple was a distant cousin of his. 'Keepin' your pens sharp?'

Temple's hair was that shade of pure copper the unkind call 'ginger', and he had the complexion that went with it. He blushed richly at being addressed, and bowed deeply from the waist. 'I endeavour to give satisfaction, my lord,' he said, with the slight stammer on the 'm' of 'my' which had held him back all his life. He had disappointed his parents, who had meant him for a high place in the Church; and his own ambition to stand for Parliament was equally out of reach. Though possessed of a quick intelligence, the shy and sensitive young man had seemed doomed to a life of penury when Lord Palmerston had intervened, taking the trouble, in his generous way, to bring him to the duchess's notice when she wanted a secretary. 'I don't forget, my lord,' Temple added in a low voice, 'how much I owe to you. I would not let you down for anything in the world.'

'Just so, just so,' Palmerston said. 'Excellent fellow. Well, well.' He waved away Temple's thanks. 'Goin' to use my prerogative now, and oust you from the duchess's side. Drop back, there's a good chap.' Lord Palmerston turned his horse to walk alongside Charlotte's, and Temple obediently dropped back to ride beside the Prime Minister's attendant, Colbert.

'How d'ye find young Temple, Duchess?' Palmerston enquired of Charlotte when they were far enough ahead to be private. 'Not regrettin' takin' him on trust?'

'Not in the least. He's very able. Apart from an embarrassing tendency towards gratitude, he's the perfect secretary.'

'But you were a good creature to take him on my say-so.'

'I assure you, my lord,' Charlotte smiled, 'he gives me all the thanks I can bear.'

'Then I'll mention it no more. That's a good-lookin' bay you're ridin'. Got your grandmama's eye for a horse. Always out early, your grandmama – one of the great sights of the Park, ridin' some damn' great fire-eatin' gelding, with that famous groom of hers behind.'

'Parslow,' Charlotte supplied the name for him.

'That's the fellow. Never told anyone this,' he added, bending his head closer, 'but I tried to poach him from her once. Didn't succeed, of course; but I always felt guilty.' He straightened up and smiled. 'Feel better, now I've confessed!'

'You were attempting the impossible. Parslow would never have left her,' Charlotte said. 'He taught me to ride. He was a wonderful old fellow. But tell me, sir, how can you find the time to be out riding? Don't affairs of state take up your every waking moment?'

'Precisely why I'm out early. I said to Colbert, I must have some air and exercise, if I'm to stay awake until three in the morning. Goin' to be another long day frowstin' indoors, and deuced hot again – can't think what's happened to the weather.' He eyed her under the brim of his rakishly-tilted tall hat. 'Glad I bumped into you, m'dear. Favour to ask.'

'I'm yours to command,' she said with a smile.

'Concernin' our friend Miss Nightingale. She's come up with a novel scheme for spendin' the Nightingale Fund.'

'The Fund must amount to a king's ransom by now,' Charlotte said.

'Well, a prince's ransom at least. Curious thing, the public,' Palmerston diverged thoughtfully. 'Catch people's attention, persuade them to act as one, and you may create a monster of brutality, or a monster of sentimentality. Bawlin' for someone's blood or pourin' thousands of pounds into a scheme of charity. Always a monster, though. But as to the Fund,' he resumed, 'the deuce of it is knowin' what to spend it on! Whatever you decide, some patron will kick up a fuss and say that's not what he meant at all. Sydney Herbert says Miss N would as lief give the whole thing up. Between you and me, there's a strong move to get her to leave military matters alone, and concentrate on civilian hospitals.'

'I can guess where that move originates,' Charlotte said. 'I know how hostile the army is to interference from outside.' When she had helped to nurse soldiers in the Crimea, only her rank and the personal intervention of Lord Raglan had protected her from the wrath of the senior officers.

Palmerston nodded. 'Quite so. Can't blame them, I suppose. But the thing is, I've known the Nightingales for ever, and I feel a sort of fatherly interest in the gal.'

Charlotte suppressed a smile. Miss Nightingale was not far short of forty; but of course to Lord Palmerston at seventy-two she probably did still seem like a girl. 'So you want to help her scheme along? What is it?'

'Somethin' in your line. She wants to start up a trainin' school for nurses. Probably at Thomas's. The Resident Medical Officer's on her side, but there's a lot of opposition. As *you* know, Duchess, most medicos think nurses are for scrubbin' floors, and they don't need trainin' for that. Besides which, the Senior Surgeon at Thomas's don't like the suggestion that his nurses ain't up to scratch.'

'Well, and are they?'

'Even if they ain't, he don't relish bein' told anythin' at all by a chit of a woman.'

Charlotte smiled. 'That I can imagine. So, what did you want me to do, sir?'

'Oh, nothin' too demandin'. Just put in a good word whenever the occasion arises. You have more contact with medical men than I do, and your surgeon feller, the head sawbones at your hospital, what's his name—?'

'Friedman?'

'That's the one! Friedman. He has a lot of influence, I understand?'

'Sir Frederick's a great proponent of women as nurses,' Charlotte said. 'I'm sure he'd be glad to do what he can to drum up support. I'll speak to him about it.'

Palmerston nodded. 'Grateful to you. I shall be deuced glad to get the army off my neck. And of course, the Queen and the Prince are mad for Miss Nightingale—'

'And you'd be happy to make *them* happy.'

'So the world turns,' he agreed with a smile.

'Well, I shall always be glad to do anything I can for you,' Charlotte said.

'You're a good creature,' he said. He looked at her a moment thoughtfully, and then said in a lower voice, 'You'll pardon an old man interferin', but I'm very fond of you, and Southport's as good a fellow as ever lived.' Charlotte looked surprised, and he went on, 'My dear, I hope you haven't quarrelled?'

'With Oliver? No, why should you think so?'

Palmerston hesitated delicately for a moment, and then said, 'The reason I ask, Duchess, is that I'm surprised to find you on opposite sides over this Divorce Bill. It happens in families, of course, but I don't like to see a husband and wife at war, especially when they've been the best of friends before. And, frankly, my dear, it ain't the thing. I mention it as a friend, you know, but it ain't the thing for a wife to oppose her husband in a public matter like this, even to support her step-father.'

Charlotte looked puzzled. 'You mean the Divorce Bill, I conclude? But surely Oliver isn't against the reforms?'

Palmerston studied her curiously. 'You haven't talked to him about it?'

'I would have, of course, but there hasn't been an opportunity since my step-father brought up the subject.'

Palmerston looked into the middle distance. 'Batchworth is treadin' a radical path. It won't earn him many friends, but I happen to know he means to retire from public life, so it don't matter to him. He's got Lansdowne and Brougham and Lyndhurst on his side, but most of the Lords have a very different cut to their jib, and Southport's emergin' as their leader. It's an important moment in his career.'

Charlotte looked amused. 'Was that why you asked me to help in the matter of the Nightingale Fund? To keep me out of mischief?'

'Crossed my mind,' Palmerston said.

'And how do you stand on the amendments, sir? Are you for or against?'

Palmerston, his eyes still tactfully on the horizon, said, 'Oh, I never stand for anythin' if I can help it, you know. My Bill aims to tidy up judicial procedure, that's all. I've no interest beyond that.' Now he bent a kindly eye on her. 'Take an old man's advice, my dear, and let Batchworth fight his own corner. A husband don't like his wife to be embarrassin' him.'

'I'm sure Oliver is far too strong-minded to be embarrassed by me,' Charlotte said.

Palmerston had delivered his warning, and would say no more. He lifted his hat and said, 'This is my gate comin' up, so I must leave you now, if you'll excuse me. Thank you for your company, my dear duchess. Colbert, come along! Temple, good day to you. Your servant, ma'am.'

Charlotte rode on in thoughtful silence. Could Lord Palmerston be right? Would her attempt to support her step-father embarrass Oliver? But he had married her against the grain in the first place – the daughter of a notorious divorcée – and must surely be supposed to be indifferent to Society's strictures. She couldn't believe he would ever put his career before her and, with this comforting thought, she dismissed Palmerston's warning from her mind.

★   ★   ★

Fanny felt a trickle of sweat down her spine under her corset; her front curls were stuck to her damp forehead. She was waiting with Peter on the landing outside the bedroom door. A mote-filled band of sunlight from the staircase window fell on the worn carpet, illuminating a darned patch, coarse blue wool amid the red-brown arabesques. Everything seemed darker beyond the straight edges of light, a stuffy dark smelling of dry dust.

It had been such an unseasonably warm spring, with little rain; flies and smells were at summer levels, and the backyard pump was bringing up brown water. She always seemed to be pumping water these days: two sick people in the house meant extra washing, and they couldn't afford to pay the laundress any more. Of all the household chores she had been reduced to – she who had been born to luxury, with servants at her beck and call – Fanny hated washing the most. She hated the tub and the dolly-legs, the harshness of the wooden shaft against her palms. She hated the touch and smell of dirty things, the stupid weight of wet washing, the grey and reasty water left at the end. Her shoulders ached and her arms hurt, and the sight of her poor ruined hands was enough to make her cry. But still the things were never really clean, and Harriet would sigh, and Peter would make excuses for her. She wished he wouldn't. Peter's sister Harriet thought Fanny should feel ashamed of not being able to do servants' work, but Fanny couldn't. To her it would always be servants' work, and she would always be a lady, no matter what reverses fortune forced upon her.

Extra work because Peter and Harriet's mother, and Harriet's son Boy, both lay sick with a high fever and stomach pains. Extra work because the tasks they usually did had to be done by someone else – and with Harriet doing the nursing, that meant Fanny and Peter. But much as she hated and resented the work, she would have compounded to do it twice over if only Mrs Welland and Boy could be well again.

As if he had heard his name in her thoughts, Peter suddenly took hold of her hand, making her start. His was damp and clammy, but comforting all the same. Dear Peter, kind Peter; father of baby Emma – oh God, keep my little Emma safe! She looked at him, and he met her eyes briefly and warily. He was afraid it was cholera – she knew that, though he had been careful never to say so aloud. Cholera! Back in that impossibly far-off time when, rich and philanthropic heiresses, she and her cousin Charlotte had gone slum-visiting, that word had been a whisper of fear, a whisper of death, in the seething, stinking back-kens. She knew enough to know this wasn't cholera; but that left other possibilities almost as terrifying.

The bedroom door opened and the doctor came out, and his face told nothing, either of hope or despair. In the slice of the room framed by the closing door, Fanny saw Harriet bending over the bed, a basin and cloth in her hands as she bathed her mother's face. Mrs Welland had been so kind to Fanny, taking her in, hardly ever looking reproachfully at her for living in sin with Peter. It pained Mrs Welland, who had always been God-fearing, but she held her tongue; and she loved baby Emma dearly. Fanny felt an upsurge of fondness and guilt. Had she been grateful enough to Mrs Welland? There was so much she disliked about her life here, but it was Heaven compared to living with Philip.

The doctor beckoned them away from the door and started down the stairs, walking into the bar of sunlight. It illuminated his face, revealing the tired pouchiness, the unshaven cheeks and chin, the rumpled necktie and soiled collar. Sykes was his name. They didn't know him. It seemed strange to Fanny not to know your own physician; but of course poor people could not afford doctors' fees, and sent for one only as a last resort. He was not 'their' doctor, in the sense that she had been used to, he was simply the nearest local physician who was willing to come.

'Well, sir?' Peter asked when they reached the hall. His voice snagged on his fear and he cleared his throat awkwardly.

Sykes turned and regarded them expressionlessly. His eyes were red-rimmed, and there was sweat amid the stubble on his upper lip. Fanny could see, now she was closer, the grease-stains on his jacket and the shininess at the seams, and she struggled with a natural, inbuilt distrust of a physician who was not wealthy.

'It's typhoid fever,' he said abruptly.

Fanny felt her knees tremble; Peter's hand clenched on hers. Typhoid was a killer, just as much as cholera, differing only in virulence. Cholera took you in hours, typhoid worked more slowly; but they cleared the slums, those two black hags, as efficiently as demolition workers.

Sykes looked from one to the other. 'You understand that this is very grave, very grave indeed? Typhoid fever is extremely infectious. You will have to isolate the sick people. I hope to God,' he added, but as if to himself, 'it's not the start of another epidemic.'

Peter wanted to ask, *will my mother die?* but he couldn't frame the words. His tongue seemed to be stuck to the roof of his mouth. At last he managed to say, 'How could they have caught it? We were never a *common* lodging-house.' He sounded near to tears. 'We were always respectable. But just lately we've had to take in God-knows-who from God-knows-where—'

Fanny intervened, pressing his hand to stop him. 'What can we do?'

'There is no cure, but good nursing can make a difference. I have given the instructions to that sensible-looking woman in there—' He jerked his head towards the bedroom and Harriet. 'The spots have appeared, so this is the second stage of the disease. You can expect the constipation to give way to diarrhoea, and distention and tenderness of the abdomen. Try to keep the patients clean, sponge them with cold water to bring the temperature down. Oil of cinnamon for the abdominal pains. A little brandy if you have it, if there are signs of collapse. Above all, on no account give them any solid food. The intestines become ulcerated, you see, and if they should rupture, the outlook is very poor.'

Peter was staring at him in blank horror, unable to respond. Fanny spoke for him again. 'Will they get better?'

He almost shrugged. 'If they pass through the second stage, there is a chance, provided no other complications arise.'

'Complications?'

'Rupture, internal gangrene, pneumonia, pleurisy, ulceration of the bones and joints, heart failure—' He stopped, as if realising the recital was pointless. 'The patient lives or dies by his own strength, and the mercy of God. The boy seems rather weakly for his age. And your mother is an old woman. Even in the natural course of things, nobody lives for ever. My fee is two guineas, by the way. I'll have it now, if you don't mind.'

When Peter came back from showing Sykes out, Fanny said, 'I've been thinking: that man who stayed only two nights, what was his name? Tebbit? Tebbins? He was a dirty man. We found fleas in the room afterwards. Maybe it was him.'

'Oh, what does it matter?' Peter burst out miserably. 'My mother's going to die!'

Fanny didn't know what to say. Too cruel to agree, but she couldn't tell the comforting lie with any conviction. She was very tired, and seemed to be having difficulty in feeling anything. She said at last, 'When is he coming again?'

'Sykes? He isn't, unless we call for him. He said there's nothing he can do; and we can't afford him. We haven't any money. Oh Fanny, what will we do?'

She looked at him helplessly, at his tired face, lined with worry, his untidy hair and shabby clothes, and had a sudden and vivid sense of him. He seemed more real to her than anyone she had ever known, more real than herself. Why was he asking her what to do? She supposed he just wanted reassurance; God knew, she wanted it too. If only Charlotte were here, she would know what to do; but Charlotte was lost to her for ever.

'Peter, we must tell the lodgers, and give them the chance to leave if they want.'

Peter shook his head, just once each way, like a tired horse. 'If they go, it will be the end of us.'

'Are we very poor?' she asked. The business was Mrs Welland's, but Peter had always been the book-keeper, and Fanny knew how anxious he had been lately. But in spite of everything she had been through, it was hard for her to anticipate poverty. She had been born to comfort and security, and though when she left Philip she had gone through a brief period of utter destitution, that seemed to her now like a distant bad dream. Arriving at the door of Mrs Welland's house, she had given herself up into Peter's care, and had ceased once again to think about money. Money had always simply been there; she hadn't any practice in supposing it wouldn't be.

Peter looked at her helplessly. 'The two guineas I gave the doctor were practically the last. We've bills unpaid to the butcher and the chandler, and we still haven't paid the laundry-woman. There's hardly anything coming in. Miss Sutton owes two months, and Mr Forbes three.'

'But why are things suddenly so bad? Didn't you always go on comfortably before?'

'Mr Tarbush hasn't sent us anyone for months,' he said. Much of their business had consisted of referrals from the solicitor, Tarbush, who paid highly for Mrs Welland's discretion, but lately that source had dried up. 'Casuals barely pay enough to cover their food and laundry, and Mother isn't tough enough with people like Miss Sutton and Mr Forbes who don't pay up.'

He stopped there. The arrival of Fanny and the baby had added to the burden on the family's purse; and as the gap between income and expenditure grew, they had had to let servants go, which meant Peter had to do their work, and so had no time for the legal copying which had earned the household extra income. It was a vicious circle. Attuned as she was to him just then, Fanny knew she was one of those with whom Mrs Welland ought to have been tougher. She was so slow and clumsy at housework that Harriet often said it was quicker to do without Fanny's help than with it. For a little while after she first arrived, Peter had tried to teach her law-writing, but she had stopped when she discovered she was pregnant, and had never taken it up again. And besides, she could not do it unsupervised, and Peter hadn't the time to overlook her work.

She stepped closer and put herself into his arms. 'I'm nothing but a burden to you,' she said guiltily.

'You're everything to me,' he said. It was true, but it didn't answer the accusation, and they both knew it. He sighed. 'All the same,' he said reluctantly, 'you ought to go away.'

'Go away?'

'For safety.'

'No, Peter!'

'Just until all this is over. You and the baby. You could go to your cousin Charlotte—'

'You know I can't go there. She doesn't know about us. No-one knows.' She felt him draw breath and added, 'In any case, I couldn't leave you and Harriet to do all the nursing.'

'We'd manage,' he said. 'I don't want you to go either, Fan, but if it was to save your life—'

She simplified it for him, tired of arguing. 'What use would it be to me to have my life saved, if you died? You're all that matters to me now, you and the baby. We go together or stay here together.'

They held each other tightly for a moment, like swimmers clinging to a rock as the sea threatened to wash them away. Then she sighed and drew herself away from him. 'Will you warn the lodgers – give them the chance to leave?'

'I suppose I must. I'll do it tonight.'

'And what about the servants?'

Peter looked as though one more burden would break his heart. 'Yes, them too, I suppose; though if they go I don't know what will become of us.'

'I keep praying,' she said. Then she looked at him almost timidly. 'Do you think God hears us?'

Peter knew what she was thinking: why would God trouble Himself over a man and a woman living in sin? In spite of all his own worries, his heart ached for her. It was he who had brought ruin on her; ruined her and loved her and given her a baby.

'If He doesn't hear sinners, He doesn't hear anyone at all,' he said.

'I wish I believed that.'

In the kitchen, in subdued mood, the servants, Mary and Bridget, were preparing dinner – neck-of-mutton stew with pearl barley, cold boiled bacon with pease pudding, a dish of bubble-and-squeak, and a suet pudding. Peter, busy with Boy's usual tasks of fetching coal, pumping water and laying the table, mourned the paucity of the meal, in a house that had always prided itself on its hospitality: the mutton was more bone than meat, and the bacon wouldn't go round, even with the help of a vast tub of potatoes; and the plum bolster, which Mary grandly called Spotted Dick, had so few raisins in it, it was almost unblemished. But when he ventured a hesitant

51

remark on those lines, Bridget, setting her jaw at its grimmest, said, 'Them lodgers don't pay enough to complain about their dinner – and I don't mind telling 'em so, Mr Peter, if you're too polite to do it!'

Mary looked across at him thoughtfully. 'Will they go or will they stay, d'ye think?'

'I don't know,' Peter said. 'I don't even know which to hope for. It would make things easier if they left, but—'

'Ah, let 'em go,' Bridget said largely. 'We can get a new lot when your ma's well again.'

Peter was grateful for the 'when', but he had to be frank. 'But without any money coming in, I can't pay your wages beyond the end of the month.'

Mary said quickly, 'Don't worry about that, now. You've enough to worry about. You pay us when you can. We're in no hurry. Isn't that right, Breege?'

'You're very kind,' Peter said, 'but I have to warn you that the disease is very infectious. You really ought to think about leaving the house until it's all over.'

'Ah, sure God, where would we go?' Bridget said robustly. 'And how'd you manage without us, with sickness in the house? Mary and me won't desert you, not when your ma's been so good to us all these years.'

'You're not afraid?' Peter asked, grateful and touched.

'The good Lord calls you when He's ready, no sooner, no later,' Bridget said. 'So there's nothing to be done about *that*.'

It was a comforting philosophy, Peter thought; he wished he could subscribe to it himself.

CHAPTER FOUR

In the Duchess of Southport's drawing-room, the company chatted as they waited to be called in to dinner. The guests had been invited for a half-past seven dinner – already rather fashionably late for some of the older sort, who expected to sit down in their own houses on the dot of six – and it was now ten minutes to eight o'clock.

Fortunately there was no lack of conversation to fill the void. The duke was in earnest discussion with two other landowners about the benefits of cattle-cake over grass and hay.

'But surely, Duke, it's an unnecessary expense, when grass grows for nothin'? Ain't it all just a trick by these millers and maltsters to make you buy up their leftovers?'

'No, no, I assure you! The difference in the speed of growth is astonishing. I wouldn't have believed it if I hadn't seen it with my own eyes at Ravendene.'

'I agree with you, Southport. We need oil-cake feeds if we're to have controlled growth and universal standards. Grass is too random. Regulation, science, exact measurements – that's the way forward for agriculture.'

'Science, pah! A good landlord's a good landlord, measure him how you like! I say the land's in your blood, or it ain't, and all your science won't change that.'

The duchess was on the other side of the room, at the centre of a group of people with medical connections who were discussing the origins of disease. But her mind was not really on what was being said. Part of it was testing the temperature of the room, to see that everyone was happy. The other part was focused on the door, expecting either her brother, or some message concerning him. They were only waiting for him to go in to dinner, and Laidler would be growing ever more frantic in his kitchen. At last she saw Ungar, her butler, enter the room. For a man who had spent his whole life developing a commanding presence, which could reduce an upstart caller to a jelly, Ungar could on occasion efface himself to the point of invisibility. No-one but Charlotte had noticed him;

the single glance he cast her across the drawing-room told her that something was wrong.

She moved quietly back from her group of companions – only Sir Frederick Friedman turned his head towards her as she left – and slipped like an otter through the river of flounced satin skirts, bare shoulders, black tail-coats, glittering jewels, and flashing orders on watered ribbon. When she reached Ungar's side, he bowed his head and gestured towards the door with his eyes. Outside in the corridor she said urgently, 'Lord Blithfield?' He nodded. 'Is he ill?'

'Not – *ill*, your grace,' Ungar said with delicate emphasis. 'But certainly indisposed for dinner.'

Her heart sank. 'Drunk,' she said. Oh no, Cavendish, not now, not tonight! she thought.

'Yes, your grace, I fear so.'

'How drunk?'

The words 'as a fiddler's bitch' hung on the air between them, unspoken. 'I do not think it advisable that his lordship should attempt to join the company, your grace.'

'Oh, this is a wretched business!'

Ungar's expression softened just a little. He had grown fond of the duchess over the years and did not like anyone but himself to upset her. 'I have consigned him to the care of his man, your grace. I have instructed *Huggins*,' Ungar's inflection told of his contempt for Huggins: Lord Blithfield had gone through three personal attendants in a year, and the trend was not upwards, 'to help his lordship immediately to bed.'

'I expect you did right,' Charlotte said. She thought for a moment. 'My secretary's left by now, I suppose?'

'Yes, your grace. Mr Temple went home an hour ago.'

'Well, it's much too late to get him back here. We must manage with odd numbers.' At a formal dinner seating forty, the glaringly empty chair would be a brand of failure on Charlotte, and she had been particularly anxious that this dinner should be a success, for Oliver's sake. But they couldn't keep everyone waiting any longer. 'I'll say his lordship has a feverish chill and won't be joining us. You can announce dinner at once, Ungar.'

In the general movement which followed the announcement, Oliver brushed against her to murmur, 'What is it? Where's Cavendish?'

'I'm afraid he's drunk,' she whispered unwillingly, and saw his lips tighten in disapproval. 'He's gone to bed. We'll have to say he's ill.'

The procession formed itself. Charlotte moved among the guests, guiding them to their partners. Ungar was standing by, ready with his excellent vocabulary of eye and eyebrow movements should she falter as to precedence. Cavendish's absence had unbalanced the pairs, of course, but she had in any case two extra men, since her cousin Aylesbury was a bachelor and her uncle Tom Weston was dining *en garçon*. The unmatched pair would have formed the rearguard of the procession, and it was the work of an instant to promote one of them when she reached Lady Cleveley, whom Cavendish was to have taken down. She hoped she had done it smoothly enough for no-one to notice.

When the pairs were formed, she returned to Lord Palmerston, took his arm, and nodded to Ungar to throw open the doors to the dining-saloon. Southport House had been built in the seventeenth century, with the principal rooms leading off one another. Many alterations had been made since, and corridors and stairs put in, but the grand drawing-room and dining-saloon had been left as a communicating pair.

Charlotte heard behind her a little starling flutter of comment at the sight of the table, for service *à la Russe* was still unusual: it required such large quantities of china, glass and silver, and so many servants, that only the very wealthiest could afford it. Charlotte was still divided in her opinion of it. It was less sociable than the old way, she thought; but there was no doubt that it complemented the food a great deal better, and Laidler was a very good cook.

The first glance, of course, told the wise that it was to be *à la Russe* tonight, for there were no first-course dishes on the table. It was decorated down the centre with an arrangement of palms, ferns and mosses, and candles in two-branched candelabra. In front of each place was a plate on which reposed a dinner-roll wrapped in a napkin, ranks of knives and forks of various sizes, and six different wine glasses. Between each two places was a menu-card in a silver holder, a salt-cellar, butter-dish and water-carafe.

Charlotte passed with Lord Palmerston to the head of the table, and Oliver remained at the foot, directing the guests to their places. Then he drew out Lady Palmerston's chair, and at that signal the servants, who had been standing back against the wall, stepped forward and drew out the other ladies' chairs. Lord Palmerston, however, waved the footman away and performed the office for Charlotte.

'All very well, these modern fads,' he said with a wink, 'but I ain't so decrepit I can't see to my companion myself.'

Charlotte accepted his gallantry with a distracted smile. Halfway down the table the empty chair seemed to scream for comment. Ungar had removed the covers and placed a low bowl of roses and asparagus fern, but to have completely re-laid the table to eliminate the gap would have taken too long, especially when dinner had already been delayed.

The servants were offering *hors-d'oeuvres*, together with thin slices of white and brown bread-and-butter: oysters from Whitstable, kippered salmon from Scotland, smoked-dried ham from Wiltshire, and caviare. When Ungar followed this by offering to fill Lady Palmerston's smallest glass with chilled vodka, she laughed and tapped Oliver on the wrist. 'Vodka, the Russian way! You learned this trick in St Petersburg.'

The comment fluttered up and down the table, and everyone waited to see what Lady Palmerston would do.

Oliver smiled. 'I'm sure you know there is no better accompaniment to caviare. The kippered salmon, too: it might have been designed for it. But I met so many Scotsmen in Petersburg, I wonder if the Scots and the Russians aren't related by blood?'

'But, my dear child,' she protested, 'what are you thinking of? Ladies do not drink spirits. It is quite shocking of you to suggest it.'

'Ladies, I suspect, do many things which the lower orders might consider shocking. Are we to be bound by their prejudices?' He nodded to Ungar to pour. 'You are known, ma'am, to be as bold as you are beautiful!'

'Wicked boy!' she said, but she nodded to the hovering Ungar.

'Why, ma'am,' Oliver said, wide-eyed, 'vodka is the purest spirit known to man. I assure you, it hardly counts as alcohol at all.'

Seeing that Lady Palmerston was game, the other ladies allowed their glasses to be filled, and the conversation rose to new heights as everyone discussed the daringness of the notion and the taste of the unfamiliar spirit, its suitability to the *hors-d'oeuvres*, where caviare came from, how and when the duke had been in St Petersburg, and whether *service à la Russe* really came from Russia. If there had been ice to break, it was now well and truly broken. Charlotte saw Oliver looking pleased as he discussed matters diplomatic with his immediate companions, and was glad that something he had planned had gone right. It might help to mitigate her brother's fault.

The dinner continued. Soup followed the *hors-d'oeuvres* – a choice of clear or pea, with sherry or madeira to drink. Then the fish – fried sole or boiled turbot – was served with Chablis.

'Damme, but I like this style of dining,' Lord Palmerston said, taking some sharp sauce to go with his fish. 'This sole is hot, Duchess, positively hot! I congratulate you. I wish Wellington were here tonight: he always said he hadn't had a hot meal since he left the nursery!'

Her other dinner companion, the Earl of Preston, agreed effusively with Palmerston, complimented Charlotte, and then said perversely, 'But the old way was better, in my view. There is something simple and gentlemanlike about helping your companion at table, and the master and mistress carving for their guests. It was a grand old tradition, suited to our straightforward English character.'

Palmerston gave Charlotte the ghost of a wink, and said gravely to Preston, 'You are quite right, sir. It ain't manly to have your food cut up for you by servants. We should tear up joints of meat with our bare hands as we did in ancient times. There's straightforwardness for you!'

Preston looked put out, and hardly knew how to answer. Sir Frederick Friedman, two places down from Lord Palmerston, took pity on him and leaned forward to say to Palmerston, 'What do you think about this proposed Medical Bill, sir? Has Sir Bernard spoken to you about it?'

Lady Tonbridge, sitting next to Sir Frederick, raised her eyebrows in disapproval and said, 'I protest, Sir Frederick, you are not going to be talking about diseases and such-like at dinner, are you?'

'No, ma'am, nothing like that! It's a proposal to replace the apprenticeship system with examinations.'

Mrs Wentworth – Preston's dinner companion – lifted her hands so that her diamond bracelets slipped back on her wrists and caught the light, a trick she had perfected over the years so that it seemed quite natural. 'Oh, do not pursue such a course, I implore you, Prime Minister! It would be the ruination of all one values in one's physician. Examinations are so vulgar, so—'

'So middle class,' Lady Tonbridge agreed quickly.

'Well, ma'am,' Palmerston said lazily, his eyes narrowing with amusement, 'but don't you want to know that your physician knows his stuff?'

'As it is,' Charlotte said, 'anyone can set himself up as a doctor without any training at all.'

'Oh, but my dear duchess,' Mrs Wentworth exclaimed, 'one can distinguish between the gentleman and the quack.'

Palmerston nodded helpfully. 'Your gentleman is just as ignorant, but he charges ten times as much.'

'What is this proposal, Sir Frederick?' Charlotte asked quickly, seeing Mrs Wentworth mottle.

'Sir Bernard suggests setting up a General Medical Council to register all practitioners, and to regulate and discipline them.'

'Quite unnecessary,' Lady Tonbridge pronounced. 'I assure you,

Prime Minister, one's relationship with one's physician is what cannot be legislated about. Such a Council would be useless.'

'You prefer to rely on a system of *caveat emptor*?' Sir Frederick asked.

'I agree with dear Lady Tonbridge,' said Mrs Wentworth. 'It is a matter of trust. One's physician must understand one's constitution; and beyond that there must be something more intangible, a – a spiritual bond. *That* is something that could not be measured by mere *examination*.'

The discussion rambled on while the plates were changed and the *entrées* – buttered lobster and chaudfroid of pigeon – were served. With them came salads, served on a crescent dish that fitted to the side of the plate. Charlotte was only half listening to the conversation: she was watching to see that everything was going as it should. But the servants, under Ungar's iron control, glided silently up and down the room, bowing, serving, moving away. It was like a ballet without music, she thought, and Ungar was the choreographer. Nothing was obtrusive. The footmen she knew so well seemed to have slipped off their personalities to become merely white-gloved hands which appeared and disappeared at the plateside like magic. It was impressive, she thought – and really rather funny.

Then the door to the corridor opened, and Cavendish came in. He was correctly dressed, but his face looked blotchy, and his eyes were glassy as they scanned the room. He swayed just perceptibly as he stood looking for his place. Ungar was already gliding towards him; Oliver, seeing the direction of several glances, turned in his seat; the level of conversation fell as first one speaker and then another paused to see what everyone was looking at.

'Sorry I'm late,' Cavendish said, a little too loudly. He smiled blankly around the room. 'That damned fellow of mine couldn't find my studs. Couldn't find a black cat in a snowfield, the villain!' His speech was slightly slurred. A few more voices dropped out. 'Dashed hard to find a decent man these days, don't you think? Mine's awful.'

Oliver half rose. 'You're not well,' he said in a low, firm voice. 'Go back to bed.'

Lady Palmerston, feeling for him, added gently, 'Why yes, you look quite feverish, dear Lord Blithfield. I'm sure you shouldn't be up.'

Cavendish looked at her owlishly. 'Not ill, ma'am. Never felt better in m'life.' He approached. 'Couldn't miss seein' you, dear Lady P. Your most humble servant, ma'am.' He bowed over her, lost his balance and had to put a hand clumsily on the table to steady himself, knocking into a glass. Oliver caught it just in time and set it upright again. Someone laughed nervously. Cavendish straightened, smiling engagingly. 'Sea's rough tonight,' he whispered audibly to Lady Palmerston, and winked. She suppressed a smile; Oliver scowled.

'Cavendish, go back to bed,' he said in a low, stern voice.

'Haven't had m'dinner yet,' Cavendish said, turning to walk up the room. 'Sorry I'm late. Oh, I said that. Where's my place? Damnit, Ungar, where have you put me?'

Mr Selhurst, taking pity on his hostess, spoke across the table to Tom Weston in a cheerful tone, as though nothing were happening. 'How is your crusade among the chimney-sweeps faring? I saw an advertisement the other day for a patent machine that ought to put them all out of business. Claimed it could be operated by a housemaid.'

'Not by any housemaid of mine, while I live!' Tom answered gallantly, and one or two people laughed. Someone else started up a conversation. Charlotte caught Ungar's eye with despair. Impossible to remove Cavendish without making more of a spectacle than his entrance had already made. She could only hope he would behave himself once he was sitting down.

'Oh, there it is,' Cavendish said. 'Is that my place, Ungar? What have you done with the eating-irons?' Ungar pulled out the chair and Cavendish sat down heavily. A footman whisked away the bowl of roses in the nick of time as Cavendish propped his elbows on the table. 'What's next on the menu?' He reached for it and knocked it onto the floor. Young Mrs Fitzpatrick, sitting next to him, laughed nervously, and looked uncertainly about her. Cavendish gave her a smile of piercing sweetness and leaned towards her to say something; he collided with the footman who was just about the replace the menu on the table and knocked it over again.

'Better sit still,' he confided to Mrs Fitzpatrick. 'Uncle Tom's glaring at me. You can tell me what's next on the bill of fare.'

'Duck, I think,' she whispered, rigid with embarrassment.

Cavendish sat back in his chair and the footman took the opportunity to nip in and lay his covers. 'Excellent. Excellent. Aylesbury duck.' He had some difficulty with Aylesbury. 'Cousin Aylesbury's duck. Burgundy with that, I fancy. Chambertin, I dare say. Keeps a damn fine cellar, my brother-in-law. Excellent fellow,' he added, leaning confidentially towards Mrs Fitzpatrick, 'but a bit on the stern side.' He leaned too far and his nose almost collided with her décolletage. 'Whoops!' he straightened himself with a genial grin. 'Steady, the Buffs! That's my wife over there, watching us. Have you met my wife Alice? Charming girl. Mad about me, you know.' All this was perfectly audible to Alice across the table, her eyes fixed on him with fascinated horror. 'It's good to have a loving wife to come home to. Everyone ought to get married, if they can find the right girl. 'Course, that's the tricky part, ain't it? Got to get it right, you know, because you only get one shot at it. Get the wrong person and you're stuck with her for good.'

It was spoken in an amiable tone, but all the same it could not but remind those who heard it of things the Southports variously did not want remembered. Alice lowered her eyes and her burning cheeks.

Old Lady Wendover, sitting to Cavendish's other side, rapped him on the wrist with her fan and said, 'Behave yourself, Blithfield! Come, turn this way, talk to me. Leave those young things alone. For shame to put them to the blush! Now, talk to me sensibly about horses, and let's have no more nonsense.'

Being old enough to command, and long beyond blushes, she kept Cavendish in tolerable order, for which Charlotte was profoundly thankful. But the dinner now seemed endless to her: roasts, game, *entremets* and the sweets followed in their appointed courses, and she was in agony the whole time, unable to concentrate on anything around her, hearing Cavendish's voice above everyone's, though it was only occasionally too loud. The other guests were resolutely ignoring him, talking animatedly – perhaps a little too animatedly – to cover any possible *faux pas*. But the whole evening was now a *faux pas*, Charlotte thought miserably, as the dishes were cleared for the dessert to be laid. It was no longer fashionable to eat dessert from the bare mahogany: when the last of the plates had been taken away, the slips were removed and the dessert plates laid on the unsoiled damask beneath. It saved some time, but Charlotte wished the formality of dessert might be done away with altogether, so that she might get the ladies out of the room before Cavendish did anything more outrageous.

The ices and wafers were served, the fruit, compotes and bonbons placed for the guests to help themselves; and then the thing happened which every hostess dreads at any time: a silence fell. Just for a moment no-one had anything to say; and in that silence Cavendish's voice rose with the sharp-edged clarity of a child's.

'Nothing will ever be the same,' he was saying to Lady Wendover. 'I went out there a whole man, came back a useless cripple. Ill all the time. Always tired. All my friends dead. Had to give up the army. What am I to fill my days with now?' His voice held a chilling misery; it was impossible to ignore.

Lady Wendover murmured something unheard by anyone but Cavendish, and he raised his voice a little, crossly. 'Oh stuff! S'all very well, talking about wives and children. They're just another burden. Mrs Bonito's my only comfort, but that's not enough to fill a man's life. And what was it for? That's what I want to know. What was it *for*? Queen and Country!' He raising his glass in an ironic toast; and then, noticing it was empty, side-tracked himself. 'Ungar! Empty glass here! Good God, service is getting slack in this house!'

The talk surged up as suddenly as it had fallen. No-one seemed to want to linger over dessert, and as soon as she could, Charlotte stood, catching Lady Palmerston's eye. Lady Palmerston was only too glad to obey the signal: she had not enjoyed the last half hour of Oliver's company. She led the way out, and the other ladies followed in order, with Charlotte bringing up the rear. It was impossible for Charlotte not to meet her husband's eye as she passed him; her look was imploring, his was steely. As she went through the door she snatched a last glance back and saw that Cavendish was sitting back heavily in his chair with his chin on his chest as though half asleep. She hoped with the ladies gone they might remove him without further upset.

The gentlemen were so long over their cigars that when they rejoined the ladies, the tea-tray appeared with them. Cavendish was not among them. Sir Frederick Friedman, having received his cup from the footman, walked over to Charlotte and said, 'We got him away all right, don't worry. Selhurst and I got him to his feet and he went like a lamb.'

'Oh, bless you for telling me,' Charlotte said, laying a hand impulsively on his arm. 'You are a good friend!'

'I hope so,' Friedman said, with a smile, placing his hand over hers. 'I took the liberty of going up to his room a little while later. His man didn't want to let me in at first, but I had my way in the end, and found him fast asleep. He won't stir until morning.'

Charlotte blurted out, 'It was so dreadful! Why does he do these things?'

'In my opinion his nerves are badly affected,' said Friedman. He gave a slight shrug. 'He is not the only one, by any means – though that's no comfort to you, I know. But there have been many more casualties from the Crimea than those who lost an arm or a leg. I think,' he added, looking at her closely, 'you know that. You all went into the mouth of hell and back. It leaves its mark.'

She didn't understand this remark, but her mind was in any case on Cavendish. He pressed her hand briefly. 'I'll call in the morning, if I may, and see how he is?'

He gave a slight bow and drifted away, as if they had been exchanging commonplaces. She watched him go, grateful for such a friend; and then saw that Oliver was looking at her. She turned her face towards him, but his gaze was withdrawn on the same instant, and he did not look at her again.

She slept heavily, full of troubled dreams, and woke later than her usual time. Norton came when she rang and silently handed her a restorative draught of her own devising. Charlotte looked a question.

'I didn't like the look of you last night,' Norton said. 'It seemed to me you were coming down with the fever again.' Since her return from Balaclava, Charlotte had been subject to bouts of ill-health – fever, sometimes nausea, and pains in the head and joints. It was called 'Crimean sickness' or 'Crimean fever', and the knowledge that so many of those who had served over there suffered from it was no consolation.

'I don't think so,' Charlotte said.

'Drink the potion anyway,' Norton said. 'You have the headache.'

'So I do,' Charlotte said meekly, and drank it. 'Is his grace up?'

'Gone out this half hour,' Norton said. 'Sent to the stables as soon as he woke, to go riding in the Park. I believe he told Mr Dinsdale he would breakfast at his club.'

Charlotte didn't know whether to be glad or sorry. *Avoiding me?* she wondered. But if there was unpleasantness to come over last night's events, she would sooner postpone it until she felt stronger.

Norton looked at her with sympathy. Of course she had heard the whole story about Lord Blithfield's disgrace: nothing else was being talked of in the kitchen regions, let Ungar ban the subject how he may. It was whisperingly canvassed that his grace meant to give his lordship marching orders this time: it was a wonder he had stood him so long. Dinsdale, his grace's man, though proud and officially as tight-lipped as Ungar, was not above dropping a sly hint to favoured servants, of whom Norton was one. 'His lordship's stopping in bed,' Norton went on, 'and Sir Frederick's been in to see him.'

'Already? Is he still here?'

Norton frowned at her lady's eagerness. 'No, your grace, he came and went while you were still asleep. But he left you his compliments and said he'd call later this morning to speak to you.'

Charlotte heard the rebuke – Norton only called her 'your grace' when she disapproved of something Charlotte was doing – but did not know what it was for. But she had too much on her mind to care, in any case. 'I shall get up,' she said. 'I must go and see his lordship before Sir Frederick comes again.'

'Yes, my lady, but Lord Batchworth and Mr Weston are downstairs, so p'raps you'd better see them first,' said Norton, turning back the bedclothes.

Charlotte jumped out. 'Why didn't you tell me? Hurry, get me something to wear. Have they had refreshments? Send to say I am coming. Don't let them go until I've seen them!'

'They'll wait, my lady,' Norton said stoically. 'No need to rush.'

Her step-father Lord Batchworth and her uncle Tom were standing by the window of the green sitting-room, their hands dug comfortably in their pockets, looking out into the sunlit street and chatting in low voices. They turned as Charlotte came in, and she was amazed at their appearance of unconcern.

'I hear that boy of mine disgraced himself last night?' Lord Batchworth said, coming forward to kiss Charlotte.

'How did you hear about it?'

'I told him,' Tom said. 'We came to make sure you weren't too upset.' He studied her face. 'You *look* upset. But really, you know, no-one can blame you.'

'Everyone will blame me,' she said. 'I was the hostess. I take the blame, even if there was nothing I could do.'

Unfair as it was, they knew this was true. Already in drawing-rooms all over Town ladies would have their heads together whispering that the duchess's dinner party had been a disaster; but what could you expect, given the way she was brought up?

'Your good Mrs Norton says that the sawbones has been in to see him this morning,' Lord Batchworth said. 'Is he ill? Not that wretched Crimean fever again?'

'I don't think so. I *think* he was just drunk. What puzzles me is why he did it. Why did he want to embarrass me so?'

The two men shook their heads, and Batchworth said, 'It was very bad of him, and I shall make sure he sees the error of his ways.'

'But that doesn't undo the damage,' Charlotte said. 'And who,' she remembered suddenly, 'is Mrs Bonito?'

Batchworth looked startled. 'Bella Bonito? Charlotte, my dear, I hope you are not cultivating an acquaintance with her. I know you have some queer friends, but that's going too far.'

Charlotte frowned. 'What's wrong with her?'

'She's a – well, suffice to say she's a vulgar woman and beneath your touch.'

'Vulgar she may be, but she's much in demand,' Tom commented. 'He must have plenty of rivals for her favour.'

Charlotte's eyes widened, and she said, 'You mean – she's his mistress?'

'Oh, is that the way of it?' Batchworth said, enlightened. 'I wonder he can afford it on the allowance I give him.'

'I fancy he doesn't,' Tom said wryly. 'He's been seen with a ripe bunch of fellows lately, and if he isn't winning at the cards and dice, he must be borrowing heavily somewhere.'

Charlotte was distressed. 'I can't believe that Cavendish would do such a thing. Perhaps it's just an innocent friendship.'

'One doesn't have an innocent friendship with the Mrs Bonitos of this world,' Tom said.

'But this is shocking! How can you take it so calmly?'

Tom shook his head. 'Really, Charlotte, have you learned so little of the world after all your experience of slum-visiting?'

She flushed a little. 'What the lower classes do is a different matter. If *we* do not behave better, with our advantages of wealth and education, what hope is there?'

'I think you're taking it too seriously,' Tom said. 'Granted Cavendish is being indiscreet, and someone should speak to him about it. He has got in amongst a noisy set, and it's gone to his head rather. But the thing in itself is of no importance. Men have certain urges, you know.'

'How can you say so?' Charlotte replied hotly. 'For a married man to consort with another woman is unforgivable.'

Tom gave her a rather strange look, and said, 'Ah, yes. Well, that is one point of view. Look here, Cavendish is making rather an ass of himself, but it will peter out soon enough. He isn't rich enough to hold Bella's interest for long.'

'In the meantime, he runs up debts and brings the whole family into disrepute,' Charlotte said. 'And who knows what trouble it might lead to?'

'I fancy you've kept him on too tight a rein,' Tom said mildly to his brother-in-law. 'He has no career, no responsibilities, nothing to do with himself, and yet he hasn't enough money to lead the idle life. Result, boredom.'

'If he had a larger allowance he'd simply waste more,' Batchworth said. 'No, the answer is to get him out of London entirely. I wish I could get him to come back to Grasscroft with me.'

'Why not insist you want him to learn how to run things?' Tom suggested. 'One day he'll inherit the title and the estate, and it will give him great power and freedom, as well as a large income. In his present state of mind, you couldn't be sure he'd use them well. He needs to be trained in his responsibilities.'

'The life of a country gentleman would be the best thing for his health,' Charlotte said. 'And if he learned to like it, he might live there permanently. I think Alice would like it better. She doesn't shine in London, but as a country squire's lady she might do very well. But would Cavendish agree to go?'

Tom said, 'You have the means to make him go, Batchworth: threaten to cut off his allowance. He can't live on fresh air – even if his suite at Southport House is rent-free.' He looked at Charlotte. 'And, after last night, I imagine that arrangement may be up for review.'

Charlotte was standing pensively by the window of her private sitting-room, staring out at nothing, when Oliver came in. She turned to look at him, but did not smile, still far away in her thoughts.

Oliver also looked grave. 'I saw Friedman leaving as I arrived. The man seems to haunt this house. If I didn't know better,' he went on lightly, 'I would think he was in love with you.'

'What?' She was startled out of her reverie, and remembering what she had heard that morning of Cavendish, she blushed with distress, and cried, 'No, nonsense!'

Oliver watched her reaction with interest. 'Nonsense, is it? The man's a blackguard if he *isn't* in love with you. What man could see you and not love you?'

There was something not quite right about his words, or about the delivery of them, but Charlotte had too much on her mind to wonder about it. 'He came to talk to me about Cavendish,' she said. 'Oliver, Cav's arm has been giving him great pain. Friedman thinks that's why he has been drinking so heavily, and probably why he behaved badly at dinner.'

'Friedman told you all that? I thought what happened between a doctor and his patient was confidential?'

'Cavendish told him to tell me.'

'And what, precisely, is wrong with Cavendish's arm?'

'It's his old wound. Sir Frederick says that when it first happened, the cut was so deep that it damaged the bone. The bone has become infected, and the morbidic principle—'

'The what?'

'Pus,' she clarified. 'It's working its way out through the tissues of the arm in the form of an abscess.'

'I see,' he said, with evident distaste. To hear such words from a lady's lips was bad enough, but when the lady concerned was one's wife—!

'He's seen it before in cases like this, where the bone is damaged. Apparently it's quite common. But he says it's terribly painful. The whole arm becomes infected, and it affects the joints, too. And they become swollen and painful—'

'Yes, I see. And what does Friedman recommend?'

Charlotte looked pale. 'The knife. He says that to cut down to the abscess and drain it would give relief and perhaps save the joints from more damage.'

'And why need you be told all these distressing details?'

'Cavendish wants me to be with him.'

Oliver turned away. 'Is that what you want?'

It wasn't a thing anyone would want to witness, she thought; but Cavendish had asked for her to be with him, and how could she refuse? She remembered her meeting with him that morning after her step-father and uncle had left. Cavendish was sitting up in bed, his dressing-gown draped over his shoulders. Huggins had shaved him and dressed his hair, but still he looked very ill, his face drawn, his eyes shadowed and puffy. She had entered his room prepared to be angry, but when he looked up she had flinched from the despair in his eyes, and accepted his bleak apology without protest. Then when Sir Frederick had told her about the constant attrition of pain he was suffering, she had yielded all resentment.

'I can't let him down,' she said now.

Oliver stared angrily out of the window. 'He had no right to ask you. The pair of them, indeed, had no right!'

'I must do it,' she said. 'If I weren't there, if I didn't nurse him, I would worry even more.'

He shrugged suddenly and turned from the window, looking at her sourly. 'You must do as you please, my dear. But then, you always do.'

'Oliver, that isn't fair—!'

'Where is this circus to take place? In my house?'

'No, Friedman wants to do it at the hospital. He believes very strongly that absolute cleanliness is important in cases like these.'

'Well, I should be thankful for small mercies, I suppose.'

Charlotte said desperately, 'Oliver, why are you so angry with me?'

'You can ask me that?'

'I'm so sorry that Cav behaved badly, but really, it wasn't my fault,' she said. 'I would have stopped him if I could. And now my step-papa is planning to make Cav go back to Grasscroft with him when the House rises, so he won't be bothering you any more.' She explained Batchworth's plan, and Oliver listened with grim lack of interest until her voice trailed away into silence.

Then he spoke. 'Do you notice, my dear, how everything that

has been said so far concerns you? This whole household revolves around your family and your affairs.'

'That's not true!' she cried. 'You must know that I would always do anything I could to support you in your career—'

'Oh, my career! We remember that, do we?'

She hesitated. 'I didn't know until just recently that you might be prime minister one day—'

'Who told you that?'

'My step-papa,' she said, and his mouth turned down again. 'You must tell me what I can do to help. Such things are not in my experience. You forget how I was brought up – how lately I've come to all this.'

'I am not likely to forget,' he said. 'It is forced down my throat every day. Your behaviour is not what is usually expected of a woman of your rank.'

'You once told me a duchess could do anything she liked.'

'I did not expect you to take such full advantage!' he snapped back. 'Your hospital, your slum-visiting, your activities in the missions—'

'Other ladies of rank have charitable interests,' she protested.

'Perhaps, but they don't go about it as you do. It's not so much what you do, my dear, but the way you do it. You show so clearly your contempt for Society and the conventional proprieties that no-one is in danger of forgetting your origins for a moment. But I don't complain of that. It's rather your contempt of *me* that I find difficult to accept.'

She was shocked and hurt. 'How can you say such a thing? I love you! I am your loving wife!'

'That, alas, is something you could not be mistaken for. Every day brings fresh evidence that you prefer to ally yourself with your family and against me. Your brother's behaviour last night was all of a piece with it.'

'But what have I *done*?'

'Specifically? I wonder I should have to tell you. Are you not quite deliberately opposing me over the Divorce Bill? Do you deny that you have been touring the drawing-rooms of the *ton* trying to drum up support for the amendments?'

'Why should I deny it?'

'Setting yourself up in direct opposition to me; allying yourself with the likes of Caroline Norton; reminding everyone daily of the scandal of your mother's adultery and divorce? And you ask me what you have done.'

She was scarlet now with pain and mortification. 'How could you throw that in my face? Was I responsible for what my mother did?'

'You need not keep it so fresh in everyone's memory!'

'So now you want me to deny my mother?'

'I have never asked you for that,' he said angrily. 'I have accepted her, and Batchworth, and your brother, even into my house, and defended them against criticism when I could. But when you directly oppose me over the Divorce Bill, that is an overt and public act which I cannot ignore.'

'I don't want you to defend my family!' she cried, beside herself. 'If they are not good enough for you – if *I* am not good enough for you—!'

'Charlotte, behave yourself. You are hysterical,' he said in a hard voice.

She closed her lips tightly and took some deep breaths. 'What do you want me to do?' she asked at last, quietly.

'Repudiate your step-father's cause. Declare yourself mistaken in having supported it. And – for a few weeks, at least – do not visit him, or receive him.'

She stared at him. If he had given her a soft look, or a soft word, she would have yielded, for she missed him dreadfully. But he only stared at her implacably, and her spirit stiffened. 'No,' she said. 'I can't do that. You can't ask me to act against my conscience.'

He looked a moment longer, and then turned away. 'Then there's nothing more to say,' he said.

She did not believe that he would walk out without any further word. Then she waited for him to come back, sure he would feel that he could not leave her like that. She waited on past the moment when she could believe he would come, because if he did not, she didn't know what else to do.

CHAPTER FIVE

Peter and Fanny sat facing Harriet across the dining-room table. The house was still. Bridget was somewhere about, weeping over baby Emma – Fanny knew that without having to check. She was glad Emma provided Bridget with some comfort, and glad, too, to have the baby looked after. She was *so* tired. It was hot, too, and humid, and her hairpins were sticking into her scalp, but she was too lethargic to go upstairs and adjust them. The table was bare except for the brown felt under-cloth, and she rested her forearms on it, and longed to lower her head onto them and sleep.

She was pregnant again, though she couldn't really feel much about it yet. When she told Peter that she had been sick, she had frightened him badly. 'Sick? Dear God, Fanny, not you too!'

'No, no,' she said quickly, 'you don't understand. I'm not feverish. I was sick for another reason.'

His frown slowly cleared as he caught her drift. 'You mean—?'

'Yes, I think so. Bridget agrees with me.'

He had folded her silently in his arms then and held her tightly. They clung together for comfort as much as in joy, for how could they really want another child now? At last he said gravely, 'This changes things. You will have to go away now. With another child on the way, we can't take the chance of your falling ill. You must see that.'

'Well, I don't,' she said stubbornly. 'Don't *you* see that, now more than ever, I must be with you?' She eyed him defiantly a moment, and then added, 'Besides, the situation is no different from before: even if I were willing to leave you, where on earth would I go?'

He had no answer to that, and so she was still here; a part, however helpless, of this family conference.

'Well?' Harriet said. Her voice was flat, without inflection. 'What do we do now?' The cruel sunlight smiled in at the window, picking out the rub-marks on the wallpaper, the chips in the paint, the lines in Harriet's face which had grown deeper over the last month, the grey in her hair which had almost eclipsed the brown.

Peter shook his head. 'I don't know. How can you ask me to think?'

Fanny slid her hand onto his knee under the table. It was meant more as an encouragement than a comfort. She wanted to say: 'You *must* think: you are the man. You must decide for us and tell us what to do.' But she still felt like the outsider when Peter and Harriet spoke together; and she hadn't as much right as them to mourn. Boy was dead; had died a terrible death, burning with fever, convulsing in the swamp of his own bloody emissions. His ulcerated intestines had ruptured and he had died within an hour. Horrible as it was – and Fanny wouldn't let herself think about it, for the baby's sake – she couldn't help wondering if it was not preferable to the way Mrs Welland had died, lingering on into the third week to prostration and collapse, her body wasted away to a parcel of bones, moaning in delirium and twitching uncontrollably as the typhoid infected her nervous system.

They had spent precious money on a funeral for Boy: as Bridget said, when someone died young, you had to give them a good send-off, because they'd had nothing else in life. Fanny remembered that evening so clearly, walking with Peter behind the coffin, Harriet and Mr Forbes the only other mourners. The other lodgers had left when Peter first told them about the typhoid, and the servants had stayed at home to nurse Mrs Welland. Two boys carrying torches before, and four bearers, were all they could afford, and they had walked all the way to the graveyard – horses cost the earth – between the curious eyes of passers-by. At the graveside Fanny remembered thinking of all the horses she had taken for granted all her life. She had been put onto her first pony when she was three years old; she had followed hounds when she was eight. Would Emma ever ride a horse? No, her daughter would never know that pleasure. And then she had thought suddenly of Boy's terrible end: would her daughter even live to adulthood?

The day after the funeral, Mr Forbes packed his bags and left – slipped out without a word to anyone, whether because he was too upset at Boy's death, or because he owed rent, was to be wondered. It meant one less mouth to feed, Peter said. Their butcher had cut them off, but they could get bones for soup from a rather inferior shop a little further off. Bridget complained about cooking 'pauper's soup', as she called it, more than about having to eat it. She complained all the time about little unimportant things, so that she wouldn't have to think about the bad one, that Mary, her companion of twenty years, had taken the sickness too.

They had had to get the doctor in to Mary: one could not do less for a faithful servant, though there was nothing he could do but repeat the previous advice. So when Mrs Welland died, there was nothing left for a funeral, and she went to a pauper's grave. Peter felt it very much; Fanny thought that by then Harriet was too shocked and weary to feel anything. At night she held him in her arms and felt his silent suffering and wished he would cry. He had grown thin, she felt that, too. Pauper's soup and boiled potatoes was what they were living on. Fanny was doing the cooking now, terrified she would burn or gash herself. Only the rich, she had discovered, could afford to be careless with their bodies.

And now Mary was dead. They had been resigned to a pauper's grave for her, but Bridget, weeping, had produced a little money she had saved out of her wages against an emergency.

'I would have given it to you for food next week,' she said to Harriet, putting the small purse in her hand and covering it with her own.

'I couldn't have taken it,' Harriet said automatically.

'Sure you could,' Bridget said, 'but now Mary needs it more.' They had come over on the boat together, Mary and Bridget, after the bad harvest of 1838; met by chance at the foot of the gangplank and took an instant liking to each other, and had worked together ever since. After Mary's funeral, Bridget said she thought she might go back to Ireland to see her brothers and sisters again: without Mary, there was nothing to keep her here. But that was three days ago, and between doing a little desultory housework she had alternately moped about the house and wept over little Emma, showing no sign of taking her leave. It was more or less what they had all been doing; a lethargy of shock and grief was on them.

But now Harriet had said, 'Well?'

Fanny waited for Peter to speak, but he just sat with his head resting in his hands and his eyes shut, so she said, 'It looks as though the sickness has passed over, please God.' There had been a couple of dozen cases, according to the doctor who came for Mary; a small epidemic, brought on by the warm weather, he thought. The Welland house was the only one in Lamb's Conduit Street to be affected, and the doctor put it down to the smells in the privy, and recommended burning tar or brimstone in there.

'We've got the house. We can get some more lodgers, can't we, and start again?' Fanny asked, looking from one to the other.

'I don't know whether Mr Tarbush would send us any more people now Mother's gone,' Harriet said.

'He hasn't sent us anyone for months anyway,' Peter said. 'I think he's done with us. I think he took offence when we asked if he'd take Boy on as a clerk.'

Harriet's eye glittered at this implied criticism: she had desperately wanted her son to do well, to be better than his father, and Boy had had a fancy for the law. It had been the obvious thing to do, to apply for help to their patron in the legal profession. 'Of course he didn't take offence,' she snapped. 'He only had to say no – which he did – and there was an end of it. You don't know much about the law if you think lawyers run on sentiment.'

'I should think I know a great deal more than you,' Peter flared in his turn. 'Doing law-writing I've met hundreds of solicitors. You've never stepped outside the house.'

'When did you last do any law-writing? If you'd kept it up, we might not be in the trouble we're in now.'

'Oh, don't!' Fanny burst in. 'Please don't quarrel! Aren't things difficult enough without that?' They both fell silent. Fanny went on, 'Even if we can't get any more people from Mr Tarbush, there are other lodgers, aren't there?'

Harriet looked at Fanny and wondered for a brief and sour moment about her use of the word *we*. What had Fanny ever done but bring them expense and worry? She was no use about the house, and with one baby already and another on the way, all she contributed was more mouths to feed. And yet she sat there looking at them, waiting for them to reassure her that they would earn a living for her, like a baby bird with its mouth open, expecting the worm.

But she didn't say any of those things. She had not been accustomed to speaking her thoughts and, besides, Peter loved Fanny, and Harriet would not willingly hurt him. So she said, 'That's all very well, but if we take in lodgers we have to feed them, and we haven't any money to buy food.'

'We can borrow it,' Fanny said brightly. 'Can't we? Surely someone would lend us money, just for a short time? They'd know we were bound to repay it.' Harriet could hardly begin to correct this statement. Fanny saw her face and added quickly, 'Or perhaps we could sell something?'

Harriet pulled herself together. 'It's plain we must do something.' Both of them looked at her hopefully. 'We must get some more lodgers. If Mr Tarbush won't send us any, we shall have to get recommendations elsewhere. And, for immediate funds, your idea is good, Fanny. If we sell the furniture in Mother's room, it should be enough to pay the food bills and extend our credit. I shall get myself some outside work – cleaning, or whatever I can – and you will have to do the work here until we're back on our feet.'

'We'll manage,' Fanny said. 'I know I'm not very good at anything, but somehow we will.' She looked a moment at her hands, and Harriet felt a small unwilling tug of sympathy for her. What constituted courage, she thought, depended very much on where you started from.

'Very well,' Harriet said. 'First of all we must clean the house from top to bottom, to make sure there's no disease lingering. Tomorrow I'll put on my best bonnet and go and see Mr Tarbush. And, if that's no good, I'll go and find a job.'

She got up, and Fanny followed suit; Peter sighed and eventually dragged himself to his feet. He felt so tired and hopeless, and he wondered how the women could be so sanguine – Fanny even looked cheerful – in the face of such ruin. He supposed that with Fanny it was a consequence of her condition, or perhaps she simply did not realise how badly they were faring; with Harriet, he could only suppose it was sheer bleak courage.

Fanny did feel cheerful that day and the next, cleaning the house. There was a sense of clearing the decks and starting afresh which suited her personality and her condition – the nesting-instinct made her want to empty cupboards, rearrange rooms and make everything tidy. The hard work also suited Bridget, who rolled up her sleeves and scrubbed floors with an energy that suggested she was scrubbing her grief out of her soul.

To Peter fell the task of sorting through his mother's belongings and setting aside what could be sold, which perhaps accounted for his continued melancholy. It was not energetic enough to be a catharsis, and it encouraged him to mourn over her little trinkets, packets of letters and personal mementoes. Harriet's application to Mr Tarbush was not a success. She could not gain admission to the presence, and when she insisted that a message was sent in to him, all that came back was a vague reply that 'he would see what he could do', which she translated as a refusal. She shrugged, squared her shoulders, and went looking for work, and without too much difficulty got herself taken on as a chambermaid and general help at a small hotel in Holborn. The wages were not large and the hours were long, but she would have two meals a day provided, and from her experience as an employer, she guessed there would be parcels of food to be taken home from the kitchens at the end of the day.

Selling Mrs Welland's walnut bed, tallboy and wardrobe pro-duced funds enough to pay the food bills and restock the larder, and while Fanny and Bridget continued with the cleaning, Peter went out to place advertisements in suitable windows, and to pass the word amongst fellow lodging-house-keepers that they were ready to take in again. He came back in the evening more cheerful, feeling better for having got out of the house and spoken to people who had not just been bereaved. They were sitting round the table waiting for Harriet to come home so that they could put supper on, when there was a thunderous pounding at the front door.

Fanny jumped up, pale with alarm, and Bridget stuck her head out from the kitchen. 'Lord sakes, what is it now?'

'It can't be Harriet,' Fanny said. The banging began again, with violent sounds as if someone was kicking the door with heavy boots. 'Oh Peter, go and answer before they break it in!'

Peter got up, picking up the poker as a precaution, for he was not a tall man; Fanny lingered in the hall behind him, and Bridget came up behind her, wiping her hands on her apron. When the door was opened, there stood two villainous-looking characters in shabby clothes and scuffed hats, one fat and bursting out of an incongruous green-velvet jacket, the other thin and greasy with a red, lumpy face and a wall eye. If they're the new lodgers, Fanny thought hysterically, we are done for!

'Name of Welland?' the fat one said. He had a notebook in his hand, and licked a pencil in a preparatory way, as though to mark down the answer.

'I am Peter Welland,' Peter said, trying to sound stern, though the apprehension was clear in his voice. 'What do you mean by pounding on the door like that? If you have damaged our paintwork—'

'Cometh right to the point, don't he, Mr Denton?' the fat one said admiringly to his companion. He had a lisp, which seemed to Fanny to make him somehow more frightening.

'He does, Mr Deggs, he does,' the thin one said, leering. 'Right to the point.'

'Becauth,' Deggs turned back to Peter, 'it ain't your paintwork, and that'th all about it.'

'What are you talking about?' Peter snapped. 'Speak sense or get out of here, before I call the constable.'

Denton pushed his hat to the back of his head and scratched his scalp. 'Tell him the tale, Mr Deggs, since he asks so civil.'

'Thertainly I will, Mr Denton, thinth *you* athk.' He turned to Peter and smiled – an unpleasant thing full of missing teeth and wet, fat lips – which sent his chins cascading over his dirty necktie. 'Mr Denton and me ith here on behalf of Mr Holland Perceval, which ith the owner of thith 'ere dethirable dwelling. It hath come to the notith of the aforethaid Mr Perceval that the tenant of thith 'ere aforementioned habitument—'

'In effect, this 'ouse,' Denton intervened.

'—Mrs Martha Welland, hath laid down the mortal coil—'

'In effect, your ma's dead—'

'—and the leathe granted to the aforementioned tenant fallth in with her thaid detheath,' Deggs finished triumphantly. 'You are therefore ithued with notith to quit. The property mutht be vacated by midnight tomorrow.'

'But you can't do this!' Peter cried. 'You can't just evict us. My wife is with child – we have a little girl. Where would we go?'

'Not our problem, cully,' Deggs said, abandoning his quasi-legal mode.

'We don't know,' Denton said, 'and we don't care. If you're still 'ere when the notice expires, we'll 'ave to chuck you out.'

'You can't do that,' Peter said again, sounding more sure of himself.

Deggs handed him a document folded legal-style, longways. 'Notith to quit.' Another, rather greasy and dog-eared. 'Denton and me'th lithenth. And notith of dithtraint if you don't cough up a little matter of rent owed. All done ath it should be, and there'th the mark o' the Bench, which you'll reckernithe, I don't wonder.'

'Mr Perceval's an understanding man, but 'e wants 'is money,' Denton said. 'That's fair, ain't it?'

Peter had been looking at the documents distractedly, but he looked up at Perceval's name. 'That's it! I'll go and see him, explain it's a mistake. We're not much in arrears, we can pay it off in a week or two, once we're back on our feet. We're carrying on with our mother's business, you see. Mr Perceval won't want to lose good tenants like us.'

Deggs grinned ever wider. 'You can *athk*,' he said, 'but it won't get you nowhere. Leathe was to Mrs W personal, fallth in on her death. Mr P wantth you out, and that'th it and all about it.'

'Got another tenant lined up,' Denton said. 'Putting the rent up. Leases like this 'ere—' he turned and spat on the ground – 'ain't worth tiddly. Keep 'em moving, keep the rent goin' up, that's the way to prosper.'

Deggs removed his smile as though wiping grease from his chin. 'You'd better thtart packing, 'cauthe you don't want Mr Denton helping you out the door when the time cometh. I'm a gentle thoul, wouldn't hurt a puthy cat, but Mr Denton'th a cruel man, and I can't guarantee to hold him back.'

'And if you ain't coughed up the owing,' Denton said with satisfaction, 'we'll 'ave your 'ouse'old goods to cover it.'

They gave one last covetous look at what they could see through the door, and went away.

When Harriet arrived home half an hour later, she found them all sitting round the table, dazed and afraid. Bridget had been crying,

75

Fanny was pale, Peter ready, as he told her what had happened, to burst into belated fury.

'I'll go and see Perceval first thing tomorrow,' he said. 'He won't throw us out. He can't!'

Harriet shook her head slowly, thinking over the story. 'If he wanted to distrain the furnishings, why did he give us notice? Whoever heard of bailiffs giving notice? We could remove everything before the deadline, and then he'd get nothing.'

Fanny met her eyes, and saw the point she was making. 'He wants us out,' she said, 'and this is his way of making sure we go without giving him any trouble.'

Harriet nodded. 'That's how it seems to me. I know Mother had this lease on very favourable terms. It was something that was arranged through Mr Tarbush with Mr Perceval's father. I don't know the details of it, but it looks as though now old Mr Perceval's dead, and Mr Tarbush doesn't want us any more, young Mr Perceval wants his house back.'

'If he just wants more rent, maybe we could still manage it,' Peter said, 'once we're back on our feet, and we've got some decent lodgers in. Mother was always too soft on the ones that didn't pay. We'll get new carpets and put our prices up. I'll go and see Perceval tomorrow, and explain it all to him. He'll see sense.'

Harriet and Fanny only looked at him, while Bridget continued to rock Emma in her arms, her head bent and her eyes closed. All three plainly thought Peter was whistling in the wind. The only difference between them was that Bridget and Harriet knew how much trouble they were in, and Fanny didn't.

Friedman wanted to operate as soon as possible, and Cavendish wanted it over with; so early the next morning brother and sister went to the hospital together. Dr Reynolds assisted, and Snow gave the anaesthetic. Once Cavendish was insensible, Snow told Charlotte she could leave the room if she wanted: Cavendish would not know whether she were there or not.

'I promised him I would stay with him,' she said. 'Please proceed, Sir Frederick. I shan't faint.'

'I know you won't,' Friedman said, pausing an instant to give her a look of warm approval before bending to his work.

It was a foul and bloody business; worse, to Charlotte, than the things she had witnessed in the Crimea, not only because it was her brother, but because it was so deliberate: such calculated mutilation was somehow more upsetting than the frenzied post-battle butchery of the field hospital. Yet there was a fascination, too, and despite her resolve not to look, Friedman's commentary as he worked drew her eyes to the operation site to see what he was doing. He worked quickly: anaesthesia was a risky business, and the longer the insensibility the greater the danger.

When it was over, Cavendish was carried to a room on the private floor below and put to bed to recover from the chloroform. Snow went with him; Charlotte accompanied Friedman to his room to hear his report.

'Well, sir, how do you think it went?' she asked him impatiently as he poured sherry for them both. She took the glass from him absently; her mind could hold nothing but her brother for the moment.

Friedman sipped thoughtfully. 'Well enough, though I had hoped for more drainage from the wound. But as you saw, I put in a bristle before I sutured the wound, so perhaps he may get further relief over the next few days.'

Charlotte managed to put down her glass before sitting very abruptly in the nearest chair. Friedman flung himself down beside her, seizing her icy hands and rubbing them vigorously.

'No wonder you are faint! I should not have let Lord Blithfield persuade me to ask you. What can I do? Shall I call for your maid?'

She shook her head. 'No, I'm all right.' But she wasn't; she felt dizzy again and wanted to put her head down in her lap. The blood drained from her face and she fell forward; there was a roaring in her ears and everything went black and red and horrid. When she recovered her senses a few moments later, she was in Sir Frederick's arms, with her head resting on his shoulder.

She gave a little cry of alarm and tried to pull away, but he held her tighter and said in a calm, sensible voice, 'No, no, just keep still or you will go off again. I suspect it was the fumes of the chloroform. Just rest a moment until your head has cleared.'

His arms felt strong and warm and reassuring, and it was a long time since she had been held close to a man's chest. She knew she ought not to, but she couldn't help herself: she relaxed again, letting her head rest against his shoulder. One of his hands was holding her wrist, his fingers curled over, feeling her pulse. At last he said, with a chuckle in his voice, 'I will tell you when your heart stops fluttering. Don't worry, it is a medical emergency, after all.'

She pulled herself quickly away, her cheeks burning. What had she been thinking of? If someone had walked in and caught her *in flagrante* she could not have been more embarrassed. 'Thank you, Sir Frederick,' she said, trying to be icily formal, but sounding, even to her own ears, merely fluttered, like a foolish girl, 'I am quite recovered now.'

'Indeed, ma'am,' he said, 'I am very pleased to hear it.' He got up at once, and his words were perfectly respectful, but there was, she thought, something in the tone of his voice. She had encouraged familiarity, and everything was now as awkward and unpleasant as could be. She didn't know where to look or what to say.

'I had better go and see how my brother is,' she said hastily.

'Allow me to escort you to him,' Sir Frederick said. He opened the door for her and bowed, his face neutral.

Charlotte suddenly felt foolish: she had over-reacted. This was Sir Frederick Friedman, the eminent surgeon, whom she had known on a professional basis for five years. There was nothing in the least impertinent in his bearing. She had fainted, he had caught her, that was all; and when he said it was a medical emergency, he was speaking the literal truth. How silly he would think her if he knew what a fuss she was making in her head over something so trivial! So she paused as she passed him, and made herself meet his eyes, to show that she was as unmoved by the unimportant incident as he was.

His eyes were very dark, and seemed unusually bright; warm and full of feeling. They held her gaze, and all her loneliness cried out for understanding and companionship, for fellow-feeling; for love. She seemed to sink into them as into a dark, warm embrace. 'Thank you,' she said faintly.

He made a little movement of his hand. 'I would do anything to serve you,' he said softly. It might have signified nothing in particular, but she knew what it meant. Just for a moment she had betrayed herself, and he had felt it. He knew.

There was little for her to do in the way of nursing. The pain was so appalling that all Cavendish could do was to lie with gritted teeth, sweating with it. There was no room in his life for anything else. He stared ahead of him blankly, lost in an iron world which only he inhabited, without hope of release. He reminded Charlotte horribly of an animal caught in a leg trap. Any movement or touch caused him to cry out with agony; when she had to do anything for him, she half thought he would bite her in desperation, as a leg-held fox will.

Huggins was of no use: Charlotte turned, as always, to the calm strength of Mrs Norton. They knew each other's ways so well now that they hardly needed to speak. Alice begged to be allowed to help, and Charlotte, who was often sorry for her, felt she had no right to exclude her, and let her make herself useful by fetching and carrying and holding things. She did not allow her to touch Cavendish, of course, and she rather suspected Alice was glad of that; and when there was anything disagreeable to do, she made sure Alice was out of the room. Alice's mental state was not of the strongest, though she was well enough if not agitated.

Cavendish had not wanted his parents told about the operation until he was over the worst, and Charlotte had honoured his wish; but it was not possible to keep such a thing private in London. Lord Batchworth arrived on the day after the operation in a state of great anxiety, having been asked at his club how his son was. Charlotte took him in quietly when Cavendish was asleep, and Batchworth stood at the end of the bed, watching his son's uneasy rest. Charlotte saw the tears sliding down her step-father's cheeks, and could not bear it. Batchworth was a wealthy man, an influential man, with a lifetime of achievement in public works behind him, but all that mattered of him and to him was lying there in the bed, suffering.

Outside, Batchworth wiped his eyes and blew his nose and said sensibly, 'We had better not tell your mother. Not yet, at least. It would upset her too much, and there's nothing she could do. When he's a little better.'

'I agree,' Charlotte said. It was necessary for them to say 'when he's better', though they both knew the dangers. It would be apparent in a few days whether he would live or die; then, either way, they could send for Rosamund.

On the second day Cavendish's temperature rose steeply. Friedman said it was 'operation fever' caused by the shock of the intrusion, and was to be expected. Charlotte tried not to worry; told herself that at least it meant her brother was less aware of the pain. There followed two days of acute anxiety which blotted out all other thought. Lord Batchworth came and went; Oliver appeared, to make enquiries and offer sympathy – a little stiffly, like one unaccustomed to the exercise, but Charlotte was glad of the attention. Oliver's mother sent a message but did not come in person: she liked Cavendish but went out of her way to avoid Charlotte.

But then the fever began to come down, and the pain became merely horrible instead of appalling, and at the end of a week Friedman expressed himself cautiously optimistic. Cavendish heard him heavy-lidded, locked in a lassitude of sickness, and barely answered his questions. When Charlotte escorted the surgeon from the room, he asked for a word with her in private, and she led the way to a small sitting-room that she and Norton had used when they had nursed Cavendish on his return from the Crimea.

Friedman did not waste time with preambles. As soon as she had closed the door he began, 'The wound did not drain as much as I expected; but, however, there are signs that the inflammation is coming down, so perhaps there was less pus than I supposed.'

'His arm still feels very hot to me, when I change the bandages,' Charlotte said anxiously.

'It will do so as long as the bristle is in. It causes an irritation to the tissue; but the wound must heal from the inside outwards, or we have done our work for nothing. I shall begin to withdraw it, and another week should see considerable progress.'

Charlotte nodded, surveying his face. 'You think he will recover fully?'

'Provided there is no mortification, I have every hope that he will. But it will be a long business,' he said. 'I wouldn't have you look for him to be out of bed in a matter of days.'

'No, I understand that.'

'He may become restless and want to resume his old ways before he is fully ready. He must be discouraged.'

'I understand.'

'And he must be kept on a low diet, and no heating liquors, or I cannot answer for the consequences.'

'You mean, he must not resume his career as a rake,' Charlotte said. 'My step-father will be going down to the country when the House rises. I hope very much that my brother will be persuaded to go with him.'

'It would be the best thing for him,' Friedman said. 'Complete rest and country air would set him up. It would be the best thing for you, too.'

It was at that moment that he stepped from being the surgeon attending her brother to being the man in whose arms, for however brief a moment, she had found comfort. She felt her heart tighten and dampness start in her palms.

'I shall do well enough,' she said.

'Your nerves are already strained by your experiences. You cannot carry the burden all alone. Let me help you.'

'No, I can't. Please don't ask me,' she said in a low voice. She knew at once she had said the wrong thing. He could have been speaking purely as a physician, but she had acknowledged that he wasn't.

'I will do whatever you wish,' he said deliberately. She did not speak, standing very stiffly, staring at him with a troubled expression. She did not know how delicately he was treading. She was a married woman, a duchess, wife of an extremely powerful man. If he made a false step, if she recoiled from him in outrage, he would be ruined, personally, professionally, for ever. Yet she would give him no sign – no clear sign, at least – and he had the choice of withdrawing the tentative step he had taken, or risking everything on his instincts. But he couldn't withdraw. She dragged at his soul. She was so strong and beautiful, and so troubled. He felt her suffering like a thorn embedded in his own flesh, and it impelled him, like the cry of a child in pain. He could not ignore it. He needed to comfort her.

He said, 'I understand that Lady Batchworth has been sent for?'

She moved her head, as though the direction of the question surprised her. 'Yes. She will be here by tomorrow evening.'

'She could take care of him, then, could she not? One of the nurses from the hospital could be sent to help her.'

'Yes, but—?'

'You ought to have a break from your cares, or your health will suffer. You ought to go into the country to rest.'

'His grace won't leave while the Divorce Bill debate is going on. Lord Palmerston means to get the Bill through this session.'

He bowed his head and said no more. She was so enigmatic, and he was terrified of offending her.

The stifling, uncomfortable weeks of the hottest summer in memory dragged by, and the House did not rise. Sitting from noon until two in the morning day after day in that airless chamber was exhausting, but Palmerston seemed determined to get the Divorce Bill through in some form, though no-one knew why he was taking so much trouble over it. Day after day the sessions went on, amendment after amendment was put up, fiercely debated, dissected, put together again, diluted, rejected and resurrected in a new body; and day by day the Bill mutated into something very different from what had first been introduced. Palmerston kept the Government benches filled, using every resource of charm, force and political barter. Over the weeks the House thinned noticeably, as the members who were not under coercion drifted away to the cool of their country seats. London was emptying as fast: the usual summer peace hung over the baking streets, and row upon row of shutters gave the great houses the appearance of having their eyes fast shut.

Cavendish improved only slowly, suffering from the heat as much as anyone. Charlotte's home circle was thinning: Lady Turnhouse had yielded to the weather and gone down to Ravendene, taking Mrs Phipps and Alice with her – Alice had not wanted to leave, but her health was poor, and she could always be bullied by one or other of the dowagers, so the two of them together were irresistible. They took also the six children – five Southports and Cavendish's son – together with the usual concomitant of governess, head nurserymaid, six under-nurserymaids, cook, laundress, two grooms, and vast quantities of luggage, which made transporting the nursery somewhat like organising a military manoeuvre.

Tom Weston had gone to Morland Place with Emily and Tommy, and not a bit too soon for his own liking, for Emily had been intermittently unwell all year. She had contracted a fever in January which seemed to keep coming back, and the doctors were unable to say what it was. He blamed her visits to the mission house. As the hot weather went on and the poor festered in their filthy slums, she went to the mission more often, he worried about her more, and the only way out of the circle was to take her away from London altogether.

Rosamund was all ready and eager to take Cavendish home to Grasscroft in July when he suffered a setback and relapsed with a high temperature, his arm again so painful that the lightest touch made him cry out in the terrible, toneless agony of the fevered child. Friedman came to examine him, and brought in Dr Snow and Sir James Clark, the Queen's medical attendant, for second and third opinions. They agreed that another operation was necessary. This time it was done at Southport House – Cavendish was too ill to be moved – and Sir James rejected any nonsense about having the duchess present. Interested parties were banished from the room, and a Southport nurse brought up from the hospital. Charlotte, her mother and step-father waited below in the green drawing-room for what seemed an endless age. Oliver came in from time to time to enquire if there were any news – he was not due at the House until two o'clock – and he was in the room when Friedman finally appeared to report.

Charlotte went to him at once. 'Tell me quickly, is he alive?'

'He is alive. His heart is strong, thank God, but the operation was difficult and protracted. It will have been a great shock to his system.'

She gave him her hand, and he covered it with his. Both of them were perfectly unaware of this gesture. 'What was it? Another abscess?'

'Several pieces of bone had sloughed from the damaged part and caused the inflammation of the tissue. But the infection was local. There was no new abscess.'

'That's good, isn't it?' she asked urgently.

'Yes, it's good. The pieces of bone have been removed, and we hope that full drainage will occur and healing will follow.'

'Thank you,' she said, and she turned away and went to her mother. 'You hear that, Mama?'

Rosamund answered her absently, having more questions for Friedman, so many they tumbled out over one another. Oliver

82

stood a little separate from the group, listening; but his eyes went from the surgeon to his wife and back again, and his attention was more on their faces than the words that were being spoken.

At last when a pause was reached, he said, with a bow to Rosamund, 'I am very glad that the news is good, and I hope it will soon be better still.'

'Yes, you must wish us at Jericho,' Rosamund said bluntly. 'After all the trouble we have been to you, you must long to have your house to yourself again. But we are very grateful.'

'You can't think I meant that,' he said. 'Ask for anything you need: Ungar will see it is provided. And now I must take my leave of you, ma'am. I am due at the House. Batchworth, will you walk along with me?'

'Yes, I should go,' Jesmond said to his wife, 'if you can manage without me, my love? It will be an important debate this afternoon.'

The two men left, and Charlotte remarked, 'Isn't it wonderfully civilised that they can walk off together like that, when they are on opposite sides of the debate?'

Rosamund made no answer – she had more questions to ask of Sir Frederick – but one small part of her mind had noticed, and was only waiting for the leisure to ponder, the fact that Oliver, after dealing so politely with her and Jesmond, had not taken leave of either Charlotte or Friedman.

By the time July turned into August, seven-eighths of the Members of Parliament had slipped away, and all but ninety peers; the rump sat, close to exhaustion, grappling with another raft of amendments to the Bill. Cavendish's improvement had been more marked since the second operation, though he was suffering from a great lassitude and general weakness. But the arm was plainly healing, and Friedman pronounced himself happy to see Cavendish removed from London and his immediate care. Rosamund had wanted to wait for the House to rise so that she could have Jesmond's support on the journey home, but since Palmerston seemed willing to keep the House sitting for ever, if need be, it seemed better to get Cavendish out of the heat and smells of London as soon as possible.

What she herself would do, Charlotte had not decided. It would depend on Oliver's plans, of course, and he had not mentioned them. She had a nervous feeling, which she pushed to the back of her mind, that they would not include her; and if they did not, it would say something very fundamental about their marriage, something she did not want to think about. Her life was in suspension, waiting for the Divorce Bill to be passed. In the weariness and heat of that summer, she sometimes confused the two in her mind, and felt that it was Parliament that would decide whether Oliver went on loving her, or whether their lives moved irreversibly apart.

Towards the end of August another outbreak of typhoid in the poor streets around Soho filled the wards of the Middlesex Hospital to overflowing, and since the Southport was not so inundated at the time, Charlotte and Sir Frederick Friedman went to the Middlesex to help. Afterwards she offered to drive him home in her carriage. As they passed the end of Soho Square she suddenly rapped on the roof, and as the carriage jerked to a halt she opened the door and jumped down before the footman had had a chance to reach her.

As she stepped onto the flagway the heat struck her ringingly like a brass cymbal. The glare coming up from the paving-stones made her squint, and she could feel them burning through the soles of her shoes. A cab was standing at the kerbside, and between the shafts the horse was drooping, its head down, its tongue protruding, its thin flanks heaving. On the box a cabman with a red and bristly face looked at her as she approached.

'Your horse is in a very poor state,' she addressed him sternly.

'It's the 'eat, mum,' the man mumbled. ''E don't like it.'

'None of us does,' she said, 'but look how thin he is. I don't think you're feeding him properly.'

'I does me best, mum,' the man protested, his voice slipping into a practised whine. 'I gives 'im what I can, but the trufe is, 'e comes 'ome too tired in this wevver to eat.'

'Then you must take him home sooner, and give him a cooling mash.'

'I got to earn me rent, mum. It's 'ard in the summer, when the nobs is all aht o' tahn, ter take enough. We juss 'as ter stick it aht, mum, me as well as 'im, till we've got enough fer the rent.'

Charlotte frowned, knowing there was truth in this. 'How much more do you need today?' she asked.

'Two pahnd, afore we can knock orf,' he said, but a gleam of hope had come into his eyes. He was watching her hand, not her face.

'Very well,' she said, digging into her reticule, 'then here's three, *if* you promise me you will go straight home and give that wretched horse some water, and feed him well when it's cooler.' She calculated that if she gave him two, he might carry on in the hope of some more good luck, but three might persuade him to keep his word.

'You're wery kind, mum. Wery kind,' he said, holding out his hand, which was as black as the reins and rather shinier.

She still held on to the money. 'Promise me.'

'Ho! Yuss, I promises all right.'

'Bible oath?' she insisted.

He seemed impressed. 'Bible oath,' he agreed. 'I'll take 'im straight 'ome. You're a Christian, mum, and I take it wery kind.'

Satisfied, Charlotte put the money into his hand, watched until he had driven off, and then turned away, finding Sir Frederick standing behind her. He had got down from the coach after her, in case she needed protection. 'That was nobly done of you,' he said.

'Noble, nonsense,' she said briskly, but he insisted.

'No suffering is too small for you to notice, and where you can help, you do so, in a practical fashion, without preaching. *That* is true philanthropy.'

'You must not flatter me, Sir Frederick.'

'I don't flatter,' he said quietly, and to her astonishment he took her hand and lifted it to his lips. 'You must allow me to tell you how much I admire you.'

It was an extraordinary thing to do in such a public place, and it forced her to consider him clearly, in a way she had not done before. He was very attractive – perhaps twenty years her senior but no less appealing for that to one who was in need of understanding and comfort: a man in full vigour, with the firm features of natural authority, and the warm eyes of one who knew how to love. Unpractised as she was, she understood that he was tacitly offering himself to her, and she did not know just then what to do about him, or with him. She remembered that Lady Friedman had died some years ago, and though it came to her as a random thought, it shocked her that she had thought of it at all, as though there were any possibility that she could be tempted to—

It was at that moment that she saw Oliver. She saw him through the carriage, through the small gap between the horses and the foot-board, through various other moving vehicles and the width of the road distant, but she would have known him anywhere, and her eye jumped to him over Friedman's shoulder as one's eye will always leap to one's own name in a page of words. He was walking along the flagway, alone, and as she watched he turned into the opening of Soho Square and disappeared from her view. He had not looked in her direction, but still she turned pale and snatched her hand back from Sir Frederick's. 'I must go home,' she gasped.

He saw her stricken face, and did not know what to make of it. She did not seem affronted or offended by him, more as though disturbed by a private thought and, on the whole, he felt that was encouraging. He must be careful not to frighten her.

'The heat is too much for you,' he said in a voice of comfortable concern. 'You should go straight home. Allow me to help you into the carriage.' The footman, Perrin, was holding the door, his face expressionless. When he had handed her up, Sir Frederick stood back. 'Don't concern yourself with me. I will walk to my house – it's only a step. If I may, I shall enquire after you later.' He nodded to Perrin, who closed the carriage door and then got up behind. Charlotte had not said a word. She was looking dazed, but as the carriage jerked into motion she looked at him quickly and smiled, and mouthed a 'thank you', and he bowed, feeling satisfied with progress made.

CHAPTER SIX

Charlotte came down early the next morning to find her step-father waiting for her. He looked pale and fagged, but his smile was triumphant.

'It's done!' he said. 'The Bill is through. The last amendments were accepted by a margin of forty-six to forty-four.'

Charlotte crossed the room to kiss him and offer her congratulations. 'You must be glad it's all over. You look horribly tired.'

'I haven't slept yet since the House rose. I've been back to St James's Square to bathe and change my linen, that's all. There's so much to do, but I thought I'd come and tell you the news first.'

'Did you get all you want?' she asked.

'Oh no – but then we knew we shouldn't. The times are not ready for complete equality before the law for women. But even a few steps in the right direction are worth while.'

'Can I offer you some breakfast? I was just going to have mine.'

'Some coffee, perhaps. I can't stay long.'

Charlotte rang, and Ungar, who had anticipated her, brought in enough for two and laid the little table in the window with coffee, chocolate, toast, muffins and fruit preserves. They ate companionably while Batchworth told her about the Act.

'Most importantly from our point of view, the property of a divorced or separated woman is now protected. So if we should ever find our poor Fanny again, she can have her inheritance back, and keep it. Anthony won't simply be able to seize it all.'

'I'm glad,' Charlotte said. That gave her something new to think about, but not now. 'Go on about the Act.'

'This comes too late for Fanny,' Batchworth said, pouring himself coffee, 'but in future the husband won't automatically have custody of the children, however vicious or brutal he may be. The new secular court will have the power to award custody to either parent, and to guarantee the right to visit to the other.'

'It's a cruel thing for a woman to be separated from her children.'

'Yes, I know,' Batchworth said. 'I watched your mother suffer all those years. And, in a different way, you suffered too, though you perhaps didn't know it at the time,' he added, looking at her across the rim of his cup. 'Your life would have been very different if you could have seen your mother, even if only from time to time.'

Charlotte acknowledged the truth of that. She had not grown up without love, but she had grown up largely without the expression of it, and she realised it had had its effect on her. These changes in the law had come too late for her, too.

'And have you managed to get rid of Crim. Con.? It is a dreadful law.'

'There will still be an action for damages available to a husband against his wife's seducer,' Batchworth said, 'though it won't be called Criminal Conversation. But the important difference is that the wife will have the right to defend herself, to have counsel and call witnesses. That I consider a huge step forward.'

'But surely an action for damages still assumes a wife is her husband's property?'

'Yes, I'm afraid so. But that merely reflects the way most people think. And a wife may still be divorced by her husband for adultery alone, whereas for her to divorce him there must be aggravating circumstances. No equality there,' he sighed. 'I wish it were not so, but, you know, the majority of people – women as well as men – still believe that different rules apply. Even Mrs Norton affirms the absolute superiority of men over women as a Christian tenet – and she has enough reason, poor woman, to think otherwise.'

'Men have the strength, the energy, the will and the education to go out and battle with the world,' Charlotte reasoned. 'How many women could do the same?'

'You have done it,' he pointed out.

'But my circumstances were unusual.'

'True, I suppose. Well,' he went on, buttering toast, 'at least we've been able to extend the list of aggravating circumstances. To bigamy and incest we have added desertion for a period of two years, and cruelty – both physical and mental.'

They discussed the details a little further, and then Charlotte said, 'Well, you have struck a great blow for oppressed women.'

'My last crusade,' he said, smiling. 'And now this very rickety knight errant can go back to Grasscroft and hang up his lance. It will be for decoration only in future.'

'I suppose you'll want to leave as soon as possible?'

'I shall stay up a few days longer. The lease continues until the end of the month, and I have some goodbyes to say.'

'I shall miss you,' she said. 'I shall be sorry not to have you close at hand. But you look tired.'

'I am more tired than you, at your green age, can have the least idea of,' he said with a tender smile. 'But the country will revive me. Will you be coming down later?'

'I don't know what Oliver's plans are,' she said, and it came out naturally enough not to sound like an evasion of the question. 'As a matter of fact, I haven't seen him yet this morning.'

Batchworth looked thoughtful. 'He didn't seem very happy at the end of the session. He walked off in a great hurry – brushed past me without even seeing me, in fact. He didn't seem himself all through the last debate. But I suppose none of us feels quite as cheerful as we did three months ago. It has been a long, hard haul.'

When Lord Batchworth had gone, Charlotte checked with Ungar, who said that his grace had not come home from the House that morning. Charlotte supposed he must have gone straight to his club, and she was surprised he had not been back to bathe and change first. But then a more unwelcome possibility occurred to her. She tried to dismiss it from her mind, but it kept coming back to haunt her. Finally, as she was dictating letters to her secretary, her voice slowed and stopped, and when he looked up questioningly she said, 'Temple, if I were to ask you a question, would you answer it honestly?'

'I would always endeavour to satisfy your grace in anything within my power,' he said.

'Yes; but that is not quite what I meant,' she said, looking at him thoughtfully.

Poor Temple blushed. 'I – I am not sure I understand, your grace.'

'I want to know something. I think it is something you may know, but may be unwilling to tell me. But if you are really eager to serve me, you will overcome that unwillingness.' Temple said nothing, but his eyes were steady, though his face was hot. 'It seems my brother Lord Blithfield, before his recent illness, was having a – a relationship with a Mrs Bonito. Did you know about that?'

A swift look of relief crossed his face, which she noted with a defeating sense of sadness. It told her almost all she needed to know.

'I – I did know it,' he admitted.

'All the world knew it but me, I conclude,' she said with a rueful smile.

'Oh no, your grace. But within his lordship's circle, it was known. It would not be a thing which would be expected to come to the ear of a lady.'

'But his lordship was not discreet,' Charlotte said. Temple seemed to assent to the rider. 'A more discreet affair, however, might still be common property within a gentleman's circle?' Temple assented to that, too, but his eyes were now wary. He sensed he was being led towards a trap. 'If his grace, for instance, were visiting a female of Mrs Bonito's mark—?'

'Oh, your grace, I'm sure—' Temple began earnestly, but she stopped him with an upheld hand.

'Don't perjure yourself, Mr Temple. I appreciate the difficulty of your position, and I understand how unwilling you might be to cause me pain. But you have often said you are grateful to me and wish to serve me. If that is so, you will tell me the truth. I assure you no-one will ever know what you have said to me. You shall not suffer for it.' He was silent, his eyes down. 'Your silence tells me that there is something to know. If there were no woman in the case, you would say so.'

He raised his eyes. 'Oh, your grace, please,' he said helplessly.

'Very well,' she said. 'I won't torment you any further. And you need not be unhappy – I knew already. I saw him myself, going to her house, but at the time I didn't make the connection in my mind.'

'Your grace,' he said desperately, 'I'm sure it doesn't mean anything to him.'

'Ah,' she said sadly, 'but it means something to me. Shall we go on with the letter? I have forgotten what I said last. Read back what we have so far.'

Oliver remained absent all day. Charlotte was on her way upstairs to dress for the evening when she finally heard the sounds of his return in the vestibule below. After some conversation with Ungar he came running up the stairs, and caught up with her at her dressing-room door.

'I would like to speak with you,' he said, stony-faced.

'Yes, and I would like to speak to you,' she said. 'But we are expected at the Malmesburys, and you're very late. The dressing-bell has gone. Where were you?'

'Never mind; we are not concerned with my conduct,' he said shortly, and taking hold of her wrist he guided her ungently into the dressing-room and closed the door.

She turned to face him. 'I heard that the Divorce Bill was finally passed this morning,' she began.

'And where had you that?' he asked unpleasantly.

'My step-papa called here this morning and told me all about it.'

'Ah yes, Lord Batchworth. What a profound influence he must have had on the formation of your character!'

She didn't understand him and chose to ignore the remark. 'The point is that I did not hear it from you. You have not been here since the House rose.'

He made an abrupt gesture to stop her, and then strode to the door between the dressing-room and her bedchamber and flung it open. Norton was moving about the bedroom, and he dismissed her curtly. 'Go downstairs. Your mistress will ring for you when you're wanted.'

Norton flung him a startled glance and went away, and as Oliver shut the door again Charlotte, angry at his high-handedness, said, 'We haven't time for this now. We'll be late for the Malmesburys.'

'Then we shall be late,' he said, turning to face her, folding his arms grimly across his chest. He stared at her with such a hard expression it was almost like hatred. 'First I want an explanation of your conduct.'

'Of *my* conduct? I have no idea what you're talking about. You can't mean to object to my receiving my step-father?'

Oliver went on as though she hadn't spoken. 'You thought you could pass unseen through London, didn't you, my lady? But you forgot how well known you are, particularly amongst the lowest forms of life. Ironic, isn't it, that the very stratum of society you pride yourself on helping should have been the one to betray you?'

'Oliver, what are you talking about?' she said, but a touch of foreboding was like a cold, empty space in her chest.

'It was not wise, madam, to get into an altercation with a cabman over your fare: your voice was overheard and recognised. Oh, yes, that startled you! An extremely vile specimen of street life, who happened to be hanging around the street when you changed from the cab to your own carriage, recognised the Duchess of Southport from her philanthropic visits to the rookeries. He noted everything and most obligingly came and told me all about your assignation – for a handsome sum, of course. He offered me first refusal, before the gossip pages of the newspapers. Though, of course,' he added thoughtfully, 'he may still go to them, when he has spent the money I gave him.'

Her first reaction was anger. 'You paid money to a low footpad not to spread vile slander about me?'

Oliver was watching her face with hooded eyes, calculating his words and her reactions. 'You must take me for a Johnny Raw, my dear. Of course I should not have parted with actual coin of the realm had it not been a confirmation of what I already knew.'

'You knew nothing, for there is nothing to know,' she said angrily.

'I've observed on many occasions how fond you are of Sir Frederick, and he of you. The lingering glances, the touch of hands – and, after all, you spend a great many hours in each other's company. What could be more natural than that you should fall in love?' What he read in her face at those words he translated as guilt, as acknowledgement that his dart had struck the target. 'But really, my dear, to be kissing the man in the street, and arranging your next tryst without regard to who might be listening—'

She gasped. 'Oliver, that is *not* what happened! How could you think it? I swear—'

'Oh, don't swear,' he stopped her, turning away with an expression of disgust. 'Spare me that, at least.'

She was silent, not knowing what to say. It was such a travesty of the truth that she did not know how to begin putting it straight. Whatever she said would only make her sound more guilty. She waited, breathing deeply, until she could be sure of controlling her voice, and then said, 'If you will take the trouble of asking Perrin or John Coachman what happened—'

'No doubt your servants will be loyal to you,' he said in a flat voice. 'I'm sure you would not have invoked their testimony otherwise.'

'But how can I answer this horrible charge if you disbelieve everything I say?' she cried in frustration. 'I am condemned without a hearing.'

He turned back to look at her thoughtfully. 'Is it so horrible? I would not blame any woman for finding Sir Frederick attractive.'

'It is horrible to suggest I would let him kiss me in the public street,' she said impatiently.

'Of course, you would prefer him only to kiss you in private.'

'That's not what I meant! You're twisting my words!'

'Careful, my dear, you are beginning to sound shrill. That is a mark of desperation. Do you wish me to believe my informant invented the whole thing? Invented the kiss? Or that Sir Frederick said he would see you at his house the next time? Quite a feat of imagination for an uneducated man.'

Charlotte was beginning to feel punch-drunk. 'He kissed my hand,' she said, 'that's all. I can't remember exactly what was said – it was a conversation too trivial to remember – but it was nothing like what you were told. And I hadn't changed vehicles. I was never in the cab. I got down from my carriage to talk to the cabman about his horse—' Oliver's stubborn, closed face showed he did not believe a word of it. The frustration of not being able

92

to make herself believed was bitter. 'Oh, I don't know why I am taking the trouble to refute such a ridiculous charge!' she cried.

'Yes, I was wondering that myself,' Oliver said. 'It can only be because it needs refuting. And really, my dear, you ought to have thought out your story beforehand. It is neither coherent nor credible.'

'It doesn't matter what I say, you are determined to believe what you want!'

He stepped closer, and his height hanging over her was menacing, like a mountain about to fall. 'Do you think I *want* to believe that my wife is having an affair? That she is bent on making me look a fool and a poltroon by conducting her amours in the harsh light of full public notice – and with a man so far beneath me it could not be a more pointed insult? And at such a time, too: knowing as you do that my future career is in the balance, you could not have made it more plain what you think of me!'

But Charlotte was no longer listening to him. Close to she could smell cigar smoke on his clothes and brandy on his breath; but more than that she could smell a woman's scent, otto of roses, hanging about him. Otto of roses – it was the proof, if she had needed it, of where he had been all day. 'You've been with *her*, haven't you?' she said in a low, hard voice. 'From the House straight into Mrs Galbraith's arms, without even coming home to change your linen! Or perhaps you keep a wardrobe there, for convenience? You have the gall to accuse me, on the flimsiest of evidence, which is no evidence at all, of what you are doing yourself?'

'Do not think to quiz me, madam!' he snapped. 'My relations with Maria Galbraith are none of your business.'

'How long?' she asked, as though he had not spoken. 'How long have you been seeing her this time?' A thought occurred to her, shocking as icy water thrown in her face. 'My God, or did you never give her up? You told me before we married that you wouldn't see her again, and like a green fool I believed you! But you've been seeing her all along, haven't you? You never really gave her up at all.'

'I will not discuss Maria with you,' he began.

'No, I'm sure you would sooner not have your own sin thrown into the balance when you wish to accuse me of the same thing.'

'It is not the same thing at all. The cases are not parallel.'

'It is exactly the same!' Her eyes filled with tears as she thought of him in Mrs Galbraith's arms. 'Oh, Oliver, how could you? When you think how it all began for us, how could you lie with her?'

He ground his teeth with exasperation. 'How? How? Because we no longer share a bed, Charlotte, or had that escaped your notice?'

He saw how much that hurt her, and it made him angrier. 'Why do you force me to say these things? For God's sake, did you expect me to remain celibate for the rest of my life?'

'*Yes!*' she cried. '*Yes!* If I have to, then so must you!'

'Oh, don't be childish,' he said shortly.

She would not cry. She forced the tears down, dragging in a deep breath. 'Childish, you call it? I call it a matter of simple justice,' she said. 'I am denied your bed just as much as you are mine.'

He lowered his voice too. 'It's different for a man. If you don't know that by now, you know nothing. A man has a different nature from a woman.'

'Are we animals, then, to be governed by our natures?'

'You have nothing to complain about,' he said impatiently. 'I give you no cause for rebuke. I am discreet. I don't flaunt my mistresses in front of you. I don't seduce the housemaids.'

'But Oliver, if you love me—!' she began, anguished.

'It has nothing to do with love,' he interrupted impatiently.

'It has everything to do with love! How can you separate the two?'

'Now you are talking like a dairymaid. Try to remember you are a duchess.'

'I do remember it,' she said. She tried to control her trembling and speak reasonably. 'Some women – most women – have no means to secure a living except by marrying; their husband provides them with everything, and they must repay him with humility and obedience. They must accept whatever he does. But that was never the way it was between *us*. I had independent means, I had no need to marry. We met and married as equals. That was *our* bargain.'

'A woman is not a man's equal, and never will be, and since everyone else in the country agrees on that, I suggest you learn to accept it.'

'I am not concerned with what anyone else thinks! I *chose* to marry you as much as you chose to marry me. I have no reason to be grateful to you. I may be a duchess now, but I was a countess in my own right before that.'

'Ah yes, how you hated to give up that title!' he said bitterly. 'If I had realised how hard it would be for you to accept my name and rank, I wouldn't have asked you. But, foolishly, I thought you would be proud to be Duchess of Southport.'

She saw the hurt in his eyes, behind the anger; there was something here she had not known about, some long hidden pain she did not understand. She softened towards him, instinctively wanting to comfort him.

'I *was* proud. And I was very happy. But lately – lately I've been so lonely. You left me, Oliver.'

'I have never left you,' he said in surprise.

'Yes, you have. In everything that matters,' she said quietly.

He looked at her for a moment, and she thought their minds were touching again. But then he said, 'And your response to this *absence*, as you imagine it, is to start a blatant affair with a public figure? To put everything at risk – my name, my reputation, my career, my children's future? If it was not lubricity but spite, that makes it even worse! You fool, don't you realise the harm that a scandal like this can do?'

'But I have not had an affair! I have not been unfaithful to you!' she cried.

'I beg leave to believe differently,' he said sourly.

She would not humiliate herself by protesting further. What use was argument? There was such a distance between them in understanding, it seemed impossible to cross it. 'How have we come to this?' she said at last.

He stared at her unhappily. 'Nothing remains the same for ever.'

'Is that all the answer you have for me?'

'It's all the answer there is.'

'Then there's nothing more to be said.' She turned away.

'Wait!' She paused, her back still half-turned to him. 'Do you mean to carry on with this Friedman of yours?'

'Do you mean to carry on with this Galbraith of yours?'

'I tell you, the cases are not parallel,' he said in frustration. 'Why can't you understand that? A man in my position is entitled to keep a mistress. No-one would expect me to remain celibate for ever – no-one but you! And I have been discreet.'

'You are mistaken,' she said coldly. 'I have known for months. I just didn't want to believe it.'

'If you insist on being unreasonable,' he said harshly, 'then understand this: you are still my wife, and you will remain my wife. I will not have a scandal.' She said nothing, waiting. 'Let us behave like civilised people,' he said in a gentler voice. 'There's no need to hurt each other.'

She turned back. 'What do you mean to do?' she asked wearily. The hurt, she thought, was already done. But he meant hurt of a different kind – the social kind. That was what mattered to him now, evidently. Her love had no value for him, her happiness was no concern of his.

'I shall go down to Ravendene for the rest of the summer,' he said. 'You may come too, of course—' He paused, waiting for her to respond, but she said nothing, and the small softening that had come to his face and voice disappeared. 'Well, then, you may do as you please.'

'Thank you,' she said. It sounded ironic.

'But I would ask you to maintain appearances,' he went on harshly. 'You will behave with circumspection; you will behave like the Duchess of Southport, if that is not too difficult for you. Speak to no-one of what may have passed between us privately. The world is not to know our business.' She inclined her head stiffly, unwilling to concede him anything, but knowing it was right. 'And if you must go on seeing—' He couldn't phrase it in any way that would tolerate being spoken aloud. 'Do what you must do, but for God's sake be more discreet. Give the world nothing to talk about.'

She found, unexpectedly, that it was still possible to feel more hurt. It hurt her worse that he was prepared to accept her having an affair than it had hurt to be suspected of it. While he had cared enough to want to stop her, there had been a little solid ground under her feet. Now she was falling through a void.

He turned away. 'We had better dress,' he said, and his voice was almost normal. How did he manage that? 'Can you be ready in three-quarters of an hour? Very well, I will order the carriage, and send a note round to Lady Malmesbury that we shall be late. Thank God at any rate that this will be the last engagement in Town!'

And he bowed and left her.

CHAPTER SEVEN

Charlotte decided to go down to her cousin Aylesbury's place at Wolvercote. 'Aylesbury's in Scotland,' she explained to Sir Frederick when she took leave of him at the hospital, 'but there's always a staff. I could be quiet there – walk and ride and recover my spirits.'

She had thought that she would feel awkward meeting Sir Frederick again after the dreadful scene with Oliver, but in fact as soon as she set eyes on him, she felt quite at ease. It was odd: he felt real and warm and near in her mind – a friend, yes, as once Oliver had been a friend and was now a stranger. She couldn't talk to Oliver any more. He had become cold, irritable, unaccountable, opaque. To Sir Frederick she could say anything – well, almost anything. She could not, of course, tell him about her quarrel with Oliver, but that was rather a function of her relationship with Oliver than of her relationship with Sir Frederick.

Sir Frederick said, 'Yes, I know the country there well. My brother has a small manor-house at Summertown, though no-one ever uses it but me, so it has come to seem like my country retreat. It's rather isolated, at the end of a lane and set about by trees, but across the fields it's only about a mile from Wolvercote.'

'I thought as the summer's almost over, I had better go some-where not far from London,' she said, grateful that he had not asked why she was not going to Ravendene. 'And what a summer it has been! I feel such a need of greenness.'

'As a medical man, even though I'm not your physician, I have no hesitation in prescribing you a course of green fields and quiet rides – and no large formal dinners or balls,' he added sternly.

'No need to worry about that,' she smiled. 'I shall be quite alone. I shall take Norton and Wildey and my horses, but no evening gowns.'

It took one more day to conclude business, give Mr Temple his congé, close up the house – Oliver had already departed – and for Norton to pack for them both. Norton approved of the plan. 'You

do look very tired, your grace. A bit of country air will set you up.'
She wanted to know why her mistress was not going to Ravendene,
and the unasked question was so naked in her voice that Charlotte
had to distract her.

'You need a rest, too,' she said firmly. 'Understand, I'm not
taking you to wait on me, but to have a holiday yourself. One of
the housemaids can do the little maiding I shall need.'

'Leave a stranger dress you and look after your clothes?' Norton
said, outraged. 'And what would I do all day in the country if I
hadn't my work?'

'Sit in the garden with your hands in your lap and make cloud
pictures,' Charlotte said, satisfied with her ruse.

By the wonders of the railway system she was transported to
Oxford in a few hours; and through the wonder of the telegraph
system, a carriage was waiting at the station to meet her and take
her to Wolvercote. They were ready for her at the house, too. Old
Mrs Loftus, the housekeeper, was almost tearfully glad to see her.
The vast, rambling mansion was sadly empty these days. Lord
Aylesbury, being a bachelor, preferred to live in Town, and to stay
with friends when he wanted the country. He only came down for
Christmas and Easter. The last two unmarried brothers, Maurice
and Clement, were as rarely at home – Maurice was in the navy,
and Clement at Cambridge – and Mrs Loftus feared that if Lord
Aylesbury didn't marry soon and start filling the nursery, the old
place would fall into ruin. Most of the house was shut up, only
the family apartments in the west wing kept ready for occupation
at short notice. With a reduced staff, already the grounds were
beginning to look neglected; and the grand stables, which had
always been so bustling, were echoing and empty. Now they
held only a couple of grooms' hacks, the pony that went to the
post, and the single pair of carriage horses for the chaise, to fetch
people from the station. The head groom, Craven – another relic
from Charlotte's grandmother's day – almost wept with joy when
Wildey arrived riding his own horse and leading Sovereign and Sir
William.

Norton had forgotten what a horrid, empty barn of a house it
was. 'Eating all alone here night after night'll be enough to give
you the megrims, my lady. There must be some families nearby
that you could invite, or go and visit,' she said as she unpacked
Charlotte's riding-habit.

'I shall come back at night so tired after a day in the fresh air that
I shall be falling asleep over my dinner. I shan't want company,'
Charlotte said. 'Besides, I'm surrounded by people all day long in
London. You can't think how I long for solitude.'

'You'll get that here, all right,' Norton said, and tried not to sound disapproving, since it was what her mistress wanted.

Charlotte woke early the next morning, wakened by the dawn chorus, which seemed riotous compared with the efforts of London birds. But more than the birdsong, it was the silence underneath it which woke her. It was like a great broad rushing river, that sound of silence, beside which all the thousand individual noises of the city amounted to nothing more than a thin, trickling stream. She lay in bed listening, watching the sunlight slither across the ceiling, and wondering why she hadn't realised how much she missed it all. For the past thirteen years she had been working to improve the lot of others, struggling against indifference, ignorance, human perversity and the sheer scale of the problems. She supposed that she had made a difference, though it was sometimes hard to believe. Now she wondered whether it were not time to do something for herself. All her life she had shaped herself to fit other people's requirements; suddenly she wanted a holiday from responsibility and care.

Norton was pleased by the hearty breakfast her lady ate. In London, Charlotte generally took nothing more than muffins or toast with her coffee, but today the cook, delighted to have such an eminent person to show off to, sent up a fried sole, game rissoles, poached eggs, baked tomatoes, devilled sausages and fried potatoes, and Charlotte was in a way to try all of them. Everything seemed to taste ten times more delicious than usual, as though it were a paradigm of itself, and eating only seemed to feed her appetite. As she ate, she thought about the ride ahead of her. A whole day to do as she liked and ride where she liked, and not be observed or judged by anyone! She had a feeling of coming alive, of spreading damp and creased wings in the sunshine and seeing them stretch and straighten out.

Wildey was at the Tudor door at ten o'clock with Sir William saddled ready for her, and was very much put out when Charlotte said she did not want him to go with her. 'You are to have a holiday too,' she told him.

Wildey looked blank. 'What would I do with a holiday, your grace?'

'Go for a walk. Take a boat on the river. Do a little fishing.' Wildey struggled with this notion, and she added, 'It would be a kindness to sit and chat to Craven, and let him tell you about the good old days.'

'But, your grace, you can't be thinking of riding alone?' Wildey said at last. That was as far as he could get.

'I shall only be riding in the park,' she said. 'There's no-one to see me. Don't worry, I won't disgrace you.' She was surprised to find herself making a little joke. She felt as if she hadn't made a joke in years.

Wildey had no sense of humour. 'Suppose you have a fall, your grace?'

'I won't have a fall.'

'Or have to dismount? You wouldn't be able to get back up.'

'Then I should have to walk home.' She took Sir William's reins and bent her leg for Wildey. 'Throw me up, please.'

He had no choice but to obey a direct order. He held Sir William while she arranged herself in the saddle, and then watched her ride away with a variety of horrible accidents in his eyes and don't-say-I-didn't-warn-you in the set of his mouth.

Away from the house, Charlotte felt her spirits bubble up in the most extraordinary way. How different the day felt here! In London the hot summer had been a curse, a thing of brazen light and glittering windows, of stifling air that was as unsatisfying to breathe as so much damp cloth. The dusty pavements burned through the soles of your shoes, the glare made your head ache, the streets smelled of horse-sweat, manure and drains.

But here the air was clear and smelled of grass, and the sunshine seemed a kindly thing. The chestnut trees shimmered a little in the heat, spreading deep indigo shadows under their skirts where the cattle had already retreated to lie in the cool grass and chew the cud. The sky was a misty mauve at the horizon, deepening to a clear chicory blue at the zenith, where swifts curved about on scimitar wings, screaming in faint ecstasy.

Sir William was plainly pleased to be here after so long in the confines of London and the Park, and put his feet down with a dancing gait, looking about him with delight. He flicked his ears back and forth, mouthing the bit, eager to gallop, and when she gave him the office he shot forward with a great bound that almost unseated her, and gave point to Wildey's warning about not being able to get back on if she came off. But she didn't care; her horse stretched his powerful body under her, the smell of bruised grass rose from under his pounding feet, the air rushed past her face. Suddenly she felt almost hilarious. What joy to be alive! Sir William caught the mood from her, and began to buck, so she pushed him on faster, feeling the thrill of speed tingle in her blood.

Holiday! To please oneself, to do something different, to forget care: in short, to escape from being oneself for a while. That's what she wanted. She *needed* it, in fact. She leaned forward and whispered exciting things to Sir William, and he suddenly found that he wasn't galloping as fast as he could after all. His muscles surged and the ground was a green blur beneath them.

The horse slowed at last, out of breath, and dropped of his own accord to a canter and then a walk, his sides heaving. He sneezed several times, tossing his head up and down and spattering her. Now there was no wind of speed to freshen them, the heat seemed to close down around them, and an army of small flies came from nowhere. Charlotte headed for the row of plane trees along the park boundary and walked her horse in under the grateful shade. After a while they came to a little gate in the iron fence; Sir William was quiet now, and stood to let her unlatch it with her crop, and then obligingly shoved it open for her with his chest. Here was a tree-shaded path edged with long grass and a froth of fool's parsley; the air was so cool it smelled greenly, deliciously damp, of moss and nettles. They crossed a narrow bridge, so little used that there were weeds growing out of its stones; the water underneath had that flat, metallic smell of canals. Now the lane joined one slightly wider, but still unfrequented – there was only very old, dried dung on the path. It had sunk a little over the centuries, and its verges rose to either side, the grass embroidered with flowers bright as a gypsy's skirt: pink and white campion, purple vetch, violet-blue cranesbill, red sainfoin and yellow agrimony. Beyond the verge to one side was a low hedge and then a hayfield, long cut, with a skylark hanging above it, throbbing with song like an exotic wind-up toy. On the other side was a high wall of old, soft red brick, crumbling quietly in the sunshine.

Sir William plodded along contentedly, flicking his ears back and forth against the flies, and sometimes sneezing as the dust from the lane tickled his nostrils. Now suddenly here was a gap in the wall, a pair of wide iron gates, one of them standing open on a stone-flagged courtyard and a Tudor house, made of the same soft red brick; a long, low house with a multitude of small latticed windows, a wavy roof, and an extravagance of wistaria in its second bloom, dripping pale mauve pendants like melting wax over the façade. Sir William seemed to stop at the gate of his own accord, as if he had known they were coming here; impossible, when even she had not known it, not really. Their ride had brought them here more or less by accident; the path had come this way, that was all.

She had a moment of painful realism: if she entered these gates, she would alter the balance of her life in a way whose consequences she could not guess. But then *holiday!* her mind cried; and she rode in at the gate, drew rein, pulled her skirts clear and jumped down – in itself an act of rebellion, for a duchess must not jump, she must be lifted off carefully, or step down in a dignified manner onto a mounting-block.

The door of the house opened and a strange man came out. Her heart bounced with fear for an instant before she saw that he was a servant.

'Good day, your grace,' he said as if he were expecting her. 'If you would be good enough to follow the path round the house to the garden—' He gestured the way. 'Please to forgive my not showing you, but there is only me to take your horse.'

There didn't seem to be anything for her to say or do, but hand over Sir William and follow instructions. The path between the side of the house and an overgrown hedge was in deep shadow, and the air struck cold enough to make her shiver. Then she was out again into the sunshine: before her a stone-flagged terrace running along the back of the house, and beyond it a wide, daisy-studded lawn. The lawn was hedged in all round with tall shrubs and trees, making it quite private; and now she saw, on the far side, a sofa and two chairs set up with a table before them in the deep shade of a copper beech. Sir Frederick was lounging at his ease in one of the chairs. There was nothing to do now but walk towards him.

He stood up as she approached. 'Ah, there you are,' he said cheerfully. 'Come and sit down in the shade.'

She had never seen him except in formal Town dress; today he was wearing a loose-fitting jacket and pantaloons, worn with a soft-collared shirt and, instead of a neckcloth, a loosely tied scarf. He was the very figure of ease; even his hair looked artfully tousled. She was suddenly aware of how very handsome he was, especially when he smiled so agreeably, as though she were all he had been waiting for to make a fine day perfect. It made her nervous. She swallowed, but since her throat was dry, swallowing only made her cough.

'You've had a dusty ride,' he suggested. 'Come, sit here on the sofa, and let me pour you a glass of lemonade. In a little while Stebbins will bring us some luncheon. I thought you'd like to eat out here; it's so pleasant in the shade of the trees.'

It was all as natural and easy as could be, nothing for her to fear, nothing to threaten her nerve or abrade her conscience. And he was pouring out a glassful from a jug of pale cloudy liquid embellished with sprigs of mint.

'Lemonade?' she said wonderingly. He could not have known she was coming, yet he seemed to have been waiting for her.

He only smiled, handing the glass to her. 'Do take off your hat and gloves and make yourself comfortable, and then we can talk.'

'Thank you,' she said, and sipped her lemonade. It felt to

her like a Rubicon, this act of accepting his hospitality: she was now officially a ruined woman, but the absurd contrast with the platitudes of seduction made the laughter bubble up again, just under the surface, where it swirled and chuckled like an exuberant stream. *Holiday!* it whispered. It made her eyes sparkle, and Friedman looked at her in pleased surprise.

'I'm glad to see you looking more rested,' he said. 'You were quite drawn last time I saw you.'

'I feel much better,' she said. 'I've decided to put off responsibility for a while. Everyone needs to do that at some time, don't you think?'

The simple, delicious luncheon – cold roast duck, salads, fresh bread and cherries – had been eaten and the table cleared away. An afternoon stillness had descended: heat shimmered on the lawn, and even the birds had fallen silent. Under the shade of the copper beech, Friedman had lit a cigar, and the blue, fragrant smoke was curling away lazily up into the canopy.

'It always seems strange to me that a tree can differ so completely in such an essential,' he said. 'Leaves are green; how can these be so different?'

'I once knew a prostitute with hair that colour,' Charlotte said idly. 'Dyed, of course.' He snorted with laughter, and she turned her head to look at him. 'What is it?'

'Oh, I'm not laughing at you, but with you. It is delightful to see you so much at ease that you don't even hesitate to use the word "prostitute" in front of a gentleman.'

'I wasn't thinking of you as a gentleman,' she said. It was true. She felt more completely at ease than at any time in her life before. Not even with Oliver had she ever felt so free – for being in love generates its own tensions. Since the strange magic of this place began to work on her, she had shed her hat and gloves, then her jacket and stock, and would even, she thought, have felt equal to removing her boots if it weren't such a fag to get them off. Sir Frederick had removed jacket and necktie. He was sprawled on the grass, resting one elbow on the seat of an armchair. She was stretched out on the sofa; when she turned her head, his face was only two feet away from hers.

'I'm certainly not behaving like a gentleman,' he said cheerfully. 'How do you account for that?'

'Holiday,' she said. He raised an enquiring eyebrow. 'I've been thinking about it all morning. That's the essence of "holiday", to leave aside everything that confines one. Look at the traditional country festivals, for instance, and how the peasants behave—'

'Drunkenness, horseplay?'

'Gluttony – all the pleasant sins. Just for a day they are let off the leash. But of course we're too civilised to give up all our morals and manners.'

'Perhaps because the morals and manners are not bound upon us, as they are upon the peasantry. We choose to bind ourselves, and if we left them off, who could make us take them up again?' He spoke lightly, but there was a seriousness underneath.

'You speak as a man,' she said. 'A woman is as much bound as a peasant. She is never free to choose or not choose.'

He looked at her. 'Don't you choose to be here?'

'Oh yes. But this isn't the real world. This is a separate place which has its own rules.'

Her words made him pause, torn two ways by his feelings. He loved her almost more than he could bear, but he was worried for her future. If he managed to convince her of the reality of her present situation, she might take fright and leave, and he didn't want her to leave; but he was older than her, and wiser in the ways of the world. He knew she was in danger; but he saw her innocent happiness and he hadn't it in him to spoil that. Eve in ignorance of her nakedness was a happy Eve.

He reached out a hand and pushed a thread of hair away from her face. 'How lovely you are,' he said, and it didn't seem like a *non sequitur*. 'Like a Renaissance angel: solemn and blissful and golden.'

She looked at him so trustingly that he could not do what he wanted and hug her to his breast, though the effort not to made him tremble slightly. 'What is it you want, Charlotte?'

If she noticed his use of her name she didn't show it. 'To be here, that's all,' she said. 'To be free.'

'Free?'

'I feel free here with you, with no-one to see us.'

'Free to do what?'

'It is a state, not an action,' she said instructively. 'If I were free to do anything I liked, I might not do anything at all, but it wouldn't alter the fact of my freedom.'

'A nice distinction, ma'am,' he said, beginning to smile.

'I am nice.'

'Very well, then I shall be more particular. What do you want to do with your freedom now, this minute?'

'Talk,' she said promptly. 'You can't think how I long to talk! But what do *you* want to do?'

He restrained himself laudably. 'I should like to draw you.'

'Do you draw?'

'I used to, rather nicely. I haven't practised the art for a long time, mostly for lack of a worthwhile subject.'

'If you think I am a worthwhile subject, I have no objection.'

'Then – might I make a further request? I should like to draw you with your hair loose.'

'Not today,' she said. 'I could never get it back up the same way. Tomorrow I'll dress it myself.'

He seemed to grow very still. 'So you will come tomorrow?' It was perilously close to the question that would break the spell, and he spoke it very quietly: the words tiptoeing past a sleeping giant.

But now suddenly she looked out at him seriously from under her playfulness, and he realised it had been absurd of him to think she did not know how things really lay between them. She had chosen not to acknowledge it or act upon it, but she was too intelligent not to know it.

'Yes,' she said quietly. 'I would like to, very much.'

He took her hand and carried it to his lips, a gesture of homage, and then he laid it carefully down and resumed a normal, cheerful mien. 'Good,' he said. And then he talked of gardens, and they discussed whether it would be better, with a new house, to have an expert lay out the garden, or to plan it oneself and live with the mistakes. They talked, and the sun moved across the lawn, and presently a little breeze got up, just enough to stir the leaves and bring the scent of jasmine from somewhere nearby. In a while, Stebbins appeared with a tray of tea, shortbread and scones, and Charlotte was astonished to find herself hungry again.

The next day she dressed herself and left early and on foot, telling Norton she was going for a long walk. She put on a simple unhooped gown of tartan lawn, light boots, and a flat straw hat, and with her hair in a long single plait down the back, she felt almost cool and comfortable. If she could have left off her corsets, she would have been entirely so, but that was a discomfort she had grown so used to that she hardly noticed it any more.

Norton saw her off with pleasure, thinking how young her mistress looked in that simple attire, and how much good being in the country had done her already. It reminded her of the time they had run away from London to live in the cottage in Norfolk – long ago, before Charlotte was married. They had lived simply, and Norton thought if it had not been that Charlotte was so unhappy, she would have been happy, so to speak. She wondered what her mistress was running away from now; and then she dismissed that thought, and substituted the memorandum to herself that Charlotte needed to refresh herself in the country from time to time, and that she, Norton, should make sure she did not forget to do it.

Charlotte walked a more direct route to the house, cutting through the hayfield, and arrived so early that there was no-one in the garden when she came round the side of the house. She didn't mind. She felt at ease here. On an impulse she sat down on the sofa and removed her boots and stockings so that she could feel the cool grass under her feet. Where the sun hadn't touched it yet, it was still damp from the dew. It felt glorious. She stared down at her bare toes and laughed aloud. How long is it since I've seen you in daylight? she addressed them. They wanted to dance, so she let them, just a few little steps in the chilly, dew-pearled grass.

Something cold touched her hand and she started and whipped round, to see a large black dog backing nervously from her sudden movement. She bent, reaching out her hand. 'Come, then. I'm sorry, I didn't mean to frighten you.' The dog came back and snuffed her hand cautiously, and then smiled up at her, swinging its tail in friendship. 'Where did you come from?' she asked. The dog barked, once, and then ran into the hedgerow and came back with a stick in its mouth, wagging not just its tail but its whole hindquarters. Charlotte laughed, 'Oh, is that it?' She threw the stick, the dog bounced after it; and the two of them began a ridiculous game, romping about the lawn in the most idiotic manner.

From a window, unseen, Friedman watched them, afraid to go down in case it broke her mood, longing to go down and seize her in his arms. He loved her so much then it was like a physical pain in his chest, and, loving her, he was glad to have given her this small time out of the world, even though to do it meant denying himself what he wanted most, so that she should feel safe and not guilty. When he did step out into the garden at last, she and the dog had run out of breath. She was standing in the shade of the tree, her head bent, her hands behind her, doing something to her hair; the dog was lying panting in the grass with the stick ready before it, in case there should be a resumption.

'What energy, and in this heat!' Friedman said as he approached. 'Is he yours?'

'No, he just appeared. I thought he was yours. I suppose he must live nearby.' She finished what she was doing and straightened up. 'Look!' she said, and swung her head from side to side, freeing the loosened hair. It fanned out, flying with the movement, and then settled around her like a golden haze. 'Well?'

Her green-gold eyes shone, her innocent mouth was made for

kissing, and he had to drag his eyes from her face for fear of losing control.

'Thank you,' he said. And then, 'I like you with bare feet. Do you know, I've just remembered, there's a little stream down at the bottom of the property, through the woods. Would you like to go and dabble in it? I'll wager it's a long time since you've felt wet mud between your toes.'

She laughed. 'I'll dabble if you will!'

'Oh, I've already more than dabbled,' he said lightly. 'I have plunged deep. But there's nothing to be done about it now.'

They lost the dog somewhere in the woods, but when they went back to the garden for luncheon, it found them again, and came and flopped companionably in the shade nearby while they sat side by side on the sofa and ate egg-and-anchovy tarts and cold chicken fritters with salads and more cherries. And when the afternoon stillness came over the garden she sat and gazed out at the heat-shimmer while he drew her, and they talked and talked, about everything and anything, feeling close and at ease.

'I feel so safe here,' she said at one time. 'This is a magic place, a secret, magic garden where nothing can touch us.'

'But it's unreal to you?' he asked.

She saw that the idea displeased him, and said, 'I don't mean that. But it's—' She couldn't find the right word. At last she said, 'It's holiday.'

'And you must go back to school,' he said. She didn't know if it were a question or a statement, and said nothing. 'Well, you will go when you want, or when you are called. One's time in Eden must always have its term. But I want you always to remember,' he went on, 'that I am your friend. Whatever you want of me is yours for the asking.'

She looked at him. 'What do *you* want of *me*?'

He turned his head too. His face was very close to hers, and he looked at her for a long time, his eyes both warm and sad; deep and dark, safe for her, and perilous. 'You know what I want,' he said.

'But you would never ask me for it,' she said, wondering at his generosity. He didn't answer that – it was not, in any case, a question. The breeze lifted the leaves above them and they rustled like a theatre audience whispering. The dog got up, stretched, yawned hugely, and wandered off into the bushes again. Friedman turned a page of his sketching-book and began a new drawing.

After a time he said, 'When I was very young – not yet eighteen – I was engaged to be married. It was a love-match on both sides. But she died before our wedding-day.'

Attuned to him, she understood. 'You used to draw her?'

He smiled assent. 'Over and over again. Through one whole summer.'

'With her hair loose?'

'Oh no, never that. We were too strictly chaperoned. But I always wanted to.' He touched a strand of hers. 'You have given me something more than anyone else on earth. God bless your generous spirit.' She didn't know how to respond to that. He hesitated, and then said, 'I will tell you one more thing you won't understand, but if you remember it, you may understand, one day.' She waited, watching him. He added a line to his sketch, then looked up at her and said, 'A beautiful thing out of its place may not be appreciated.'

'Is that all?'

'That's all.'

When she got back to Wolvercote, Norton was waiting in her room. Charlotte took one look at her expression, and wondered how she could have found out. 'I suppose I was foolish to think I could keep anything from you,' she said.

Norton would not meet her eyes. 'It's none of my business, your grace,' she said stiffly, but then her feelings broke through. 'Oh, your grace, be careful! If his grace should come to hear of it—'

'His grace already knows about it. In fact, he knew about it before it ever happened. Why do you think I came here?'

Norton was silent, cold with foreboding. Now what would come of them all? Divorce had been so much a topic of conversation recently that it might well be on the duke's mind. Had he packed her off into the country in disgrace? Or simply to get her away from Sir Frederick? If the latter, her mistress was playing with fire to be seeing him again. But how could she? It was so out of her character.

'You don't speak,' Charlotte said at last. 'Does that mean you are against me too?'

'Not against you, never that,' Norton said quickly. 'I don't understand why you . . . But it's not my business to judge. I'm yours to command, my lady, always, you know that. I just don't understand.'

'His grace has a mistress,' Charlotte said. She had meant to say it lightly, but the bitterness in her voice surprised even her. 'That woman that he was visiting before, when we were first engaged.'

'Mrs Galbraith?'

'You remember her name.'

'I could hardly forget, my lady, seeing how much it upset you. So he's been seeing her again?' Norton studied Charlotte's face

108

and sought for comforting words. 'But, my lady, it's not unusual for a married man, especially one in his grace's position. After all—' She could not say what came next, but they both knew it: after all, he can't sleep with you any more. In any case, Norton was not much interested in the duke's personal entanglements, taking it as read that men would be men; it was her mistress she was worried about.

'Yes, that was what his grace said about it,' Charlotte said.

'But what did he say about you?'

'He said I must be more discreet.'

'Just that?'

'That was the essence of it.'

Norton scanned her face, trying to understand. If that was all his grace had said, it might have seemed on the surface that they had got off lightly. The consequences might have been appalling; instead she seemed to be being left to do as she pleased. So was she seeing Sir Frederick to pay his grace out, or because she really liked him? Norton tried to put herself into her mistress's mind and understand how she was feeling, but she couldn't. It seemed, she sighed inwardly, as though since they had come back from Russia they had all been a little strange.

'You don't ask,' Charlotte went on, 'what I meant when I said his grace knew about it before it ever happened.'

'What does that mean, then?' Norton asked obediently. And, with relief, Charlotte told her about the false accusation and how he wouldn't listen to her defence. 'Oh, my lady, that was a cruel thing,' Norton said with quick, warm sympathy, when the tale was done. 'But, all the same—'

'We talk,' Charlotte said quickly. 'We sit in the garden and talk, and he sketches me. That's all.'

Norton looked at her for a long moment, frowning a little. 'But, my lady,' she said at last, 'it doesn't make any difference.'

'You mean that the world will still condemn me? Yes, I know, but what do I care about the world, when his grace has condemned me already?'

'I didn't mean that. What matters is how you are inside, with yourself. I know you, and you won't be happy if you're not comfortable with yourself.' Charlotte removed her face from that clear, penetrating gaze. 'Do you love Sir Frederick, my lady?' Norton asked softly.

Charlotte was a long time answering. 'I love Oliver,' she said at last, 'but I can't have him. Sir Frederick is my friend. I'm happy when I'm with him.' She wanted to explain about the magic place, to assure Norton that she knew it could not go on, that in London things would be different, that it was just something she wanted now, for a little while, before she returned to the real world. But she could not have put it into words that Norton would understand; and she was afraid that if she talked about it, the magic would rub off.

So in the end she just said, 'No-one else must know.'

'I know how to hold my tongue,' Norton said with wounded dignity.

'I know you do. Dear Norton! Just be patient with me for a few weeks. It can't last long.'

Norton's sympathy was touched by the sadness in her mistress's voice. She put out an impulsive hand. 'I'm on your side, you know I am. I just want you to be happy. You deserve to be happy.'

'Don't all of us?' Charlotte said.

At the end of the week came a cooler day, when the sunshine had a different quality, seemed a darker gold, the sky a more transparent blue. Charlotte rode over on Sovereign, and noted with a sharp pang that one or two leaves of the plane trees were turning yellow. Summer was easing over into autumn; time was drawing away from her like a receding tide, and soon she would be left beached and stranded. Sir Frederick sensed her mood, seemed to have sensed it before she arrived, for he was waiting with his own horse saddled, and they rode out together, not talking much, but cantering side by side, easing her restlessness with movement.

In the afternoon they sat in the garden, but he did not draw her. It had grown still, and the light was strange: there was going to be a storm. The air seemed sticky, and there was a quantity of tiny black thunder-flies to annoy them. Charlotte waved them off her face with an improvised fan of paper; he merely sat and watched her, consuming every feature, every movement, knowing that he would lose her soon.

'I wish we could go away,' she said at last. 'Right away from everyone, from everything we know, and never come back.'

'The thought of London appals you?'

'Doesn't it you?'

'Just now – yes. But my work is there. Yours, too. Could you leave your work? What about the hospital?'

'It doesn't need me any more. It can get on without me – without you, too. Let others take up the slack. We have done enough. It's time to have something for ourselves.'

'And what would you like to do?'

'To take a house – a small house, or a cottage, even – in some remote place. Near the sea, perhaps, or on the edge of the moors.

Somewhere where there is a wide horizon and a great deal of sky, and where the wind comes to you fresh and unused.'

'Yes, I see it,' he said. 'A snug, neat cottage standing all alone at the edge of the world, on the brink of untamed Nature. No neighbours to spy and pry. In fact, I dare say no-one knows who we are.'

'We've changed our names,' she agreed. 'And Stebbins and Norton take care of us. We don't need more.'

'Just a groom to take care of the horses. There must be horses?'

'Of course! We ride or walk all day—'

'Swim, too, if we're near the sea.'

'I've never swum. Is it nice?'

'Indescribably. We'll find a little cove where no-one ever goes, and I'll teach you.'

'I should like that. And in the evenings we just sit and talk.'

'Strange how we never tire of talking,' he said.

She looked at him desperately. 'It's ending, isn't it? I don't want it to end.'

'Oh, my dear,' he said. He left his seat, slipped to his knees beside her, gathered her two hands into his. 'What can I say?'

'Kiss me,' she said. He took her face in his hands and closed his eyes and laid his lips against hers, and bore the agony of love and longing that swept through him. Then his control wavered, and he kissed her passionately, one hand sliding up through her hair to cradle her skull and hold her still; and he felt a little shudder of reaction go through her, and she stirred towards him. Very gently he released her, as if afraid a sudden withdrawal would make her fall; her eyes opened, and she tried to smile at him. Inwardly he said goodbye then, smiled kindly at her, resumed his seat. The little shudder of longing he had felt was not for him but for her husband; he knew that, and so now, he saw, did she.

'I'm sorry,' she said.

'Don't be. We can none of us help the way we feel.'

'He doesn't want me,' she said sadly. 'He has betrayed me and left me, but it doesn't seem to make any difference.'

'I know.' He waited a moment. 'But we have a while longer yet?'

'Yes, a few days more. And, Frederick—' It was the first time she had used his name, and it moved him absurdly. 'I didn't come to see you because of him. I came because of you. Really, really. I want you to know that.'

Now his smile for her was unshadowed. 'I do know it. And I want you to know that I am your friend, always, and nothing can change that.'

The skies closed in as she rode home, the clouds easing together into a single blanket, plum-coloured with approaching dusk; the sunset light was coppery, the air tasted slippery and salt. Sovereign hurried homeward, his ears flickering nervously, but Charlotte felt calm, and happier than she had been for a long time. She knew herself now, and was glad at what she knew. Loving Oliver might not make her happy – was sure, indeed, to give her grief in the future – but Norton was right, she needed to be comfortable with herself. And she was glad, so glad that she had Frederick as her friend. Tomorrow they would talk again, and she would take comfort from him without feeling guilty, because all was fair and open between them now, and whatever the world might wish to think, there was no wrong in it.

She rode straight to the stableyard, and got in before the storm broke. Craven came hobbling out at the sound of hooves and was scandalised that she had given herself the trouble of coming round. 'It's going to rain cats and dogs any minute! Get you indoors, your grace, do, before it starts. Oh dearie me, there's the first drop! I'd have fetched him from the house, your grace, rather than see you get a drenching.'

She handed over the reins and hurried in by the Tudor hall, as the first large, separate drops were smacking onto the cobbles and leaving dark circles in the white dust. She got up to her room unseen, and rang for Norton, and had got as far as removing her jacket and stock when her maid came in with trouble in her face.

'I didn't know you were back, your grace, until you rang,' she began.

Your grace? Charlotte thought. 'I took Sovereign straight to the stableyard. I didn't want him to get soaked, and give Wildey extra work drying him off.' She stopped as she saw that her trunk had been pulled out and was half-packed, and then Norton's expression took on a different significance. 'What is it? What's happened?'

'A telegraph came half an hour ago, from Grasscroft,' Norton said, her face terrible with sympathy. 'Those fools in the village had it last night and didn't think to bring it up to the house. The postmaster didn't know you were here and thought it was a mistake. Someone will pay for their stupidity, I warrant you!'

Charlotte felt a cold emptiness open up inside her, a vast black space like the night sky. 'My mother?' she said.

'Lord Batchworth, my lady. He died yesterday, quite suddenly.'

CHAPTER EIGHT

Her mother seemed to have shrunk in the few weeks since Charlotte saw her last. All in her blacks, she sat very still in the shaded drawing-room, her crooked hands lying in her lap like knotted sticks, like kindling, no use for what hands were for.

'It was his heart,' she said to Charlotte. 'He was worn out with the Divorce Act, sitting through the night in that terrible heat, rushing about trying to get people to support his amendments. It was too much for him, at his age.'

Charlotte nodded, afraid to say anything yet. Her mother seemed not really to be paying attention to Charlotte, or to what she was saying. Her eyes were always elsewhere, as if she were listening for something; waiting for something.

'He seemed to revive when he got back here,' Rosamund went on. 'We were out riding together the last morning. When we got back to the stable he stayed behind to talk to Padworth about getting the hunters up. I went on to the house. I happened to be standing at the window in our room when he came along the path, and he stopped and looked up at me as if he knew I'd be there. And then he just – fell. Like a tree.'

Charlotte nodded again. Her throat hurt so much she couldn't swallow.

'I ran downstairs,' Rosamund said, still in that absent, listening voice. 'When I reached him, he opened his eyes and looked at me. And then he sighed, and died. He was only waiting until I got there.'

The stillness that surrounded Rosamund was the only stillness in the house. There was a constant stream of visitors and messages, letters and telegraphs, and the funeral to arrange besides. Charlotte was grateful for the activity, for it seemed kinder to have people coming and going, and things to do. The servants were all in floods: Batchworth had been loved. His man, Sopwith, who had been with him since he first got his colours and went off to fight Boney, was beyond consolation; and Padworth could only find relief in grooming the horses over and over, wetting down their manes with his tears. Batchworth's renowned chef, Monsuchet, kept cooking things that no-one wanted to eat and sending up little trays of delicacies to tempt Rosamund's non-existent appetite.

Cavendish, grave in his new dignity of twelfth Earl of Batchworth, seemed to have grown up with cruel suddenness. On the day after she arrived, Charlotte went out early after a sleepless night to walk about the gardens and clear her head, and found Cavendish there, sitting on a damp stone bench staring at nothing. She sat down beside him and took his cold hand into her lap, and looked at his stern profile for a while. She remembered the charming, high-spirited, elegant Hussar who had embarked for Varna in April 1854, and ached with pity for him. No-one would ever again mistake Cavendish for a boy. The lines around his eyes were cruelly deep-etched in the low sunlight, and his hair was receding, revealing the scar on his forehead, and the furrows of long-endured pain on his once-smooth brow.

At last he spoke, not looking at her. 'So often in the last two years, since I was brought back from Sebastopol, I've wished to die. My life was useless to me.' She made a little movement of protest and he shook his head. 'No, ever since I was a little boy, all I wanted was to be a cavalryman. I came back from the east a useless cripple, in constant pain, my career over, with nothing to do but gamble and get drunk and make everyone around me as miserable as I was.'

He moved his eyes sideways to glance at her, without turning his head. 'I don't know whether you know it, but when your Dr Abernethy first came to see me after I woke up, he said that I should be very careful in future because another blow on the head could prove fatal.'

'Yes, I knew that.'

'You don't know how often I thought of crawling out of bed and throwing myself head-first down the stairs, just to end it.'

'Because of the pain?'

'No!' he said with some emphasis. 'I could bear the pain – even when this arm got really bad. It wasn't the pain; it was because, try as I might, I *couldn't remember*.'

'You mean, about—?'

'About the year I was missing from my life. I remember starting to ride off towards the guns, and then, nothing. Suddenly I was back here, lying helpless in bed. You can't imagine what it's like, Charley. I went out there a young man and came back like this, and in between there's a great, black gulf. I felt so cheated. I'd lost a piece out of my life. My healthy body had been stolen from me and replaced with this damaged one – and I *couldn't remember its happening.*'

'I understand,' she said.

'Do you? It was like being trapped in a recurring dream. In my head I would see all my friends, and my own men whom I was responsible for, riding away down the valley towards the guns, knowing they were all going to be killed, without being able to do anything to stop them, or save them. I should have been killed, too, and because I wasn't, I felt so guilty, as if I'd let them die. Often it seemed to me that only by dying as I should have, could I expiate the guilt.'

She squeezed his hand. 'Oh, Cav,' she said helplessly.

'I couldn't bear to be with anyone I'd known from before. I couldn't bear their eyes on me – pitying me, condemning me.'

'I'm sure they—'

'I'm just telling you how I felt. So I found a new circle of friends, people who didn't know me. People I couldn't let down.'

'Like that horrid man Nagel and his low cronies? And Mrs Bonito?'

He shrugged. 'I drank, I gambled, I made merry – anything to try to blot out that image in my head, and the terrible feeling of having lost myself. I knew how it was hurting Papa and Mama, but I didn't care. And now—' He paused, and she saw him swallow hard, and his eyes fill with tears. 'I shortened his life, Charley. Not the Divorce Bill, or the hot summer. Papa's dead, and I can't make it right.' The tears rolled over. 'I keep thinking,' he said between gasps of tears, 'of all the things – I wanted – to say to him – and now it's – too late!'

He turned abruptly and buried his head on Charlotte's shoulder, and she put her arms round his brittle shoulders and held him while he sobbed, his hot tears soaking through her gown. She rested her cheek against his hair, not speaking, for there was nothing she could say to comfort him. All the way up on the train, she too had been thinking of the wasted opportunities, how little she had seen of him in recent years and how much time she would have spent with him and her mother, had she known; going over their last farewell and tormenting herself with whether she had kissed him warmly enough, whether she had really let him know how much she appreciated his qualities and valued his affection.

And she was only his step-daughter, and had no major sin to reproach herself with. Poor Cavendish would bear this guilt for ever.

At last his tears eased, and he sat up and fished in his sleeve for his handkerchief, wiped his eyes and blew his nose. Charlotte silently provided her own as supplement. Eventually he said in a much more normal voice, 'Well, that's over. You must be impatient with my self-pity, but I promise that's the last time I'll indulge it.'

'Dearest, I do understand.'

He looked at her for the first time, and nodded. 'Yes, I know you do. Thank you. And I know what I must do in atonement: I must be the son Papa wanted me to be.'

'The country squire?'

'The good landlord, the good mill-master, the good father. The good husband, too. Oh Lord, Alice! What a mess I've made of my life! But I mean to do right by her from now on.'

'A worthy resolve,' Charlotte said, and offered him her own comfort. 'She wasn't very good at grand society, but I think you may find she does very well here, away from Town, in the quiet of the countryside.'

'Especially if I can get rid of her mother. No, it's all right, I shan't quarrel! I'm a reformed character, I tell you. And William shall have a brother – several brothers. That ought to keep Alice busy. I know what to do, Charley,' he said, squeezing her hand again. 'I'm to be the Earl of Batchworth in Papa's mould, for however long is left to me. It's the only way to assuage the guilt.'

'And it's the right thing to do,' she said, 'in absolute terms.'

He nodded. 'If you say it's right, then I have confidence that it is. You've always been so good, dear Charley. Such a paragon of virtue, indeed, I count it exceeding generous of me not to hate you for it!'

'Foolish!' she said, and kissed his cheek.

'And now we ought to go back to the house, before we alarm anyone by our absence and have them sending out for us.' He stood up and offered his good arm. 'Thank you for letting me spout. I feel better for it.'

'My shoulder is always at your service,' she said gravely, and they set off towards the house.

Tom and Emily Weston came from Morland Place where they'd been spending the summer. Tom confided to Charlotte that he'd tried to persuade Emily to stay behind, for she was still far from well, and he thought the upset of a funeral would not be the best thing for her, but she would not hear of it; and certainly Rosamund was glad to see her. Emily had a quiet way of being good company, and of encouraging people to talk without badgering them. She sat long hours with Rosamund, the two of them conversing in low voices. Charlotte never heard what was being said, but some of her mother's strained look of waiting left her, and she seemed merely tired. Emily got her to eat, too, without making a great fuss about it, and everyone was glad of that.

Benedict followed the next day, when he had settled things to run smoothly in his absence. He did not bring Sibella, who was pregnant again and rather *souffrante*. 'She didn't mean to have another so soon,' Emily confided to Charlotte, 'and I think that makes it harder for her. She's sick all the time, poor thing, so the journey would have been quite beyond her.'

Alice came from Ravendene with her mother, Mrs Phipps struggling to conceal her fermenting excitement that her daughter was a countess at last. She had never been to Grasscroft before, and her acquaintance with the modest house in St James's Square had given her a false idea of the Batchworths' substance. The sight of the house and grounds, the vast park, the army of servants, the stables and horses and coaches, the furniture and silver and ancestral paintings, sobered her, and when she reminded herself that there was also Batchworth House in Cheetham Hill and the Ordsall Mills to take into account, she was cast into an agony of deference towards her son-in-law and his family which, fortunately, robbed her of speech.

Cavendish was rather annoyed that Alice had not brought William back with her, for he wanted to make a new start at once with his family around him, and had expected to be showing his son-and-heir to the tenantry after the funeral. Now someone would have to be sent to fetch the boy. But through discreet questioning Charlotte divined that the real culprit was Lady Turnhouse, who had insisted on keeping him, telling Alice that he would only be in the way at Grasscroft. Charlotte guessed the reason behind it. Lady T adored her grandsons and did not wish them to be deprived of anything they found pleasant. In her eyes, William was *their* playmate and attendant, and any other function he had as someone's son or grandson was subordinate to that. Furthermore, she hated the late Lord Batchworth and Charlotte's mother almost as much as she hated Charlotte, and was glad of any opportunity to thwart and snub them.

Charlotte's interest in Alice, Mrs Phipps and Lady Turnhouse shrivelled abruptly when a telegraph arrived from Oliver, to say that he was on his way, and asking for a carriage to meet his train.

She was in the morning-room with Rosamund, Emily and Tom when the carriage was heard outside. They carried on talking, but she heard no further word that was said, all her senses focused on the sounds of arrival – doors, footsteps, voices – and her imagination providing the picture of him, sweeping off his hat, looking round the hall, being greeted by Raby and told that his lordship was unfortunately engaged with his agent but that her ladyship, that is to say her *dowager* ladyship, was in the morning-room. Booted heels approached across the marble and the door-latch clicked as the handle engaged. Charlotte's nerves stretched agonisingly. The door opened and Raby announced, 'His Grace the Duke of Southport, my lady,' and then *he* was there, stepping through the doorway without hesitation as if he were making any ordinary entrance to any ordinary scene.

Well, perhaps to him it was ordinary, Charlotte thought. Her heart was knocking foolishly, and all her senses yearned towards him as though he were a very strong magnet and she a very weak pin: the first sight of him told her that she still loved him, and that nothing had changed. His eyes scanned the room rapidly, taking them all in – her no more than anyone else – and then he walked straight over to Rosamund and bowed gravely over her hand and spoke the formal words of greeting and sympathy. He nodded to Tom and Emily and then looked at her and said, 'Madam.'

That was all. Charlotte curtseyed in response, but bowed her head to hide her face, which she felt was tingling as if it had been slapped. His eyes had rested on her with utter indifference, he had greeted her as if she were a common acquaintance. She wanted to howl and break things and bite the carpet, but instead she merely resumed her seat and listened quietly as commonplaces were exchanged. At last Tom and Emily rose to go, and Rosamund, intercepting an anguished look from her daughter, also stood and said, 'I have letters to write, if you will forgive me, Duke. I'm sure Charlotte will look after you. I expect you'd like a moment together, anyway.'

Oliver did not exactly demur, though he did not look as though the prospect invited. He bowed and opened the door for Rosamund, and Charlotte half feared he would follow her out; but he closed it again and came back to the table where she was sitting.

She looked up fearfully. 'How are the children?'

'Well enough. Venetia fell off her pony and cut her lip, but not badly, so I understand.'

There was nothing in his face for her, no light, no warmth, no hostility either. It was as if he had nothing to do with her. 'I'm glad you came,' she said, hoping to break through the barrier. 'I didn't think you would.'

'Since you were here, I could not do otherwise,' he said with faint impatience.

'I don't suppose your mother would have agreed with that,' she said, with an attempt at playfulness.

'It would have been rather too public a snub if I had not come,' he said.

She couldn't bear it. She appealed to him directly. 'Oliver—'

'You enjoyed your stay at Wolvercote?' he interrupted her harshly. Now there was expression in his face. Negative as it was, it was better than stony blandness. At least he was feeling something!

'Yes, thank you – though it was interrupted too soon.'

'Oh yes, I can believe that!' he said. 'You had better company there than you now find yourself in.'

'I didn't mean that—'

His mouth curved down. 'You didn't waste much time, did you, my lady? I was barely out of the house before you were rushing off to an assignation with your lover!'

Her temper frayed a little. 'You told me to be discreet. You made no other conditions.'

'What use if I had? Nothing, it seems, would keep you from his elderly embraces.'

The combination of words was so ridiculous it almost made her laugh, and her temper sank again. 'How on earth did you find out?' she asked in sheer curiosity.

'You are not invisible, and neither, unfortunately, is he. You were seen by half a dozen people riding out with him.'

They had seen no-one, and she reflected how populated a seemingly empty country scene always was.

'And of course that gave rise to ample speculation as to why you were staying alone at Wolvercote just when *he* happened to be staying at Oakthorpe Manor.'

'That isn't why I went to Wolvercote!'

'My dear, you have no need to explain anything to me,' he said harshly. 'The details of your affair are beneath my interest—'

'Oliver, he is not my lover! Why won't you believe me?'

'I prefer to believe the facts. You visited him alone at his house. Whether the arrangement was made before or after you left London is unimportant.'

'Yes,' she said thoughtfully, 'I did visit him.' Well, she had known that it would change her life; but she had been condemned before the fact. 'But we are not lovers.'

He turned away. 'This is a singularly distasteful and pointless conversation, especially given the present circumstances. I wish you will refrain from renewing it. I shall leave an acceptable time after the funeral and go back to Ravendene.' He paused a breath, and then added with studied indifference, 'You may come with me if you wish.'

She almost snapped a refusal, but just in time heard under the indifference the little quiver he was at pains to hide. It was possible that he was hurt by all this, wasn't it? That it wasn't just his pride that objected to her supposed infidelity?

'I should like to see the children,' she said. He didn't look at her, but she saw his shoulders go down. She was glad she had said it; and she would be glad to see the children, and to be near Oliver, however cold he was towards her. It was only the thought of facing Lady Turnhouse that made her doubt how long she would be able to stay at Ravendene.

The day of the funeral was grey and overcast, but it did not rain: rather, it was a blank and windless day, neither hot nor cold, as if all of Nature were holding its breath until the business was over. The cortège moved slowly from the house down the long drive to the church where Jesmond had been christened, and where he had married Rosamund, his first and only love. Villagers and tenants lined the route and fell in silently behind as the carriage passed to the muffled drums of the band of the county militia, sent by courtesy of its present colonel, to remind everyone that Batchworth had been a hero of the French wars. As well as the county neighbours there were dignitaries from Manchester, representatives from the mills and from the various civic committees he had been active upon; representatives from the Government; even the Queen had sent a message. Charlotte was glad to see Mr Temple, who arrived that morning, and was touched to learn that Oliver had sent for him, in case there should be matters arising from the reading of the Will. Temple took off his hat and bowed his autumn-leaf head as Charlotte greeted him under the grey sky, and murmured that Lord Palmerston had asked him to give her his deepest condolences, and to say that they had all lost a good friend.

Charlotte represented her mother at the funeral, while Emily stayed at home with Rosamund – it was not customary for the widow to attend the interment, and Rosamund was glad of it. She didn't want to think of his empty body being lowered into the crypt. That was not the Jes she had loved so long. She sat quietly with Emily's silent, undemanding presence warming her sad heart, and thought of the first time she had ever seen him, on the strand at Scarborough in the summer of 1816. He had been convalescing from a wound got during the final defeat of Boney's army outside Paris; she and her cousin Sophie (poor Fanny's mother) had been convalescing from broken hearts, their fiancés both having been killed at Waterloo.

Batchworth had been plain Jesmond Farraline then, a penniless soldier without prospects; she was the wealthy Lady Rosamund

Chetwyn, pledged to marry her cousin Lord Chelmsford (Charlotte's father). But she had known from the first moment that Jes would be very important to her; more than forty years later she could still see in her mind's eye the way he had looked that day as he took off his hat and bowed over her hand, with his fair hair ruffled by the sharp east-coast breeze and his eyes bluer than the sea. He was that Jes still, and would remain so for ever, as long as her heart remembered him.

When the interment was over, the carriages and walkers processed back to the house, and now the band played, not mournfully but cheerfully, not dirges but triumphant tunes. Jes had decreed it so in his Will, to remind them all that Death is the Great Victory, and that nothing is ever lost. So those who had loved him did their best to obey his wish and walked with their heads up to his farewell party.

The reading of the Will did produce a surprise, and Charlotte was glad that Mr Temple was to hand. Most of it was straightforward – and indeed the terms of it, as Mr Culverhouse, the solicitor, said, had not changed in years. Rosamund's portion and the use of the dower house (though Cavendish assured her earnestly that he would much sooner she stayed on here), together with various small bequests to relatives, servants, pensioners and charitable organisations, had all been laid down long ago. There were personal mementoes to various friends and relations – to Charlotte he left a very pretty Sèvres clock and matching pair of vases, which he had bought in Paris after the surrender, and were reputed to have come from Versailles – but of course the bulk of the estate went to Cavendish. The house and park at Grasscroft, together with the attached farms, were entailed along with the title. The house at Cheetham Hill, the Ordsall Mills and the town property in Manchester and London were not entailed, but Batchworth had left them, together with various securities, to his son. Batchworth had been a good caretaker, and the estate was worth a great deal more now than when he had inherited it from his carefree, spendthrift brother, who had broken his neck while out hunting.

But the big surprise came at the end. The late earl, said Mr Culverhouse, had recently completed the purchase of a half share in the three Hobsbawn Mills from Mr Benedict Morland, together with a half share in some workmen's cottages known as Morland's Rents, and the entire freehold of a mansion known as Hobsbawn House in St Peter's Fields. This property the late earl had left to his step-daughter, her grace the Duchess of Southport. There were two sealed letters, one for her grace, and one for the duke, explaining his action and framing a request for the subsequent disposal of the property.

Mild sensation. 'My original share was only a quarter,' Benedict explained to Charlotte through it, 'but I have a fancy to interest myself in manufacturing, and Lord Batchworth had no objection. In fact he thought it would be more comfortable for you to have an equal partner to share the responsibility of running the mills. But he wanted the whole of Hobsbawn House, and—' he shrugged, 'I had no particular desire for it, so I let him have it.'

'You knew he was going to leave it all to me?' Charlotte said in astonishment.

'I knew he wanted to make you trustee,' Benedict said, 'but I suppose—' he hesitated and lowered his voice, 'the trust would have taken time to set up, and I wonder if he had a premonition? He knew he could trust you to do what he wanted, however it was set up.' And he slid his eyes briefly in Cavendish's direction. Charlotte felt a pang for her brother. If Batchworth had died before Fanny's Portion, as she thought of it, had been put into a trust it would have fallen in with the main estate and passed to Cavendish; and Cavendish had been behaving badly. Did Batchworth really not trust his son to keep it for Fanny? She could only hope Cavendish would never draw that conclusion.

But leaving Fanny's Portion to Charlotte did not eliminate all difficulties. Charlotte was a married woman, and all her property automatically belonged to Oliver, except that which had been reserved to her by the terms of their marriage contract – which could not, of course, include Fanny's Portion, since she had not owned it at the time. That, she supposed, was what the letters were about. She turned to look at Oliver, and saw that he was looking at her, the letter in his hand, and an eyebrow raised in enquiry. But his mouth was grim. For some reason, she saw with a sinking heart, this bequest was a new source of disapproval for him.

'Perhaps we had better talk, you and I,' Oliver said.

They retired to the library. Oliver closed the door behind them. 'Life with you at least has the charm of unpredictability.'

'Perhaps we should read the letters first,' Charlotte said nervously, but he shook his head.

'The letters can wait. First I should like to be put on an equal footing with Mr Benedict Morland, who plainly has the advantage over me. But then I am merely your husband.'

'Oh, Oliver, don't be cross! I didn't know this was going to happen – or at least, I didn't know it was going to happen like this.' Oliver merely waited expressionlessly. 'It's quite simple. Papa heard that Dr Anthony was planning to sell all the Manchester property that he acquired when he married Fanny. Papa wanted to buy it so that, if he ever found Fanny again, he could restore her inheritance to her. But he knew Anthony wouldn't sell it to him, so he got cousin Benedict to buy it, and then *he* bought it from *him*.'

Oliver nodded understanding. Thank God, at least, she thought, for an intelligent man. 'That explains Batchworth's passionate espousal of the Divorce Bill amendments. Before the present Act, anything he gave Fanny would have automatically become Anthony's.'

'Just so,' Charlotte said eagerly, 'whereas now—'

'Whereas now, it becomes mine,' Oliver concluded for her. 'I wonder Batchworth didn't think of that. For a conspirator, he has been extremely clumsy.'

'Perhaps we should read the letters now?' Charlotte suggested meekly. 'They may explain everything.'

Hers read:

My dearest beloved Daughter – for so you are to me, and could not be more dear if you were indeed the flesh of my flesh. If you are reading this, it is because I have not had time to mature my plans. I feel the Reaper's breath on my neck, and so I must make an interim arrangement in case he catches up with me too soon. Fanny's inheritance is now in your hands, and you know what I want you to do with it. I think it likely that if she comes to anyone, she will come to you, who were always her closest friend. Preserve it against that day, and give it to her, as I would have. Anthony can't touch it now. If you find out that Fanny is dead – and we must acknowledge it is possible – do with it as you think fit. I trust you entirely. I leave a letter to your good husband, too, explaining my wishes. He is a just man, and I am confident will do what is right. I am so very glad you have him: I could not have been content to leave you to anyone who loved you less. Your loving Papa, now and to Eternity – Batchworth.

She read the last part with tears in her eyes. If he had known how things stood between her and Oliver! Oliver might have loved her once, but he did so no longer, and what would happen to Fanny's Portion now?

Oliver's letter read:

My dear Southport, you will be surprised at my leaving such a property to Charlotte, which means, in effect, to you. She will explain how it comes about. I had meant to leave it in trust for Fanny, but approaching Death has altered my plans and I must trust to your love for my dear Charlotte, and your sense of justice, to see that it goes to Fanny at last. Thank God! we were able to change the law in time, so that now it will be possible for Fanny to keep what should always have been hers. I know that you and I were on opposite sides during the late struggle, but I know also that you have a compassionate heart, and I believe, were it not for your Government commitments, you would have found yourself fighting alongside me. I respect and admire you more than any man I know. Your servant, in this world and the next – Batchworth.

He looked up from his reading to find Charlotte's eyes fixed on him in urgent enquiry. 'He trusts me to let you keep this property and hand it over to Fanny, if ever she reappears,' he said at last.

'Yes. So he says here.'

'It is a pity, in that case, that he did not tell me about it before.' He shook the letter as if it were something unpleasant sticking to his fingers. 'All this talk of *trust* and *respect* – yet he conspired with you behind my back, and would never have told me of it at all if he hadn't felt himself failing. So much for trust!'

Her heart sank. Why must he see everything in such black terms? 'I'm sure he didn't mean it that way,' she began.

'Are you? I can't see how else the facts can be interpreted.'

'But, Oliver, surely what matters is that Fanny should have what's hers? What does it signify how it is done, or who should have said what to whom?'

'What *signifies*,' Oliver threw the word back at her, 'is that this is another example of your attitude of mind – in which your late beloved step-father encouraged you. An attitude that puts the contract of marriage at nought. An attitude that says a woman should take all the advantages of marriage but renege as she pleases on the duties.'

'No! it isn't like that!' she protested.

'Isn't it? You were such a reluctant bride, madam, or don't you remember? You wanted my name and title and my position in society – my protection and sanction – but you wanted to keep your own fortune, and the freedom to do exactly as you pleased! Well, it doesn't work like that! There are responsibilities to fulfil. A married woman is not free, and no matter how you and your step-father rail against that, it is a fact and can't be changed.'

'But it can be changed!' Charlotte said, trying to speak reasonably, though her heart was pounding and her palms were damp.

'You see how this new Act has changed things. Injustice doesn't have to be borne for ever, just because it existed in the past!'

'Injustice?' he exclaimed furiously. 'You call it injustice?'

'That a separated woman should not be allowed to keep what she earns or is given – yes, I would say that's injustice! That men and women are not equal before the law—'

'Men and women are not equal in any respect! *Why* can't you understand that?' he cried in frustration. 'if you wanted so much to be a man, why in God's name did you marry me?'

'Because I loved you,' she said. 'And love you.'

'You have a strange way of showing it,' he said bitterly.

She flared. 'I have never betrayed you – not as you have betrayed me!'

He was silent, but there was no softening in his face; rather, she thought, he did not want to go on arguing on a subject in which she was unteachable. For an involuntary instant she saw him in bed with Mrs Galbraith, and the pain scorched through her agonisingly before she dismissed the vision angrily. Their loving lives together might be over, but at least they could learn to deal justly with each other – must do so, since they were to stay married.

'Oliver,' she said gently, 'don't let's allow this piece of business to become a new thorn in our flesh. It really isn't anything to do with us. Let me keep Fanny's Portion until I can give it to her. It can be added into our contract any way you like.' He didn't speak. 'You don't want the property, I'm sure, any more than I do. You wouldn't want to profit unfairly by Papa's death, would you?'

He sighed, and she saw the resistance go out of him; and in a strange way that was worse, because what was underneath seemed to be sadness, and she would sooner he was angry than sad. 'Do as you please,' he said. 'I want nothing that was Batchworth's, and nothing that was Fanny's. You're right about that, at least.'

Cavendish had no objection to the arrangement. 'It will mean you have to come and visit us often. You'll have to keep an eye on the mills and make sure they're being run properly, won't you?' he told Charlotte.

'What do I know about mills? An agent will do that for me.'

'Tush!' he said. 'Here I am giving you the excuse and you're busy throwing it away with both hands!'

'Darling, I would come and visit you anyway. Do you think I'd need an excuse?'

'I thought you might. I don't like the way Southport looks at me. I think he don't approve of our family much.'

'Nonsense! When our children are all growing up together? What greater sign of approval do you want than William sharing a bed with Henry and Marcus?'

Rosamund was glad, too. 'My poor Fanny! If only you can find her and restore her fortune to her, maybe she will come back here to live. She and I could share the dower house and be comfortable together. Oh, I hope you find her soon! I should hate to die not knowing how it came out.'

'You're not going to die, Mother,' Charlotte said, alarmed.

'I have to one day,' Rosamund said reasonably.

'But not yet, not for a long time. I can't do without you.' Rosamund patted her hand comfortingly. 'Do you really believe that I can find Fanny?' Charlotte asked curiously.

'Jes believed she's still alive. He said he could feel it in the back of his mind, like a faint, distant sound, like the wind. He said when it fell silent, he would know she was dead.' She shrugged. 'In the absence of any other evidence, I could only trust his instinct. So I hope you can find her soon.'

'I'll do my best,' Charlotte said, but she was apprehensive about it. She supposed now she would have to contact Fanny, but she still felt it would be better for Fanny to be left alone. Would even a large fortune compensate Fanny for having her shame dragged out into the glaring light of day? She could not now re-enter Society; indeed, restored to her own stratum she would have to live in greater retirement than she did now. Besides, if Fanny had wanted to be found, she could have come to Charlotte at any time, for she was less than a mile away.

But Charlotte went over and over the matter in her mind, coming always to the same unhappy conclusion that it was not for her to choose to withhold Fanny's fortune from her. A duty had been laid upon her by her step-father and she must carry it out, whatever the consequences. But she wished with all her heart that Anthony had never thought of selling the property, or that Batchworth had not heard about it, or that, best of all, Anthony had never met Fanny in the first place. And that, of course, was Charlotte's fault. It was she who had taken Fanny to the Welland house where she had first met Dr Anthony, and everything that had happened to Fanny afterwards was therefore her responsibility. There was no way out for her but to shoulder this new, unwelcome task and see it through.

Oliver stayed two days after the funeral and then went back to Ravendene, and Charlotte promised to join him there in a week or so. He seemed satisfied with this, and parted from her more kindly than he had been used to speaking to her for some time. 'The children will be so excited when I tell you you're coming,' he said.

To save Cavendish trouble – he was busy from morning till night with agents and tenants and lawyers – Charlotte offered to arrange William's return to Grasscroft when she got to Ravendene, which he accepted gratefully.

Emily went back to Morland Place on the same day Oliver left, feeling Sibella needed her now more than Rosamund. Tom went with her, never wanting to be far from her side; but Benedict stayed on, saying he'd like to begin looking at the mills and Morland's Rents to see what condition they were in and how they were being run. He suggested Charlotte join him, but she said she would be glad to leave everything to him for the time being, though she would certainly wish to make an inspection some time soon, when her immediate and pressing business was concluded.

This immediate and pressing business was to go to London on the way to Ravendene, and get the first interview with Fanny over. She left Temple to sort things out with Mr Culverhouse, and when she got to London she shed Norton by leaving her at Southport House to unpack and repack for Ravendene. She told her maid that she was going to pay a brief visit to the hospital. Since the house was officially closed up, she would take a cab. She would be quite all right on such a short journey, and to such a destination. Norton supposed, glumly, that Charlotte was going to see Sir Frederick, and the less she had to do with that situation the better.

Charlotte had not thought how it would appear to Norton; her mind was on other matters. Once the cab had turned the corner she rapped on the roof, and when the driver's face appeared in the hatch she said that she had changed her mind, and told him to drive to Theobald's Row. There she got out, told the driver to wait for her, and set off briskly to walk to Lamb's Conduit Street. Her feet slowed with reluctance as she neared the house, thinking of the pain, shock and embarrassment she was about to visit on them. But Peter was a good soul, she thought, and surely would not abandon Fanny and their baby out of false pride? And, oh, the baby! It hurt her even to think about it. But at least now it would be properly clothed and educated; and money could go a long way to making a bastard child acceptable, at least in certain sections of Society.

She walked up to the door of the house and, straightening her shoulders with determination, rapped on it. She had a moment of panic as she waited, wondering whom to ask for. What did Fanny call herself? But if she asked for Mrs Welland, that would cover Peter's mother too, which would do just as well. The door opened, and Charlotte's heart did a somersault, but it was not necessary: it was a servant who stood there, a slatternly kind of servant in a dirty apron.

'Good afternoon,' Charlotte said. 'Is Mrs Welland at home?'

The girl stared stupidly. 'Who, miss – mum?'

'Mrs Welland. The lady of the house.'

The girl shook her head, slowly, like a cow. 'I dunno no Mrs Welland,' she said at last.

'Who lives here, then?' Charlotte said impatiently.

'Who is it, Patsy?' came a sharp voice from inside the house. 'Don't stand there gossiping on the doorstep.'

The maid began automatically to withdraw, and seeing the door was about to be closed on her, Charlotte said quickly, 'Go and ask your mistress if I may speak to her for a moment.'

'Who shall I say, mum?'

'Say Mrs Morland.'

The girl went away into what used to be the dining-room, and a moment later a strange woman came out, brisk, shrew-featured, and dressed rather too brightly for her age. Her eyes were sharp with suspicion. 'What do you want?' She looked Charlotte up and down, noting the quality of her clothes, which seemed oddly to increase rather than allay her suspicions.

'I beg your pardon for disturbing you, but I'm looking for Mrs Welland. I am an old friend.'

'The Wellands don't live here any more – which you'd know if you were that much of a friend,' the woman replied gracelessly, and began to close the door.

'Wait!' Charlotte said. 'Please! Do you know where they went? I'm sorry to trouble you but it's very important that I find them.'

The woman sighed as if it were a great imposition, but she said, 'I'll ask Cook. She might know. Wait here.' She closed the door and Charlotte waited, aware that a small knot of children was gathering in the street behind her, interested in her appearance and hoping the situation was going to become exciting. At last the door opened again, and the householder appeared with a stern expression. 'Cook says Mrs Welland died, and the rest of them had to leave under the bailiffs, and if that's the sort of friends you've got, the more shame on you!'

'Where did they go?' Charlotte cried against the closing door, but this time there was no relenting. She turned away from the door, and the children backed delicately before her. She caught the eye of the oldest and brightest-looking, and said, 'Do you know where the people went who used to live here? The Wellands?'

The child stared a moment, and then stuck out her tongue, and the whole gang scattered, shrieking with hilarity, and disappeared round various corners. Charlotte started back towards her waiting cab. She foresaw long investigations ahead, and that would mean hiring an agent. Plainly she could not herself tramp the streets asking questions. But which Mrs Welland had died? Surely the elder – surely not Fanny? And why had the bailiffs been called? She would worry now until she found out, and finding out might be long delayed. Her step-father had left her a troublesome burden.

CHAPTER NINE

One spring day in 1859, Lennox was coming back across Low Moor towards Harewood Whin. He had been out as far as Redhouse Wood, and now he was tired and heading home. Home! he thought. Would that it were! He loved the handsome old house with its mellow bricks and stones, the lovely gardens and the fertile fields all around; but it did not belong to him and never would. Likewise he did not belong to it, as everyone seemed constantly to be reminding him – as if he were likely to forget! Georgie seemed to live in a ferment of anxiety that Lennox should ever settle for a moment, feel a moment's ease or comfort in what was 'Georgie's inheritance'.

He did Georgie the justice to believe that he wouldn't have thought of it for himself – not from the beginning. It was Mr Wheldrake who really hated Lennox, and who encouraged George to do likewise; and Teddy merely followed where George led. If ever he was alone with Teddy, he got on quite well with the younger boy, who was good-natured and lazy and would as soon like everyone as make the effort to dislike them. But there was no pleasing Mr Wheldrake.

He no longer did lessons with the younger boys, which was a relief to all concerned. Lennox had been ejected from the schoolroom on the grounds that he was disruptive and a bad influence. The injustice of the accusation burned him, as did the cold looks it won him from Mrs Morland. Still, it was a relief to be able to work alone and at his own pace. The family's library of books was kept in the Long Saloon, and there Lennox worked on a project of his own: a translation into verse of the *Carmina* of Catullus. He had a rather inferior eighteenth-century translation, plus a Latin dictionary and grammar to help him; the problem was that when he did have a difficulty, there was no-one to ask for guidance. But still, he worried away at it and the end result he was modestly pleased with. Mr Wheldrake insisted on seeing the work as it went along, and now took each instalment away into his private room where he kept it for a time before handing it back. He did not precisely praise the work, but he gave Lennox a curt nod and told him to carry on.

As well as the Catullus, Lennox was reading his way through every book in the library, and devising a course of study for himself with the materials to hand. He learned large pieces of prose and poetry by heart; memorised lists of dates, capital cities, Roman emperors, elements and metals, constellations – anything, indeed, that leant itself to memorising. He re-fought historic battles on paper with the help of books on military strategy; and with a book on the principles of architecture he designed houses, churches, factories and railway stations of airy simplicity or Gothic elaboration.

His mathematics he kept exercised by doing the household accounts. During her last pregnancy Sibella had found them too much of a struggle and had given them to Haxby, the steward. In the face of the mistress's drawn looks Haxby could not refuse, but he was no more of a mathematician than she was. He disliked the job so much he kept putting it off, until Lennox stumbled upon him one afternoon in the stewards' room, crouched over the books with ink on his forehead and a snarl of desperation on his lips. It took Lennox two weeks to sort out the muddle, and after that he did the accounts daily with the information Haxby and Ketton, the agent, brought him.

When he was not occupied with any of these mental pursuits, he took himself out of doors for long walks, finding comfort in the indifferent bosom of Nature. He had missed the sea very much at first, but now he liked the moors almost as much, with their wide expanse of sky and the strange, fluky light which made things look sometimes very close, sometimes impossibly far off. He came to know the countryside and its people very well, the hedgers and ditchers, the ploughmen, the cowmen and shepherds; he visited the Morland farms, and found that he was more accepted away from Morland Place than he was within it. At White House, Woodhouse, Huntsham and Prospect he got a cordial welcome rather than a scowl; and if he happened to arrive at dinner-time, he'd be invited civilly to sit down at the big table.

They were not great talkers on the whole, and he liked them better for it. Speech was full of traps and dangers; in silence was safety. Farmhouse dinner was a serious business: men who had been working hard all morning had solid food to get outside of, which left no time for chattery. At Thickpenny, the most outlying of Morland farms, where he had luckily happened upon dinner today, they did not even bother with plates. The huge oblong scrubbed table in the kitchen had circular recesses carved out, a foot in diameter, at regular intervals along the sides. When the house bell was rung for dinner, the men came in and took their places along the benches, and into each recess the farmer's wife and her girls dropped a thick round batter pudding of the same size. Onto this would be served the meat and potatoes and cabbage or whatever was the day's fare; and when the men had eaten the meal, they ate the 'plate' as well. Afterwards a massive slab of an apple pie would come round in its dish, each man cutting himself a wedge with his knife and passing the dish on; and this was generally taken with a same-sized slice of cheese. It was good, solid, nourishing, tasty food, and the men looked well on it.

He called at the farms at dinner-time as often as he could, not for the food but for the acceptance. They did not question who and what he was: he was from 'up the House', and that was good enough. On an even simpler level, Lennox understood that he was benefiting from an older tradition that had sunk deeply and wordlessly into the Yorkshire character: to give hospitality to the passing traveller.

Skirting the Whin, Lennox was drawn from his inner monologue by a commotion going on just out of sight beyond the incurving edge of the wood – a trampling and cracking and cursing that sounded like someone in trouble. He broke into a run, and came round the corner to find that it was Georgie, beating his pony. The boy was hatless and dishevelled and red in the face with fury, grasping the bridle tight up by the bit-rings, while he hit the pony about the head with the shaft of his whip. The pony was trampling on the spot, desperately trying to free itself, its eyes rolling whitely and foam dripping from its lips.

Lennox reached them in a couple of strides, snatched the whip from George's hand and flung it as far away as he could. 'Stop it! Stop that!'

George turned a furious face on him. 'Give me back my whip, damn you!'

'So you can beat the poor brute again? Not likely!'

'What the devil is it to do with you? Let go my arm!'

'I will not, until you let go the bridle,' Lennox said. 'I won't have you hit the pony like that.'

'I'll hit him any way I like! He's my pony. He wants a lesson, and I'm the man to give him one!'

Lennox had interfered out of pure instinct, but now his resentment was boiling up. He had suffered a great deal at George's hands, one way and another. George was inclined to pass off his sins on Lennox, secure in the knowledge that Mr Wheldrake would always believe him, and that Lennox had been brought up not to tell tales. Lennox was helpless in the situation: if he denied the charge

– and sometimes the crimes were so mean he simply couldn't stop himself – he was accusing Georgie of lying, which was an even worse sin. And George liked to torment Lennox by picking fights with him, knowing Lennox could not hurt him. Lennox did not like to fight, thinking it a pointless and ugly pastime, but in any case he would not have fought with a boy four years his junior. So Georgie would attack him, and Lennox could do nothing but try to defend himself without hurting George. George, of course, had no compunction about hurting *him*, but far worse than the physical pain was the pain of humiliation.

It was part of the reason he went on his long walks, so as to be out of George's way as much as possible. But he had a lot of scores to settle, and was fast reaching the point where he no longer cared about the consequences. Seeing the boy thrash this pretty pony was the last straw. George had a short way with anything he thought his inferior, like servants and animals – particularly animals.

'So you're a man, are you?' Lennox said now scornfully. 'Man enough to curse, and man enough to hit a defenceless brute for nothing!'

'It wasn't for nothing! He tipped me off,' George said. 'I put him at the gate into the wood and he refused and refused and then he tipped me off. I won't brook disobedience, I can tell you!'

Lennox looked round. 'That gate? But it's far too high for him! Good God, you'd know that if you were anything of a horseman.'

George's eyes narrowed, and a hot, red light burned deep down in them. But he spoke in a reasonable voice, saying, 'Well, perhaps you're right. Just hold him, will you, while I go and pick up my whip.'

He let go the reins and Lennox took hold of them automatically. 'You'll not hit him again,' he said.

'No, I'll not hit him,' George agreed, turning his back so that Lennox would not see his smirk. He walked off to where the whip had landed, while Lennox tried to soothe the pony. He could not touch its head – it was too upset for that – but he spoke to it gently and examined it as best he could, noting that its lips were raw from the curb bit, and that it had a cut across one eye from the blows it had received. It would not stand still, but fretted about him, trembling and sweating.

He was so preoccupied with the pony that Georgie's attack took him completely off guard. Suddenly he was hit on the side of the head with the whip-stock; the pony jerked away from him and was off, galloping for home with reins flying and stirrups banging. Lennox reeled, his hands going up to his head, and George hit him again, shouting. 'That's for you, pauper! How dare you interfere, you damned penniless upstart!' Lennox stumbled and went down on his knees while the blows rained on his head and hands; but only for a moment. He gathered his wits, and at the same time lost his temper. He managed to grab the whip as it came down on him again, and as Georgie wrestled for control of it, he used it to pull himself to his feet, and then wrenched it from George's grasp and with a convulsion of anger broke it in two across his knee.

'There!' he said, throwing the pieces violently away. 'Now we're equal!'

'Equal?' George panted in rage. 'You're not my equal. I am a gentleman!'

'That's something you'll never be,' Lennox said, and hit him. Even as he did it, he was ashamed of himself, and pulled at the last moment, so that the blow only grazed George's chin and made him stagger backwards, his eyes flying open with surprise.

'You'll pay for that!' he cried shrilly. 'You hit me! You shall know all about it, cully, when I get home!'

Lennox found himself trembling with emotion. His head hurt abominably from the blows, but his heart was even more sore. 'Oh yes, now we see how much of a man you are! You'll hit a dumb brute of a pony – you'll hit me as long as I'm off my guard – but you won't stand up with your fists in a fair fight. Run home then, tattletale! I know about you now – Mary Ann!'

'Mary Ann?' Georgie screamed in fury, and came at him, fists flying.

Despite the difference in age, and Lennox's advantage in height, they were about the same weight, for George was a good trencher-man and had first pick of everything on the nursery table. And both were furious enough not to heed the blows they received. They circled and hit and grappled, stumbling on the rough grass, panting with exertion, silent except for grunts and gasps. Then George tried to kick Lennox, and when Lennox pulled him in close to prevent this, George bit him. This broke the last barrier of restraint in the older boy. He thrust George away from him with a cry of anger, and followed it up with a blow which landed fair and square on George's nose. Maddened with pain, George hit Lennox in the stomach, and when he doubled up, punched him in the eye. Lennox saw stars, reeled away and sat down hard. George subsided onto the grass too, blood flowing over his mouth and chin while he fumbled for a handkerchief.

After a while Lennox stopped feeling sick and looked up. George, with a stained handkerchief to his face, was sitting a little way off, surveying him speculatively. Ugly and unpleasant as the fight had been, Lennox thought, there was a sort of satisfaction to it. His eye was throbbing and seemed to be closing up, but George was going to have a very tender nose. In the strange euphoria of the moment, he felt they had passed through something together, and perhaps now could make a new start.

'Well,' he said. George watched him cautiously over the handkerchief. 'I'd say we came out about even. What say we declare friends?'

George lowered the handkerchief. His nose was red and swollen, and the blood was crusting on his lips, giving him a rather nasty look. 'Friends?' he said. 'Friends with a thing like you? You'll catch it when I get home and show what you did to me!'

Lennox was so surprised he only stared, unable to realise George did not feel the same catharsis. 'But – but what about my eye? It was a fair fight.'

'You set about me for no reason,' George said, enjoying his power. Lennox had hurt his nose and his pride, but he was going to hurt Lennox far more. 'You dragged me off my pony, took my whip out of my hand and set about me. I had to defend myself – managed to get in a lucky blow to your eye, otherwise you might have killed me.' He got slowly to his feet, staring down at Lennox with a gloating smile. 'Oh, you'll catch it *all right*! They'll send you away for this – and good riddance, I say!'

'He'll have to be sent away,' Sibella said, watching her husband pace about the room. 'You must see that.'

'I dare say it wasn't all one-sided,' Benedict said unhappily. 'Boys will be boys. I was always scrapping with the farm lads when I was Georgie's age.'

'But this wasn't a scrap. And Lennox isn't a farm lad,' Sibella said. She had been supervising egg-pickling all afternoon and felt tired and worn and had a nagging pain in her back that she always got when she stood for too long. It made her feel irritable. 'He's a member of the household, and one, moreover, who ought to be grateful to us for giving him a home. But how does he show his gratitude? By setting on our little boy!'

'He got a black eye for his pains,' Benedict pointed out.

'He's four years older than George!' Sibella said, outraged. 'It's unforgivable, to pick on a boy so much younger – and for no reason! It's cowardly and wicked and I cannot understand why you stand up for him instead of your own son!'

'Oh, I'm not defending him,' Benedict said hastily. 'It's not right to hit a younger boy. I was only saying perhaps he was provoked. But of course he must be punished. One can't turn a blind eye to that sort of thing.'

'Punished? He must be sent away,' Sibella said. 'There's no alternative now. I was always against having him here, and now you see how it's come out. What will he do next, if he stays here? Are you going to wait until he hits Teddy, or one of the girls?'

'Oh, come, he wouldn't do that!' Benedict said.

'You don't know what he's capable of!' Sibella cried. 'With such a mother and father he's bound to turn out wicked. You can't expose our children to his bad influence.'

Benedict came to sit beside her, looking anxiously at her. 'My love, you're making too much of it. He's just a boy. Why do you hate him so?'

'You can ask me that?' Sibella said. 'Are you deaf and blind, that you don't know the gossip that goes on about him? Do you think people don't wonder why you have him here? They say he's your love-child and you're besotted with him. They even say you're going to leave Morland Place to him instead of to George. Well, maybe you are! If you let him hit my child with impunity, what else might you not do? Her child means more to you than mine, it seems!'

She burst into tears, surprising them both. Benedict took her into his arms, patting her shoulder awkwardly and making soothing noises. 'Promise me you'll send him away,' she said at last when she was able to frame words among her sobs. 'Promise me! I don't want him here.'

It seemed unfair that she should hate the boy so much because of who his parents had been. Benedict had begun by being in Lennox's favour because he was Mary's brother, but now he thought he was a likeable lad, for what little he knew of him, and it saddened him to see every hand against him. He had wanted to give Lennox a fair chance, but he saw that Sibella was at the end of some personal tether, and she must be his first consideration. And his children and his household must be his second. Fairness to Lennox could not take precedence over all that.

'All right, I'll do something, I promise,' he said. 'But you must let me think about it. I've taken responsibility for the boy, and I can't shrug it off. I must do what's right by him.'

Sibella reached for her handkerchief. 'Just as long as you remove him from my house, I don't care. But don't take too long over it. And, meanwhile, he's not to go near my children.'

'Very well,' Benedict said. A good thought occurred to him. 'He can go round with Ketton. Ketton seems to like him, and he can make himself useful to him, while I think what's to be done.'

Since her step-father's funeral, Charlotte's life and Oliver's had spun apart like two planets taking up orbit around separate suns.

It was easy enough to keep herself busy. She had the hospital, in which she could interest herself as much or as little as she pleased. The Medical Act had been passed the year before, in 1858, and apprentices had transmuted into medical students. New arrangements had had to be made for teaching, examining and disciplining them, but they were worth having at the hospital, since they paid eighty-four guineas a year for their instruction, while continuing to do much of the hard work. Students had to be lectured in anatomy, histology, pathology, chemistry, botany, physiology and materia medica, plus daily teaching in morbid anatomy. A new wing had to be built onto the south-west corner of the Southport, with examination rooms, laboratories and offices on the ground floor, a large and a small lecture theatre on the first floor, and a post-mortem theatre and morgue in the basement.

The new building had presented Charlotte with the space to add another ward on the second floor, and the chance to do something she had long been discussing with Sir Frederick: separating the surgical cases from the medical. While the use of anaesthesia had greatly reduced surgical deaths, infection still took a huge toll, and isolating the surgical patients made it easier to monitor the cleanliness of their surroundings.

When she wanted a change from medical matters, there was her work in the slums, and on her various other committees. No, it was not difficult to keep busy: the difficulty was rather finding enough hours in the day. Oliver had his own round of business, and Southport House was large enough to accommodate them both so that they need not see each other unless they wanted to. There was no official separation, and they appeared together in public a regulation three or four times a year, on which occasions they would smile and be gracious to each other; and Society, which understood perfectly how these things went, made nothing of it. The duke, who was an attractive and amusing man, was invited *en garçon* and provided with a well-born, well-behaved 'flirt'; the duchess, it was given out, went little into Society, being now entirely given up to good works.

Charlotte had thought she could carry on in that way for ever, but she had reckoned without the loneliness. She had always wanted to lead a useful life, but when the whirl of activity dropped her with time to spare before going to bed, the pain caught up with her. She didn't even have the children to distract her: they now lived permanently at Ravendene with Lady Turnhouse, who, in her sixties, had at last given up London Society. The official reason for the removal of the nursery was that the air of London was bad for them, but Charlotte knew that it was she who was bad for them, in their grandmother's opinion. Officially she could go down to Ravendene at any time; in reality she was not welcome there.

Her three regular companions each had an area of intimacy with her. Norton, of course, was her personal maid, with all that that implied. Temple, besides dealing with her business and correspondence, was her agent in the matter of Fanny's Portion. She had told him everything under pledge of secrecy, and Temple it was who interviewed the landlord, the firm of bailiffs, and the late Mr Tarbush's clerk; who tramped the streets knocking on doors and asking questions; who carried a miniature of Fanny in his breast pocket which he showed to jarvies and railway clerks and hotel porters in the hope of sparking recognition. But in almost two years he had found no trace of them. Mrs Welland had died of typhus – that much the landlord vouchsafed. Sometimes Charlotte wondered whether they had taken the typhus with them when they flitted, and were now all dead. They might as well have been, for all the luck Temple had in finding them.

As to Sir Frederick Friedman, after her step-papa's funeral and Oliver's condemnation, Charlotte had wondered how she would cope with meeting him again. But when she first saw him at the Southport in his formal frock, high collar, black cravat and top hat, he seemed a different Sir Frederick from the one she had talked with so long and intimately under the copper beech, and she fell naturally into her old form of dialogue with him. Yet it *was* different, inwardly if not outwardly. Wherever she saw him at the hospital – in his office, in the committee-room, on the wards – she was intensely aware of him in the room; she felt almost palpably the warmth of his interest, the sureness that everything she did and said would be accepted by him. She developed, though she was not aware of it, a shorthand way of talking with him, which was normally the province of childhood friends or long-term lovers. There was nothing improper in his behaviour, nothing arch or sidelong, nothing to make her uneasy. He was her frank and cordial friend – the more precious to her for being singular – but never by word or look did he hint at what more he would have liked there to be between them. Yet all the time she was sinking deeper into intimacy with him, and taking comfort from his unspoken love. They shared so many ideas and interests, and a day when she did not see him left her unsatisfied.

The day came when she called at his rooms in the hospital to discuss student discipline with him – the former apprentices were a rough, unruly and frequently drunken lot – and from there went on to discuss other, everyday, matters. London was emptying fast, and the smells were beginning to concentrate. Summer in London had always been unpleasant, but the plan to provide a sewerage system for the capital had paradoxically made things worse, since the sewers all emptied into the Thames. It now resembled a huge open kennel, and in the dry summer the year before, the stench had been so bad at Westminster that the Houses of Parliament had had to be evacuated.

So in the course of conversation it was natural for Charlotte to ask Sir Frederick if he was going out of Town, and where he meant to go.

'I haven't decided yet,' he said. 'Some clean country air is an essential. What about you? Will you be going to your brother again?'

'No – I don't know,' she said. 'I sometimes wish—' She stopped, deep in thought. Much as she loved Cavendish, she felt uncomfortable there without Oliver. Last summer so many questions had been asked about him and the children that she had almost told the truth. But it would be the same wherever people knew her.

He looked at her unobserved for a while, then said, 'Do you remember how you said once you wished we could go away somewhere remote, and take a little cottage by the sea or on the edge of the moors?' The focus of her eyes changed. She looked startled. 'We still could,' he said. 'There's Oakthorpe. Or, if that isn't remote enough, there's the whole country to choose from.'

She seemed to be thinking very slowly. 'You mean—?'

'Freedom is a state, not an action, so you said,' he smiled. 'Why shouldn't it be both? Let's find that small house. Stebbins and Norton shall look after us, and you shall talk and I shall draw. I want you to be happy. Why shouldn't you be?'

'No reason that I know of,' she said rather blankly. 'You've never asked me before. Why now?'

'Because the time is right,' he said. 'I see how lonely you are; but there's no need to be. Why should we spend the summer in two different places, each alone, when we could spend it together?'

His eyes were dark and insistent, and she felt as if she were falling into them, sinking effortlessly through deep, cool water. She wanted so much to be comforted, to be loved; her need for it was greater than her need to love. And who cared now what she did? Who would be hurt?

A mile across the fields from Morland Place was the manor house of Shawes. It had been built by Sir John Vanbrugh, a small but perfectly proportioned house, which had been much admired. It was described in the old guidebooks as 'Vanbrugh's Little Gem', and was thought to be one of his finest works.

The house had no estate, only a small area of pleasure grounds. Yorkshire being rather remote from London until the railways came, the owners had not used it in generations. It had been leased out, but nine years earlier the last tenants had departed and it had not been let since. It had fallen rather into disrepair and would need money spent on it before it would be fit to let again, and apparently the present owner was not inclined to bother.

It was one of the places Lennox liked to go, particularly when he was unhappy. Quite by accident he had found a door in the high perimeter wall which had been left unlocked. It was almost completely hidden by the rampant ivy which grew all over the wall, and he was careful to squeeze in without breaking the tendrils, pushing the door closed behind him so that no-one should know where he was. The door led into a corner of the walled kitchen garden behind the glass-houses, a dry place of broken flower-pots and seed-boxes, long-dead weeds and ghostly grass growing through an abandoned and rusty fork. The glass-houses had broken panes outside and nettles and bear-bind growing inside; the kitchen beds were a wilderness of thistles and brambles and fruit bushes gone back to Nature.

All the pleasure grounds were like that, gone to seed, with tall grasses and wild flowers obscuring the lines. Lennox liked it in summer: it was like a lovely, wild woman, a gypsy princess perhaps, with whirling skirts and long, flying hair, unkempt and beautiful. In winter it was sad rather than beautiful, and the house looked forlorn in its neglect.

It was a beautiful house, though. He had read about it in an old guidebook he had found, a local directory dated 1780; and it was mentioned, too, in a book on architecture. The original owner – Annunciata, Countess of Chelmsford – had been a close friend of Vanbrugh and he had designed it to her exact requirements. Last summer Lennox had brought drawing-materials here and sketched it from various angles, and it had so entered his imagination that he found it featured in many of the fancy houses he drew during the long winter evenings.

His favourite place was the bathing-house, which made a separate little wing. There were two rooms, a bathroom and a dressing-room, with floors of black and white marble squares. The ceilings, supported by porphyry columns, were painted with the most wonderful frescos of tritons, naiads and dolphins, full-breasted mermaids and fat cherubs spouting water from their puffed cheeks, with a centre-piece of a grey-bearded, wild-haired Neptune, furiously driving his chariot drawn by four white-maned sea-horses in a sea of deepest blue. The bath itself was an enormous white marble scallop shell, and above it on the ceiling was a massive white marble rose.

Of course it was all a little shabby now: some of the window-panes were cracked and one was broken; dead leaves had blown in and gathered in the corners. The floor was grimy, the looking-glasses spotted, the veined marble of the shell-bath streaked with rust-stains, the bright colours of the ceilings were dulled and here and there patches of plaster were coming away. But Lennox saw it as it must have looked when it was all new. He imagined the Lady Annunciata bathing in the shell and lying on a couch in the dressing-room, swathed in something diaphanous, while musicians played to her and servants brought her tall glasses of sherbet . . .

He was standing staring up at the rose on the ceiling above the bath, wondering again why it was a rose and not, say, a whale or a whelk-shell, when a voice behind him said quietly, 'I used to wonder about that, too, but in fact it's a shower-bath. For all I know, it may be the earliest one in existence.'

He turned so fast that he almost fell over. A woman was standing there in a grey dress with a shawl round her shoulders. The dress, though only lightly hooped, was expensively cut, and the shawl was silk. Her head was bare, but her pinkish-gold hair was put up by the expert hand of a lady's maid. This was certainly a gentlewoman, as he would have known by the voice and the demeanour, but what he noticed most were the sad grey-green eyes. He didn't think he'd ever seen eyes so sad, and it stopped him being afraid or shy or embarrassed, or anything else he might appropriately have felt at being caught here.

She went on in a perfectly neutral voice, as if he were an old friend she was showing round, 'If you look closely you can see the holes drilled through it, and there, in the centre, is the ring that once had a chain attached to it. You pulled the chain and up there, above the ceiling, it moved a lever which uncovered the holes and let the water through from the cistern.'

'Have you been up there?' he asked, fascinated.

'No, but I found a book about it in the library. It's got all the original drawings. It was very ingenious. There's a staircase in the boiler-house for the servant to go up and fill the cistern. It had to be done with buckets – rather primitive – but at least there was a pulley.'

He nodded, and looked around him again. 'It must have been gorgeous when it was all new and bright.'

'Yes, and there were marble containers all around with orange trees and myrtle and white roses growing in them, and a white-and-gold brocade daybed in there.' She nodded towards the dressing-room.

'She must have looked wonderful, rising from the bath – like Venus,' he said unguardedly, and added hastily, 'The one it was built for.'

The woman nodded. 'She was very beautiful, apparently. She had long black hair, and the King was supposed to be in love with her.'

They were silent a moment, looking around. 'It's such a pity to let it go to ruin like this,' Lennox said. 'If it were mine, I'd want to make it perfect again. I wonder who owns it now.'

The woman almost smiled. 'I do,' she said.

He felt himself blushing. 'Oh! I'm sorry.'

'For what?' she said indifferently. 'I've never been here before. This is a secret visit. Don't tell anyone you've seen me here, will you?'

'No – not if you don't want me to.'

'What are you doing here, by the way?' she asked, but not as if it mattered much.

'I'm running away,' Lennox said, a little mournfully.

'Where from?'

'The house over there. Morland Place.'

'Oh. You haven't got very far, then.'

'No. I suppose I'm not really running away – more sort of hiding.'

'Why?'

'Because I was accused of doing something I didn't do, and no-one will believe me, and I hate it, *hate* it!'

'Ah, yes, I know just how you feel.' The woman shivered suddenly. 'It's chilly in here. Come outside and walk with me. There's supposed to be a pond somewhere, if we can find it.'

'I know where it is. I'll show you. I come here quite often,' Lennox said.

'I see you do,' she said mildly. 'Come, then.'

Outside, the sunshine was golden and furry and the air was shimmering with gossamer and floating seeds; the long grass was lion-coloured with late summer, whispering softly to the little passing breeze. The sky was a dense blue, with a few large achingly white clouds which seemed beautiful and remote as if they had nothing to do with the earth below. The chestnut trees stood silent and heavy in their dark green skirts that came almost to the ground: they had nothing to say to the breeze.

The unlikely couple walked. Lennox noticed with approval that the woman pushed through the grass like one accustomed to the country, not minding seeds and burrs, not fussing about her skirts or hair. After a while she said, 'I'm running away, too. Just like you, I was accused of something I didn't do.'

'I thought grown-ups could do anything they liked,' he said.

'There are always rules,' she said.

'It's hateful not to be believed!' he said passionately.

'Yes. I think it's the worst pain there is.'

'It makes me want to – want to—' He balled up his fists. 'Oh, I don't know – to do something bad, just to show them!'

'No, don't do that,' she said. 'It doesn't work.'

He was interested. 'Is that what you did?'

'I almost did the thing that I was falsely accused of doing. Not to spite them – for another reason. In the end I didn't do it, but I was tempted, and now I don't feel easy with myself any more. How can I blame them for anything they do or say to me?'

He was puzzled. 'But you *didn't* do it – whatever it was.'

'No, but I was angry that they thought me capable of it; and now I know I am. So I've lost the right to be angry. I was innocent when I was first accused, but I'm not innocent now.'

It was a sophistication too far for him, but he absorbed the main thrust of her argument. He sighed. 'But, then – what *can* a person do?'

They were silent a while, walking under the still, dark trees. After a bit she said, 'What are they going to do to you?'

'Send me away,' he said, and added bitterly. 'I'm supposed to be a bad influence.'

'Yes, I know how that feels,' she said. 'But for you – maybe it will be better to get away, right away? You might have a new start.'

'But they're bound to tell everyone I'm a bad person, and I'll start off in the wrong, and never get right again.' She nodded, accepting the likelihood. 'So what *can* I do?' he asked again.

'Just be true to yourself. Care for yourself, if no-one else cares for you. And do what's right, always, because a quiet conscience is the one thing no-one can take from you but yourself.'

'Is that all?' he said, disappointed. Somehow this meeting had been so odd, almost magical, that he had expected it to provide the answer to his problems.

She turned her head to look at him, and he saw that her eyes had flecks of gold in them, now she was out of doors. 'You are better off than I am. You're young now, and you have to do what you're told. But one day you will be grown up, and then you can leave the people who don't approve of you and find some who do. You'll have a measure of freedom.'

'But you're grown up,' he said, puzzled.

'I'm a woman,' she pointed out. 'You'll grow up to be a man, and that's quite different.'

'Oh,' he said. And then, 'What will *you* do?'

She sighed. 'Go back, I suppose. I shall hide here for a little while, but someone will find me, and then I'll have to go back.'

'I won't tell,' he assured her.

'I know you won't,' she said, and held out her hand. 'It's good to have a friend, even if we won't know each other for long.' He took the hand gingerly, hardly knowing what to do with it. 'What's your name?' she asked suddenly.

'Lennox Mynott,' he said.

'Well, friend Lennox Mynott, where's this pond you were going to show me?'

'It's just down the end here. You can't see it until you get right up to it because of the grass. Of course, there may not be much water in it. There isn't, sometimes, in the summer.'

There wasn't. 'Hardly worth the finding,' she said, 'but there were fountains once. I saw them on the plans. It would be nice to restore it to the way it should be.'

'I'd really like to see those plans,' he said.

'You must come again, and I'll show them to you. There are lots of books here you might find interesting.'

'May I? Come again?'

'As long as you can do it without being found out. I shouldn't like you to get into trouble.'

'I don't think I could be in more trouble than I am,' he sighed. And then, shyly, 'What's *your* name?'

She didn't answer immediately. 'I used to be Charlotte Morland.'

His eyes widened. 'Morland? But then—'

'Don't be alarmed. I was cast out from the family at birth. I've been an outcast all my life, I think.'

'Me, too!' said Lennox feelingly.

It was a letter from Mary, arriving opportunely while Benedict was racking his brains for a solution to the problem of Lennox, which gave him his Great Idea.

'What better place than the New World for a bright lad to make his way? He will have a fresh start there, where no-one will care about his origins.'

Sibella was impatient to have the thing settled as it had been dragging on for months. But the mother in her said, 'He's only fourteen, far too young to take care of himself, all alone in such a wild place.'

'All of America isn't wild,' Benedict said indulgently, 'and I didn't mean him to be alone. I gave him a home in the first place because he's Mary's brother. What could be more fitting than to send him to Mary?'

'How do you know Mary's people will take him in?'

'Well, of course, I'll ask first. But Americans are very hospitable, and have a great reverence for family. And though you don't like Lennox, he's intelligent and quick, and he's been a great help to Ketton and Haxby. I'm sure he could find work for himself as a secretary or a land agent, if he were just helped along a bit. It's gentlemanly work, and some land agents do very well for themselves.' He was more pleased with the idea as he expanded it. 'I know he and Mary will take to each other, and it will be such a comfort for her to have a blood relative with her.'

'They don't know about each other,' Sibella pointed out.

Benedict paused. 'Well, then, I'll tell him. It's only fair that he should know the truth, especially if he's going to start a new life on the other side of the world.'

'And are you going to tell Mary that she's not your child, that her mother was an adulteress and her father a wicked, unprincipled seducer?'

Benedict looked hurt. 'I wouldn't put it in those terms.'

'Whatever terms you put it in, that's the truth,' she said impatiently. 'Would you break her heart?'

He frowned in thought. 'I've got it! I'll say they're cousins: their mothers were sisters. That will cover the obvious resemblance. And then, when I've had a little time with Mary and seen how the land lies, I might find a way to tell her the truth, if I think she can bear it.'

'When you've had a little time with her? You don't intend going over there yourself?'

'Well, of course!' He looked surprised. 'I thought you realised that. I couldn't just send the poor boy all that way on his own. Now, Sib, don't look like that! I can easily afford it, and I'd always hoped to go and see Mary one day. And, you know, now that I'm a mill-owner, I ought to know something about the production of cotton.'

'What on earth for?' Sibella asked, amazed.

'Oh, I just think it would be useful,' he said vaguely. 'And Mary said in one of her letters that her father-in-law has a mill that's fallen into disuse and no-one there understands how to repair it. I could help with that. He's got a factory, too, that probably needs improvement. And think of those huge plantations with no machinery! It would be a perfect chance for me to try out some of my ideas for agricultural machines.'

The multiplicity of excuses Benedict advanced only convinced Sibella that the real reason was simple restlessness. He wanted new adventures; and of course there was his strange, painful relationship with Mary, which would never let him be quiet. She looked at him hopelessly, knowing that whatever she said, he would go. He would do what he wanted, because he was Master of Morland Place, and though he loved her, he loved his freedom more.

'How long will you be gone?' she asked at last, so miserably that he felt a prick of conscience.

'Well, you know,' he said apologetically, 'one could hardly go all that way and not stay a reasonable time. Three months, perhaps.'

'Three months.' It was better, or rather less bad, than she thought.

'Then there's the journey – three or four weeks to get there. That adds another two months. Say, six months in all.' He reached out and patted her hand. 'You'll hardly have time to miss me. The estate's running smoothly, and Ketton and Haxby can do everything between them. In fact, if you leave all the housework to Mrs Hoddle, you can have a good long rest while I'm away and get your strength back. You're looking awfully tired still.'

Sibella didn't answer. It seemed a lot of expense and trouble to get rid of Lennox; but perhaps when Benedict came back from America he would finally have purged That Woman and her offspring from his system, and they would then be able to settle down and have some real peace together. If so, six months alone and whatever small fortune the passages would cost would be a reasonable price to pay.

BOOK TWO

The Vision

> Thou, bethink thee, art
> A guest for queens for social pageantries,
> With gages from a hundred brighter eyes
> Than tears even can make mine, to play thy part
> Of chief musician. What hast thou to do
> With looking from the lattice-lights at me –
> A poor, tired, wandering singer, singing through
> The dark, and leaning on a cypress tree?

Elizabeth Barrett Browning:
Sonnets from the Portuguese

CHAPTER TEN

April 1860

The city of Charleston was built on the long spit of land shaped like an ox-tongue which lay between two broad rivers, the Ashley and the Cooper. The rivers joined around the tip of Charleston and, combined, flowed on into the sea. The mouth of their estuary had been narrowed by the growth of sand-spits from the low, marshy seashore, turning the estuary into a sheltered bay called Charleston Harbour. The mouth was further narrowed by an island that sat right in the middle, a natural defence which had been strengthened by the building of a fortress, Fort Sumter.

As the *Martha Bradstock* crept in through the passage, Benedict, standing at the rail, pointed out to Lennox another fortress on the northern shore, over which the distinctive 'stars and stripes' flag of the United States was fluttering. 'I believe that's Fort Moultrie,' he said. 'There were a lot of defences built here during the Revolutionary War. It was an important city even then. It's all very peaceful and prosperous now, though.'

Lennox could feel his companion's excitement almost like a vibration carried through the rail and up through his own hands and arms. He was excited too, but there were other things to think about. Benedict had not meant to tell Lennox the real story of his birth, but in the weeks of enforced intimacy of the journey it had come to seem inevitable. It had been hard for Lennox to hear the truth, that he was the child of shame, that his parents, and particularly his adored father, had been bad people. 'No-one can blame you for that,' Benedict had said, but it seemed to Lennox on the contrary that that was exactly what people were blaming and would always blame him for. Why else was he being cast out from England? What capital would his former tormentor George make of it, if he knew? Was it not the source of Mr Wheldrake's scorn and Mrs Morland's coldness?

And yet, once he had begun to be used to the idea, he had found a kind of relief in knowing. Better to face the bared fangs of a known danger than the sinister shape behind the curtain that might be anything. He remembered from his reading of Chaucer the words: 'And trouthe shal delivere; hit is no drede.' He felt that if he were a knight of old he would have that on his banner; he would ride out and fight for that, the right to know.

And it meant that the cousin he was to meet was in fact his sister! He who a few weeks ago had no relative in the world now had one of the whole blood. Of course there was the complication that Benedict had not told *her* the truth, and in justice Lennox could see how it would be difficult for him. But when he had gone back to England and it was just Lennox and Mary (how good that sounded!), Lennox thought the way would present itself. *Hit is no drede*, he thought. If Mary was intelligent and wise, as Benedict said she was, she would see that too.

As the ship came down the harbour, the details of the city gradually emerged from the faint bright mist of morning: a strong, straight jetty wall, a broad promenade, a public garden with fountains and handsome trees; then a row of large, splendid houses set amid shady gardens and behind, a neatly laid-out city with wide thoroughfares and a glimpse of several fine church towers. Most of the houses had wood or stucco façades, and they were painted in an unexpected variety of colours – pale yellow, saxe blue, terracotta red, rose pink, apple green. In the hazy light of a warm spring morning, the whole town looked as though it were made of coloured marzipan.

'It's beautiful,' Lennox said.

'It looks almost unreal,' said Benedict. Somewhere in that fairy-like city, he thought, Mary was waiting.

Mary was waiting on the quayside, remembering her own arrival six years ago. She had always liked Charleston. It was a cheerful, vibrant city. The grand houses of the wealthy, beautiful churches, fine gardens and public buildings, hotels, clubs, theatres, the racecourse with its handsome new grandstand, built by public subscription – these were its splendour. But it was also a great commercial centre, the largest and most important city in the South, and one of the five or six largest in the whole United States. Along the Ashley River side of the city were mills, factories and workshops; along the Cooper River side, where she now stood, a long succession of wharves and warehouses; and one of the few railroads in the South ran right down the Neck to a depot in the city itself. Charlestonians had built that railroad to the trading city of Hamburg going on thirty years back, and mighty proud they were of it. When it was first opened, it was only the second railroad in the whole of the United States: that's the kind of go-ahead people Charlestonians were!

Charleston's wealth was built on trade. The great rice and cotton plantations of South Carolina sent their produce into Charleston to be distributed, and the multitude of goods the South could not produce arrived there from the rest of the world for inward distribution. Carolinian planters spent freely on luxuries, spreading their wealth downwards through traders and purveyors of pleasure, through innkeepers, shopkeepers, shirtmakers, cobblers, pastrycooks, bath-house attendants, hairdressers, actors – it was said that Charlestonians knew more ways of amusing themselves than anyone else on earth. The idle sons of planters – and sometimes the planters themselves – came to the city for a taste of dissipation, and many of them never went away again.

Behind her, Patty sighed and changed her weight from one foot to the other, and the shadow of the large parasol she was holding over Mary swung back and forth. 'It won't be long now, Patty,' Mary said. 'You can see the tide's turned and the boats are coming in on the make.'

'Yassum,' Patty said resignedly, not understanding a word. Patty was a reminder to Mary of the other foundation of Charleston's wealth, the older, darker seam of riches that Southerners mined. Some of the leading families of Charleston were 'brokers' – the polite term for slave-traders. The slave trade with Africa had been abolished fifty years ago, but still thousands of home-grown negroes changed hands every year, and Charleston was an important centre for the business. To Mary it was like a hideous blemish on a beautiful face. No, worse: Charleston was a beautiful face concealing an ugly heart. Slavery was an evil, and Mary, by marrying into it, had made herself guilty by association.

What a fool she had been! She looked back now and saw how the mistake was made, and yet at the time her delusions had seemed to have all the substance of reality. Of course, she had been very young, only fourteen when she first met Fenwick. With her head stuffed full of the Classics, he had seemed the epitome of romance, like Odysseus, the mysterious, godlike stranger from across the sea. How could she not fall in love with him?

He had been dazzled by her, too, her youth notwithstanding, and for the weeks of his visit he had been courting her in all but name. Then he disappeared again. For three years she had kept the image of him fresh in her heart. At fourteen, at fifteen, it is easier to be in love with the absent than with the red-faced, clumsy, tongue-tied reality of one's actual and present admirers. And when Fenwick had come back for her, against all her expectations and hopes, and offered to carry her off to America and a new life in the land of wonders, she felt she must be allowed to marry him, or die.

But *why* had Papa allowed her? That was the mystery. Even at the time it had surprised her, though her surprise had been over-whelmed by her gratitude. She had always been Papa's favourite, and she believed that parting with her hurt him dreadfully. Why had he let her go without word or warning? Within a month of Fenwick's reappearance she had married him and left her native shores for ever, entrusting her honour and happiness to a man she hardly knew.

The sailing-boats that had been waiting outside the bar for the tide were coming down now, and behind them were the steamboats which timed their arrival to take advantage of the flood. The harbour was always busy. Coasters, fishing-boats, cargo ships, luggers and private yachts were making their way in; and there was the Wilmington Steam Packet, which had its own wharf connected with the railway, just nosing in past Fort Sumter. Another steamer was behind her, which could be the *Martha Bradstock*. Mary's heart beat faster at the thought that her father would soon be here, in the flesh, holding her in his arms; dear, familiar, long-missed Papa, with all his resonances of Morland Place, of England – of Home.

A newly married woman of seventeen, she had made the long journey Papa had just made, across England to Liverpool, across the Atlantic to New York, down the coast to Charleston. The thrill of being in love, of being married to her hero, had survived the journey. She adored him on the train, she adored him in the Liverpool hotel, she adored him on the *British Queen*, despite every effort of the North Atlantic and seasickness to spoil the dream. She worshipped him in New York, where it seemed he knew the name and history of every building; and she went on loving him on the long coastwise leg, in their cramped cabin that smelled of oil and bilge and damp blankets.

It was only after she had arrived that she had discovered how unsuited she was to the life she had chosen. In the South, a female was supposed to be a delicate flower easily crushed by the harshness of the world; ignorant of everything but needlework, innocent, bewildered and clinging. The man was the fount of all power: strong, just and wise, God's representative on earth and only a short step below Him. If he were so good as to grant a female his protection by marrying her, she must repay him with obedience. She must run his household, bear and raise his children, minister to his physical needs, and be virtuous, gentle, meek, pious, and above all silent, bathing her menfolk in a constant stream of uncritical adoration.

Southern women were used to the game, and since they were

denied education and never allowed to step out of doors unchaperoned, most of them believed in the superiority of men. But Mary, extensively educated, and brought up by dear old Father Moineau to think and to debate, was out of her place. She gave her opinions vigorously, joined in with conversations and, where she disagreed, said so. Company was reduced to embarrassed silence around her; ladies were shocked, gentlemen made uncomfortable, elders scandalised by her unfeminine boldness.

Fenwick had loved her eager mind in England, enjoyed it when alone with her on the boat, but at home he was under his father's subjugation, and he saw at once that Mary's behaviour wouldn't do. Charles Morland, master of all he surveyed, as much an autocrat in his own household as any Russian tsar, frowned on Mary, and told Fenwick coldly to correct her behaviour. Fenwick passed on the rebuke with a vigour that owed something to his resentment at being made victim of his father's scathing tongue.

Mary, not understanding then how things worked in the South, thought that Fenwick ought to have defended her. Time and many reproaches taught her to keep her opinions to herself – at least most of the time – but it was too late. To tell a man he was wrong was the unforgivable sin, and the first time she said so to Charles Morland she was cast forever into outer darkness: he would always dislike her now. And her love for Fenwick had withered and died under this perpetual frost.

It was a bitter realisation to make at the age of seventeen – that she was tied for life to a man she no longer loved nor esteemed – but she had made a vow and must keep it. Fenwick was not a bad man, and when she conformed, he was kind. With all the resources of her mind she determined to adapt to the circumstances, and be a good wife to him. Six years and three children later, she felt she could have succeeded, and could even have been happy, if it were not for the curse of slavery. Its poison entered every aspect of life, and while its benefits accrued only to the men, its burden fell almost entirely on the women. Few dared say so, of course. Slavery and women's silence supported the way of life the men enjoyed, of idleness and pleasure, billiards in the morning, cards and segars in the evening, gentlemen's clubs, gaming, brandy, fast horses and loose women – white, black, or any shade in between. The women were owned by the men just as surely as the slaves were. They had no power to change anything, and no means of escape.

There was the *Martha Bradstock* now, and there was a man standing at the rail that her heart told her was her father. Beside him was a slighter figure with a bare head, pale gold in the sunshine

– her mysterious cousin Lennox, son of an aunt she had never known she had.

'There they are,' she said to Patty. 'Not long now.'

'Which boat is it, Miz Mary? Kin you see dem?'

'Yes, I see them. That boat there, with the red stripe on her funnel.'

The *Martha Bradstock*, her great wheels churning, sidled crablike into the quay. There followed one of those mysterious delays that always seem to attend the docking of ships, when they have bumped against the quayside and yet the gangplank does not go down and no-one seems to be doing anything about it. But at last the passengers began to descend, and there was Papa, hurrying as fast as his sea-legs would let him across the cobbles, snatching off his hat, his face wreathed with smiles. He'd grown older, she saw with a pang, more than six years older, as if Time were running faster with him than with her. Oh, she didn't want him to grow old! When she had left him, she was still of an age to think him immortal; now motherhood had taught her that children steal life from their parents, that the very fact of them guarantees one's own mortality. But there was no time to think about that now. He was there, smelling of salt and ship's smoke, his arms wide, and she was enfolded, and both of them were shedding ridiculous tears of joy and loss on each other's shoulders.

'Let me look at you. Oh, my precious one!' When he was finally capable of coherent speech, he set her back and looked at her wonderingly, and touched her face with his fingertips, and she saw that she had changed to him, too. 'You've grown up,' he said. They had lost each other when he let her go to America, and to that extent they could never go back.

'I'm so glad to see you!' she said. 'We've been waiting hours, haven't we, Patty? We had such a complicated relay set up so that we'd know when your boat was coming in – the telegraph system's been completely given over to it – but then in the end it all came down to standing here watching the horizon. Oh, Papa!' Another long, hard hug, and she was ready to release him and be introduced to Lennox.

It was a shock. Outsiders are always more able to see the resemblance between two people than the people themselves, but unless Mary had lived her entire life without a looking-glass, she could not have missed it. Lennox was only a little taller than her, and at fifteen still slight and tender-skinned, with a delicate complexion not much tanned by the long journey. These things made the likeness more obvious than if he had been a full-grown, bearded and muscled man; but there would still have been no mistaking the sculpted features, the golden hair and bright blue eyes that made Mary a beauty.

Lennox was looking at her with much the same shock in his expression. Mary pulled herself together, held out her hand and smiled warmly. 'Cousin Lennox, welcome to Charleston! I'm so glad to meet you.'

Lennox took her hand and held it as if he didn't know what to do with it. Not one word managed to escape him.

The carriage was waiting outside, together with a buggy for the luggage. Mary gave swift orders to the two footmen for collecting the trunks from the ship; Patty set off to walk home, with the furled parasol across her shoulder like a rifle, and the white folks climbed into the carriage and rolled away. The spring sunshine fell straight and clear from a fresh blue sky, making the colours of the houses and the blossoming trees seem more brilliant than life. Benedict stared eagerly about. The road was neatly cobbled, the footpath paved with handsome large squares of stone, the buildings all seemed freshly painted, and everything gave an impression of prosperity. The startling thing to English eyes was that every second person seemed to be black, varying from near-ebony to pale honey, through every hue in between. They varied in dress, too, from women in plain calico dresses and head-rags to dandyish men with frilled shirts, shiny boots and top hats, who might have been Bond Street Beaux had it not been for the dusky face between collar and hat-brim.

Mary said, 'It takes you by surprise at first, doesn't it? But you'll quickly get used to it.'

'I didn't expect there would be so many,' Benedict said.

'Charleston's different from other cities,' Mary said. 'There are almost equal numbers of blacks and white people here. And we have a large population of free negroes. Lots of the tailors and barbers are freemen – most of the dockyard workers and fishermen – cooks, carpenters, blacksmiths, shopkeepers. Some of the free blacks have their own businesses, and do very well for themselves. Some even own slaves.'

'Negroes owning slaves?'

'I'm told it's quite common in Africa. Slaves have a much freer life here than in other places, too. They have "free time", when they can go out of the house and visit amongst each other. Some even live apart from their masters, which is unheard-of anywhere but Charleston, and go in and work by day like ordinary people.'

Lennox seemed not to be able to take his eyes off her, and sought for a question to ask which would make her look at him. 'Do you like Charleston?'

'Yes, very much. It's a pretty place, don't you think?'

'I like the way the streets are all straight, down and across. It's very neat.'

'It was laid out on the chequerboard plan that Sir Christopher Wren drew up for London after the Great Fire,' Mary said. 'D'you remember, Papa, the engraving in that book at home, of what London would have looked like if Wren had rebuilt it?'

Before Benedict could answer, Lennox jumped in eagerly. 'I know it! It's in the end bookcase in the Long Saloon at Morland Place. It's signed by Wren himself – there's an inscription on the flyleaf.'

'Yes, that's the one! How nice that you know it, too. Are you very fond of reading?'

'Yes, I love to read,' Lennox said. 'Do you have a library here?'

'There's a large library at Twelvetrees, but we don't have one here in Charleston,' Mary said abruptly. This was a subject better not pursued. Southern women were not supposed to read, except for the Bible; erudition was a grave fault in a woman. As a matter of fact, it was not much admired in men, either – to be popular, a planter had far better be a hard rider, a hard drinker, a fine shot, and a skilled card-player. But Charles Morland did not much care about being popular: he was an educated man, and had collected a large library at Twelvetrees. The room itself, like a gentleman's club, was forbidden territory to women. Mary could not go in there and read even when Charles was away, for one of the slaves would be sure to betray her. Her resort was to take the books in secret and read them at night in the privacy of her own room. She resented the necessity for subterfuge, but she could no more live without books than without air.

To change the subject she said, 'We're nearly there. It's a nothing of a journey, really, just a step, hardly worth putting the horses to, but of course I couldn't make you walk.'

'And whom shall we find there?' her father asked her.

She glanced sideways at him. He looked tired, pale under his tan from the long journey. 'Most of the family is at Twelvetrees, except Fen's Uncle Heck, who's in Savannah on business. Only Fenwick and I came up to meet you – he's waiting for us at home. Charles Morland was already here, and Aunt Belle – that's Charles's sister – lives here all the time. But Martial's on a trip to New York, mostly social, I suspect, though one never really knows what Mart is up to. He's independently wealthy and accountable to no-one.'

'Martial?' Benedict queried.

'Fen's cousin, Martial Flint, son of Charles's sister Louisa. She's dead now, though. He only lives at the Morland House through historical accident, really.'

'And that's all?' Benedict enquired.

'Apart from the servants,' Mary said. 'There's twenty-four of them.'

'Slaves?' Benedict asked.

'Mostly,' Mary said. 'Fen's body-servant Abel is a freedman, and so is the coachman, Ben, though he was freed before he came to us. And my groom Cedar is a free black. But Cedar and Ben both live out, and Abel sleeps in Fen's dressing-room. It doesn't generally pay to mix slaves and freedmen in the same household – causes resentment, according to Aunt Belle, and puts ideas in heads.'

'It's a strange way of life you have here,' Benedict said.

'It's stranger still when you live it,' she said. 'Here we are. This is the Morland House.'

It was a square house, three storeys of butter-yellow stucco with white copings and dark green shutters. Deep balconies ran the whole length of each storey on the south side, creating a shady verandah on the ground floor and two loggias on the upper floors. Above them a balustrade, mimicking the balcony railings, ran all the way round, projecting above the façade to hide the pitch of the roof and make the house look even more imposing. A narrow strip of garden, filled with glassy-leaved shrubs and small palm trees, divided the sweep and the wide, shallow front steps from the street. Along the south side was a wider and more densely planted piece of garden behind wrought-iron railings. Along the north side was a gravelled drive leading to a group of white-painted wooden buildings at the rear – the slave quarters, the stables and the coach house.

As they descended from the coach the huge double front doors were opened by the butler, Matthew, a large, impressive man in tail-coat livery and a striped waistcoat. Benedict thought he was wearing a powdered wig as well, but as they trod up the steps he realised that it was the man's own white hair, a strange contrast with his black face. He bowed, and beamed, and welcomed them, but was evidently anxious about something, and as soon as they were over the threshold he bent over Mary and said in a penetrating whisper, 'Miz Mary, Master hain come back from de crub. Should Ah sen' word dat de vis'tors is arrove?'

'No, Matthew, that's all right,' Mary said. 'Master knows they're coming today. He'll come when he's ready.'

She turned to conduct her old family upstairs to meet her new one. Benedict saw the hurt and anger she was trying to conceal. All was not well here, he thought, and his old guilt revived itself, ready to twine round a fresh new crop like two vigorous shoots of bindweed.

Aunt Belle, Mary discovered, had put on a go-visiting gown of puce silk for the benefit of the visitors, along with her best cap of (reputed) French lace with the long lappets. Neither did anything for her face, which, in colour, flatness and hardness of expression, pretty much resembled a brick. Aunt Belle had never married: according to Fenwick, she had been deliberately kept unwed to act as housekeeper to Fen's great-grandmother, the formidable Eugenie. Eugenie and her husband had backed the wrong side in the Revolutionary War and been forced to flee from Maryland all the way to Canada. Eugenie returned by stages, first with her son and then her grandson, and to end her days as a Grande Dame in Charleston. Such a legendary figure might well demand human sacrifice, and the sacrifice concerned might well resent it; but though Aunt Belle cultivated a sharp tongue and an air of being put upon, Mary had a shrewd idea that she liked showing herself mistress of the board, bullying the servants and fishing for compliments from admiring guests. Certainly while the family was in Charleston she never permitted Mary the slightest say in the household workings. She never went to Twelvetrees if she could help it: the pains and privations of country housekeeping were all Mary's.

Aunt Belle greeted the visitors, subjected Lennox to a piercing scrutiny, and then remarked, as though it were a criticism, 'My, you are like Mary to look at. Two peas in a pod couldn't be liker.' Lennox blushed and looked at his feet. Aunt Belle went on, 'I declare it's too bad of Charles to be so late! If there's one thing I can't abide it's unpunctuality, and what I've suffered from that over the years no tongue can tell. Of course, I don't complain, and I never have – that's my downfall. But when a person goes to a lot of trouble to order a special meal and have everything nice – but there, one shouldn't expect to be thanked for doing one's duty. Lord knows it's the easiest thing in the world to run a household this size, and take account of everyone's likes and dislikes, and arrange things to suit everyone! A child could do it! I don't pretend to have any special talent.'

Fenwick obliged by jumping in with the expected compliments, and after a pointed look from him, Mary joined in, though not forcefully enough for Aunt Belle, who was soon obliged to take her praise into her own hands by describing some of the occasions she had made more special by her nice arrangement of domestic details.

They went in to luncheon eventually without Charles, and when they were seated Mary asked after her step-mother, and then her brothers and sisters, the servants, neighbours, dogs and horses and everyone else she remembered. Listening to her father's replies, she thought what a contrast her upbringing had been with that of Fenwick and his siblings Eugene, Maybelle and Ruth. Mary had lost her mother when she was seven, but had gained the kindest step-mother in the world, and had never lost the affection of her father, or the attention of her wise, loving tutor, Father Moineau. These Morlands, by contrast, had a mother whom not even Fenwick remembered as anything other than sickly and ailing, and a father whose attitude towards his children might well have been *oderint dum metuant* – let them hate me as long as they fear me.

Mary wondered what had happened to Charles to make him so hard. He must once have had softer feelings, for it was a matter of recorded fact that he had married for love. Emily Fenwick was only fifteen and not wealthy, but, as Aunt Belle sourly affirmed when asked, he had fallen madly in love with her and married her within weeks of their first acquaintance; and after marriage had remained enough in love with her to beget seventeen children. Was it, Mary wondered, the sight of Emily's suffering, the endless miscarriages and consequent destruction of her health, that changed him? Emily had died soon after Mary's arrival in America – indeed she hardly remembered her, for in the weeks between Mary's arrival and her departure she was nothing more than a wraith-like presence upstairs; a brooding sense of futility and pain round which the house circled uneasily, trying to avoid talking about her, as one tries to avoid touching a painful bruise.

Married at fifteen and dead at forty, and, in between, seventeen pregnancies. Seventeen! The horror of it shook Mary. Four children remained alive; a fifth, a daughter between Fenwick and Eugene, had died at thirteen. And then there had been the bloody toll of miscarriages and stillbirths: four between Eugene and Maybelle; four between May and Ruth; four more after Ruthie. If nothing else had made Mary hate her father-in-law, she would have hated him for inflicting that on his wife.

The principal effect of Emily's death on Mary was that at a difficult moment of her own life she had to try to comfort her husband and her new family. Ruth had been only eight years old then, and needed Mary even more than Fenwick did. She was now Mary's greatest ally, purveyor of the only uncritical love Mary had known since she landed in America. Whether Charles had mourned his wife, Mary had no way of knowing; but it was certain that he was a bitter man, and that he took himself away from his family as much as possible, spending all his time at his clubs when in Charleston, and locked in his library or out on solitary rides when at Twelvetrees. He emerged from his remote fastness only to criticise and punish: no wonder the children, even rebellious Eugene, were afraid of him.

Later that evening, Mary was about to go upstairs to dress for dinner, when, passing the morning-room door, she saw Charles Morland standing by the empty fireplace, one elbow on the mantelpiece, reading a letter. He was in rather crumpled day clothes, and even from here she could catch the scent of brandy and segars hanging about him. He had not noticed her, and she ought to have walked on, but the sight of him, so casual and comfortable, free to do exactly as he pleased, reminded her of the insult to her father, and she paused in the doorway, looking at him resentfully. His English setter, Brenda, who was lying at his feet, noticed her, got up with a little whine of welcome, and came towards the door, her tail swinging.

'Here,' Morland snapped in a hard voice, and the dog, halfway to Mary, veered away at once and went back to him, and stood waiting for the next command. He snapped his fingers, and she lay down at his feet again; then he looked up at Mary. He was sixty, but looked to Mary older, with his bald front surrounded by bushy white hair, his weatherbeaten face marred by deep-etched lines of disappointment. Above a pair of gold-wire half-glasses, his pouched eyes of faded blue were cold and unfriendly. He wanted her to go away, but the fact that he could not even be bothered to tell her so irritated her further, and she stood her ground.

'Well?' he said at last in a tone of utter uninterest.

'My father is here,' she said. Strength of emotion prevented her from expanding.

'Yes,' he said – the merest acknowledgement that she had spoken. But she did not go. 'What is it to me?' he said harshly.

'You invited him, but you weren't here to greet him,' she said.

'I did not invite him.'

It infuriated her to be so flatly contradicted. Her voice shook with the effort of control. 'You are master of this house. Therefore the invitation was from you, even if I wrote the letter.'

He made a quick, restless movement. Had she been a child, and standing nearer to him, it might have ended in a slap for her. 'Master of this house, am I? Then you should remember it!'

'And so should you,' she retorted before she could stop herself.

His eyes narrowed, and for a moment she quaked. Then he said, '*Must* you always argue? God preserve us from barking dogs and disputatious women!' It was spoken with weary contempt, but the mere fact that he had not bellowed at her meant that he accepted her rebuke. Surprise silenced her. It was almost more frightening to win than to lose.

A faint malicious gleam came into his eyes as if he knew exactly what she was thinking. He put the letter aside and turned to face her, putting his hands behind him under his coat-tails as if the fire were lit and was warming his seat. 'Well,' he said with mock geniality, 'so your father is here – bringing with him the boy he wants to get rid of. I wonder why?'

Mary felt confused, not knowing from which direction the attack was coming. 'My cousin—' she began.

'Ah yes,' Morland interrupted. 'Your cousin. What's his name?'

'Lennox Mynott.'

'How old is he?'

'Fifteen.'

'A mere youth. And this youth I am supposed to find a use for?'

'Papa says his abilities are remarkable, and he has already had some training in estate duties.'

'If his abilities are so remarkable, why does your father not make use of him at home? Because, I conclude, there is a very good reason to want him out of the way.' Mary began to protest, and Charles smiled coldly and cut her short. 'I can guess what the reason is. A man would need to be a fool not to. Lennox Mynott, eh? A cousin on your mother's side?'

'Our mothers were sisters,' Mary said.

'I saw him on the stairs as I came in. I couldn't mistake who he was – you and he are so alike, you might be twins. And this aunt, his mother, you knew nothing about until now?'

Mary said nothing. She felt apprehensive now. He was enjoying himself, and that meant trouble was coming. But Charles seemed to tire of it quite suddenly. He turned away from her, waving his hand in dismissal. 'Well, well, as long as he behaves himself, it's nothing to me. You may tell your *cousin* welcome. Family is family after all.'

Mary didn't understand what he would be at, but she knew better than to believe the geniality of the words. *Reculer pour mieux saulter*, that was her father-in-law – like a snake, she thought. He had given her her dismissal, and as soon as she could command her feet, she took it, and hurried up the stairs to her room. He had planted a seed which he would expect to bear fruit, and she had no wish to know what it was, but she feared that her intelligence would worm it out at last, despite herself.

CHAPTER ELEVEN

On the third morning of the visit, Benedict came downstairs early to breakfast and found Mary alone on the verandah. It was a lovely morning, clear and fresh; a little chilly still from the night's dew, but with an unblemished sky that promised heat later. She was sitting in her rocking chair, moving herself gently with the tip of one toe, staring out into the garden. Her hands were folded in her lap and she was very still, giving the impression she had been there for some time. Benedict paused in the doorway to look at her for a moment unobserved. She was all in white muslin with full bishop sleeves, her golden hair neatly smoothed back into a thick plaited coil under the merest spider's web of a 'breakfast cap'; her face was serene and lovely. He looked at her with the usual mixture of intense love and pain: *not his own*, said the pain, but the father in him who had raised her and cared for her since her birth could not feel less her father because of that. Mostly he hated her mother for what she had done to them both, but if he had not married Rosalind, either Mary would never have existed, or he would never have known her. His thoughts on that subject always tormented him, swallowing their own tail in an agonising circle.

A mocking-bird flew into the figwort just beyond the verandah rail and hopped about, crying its strange, human-sounding call, and the long, pale, funnel-like flowers shook and shed blossoms. Mary's train of thought was disturbed. She turned her head and saw him. 'You're up early,' she said, and, studying him, added, 'You look more rested this morning.'

'The bed stopped going up and down at last,' he said. He pulled a chair over to sit beside her. 'I don't seem to have seen much of you yet, except looking lovely on the other side of a room full of people. Charleston folk are very sociable, aren't they?'

'They love to have visitors,' she smiled. 'Especially visitors from England. I'd have liked to take you straight to Twelvetrees, but it was absolutely essential for us to give a dinner for you, and to let at least a few of the important families give one back. And naturally you had to see some of the gentlemen's clubs: Charleston has more clubs than any other city on earth. Are you enjoying the attention? I imagine you the centre of an admiring circle everywhere you go.'

'Oh, I'm not such a wonder as you seem to think,' Benedict said. 'No sooner do I begin to answer a question about agricultural improvements in England, than someone veers off onto the subject of tariffs. Tell me, my love, what is all the fuss about? Everyone seems incensed about it, but I never get a clear answer from anyone.'

'Import tariffs,' Mary said. 'You should speak to Charles about it – he's very knowledgeable, coming from the North originally. The tariffs were imposed back in, oh, 1815 or 1816, I think, to protect the manufacturing trade from competition with foreign goods. In those days they were just beginning to set up mills and factories in the North, in New England mostly, so it seemed a good idea to give the young industry some protection until it got on its feet. But the tariffs have never been removed, and there's even talk of increasing them.'

'A very bad notion,' Benedict said. 'Speaking as a convinced free-trader, tariffs are bad business in the long run.'

'Well, the North likes them, but the South never developed any industry, and all it means for us is having to pay higher prices for manufactured goods. It's one of the bones of contention between the North and the South.' The other was slavery, but six years had taught Mary reticence on that subject, which had become so instinctive she did not mention it even to her father.

'I see,' he said. 'And what's all the excitement over the Democratic Party Convention, which I understand is to take place here? I look to you to guide me, love – the men all seem too overwrought to make sense.'

Mary laughed. 'I don't know if it will make much sense however I explain it, but I'll try. The purpose of the Convention is to choose a candidate for the presidential election in November.'

'Yes, I gathered that.'

'Very well. It's usually just a matter of confirmation by this stage – everyone knows who's going to be Democratic candidate long before. This year it's supposed to be Judge Stephen Douglas, but most Southerners don't like him because he's suspected of being not quite sound on the question of slavery, and a large number of delegates say they won't vote for him.'

'And what will happen then?'

'That's what's causing all the excitement. Some people say there ought to be an alternative candidate that Southerners can vote for – but then the Northern Democrats might not like him. Others still want a compromise candidate that both lots will accept; but the trouble there is that a compromise would most likely please no-one. Of course, the anti-Douglas-ites might change their minds and vote for him rather than give the Republicans a chance to win. The excitement comes from simply not knowing what's going to happen.'

'It sounds as though Charleston's the place to be,' Benedict said.

'For the men,' Mary said. 'Women have no say in politics.'

'But you seem to understand it all.'

'I listen when the men talk,' she said. 'And Martial explains thing to me – when he's home.'

'Martial? Oh, yes, the cousin.'

'Fortunately he has rather different ideas about women – no doubt from spending so much of his time in the North. Most Southerners think that if a woman has the misfortune to know anything, she had better forget it as quickly as she can. Adoring ignorance is the key to happiness here.'

As soon as she said it, she regretted her vehemence. Her father looked disconcerted, and his lips rehearsed some question or protest, which she forestalled by continuing lightly, 'I must say, it is nice to have a few moments alone with you, Papa. I hope we can go riding together when we go down to Twelvetrees.'

'I hope so, too. When is that likely to be?'

'At the end of the week,' Mary said. 'I shall be glad to get back and see that my boys are all right. Mammy isn't awfully reliable, and she has some bad old-fashioned ways, though I can't say anything because she was Fen's and the other children's mammy before, so she's a family institution. I have a good girl, Rosa, whom I trust, but Mammy outranks her, and she interferes if I'm not there to back Rosa up.'

Benedict smiled. 'It seems strange to see my little girl a mother of three. You look far too young.'

'And you're too young to be a grandfather,' Mary said, smiling back, quite unconscious that she was planting a dagger.

The Democratic Convention produced high rhetoric and intemperate speeches in the Institute Hall, fierce argument and hard drinking in the gentlemen's clubs, harangues and threats in the newspapers, and ultimately a deadlock. Judge Stephen Douglas could not get enough votes in Charleston to secure the nomination, and the Convention was forced to adjourn with the intention of reconvening in Baltimore, where a more moderate, or perhaps a more Northern, slant on things might be obtaining.

After all the excitement, the move to Twelvetrees seemed like stepping into a rural haven of peace. The family decamped there without Charles, who remained in Charleston for purposes of his own, unexplained, as was everything he did. Benedict was eager to see the plantation, and since Fenwick was to show him round, Charles was no loss to him. Lennox was also eager to see the place which would be his home, at least for the immediate future, and meet the rest of the family and find out if they were going to like him. So far it seemed to be two for and two against. Charles Morland and Aunt Belle were cold towards him, but he could not see that they were much different to anyone else. More importantly, Mary was kind and affectionate, and he already loved her – he didn't see how anyone could do otherwise – and Fenwick seemed genial and pleasant and prepared to accept him for Mary's sake.

The journey didn't take long, by train and then carriage. Twelvetrees was approached along an avenue of limes – the original twelve augmented by later plantings so that the avenue was now fully half a mile long. At the end of the avenue a wide sweep opened up around an area of grass, which was painstakingly cared for by an old negro: Moses was reputed to have been owned in his youth by an English aristocrat in Jamaica, and was supposed therefore to know all about the tending of an English-style lawn. It was Fenwick's dearest ambition to have the sort of immaculate velvet sward that he had read about from childhood and seen occasionally on his visits to England. Moses, infected by his master's enthusiasm and the legend of his own past, brooded over his grass like the tenderest of mothers, watering and weeding it by hand, and mowing and rolling it with the aid of a morose and equally aged mule, Thunder. Thunder wore leather boots to prevent its hooves marking the turf, and resented them bitterly. Putting them on in the morning was a daily-renewed battle in which honours remained about even: the mule always went to work booted; but Moses' behind was so scarred with teeth-marks it looked like scrimshaw work, as he proudly assured anyone who would listen.

Beyond the sweep, the house was a three-storey plain oblong with many windows, embellished with a porch of four vast columns supporting a classical pediment and entablature, which covered the middle third of the façade and rose the full height of the house. It was an impressive feature, but sat rather oddly, Lennox thought – like someone wearing a fancy hat with workaday dress. The reason became clear on further acquaintance with the house, which from very modest beginnings had been extended by degrees over the years, with the columns arriving last, added for Fenwick's marriage to impress the English heiress Twelvetrees thought it was getting.

At the back the house was much less grand, but more comfortable, life centring on a long verandah which looked out onto the parkland area of the plantation. It was here that the English visitors first met the rest of the family. The eldest daughter of the house, Maybelle, was nineteen, shy, and not quite pretty, having inherited from her paternal grandmother the same Scotch flatness of face and sandiness of hair as Aunt Belle. Within a few minutes of being introduced to her, Benedict and Lennox found themselves discussing her forthcoming marriage to Conrad Pinckney Ausland. They were soon to learn that she had developed a skill for working any subject round to her beloved that was almost uncanny.

May's red cheeks grew redder and her face took on animation as she explained that she had known Conrad for ever, because he had been at school with her brother Eugene and ran tame about the Morland House most of May's life. She had been content to be treated merely as Gene's-little-sister until her coming-out ball three years ago, when, either through an idle fancy or because his parents had insisted, Conrad had danced with her. May had fallen instantly and hopelessly in love, and had worshipped him from afar ever since, without any hope of a return. His proposal to her during race week had surprised her more than anyone else in Charleston.

When May stumblingly and adoringly reached this point in her narrative, Eugene interrupted to suggest unkindly that the proposal had been made only because Conrad had been drunk at the time.

'Con had what I'd call a Claret Conversion,' he said, and added as if thoughtfully, 'Wonder how many bottles it would take to make me propose to Tomsy Trent.'

'Tomasina Trent's only twelve years old,' Fenwick said blankly.

'Exactly,' said Eugene, pleased with himself, and then, seeing that no-one but Mary had got the point of the gibe, elaborated. 'Well, and Con's known May since she was a snot-nose kid. Only be natural for him to see her as a sister rather than a wife.' He looking sideways to see if he was upsetting May. 'Good job you didn't ask for a long engagement, May. No sense in testing a man's constancy too far.'

His remarks brought Maybelle close to tears, which seemed to amuse him mightily. Eugene was twenty-six, a loose-limbed young man with the same flat-nosed face as May. He had brown freckled skin and wiry blonde hair like Fenwick, but whereas Fenwick had a frank openness of expression which made him almost handsome, Eugene had a pinched face, a sulky mouth and secretive, watchful eyes. Lennox didn't like the look of him; there was something in that mouth and those eyes that reminded him of Georgie.

'Spoilt,' said Aunt Nora Hempton abruptly, reading Lennox's

face. Lennox turned to her with a start and a blush. Aunt Nora Hempton was the aunt of Fenwick's mother, an old lady of walnut appearance and strange garb who migrated between the various branches of the family, staying with each as long as the fancy took her, or their patience lasted. She was an unreformed, contrary, snuff-taking, care-for-no-one from the pioneering days, who had farmed single-handed after her husband died, fought Indians, and now was not to be glared or tutted into mimsy-pimsy society manners. She liked Mary better than any of the other relatives because Mary did not expect her to be a Grande Dame, and seemed to like her plain speaking, so she spent more time with 'poor silly Emily's fambly' than anywhere else. Her *bête noire* was Aunt Belle, whom she called 'that plum-in-the-mouth counterfit', and whom she delighted in embarrassing in front of her fancy Charleston friends.

'Spoilt, is Eugene,' she repeated to Lennox, with a fierce nod at her great-nephew. 'That unspeakable fool Belle Morland spoiled him – her and Charles. He was 'way too strict and she was too 'dulgent, and they messed him between them. Look at him, sulkin' at me!' She waved her stick at Eugene. 'I've shot Injuns for looking at me less provokin' than that, so mind, you!'

'Now, Auntie,' Fenwick protested mildly, while Eugene glared.

Benedict, feeling a little sorry for Eugene, kindly asked him about himself, and by ungracious inches elicited that Eugene had been given the choice, after he finished school, of West Point or the law. He chose the law.

'You were silly. I'd have gone to West Point,' Ruth said smartly.

'I dare say you would,' Eugene replied. 'That's because you're a horrible little hoyden.'

'Either is a perfectly gentlemanly pursuit,' Fenwick pointed out.

'Oh yes, suitable for younger sons,' Eugene muttered, giving him a resentful look.

'That fool Belle was glad you didn't choose West Point,' Aunt Nora said, and shot into a falsetto parody. 'Oh my, all those nasty swords and guns – so dangerous! Much safer you stay home, puss-cat, and be a lawyer!'

'Now, Auntie,' Fenwick said.

'Anyway, West Pointers have to get up much too early, don't they, Gene?' Ruth interposed smartly. 'Too much hard work being a soldier.'

Eugene made a face at her. 'Much you know about it, miss.'

Benedict, amused, said to Ruth, 'I'd have thought the law was hard work too. Don't lawyers have to get up early?'

'Lord, no!' Ruthie said. 'Not in Charleston. "The law is an overcrowded profession which guarantees comfortable idleness to anyone not determined to be busy." I read that in Pa's paper once. It means Eugene can pretend to have a profession and never actually have to work at all.'

Mary felt she ought to intervene. 'Ruthie, don't tease,' she said mildly. 'It isn't ladylike.'

Ruthie opened her mouth to protest, but caught Mary's eye and a slight shake of her head, and subsided. She was the one who most interested Lennox, not only because she was nearest his age, but because she was bold, vivacious, and full of fun and frolic. And even at fourteen she was remarkably pretty. She, alone of the children, looked like her mother, with the same pointed little fox-kitten face, though her hair was not dark like her mother's but a fascinating, burnished auburn. But at present she had little interest in her looks: her pleasures were all to do with horses and dogs and going off on the sort of jaunts her male cousins enjoyed – fishing, swimming, tree-climbing and the like.

It was Ruthie over the next few days who showed Lennox over the plantation. She seemed to take it for granted that he would be her companion – at times seemed almost to regard him as an amusement provided specifically for her, like a rather superior pet – but Lennox was perfectly happy to be annexed in that way. She accepted him so freely and uncritically that he felt at ease with her as he had never been with anyone else. So it was at her side he discovered the lie of the land at Twelvetrees. To one side of the house were the stables and coach-houses, and on the other an extensive jumble of various farmyards and barns, and beyond them the long double row of wooden cabins which were the slave quarters. A path, beaten white by the passage of feet, ran down the centre of the grass between the rows, and each cabin had a little strip of garden behind it, where the slaves might grow vegetables or keep chickens to augment their rations.

At one end of the rows stood the square wooden house of the overseer, Hazelteen – placed so he could keep an eye on whatever went on. At the other end were the other 'slave-lot' buildings: the nursery where two mammies took care of the black children all day, the cookhouse, the laundry, the mule stables, the washerwoman's house, a tiny cabin where Moses the gardener lived, and finally the brig – a grim, windowless shed where obstreperous slaves could be incarcerated, or might be penned to await punishment. In front of the cookhouse was a beaten area planted with shade-trees where the slaves gathered of an evening to talk and smoke, and where many carried their meal to eat al fresco and in company, rather than in their cabins. And behind Moses' cabin lay the main vegetable plots, which he was almost as proud of as the lawn.

Beyond all this the plantation spread away over gently rolling countryside, punctuated by mixed woodland, and streams – some of them deeply indented into the land – which everyone called 'cricks'. The nearer fields were under cultivation for food, some arable and some pasture, while the further-away fields were under cotton. And beyond the stables were extensive paddocks and a level grass gallop: Charles Morland bred horses, and frequently had winners at the Charleston races.

Ruthie knew it all, and had places in addition that were special to her: a particular climbing-tree, a rock in the middle of a certain crick where she liked to sit, a still pool where the biggest fish in the world lived and refused to be caught, the ruin of a mill where 'hants' were known to come at night. She took Lennox to see them all, and he was sensitive enough to understand that they were a series of gifts to him, of incalculable value, and received them with her in the proper spirit. In addition, Ruthie told him about the family and the neighbourhood with the most valuable degree of indiscretion.

They were in the old apple barn one day – a favourite resting-and-talking place for Ruthie. Someone long ago had fixed up a swing to the big beam across the centre, a handsome affair with thick ropes and a broad, solid, wooden seat, polished smooth by successive trousers. The barn was not used for apples any more, serving out its time as a supplementary woodshed, and at this time of year there was not much wood in it either. Ruth sat on the swing, pushing herself idly with one foot, while Lennox sat nearby on a small stack of logs, watching her. It was dim in here, and after the warmth outside almost shivery-cool, with a secretive smell of earth and wood-mould, and the faint scent of apples lingering somewhere like the ghost of autumns past. The bare earth floor had a long shallow scuff under the swing, where Ruthie's foot now struck rhythmically, shoving her backwards and stopping her return, to the swing ropes' creaking accompaniment.

Ruthie was talking about May's wedding, which had taken over from the Convention as everyone's most-discussed topic.

'I don't mind being a bridesmaid,' she was saying, 'even if it does mean wearing a pink dress. I hate pink, but May loves it – she thinks it suits her, the simpleton! But when she said she was asking Kitten Ausland as well, I told her I was not going to carry her train with that simpering idiot, no matter how she begged me!'

'Who is Kitten Ausland? Conrad's sister, I suppose?' Lennox said. He was getting better at keeping up with Ruthie's chatter.

'Yes, and she's the silliest female in three counties. She's got a perfectly sensible name, Katherine, but she's made eveyone call her Kitten because she thinks it's prettier.' She made a face of violent nausea. 'I can't think why Cousin Hamilton's sweet on her.'

'Cousin Hamilton?'

'You must've met him in Charleston? Uncle Hemp and Aunt Missy's eldest son? Oh well, you'll meet them all at the wedding. Ham's been spoony on Kitten for years. You'd think just her being an Ausland would put him off.'

'Don't you like the Auslands?'

'Who could like them?' she asked in simple amazement. 'Judge Ausland and Mrs Judge – oh my, don't they think themselves grand, just because *she* was a Pinckney! I believe May's chosen the worst possible in-laws in the whole of South Carolina.'

'I expect she chose her fiancé, rather than his parents,' Lennox suggested reasonably.

'I don't like Conrad either,' Ruth shrugged. 'You've only got to see how his dogs cower when he speaks to them to know he's cruel to animals. Well, if he ever does anything in front of me I shall say something, I don't care if he is half a Pinckney and horrid rich.'

'Why does Maybelle like him, then?' Lennox asked reasonably.

'May always does what she's expected to. Conrad's supposed to be a good match. The Auslands' plantation is next to ours – Camelot, that's what they call it, did you ever hear anything so silly? – and he's the eldest son, so he'll inherit it all. Pa and Judge Ausland belong to the same clubs and play golf together and breed racehorses so they're supposed to be friends, though I don't think Pa really likes him any more than I do,' she added thoughtfully. 'But they've got together to decide May and Conrad ought to marry, and that's that.'

'Didn't Conrad have anything to say about it?' Lennox asked. 'He's a grown man, isn't he? Or is he in love with your sister?'

'I don't think he *could* be in love, except with himself, maybe!' Ruth twisted the swing-ropes together, and then let them untwist themselves, over and over, so that the swing did a half turn back and forth. The action gave her a little jolt each time, which she found pleasurable. 'He and Eugene have been chasing girls for ten years and never cared a jot for any of them. But the thing is, Conrad is a catch, and sooner or later he was going to have to get married to some girl or other. I think he thinks May'll be the least trouble. Poor May,' she added. 'He's such an ugly old thing, and not interested in anything except silly cards and brandy. How dull he'll be for a husband!'

Marriage, Lennox thought, was still something unreal to her, just a ceremony followed by a loss of scrambling-about privileges.

He felt tender, protective towards her in her innocence. No-one brought up on the classics as he had been could be ignorant of the facts of life, or of the power men wielded over their wives – rarely, it seemed, to the wives' benefit. 'Perhaps it won't be so bad,' he said comfortingly.

'Well, I'll tell you one thing,' she said firmly, 'when I marry it will be to someone who loves me quite madly, and I'll love him just as much. Otherwise I shall refuse to do it.'

'What if your father insists?'

'Then I'll run away. I'll take a few things and get my pony and ride away up into the mountains where no-one will ever find me, and live in a log cabin and shoot things for food and eat berries and birds' eggs and such.'

'Wouldn't you be awfully lonely?' Lennox asked seriously.

'I suppose, maybe,' she said, thinking about it. 'Well, then, you could come too. I expect two would be better than one for building a log cabin, anyway, because I'm not sure one person could lift a whole tree-trunk.'

At this interesting moment they were interrupted by Mammy, who appeared in the doorway beaded with sweat and clothed in indignation.

'Dyah you is! Miz Ruthie, you come on in de house so's Ah kin mek you diss'nt. Don't you know we got comp'ny to dinner? Huccome you makin' me traipse all de way down heah lookin' for you, 'stead o' comin' in when you spose to? Ah tole you ter come in at t'ree o'clock, an' Ah bin callin' and callin' out de winder for you.'

'Well, I couldn't hear you from here, could I?' Ruth said, unwinding herself from the swing with a show of reluctance. 'Why didn't you send Rosa?'

'Rosa lookin' after de li'l boys, she busy. Deah on'y me, an' you knows Ah hain fit to go climbin' up an' down stairs all day, chasin' after you. Hit gib me de spasms in ma side. You knows Ah is po'ly.'

'You are not,' Ruthie said. 'It's all a make-up. Aunt Belle says so.'

'Ah *is* po'ly, t'ank God, an' Miss Belle hain got no right to say such a t'ing. Ah bin po'ly all ma lahf, which she knows is de trufe, becays ma maw wuz her Mammy, an' we growed up together. I was a po'ly chile an' Ah's gettin' po'lier ever' day!'

Ruth sighed, rolled her eyes at Lennox, and went off towards the house, followed by the diminuendo grumble, which issued from as stout and active-looking a woman as Lennox had ever seen.

★   ★   ★

On arrival at Twelvetrees, Mary put off the white muslins and fine Sea Island cottons, the delicate breakfast caps and wide-hooped petticoats that were her Charleston-wear. She folded away her two silk gowns, to be got out only for 'company dinners', and got out her Twelvetrees apparel. Twelvetrees caps were designed not to decorate but to cover the hair completely and keep it clean. Twelvetrees dresses were lightly hooped, and of wool or bombazine, in plaid or close-printed dark patterns that didn't show stains. They were covered all day by a capacious apron of linsey-woolsey, which was not only hard wearing but did not easily catch fire. Burning to death was the most common domestic accident to befall women, after death in childbirth, and linsey-woolsey smelled abominable when it began to scorch, which was a useful warning system.

Thus clad for the fray, Mary got to work. Maybelle's wedding was to be celebrated on the 28th of July, but preparations had begun the moment the engagement was announced in February. Five months was all she had to get everything done, and she would have been glad of twice as long. Aunt Missy had sniffed a little that so short an engagement was nigh-on indecent, but Aunt Belle, outraged, demanded if she thought a son of Mrs Judge *Pinckney* Ausland could be capable of anything less than perfect taste.

The fact of the matter, Mary thought privately, was that the Auslands as much as Maybelle herself wanted to make sure of Conrad before he could change his mind. It would be a shocking thing, practically unheard-of, for a man to break an engagement, but if any man could be thought capable of it, it was Conrad. A man who did such a thing would be utterly condemned and outlawed by polite society, but Mary had yet to discover that Conrad cared a jot for the opinion of polite society. Better therefore to get him hog-tied before he jettisoned Maybelle as capriciously as he had taken her up.

Poor May had been gazing longingly at Conrad at every party and picnic, ball and barbecue – ever since, prompted by who knew what devil, he had told her, while dancing with her at her first ball, that she was beautiful. Mary thought that that had probably been his idea of a joke: gingery-haired, red-cheeked Maybelle had wanted pink satin for her first ball-dress. It was what all the other girls had. Mary had tried to talk May out of it, but Aunt Belle and Fenwick between them had overruled her. Pink satin was the traditional stuff of the débutante, and May would look sweet in it, they said.

In fact, May looked pretty much like a prawn in it, in Mary's opinion, and Conrad, well lubricated from iced punch liberally reinforced from his hip-flask (Mary saw him covertly swigging behind the potted palms), probably thought he was being wonderfully funny in first solemnly soliciting a dance from Maybelle and then telling her she looked like an angel. Mary imagined him and Eugene sniggering themselves silly afterwards about it. Until the very moment of his proposal May had thought her love hopeless; and from what Mary could gather from May's misty-eyed description, the proposal itself had been as un-loverlike as it was possible to be.

Conrad: Well, May, Gene says you're pretty much in love with me?

May: (blushing) Oh, Con, I – I do think you're wonderful!

Conrad: All right then, say we get hitched? But no mushy stuff, mind!

Mary suspected Conrad had been pushed into the proposal by the Judge, who wanted his son married at any cost, before there was a public scandal. Mary doubted he had any real affection for poor May, but a girl had to marry someone, and at nineteen she was already old to be a spinster, when some Southern girls married at fifteen, and even fourteen was not unheard-of. At least at Camelot she would be near her childhood home. Probably Con would spend most of his time in Charleston, and with luck May would never get to know him well enough to have her heart broken.

After the wedding itself, the couple would visit around the neighbourhood for a week, having a dinner or ball given in their honour at every notable house, before beginning the wedding tour of more distant relations who could not come to the wedding. Hospitality in the South was such that a wedding tour could easily last a year, and Mary had heard stories of 'honeymoon' couples who had finally arrived back home at the parental hearth with two children in tow. Mary didn't think Conrad would want to be out of circulation very long. Perhaps he would deposit Maybelle with some distant relative and head for the bright lights of New Orleans or Atlanta for a private debauch. She wouldn't put it past him.

In the meantime, however, there was the wedding to prepare for, and most of the work and responsibility fell on Mary's shoulders. Although the wedding dress itself was Miss Emily's, laid away in a trunk in the attic for this day, it had to be fitted and altered for Maybelle, and all the rest of her trousseau was made at Twelvetrees. There were the second, third, fourth and fifth day dresses, two ball-gowns, two new carriage dresses and the rest of May's wardrobe to be looked over and refurbished, plus a stack of new linen – underwear and nightgowns – to be made and trimmed, a new gown for Mary for the wedding, and the three bridesmaid's dresses. (Ruthie remaining adamant that she would not share train-holding duties with Kitten Ausland, cousin Cecilia had been asked to be a train-bearer, while Ruth was to walk before the couple scattering rose-petals from a basket.) Virtually every female in the house had to be recruited for the needlework, but Mary and her head woman, Julia, did all the measuring and cutting out, and most of the fitting. Hats, gloves and outer wear, thank God, were ordered from Charleston.

As well as the clothes to make, there was the house to be cleaned and polished, invitations sent out and checked off, wedding gifts received, acknowledged and displayed, and the wedding feast planned and prepared, including the massive wedding-cake, for which a special oven had had to be built out of doors, the kitchen bread-oven not being big enough. Twelvetrees, as Mary had had painfully to learn, was not Morland Place. What you did not have, you could not simply order from the nearby town. You wanted ham for your feast? Be sure to butcher your hogs in time to cure them. Fried chicken? Make sure you set enough eggs under the broodies to have the poults to fatten in time to slaughter the day before. Cakes and bread? Hope you've made enough yeast to last. Melons for July? Don't forget to sow the seed in March.

Mary had responded to the challenge in the same way that she had responded six years earlier to finding herself, at the age of seventeen and utterly untried, mistress of a plantation and in charge of the feeding, clothing and nursing of a family of eight and a hundred negroes. She subdued her emotions, put aside incipient despair, and made lists. 'A horse has stronger muscles than a man, but it is the man who rides the horse,' Father Moineau used to say. (Oh, how she missed him!) If you used your brain, you could solve any problem, complete any task. Mary applied order and logic to the mass of work and responsibility she found herself faced with, and survived, but it was a heart-breaking task.

She had slaves aplenty to do the actual work, more pairs of hands than an English lady could hope to command. But slaves were not like servants. Servants you could train to the point where they did their duties without being told; any that were untrainable you could weed out and dismiss. But slaves would not work without constant supervision. Nothing could be initiated without her presence, and even once they were started, only the best of them could be left alone to get on. In most cases, as soon as she left the room they would slack off, or stop altogether, or even sneak out of the house, to be tracked down later at enormous expense of time, and found snoozing somewhere under a tree, or idling about their own purposes.

Between February and April, when she went to Charleston to

meet her father, Mary thought she had accomplished a small miracle. Then just as the household was preparing to decamp for Twelvetrees, Aunt Belle threw a clog into the machine by 'reminding' Mary that it was customary when a marriage was celebrated in the house to give the negroes new clothes to wear at the wedding.

Mary almost tore out her hair. 'Why did no-one tell me?' she cried to her husband.

'I thought you knew,' he said. 'The slaves have their own feast out at the cabins while we're having ours—'

'Yes, I know that. Chitterlings and pork belly, fried yams, water-melon, lots of corn-meal with molasses – Uncle Heck told me what was expected – and then they dance. But nobody mentioned new clothes.'

'Surely you can manage?' Fenwick said. 'If you haven't enough cloth, you can order it before we go back to Twelvetrees.'

'It isn't the cloth,' Mary said grimly, 'it's that everything will have to be cut out either by me or Julie. No-one else can be trusted to do it right. Have you any idea how much work that means?'

'P'raps you could get Mrs Hazelteen to help,' Fenwick suggested brightly.

Perhaps she could; but three into a hundred still came out at enough work to keep them occupied without a wedding, never mind with one. Out came the great bolts of white jean and calico, red flannel and pink gingham; out came the muslin patterns – standard sizes, and the odd individual patterns for the very tall or the very fat; out came the french chalk and the cutting-out shears. To save time Mary would lay out a pattern on top of several layers of material and chalk it round, and she or Julie would cut out. Added to the rest of the work, it left Mary exhausted at the end of each day.

But still she was determined to find time to ride out with Papa, even if only once, and show him the plantation; see with him and through his eyes her new kingdom, so that she would know what images he would take away with him when he went back to that small green island with the soft skies that was her heart's home. So as soon as the first flurry of arrival had calmed down, Mary arranged to ride round the whole estate with her father, starting off early in the cool of the morning, and having a picnic lunch taken to a prearranged place to meet them in the middle of the day. Mary was to ride Golden Oriole, a very pretty chestnut and her favourite horse, and she ordered the bay Kingcup to be saddled for her father. Then, as they were waiting for the horses to be brought round, Fenwick appeared, carrying his hat and whip, with his pointer, Mag, at his heels, and announced he was coming with them.

'I assume my company will be welcome?' he said.

Mary was pleased that he was showing her father the attention. 'Of course,' she said quickly. 'You know so much more about everything than I do, you can answer Papa's questions more fully.'

The luncheon-spot Mary had chosen was where the track to the old flour-mill crossed a crick in a little wood. Here the crick ran over an outcrop of stone, broad and almost flat and scored by deep grooves into the appearance of a huge natural pavement. Just above the fording-place there was a drop of about four inches between one section of the pavement and the next, forming a natural weir over which the water rushed smoothly like curved glass; further up again the banks rose steeply, so that the crick ran between hanging woods into a deep green shade, before bending out of sight.

The picnic-wagon was waiting for them. The place Mary chose was just beside the weir, where there was a small natural lawn and the remains of a huge fallen tree, a section of trunk which had been there so long the bark had all worn away, leaving a smooth and silvery bench. Here they sat, while the slaves laid out the cloth before them. Mag lay down in the thin grass at Fenwick's feet and draped her pink tongue gracefully over her sharp white teeth. A tall marshall tree behind them cast its shifting shade and whispered to itself in a breeze no-one else could detect, a sound that made the cool feel cooler; the waterfall rushed and roared softly, and invisible birds called and echoed from the gold-green dapple of the woods.

They ate, and chatted a little; and when the slaves had cleared everything away and left them again in peace, Fenwick felt in his breast pocket and held out a battered metal case towards Benedict.

'Segar?'

'Thanks. You don't mind, Mary?'

In a moment the blue wreaths of smoke were winding up slowly into the branches above them, and the marshall leaves trembled all together as though in ecstasy at the fragrance. The crick pattered over the stone causeway, flicking spangles of light into the air, and a dove called liquidly and monotonously from the deep shade of a chestnut.

'Do you know,' Benedict said after a while, 'I'm beginning to like this place. There's a magic about it . . .'

'There is,' Fenwick agreed. He sounded pleased.

'All the same, I can see just with the most cursory glance that great improvements can be made. Your farming methods are very primitive, if you'll forgive me. Quite extraordinary numbers of hands at work, not seeming to achieve very much, and only the most rudimentary of machinery.'

'Well, sir,' Fenwick said, 'what we have a great deal of is labour.'

'But they don't work effectively. That's my complaint.'

'They're slaves,' Fenwick said, as if that answered it all, and then added, for Benedict's further enlightenment, 'You must understand that negroes are naturally stupid and lazy. You can't expect to get the same work out of them as out of a white hand back in England. You have to remember that in their natural habitat they don't work at all. In Africa they wander about amongst the trees picking up their food as animals do.'

'It's a pity you didn't leave them there, then,' Mary said. Fenwick shot her a sharp look of disapproval, but Benedict turned to her for her opinion.

'Do you think they are lazy?' he asked.

'Why should they be otherwise?' she said. 'If they finish a piece of work, there's more to be done afterwards – always more, until the day they die. One task is much like another, so what good does it do them to work hard? What can they gain by it?'

'Pride in a job well done, perhaps?' Benedict hazarded.

'Pride?' Mary said. 'They must live and die as property – where's the pride in that? All responsibility is taken away from them, and all hope. Their sole desire, the aim towards which every waking thought is directed, is to do as little as possible. The ambition of their lives is to be thought too "poorly" for heavy work.'

'In other words,' Fenwick said angrily, 'they are idle, ignorant darkies. In their position, would you or I fall so low? Of course not. We would have some respect for ourselves, because we are different from them. That's why God placed us in authority over them, as He did over the animals. Why, left alone they couldn't even fend for themselves. If they couldn't pick their food off the trees, they'd starve to death.'

Benedict felt embarrassed by this turn of the conversation. 'You speak as if they are all the same. But surely they are different from each other, as we are?'

Mary answered before Fenwick could. 'They are all alike in being slaves. Slavery is like an identical box each is locked up in. It immobilises the South, freezes it into an unchangeable shape like a fly caught in amber.' Her voice grew more agitated. 'Nothing can grow, nothing can develop. Slavery is a curse, a burden, a weight round our necks. You'll find out!' She stopped abruptly, hearing her own voice. Her father was looking upset; Fenwick's eyes were hard.

'My wife seems to have been reading Abolitionist pamphlets,' he said with an attempt at a laugh. 'But you mustn't take it all so seriously, my dear. Pamphlets are always full of extreme language, but they don't reflect real life. You've only got to look at our darkies to see how contented they are. No responsibility, plenty of food and just enough work to keep them healthy. It's an idyllic life for the uneducated, wouldn't you say, sir?'

'I know a great many factory workers who would consider it so,' Benedict said agreeably.

'Just so,' said Fenwick, and turned the conversation to horse-breeding. Nothing more was said on the subject on their ride round the plantation, but Mary knew the last word had not been pronounced.

Sure enough, while she was dressing for dinner, Fenwick came in, and dismissed Patty tersely. He sat himself down on the edge of the dressing-table, looking stern. Mary, sitting before the glass, not looking at him, turned a hairbrush around and around in her hand. She had on a gown of lavender, trimmed with white lace, very low cut, with short puffed sleeves, displaying her lovely shoulders and arms. Her golden hair was still loose, hanging in shining coils over her shoulders and down her back: Patty had been about to dress it when she was interrupted. Fenwick thought how beautiful she looked, and his senses were stirred by the combination of naked skin and loose, tumbled hair. He remembered, involuntarily, their love-making – discontinued this long while, ever since she announced her last pregnancy. He was not a very sexually active man, and his full life left him tired at night and ready to sleep. He didn't miss the physical side of marriage; the exploits and boasts of other men left him puzzled. But just now she looked so beautiful and so sad that he wanted to touch her, to stroke the ivory flesh of her shoulders, to turn a strand of her hair between his fingers, perhaps to kiss her warm neck—

But he was forgetting that he had to rebuke her. That lovely golden head contained unacceptable thoughts, even more unacceptably expressed. If his father had been present when she was talking in that terrible way, what would he have said? Fenwick was conscious that he had let her off lightly. His father would have stopped her in a word or two, not allowed her to go on pouring out that poison.

She looked up suddenly, interrupting his thoughts; her gaze was as blue and as blank as the summer sky. 'Well?' she said. 'Shall we have it over with? Don't keep me waiting for the lash.'

He disliked the imagery, and her seeming lack of shame for her behaviour angered him. 'If you are apprehensive, you have only yourself to blame. How dare you air your trashy opinions in front of me? How dare you contradict me in front of your father?'

'I didn't contradict—' she began.

'You're doing it now!' he snapped, making any further response from her impossible. She lowered her head before the storm. 'I warn you, if ever I find any literature of that sort in the house, I shall take it straight to Father! I will not have you spout such ideas, and shame me like that.'

'How does it shame you?'

'What you say reflects on me. There must be one mind between man and wife, and one only.'

'Yours,' she said, so much without inflection that he was able to take it as consent to his will.

'Naturally,' he said. 'A woman can have no opinion on things which do not concern her, of which she has no experience. That is why she has men to protect her. Listen to me and to my father and learn from us, be guided by us, and all will go well with you. Don't forget it is your divine as well as your human duty to obey. Obedience and humility to your husband is a rehearsal for obedience and humility before the Throne of God.'

'I'm sorry,' she said when he had stopped. 'I will try not to disappoint you again.'

She sounded genuinely unhappy, and he was touched. 'Do,' he said. 'Do try. I don't like to have to speak to you like this.' Her bowed head looked so childlike that his feelings stirred again. He remembered the little girl of fourteen he had fallen in love with, so innocent and pure; and before that, long ago, his little sister Hero – next to him in age, constant companion of his plays, snatched from him by the fever when she was just thirteen years old. His grief then had been inconsolable; he sometimes thought that she was the only creature he had ever really loved – until Mary. That was why it hurt him so much when Mary let him down, proved not to be meek and innocent and perfect as Hero had been. But when she looked sad and humble like this, it stirred him. 'Mary, my dear,' he said, and a husky note entered his voice, 'let's not quarrel, you and I. Be my dear, obedient little wife, and let's be happy together. I do love you.'

His fingers rested lingeringly on her shoulder, and after a moment Mary laid her own hand over his, turning her head the other way, so that he should not see her eyes. He took it for an invitation, and bent to kiss her neck. She waited, schooling herself to accept him. She was his wife; she had loved him once; she so desperately wanted to love him again. And she was lonely – just this brush of the lips touched her unbearably. But he was not one for spontaneous gestures or unconventional actions; and besides, the dressing-bell had gone, and they must not be late for dinner. Later, when they had retired for the night – that would be the time for him. If he came to her then, she thought, she would welcome him with affection, make him feel loved. *If* he came to her: she knew that he got very sleepy after dinner. By the time Abel had undressed him the urge would probably have passed, and his bed would beckon him more warmly than hers.

And at the thought of his human foibles she felt a spontaneous burst of affection, and was able to say, 'I love you, too,' in a natural enough tone to satisfy him. He removed his hand and went away, and presently Patty crept back and took the hairbrush quietly from her mistress's unnoticing fingers.

CHAPTER TWELVE

A wedding was an important occasion in the South, and friends and relatives came from far and wide to celebrate it. Those who lived near enough would go home at the end of the day, but many had to be put up, calling into service every bed, couch, mattress and palliasse in the house, and farming the surplus guests out to neighbours. On these occasions, everyone threw in their lot together, and no-one was too particular where he laid his bones; indeed, most of the menfolk hoped to be too drunk by the end of festivities to notice.

Arrivals began well beforehand with a family of cousins several times removed who lived in Georgia and wished they didn't. They arrived like desert wanderers at the oasis of urbanity and plenty that was Twelvetrees, and at once unpacked and arranged around them a worrying quantity of personal items, of the sort that refugees shove into their bundles when they know they are leaving home for ever: ma's silver teapot, the plait of grandma's hair, the baby's first shoes, great-granpa's medal from the Revolutionary War. Aunt Nora eyed them with contempt and took to shrieking 'Locusts!' at them every time she passed through, which made them jump, but on the whole that was a small price to pay for three square meals a day and a wedding-feast to come.

Uncle Heck arrived home from Savannah, smiling and genial, and greeted Mary's father and cousin with a hard shake of the hand, and a quick, noticing look-over. Of Miss Emily's brothers, he was the nearest to her in age, and they had been so close that when she married he had moved with her to Twelvetrees and never gone away again. He was small and dark and bandy-legged from riding; not a great talker – though when he spoke it was worth listening – but a great contriver, who would look at a problem for a moment or two, whistling silently through his teeth, and then fix it magically with a bit of string, two nails and a piece of bent tin. He was also wonderfully musical, could play any instrument ever invented, and knew the words of every song ever written – according to Ruthie, who adored him.

Hill was with him, but he only glowered at the newcomers and then stumped away to stable the horses, since he wouldn't trust them to the slaves. Heck was the only person Mary knew who had a white servant, though he called Hill 'my friend'. Hill would have none of that. 'I ain't nobody's friend,' he growled, but he was fiercely loyal to and protective of Uncle Heck, and no-one had any doubt he would die for him without a second thought if required.

Hill was a villainous-looking, skinny old man, with a face so wrinkled and tanned from years of exposure to the weather that it was impossible to tell how old he really was. He always had an ancient greasy hat jammed on his head, indoors and out, and the stub of a cold cheroot clamped between his teeth. Mary would have bet that he slept with these two accessories, if she could have believed he ever slept at all. His background was obscure. He came from the mountains somewhere beyond Tennessee; his parents and brothers and sisters had been killed by Indians when he was about twelve, and he had fled into the hills and taken care of himself for many years, so that by the time Heck came across him he could barely remember how to speak, and had forgotten his age and even his name. It was Heck who named him John Hill, since all he knew about himself was that he came from the hills. But everyone now called him Hill, since he seemed too wild and fierce for anything so civilised as a Christian name.

Heck had saved his life, in circumstances neither would talk about, Heck because of modesty, and Hill because, he said, 'it was none of anybody's damn business'. But Hill had been with him ever since, part body-servant, part praetorian guard, acting as valet, footman, cook and groom, and sleeping on a blanket across the door of whatever room Heck was occupying with his hand on the hilt of his huge bowie-knife. He rarely spoke and, when he did, the listener would usually have preferred that he didn't, since his language was mostly profane and never complimentary. He hated negroes with a fervour rare in the South, saying that 'niggers was jist Injuns without feathers', and if you asked him if there was anything he hated worse than Indians, he would say, 'wimmin'.

Another early arrival for the wedding was cousin Cecilia – another of Uncle Hemp's brood – who came the day after Heck got back. She had to be fitted with her bridesmaid's dress, and was to stay as a companion to Maybelle, whose state of nerves required constant reassurance. She was accompanied on the journey by her brother Hamilton, who needed very little persuasion to stay on as well, since bridesmaids' fittings meant he was pretty well bound to bump into Kitten Ausland.

Aunt Belle would remain in Charleston until the last minute, which was a little relief to Mary, for whom every new arrival made extra work. To her surprise, Charles, whom she would have expected to do the same, came at the beginning of July, with still three weeks to go before the wedding. Also surprisingly, he spent a lot of time with Benedict and Lennox, talking about the mill that needed renovation. The initial scheme soon spawned a number of schemelets, and the library table was covered in pieces of paper on which they worked out the feasibility of them, and drew up designs and lists of materials required. Lennox entered these séances nervously at first, and was not reassured to discover that both men seemed to be trying to probe his mind and gauge his abilities. But the work itself soon took hold of him: his nervousness faded, and he found he was able to contribute ideas that the older men accepted with approval and even respect. Benedict was surprised and gratified to discover how sound the boy's understanding of architecture and the principles of building was. 'You'd have made a fine engineer,' he said once – his highest accolade.

And then, a few days after Charles, Martial came home. He came like a breath of fresh air to Mary, bringing the sense of a wider world into the stifling round of slave talk and wedding talk. She greeted him with fervour, surprising herself a little: in the excitement of her father's visit she had not realised how much she had been missing him, for, though he was politic to the death, she could not help feeling that in him she had an ally against her husband and father-in-law, that he liked her, and for the very things that they disapproved of so much.

He came bowling up to the house one day in a cloud of dust and the station buggy, his luggage piled high in the back and his slave Ratty perched on the top, clutching his hat. Mary happened to be out at the front at the time, talking to Moses, and as the buggy jounced round the sweep Martial made a flying leap from it onto the grass, ran the last few steps and grabbed Mary round the waist and swung her round. It made her shriek, scandalised Moses, and so shocked Thunder that he felt he had no alternative but to bite somebody really hard, and sank his teeth into Moses' side at the waist where there was loose flesh he could get a good grip on.

Ignoring the commotion, Martial set Mary back on her feet, and smiled down into her flushed and breathless face. 'Home is the sailor, home from sea,' he said.

'You *devil*!' she gasped. He still had his arms round her waist. 'You startled me!'

'No wifely kiss?' he asked. 'Oh, I know you're not my wife, but I'm sure when Odysseus had been gone so long he wasn't particular either. Very well, then, how about a cousinly kiss? Here, chastely upon the forehead. You're looking very pretty, Mrs Morland; but, then, you always do.' He released her at last, and not before time, she thought, as she saw from the corner of her eye the door of the house open and people begin to come out. 'My quotation was not apt, I realise, since I've not been to sea, but since you show no desire to play Penelope, I suppose it doesn't matter.'

'Weaving is one of the few things I don't have to do,' she replied.

'Not for cloth, I grant you, but you do cast a very pretty web all the same. Well, if I can't be your Ulysses, what about the Emperor Caligula? He had a horse called Penelope.'

'Penelope was a mare, not a horse,' Mary said firmly, 'and a married mare at that.'

'How shocking of you, Mrs Morland, to use the word "mare". Aunt Belle would have a conniption.' He smiled down at her. 'How refreshing it is to talk nonsense again! I love Yankees, but they're so terribly earnest, it makes one's head ache.'

Mary thought, though she did not say it aloud, how refreshing it was for her to talk to someone who used classical allusions and didn't mind that she understood them. She looked up at him with a sense of ease and gladness, as one might feel on finally coming in sight of home after a long and tiring journey. Martial was not handsome, but somehow one never noticed it, for his face was one that you could not look away from, and could not forget, it was so full of life and humour and intelligence. Looking at him now, Mary found that she knew every line and plane of it, every tiny crease and mark, every brush-stroke in his eyebrows, every movement of his lips and expression of his eyes. He was so familiar that it was almost like looking in a mirror.

'It's good to have you back,' she said quietly.

He only looked at her, but his smile suggested he understood all sorts of things that she didn't say, perhaps that she wasn't yet aware she thought. 'Hush,' he said, 'the barbarians are upon us', and turned away from her in time to receive Ruthie full in the chest. She was well in the vanguard, and breathless, having run from the farmyard whence she had seen his buggy pass in the distance. 'Cousin Mart! Cousin Mart!' was all she managed to pant, but she plastered his cheek with kisses, a gesture she offered to no-one but him, for she was sparing with her embraces. Martial heaved her, large as she was, onto his hip, and with the other arm casually draped round Mary's shoulder, walked with them towards the approaching welcoming committee.

Mary sighed and put down the bodice she was sewing, and stretched out her hands, flexing her fingers. She had been up at five that morning, and had not stopped since, except to eat; and even now, after dinner, she could not sit down without some work in her hands, though she was sewing almost by feel by this time. She looked around the room, and marvelled at the difference Martial's return a few days ago had made. There was a new animation in the house. No more deadly evenings of circular talk, the same comments on the same subjects made almost in the same order by the same people, but proper, amusing conversation, with everyone joining in, and games, and songs.

At the moment Martial was not in the room – he was in the library talking to her father and Charles – but his influence was still apparent. Aunt Nora Hempton was sitting in the big wing-back chair by the fireside preparing to nod off after the large meal she had just consumed, but the others, Fenwick, Eugene, Hamilton, May, Cecilia, Ruth and Lennox, were gathered round the piano where Uncle Heck was playing favourite songs for them all to join in with. He had begun with the jolly songs – they had had 'Seven Pigs' and 'The Jolly Ploughman' and 'Phyllida Flouts Me' and 'The Tramping Man' – and now he was getting on to the sentimental ones with the slower beat. They were all singing 'My Carolina Home', Eugene putting in the tricky tenor descant above Fenwick's light baritone.

Mary was amused to see Eugene for once enjoying such an innocent pleasure; when Martial was around he always behaved better, stopped looking sulky and superior and aping the cynical debauchee. She supposed that even in his vanity, Eugene realised that Martial was a real man, of the sort he ought to aspire to be, not the hollow sham that Conrad represented, which he copied. Fenwick was pleased, too, at the change in Eugene, though Mary doubted he attributed it to the same cause. But he smiled affectionately at his brother as their voices twined through the chorus, remembering shared pleasures from their early childhood, when it had been just the three of them, Fenwick, Hero and Eugene, and their mother was alive and their father had not yet turned sour.

Lennox didn't know the songs, of course, but he sang the choruses, and was quick enough to sing some of the verses, too, by mouthing the words a fraction after Ruthie. He caught Mary watching him do it, and blushed; Fenwick looked to see what he was looking at, and invited Mary by a smile and a gesture to join them, but she shook her head. She did not feel part of it, just then; she preferred to remain on the outside looking in. Then, by way of advancing a reason for her refusal, got up and went out onto the verandah.

It was a balmy evening. The air was softly perfumed with the scent of the roses which scrambled, invisible now, over the verandah roof like a pink-white snowfall; crickets scissored away in the dark all around. The night beyond the porch lamps was velvet, dense and smoothly black; leaning on the rail, she felt she could simply have slipped into it as into warm water, and it would have borne her weight. She imagined herself lying back and floating away – where? She didn't know. Just away, that was all. She was tired, and she longed to get away from the endless work; most of all, away from the endless preoccupation with negroes. Oh, to be free of slaves! She felt them like a weight constantly dragging at her, hampering her movements like a weight of chains. It seemed terrible to waste all the days of her precious youth following after them: cajoling and berating, dispensing justice, answering their maddening, repetitive questions, settling their silly, childish feuds. Oh, the complications and frustrations of directing their labours! The tedium of their company, from which she was never free, day or night! Their endless ailments and complaints and excuses and lies!

For some reason, she began thinking about Miss Emily. Her ghost seemed somewhere near, a thin, frail thing, like the sweet, sad tune Uncle Heck was playing, which was twining itself like mist around her thoughts. Perhaps Miss Emily had sat here, on the verandah, listening to these same songs; sat here pregnant, more likely than not, tired, as Mary was tired, and dreading another childbirth to come. Mary was safe from that, at least, for another month: her bleeding had started that morning. But for Miss Emily, no relief, just that endless tax on her body, paid in pain and blood and weariness, until she had no capital left, and she died.

Here in the South, of course, such a view would have been considered blasphemous, if not plain daft. Marriage was for begetting children, women were created by God to be wives and mothers. Frequency of pregnancies, indeed, was proof of love. Did he love you, Miss Emily? she thought into the dark, sending the question coiling away like segar smoke in the direction of the faded ghost. When you were alone together in bed, was what he did to you a proof of love, did it feel like love to you? The ghost seemed to shiver on the warm night air. Was that an answer?

Mary thought of Fenwick's shy, rather puppyish love-making; always with the lamps out, and without words, just a fumbling and a panting and a dampness of hands. It did not touch her in any way.

There was no tenderness of words and, without words, nothing was real to her. When he lay on top of her for those infrequent and brief contacts, she waited like someone outside in the dark looking into a lighted room.

Mais que voulez-vous? She didn't know; yet she thought of the classics on which she had been reared, all the passionate, yearning, devastating literature of love – did it really refer only to that damp little act of procreation? Surely there must be something more to feel, something others had felt before her? Well, she would never know. It was no golden shower that had fallen about her shoulders, but Miss Emily's leaden mantle. She had inherited her husband, her children, her household and her duties. This was what her life was to be: endless toil, and perhaps an early death. And all because as an ignorant, foolish girl, she had insisted on having her own way and marrying Fenwick. Perhaps instead of preparing for Maybelle's marriage she ought to warn her on no account to marry Conrad? Was that what Miss Emily's lingering ghost wanted of her – to warn her child away from the danger? But Maybelle wouldn't listen, of course, in thrall to the Marriage Myth. And, in any case, what else could Maybelle do? Her father had arranged this marriage, and she had no choice but to comply.

A soft footfall on the verandah behind her brought her from her deep thoughts. Within, there was a soft patter of conversation, while the piano ran idly here and there, picking up a few bars of a tune and dropping them, like a casual shopper running skeins of silk through her fingers. The footstep did not belong to one of the drawing-room party: it had come from the other end of the house; nor was it the shuffling tread of a slave. Mary did not turn to see. She knew who it was. All her senses seemed to be on tiptoe, like a child when a parade is approaching.

A cheerful voice close behind her said, 'All alone out here? What a terrible waste!' And then there was – or did she imagine it? – a breath of a touch on the back of her neck that sent a shudder all down her spine. Miss Emily's ghost dissolved; the night was dense and velvety again, and inhabited by shrilling crickets and the suddenness of bats.

'Well, Martial?'

'I've left your father to entertain Uncle Charles. I'm too young for such *sages conseils*. I was designed by a beneficent God to laugh, to sing, to dance – to make others happy!'

'You are twenty-seven years old,' Mary reminded him.

'Twenty-seven years,' he interrupted, 'three months, ten days and, oh, let's just say six hours in round figures, rather than force me to get out my watch and make the calculation.' He came round from behind her to lean on the rail beside her. 'How charming of you to know so exactly how long I have graced this orb!'

'Twenty-seven years and etcetera,' she waved a hand, pretending sternness, 'master of your own fortune, and *not married*! You are far too handsome and rich to be a bachelor, let alone a singing, dancing, laughing one. It's not fair. It's not decent. Have you no shame?'

'None at all,' he said lightly. 'When I see matrimony all about me, I feel it is my duty to remain single so as to warn the young people of the awful consequences.'

'Awful consequences which way?' she asked suspiciously.

He laughed into her eyes. 'That's an interesting question! Take your choice, my sweet cousin. Oh, and thank you, by the way, for the "handsome"! Yankee ladies think me piratical and exciting, a Southern devil, but they never notice my extraordinary good looks. But what are you doing out here all alone?'

'Looking into the dark and thinking,' she said. He leaned his forearms on the verandah rail in the manner of one settling for a long chat and so she did the same, dragging her eyes from his face reluctantly, but with the feeling that it was her duty to do so. It didn't make a great deal of difference, anyway. Side by side with him, close enough to feel the heat his body radiated, she could see his face in her mind as clearly as in reality.

'Thinking about what?' he asked.

She selected the beginning point. 'That it was like dark water. That I should like to slip into it and be carried away.' She could say such things to him. To anyone else she would have made a commonplace answer.

'Yes, Helle, I can see you breasting the great flowing ocean of night like a swimmer, your pale hair trailing behind you. But where will the current take you?'

'Not to; just from.'

'Ah,' he said, and she almost heard him following the spoor of her mind to find what she had been thinking. 'It's a great deal of work for you, all this, isn't it?'

'The wedding, you mean?'

'Particularly, but not exclusively. I've visited many plantations, stayed with friends and relatives. I've seen what it entails.'

'It's not the what,' she said, 'but the how. In England I could have enjoyed it, every bit, even the pricked fingers, in a good cause.' She held up her hands to display the reddened tips. 'But here—' She shook her head, but the words burst out of her anyway. 'Oh God, but this slavery is a curse!'

He caught her nearest hand and carried her fingertips to his mouth and kissed them softly, and let them go. 'You mustn't hate *them*,' he said.

'No, no, I don't! How could I? I pity them so, even those who exasperate me most! And with some of them, working with them all day, there's a great affection between us. Julie, for instance, and my little girl Patty. I think they even like me – though God knows how they can! Their forgiveness is heartbreaking.'

A burst of laughter behind in the room stopped her. She heard Maybelle's voice lift brightly above the rest with an 'Oh, but Conrad says—' before it sank below the conversation line again.

She went on, very quietly, 'It must end. It must end, Martial. We are slaves as much as they. How can it go on? How can men let it go on?'

'Because they don't feel it and see it as you women do. You are the ones who have to bear the pains day by day.'

'But I've heard them talking – God, how often! – about the inferior nature of the negro, and how God placed the white man above him. You know how men go on.'

Martial stirred uncomfortably. 'I'm a man, too, you know!'

'Not you, Martial,' she said quickly.

He smiled ruefully. 'Thank you, you don't know how that touches me! But look, they believe it because they have to – some of them – because there's no other way. And some are just stupid enough really to believe it. Superior to women, to children – self-evidently, because society says so, everything in their day-to-day life confirms it – and so why not to darkies? But underneath we all know it must end. It *will* end.' He turned to her, and looked down seriously into her face. 'I'm telling you this, my beautiful cousin Mary. No, beautiful Mrs Fenwick Morland, let me say rather: there will be enough peril soon to satisfy the most foolhardy spirit, I need not seek out more. I'm telling you it will end, this abominable system. The question that remains to be answered is how – quick and painful, or slow and easy?'

'What do you mean?' she searched his face, suddenly foreboding.

'I mean that we mustn't let the North force us into abolition. In a few years, if we're left to ourselves, it will die naturally. Already thinking men in the South say so privately, and where they lead all must eventually follow. But if we try to make a sharp cut – if the North forces our hand – the pain will be terrible, and I fear it will never end.'

'You frighten me,' she said. 'What do you know?'

He looked at her for a long moment, and then drew back; not physically, but behind a laughing mask. 'Not yet, love, not yet.

Es ist nicht Zeit. Trouble is beginning and some of us will not see the end of it, but *carpe diem*, let us laugh while we can, and sing – especially sing. I can't believe, Mrs Morland,' he went on in a different voice, 'that you can be content to stand out here and listen to those inferior performers inside. Come, I insist you go back in with me and show them how it's done.' He turned away from the darkness and held out his hand to her, flat-palmed, as one ushers a child through a door.

'I don't want to sing,' she said, but she was already obeying him, moving towards the door.

'Oh yes, you do, more than you can possibly help, because I am going to sing with you. A duet.' They stepped through the long doors into the stuffy, lamp-lit interior, where the erstwhile singers were clustered about the piano, leafing through music and arguing about what to have next. Only Uncle Heck saw them come in; looked up above his quietly moving hands, took in Mary's face and exchanged a silent question and answer with Martial.

'Now, good people,' Martial announced authoritatively enough to cut through the chatter, 'by special request, for your fortunate ears and for this one performance only, Mrs Fenwick Morland and I are going to sing you a duet. I shall begin, dear madam,' he bowed to Mary, 'and you and Uncle Heck shall join in when you have the idea of it.'

> *So we'll go no more a-roving*
> *So late into the night,*
> *Though the heart be still as loving,*
> *And the moon be still as bright.*

His voice was dark and velvet as night or black water. Uncle Heck picked him up in the second bar, and Martial turned sideways on to the piano and collected Mary's eyes as he sang, drawing her in.

> *For the sword outwears its sheath*
> *And the soul wears out the breast,*

Mary joined in, suddenly free of self-consciousness, free of worry for the first time since waking, enjoying the simple release and power of the act of singing.

> *And the heart must pause to breathe,*
> *And love itself have rest.*

Their voices were good together, and the others stood silent, enjoying it, leaning into the sound as a dog leans towards the warmth of the fire. Benedict appeared in the doorway of the drawing-room, smiling with paternal pleasure; Charles, who had been behind him, paused only an instant, looking on with indifferent eyes at the family party before slipping quietly away, collecting a lamp from the hall and going out by the side door.

Only Heck, at the piano, saw him go; only Hill, sitting alone in the dark on the far end of the verandah, saw the lamp bobbing through the darkness towards the negro cabins.

Mary was up at four o'clock on the day of the wedding, an hour earlier even than her usual time. She felt little rested. She had been disturbed in the night by a call to the slave cabins where one of the women had gone into labour, but it turned out to be a false alarm. She was hoping the woman would manage to hold off for the rest of the day: it might prove the straw that broke this camel's back.

In the kitchen Julie, bless her, was already at work, stoking up the stove and chivvying Cookie into getting the biscuits in for breakfast. Cookie's eyes were still half closed and she grumbled constantly as she moved about the kitchen, her large bare feet flapping against the stone floor with a sound like pastry. Mary was used to the grumble, found it almost soothing now, like the sound of a waterfall. Julie smiled at Mary as she straightened up.

'Goin' to be a nice day, Miss Mary.'

'Do you think so?' Mary said gratefully. 'It looks awfully grey to me.'

'Dat'll burn off by nine. Everyt'ing goin' to be nice as nice for Miss Maybelle, don't you worry.' She eyed Mary shrewdly and said, 'An' dat no-good Myrtle ain' goin' have her baby in de middle of de weddin' neether, not if Ah has to git over there an' shove it back in maself.'

Mary laughed, and felt a little of the tension ease. 'Oh, I can't do without you at my elbow today, Julie. If anyone has to go over and bully Myrtle, I'll send Mammy.' That made Julie and Cookie both laugh, for Mammy had been in a pet about the wedding for days, ever since Maybelle told her that she wanted Mary's Patty to dress her hair on The Day. Since then Mammy had been ostentatiously ignoring the preparations and telling anyone who asked her to do anything that 'Dis weddin' hain' none o' *ma* business. Ah hain' eben comin'. Miz Maybelle done growd up now, she don' need dis ole nigger no more. Ah stoppin' in de house wid ma chillun while she git mah'd, an' Ah hopes she don' speck me ter help her git undressed tonight needer, coz dat hain' *ma* job no more.'

'Well, I'd better go and see that nothing's happened to the cake,' Mary said, 'and check that the men have started on the marquees.'

'Ah looked at de cake before you came down, Miss Mary, and hit fine,' Julie said. 'An' Mist' Lennox, he already gone out to hep git the tents up. He say ter tell you dat he'll tek care of ever't'ing outside, so you don' need ter worry 'bout none o' dat stuff.'

Mary smiled. 'Well, God bless all of you! Let's get the breakfast out of the way then. That's the biscuits and the grits. Is that you frying ham, Cookie?'

Cookie swivelled at the stove and opened her eyes a fraction more to register surprise at the question. 'Marse Morland got to hab he's ham an' eggs, Miz Mary, weddin' or no weddin'.'

'I suppose you're right,' Mary acknowledged. The Master's will was the fixed point in the universe, and, let the skies tumble, his preferences must be attended to first. 'Lord, how can people want breakfast with all those mountains of food to come later? I don't feel as if I ever want to eat again.'

She plunged then into a sea of work, and afterwards recalled little about the early part of the wedding day, only isolated moments that became embedded, randomly as flecks of grit, in her memory. There was Mammy, for instance, picking her way massively through the frenzied kitchen with Rosa hopping behind her, complaining bitterly that she had been forced to come all the way downstairs herself for gripe-water for her baby because it wasn't in the usual place in the pantry and Rosa couldn't find it. 'Whut all dis stuff doin' hyah?' she demanded, poking disdainfully at a coloured jelly and bringing Cookie flapping over in outrage. 'Ma baby got de cralick, an' Ah come fo' de gripe-water, and whut Ah find? Miz Mary, huccome you move ma baby's messipunt for all dis trashy sweet stuff? Hit ain' Christmus dat *Ah* noticed!'

Julie intervened before there was a fight and drove Mammy away, telling her she would give the gripe-water to Rosa to bring up. Julie was as omnipresent as Mary that day – Mary couldn't have done without her. She couldn't have coped without Lennox, either, who was always quietly where he was most useful, seeing the tents and trestles were set up, that the barbecue pits were ready, that the dance-floor was dry and properly chalked. Mary saw him at one moment holding the slack of a flower garland while Tammas nailed the other end to the drawing-room cornice; at another settling a quarrel between two of the musicians who both wanted the same chair on the bandstand; at yet another directing the rounding-up of a particularly characterful sow who had escaped her pen and chosen a cool corner of the verandah to snooze.

Images isolated like photographs, but photographs come strangely to life: the fracas when a dog ran off with one of the cold roast turkeys which that imbecile Tina put down on the floor 'jus' fo' a minnit, Miz Mary, Ah sweahs!' while she admired the way a colleague had plaited her hair; Tammas's dance of rage when Isaac, who had taken his place up the ladder, dropped the hammer from a great height onto his foot; Uncle Heck on the bandstand showing one of the musicians a different fingering for a difficult passage on the bassoon; Cedar like a grim Charon standing on the sweep directing the carriages as they arrived, pointing alternately to the left and the right; her five-year-old Preston – a surprising one, this – walking along in deep conversation with Hill, his little hand wrapped around one tobacco-brown finger, as Hill apparently kept him from getting into mischief and dirtying his spotless wedding suit of cream linen.

Oddly enough, she remembered nothing of the wedding ceremony itself. She ran upstairs and changed into her new dress of moss-green merino with the velvet ribbon edging, discarded her cap and bent her head to Patty's hurried fingers, and managed to get back down to the drawing-room before Uncle Heck struck up the march. The drawing-room had been thrown into the dining-room by opening the double doors, and all the furniture of both removed to accommodate the family and guests. The room was decorated with ropes of smilax and ivy and sheaf on sheaf of roses, and the doors to the verandah were open to allow as many slaves as possible to witness it, the house slaves crowding the verandah and the field hands massed behind, hats in their hands and sentimental tears at the ready for the moment the bride would appear and show herself to them.

Mary had seen Maybelle many times in the wedding dress while she was fitting and altering it, and the night before had seen the whole effect with the veil as May tried it on for one last time. And she had popped in several times during the morning to check on progress, and seen how Patty was doing her hair; but afterwards she had no image at all of Maybelle the Bride standing before the minister in the drawing-room. She didn't remember Conrad standing waiting with his groomsman Beaufain Raven, or Maybelle arriving on her father's arm, with Ruthie scattering petals before and Cecilia and Kitten carrying her train. She didn't remember the sound of the couple's voices making their vows, or whether Conrad had sounded as if he meant any of it, or whether Eugene had behaved himself, or who had cried. She supposed that by the time the ceremony began she was so exhausted she had simply blanked it all out.

Later, when the feast was under way, Martial appeared beside her with a glass of claret cup and said, 'Have you eaten anything? You look pale. Anyone would think you were the bride and facing the thought of going to bed with Conrad Ausland.'

That startled Mary out of her numbness. She looked round in alarm and hissed, 'Don't say such things to me! What are you thinking of?'

'Oh, I can say anything to you,' he said easily. 'That's the joy of it.'

'Not in public! You'll ruin me.'

'Would that I had the chance,' he said, and before she could wonder what he meant by that, added, 'But no-one's listening. So tell me, frankly, if Maybelle were your child, would you let her marry a man like Ausland?'

'I think I'd advise her not to marry at all,' Mary said. 'When I think what's before her! We fill girls' heads with nonsense, and tell them that as long as they are nervous, delicate and dependent, men will adore them. We tell them that they must cultivate their weakness, to cast a "magic spell" over a man, and so spend the rest of their lives in submission to a superior creature who will secure their perfect happiness.'

Martial laughed soundlessly at her, as a dog does, his mouth wide and his eyes crinkled. It was a way he had, which she found rather endearing. 'You forget, ma'am, that Maybelle is better situated than you to find perfect happiness, because she really does believe men are superior. *You* have the misfortune to have a brain and the education to use it. Lucky May is both ignorant and meek.'

'She's in love,' Mary replied. 'Still, I suppose she will be no worse off with Conrad than any other man. When she sees him in a temper over some trivial disappointment, or irrationally demanding, or holding his opinion against all reason – when she finds him in drink, or – or doing other things that men do—' She had made herself blush now.

Martial looked grave. 'Not all men do that,' he said.

She looked at him steadily. 'Conrad does.'

'Good God, how do you know?'

'Eugene told me.'

'The devil he did!' He longed to horsewhip the little swine. He longed to ask her if Fenwick did that thing, but that was certainly not possible. 'I don't wonder at your poor opinion of men. But we are not all the same. Believe us all capricious, conceited and tyrannical, but not all vicious.'

Mary looked away and sighed. 'But it is not considered vicious here, is it? By miscegenation a man may satisfy his urges and increase his property all at the same time. That's not vice, that's good husbandry.'

'You do things better in England, I dare say,' he said quietly. 'You must wish so much to go home. Now that your father is here—'

'I may not think about it,' she said. 'I'm a married woman. And you forget, the South has taken hostages.' She nodded to where Preston and Ashley were capering about with their hands full of cake. 'No, I can never leave now.'

'"Never" is a large, hard word, like a boulder,' Martial said. 'Fate has a particular liking for dislodging it and sending it bouncing down the side of the valley and onto the head of the impudent traveller.'

Mary smiled, allowing him to lighten the mood. 'And what "never" has fate dropped on you?'

'I said once that I would never fall in love and marry,' he said solemnly, 'and that started a landslide.'

'But here you are, still a bachelor,' she said, not understanding; but he only laughed his silent laugh, and offered to go and get her something to eat.

CHAPTER THIRTEEN

The heat shimmered over the land, and the great trees stood motionless with their feet in their own deep shadow like cattle in water. An afternoon stillness fell; the roses hung limp along the verandah roof, their petals browning in the baking sunlight; the birds were silent, hidden in the trees; only the crickets endlessly shrilled in the long grass, tireless as mechanical toys.

Every creature sought shade. The dogs wriggled under the verandah and lay with their bellies against the cold, mushroomy earth, becoming just a glow of yellow eyes in the shadows, a gleam of white teeth and dripping tongues. In the yard, the pigs stretched out like corpses in the strip of shade along every wall; the geese shuffled into the cool of the barn, lifting their wings to let the air under them; every tree branch was decorated with roosting brown hens, their eyelids rolled up and their beaks gaping a little as if they were gasping for breath.

Children slept where they had fallen, heads pillowed on laps, on dogs, on rocks, on each other, cheeks flushed and hands sticky with the morning's pleasures. Young people gathered under the trees to talk about each other and their own fascinating preferences; matrons lined the verandah and talked about servants and children; the older people went indoors to rest, doze, smoke or chat, according to preference.

Mary went upstairs with May to help her bathe her hands and face, tidy her hair and adjust her wedding-dress, which had become rather disordered by the jostling it had sustained.

'Well, love, are you having a nice time?' Mary asked.

'Oh yes,' May said. 'Everything's been wonderful.'

Mary cocked her head. 'And now you're feeling a little bit let down? That's natural, after so much excitement.'

'Oh, no, not let down.' May licked her lips. 'Just – rather – nervous, I guess. I mean about – about—'

'What comes later?' Mary helped her out.

May nodded. 'Some of the girls were talking before, when

I was showing them my ring.' Mary had seen May with her head together with Adeline Raven, Kitten Ausland, Sarah Trent, Annabella Lawrence and one or two others. May lowered her voice and her head, and whispered anxiously, 'Addy said that it's so terrible – you know, the afterwards thing – that some girls go stark mad.'

'Oh, no, really, May!'

'But Kitten said she knows it's true, because her ma had a cousin whose hair went white overnight, and her mammy found her like that in the morning, just shocked white-headed like an old woman!'

Mary suppressed a smile. 'Oh, May, you mustn't believe what those girls tell you. *They* don't know any more than you do.'

May became earnest. 'Well, I guess so – but *you* know, and that's why I thought – I hoped you might—' She stopped, her cheeks mantling. 'Is it really so terrible?'

Mary wondered what to tell her. She thought of Conrad and what Eugene had said about Conrad. She thought of Charles Morland's nocturnal trips across the yard. She thought of Fenwick's diffident approaches and the long loneliness of the night afterwards, as he slept and she lay wakeful. And the consequences of those approaches, diffident or otherwise: three children in less than six years of marriage – and she had been lucky, by most standards.

But she had to say something, and what was the point in even trying to tell May the truth? There was nothing to be done about it. What Conrad would do to her, he would do, and the best thing would be to reassure her, and let her remain happy as long as possible.

'No, dear, it isn't terrible,' she said kindly. 'Just a bit strange.' Not terrible, she thought, just sad. 'You love Conrad, don't you? Of course you do, and you want to please him; so I'm sure you'll find everything is all right.'

May lowered her head and her cheeks flamed on. 'Sarah said that her brother said that there were some women who liked it; but he said no man would want to marry a girl like that. So I guess I won't like it.'

'No, love, I guess you won't,' Mary said, thinking of Conrad. If half what Eugene said was true, Conrad had had plenty of practice with women who 'liked it'. But did they really? Did anyone? Perhaps, she thought, some women were required to pretend they liked it.

'But it's my duty to my husband, isn't it?' May persisted anxiously.

Perhaps that was the best approach. 'Do your duty, and all will be well,' Mary said. 'I'm sure you'll be very happy.'

May's watery smile of gratitude for the reassurance was her reward.

In the library, the segar smoke had formed a cloud stratum just under the ceiling which the central fan stirred only languidly. Below it the elders of the gathered tribes were growing red-faced with heat both calorific and emotional; the conversation which had begun diffuse was coalescing, and slipping inevitably into the well-worn grooves. The Kentucky-Nebraska Act. Railroad subsidies. The Dredd Scott Case. John Brown. Tariffs.

Inevitably came the moment when Mr Raven pronounced, as if stumbling upon an original thought, 'The plain fact of the matter is that the North never did understand Southern ways, and there's an end of it.'

'Free farms in the west are just another symptom—'

'I said back in 1820, at the time of the Missouri Compromise—'

'Compromise be damned! Does a man compromise with a wolf or a bear?'

'You can't compromise with a damn', dirty, low, blood-sucking, money-grubbing—'

'Northern gentleman?' a wit suggested slyly. There was a burst of hard laughter. 'Ain't no such thing!' someone shouted through it.

'But that's exactly my point! Precisely my point!' Mr Ratliffe said excitedly. 'All a Northerner cares about is money; that's all that matters to them. We know that. So you'd think, wouldn't you, that they'd at least have respect for another man's property? But the Fugitive Slave Act's a dead letter in the North. They have *organisations*, damnit, for smuggling runaways out of the country! And the Federal Government knows it. Congress knows it. The whole damn' District of Columbia knows it, but do they do anything about it?'

'Damn' right they don't!'

'No, no, you're missing the point! You're missing the point! Judge Douglas said—'

'Douglas is a fool. Lincoln walked rings round him in the debates.'

'Douglas is no friend to the South, that's what I say.'

'Well, he ain't my nominee, that's all!'

The Convention which had reconvened in Baltimore, with its more Northern outlook, had finally managed to select Judge

Stephen A. Douglas as Democratic Presidential candidate, to the savage disgust of most Charlestonians.

'I won't vote for him. I've been a Democrat all my life, but if Douglas is a Democrat, then I'm a – a—'

'Blowhard?' suggested the wit, laconically. More laughter.

'So now we've got two Democratic candidates,' Uncle Heck said, 'Douglas and Breckinridge, who'll split the Democrat vote between 'em. And the result of that, my friends, is that the Republicans will win the election. This time next year we'll have a President Lincoln, first Republican president in the history of the United States. And I hope you'll all be very happy together.'

There was a brief silence, and then Mr Lawrence said, 'It's not a joking matter, Heck. Lincoln's election would mean slave insurrection. It would follow like night follows day.'

'It's *not* inevitable,' Pick Manning, Martial's friend, said reasonably. 'Lincoln's no friend to abolition—'

There was a roar of dissent. 'He's a Republican, damnit!' 'And a Northerner!' 'He's a damned Yankee Abolitionist!'

Manning waited for it to die down. 'The Republicans chose Lincoln instead of Seward or Chase because he's a moderate on the slavery question. He's on record as saying that he's got no desire to interfere with slavery where it already exists.'

'Well, that doesn't mean—!'

'Once a Yankee always a Yankee!'

'He wants to bathe in our blood like any damn' Northerner!'

'Slavery is not the issue here,' Charles Morland said, lifting his voice above the indignation. 'The Republican platform, abolition or no abolition, is a threat to the Southern way of life. It will mean a pro-Northern programme of legislation from the word "go". Take the upward revision of the tariff—'

He got no further. Slavery was what they wanted to talk about. Through the clamour Judge Ausland said, 'What it comes down to is this,' in such a weighty tone that everyone stopped trying to talk at once, and into the ensuing silence he laid down his words like Moses back from the mountain with fresh tablets.

'What it comes down to is this: whatever the next Government decides to put through by way of legislation, an Act of Congress is only valid in any State if that State enacts it. And any Act can be nullified unilaterally,' he liked the word and said it again, with emphasis, '*u-ni-laterally* by an individual State, if it's against that State's interests. That's what Judge Douglas was saying when he put his foot in it over the free farms and everybody stopped listening to him. Now I've no brief for Douglas – the man's a fool and a traitor – but he was right about one thing: the Federal Government can't force any measure on us. It's a matter of democracy. We entered freely into the Union, but in the interests of mutual defence only. Mutual defence, my friends, that's all.'

Everyone was nodding now. They liked this sort of talk.

During the last few exchanges some of the younger gentlemen had gathered at the door to find out what was going on. Now Fenwick said, 'But it's gone a lot further than that now. The Union covers more than mutual defence.'

The Judge turned his mighty gaze on the small fry. 'Just so,' he acknowledged generously, 'but we're a free people, my boy, a freedom-loving, democratic people. With a small "d",' he added, as a little pleasantry, and Fenwick smiled dutifully. 'And in a democracy, the benefits are shared equally by all, and the burdens are borne equally by all. Congress can't pass a law that helps one State by injuring another, and if it does – as in the case of the Tariff reforms – then the injured State has every right to nullify it.'

'And what if the Federal Government just doesn't understand about States' Rights?' Manning said. 'What if they simply decide to force the issue?'

'Then we leave the Union. South Carolina entered into it as a free sovereign state, and by God we can walk out just the same way!'

'Right enough!' said Mr Trent, seeing the point at last. 'If Mrs Trent buys a hat and finds she don't like it, she takes it right back to the damn' milliner's!'

Everyone laughed.

'The South will never find happiness except by leaving the Union and setting up an independent nation, that's my view,' said Raven, looking around him for approval. 'The plain fact of the matter is that the North never did understand Southern ways, and there's an end of it.'

'It's States' Rights, or it's secession, gentlemen,' the Judge pronounced, 'and my money's on secession.'

'And Lincoln's election will give us the excuse,' Trent said gleefully.

'You can't make Lincoln's bare election a *casus belli*,' said Charles Morland impatiently. 'If planters were in debt or cotton was at five cents—'

Lawrence interrupted. 'It's no use talking about Lincoln being a moderate. He's a Yankee. Whatever he *says*, it's slave insurrection he'll bring behind him. Secession's our only choice.'

'And what makes you think,' Martial asked, 'that the North will simply let us walk away?'

All heads turned towards him. The Judge spoke for everyone, as he always did, whether he was asked to or not. 'Ah yes, Martial, my boy! You've just been up North, haven't you?'

'Northerners don't believe you can have slavery in the South and not the North,' Martial said. 'The two systems can't co-exist. They say either they'll have to abolish slavery in the South, or accept it in the North; that either our rice and cotton plantations must be tilled by free labour or the wheatfields of New York will be worked by slaves, while Boston becomes a slave-trade port.'

'Those Yankees are so dumb they believe anything they're told. They think they're going to catch slavery like influenza!' said Mr Ratliffe disgustedly.

Martial turned to him. 'Maybe so, but they do believe it, and it means that secession isn't a possible answer in their books.'

Judge Ausland didn't like other people having the stage. He took Martial's attention back to himself. 'Tell us what the mood is up there, Martial? What do they think of our position?'

'That we're engaged in a political game of poker – without a winning hand. Our talk of secession is a bluff. They don't believe for a minute that we would do it.'

Amongst the voices of protest, Fenwick managed to ask, 'Why not, Mart? What makes them think we wouldn't go?'

'Because we couldn't do without them,' Martial said. 'We haven't the resources. We couldn't survive on our own.'

'Couldn't we, by damn!' said Mr Ratliffe. 'They couldn't do without us, more like! They want our cotton, don't they, to keep their damn factories open? But we don't have to sell it to them. We can sell it to anyone. That's what I call a winning hand!'

'The whole world wants cotton,' Mr Ogles agreed. 'Why, in England alone the demand is—'

Martial interrupted. 'The North would face a cotton famine and close every factory in New England rather than let us walk away.'

There was an uncertain pause, and then Mr Trent said, 'Why, how could they stop us?'

'They would be unwise to mistake our strength of feeling,' the Judge said weightily.

'And we would be unwise to mistake the strength of theirs.' Martial looked around the room, gathering all eyes. 'The Union is as sacred to them as States' Rights are to us – perhaps even more so. Be very sure they are just as serious as we are when they say they won't let us secede.'

'But, why, they hate slavery and they hate us: they'd be glad to be rid of us,' said Mr Trent, puzzled.

'If we try to leave, they'll try to bring us back,' Martial said. 'If necessary, by force of arms.'

'War, d'you mean?'

'They'd actually go to war to preserve the Union?'

'I don't believe it!'

'People don't fight wars for stuff like that.'

The general mood was of disbelief, but Mr Ogles added combatively, 'If it's a fight they want, why, we'll just give it 'em!'

'Is slavery something you want to die for?' Martial quizzed.

'If there's any dyin' to be done, we'll let the damn' Yankees do it,' Mr Ogles growled to general approval.

'We don't want war,' the Judge translated, with more regard to Southern dignity, 'but if it came to it, well, need I remind you gentlemen of the great Poet's words: *dulce et decorum est pro patria mori?*'

Martial gave a cynical smile and turned away from the renewed outbreak of comment and argument. Fenwick, standing beside him, caught his eye. 'Rather,' Martial said, 'it's a case of *dulce bellum inexpertis.* How sweet is war to those who haven't experienced it.'

'You've never experienced war,' Fenwick pointed out.

'Unlike those woodenheads, dear cousin, I have an imagination,' Martial said. He was smiling, but his eyes were grave.

The screen Charles used in winter against draughts when he was working in the library had been removed temporarily to make room for all the male guests, and was standing half-folded beside the door in the hall. Mary had been sitting unseen on one of the small hard hall chairs just beyond it. She had sat there to begin with just to get away from being bothered: she desperately needed to sit down, but every time she did someone came to her with a request or a problem. But once the babble inside had resolved itself into individual voices, she began to listen; and when Martial walked past her, she waited to see if anyone else would come out, and then followed him.

He turned down the gun-room passage, but to her relief went past the gun-room door – another forbidden temple to women – and out through the side door towards the stables. She caught up with him under the plum tree by the paddock gate where he stopped to light a segar. With his face bowed over his cupped hands, he saw her at last, and cocked his head, raising an enquiring eyebrow, screwing up the other eye against the rising smoke.

'I was listening,' she said abruptly.

'The devil you were,' he said mildly, puffing the smoke into life. He straightened up, shaking out the match. Above him the plum tree spread veined translucent leaves against the afternoon light, and the nascent plums hung like jade earrings, seeming to quiver as the smoke drifted past them.

'Where were you going?' she asked, seeing he didn't seem disposed to say anything more.

'Nowhere in particular. To borrow someone's words: not to, just away from.'

She made a little gesture of the hand back towards the house, her fingers spread, and the image captured his attention as one of those hooks of experience that always accompany memory. Against the dark background of the barn behind her it was like a small white starfish. 'They're all fools,' she said.

'Jackasses,' he concurred agreeably.

'But, Martial, you don't think it could really come to war, do you? However strongly both sides feel, they are all Americans. How can they fight each other? Brother killing brother – and for something so intangible?'

'They?' he queried. 'You forget I'm one of them.'

'No, not you,' she said quickly. 'You stand outside it all. You are Shakespeare's Fool, who always sees clearly. If it comes to a choice, the North will have to let the South secede, won't it?'

'I hope so. I truly hope so,' he said.

She stepped closer. 'If people like you came out in the open and said slavery was wrong – started an abolitionist movement—'

'Abolition is not the answer.'

'How can you say that?' she cried passionately. 'You don't believe in slavery! You hate it, I know you do!'

'Do you really want me to explain? Or do you just want to fulminate? I'd just like to know,' he said with a faint, mocking look.

'Of course I want you to explain,' she said indignantly. 'Don't talk to me like that – not you.'

'Very well, then. Firstly, there's the question of money. Slaves are property, and therefore part of the owner's wealth. If the North set the slaves free without paying the South for them, it would be robbery, and the North has neither the money nor the inclination to pay for them. Suppose the South took away all the North's horses and turned them loose? It would be just the same thing.'

She frowned. 'But—'

Martial stopped her with a shrug. 'You asked me. D'you want the answer?'

'Go on,' she said meekly.

'If you took away all the North's horses, what would pull their vehicles? Trade would collapse, poverty and anarchy would follow. If you take away the South's slaves, who would do the work?'

'The freed slaves, of course, for a wage,' Mary said promptly.

'And where does the money for wages come from, to pay for work that's always been done for nothing?'

'Machinery, then. Papa says that's the answer.'

'Yes, in the long term,' Martial agreed, 'but immediately? There are no machines and no factories to make them. No money to buy them, either, except by selling the crops which couldn't be got in without slaves.'

'*Impasse*,' Mary acknowledged. 'Yes, I see.'

'And the biggest problem of all – the one that I have most trouble with in the North when they ask me the same questions – is what do you do with the slaves when you've freed them? You can't just turn them out into the road and say, you're free now, go and fend for yourself. Most of them have less idea than a kitten how to look after themselves.'

'That's not their fault!'

'Don't rail at me, Boadicea. I didn't say it was, but it's still a fact. What would they do with their freedom? Some would sit down under the nearest hedge and starve. Others would wander away without any clear idea where they were going, begging or stealing when they got hungry. Others still would simply decide to take what they wanted by force. Would you really like to see disaffected slaves, possibly armed, probably drunk, roaming the countryside unrestrained? You'd have robbery, arson, looting, pillage, rape, murder and pestilence.' He looked at her white face. 'Am I frightening you, my dear? I wish I could frighten the people who have some influence in these matters.'

She shook her head, grasping after possibilities. 'But wait, wait. Couldn't you give them their old jobs back, as free labour, paying them in kind until there was money to pay wages?'

'Yes, you could,' he said, 'provided it was done gradually over a long period. Release them all suddenly, and there would be chaos. What about the ones who didn't want to stay – how would you stop them? They'd naturally tend to be the worst of them, the bad ones who would turn to robbery and murder. As to the rest, they haven't yet got the habit of work. You know that, as slaves, their whole purpose is to do as little as possible, knowing they'll be fed and housed whatever happens. You can't change that attitude overnight, and once they were free you'd have no way of coercing them. The work wouldn't get done, and you'd have the choice of going on feeding and housing them for no return, or turning them out to starve or join the robber-bands.'

How clearly he saw it all! Mary stared through him at the hopeless scenario. 'Then you're saying there's no solution?' she said at last.

'No, I'm not saying that. Slavery must be done away with, but it must be done slowly, the negroes educated into a new way of life and freed little by little. And if we are left alone, it will happen. Attitudes *are* changing. If we are allowed to secede, slavery will be gone within a generation. But if we are not—'

He stopped, unwilling to release words into the air, in case they took power. His mind was full of images he would rather never have conceived of. Mary was looking up at him earnestly, and he wanted to snatch her to him, to saddle the nearest horse and ride hell-for-leather with her as far away from this place as possible. But she was not his to snatch. He cursed her father for ever having allowed her to be brought to this insanity, cursed him for marrying her to Fenwick. Better that he had never known her, than to see her exposed to the brutality of slavery and the violence that would attend its abolition.

Mary saw the tension in his face, felt the vibration on the air of his thoughts, but could not see the visions he saw. He was anxious, she knew, but she could have no idea how anxious. 'I can't believe Northerners would actually kill Southerners rather than let them leave the Union,' she said at last. 'That would be madness.'

'Yes, it would,' he said, and she took it for reassurance. He saw her misunderstanding him, and was about to try again to warn her – though God knew there was nothing she could do with a warning – when they were interrupted. Patty came round the side of the stable block, picking her way fastidiously with a house-slave's distaste for 'outdoors'.

'Oh, Miz Mary, dyah you is!' she cried eagerly, and then short-circuited herself with a frown. 'Miz Mary, huccome you stan'in' out in de open ayar widout yo' sunshade? Hif you gits freckles, Ah's de one dat gits de blame!'

'I'm in the shade of a tree,' Mary replied, seeing Martial laughing his silent laugh out of the corner of her eye. 'Don't fuss, Patty. Is that what you came here to say, or was there something important?'

Her mouth and eyes went round. 'Miz Mary, Julie sent me ter fin' you. Dat Myrtle goin' ter have her baby right now, an' Julie she need you ober at de quarters dis minute ter he'p fitch it.'

Mary's mouth turned down, but she said, 'All right, Patty, go and tell Julie I'm coming. And then find Rosa and ask her to take the basket over to the cabin – the big basket with all the baby-fetching things, she'll know which one. Tell her to hurry.'

Patty went away, and Mary turned to make an excuse to Martial, and found she didn't need to. Everything that she knew about this situation, he knew; and everything she felt about it, he felt.

'How all occasions do inform against him,' he said. 'Try not to let it upset you too much.'

She shook her head. 'I sometimes think I'm in a dream. But not a very good one.'

In the big cedar that dominated the rear lawn of the house was a tree-house, sturdily built by Uncle Heck for Fenwick and Eugene when they were young. Here Ruthie and Lennox had retreated from the heat of the day and from the flocks of younger children they were just of an age to attract and to find annoying. Lennox sat in a corner, his knees drawn up and his chin thoughtfully resting on top of them. Ruthie sprawled on her front on the platform, to the detriment of the pink satin, staring down over the edge of it, idly picking off bits of bark and moss and watching them drop.

Lennox had enjoyed preparing for the wedding much more than the wedding itself. He liked to see something taking shape and growing, the sense of achievement that came with executing plans. Of course, it was difficult here on the plantation to get things done. In the time he had been here he had had plenty of chance to observe the problems that arose from the slavery system. Used to brisk, self-reliant Yorkshire servants, he had been amazed at the slowness of the negroes: not just their apparent slowness – he could not have walked as slowly as they walked even if he tried – but at their capacity to appear to be doing something while actually doing nothing at all. You would set a gang to erect a length of fence, supervise the hammering in of the first post yourself just to get them started, and four hours later come back to find them still diligently fiddling about with the first rail.

As Mary had said to him, there was no incentive for them to finish a job, since there was always another to replace it. And you couldn't even punish them. What could you do, after all? You couldn't fine them, because they didn't own anything. Lock them up, and you lost their labour, which was more a punishment on you than them. You could beat them, but you couldn't give them more than a light licking because they were property, and only a madman damaged his own property; and though they naturally disliked being beaten, the prospect of a light licking was not enough to make them work harder, since it could not be kept in the forefront of their minds all day. Besides, promise a man a licking for slacking at nine o'clock, and what was to make him work hard the rest of the day, with a punishment already earned?

Lennox saw the problems as he worked alongside Benedict to try to bring at least one of the projects to fruition before Benedict had to go home again. He wondered what his rôle would be here afterwards. Nobody seemed much to mind what he did, or whether he did anything at all. As far as estate management went, it was a very different matter here from England, and what he had learned there was no use to him here. Land was in plenty, and hands, but plans for soil improvement and new methods of cultivation were always hampered by the sheer size of the place, the lack of skills, and the impossibility of getting the negroes to work differently.

Fenwick made the large-scale decisions about the plantation – referring them to his father as a matter of form, since Charles was really only interested in the horse-breeding side – and handed them to Hazelteen to implement. Hazelteen was a big, lean man with an unfinished appearance, barely able to read and write, and not too strong on mental accomplishments. Lennox had learned from conversation that overseers were usually pretty hopeless people, which was in the nature of their calling: they were there to be a filter between the white master and his black slaves. The master despised and relied on his overseer, the overseer despised and relied on the slaves, the slaves hated the overseer and were as much of a trial to him as they could be, since they could never get back at the master. It was a horrible system, degrading to all; and the overseer was in the middle, the whipping-boy for everyone's discontents.

From what Lennox had heard, Hazelteen was not too bad a specimen. As a rule they were uneducated, thriftless men who couldn't get any other kind of work, but sometimes they were also sadistic brutes, drunkards or thieves. They rarely lasted long in one job, a constant passage of overseers in and out being a feature of plantation life. But Hazelteen was only stupid and rather lack-lustre, and had been at Twelvetrees for some time, which accounted both for the stability of the place, and the impossibility of getting the negroes to hurry themselves. Lennox guessed that insofar as he himself had a job after Benedict's departure, it would be as a filter between Hazelteen and Fenwick, leaving Fenwick at one further remove from the field-hands he disliked, and with a little more freedom to enjoy himself.

For the moment, it seemed that his most useful occupation was to keep Ruthie company, and in this he was encouraged tacitly by the rest of the family and openly by Mary. 'She's so wild, I'm afraid she may hurt herself, or get into trouble. If you could keep an eye on her, stop her doing anything too outrageous, it would be such a weight off my mind. And talk to her, too – she's lonely, poor little girl, and I simply don't have the time to spend with her that I would like.'

It was a task he had enjoyed. Of all the people at Twelvetrees – apart from Mary herself – he liked Ruthie best. She was full of fun, bubbling over with energy, and as clear and open in her character as fresh spring-water. What she thought, she said, and she could no more have done a mean or underhand thing than fly. She confided completely in Lennox, gave him her absolute trust and friendship from the beginning, a generosity he knew how to value; and as he knew her better, he saw that Mary was right, and that she was lonely. She had never had a regular companion, and except when cousins or neighbours came to stay, she played alone.

So he spent his time, when he was not helping Benedict, in riding all over the estate with Ruthie, walking with her, fishing, paddling in the cricks, stalking the various kinds of wildlife, and, in the heat of the day or after their more strenuous exertions, sitting in the shade with her and talking. He was appalled at her ignorance. She had been taught to read and write, but did neither with any facility, and since she had been left pretty much to her own devices because of her mother's illness and death, she had hardly read a book in her life. The pity of it was, he thought, that she was naturally intelligent, and he set to work to waken her curiosity and lead her gently to acquire some information. Like many people who don't read, she had a tenacious memory, and could repeat back to him what he said almost word for word. He led her through as much of the world of wonders as he could without books, and was humbly proud to see the difference he was making to her. She was less wild as she had more to think about, was gentler in her speech, and began to ask more directed questions. Her affection for him grew as she depended on him more and more, and he loved her best of everyone in the world, except Mary.

Ruthie rolled over and looked at him across the dimness of the tree-house platform, and said, 'What was that?'

'I didn't say anything.'

'But you were thinking something about me – and Mary,' she said.

He was fascinated by this ability of hers which she had displayed from time to time. It was disconcerting – though she was growing more discreet about where she displayed it, and no longer embarrassed people in the drawing-room. His affection for her just then made him unguarded, and he said, 'I was just wishing you were my sister, too.'

He heard the word just too late to take it back, but hoped Ruthie wouldn't notice it. Vainly! She looked hard at him and said, 'What do you mean, *too*?'

'Nothing. I didn't mean anything. It was a slip of the tongue.'

But it was no use. She was reading his face and his mind, and sat up now, smiling triumphantly, and said, 'You and she are sister and brother! No wonder you look so alike! Well, I wonder I didn't guess it before! But why do you pretend to be cousins?'

'Because Mary doesn't know. Ruthie, you must promise me not to tell anyone, anyone at all. Please, it's really important.'

'Oh, I won't tell if you don't want me to,' she said carelessly.

'Promise,' he insisted. 'Solemn vow.'

She folded all but the first two fingers of her right hand and laid them in solemn rigmarole to her throat, her lips, and then to the side of her head, sticking up to represent Indian feathers. 'Injun promise,' she said. Her face was all curiosity. 'So tell me why, then,' she urged.

He told her, because if she understood it might put her more on her guard against slips, and she listened with her whole attention, her eyes fixed on him and even her skin seeming to absorb his words. 'So you see,' he said at the end, 'why it's a secret.'

Ruth nodded. 'But, goodness, it's exciting! Fancy having a brother you don't know about, and your father isn't even your father. Do you ever mean to tell her?'

'I don't know. I don't see how to, without breaking her heart. She loves her father so much, and he loves her, and if he doesn't tell her, then how can I? It was hard enough when he told me.'

Ruthie laid a slender, brown hand on his arm. 'Poor Len! But at least you know your ma and pa loved each other. And you've gained a sister, so you're better off than before, even if you can't tell her.'

He put his hand over hers. 'I've gained more than a sister,' he said. 'I've got a whole family now. That's riches.'

She gave his arm a friendly squeeze and then said in practical tones, 'Yes, and you'd better be sure Pa and Aunt Belle never find out the truth, or they might take your new family away from you! They care about silly stuff like that. I see now why you want to keep it secret. Well, I've said "Injun promise", and you know I never break that.' She considered him a moment. 'I wish you were my secret brother,' she said at last. 'I like you much better than my real ones.'

As dusk fell, the lamps were lit, the band tuned up, and the lowlier neighbours, who had not been invited for the wedding ceremony, arrived for the dancing. The bridegroom, who had unwisely topped the punch and brandy he had consumed earlier with a large quantity of rum smuggled to him by Eugene, had been partially sobered up, provided with a clean jacket, and was opening the dancing. Propped against his lovely bride he circled slowly, a little green of visage and smelling faintly of vomit, but from a distance still an acceptable figure of Hymen.

When they had completed a circuit without accident, the applause from the matrons signalled that other dancers might join in. The two eldest Lawrence boys, Quincey and Fontaine, were first off the mark, leading out Sarah Trent and Adeline Raven; and Eugene, mostly to annoy his cousin Hamilton, captured the not entirely willing hand of Miss Kitten Ausland and dragged her into the fray. She had been hoping to be asked by Martial Flint, who had the kind of dangerous good looks and cynical eyes that gave her a pleasant shiver; the sort of danger Eugene brought with him was all too well known to her.

Martial was showing no immediate desire to dance. When Fenwick led out Cecilia for a duty dance, he took the excuse to drift up to Mary. They stood close but not talking for a while, until he said, 'Was it very bad?'

Mary didn't answer directly. 'Mostly they give birth easily, thank God. The mother had got herself over-wrought, but once she calmed down, the thing was soon over. A boy,' she added, in case he wanted to know. He looked down at her, saw the tense unhappiness of her lips, her pallor, the tired lines about her eyes. He did not need to ask if it was a mulatto. The story was there in her face.

He sought for something to distract her. 'Look there,' he said. She glanced up at him, saw his eyes fixed on the dancers, and looked that way herself. 'It reminds me of *A Christmas Carol*.'

'Charles Dickens?' she wondered, not understanding yet.

He gestured towards Uncle Hemp and Aunt Missy, solemnly circling in complete harmony with each other and utterly oblivious of the music. 'There you have the Ghost of Matrimony Past; and there,' he indicated the livid Conrad drooping over the flushed and nervous Maybelle, 'the Ghost of Matrimony Present. You women have the devil of a life, don't you?'

'You mustn't include me in that generality,' Mary said, and he looked down at her.

'A conventional answer, Mrs Morland. I'm disappointed in you.'

Her lips twitched in answer to his sally. Ruth and Lennox went past, Ruth hopping and chattering, Lennox obviously concentrating hard on the steps and avoiding Ruth's feet, which were never where they should have been. 'And what do you say to the Ghost of Matrimony To Come?' she said.

Martial watched them go. 'Not very much. Your father-in-law would never permit it. Who is he, after all?'

'My cousin,' she said, with a touch of indignation.

'He has no money. An able young man,' he added judiciously, 'but wasted here. There's not much opportunity for a man of ability, unless he also has money. He should go to the North.'

'I hope not. I'd miss him,' Mary said.

Martial still watched the dancers. 'He'd do well there. He could make his fortune, marry well, go into politics. The North would be his oyster. He *ought* to go, and,' he looked down at her suddenly, 'you should persuade him to go quickly. Things are going to get very bad here, and it won't be the place for a sensitive young man like him.'

She stared at him, trying to read his meaning, and suddenly she caught the flash of those images in his mind he had not let her see before. Her lips paled.

'Damnit!' Martial exclaimed softly as she buckled at the knee. He caught her elbow, and tried to slip his arm round her waist to support her, without being too obvious. 'Why will you women wear such tight corsets? Don't look up at me, fool! Put your head down. That's right. Pretend to be looking for something you've dropped.'

In a moment the faintness passed, and the drumming in her ears receded. 'I'm all right,' she said.

'You are not. Have you eaten today?'

'Yes, quite a lot, really. I'm all right now. As you said, it was just my stays.' He withdrew his arm, and she steadied herself, and asked what she did not really want to know. 'What did you mean about things getting bad?'

He was not going to make the same mistake again. 'Oh, just that your father-in-law is not going to like to see Ruthie and Lennox running about together like that,' he said lightly. 'If Ruthie isn't careful, she'll get him into trouble.' He smiled. 'An odd phrase, that! But he's the vulnerable one in that situation.' The dance had finished and out of the corner of his eye he saw Fenwick approaching, probably with the intention of dancing next with his wife. Martial turned her in the other direction. 'Would you care to dance, Mrs Morland?'

She allowed him to guide her onto the floor, and he edged them both through the couples until they were right in the middle and beyond reach of pursuing husbands.

'That's better,' he said as the sweating band struck up again. 'There's no better place for a private conversation than the middle of a dance-floor. Here we are, pressed together by the crowd, my mouth practically against your ear, and no possibility, as long as the band keeps up that racket, of being overheard. You dance very sweetly, by the way,' he added, and the way he smiled made her uneasy.

'Don't,' she said, not quite sure what she was saying 'don't' to. 'What did you want to say to me?'

Martial became serious. 'Just that if there is any trouble over Lennox, send him to me. I can always find use for a young man of abilities.' She nodded slightly; her hands tightened on him. 'And I want you to know,' he went on quietly, 'that you both have a friend in me. In any trouble, turn to me. Remember that, Mary.'

She searched his face solemnly, trying to analyse the warning she felt under his words. 'What trouble? What is it you fear?'

He smiled suddenly. 'Don't look like that, or people will wonder what I'm proposing to you. Smile, cousin! I don't mean anything in particular, it's just my sense of drama coming out. I saw a great many plays while I was in New York. Do you care for the theatre? Not the whipped-taffy productions they put on in Charleston, but I mean real theatre. I sometimes think I should have been an actor – or, as some of my more unkind Yankee friends suggest, a mountebank.'

She was smiling now. 'Can you still do that trick with a horse – jumping on and off at full gallop? You promised you would teach me how to do it.'

'Mrs Morland! What are you suggesting? It would be most improper! Civilisation as we know it would have to crumble to nothing before I could do something as outré as teach you circus-riding tricks. On the other hand,' he added, as though having second thoughts, 'the crumbling to nothing of civilisation would make tricks like that a valuable resource. We shall have to see.'

He was joking, teasing her, of course; so why did she feel there was an underlying vein of seriousness to his words?

CHAPTER FOURTEEN

It was some time before all the visitors departed after the wedding: Conrad and May, together with Kitten as bride-companion, had left on their honeymoon before Twelvetrees got back to normal. Martial went back to Charleston, and Fenwick went with him, taking Benedict to show him the factory on the Ashley River and ask his advice about it. Mary would have expected Charles to want to take her father himself, but he stayed at Twelvetrees, pursuing his own mysterious round. She wished he had gone: housekeeping could have dropped to a slightly less exacting level with both Charles and Fenwick away. The house-slaves were inclined to be fratchy after all the excitement, and autumn was always a busy time with all the salting and bottling and pickling to do, and a big wash, and hog-killing coming up.

Mary found to her surprise that she missed Maybelle. In the last few months, since she had become engaged, she had become more of a companion. Aunt Nora was still there, having forgotten to leave after the wedding, but she was no company; Ruthie was too young, and in any case was hardly ever at home. When she was not out on horseback with Lennox, she was playing with the children of her own age from the neighbouring plantations – principally Knox and Effie Fairfax from Fairoaks and the three youngest Lawrences from Pinelees. Eugene had friends at both plantations, and could usually be prevailed upon to escort Ruthie to spend the day there, as long as he didn't have to undertake to bring her back.

Mary had expected Eugene to miss Conrad, his former second self, but in fact he transferred his allegiance easily enough to Beau Raven, who had been Conrad's groomsman. Beau was younger than Eugene, and perhaps because of that was inclined to take him at his own valuation, which accounted, Mary thought, for his attraction for Eugene. Beau and his sister Adeline seemed to be often at Twelvetrees these days. Mary had no objection: they were handsome, stylish, nicely mannered young people. Beau had long been considered one of the 'catches' of their circle, a handsome, dashing young man who would inherit his father's considerable fortune; Adeline was a beauty, and would have a large dowry. The two of them, being the only children, were very close and went everywhere together.

A surprising consequence of May's wedding was that Mrs Judge Ausland, who had never noticed Mary much, took to 'dropping in' on her, usually at the busiest part of the morning. It meant she had to stop what she was doing, take off her apron and cap, tidy her hair, and sit in the parlour or on the verandah and order refreshments. Mrs Judge was a large woman, and once having settled into a chair was in no hurry to extricate herself, so these visits were never short. Mary had to use all her self-control to sit still when a thousand jobs beckoned from the corner of her mind.

Mary did not understand to begin with what the attraction of Twelvetrees was for Mrs Judge, but after a while she worked out that it was simply a lack of anything else to do. Conrad, who had occupied her mind and emotions for twenty-six years, was married and gone; Kitten, her closest companion, had left with him; and her other children did not interest her, Chesney because he was no trouble and Clara, Sneed and Juvenal because they were too young. Mrs Judge had, besides, no household duties, since a spare and sour-tongued maiden cousin of the Judge's, known as 'Aunt' Margaret Bohuns, acted as housekeeper at Camelot and did everything that Mary did at Twelvetrees.

'I wouldn't be in your position for the world, Mrs Fenwick,' she said once, overflowing a chair on the verandah, with a cup of tea perched on the ample curve of her stomach. She always asked Mary for tea, which she regarded as evidence of a sophistication peculiar to the English upper classes and high-born planters. 'I wonder your husband doesn't find you some cousin. The Fenwicks and Hemptons are numerous enough, surely? Or isn't there a Flint somewhere?'

'Martial only has one cousin, and she's about to marry a Congressman, so I don't think she'd want to come and do my housekeeping.'

'Well, yes, and you are short of relations on the Morland side, aren't you? We're quite numerous on both sides, of course. I could have taken my pick. Thank you, dear, I'll have a piece of that cake. Your own, is it? Yes, very nice. You can't get a slave to make anything so light. I always had to do my own fancy baking until Aunt Margaret came to us.'

Under the influence of ease and refreshments, she grew fascinatingly indiscreet about Conrad. 'He's off my hands, thank God! And I can tell you I've been on tenterhooks these last four years for fear of what he might get up to. I was so relieved when he made an offer for your May – and I wouldn't like to guess what pressures Judge must have brought to bear on him.'

'You don't think he was in love, then?' Mary said, swallowing the insult to May.

Mrs Judge snorted. 'That boy's as cold as a rattlesnake, though I say it who's his mother. But May's lucky to get him, all the same, for a more milk-and-watery girl never came out in Charleston. Judge pushed Mr Morland for a pretty good dowry, I can tell you! Well, if he was paying down hard cash to get rid of Conrad, it was only fair that Mr Morland should do the same to get May off his hands.'

'Do you think Conrad will settle down now he's married?'

Mrs Judge took a second piece of cake and settled a little lower into the chair. 'In my experience, what a man is when he's sixteen he'll be all his life. There's no changing men's natures. But the thing is, now Con's married, it won't matter how he behaves. While he was single we were in terror he'd compromise some unsuitable girl and have to marry her, or have a scandalous affair with a married woman and bring the husband down on us. But now if he does debauch a female, married or unmarried, it'll be her fault for not knowing better. No-one will blame him. And no-one will blame us, more to the point.'

Mary was silent, as interested as scandalised by this view. Mrs Judge looked at her sharply. 'And if I were you, dear,' she said firmly, 'I'd get your husband to persuade Mr Morland to make Eugene marry before he gets you all into a heap of trouble.'

'I have no influence with Fenwick,' Mary began, and Mrs Judge threw up her hands in protest, showering Mary lightly with cake-crumbs.

'No influence? Never say it! It's the only thing that keeps men civilised at all! And, besides, Fenwick worships you. Everyone knows it was a love-match, and if a woman can't make something out of that . . . ! Well, my Pa arranged my marriage, and a good one it's been. I've no complaints. But if a woman can marry for love, it stands to reason she has a head start. So get Fenwick to make his father force Eugene to marry. Twenty-five, or is it twenty-six? is a shocking age to be keeping a bachelor at home.'

'Martial's twenty-eight,' Mary said.

'Martial Flint has his own fortune,' Mrs Judge said firmly. 'And he never did care a thing about any woman, unless it's some Yankee female he's met on one of his trips north and doesn't dare mention. In any case, he's a close hand, is Martial: he knows how to keep his affairs private. No-one will ever know what *he* gets up to after dark. And another thing,' she went on. 'If I were you, I'd send young

Ruthie to school. All this scrambling around the countryside has to stop some time. I'm sending Clara this fall, to an excellent seminary in Savannah, to learn deportment and such-like. You should do the same, or she'll be so fixed in her ways she'll never get a husband. Yes, I'll have one of those, dear, thank you. Cinnamon jumbles, are they? Yes, and some more tea.'

A fly was walking round Lennox's neck just under the line of his open collar, stopping every now and then to sip his sweat. He was unable to do anything about it because both his hands were occupied, trying to get a line through the ring on the end of the timber, which had slipped under water. The water was low, but now so clouded with mud that he had to feel for the ring, fumbling in the grey-brown soup, while little fishes nibbled curiously at his pale fingers.

With Benedict's departure, Lennox had taken over complete control of his building scheme, but progress had been desperately slow. The original plan simply to get the old mill into working order had rapidly expanded: Benedict thought that, while he was about it, it made sense to enlarge the mill building and install a mechanical thresher as well. A second wheel on a lateral race, closed off by sluices when it was not needed, was all that was needed; and then it seemed to him that it would not be difficult to adapt the thresher to operate a roller for crushing peas, beans and maize as well. It was simply a matter of gearing.

But all this work at the mill required a great deal of material to be carted to the site, and it wasn't long before Benedict saw that a new straight track was needed to cut off a loop of the crick and avoid the muddy bottom where the carts kept getting stuck. The new route only required a simple timber bridge to be built, and the approach down the bank to be levelled and paved with stone. It was the bridge that Lennox was working on now, and which was proving no simple task. He had never cursed in his life before, but he was getting close to it now.

His groping fingers found the ring but, even as he was poking the end of the line through, he felt the timber give a little and slump further into the water, snatching the ring from his grasp.

'Keep that line taut!' he shouted. He tried to turn to see what was happening behind him, but his boots had sunk into the mud, and the effort almost lost him his balance. He floundered inelegantly, and twisted round to see the team on his side of the crick sitting down in the shade of a Spanish oak, smiling their wide, white smiles at him as if he were sweating and splashing under a hot sun for their entertainment. Exasperation overwhelmed him. 'Stop grinning at me, you imbeciles!' he shouted. 'What the deuce do you think you're doing?'

He knew what had happened. The other end of the supporting line was attached to the harness of a mule, and the mule-holder and the team between them were supposed to keep pulling on it while he attached the drag-line. Once they let their line go slack, the pull of the team on the opposite bank had swung their end of the timber up, so that it slipped backwards and dipped his end further into the water from which he was bent on rescuing it.

This was beyond endurance! They had been hardly into the day's work when the timber first slipped, and now the sun was high. They would get nothing done today, nothing! He floundered out onto the bank. 'What are you sitting down for? D'you think you're here for a picnic?' he bellowed. The smiles slipped away like mice behind the skirting-board. 'You, Jedda,' he shouted at the mule-holder, 'don't let that animal graze! Get his head up! Didn't I tell you to keep him up to his collar?' Jedda gave no answer, merely looked at him stupidly. He *was* stupid, Lennox acknowledged, but Jeb, leader of the team now taking its ease under the tree, only pretended to be. Lennox rounded on him furiously. 'You, Jeb, didn't I tell you to keep this line taut? Well, didn't I? Answer me!'

Jeb's grin inverted itself into an expression of bewildered woe, as of one who despite noble effort was unfairly berated. 'Yessuh, Mist' Lennuck. But dat wuz hages ago.'

'Ages ago? Did I tell you to stop? Did I tell you to sit down and enjoy yourselves?'

'Mist' Lennuck, suh, hit pow'ful hot, an' de flahs bitin' fit ter kill! Ah di'n know we wuz meant keep pullin' on de rope for evah.'

'Good God, man, you could see what I was trying to do! Now we'll have to start all over again!'

A tremendous splash made him whip round the other way. The far bank team, still diligently hauling on their line, had managed to dislodge the timber entirely from the pivot wedges, so that, its unsupported weight being too much for them, they had perforce to let it fall into the crick.

Lennox almost danced with fury. 'Slack off that line! Oh, good grief, now look! You senseless clods! You hen-witted lunatics! You – you—!' He wished he knew some really powerful oaths: he longed for such a store of ripe vocabulary as Benedict had learned over years of working on the railways. But he had seen with Hazeleen that if anyone really cursed the darkies full-bloodedly, they withdrew into pious hurt and revoked what little co-operation they had given.

They were Evangelists to a man, and religion was a powerful force in keeping them under control.

They were all standing looking at him now, with the immovable patience of cows whose usual route to the milking-shed has been blocked. They could outlast him, those stares said; they could simply stupid him to death. The mule, now asleep with one long hoof cocked and his lower lip drooping, had more natural propensity for co-operation than the field-hands he was facing.

Jeb spoke up for the group. 'Hit pow'ful hot, Mist' Lennuck,' he said again, his face taking on the air of pathetic suffering which, out of a range of unhelpful expressions, most irritated Lennox. 'Marse Morlan', he don' mek us stan' out in de fiel' when de sun dis high. An' Jedda, he po'ly wid de stummick crams. He gwine hab a fit hif we don' git in de shade.' Jedda rolled his eyes to confirm the point, and the mule groaned in its sleep as if in agreement. 'Marse Morlan', he won' lahk it hif Jedda git sick,' Jeb added persuasively. 'Hit dinner-time, nigh on, suh. Say we quit for dinner now?'

The desire to give up was strong in Lennox but, on the other hand, he was damned if he would be defeated by a bunch of darkies. 'You'll stop when I say it's dinner-time, and not before,' he said, surveying the scene and wondering what was the best way of getting the timber out again.

But a different atmosphere seemed to be creeping over the slaves; their expressions were not merely blank now but actively stubborn, and Lennox suddenly realised how exposed he was out here, several miles from the house. He was alone, weaponless in the face of twenty negroes, all older and stronger than him. Don't be a fool, he adjured himself. They wouldn't harm you – it would be more than their lives were worth. They'd be hunted down and hanged if they so much as raised a hand to you. Well, that was true – but not entirely consoling. If they were stupid enough, they might not weigh the consequences; if they were desperate enough, they might not care; and if they were hanged afterwards, it wouldn't help him, would it?

'Hit always dinner-time when de sun git dis high,' Jeb said. He took a step forward, and the two big men either side of him stepped with him.

It was merely coincidental movement, Lennox told himself, and resisted the urge to take a corresponding step backwards, which in any case would have put him back in the water. 'You men get hold of that line again and take up the slack,' he said. Was it just his imagination, or were they hesitating, as if considering disobedience? He was never to find out, for at that moment a gunshot rang out, and there was a ping and whine as a rifle bullet skimmed just above

Jeb's head and nipped a small chunk of bark out of the trunk of the oak. Everyone, including the mule, flinched, and Jeb and his two companions dropped to the ground, displaying commendably quick reactions.

Lennox whipped round, to see Hill at the top of the bank with his mongrel hound, Yaller Dawg, sitting unconcernedly at his side. Hill stood quite still, his rifle in his hand, but held down at his hip, as if he were just carrying it – though there was a snip of smoke rising from the muzzle. His face under the brim of his revolting hat was impassive, and as Lennox turned he calmly removed his cheroot from his teeth, spat a fragment of tobacco sideways, and said, 'Beg pardon if I skeered you any. Damn' thing just went off in m'hand.'

Jeb and his companions scrambled to their feet and began an agitated jabber in Gullah, the private language of Carolinian blacks. On the other side of the crick the other team were pointing and laughing at their fellow labourers' discomfiture. Hill raised his head and his voice slightly and said, 'Shut that niggery row!' The chatter and laughter subsided abruptly, leaving a quiet in which the slow gurgle of the crick and a distant, monotonous cawing of a crow were the only sounds.

Hill came down the bank. Yaller Dawg went past him to crouch and lap the cloudy water with a noise like wet leather being slapped – a thirsty sound that made all the blacks lick their lips involuntarily.

'Sorry 'bout the gun going off like that, Mr Lennox Mynott,' Hill said. Lennox found nothing to say in reply. He dabbed at the sweat on his upper lip with his damp handkerchief, and wondered how it was that Hill didn't seem to sweat at all. Maybe his skin was just too weathered to allow moisture through. 'I jist passed the dinner-wagon, thought I'd come down and tell you it'll be here in ten minutes. Don't let me disturb you none, though.' His flat eyes roved quickly over the scene. 'Jist got time to secure that timber 'fore the wagon gits here, ain't you?'

'That's what I've been trying to do,' Lennox said.

'I seen you,' Hill said neutrally. He turned and shouted across the crick, 'Here, you Habbuk, you Simmy, git on that pole and lever that timber back on the pivots. The rest o' you take up that line, hold it steady.' He swivelled to the team this side and said, 'Take up the slack, you grinnin' black Injuns, an' if you let it slip I'm gonna shoot one of ya, but I ain't sayin' which one.' The threat sank in, and they scampered to the line, still commenting, but quietly, in their own language. 'Now, you darkies, when I say pull, pull. And you, Jeb, git in the water and git that line through the ring when it comes up.

F'anyone goin' to get their fingers caught, ain't goin' to be me or Mister Mynott. Come on out o' there, Yaller. Right, now, *pull*!'

The difference was amazing. By the time the ox-cart came creaking into sight, bringing the hands' dinner, the timber was in place and secured, and the hard part of the job was accomplished.

'All right, Habbuk, bring the men over this side. Dinner-time,' Lennox called. Habbuk signalled his understanding, and Lennox nodded to Hill, and the two of them walked a little apart, out of earshot of the slaves.

'I want to thank you for getting them moving again,' Lennox said. 'That was pretty fancy shooting, just skimming Jeb's head like that.'

Hill stared into the middle distance with laconical eyes. 'Meant t'hit the bastard,' he said. 'Never was much good shootin' from the hip.'

Lennox didn't know whether to take him seriously or not. Yaller Dawg came sniffing round his trousers and raised yellow lamp eyes to his face, and when Lennox smiled and put down a cautious hand he was allowed to scratch the floppy ears. 'Nice dog,' he said. 'They have hounds back home at Morland Place with eyes like his.'

'He don't take to folks much as a rule,' Hill said, and his voice had warmed very slightly. 'You havin' some trouble with them niggers?'

'More than some,' Lennox said. 'This is such a simple job, but I've been getting nowhere – until you came along, that is.'

Hill grunted. 'You're a gentleman. I ain't got your handicap. They know I'd shoot 'em soon as look at 'em.'

Lennox frowned. 'You wouldn't really, would you?'

'What's to stop me?' Hill said. 'Nobody ain't goin' to hang me for shootin' a goddam uppity nigger. More like to give me a medal. Since Harper's Ferry they're all too skeered o' slave rebellion.'

Lennox had heard about that episode: it was much on people's minds. Last October a fanatical Abolitionist called John Brown had led an assault on the Federal arsenal at Harper's Ferry near Washington, intending to use the weapons to kill slave-owners and start a servile uprising in Virginia. Fortunately a detachment of Federal marines had cornered Brown and his men in the arsenal, and they were eventually taken, tried and hanged. But Lennox had heard much about the horrors that would have followed if Brown had succeeded in his plan: pillage, wholesale murder, plantations burned, women violated. It was well known that a lot of Northerners regarded Brown as a martyr, which made more volatile Southerners believe that what the North really wanted was a slave revolt throughout the South, and the death of the whole planter class. Harper's Ferry was often cited as a powerful argument for secession.

'You goin' on with this after dinner?' Hill asked next.

'I must. I can't let them beat me – though I don't know what I'll do if they—' He didn't like to specify, in case the words had power.

Hill rolled his cheroot to the other side of his mouth, squinting against the river's brightness. Now it was undisturbed again, it had re-established a pattern of flashing diamonds down its centre, magnificent as an empress's collar. 'That's where they got you,' Hill said. 'Ain't nothing you can reward 'em with that's worth the effort of winning. Ain't no way you can punish 'em that's worth the effort of avoidin'.'

'They take heed of you,' Lennox said wistfully. 'I wonder—?'

'I'll git 'em started,' Hill said tersely.

'Thank you,' Lennox said fervently. 'You're very kind.' The words struck him as odd, since everyone said that Hill hadn't a kind bone in his body, and he said apologetically, 'I don't know why you should bother with me.'

'You're her brother, ain't you,' he said, not as a question, but as an answer. Lennox felt himself blush. Hill went on, 'I jist guessed it. Like as two peas.'

'You wouldn't—' Lennox began and then wisely corrected himself. 'No, of course you wouldn't. You're fond of Mary, aren't you?'

Fond was not a word in Hill's vocabulary. 'Never met a female worth spit,' he said, 'but she's different. Got a mind. Got a sense of honour. So I take care of what's her'n.' He looked Lennox up and down like a recruiting sergeant faced with an unpromising intake. 'Nex' time you come out alone,' he advised, 'bring y'self a pistol.'

A few days later a letter came from Benedict for Mary, enclosing one from Sibella to Benedict which he thought she might like to read. Mary opened it as they sat around the breakfast table in the quiet time between eating and starting the day's work, and read bits aloud to Lennox. 'George is getting very good with a gun – shot ten rabbits in one morning, and half a dozen pigeon. Regina's had her first riding lesson – goodness, how old is she?'

'Three,' Lennox said. 'She was three in April.'

'The corn harvest was good again, and the sheep fetched a good price, but they've had three cows with wooden tongue and two with milk fever. And a gale brought the weather-vane down through the stable roof. No-one was hurt, though.'

Lennox listened, transported for a little while to that place which had never been his home, but which he had loved. He heard the wistfulness in Mary's voice as she devoured the home news almost greedily. 'Poor Mama is having to do everything,' she said. 'I wonder Papa hasn't said anything about when he's going home. Not that I want to lose him, of course, but I'd have thought he'd be anxious.' She didn't say any more with her father-in-law listening – or at least, at the same table – but it seemed the longer Benedict was here, the more he slipped into a Southern rhythm of life. At first he had been always active, rising early and wanting to be doing all the time, but lately he had slowed down so much that not getting the mill finished didn't seem to bother him. She wouldn't be surprised if in Charleston he was leading a life of idle pleasure with Fenwick and his friends, and never got round to looking at the factory at all.

She read on, and then said, 'Oh, here's something to interest you, Lennox – about your tutor, Mr Wheldrake.'

'He was more Georgie and Teddy's tutor,' Lennox corrected.

'Well, at any rate, he's come in for quite some distinction, it seems,' Mary went on. 'Mama says he's about to have a book published, and two very distinguished scholars have read the manuscript and said flattering things about it. Did you know he was writing a book?'

'No, I didn't,' Lennox answered, puzzled. He wouldn't have thought that was a thing Wheldrake would have kept to himself; but then he wouldn't have thought Wheldrake capable of writing anything scholarly. 'Does she say what the book is?'

'It's a translation of Catullus into verse – the *Carmina*. Mama says she doesn't know any Latin, but the English poetry is quite beautiful.'

Lennox rose abruptly from the table. 'I didn't realise what the time was. I'd better be getting on with my tasks. Will you excuse me, please?'

He left the room quickly, before he gave himself away. Mary, still reading her letter, only murmured vaguely, but Ruth looked at him sharply, and a moment later excused herself and slipped out after him. Her father's eyes lifted from his newspaper briefly, and then returned to the page.

Ruth caught Lennox up in the barnyard. He stopped when she called, but did not look at her. 'What is it?' she said. 'You look so grim!' Lennox was silent, and she grew impatient and tugged his arm in a child-like gesture. 'Come on, you might as well tell me. You know I'll worm it out of you in the end.'

'It was that bit in Mary's letter about the tutor,' he said reluctantly.

'Mr Whale, or whatever his name is? What was wrong with that?'

'Wheldrake,' Lennox said. 'He wasn't my tutor. He was supposed to be, but he took a dislike to me the moment he saw me, and sent me off to study on my own.'

'Well, he was a fool, then,' Ruth said stoutly, slipping her arm through his and giving it a hug. 'Why should you care about him?'

'Oh, I don't.' Lennox hesitated. 'The thing is, Ruthie – I don't want to make you think I'm conceited, but my father educated me, and he was a very wise and clever man, and – well, the fact is, Mr Wheldrake was not a clever man, or well read. I think that's why he hated me, because I knew more than him. Does that sound horribly boastful? I don't mean it to, but I want to tell you the truth.'

'It doesn't sound boastful. *I* know how clever you are. Goodness, I never knew a person who knew as much as you – apart from Mary.'

'Thank you for that,' he said. He took a deep breath and said, 'Mr Wheldrake has stolen my work.'

'You mean this book of his?'

Lennox was grateful for her quickness. 'When I studied alone all day, I had to have something to work on to keep me from getting bored, so I started translating Catullus into verse. I showed the pages to Mr Wheldrake every day, to prove I'd been busy. He took them away with him into his room and gave them back the next day. I was pleased to think he was taking the trouble to read them—'

'And all the time he was copying them!' Ruth cried. 'The old thief! Poor Lennox, no wonder you're upset!'

Lennox tried to be just. 'I don't know for sure that's what he was doing. Maybe he did a translation of his own. After all, if scholars have said the work is good—'

'Oh, don't be so saintly!' Ruth said. 'You are as clever as a circus horse, and you know it! It's obvious this mean old man has cheated you, and if I were you I'd write to that publisher fellow and tell him that the work is yours. Serve this Whale person out!'

Lennox shook his head. 'How could I prove it? It would do no good, and make me look a fool. But, oh Ruth, he held me in such contempt that he simply stole my work, as if because I had no name and no fortune I had no right to own anything, not even the contents of my own head!' He clenched his fists down at his side with frustration. 'You don't know how terrible it is to feel so helpless!'

'Don't I?' she said. With an effort he detached himself from his own troubles and looked at her. With someone you knew well and saw daily, you didn't tend to notice change in them until something unusual made you look at them with fresh eyes. Now in this moment of deep upset he saw that she had grown up during the summer, and that the little girl she had been when he first met her was now hovering on the brink of womanhood. Her manners were gentler and her movements less angular, and she carried her head differently – like a schooled horse, he thought absurdly, instead of an unbroken colt. No, not so absurd: she was more aware of herself, that was all, and aware of how she appeared to others. That's what gave her new poise. And she was more than pretty: one day she was going to be very, very beautiful.

'Just think about what it's like to be me,' she said. 'You saw May married off to that horrid Conrad. Well, she thought she was in love with him, so she didn't mind, but it wouldn't have made any difference if she had. And that's what will happen to me. One day Pa will send for me and tell me he's arranged for me to be married, and that will be the end of all my fun and freedom.'

'Yes, I hadn't thought about that,' he said, and thinking about it now made him depressed. 'Your father wouldn't marry you against your will, though, would he? He wouldn't marry you to someone you didn't like?'

Ruth almost laughed at that. 'He wouldn't even think to ask me. It'll be a business matter, something to do with land or trading rights or cotton mills. I suppose,' she said with a shrug, 'it doesn't matter too much who you marry, as long as they're not really horrible, like Conrad.'

'Oh, Ruthie,' Lennox said helplessly. It seemed dreadful that Ruth should be an element in a business deal. It was as bad as buying and selling slaves.

'It's nice of you to worry for me,' she said. 'But it might just as easily be someone nice – like Beau Raven, say. Think of that!'

Lennox obediently thought about it, but it brought no comfort.

Charles Morland departed without warning for Charleston, was gone a week, and returned to announce that Ruthie was to go away on an extended visit to Alexandria, to stay with Martial's only cousin, Phoebe, who had just married. Alexandria was a pretty, sophisticated Virginia town just across the river from Washington, and the new Mrs George Canfield was a lively, sociable young woman just in the way to enjoy a young girl's company and take her about.

Ruth turned a little pale at the news and even dared to voice a protest. 'I don't like towns, Pa. Must I go? I'd much sooner stay here in the country.'

For a wonder Charles didn't scowl at her. Mary suspected that Ruth was something of a favourite with him. 'The Canfields go everywhere,' Charles said. 'George Canfield is in Congress, so they're well known in Washington, and dine with the President and his circle. After a few months of the civilised round, you'll come home with your skirts down and your hair up, and manners, it's to be hoped, a little less rustic.'

Uncle Heck spoke. 'You're sure to have a good time, Ruthie. Phoebe Canfield's a peach, and full of fun. There'll be theatres and parties and all sorts.'

'It's Alexandria or school,' Charles said impatiently, 'and from what I've seen of the products of these schools, you've more chance of coming back a lady from the Canfields.'

Mary was only surprised at the suddenness of the decision, and when she was alone with Ruth encouraged her to think well of the idea. Ruth was persuadable. She didn't want to leave home, and she preferred riding and country pursuits to town things like dinners and balls; but on the other hand it was a novelty, and Mrs Canfield might be nice, like Mary, and it would be fun to see the President (even if he wouldn't be President for much longer) and all the famous buildings in Washington one heard so much about.

Mary had to get to work on Ruth's wardrobe for the trip. Though part of Mrs Canfield's brief would be to buy new dresses for Ruth, she had to have something to wear to begin with. So Mary had to inspect her frocks, mend them – Ruth was hard on her clothes – and in some cases alter them, for she had grown a lot during the last summer. Her second-best frock was now much too short, and Mary had to sew a deep double frill on the hem to lengthen it; her best – the pink dress she had had as a bridesmaid – was so dirty that Mary decided, sighing, that there was nothing for it but to wash it. This was a tedious business which involved unpicking the stitches and taking the dress to pieces, washing the separate pieces carefully and laying them flat to dry, then sewing the whole thing back together. Dresses were rarely washed: often the fabric would not stand it and, with linen underneath and apron on top, they were never supposed to want it.

As this was to be her first grown-up visit, Ruth was not to be accompanied by Mammy, but by her 'own' slave, Frank – Francesca – a slim, yellow-skinned, straight-haired mulatto. All the children were allotted a slave of their own as soon as they were born, usually one of their own age – sometimes even a milk-brother. They attended and played with them all through their childhood, and would eventually become their body-slave when they reached adult status. Mary's own boys each had a little darky in the quarters, much as she disliked the idea. Frank was two years older than Ruth. Mary suspected she was one of Charles's bastards: her mother was an attractive woman who certainly seemed to enjoy some special status, since she never did any work that Mary could see. Mary considered it a revolting piece of bad taste to assign to Ruthie her own half-sister as a body-slave, but it was the kind of thing she would not put past Charles, who probably never thought of his mulattoes as 'his' in any but the commercial sense.

Perhaps because of her mother's position, Frank had grown up into what Julie described as 'de mos' wofless gal on de place', lazy and unreliable to a remarkable degree, and possessed of an enormous personal conceit, which had her forever dawdling in front of mirrors, combing her hair with her fingers and making simpering faces. She had been found once or twice in people's bedrooms trying on white folks' clothes – a heinous crime, even if she hadn't meant to steal them. Ruthie had an odd affection for Frank, and wouldn't let her be beaten, so the punishment usually involved extra work, which she never did, or removal of privileges, which she ignored.

When Mary started packing for Ruth, she called on Frank to help – not because there was any prospect that she would be useful, but because Mary wanted a chance to drum into her some elements of a code of behaviour, and give her some notion of what her duties would be in Alexandria. But Frank was much too excited at the idea of going away to listen, and she wandered round the room, picking things up and putting them down, and interrupting Mary now and then with a comment or question in her high, sing-song voice that proved she had not heard a single word Mary said.

All was done at last, and Ruthie was packed off in the carriage with Frank perched on the edge of the seat beside her, on their way to Alexandria via Charleston. Mary thought that, of the two, Frank looked more expectant of pleasure.

Soon after Ruthie's departure, Maybelle and Conrad returned to Camelot. Mary was surprised that they were back so soon, but she learned through the usual indirect sources that Conrad had outrun his purse and outstayed his welcome with all well-placed relatives, and Maybelle was pregnant. Eugene was excited that his old friend had come back, feeling that Ravens and Lawrences and Fairfaxes were not a substitute, and rode over at once to see if Conrad had lost his taste for getting drunk. Conrad reassured him on that point to such effect that Eugene did not come home for two days but, when he did, he seemed oddly subdued. Mary wondered whether he had found Conrad changed in some way; certainly in the weeks that followed Eugene did not call at Camelot again, and Conrad never came to Twelvetrees.

Maybelle came to see Mary, however, and Mary was surprised and relieved to see how well she looked: a proper little woman with a quantity of smooth golden curls (which puzzled Mary until she realised they were false – quite the fashion in New Orleans) and a very stylish, wide-hooped gown of foxglove merino with enormous cambric undersleeves. Undersleeves were very much a mark of the lady of leisure, for they were wildly impractical for any kind of work, and Mary looked at them, as at nothing else, with some envy: she never wore undersleeves herself. May had also developed a society manner, smiled a lot, chatted, and fiddled with her curls and her cuffs, while her eyes wandered restlessly about the room, looking, Mary supposed, for changes.

She asked after her sister, and said, 'She's lucky to be going to Alexandria. She's bound to visit in Washington, and the society there is the best – plays and balls and dinners every single evening. We wanted dreadfully to go to Washington this fall, but Conrad had to go home. His father couldn't spare him a moment more.' She looked conscious of the lie, and added defiantly, 'But he says we might go in the New Year. There's sure to be lots going on then.'

'But May, dear,' Mary said, 'you won't be fit to be seen by then. You know you can't go out anywhere when your condition starts to show.'

May blushed, but then dropped her affectations and began to talk eagerly about the baby and her hopes for it. Mary watched her closely and listened for nuances in her speech. There was a look in her eyes, a sort of feverish brightness, coupled with an occasional failure to meet Mary's gaze, that was worrying. But Maybelle said she was happy, and Mary could not pinpoint anything to justify her uneasy feeling.

CHAPTER FIFTEEN

The year advanced. The cotton-picking was finished, the hands had their annual three-day holiday – two days of relaxation and merry-making, and one of quarrelling and misbehaviour which Mary had to deal with. Charles went back to Charleston. Mary's son Ashley had his fourth birthday and was breeched and had his baby curls cut off. Adeline Raven went to stay at Fairoaks, where one of the daughters, Barbara, was of her own age, and Eugene rode over there most days to 'mess around' with the elder Fairfax boys, Clay and Drew, and Beau Raven. One of Moses' mule-bites turned septic and the grass didn't get cut for a fortnight. Lennox's horse slipped down a bank during a rainstorm and fell, and Lennox got his foot caught in the stirrup and ended up with a nasty sprained ankle, which he was lucky not to have broken.

Ruth's letters home were of great interest to Mary. At first she only offered descriptions of the Canfield house, of Mrs Canfield ('She asked me to call her Cousin Phoebe right off, in just the nicest way!') and of Alexandria ('Everyone knows everyone else, so they know all about me already, and everyone calls me "Miss Morland" as soon as they see me, whether I've met them or not'). To begin with, her time was taken up with mantuamakers and fittings, which she claimed to find a great bore; but, even so, there seemed to be a certain amount of enthusiasm in the descriptions of 'a tartan walking-dress with lilac ribbon and black fringe trimming', and 'a white transparent wool that looks just like muslin, and the sleeves piped with black lace over bright green ribbon'. Soon Mary was being advised solemnly that 'basques are not much worn now', and 'flounces are completely out – my old dress you lengthened won't do at all', and 'the fullness of the skirt must be more towards the back, with five or six pleats at the side and three or four large box pleats in the rear.'

However, when the wardrobe was arranged, Mrs Canfield began to take Ruth about not only in Alexandria, but to Arlington and Georgetown and Washington too, and Ruth's subject-matter became more varied. She had some sharp observations to make on the situation in the capital city that fall and winter.

The lines are pretty much drawn between North and South now, and a lot of people who used to be friends have 'fallen out'. You have to be careful which occasions you go to, and who you ask to yours, in case enemies get sat together. It's real difficult to remember. Sometimes even old friends don't see each other any more, which I call silly. But Cousin Phoebe don't 'take sides' and since she is very nice and popular, she still goes most everywhere, so I get to see both sides of the line.

One day she wrote,

We went to the theater Tuesday, guests of Mrs Douglas — you know, Judge Douglas's wife? She has a box there. Seats are hard to come by, so Cousin Phoebe said we was lucky to be asked. So in the interval the door opened and Mr Porcher Miles stood there. Judge Douglas hates Mr Miles because Mr Miles opposed his Nommernation, so Mrs Douglas comes up all frosty and says, 'Sir, you have come to the wrong door,' so Mr Miles comes right frosty back and says, 'Madam, I hope I might pay my respecks to Mrs Canfield, for whom my visit was intended.' So after he went away Mrs Douglas couldn't stop grumbling about him. She said, 'Is that what they call Southern chivalry? I call it more like ill-bred impertanunce.' I had to bite my cheeks not to laugh! But so the day after we called on Mrs Miles, who is also an old friend of Cousin Phoebe's, and Mr Miles come in and he says he was serprised what he had learned of Mrs Douglas that night. 'I had serposed her a lady, but she behaved like a rustic.' Do you call that really funny? Cousin Phoebe and me laughed fit to bust in the carriage on the way home.

Another time she wrote,

Everyone is back from the country early this year. The season don't really start until January, Cousin Phoebe says, but with Mr Lincoln elecked no-one knows what's going to happen next, and no-one wants to miss anything. Cousin Phoebe and Mr Canfield and me were invited to call on President

Buchanan at the White House, which was real interesting. You can guess I was excited! It is a real nice house. Cousin Phoebe says Mr Buchanan has aged terribly since last summer. He calls her 'my dear Phoebe' because he has known her since a child. We sat out on the verander and the Marine Band played in the grounds. They made a fine noise! Cousin Phoebe asked the President if he was quite well but he said he slept finely and enjoyed the best of health. So then Mr Canfield said something I didn't catch, and Mr Buchanan looked real upset and said, 'Not in my time. My dear country to be drowned in blood? Not in my time.' Cousin Phoebe said afterwards Mr Canfield had asked if he thought the South would secede. You can guess how queer those words sounded. They made me shiver, even though we were sitting in the sun.

As time passed, Ruth's spelling and her felicity of expression both underwent an improvement that Mary hoped her father would note with approval. She was obviously getting about and seeing a great deal.

We drove out in the carriage yesterday to visit Mr and Mrs Robert E. Lee at Arlington, and you'll never guess who was there! Well, it was Martial, and it turned out that Phoebe knew all along he would be there, but kept it secret as a surprise for me. I was so glad to see him. He was just the same old Mart. He gave me a big hug and said I looked grown up. His friend Pick Manning was there too. Mart talked a bit about home, but he says he's been in Charleston all the while, so he couldn't tell me about Twelvetrees. When I said I wrote you often, he said to send you his love, in case my letter got there before he did.

Mary was touched that she had been remembered at that distance.

It turns out that Mr Lee was Martial's superintendent at West Point, and that's how he knows him. Mr Lee is a very nice gentleman, very tall and straight up, with nice brown eyes, kind of twinkly, and gray hair and mustache. He was so kind and pleasant to me. Poor Mrs Lee is an invalid, and doesn't get out of her chair with arthritus, but she is a real lady and makes nothing of it. Phoebe says that is the mark of a lady, never to show discomfort or temper. What do you say to that, Mary? Martial flirted with Mrs L and made her laugh, and you could see she was pretty once. Mart and Pick and Mr Lee talked a lot about secession. They were very grave about it. Martial said it had to happen and Mr Lee said it is not the answer. It would make Pa stare to see how Mr Lee hates slavery! He recently inherited his father-in-law's estate and now he's busy freeing all the slaves on it! But though he hates slavery, he doesn't want enforced abolition. And he thinks secession will lead to war. I heard him say to Martial, 'I don't want to have to grow my beard again.' Phoebe said afterwards that meant 'go to war', because old soldiers always grow beards on campaign so as not to have the bother of shaving. Do you call that interesting?

Another letter:

I guess I don't need to tell you the news, for you must have had it before we did, though we heard it pretty well right away. We were at Mr Parker's house, at a wedding-reception, and suddenly a hullabaloo broke out in the hall. It was Mr Keitt waving a telegram in the air and crying, 'Oh thank God! South Carolina has seceded!' Well, that was the end of the wedding! President Buchanan, who was the guest of honour, fell back in his chair in a shock and had to be taken home right away. Mr Canfield disappeared with Mr Keitt, so we couldn't leave for ages. Phoebe and I huddled together in a corner feeling very shocked, and very sorry for the poor bride, who was crying fit to bust over her wedding-cake, which nobody had an idea of cutting now. When Mr Canfield came back there was no thought of going back to Alexandria. We just went from house to house, telling the news and being told it about equally. In the evening, which was horrid wet and drizzling and the streets a sea of mud, we fetched up at Mr Conybeare's. Mrs C had a huge bowl of punch going, and buttered biscuits and chipped beef. With so many people dropping in, it was like a party, but a strange, nervous one. One old lady said, 'The comfort is that South Carolina is a fickle young girl and may change her mind. You recall you said once before she would walk out, but then she took off her things and decide to stay.' But Mr Conybeare said, 'She is gone for good this time, depend upon it,' and Mr Canfield said, 'Even if she stays away, there's no need for Virginia to follow her.' Then a young man came in and said he had just been to the White House to tell the President, but that he knew it already, and Mr Canfield said, 'Certainly, he was at the Parker house when the telegram came.' 'Why, sir, how can you know that?' the young man asked, and Mr Canfield said, 'Because I was there myself,' and the young man looked so stupid, as if it was the greatest conundrum in the world! You would think people had been knocked on the head like great fish, they are so overset by this news.

By the time Mary received this letter, she had indeed heard the news. The trouble had begun on the 7th of November when it was known for sure that Mr Lincoln had won the election and would be the next President of the United States. It had long been expected, of course, but the reality was still a shock. It was firmly believed by almost everyone that Lincoln's first act on his inauguration in March would be to abolish slavery in the Southern states, and that the immediate consequence of that would be a slave revolt. It was widely believed among the negroes too: Mr Lincoln would come to Charleston to free them, they said. They were very calm about it, and there was no suggestion of their giving any trouble, but still the white community expected the worst. There was only one opinion which was allowed to be expressed in Charleston for the next month, and that was that South Carolina must and would secede from the Union in order to protect her way of life.

The Secession Convention met in St Andrew's Hall on the 17th of December, led by the delegates who had walked out of the Democratic Convention in April. Mr Robert Barnwell Rhett, editor of the radical *Charleston Mercury* and well known for making inflammatory speeches, had very little left to achieve, and on the 20th the vote was passed unanimously, and the Ordinance of Secession was signed.

There was rejoicing in Charleston, the church bells were rung, a salute of guns fired off across the harbour, and the Palmetto state flag hung from every public building. The news spread rapidly outwards into the countryside, met everywhere with euphoria. South Carolina had removed her neck from under the Northern heel! Indignity and injustice were over: she was free at last!

Mary was alone when the news reached her by letter. The great events in Charleston had called all her menfolk away; even Uncle Heck had gone to attend the Convention which must alter all their lives. Only Lennox remained at Twelvetrees, and he would have liked to be elsewhere, though he was too loyal to say so. As soon as she received it, Mary sent a note over to Camelot, in case they hadn't heard it there, and the following day May and Mrs Judge both drove over in the carriage.

'Well, I call it a great cause for celebration, don't you?' Mrs Judge said, settling herself into the most comfortable chair and looking around her with hungry eyes.

'Freedom is a lovely thing,' Mary said. 'The freedom of a whole state must be doubly special.'

This wasn't enough for Mrs Judge. 'Doubly? A hundred – a thousand times so! Well, Judge says we had to show them we meant what we said. If and when they meet our conditions, we may think about going back in. There's been too much talking. They needed to be shocked out of their complacency.'

'But suppose other cotton states follow suit?'

'I should hope they will! We have a community of interest with the Southern states. That's what the North can't and won't understand. Well, we've concentrated their minds for them. The South could never be happy under the Northern yoke.'

These words, Mary could tell, were not Mrs Judge's own. She suspected Mr Raven had been visiting. She said, 'What I meant was that if other states follow us out, if there's a general secession, the North may feel obliged to resort to force to bring us back, and that would mean war.'

'It won't come to that,' Mrs Judge said briskly. 'Did you send for tea, dear? Ah, yes, here it is! And is that your plum-cake I see there? Oh, and gingerbread too. Both, please.' She gave a little laugh. 'I really couldn't bring myself to choose between them.'

May hardly spoke during the whole visit. At five months pregnant, she was beginning to show. Mary thought she had chosen the right season to carry through: she would have the baby in April, before it got hot. Mary's first had been born in August. When Mrs Judge had talked herself to a near standstill, Mary took the opportunity to say, 'You're very quiet, May dear.'

Mrs Judge said at once, 'She's missing her husband, of course, the silly goose. But it's natural all the men want to be in Charleston at a moment like this. He'll be back in a week or two.'

May kept her eyes on the carpet. She seemed a little flushed and not quite well, and when Mary was able at last to ask her how she felt, she admitted to having the headache. Mrs Judge seemed inclined to be sharp about that. 'Headache, phooey! A young thing like you? It's the mopes, plain and simple, Mrs Fenwick. Don't be taken in by it.'

There was something in the edge of her voice that Mary couldn't fathom, some cause between them that she was evidently not meant to know about. She couldn't pursue it, of course, but she ignored Mrs Judge's advice and quietly went to her medicine cupboard for a powder which she obliged May to drink. May took it without fuss, and when she tilted her head back to drink, raised her eyes for a moment to Mary's, with a look of gratitude.

On the 27th of December, Mary was going through the store-cupboard with Grace when Martial walked in.

'A nice, womanly pursuit, Mrs Fenwick Morland. And how fetching you look in that apron – though I can't say I admire the cap.' He reached out and twitched off the offending article which, unadorned like a large cotton flour-bag, covered all her hair.

Mary could have blushed with vexation to have been caught like this, in working-cap, her least attractive gown and the all-enveloping dull-purple apron which had the unbecoming scorch-mark down the front. In his mud-splashed riding clothes and with his dark hair ruffled, he was devastatingly attractive. She hadn't seen him since the wedding, and the sight of him, suddenly, and in this manless place, made her heart thud in an unruly way. Amid the fust of women and slaves and household things, the pungency of a man's smell assailed her senses: sharp tangs of leather and tobacco, good clean sweat, horses, and the earthy-leafy smell of the outside air. It almost made her mouth water. It was like being woken up from a heavy sleep by the smell of fresh coffee.

'What are you doing here?' was all she managed to stammer through her confusion.

He smiled down at her in that way that made her feel her head was transparent; his smile was sly, his eyes bright and knowing. 'What sort of a greeting is that?' he said. 'Should we not begin with, "Welcome, Cousin Martial Flint. How good it is to see you again. Would you care for some refreshment?"'

'I am heartily glad to see you,' she said, and he could have no doubt from her face or her voice that she meant it.

'That will do for now,' he said. 'Shall we remove the apron, too, and go into the parlour?'

'Yes, of course.' She began to move that way, fumbling behind her for the apron strings, and then turned back to say, 'Grace, we'll finish this later. Some refreshments for Mr Martial in the parlour.'

'Yassum.' Grace looked towards Martial. 'Is dat coffee, Mist' Mart, or brandy?'

'Both. And something to eat. I've just ridden from Charleston and I'm cold and hungry.'

'Shall I have a meal cooked for you?' Mary asked.

'No, I'll wait and have dinner with you later. Just some bread and meat to tide me over.'

Mary confirmed the instruction with a nod to Grace, but her

mind was on the first part of his last sentence. He was not rushing straight off somewhere: she would have his company at least overnight!

'Here, let me. You're making a mull of that,' he said, stepping behind her as they crossed the hall towards the parlour. She paused, bending her head forward, while he attacked her strings. 'You've got them in a knot, fool,' he grumbled. 'Stand still.' He worked in silence for a moment, and then said in a different voice, 'You know, this is just like undressing a child. You're so small that with your golden head and your neck bent like that you might be a ten-year-old little girl. There, that's done it.'

The strings yielded and he pushed the straps down off her shoulders, but his hands remained on her upper arms. She stood very still. The moment seemed to catch its breath: in the sudden pause she could hear his breathing and the slow tick of the long-case clock in the corner, and both sounded unnaturally loud. And then he chuckled softly, and said, '*That* is not, however, the sensation of a child.' His hands removed, she pulled the apron away from her, and the moment moved on again. What did he mean by that? she wondered. But Martial was such a tease, and so unaccountable, that it was dangerous to start speculating. She led the way to the parlour, glad to have time to compose her face before facing him. When she did, she found his expression was grave. He went straight to the fire, and stood with his back to it, warming his tail. She sat down on the sofa facing him, and he regarded her thoughtfully for some moments before he spoke.

'Something happened yesterday which I think we may find was the deciding moment when we went to war.'

She jumped. 'Are we at war?'

'Not yet, but I'm afraid it's now almost inevitable. I would say quite inevitable, except that, human as I am, I am cursed with a propensity to hope for the best, even against all the evidence.'

'But what has happened?'

'You knew, I assume, that there was a body of Federal soldiers garrisoned in Fort Moultrie under Major Robert Anderson? Last evening, apparently on his own initiative, Anderson moved his men from Moultrie across to Fort Sumter.'

Mary waited blankly for more, and he gave a grim sort of smile.

'Yes, I see you don't catch the significance; you and most of Charleston. Listen: Moultrie is an old fort, really nothing more than a sea battery. It has only low brick walls, and in places the sand has drifted so high against them you can hardly see the masonry. At the rear it is virtually defenceless. In fact, a lot of civilians have built cottages right up against the walls; the sentry walking the rampart has to turn his head so as not to look in at their bedroom windows! But Sumter, now, Sumter is new, well fortified, situated on an island, with an impressive armoury and a large magazine down below.'

Mary said slowly, 'You mean Major Anderson thinks he may have to defend himself against attack?'

'Now you are following,' Martial said approvingly. 'It's a passive act of aggression, if I may permit myself a paradox. Since he's taken that course, it's hard to see how he can back down.'

'We could just leave him to sit there,' Mary hazarded.

'Sumter commands the entrance to the bay. If he wanted to, he could besiege the harbour, destroy our shipping.'

'If he wanted to.'

'Yes, and I don't suppose anyone *wants* to start a war. But as long as he is there, he wields a threat of force against South Carolina: how can any independent state tolerate that? And if he withdraws, he admits that the Union accepts our secession.' He moved restlessly away from the fire, his brows drawn down. 'Anderson is a nice fellow, a civilised fellow, and I have dined with him pleasantly on several occasions; but I could wish he had never been born. He has made it impossible for either side to draw back.'

The door opened and Isaac carried in a tray. Martial said in a light, social tone, 'So, let's eat, drink and be merry while we may. Tell me, Mrs Fenwick, what news from Alexandria? How is your young correspondent getting on?'

Mary went along with him, chatting brightly about Ruth's latest news while Martial slaked his first thirst and hunger. Then he interrupted her to say, 'She will have to come home, of course.'

'Now? At once?'

'No, not yet. But I've asked Canfield to keep a close eye on things, and to telegraph me as soon as there is anything to fear. He's a shrewd fellow. I can trust him. I suspect things may last as they are until March, but there's bound to be trouble at Lincoln's inauguration – demonstrations, even riots – and the trouble may spill over into neighbouring areas. Alexandria's too close to Washington for comfort. If need be, I'll go up myself and fetch her back.'

'What does her father say about it?'

'I haven't consulted him. In any case, he doesn't believe Lincoln will go as far as to declare war.'

'Could he possibly be right?' Mary said tentatively.

'It's coming, Mary,' he said abruptly, and she felt the cold touch of fear on her neck. 'That's why I'm here,' he went on. 'If – when – it comes, the men will go away to fight. All that will be left here will be slaves, old men and boys. And you women will be vulnerable as you've never been before.' He paused, looking into her face with a searching, questioning look, but she didn't know what he was searching for.

'I understand,' she said at last, to help him on.

He made a strange grimace. 'I hope to God you don't. I hope to God you never do. But, just in case, I'm going to teach you to shoot.'

Her eyebrows went up. She hadn't expected this. 'To shoot?'

'Oh yes,' he said with a savage sort of grin, 'and it will make you more dangerous to men than you are now, which is quite a feat! But I know that in England ladies do shoot – high-born ladies, at least – so the idea will not be as foreign to you as to a Southern belle. I will teach you to shoot, both a rifle and a pistol, and before I go I will give you a pistol and some ammunition, which you must conceal somewhere safe – but somewhere you can get to it easily.'

'What does Fenwick think about this?'

'I didn't tell anyone I was coming here. Tomorrow we will go out somewhere far from the house for your lessons, where we shan't be overlooked. You mustn't tell anyone about it, because I doubt they would understand or approve. The time will come when they change their minds, of course, but by then it may be too late, and I'm not willing to take the chance. You shall have a secret skill and a secret weapon. Make sure you put the pistol where Fenwick won't find it, that's all.'

They went out on horseback the next morning, accompanied by Martial's slave Ratty, and Mary's groom Caspar. They told Lennox they were going for a ride, and asked if he would like to accompany them, but he declined, having his own work to do. He did not remark on the rifle on Martial's saddle: most gentlemen carried a gun when they rode out, in case they spotted something for the pot.

'What if he'd said yes?' Mary asked as they walked the horses down the track.

'It wouldn't have mattered. I'm sure we could trust him.'

It was a cold, grey morning, rather damp, but with little wind. They rode in silence for a while, Mary enjoying the delight of being out of doors again after so long. Then she said cautiously, 'There is something I want to ask you.'

He looked at her warily. 'Be careful, Madame Bluebeard. What is it?'

'Just this: yesterday you seemed familiar with the action of undressing a child, yet you are unmarried and have no little brothers or sisters. Where did you have your experience?'

'What an indiscreet question, Mrs Fenwick!'

'Oh, is it indiscreet? But you once said you could tell me anything.'

He was laughing, but to himself, almost ruefully. 'I should mind my poetic tongue with you in future. It's most unfair to be remembering against a man what he may say in the heat of – of whatever heat it was.'

'You don't answer the question.'

'Very well then, out with it. There is a certain lady in New York whom I met during my time at West Point, and she has a little girl just ten years old, with a neck, I may say, remarkably like yours. Life is very much more informal up there, especially when you live in a small house with only one servant. A man may help put his daughter to bed without outraging the manly image or the great hierarchy of servants.'

Mary's cheeks reddened, and the words struck at her in a way she could not have anticipated, and hardly understood. 'You have a daughter?'

He chuckled. 'Several, for all that I know. I may be a bachelor, ma'am, but I am not a Catholic priest!'

'Don't joke about it!'

'Why, Mrs Morland, what is it to you? I assure you I never debauch gentlewomen or green girls. The females of my more intimate acquaintance are all perfectly aware of the rules of the game, and happy to play by them.'

She turned her face away stiffly. 'You don't have to assure me of anything.'

'I know I don't,' he agreed cheerfully, watching her with great amusement. 'I didn't say,' he added after a moment, 'that the little girl in New York was *my* daughter. I just said that, in the North, a man may help put his daughter to bed.'

Mary frowned. 'But is she?'

'You just said I don't have to assure you of anything.'

'No, you don't,' she said. He waited for her next outburst. 'I suppose you have Yankee women tucked away all over the North,' she said crossly, 'like a – a—' She couldn't think of the word harem.

He offered her helpfully, 'Like eggs laid hither and yon by a particularly peregrinating hen?' She couldn't help it, but burst out laughing, and he smiled and said, 'That's better. Laughter is the watchword for today.'

'I don't think you meant any of it. You've been teasing me,' she said.

'You began by being indiscreet,' he reminded her.

'Well, I've learned my lesson,' she said. And when she thought it over, she realised she still knew nothing, which was obviously what he wanted. If there were Martial women all over the North, it was none of her business – and she would sooner not know about it.

It was evident that Martial had a particular place in mind, and when they reached it, she saw why. It was a small flat-bottomed quarry with steep sides, hidden until you came suddenly to the rim of it by a belt of trees. There was only one path down, a steep zig-zag down the shallower side, and in the bottom was nothing but a few stunted pine trees and a derelict wooden hut.

'The charcoal-burner lived here a long time ago,' Martial said, 'but now no-one comes here. When I was a little boy, I was taught to shoot here.'

'By whom?'

'Oh, by your father-in-law. He was very kind to me when I was young. He was a different sort of man then.'

They left Ratty and Caspar up in the wood, and went down alone for the shooting lesson, tethering the horses under the thorn trees. There was a rough target marked on one of the walls of the derelict hut, which Martial improved with a lump of chalk he took from his pocket. He made her take off her cape and bonnet – it was sheltered down here in the quarry – and began.

'Now, fit it into the curve of your shoulder. Cradle it. That's right. Gently. Now look down the barrel . . .'

Once she got used to the weight of the rifle and the kick, she proved a fair shot, and he was interested to note that she could look with one eye without having to close the other. 'That's a great advantage when you're in a dangerous situation,' he said. He taught her how to load, unload and clean. 'Always keep your rifle clean. It deserves loving attention if it is going to save your life one day.'

Then he went on to the pistol. 'I'll teach you how to aim, but it's best to be as close to your target as possible with a pistol. They are never as reliable as a rifle, and above a few yards you'll be lucky to hit anything you're aiming at. In fact, if you can have the muzzle against your enemy's ribs before you pull the trigger, so much the better.'

Until that moment she had been enjoying herself. Now she lowered the gun. She looked pale. 'I couldn't shoot a person,' she said.

'What do you think we are doing here?' he said impatiently. 'Do you suppose a need to defend yourself against log cabins?' She only looked at him, green-pale. 'Don't you dare swoon,' he said sharply.

'I don't swoon,' she said, annoyed. 'Or hardly ever. But, Martial, I couldn't kill a man.'

'If it was him or you?' he said steadily. 'If he was going to rape you? If he was standing over your little boys with a knife?'

Her expression hardened. 'Don't talk like that.'

He looked serious. 'I didn't want to frighten you. I didn't want to tell you what can happen in war, but now I have to. War changes people. Men become beasts. He won't see you as a human being, or treat you like one. If you have to, you will pull the trigger. You *will*.'

She held his gaze a moment longer, and then bowed her head. 'God forgive me,' she said, so quietly he hardly heard her. She looked so forlorn that his instinct was to say, 'Don't worry, it will never happen,' but he could not tell her comfortable lies.

'Be strong,' he said. 'You will do what you have to. You always do, you know.' She looked up at that, and saw the teasing light in his eyes, and something else, a seriousness that made her heart quicken. And then he said, 'Come, we have work to do. Let me see you load and fire six rounds. And remember to come down onto the target, and allow for the kick. And this gun throws a little left, so correct for that, too.'

The grey cloud grew more dense and it grew colder as the winter day darkened. They rode back to the house with a feeling of something accomplished; that evening they were very merry over dinner, and when Mary left the table Lennox and Martial did too. They sat by the fire in the drawing-room and talked and laughed like three old friends who had grown up together – as in a sense they had, for they had read the same literature, and there are no closer companions than the dear friends found between the pages of books. Later, Mary played the piano and they all sang. Their voices worked well together, Mary's soprano, Lennox's light tenor, Martial's powerful baritone, three strands weaving together to make a satisfying texture. The fire crackled quietly, and the room glowed like a golden cave where they sheltered, safe from the winds that were blowing death towards them like a great, looming storm.

When Patty was undressing Mary's hair that night, she said, 'Miz Mary, Ah wiz t'inkin'.'

'I always encourage that wherever I find it,' Mary said sleepily. It never mattered what she said to Patty, because the girl understood so little of it, and what she didn't understand she generously ignored.

'Well, ma'am, Ah wiz t'inkin', when Mist' Lincum come here ter set us free, kin Ah keep on bein' yo' maid? Ah lahks takin' keer o' you, Miz Mary. You is kahnd, and you has real purty hair.'

'Thank you, Patty. But what makes you think Mr Lincoln is coming here?'

Her eyes widened. 'Lawd, Miz Mary, ever'body knows dat! Mist'

Lincum, he pormis he gwine come an' free us all, an' he comin' all right, soon as soon! On'y,' she sighed, 'Ah don' want ter go be some other white lady's maid, caws white folks is mos'ly not so kahnd as you, an' Ah lahks it here.'

'You wouldn't have to be anyone's maid if you were free,' Mary said.

Patty looked puzzled. 'But dat all Ah knows to do. You ain' sayin' Ah got ter be a fiel' han'?'

'Of course not, but you could work in a shop, perhaps, or a laundry.'

Patty considered this. 'Ah don' know how ter do dem t'ings. An' where Ah gwine live? Ah cayn stay on ma own, by mase'f. Who gwine safe me form de Yankees, if Ah's all by mase'f?'

Mary suppressed a smile. 'I thought you wanted the Yankees to come? You said they were going to set you free.'

Patty put her hands on her hips in outrage at this wanton stupidity. 'Miz Mary, Ah never sayd dat! It *Mist' Lincum* who gwine set us darkies free!'

'But Mr Lincoln is a Yankee.'

'Nosir, ma'am, he is not!' Patty said indignantly. 'Miz Mary, huccome you say sich a t'ing? Mist' Lincum, he a *good* man! Dem Yankees is awful bad, bad as de debil himse'f, dey say! Ah don' want no Yankees ter come here, no, ma'am!' She looked round nervously, as if they might be creeping up on her already, and shivered.

'Well, Patty, you can certainly stay with me and be my maid,' Mary said reassuringly. 'You're a good girl, and you do my hair very nicely.'

'T'ank you, Miz Mary,' she said with dignity, and, comforted, turned her attention again to Mary's hair. 'Hit bees all right hanyway,' she murmured to herself as her nimble fingers moved amongst the pins. 'Ah guess Mist' Lincum won't let no bad Yankees git us. He'll whup 'em *good*.'

The men came back from Charleston, and the mood was one of euphoria: at this very minute, representatives from South Carolina were taking the news to the leaders of other states, inviting them to emulate her and secede from the Union. Expectation was high that many would follow where she led. A new country was in process of being born, an independent nation, free to make its own laws without the interference of those arrogant, money-grubbing, vulgar Yankees!

Mary's isolation ended. Now there were visitors every day, notes sent back and forth, meetings in the library, guests for dinner.

People talked so late into the night that beds had to be made up for them, and visits of a day turned into two and three days. Mary was amused to see that her father was as steeped in it all as any Southern gentleman. He even began to look like a planter: he'd had a new suit made while he was in Charleston and bought a pair of smart new boots in the Charleston style; his speech had slowed to Southern pace, and had taken on just a hint of an accent.

Matters moved quickly during January. Other cotton states were ready to throw in their lot with South Carolina. 'They know if *we* are forced back into the Union, they need never think of lifting *their* heads again,' Fenwick said.

A date for a first meeting was set for the 4th of February 1861, at Montgomery, Alabama, and as the date approached it was known that five other states would be sending representatives: Georgia, Alabama, Mississippi, Louisiana and Florida. The notable absentee was Virginia: the Old Dominion regarded herself as the cradle of American settlement, and called a 'peace convention' in Washington to try to find a compromise that would allow the cotton states to remain within the Union. South Carolina did not send delegates to that: things had gone too far now for reconciliation.

Meanwhile, South Carolina's Governor Pickens ordered state troops into the abandoned Fort Moultrie, to restore the guns bearing on Fort Sumter, which Major Anderson had left spiked and dismounted. State troops also took over Castle Pinckney, the fort situated on the island that lay between Sumter and Charleston, and the United States Arsenal, capturing twenty-two thousand pieces of ordnance. There were no casualties: both places had been guarded by very small forces of Federal soldiers, who surrendered without a fight and were allowed to return to Washington.

Most people were pleased with this initiative, but Charles did not approve. 'It's an act of war to seize Federal property under force of arms,' he said at dinner one evening. 'I don't see how we can avoid conflict now. Pickens is a fool.'

'Pish and tush!' the Judge said. 'He had no choice, man! When Anderson disabled the guns at Moultrie and cut down the flagpole, that was wanton destruction of public property! Pickens had to order Moultrie to be taken to restore the damage, and took over Castle Pinckney and the Arsenal to prevent the same thing happening there.'

Charles looked scornful. 'You can't really believe that?'

The Judge dropped a solemn wink around the table. 'Don't signify what I believe. Pickens has covered his back. He's got the forts, but if it all goes sour, he's got a legal defence. I don't call those the actions of a fool!'

'I take leave to call them the actions of a poltroon,' Mr Ogles said disgustedly. 'All this shilly-shallying and finding excuses!'

'That's right,' Lawrence said. 'If we're going to have a war, let's get it started, the sooner the better.'

Charles looked at him in undisguised contempt. Mary disliked her father-in-law unremittingly, but she envied him the social licence he had to make his feelings plain. 'What hope do you think South Carolina alone would have in a war against the whole of the North?'

'We aren't going to be alone,' Lawrence said. 'What about the rest of the Southern states? They'll come in with us.'

'Then don't you think you had better wait until you know what strength you have before you start tweaking Northern noses?'

'I don't know about that, Pa,' Eugene put in eagerly. 'What I want is to have a crack at the Yankees, and I don't care when I start. I dare say every man in South Carolina feels the same – eh, Conrad?'

'Eh? What? Oh, yes, of course.' Conrad seemed less than enthusiastic – or perhaps, Mary thought, he was drunk. He had certainly been drinking deeply all through dinner, and he was half slumped in his seat and did not seem to be paying attention. He looked dreadful, Mary thought, his complexion muddy, his eyes poached, his skin slack.

'But you have no army, have you?' Benedict asked. Everyone looked at him as if he'd said something indelicate. 'Presumably the national troops – Federal, I believe you call them? – will belong to the North?'

Everyone looked at the Judge to answer, and he of course obliged.

'We are not quite helpless, sir,' he said with irony which pleased his listeners. 'Every state has its own militia – all male citizens between sixteen and sixty are liable for service. And when the call goes out, I guarantee you every man of them will volunteer – volunteer, mark you! The North will have to rely on bribery and coercion – and I'm sure I don't need to tell a gentleman of education like yourself,' he bowed to Benedict, 'that one volunteer is worth ten pressed men!'

'Hear, hear,' said Mr Ogles, thumping the table.

'I'll tell you what else, sir,' Mr Lawrence said, his voice rising in excitement. 'One Southerner is worth ten Yankees!'

'Which means that one Southern volunteer is worth a hundred Yankee pressed men,' concluded the Judge. Everyone at the table seemed satisfied with this arithmetic, which suited their emotions if not their intellect.

'Well, if you are sure it will come to war,' Benedict said next, 'you had better have some plan for getting Major Anderson out of Sumter.'

'It certainly can't be left in Northern hands,' Charles agreed. 'But an assault would be hard to mount, and costly of lives.'

'Of course we don't know how far Anderson would go to defend it,' Fenwick said. 'If we could pound it hard enough with heavy artillery, he might surrender rather than sacrifice all his men.'

'Perhaps you should consider bombardment from a fortified vessel,' Benedict said.

There was a murmur of interest. 'Have you seen such a thing?' Fenwick asked.

'Oh yes. The French have been experimenting for some years, and I saw one when I was in the Black Sea: a wooden ship, clad all over with iron, and mounting heavy guns. Quite a formidable sight.'

'Yes, I've heard about "ironclads", but I thought they were terribly unseaworthy,' Martial said. 'I read somewhere that they were so unwieldy and slow that conventional ships had no difficulty in keeping out of range.'

'Yes, that is their great drawback, but in this case, however unwieldy the vessel, it would still be more manoeuvrable than Fort Sumter!'

Martial grinned. 'A touch, a very touch.'

Fenwick joined in. 'Do you think we could build one here?'

'I haven't a doubt of it,' Benedict said. 'You've wood in plenty, dockyard space and skilled workers and, as for iron, you make plenty of parts for your railways, I'm sure something could be adapted.'

'It would take years to build such a thing,' Charles said impatiently.

'The kind of vessel I'm thinking about could be built in two or three months. You hardly need to sail it at all, just float it close enough to Sumter for the guns to bear. A floating battery is all you need, a sort of fortress-on-a-raft.'

'And would such a thing be effective?' Martial asked.

'I see no reason why not.'

'Would you come to Charleston and explain the principle to the Governor?' Martial said urgently. 'If it's approved, would you undertake to design it, and show us how to build it?'

Benedict didn't hesitate. 'With pleasure, sir. Whenever you like.'

'There's a good man in Charleston, a Lieutenant John Hamilton,' Martial said. 'Used to be an officer in the Federal navy. He's intelligent – he'll be quick to understand what you want. I think you'd be happy to work with him.'

The men sat long after the ladies had withdrawn, and Mary was growing abominably sleepy and longed for her bed. Eventually they appeared, redolent of segar smoke and still talking as they came through the door.

'You'll need more than good intentions,' Benedict was saying. 'If you are to be a nation independent of the North, you have to acquire some of their skills. You depend on them for so much.'

'Such as factories, ironworks and so on,' Martial said. His eyes met Mary's across the room for an instant; it was like a touch on the shoulder from someone passing behind your chair.

'Just so,' Benedict said. 'To be purchasing every manufactured good from outside the country puts you in a very weak position.'

The Judge looked piqued. 'The South will not be weak, sir, I assure you. We have everything that matters to a gentleman.'

'I do not mean to touch your pride,' Benedict said, 'but, materially, all you have is what you grow in the ground. Food, tobacco and cotton.'

'We are in the right, sir,' the Judge said magnificently, 'and God is on our side. Even Mr Lincoln yields to God.'

Martial shrugged. 'Once you bring God into it, there's no arguing against you,' he said.

CHAPTER SIXTEEN

The first Confederate Congress opened on the 4th of February 1861 at Montgomery, and on the 8th a separate, sovereign, free and independent nation was born: the Confederate States of America. The original six states were joined on the 13th of February by Texas. A temporary Constitution was adopted, and Jefferson Davis of Mississippi was made President – deeply to the disappointment of Mr Rhett, who had wanted the job himself and hinted hard in the *Charleston Mercury* for it.

On the 4th of March President Lincoln made his inaugural speech in Washington, the matter of which was soon being discussed by the South. He promised not to interfere with slavery where it already existed, but said that he would not brook secession. What he would do to stop it was unclear. On the one hand he said, 'In your hands, my dissatisfied fellow-citizens, not mine, is the momentous issue of civil war. You can have no conflict without being yourselves the aggressors.' Yet he swore 'to hold, occupy and possess' the Federal government property which lay in Confederate territory, by which he must have meant principally Fort Sumter. And how was Mr Lincoln to repossess that without being the aggressor and starting the civil war himself? On the whole, the South thought that Lincoln would have to accept the *fait accompli*; but, if he didn't – watch out!

On the 11th of March the permanent Constitution of the Confederacy was adopted. President Davis sent a polite request to President Lincoln for Fort Sumter to be evacuated peacefully, which President Lincoln as politely refused, saying it was Federal property and lawfully occupied.

'How long are we going to tolerate that Yankee flag flying over Sumter?' Eugene demanded irritably one day at breakfast.

The family had come to Charleston for the usual 'season'. Their stay this year would be extended to include Ruthie's fifteenth birthday, an event Charles planned to mark with a grand ball, since Ruth had missed the St Cecilia Ball at which young ladies were customarily presented for the first time to Society. Phoebe and Ruth had left Washington a couple of weeks before the inauguration – which had gone off peacefully after all – and gone back to Alexandria. But with the failure of Virginia's Peace Commission, things in the old colony were growing tense, and Ruth was to be fetched home by Uncle Heck in a few days' time.

'I must say, I hate the sight of that flag as much as the next man,' Fenwick said, 'but I can see President Davis's problem.'

'Can you? Well, I can't!' Eugene said belligerently. 'We've got the whole place ringed with fire. We don't need to wait for the Boomerang to be finished.' He gave a scant bow in Benedict's direction, which Benedict, who was engaged in extracting the bone from a fish and wasn't listening, returned with puzzled politeness. 'If Lincoln won't give Anderson the order to evacuate, let's just blast them out of there!'

Uncle Heck gave a sigh. 'Listen to the boy! Just use your noddle, will you? If Jeff Davis gives the order to fire on a small band of soldiers who've given no provocation, he'll go down in history as a bloodthirsty warmonger – and give Northerners a good cause to fight us for.'

Benedict, attending now, said, 'On the other hand, if Mr Davis does nothing, he admits he's head of a country so weak it allows a foreign power to occupy a fort in the harbour of its most important city.'

Martial said, 'The situation ought to resolve itself before too long. Anderson's running short of food. Even on short rations he'll have to evacuate his men by the middle of April.'

'How do you know that?' Fenwick asked in surprise.

'Because I went over there and asked him.'

There was a mild sensation. Benedict said, 'I suspect this is something to do with General Beauregard. Am I right?'

Martial grinned. 'You know what a fire-eating little devil Peter is. I'm the only thing that keeps his combustibility from blowing us all into the middle of next year.'

General Pierre – 'Peter' – Beauregard was a short, swarthy, dour Creole from New Orleans, where Martial had dined well and drunk deep with him on many occasions. Beauregard was a West Pointer and former US army captain, whose ferocious attachment to States' Rights had hindered his progress up the ladder of promotion. When Louisiana had seceded he had resigned his commission and hastened to Montgomery, where Jefferson Davis had at once made him a brigadier-general. Now Beauregard had been sent to Charleston to organise its defences.

Beauregard was a skilled engineer. Benedict had been introduced to him by Martial as soon as he arrived on the 3rd of March, and Beauregard had seen the value in Benedict; so that from merely working on the floating fortress – which had been dubbed 'The Boomerang' because it was going to fling shot back whence it came – Benedict was now involved in all the defences of the city.

The odd thing was that Major Anderson and General Beauregard were old friends. Anderson had been Beauregard's superintendent at West Point, and both had served with distinction in the Mexican War. But Anderson was from Kentucky, which, though a Southern state, was on the border with the North and had not seceded, and Anderson's loyalties were with the Union.

'I'm surprised Beauregard sent you to treat with Major Anderson,' Benedict said.

'Oh, he didn't,' Martial said. 'Peter's logic says if he has to fire on his old friend for the sake of the South, he'll just have to get on with it, but I thought it would be nice to save him the necessity. So I sent Ratty to hire me a boat, and had myself rowed over there. Poor Anderson,' he mused. 'I never saw a man so haunted. He has no doubt where his loyalties lie, but the idea of firing on fellow Americans fills him with horror. I went there to try to save Peter's feelings, but I came back with Anderson equally on my conscience.'

'So you think there's a chance he may surrender?' asked Pick Manning, who was breakfasting with them, having called early on Martial.

'He's under orders from Washington, so it's not up to him,' Martial said. 'But he hopes that Lincoln may be just as glad to take the excuse of the supplies running out to evacuate him, rather than be the aggressor in a war no-one wants.'

'You speak for yourself!' Eugene said vigorously. 'You may not want to fight the Yankees, but every other man in Charleston does!'

'Don't worry, I'm sure you'll get your war. But if I can do anything to make it later rather than sooner, I will.'

Eugene sneered. 'Scared, Mart? And you a West Pointer! What would your precious Major Lee think?'

'It's a matter of common sense,' Martial replied calmly. 'We need time to get our men recruited, trained and drilled. At the moment we are completely unprepared.'

'The only comfort is that the North is, too,' Manning agreed with him.

'Who needs preparation?' Eugene said. 'What sort of army can the North raise anyhow? A nation of mud-farmers and immigrants ruled by money-mad Yankees! Any rag-tag army they manage to muster will dissolve like mist as soon as it runs into real Southern soldiers, commanded by gentlemen.'

'That doesn't sound like your own oratory,' Uncle Heck said. 'Have you been round at the Ausland house?'

Eugene flushed a little. 'I hear more sense spoken there than I do in this house! The Judge says he undertakes to mop up with his handkerchief all the blood that's likely to be spilled because of secession. My only fear is that it'll all be over before I have a chance to kill me any Yankees.'

After breakfast the men went their various ways, and Mary set off to visit Maybelle, in response to a note sent round first thing asking her to call. The Auslands had come to Charleston at the same time as the Morlands, and had stayed on, despite the Judge's losing the Nightingale Cup to Charles. May's time was approaching, and Mrs Judge preferred to have the facilities of the city available for her first grandson, rather than depend on the plantation mammies.

Mary arrived at the Ausland House to find May alone, sitting in the parlour with the shutters closed. Above her the big palmetto ceiling fan flapped back and forth, pulled by the little four-year-old moppet who had already been assigned as body-slave to Pinckney Jefferson Ausland – the name the Judge and Mrs Judge had bestowed on the child in Maybelle's womb. Judge had wanted Jefferson Pinckney, but Mrs Judge thought it more distinguished the other way around, and had persuaded her husband by dint of gently repeating her opinion every time she saw him until he gave in rather than hear it again. May had not dared to raise the possibility of the child's being a girl.

'Oh, thank you for coming,' May said as Mary was announced by the Ausland butler, Hoccles (a negro corruption of Hercules). 'Hoccles, bring refreshments for me and Mrs Morland.'

'Yasum. Mint tea, was it, Miz Maybelle?'

May shuddered. 'I can't bear that awful, muddy drink. Bring me coffee.'

Hoccles looked stern. 'Miz Maybelle, you knows you hain' spose ter have cawfy. Hit too heatin'. You best tek tea like Missus say you should.' He looked at her drawn brows and said wheedlingly, 'Ah could mek Henglish tea, and preten' hit mint, hif Missus ask me.'

Maybelle agreed to the compromise and Hoccles left. Mary thought she looked very unwell. The baby was only a few weeks off, and it was a stage of pregnancy at which no woman looked her best. May was dressed in a voluminous all-enveloping skirt and caped top, which did not quite conceal the forward jut of the child, and she sat awkwardly, leaning back in her chair and fidgeting uncomfortably from time to time, seeming to be trying to raise her weight off her buttocks and support it with her hands on the chair-seat.

'Are you in pain, May dear?' she asked. 'A horrid sort of needling pain in the place you sit? I had that with Ashley.'

May shook her head. 'It isn't a pain, it's a rash. It's worse when I sit, but standing hurts too much now.' She looked up fleetingly. 'But, please, don't tell anyone. Conrad said it was nothing and I mustn't complain. He'd be so angry if he knew I'd said anything.'

'But you look flushed to me,' Mary said. 'Have you a fever?'

'Oh, it's just the heat. That's why I have Jack to fan me, but he isn't much use. He doesn't fan fast enough.'

'He's only a baby,' Mary said, seeing the little thing pulling on the fan-rope with such effort, his pudgy arms without strength yet for such constant, unremitting work.

May said indifferently, 'He's just lazy. They're all born lazy, Conrad says. That's why God put us in authority over them.'

Mary didn't want to go down this route; May's thoughts had evidently been guided by Conrad and his father. She was more worried about May's health. 'Wouldn't you be more comfortable lying on the sofa?' she asked.

'No, it's worse like that. The rash is down my legs as well, you see.'

'Would you let me look at it?' Mary asked carefully. 'I might be able to send something over. Let me just open the shutter a bit—'

'Oh no, don't,' May said quickly. 'The light makes my headache worse.'

'You have the headache too?'

'It's not bad now, as long as I stay in the dark. It gets worse at night,' May said, and then, catching herself up, 'But it's nothing, really.'

'My love, this isn't right. What does Dr Trevelyan say?'

'Con doesn't want me to bother him about it,' May said in a quick, low voice. She seemed apprehensive. 'I'm all right, Mary. Please don't fuss. And don't say anything to anyone.'

Hoccles came in with the tea, and she abruptly stopped speaking and waited in silence until he had poured and handed it, and gone away again. Mary was surprised at this reserve. Most Southerners spoke exactly the same in front of slaves as when they were alone, treating them as if they were tables or chairs. But when Hoccles had gone, May leaned forward and whispered, 'I'm sure he spies on me, and tells Mrs Judge everything I say. I expect he was standing outside the door for ages before he came in. This tea's quite cold.'

It wasn't, but Mary could see she wasn't rational on this point, and could only hope it was her advanced pregnancy that was unsettling her. It wasn't particularly hot in this shaded parlour, but even in the dim light Mary could see May looked flushed, and that her eyes were a little glassy. But talking about her health only seemed to agitate her, so she said instead, 'Well, then, May, what did you want to talk to me about?'

'Talk to you about?' May asked vaguely.

'You sent me a note asking me to come round this morning.'

May frowned and put her hand to her head, and then her brow cleared and she said, 'I remember now! I wanted to ask you if you will be with me when the time comes. I'm to have the doctor and a midwife, but I'd really like someone of my own to be there.' She met Mary's eyes with naked fear. 'I'm awfully scared.'

'Of course I'll be there, if you'd like it.'

'You'll come as soon as it begins and stay all the time?'

'All the time,' Mary promised.

'Oh, thank you!' May sighed. 'It won't seem so bad if you're with me.'

'It won't be so bad, you know. Thinking about it beforehand is the worst bit. Once you start, there's too much to do to be scared.'

May didn't seem entirely convinced, but with a visible effort to pull herself together, she said, 'Tell me all the news. I haven't seen anyone for days. Have you heard from Ruthie? Is she coming home soon?'

'Yes, on Thursday. Uncle Heck's going to fetch her. I expect she'll want to call on you right away.' May didn't say anything, and by way of a little joke, to lighten her gloom, Mary added, 'One thing, though, you mustn't have your baby on the 11th of April. I don't think Ruthie would forgive you if you took the attention from her on the day of her birthday ball.'

May smiled faintly. 'No, I won't do that,' she said, but Mary wasn't convinced May had heard or understood what she had said.

Ruth came home, and, despite the change that had been evident in her letters, Mary was not prepared for the smart young woman who came through the door. She felt a momentary pang of loss. The new Ruth moved gracefully, with her back straight and her formerly whirlwind elbows close to her sides. The tangle of loose curls was transformed into a neat plaited coil at the nape of the neck, and the front hair was smooth as burnished bronze. Mary would even have sworn that Ruth's eyelashes were longer and her lips fuller and redder.

'I can't get over the change in you. You look every inch a lady,' Mary said. On the day after her arrival, she and Ruth were upstairs together, going over the contents of her trunk.

'Do I?' Ruth seemed pleased with the comment. 'Well, Phoebe taught me such a lot – and it's easier taking an interest in being grown up when the grown-ups around you are interesting.' She caught Mary's eye. 'Oh, I don't mean you! But in Washington everyone has something to do with the Government. In Charleston the men think of nothing but horses and billiards, and the females of nothing but clothes.'

Mary smiled privately, lifting out a gown of slate-blue wool, plain but beautifully cut. 'Your new clothes are quite lovely. This gown is so elegant. It's like nothing you could get here.'

'Phoebe has a mantuamaker in Georgetown who's a real French-woman, from Paris. She makes all Phoebe's clothes. It's all in the cut and the seams, you see,' Ruth added instructively. 'But Phoebe says it's the mark of a lady to see that she's well dressed, and then to ignore the fact. She says it's vulgar to talk about clothes all the time.'

'It certainly makes for dull conversation,' Mary agreed. 'But don't let this new-found sophistication of yours lead you to speak out in men's company. It may be all right for Washington, but it won't do for Charleston.'

'Oh, I wouldn't do that,' Ruth said quickly. 'I couldn't in any case, because I really don't know anything. I felt quite ashamed sometimes when I was in company with Phoebe, to realise how ignorant I am.'

'Men like women to be ignorant. Is this your blue muslin? What a strange colour it's gone.'

'I spilled raspberry shrub on it, so Phoebe tried to dye it for me, but the dye wouldn't take. But, Mary, it can't be *right* to be ignorant, can it? I mean, I've hardly ever read a book in my life, and I don't know anything about Europe except what Lennox has told me. Everyone in Washington talks about England and France as if they were right next door!'

This was a delicate subject. 'No, I don't think it is right for any person to be ignorant, if they can help it. And if I ruled the world, I would see to it that everyone was taught to read and write, and was put in the way of as much education as possible.'

'Even slaves?'

'Yes, everybody. But, darling, I *don't* rule the world, and neither do you. We have to get along with what there is.'

'Even if that means pretending to be ignorant, as you do?'

Mary was wrong-footed. 'What makes you say that?'

'I've seen you bite your tongue when someone says something stupid – not that I knew it was stupid, but I could see that *you* did.'

'Then it was very wrong of me, and I must endeavour to do better,' Mary said sternly. 'I should have better control.'

'Oh, it's only me that notices,' Ruth assured her affectionately, 'because I always look at you, and I know you very well. No-one else sees – except maybe Mart, because he thinks like you. And I've seen him look the same way when Judge Ausland is habber-gabbering away about something he knows nothing about!'

'Martial is a man and may do as he likes. You and I, love, may not. When we marry, we make a vow to respect and obey our husbands, and that means not disputing with them.'

Ruth took up a little scarlet jacket and inspected it. 'I wore this ice-skating on the canal ponds last winter with Mart and Mr Manning. I can't think what this spot can be. Yes, I do know about not disputing, and I wouldn't. But it will be much easier to be good if I marry someone clever and book-learned, like you and Lennox. Where is he, by the way? I thought for sure he'd be here when I came home.'

'He's at Twelvetrees. I'm sure he'd have liked to be here, but he has his work to do.'

'Are we going back to Twelvetrees before the birthday ball?'

'I don't think there are any plans for it. I must stay here in any case, until May's baby is born – it could come any time now – and the men won't want to go when everything on the political scene is so exciting.'

'I suppose you mean the war?' Ruth said impatiently. 'But there isn't going to be any old war. Mr Canfield says Mr Lincoln has friends in Charleston who send him reports, so he knows exactly what people here are thinking. So he knows that the South won't come back into the Union, no matter what, and there's no point in him making a fuss. Mr Canfield says Mr Lincoln doesn't want to go down in history as the man who started a civil war; so, you see, nothing's going to happen.'

'I hope you're right,' Mary said. But she thought of fiery 'Peter' Beauregard, of the defences her father had been helping to build, of the Floating Fortress, of the bloodthirsty young men like Eugene longing to 'kill them some Yankees' – and she wondered if everything hadn't gone too far now.

There was a tap at the door. It was Aunt Belle's little servant Jippy, who went everywhere with her to run messages. She came to say there was a visitor downstairs for Miss Ruthie.

Ruth said, 'For me? Who is it, Jip?'

'Hit Mist' Mart's fren' Mist' Manning. He settin' wid Miz Belle in de parlour, but he axed for you pertickler, so Miz Belle says t' fitch you down.'

'Very well, go and say I'm coming,' Ruth said. When Jippy had gone, she went over to the glass, smoothed her hair, pinched up her cheeks and bit her lips to make them redder.

Mary watched her in amusement. 'I didn't know Patrick Manning was such a particular friend.'

Ruth smoothed her dress at the waist and answered with elaborate nonchalance. 'I'm sure I mentioned in a letter that he came with Mart to visit Mr Lee. After that he stayed in Alexandria for about a fortnight, and we saw him every day.'

'It's prodigiously civil of him to call on your first day back. Is he an admirer of yours?'

'Oh, Mary! How could he be an admirer? He's so old!'

'He's the same age as Martial. They were at school together.'

'He's a year older than Mart. And what do you call thirty, if it's not old?' Ruth said, hurrying to the door.

'I thought you'd grown up,' Mary laughed, 'but you're just the same inside!'

'I told you so,' Ruth said. But, all the same, Mary could see it wasn't true. The fact was that the inheritance of Ruth's blood had caught up with her. The wild Scottish and stubborn Yorkshire streaks had been subdued by her Southern half; she was Emily Fenwick's daughter in more than looks.

On the 8th of April Governor Pickens was handed a message from President Lincoln. Martial brought a copy home.

'I am directed to notify you to expect an attempt will be made to supply Fort Sumter with provisions only; and that, if such an attempt be not resisted, no effort to throw in men, arms or ammunition will be made without further notice, or in case of an attack upon the fort.'

'You have to call him clever,' Martial said. 'You see how ambiguous the wording is?'

'It seems plain enough to me,' Fenwick frowned.

'That's the beauty of it,' Martial said. 'Everyone will read it his own way, and think it can only mean one thing.'

'It says that if we prevent them from supplying the fort, they will do so by force,' Fenwick said. 'What's ambiguous about that? It's a clear threat to our sovereignty.'

'But a Northerner reading it in his morning paper in New York or Boston will see a request to take food to starving men, while avoiding force if at all possible. What reasonable man could object to that?'

'You needn't sound as if you admired him so,' Fenwick said crossly.

'Do you think it's just a hum?' Mary asked.

'It's no empty threat. A large naval expedition left New York two days ago,' Martial said.

'How do you know that?'

'My dear Mrs Fenwick,' Martial laughed, 'how can there be any secrets in a situation like this? Half the populations of Washington and Charleston are related, and write to each other regularly. But this news puts President Davis in the deuce of a spot,' he added seriously. 'Our one hope lay in starving Anderson out. Now we can't prevent Sumter being relieved except by firing the first shot.'

'How long will it take the ships to get here?' Mary asked.

'Three, four, five days. Who knows?' Martial shrugged.

'I'm thinking of Ruthie's ball on Thursday. Will we have to cancel it?'

'I should say not,' Fenwick said robustly. 'We aren't a pack of children to be frightened by empty Yankee threats.'

'Oh, I agree,' Martial said. 'Besides, judging by the number of young men who've been calling here daily ever since Ruth came home, we should be the most unpopular family in South Carolina if we cancelled.'

Fenwick laughed. 'Young men calling? What nonsense!'

Martial looked grave. 'My dear fellow, you obviously don't know what's going on in your own house. I tell you I can't sit down quietly to read the paper without being interrupted by some love-sick, spaniel-eyed booby being shown in with a wilted posy clenched in his hot fist.'

'The only young man I've seen is Beau Raven,' Fenwick said, 'and he only came to accompany his sister, who's a particular friend of Ruth's.'

Martial rolled his eyes at Mary. 'The man's such a simpleton, how ever did he manage to propose to you? Adeline Raven was Beau's ticket of entry,' he explained to Fenwick kindly. 'Ruth's never cared a jot for her. In fact, until she was taken in hand by Cousin Phoebe, Ruth never cared a jot for anyone with less than four legs. I must say, Phoebe's done wonders,' he added approvingly.

'And about time, too,' Fenwick said. 'Pa's anxious to get her married.'

'She's only fifteen,' Mary protested.

'You were only fourteen when you fell in love with me,' Fenwick pointed out. 'But I hope you're right about Beau Raven,' he added.

'He's just the kind of young man I'd like to see Ruthie marry: an eldest son with a good property. And he's a gentleman: a fine shot and a fine horseman.' He caught Mary's eyes on him and went on hastily, 'He's handsome and charming, too, if you care about that sort of thing. All the girls rave about him.'

'He seems a very nice sort of young man,' Mary allowed. 'I just don't see why Ruth has to be hurried into marriage so young.'

'Best thing for her,' Martial said. She looked at him in slight surprise, and read a complexity of messages in his eyes. 'The way things are,' he added, gesturing with the paper in his hand, 'better she has a husband as soon as possible.'

The ball-room was a separate building, to the side of the Morland House. It was on two storeys, the lower floor containing a supper-room and kitchen, with an enormous entrance hall and grand staircase in the middle. The ball-room itself was on the upper floor, flanked at either end by ante-rooms for cards and sitting-out.

Aunt Belle was in a frenzy of preparation. She was determined that Ruth's ball would be better than Kitten Ausland's last year; so good, in fact, that Mrs Judge would not be able to top it when she came to hold Clara's ball in the autumn. The ante-rooms were decorated with shrubs in huge pots, the floor french-chalked just so, the rout-chairs regilded, the chandeliers washed until they sparkled like diamond. There was to be champagne and iced fruit punch, a magnificent cold supper, and hot soup when the ball ended. The best orchestra in Charleston had been booked: they were free blacks, which Aunt Belle did not approve of, convinced that all free blacks were bent on corrupting slaves and starting rebellions, but they were the best, so she had to have them.

Too many females were death to a ball, so Belle invited every eligible young man of their acquaintance: Clay and Drew Fairfax, Quin and Fontaine Lawrence, Bob Trent, Beau Raven, two Ratliffe boys, three Ogles, two Mileses, Pick Manning, Jack Preston, John Green – every unmarried gentleman's son within reach received his card.

Ruthie's ball-gown had already been made by Cousin Phoebe's French mantuamaker – and all the better for it, Mary thought, for if she had gone to anyone in Charleston she would have ended up with something pink covered in frills. But Madame Moltessier had taken one look at Ruth's copper-beech hair and said firmly, '*Il faut être jaune pour une telle p'tite renarde!*' And yellow it was, a creamy yellow silk taffeta, embroidered round the hem four inches deep with white silk thread and seed pearls. The bertha was of ruched spider muslin so delicate that Ruth's shoulders and neck seemed wreathed in mist, and Cousin Phoebe had forwarded Madame Moltessier's detailed instructions on how to dress 'la tête de mademoiselle', as she grandly put it. Mary had spent some urgent hours poring over these with Patty to determine if they could manage the required effect between them. It was of no use to consult Frank, who had come back from Alexandria worse than she went, so above herself after her sojourn in the capital city that she would do nothing but lounge about and regale the other slaves with improbable stories of her experiences there.

'You're going to look beautiful,' Mary said to Ruth. Lennox, who arrived on the Wednesday from Twelvetrees, evidently thought she did so already. He came cheerfully into the morning-room where they were entertaining visitors, and then was struck dumb for a telling instant at the sight of Ruth, with her newly grown-up figure and smooth hair. Ruth's face broke into her old grin at the sight of him, and Lennox bowed over her hand with a nicely judged mixture of admiration and self-mockery. Mary couldn't help thinking how handsome Lennox looked, even ruffled and dusty from his journey. In the year since his arrival he had grown two inches taller, and had filled out in the shoulders and chest while keeping his gracefully slim flanks and elegant legs. He was such a contrast to Eugene that she thought again what a thousand pities it was that he hadn't Eugene's name and fortune.

On the morning of the ball, when preparations were well in hand, Eugene came running into the parlour, where Aunt Belle, Mary, Ruth, Aunt Missy and cousin Celia were busy making posies and buttonholes.

'Here's a go!' he cried in great excitement. 'Why are you all sitting there? Haven't you heard the news?'

'What news?' Aunt Belle frowned. 'Don't shout, dear.'

'What news? We are invaded, that's all!' Eugene cried.

Aunt Belle dropped the scissors with a clatter and clutched her hands to her chest with a little shriek. 'The Yankees are here!'

'Eugene, stop romancing and tell us what's happened,' Mary said sharply.

'There are six Yankee ships outside the harbour bar,' Eugene said. 'No romance about it. Six men-o'-war from New York, bristling with guns, and you know what that means: the war has started!'

'Wait, wait!' Aunt Missy cried as he began to turn away, evidently longing to spread his news to a wider audience. 'Who told you this? It could be all a hum.'

Eugene paused to say self-importantly, 'I met Governor Manning on his way from headquarters and he told me so himself. His son's an aide-de-camp to General Beauregard, so that proves it, if you like.' And he skidded away out of the room, more like an excited nine-year-old than a man of twenty-six.

The women looked at each other. Aunt Belle's lips were white and she was swaying gently in her seat, having no doubt of anything Eugene told her.

'Ex-Governor Manning ought to know,' Aunt Missy said to Mary.

'But Eugene might have misunderstood. You know what he's like,' Mary replied.

They were not left long in doubt. Uncle Hemp was the next arrival, his agitation revealed by his coming in against all custom with his pipe still lit and in his mouth. 'Have you ladies heard the news? The Yankee fleet has arrived.'

'So it's true?' Aunt Missy said. 'Then the war has begun?'

'Oh, I don't want to alarm you. They can't get the warships across the bar. I met Mr Benedict Morland down at the White Point and he says Jack Hamilton assured him the bar is a very effective defence. In any case, they've come to relieve Sumter, that's all, not fire on the city.'

But other visitors were less reassuring. Mrs Means and old Mrs Wigfall believed that a full-scale invasion was on its way. Aunt Belle jumped up, her cheeks ashy. 'Civil war with all its horrors is upon us!' she cried, and went over to clutch Ruth's unwilling head to her camphor-scented bosom. 'Oh, you poor child! On this day of all days! Your ball ruined, the lives of all the young men in jeopardy! What future is there now for any of us?'

Ruth paled, and Cecilia burst into tears. 'Oh, do stop it, Belle,' Aunt Missy said crossly. 'There's no call for such talk.'

'Bunch of ninnies!' Aunt Nora said inclusively.

'But civil war turns men into beasts,' Aunt Belle said with interested horror. 'All decency flies out of the window.'

'And that's not all,' Mrs Wigfall capped her. 'We must expect servile insurrection too. It'll follow like night follows day. With the Yankees in front and the slaves to the rear, we shall all be slaughtered.'

'Or worse,' Mrs Means added cryptically.

'Servile insurrection? Better we had all died yesterday, than live to see this day,' Aunt Belle cried.

They all instinctively turned to look at Jippy, who was sitting on a footstool by the fireplace, Belle's basket of keys in her lap, her hair in numerous short plaits sticking out round her head like a child's drawing of the rays of the sun. Finding all the white folks looking at her, she stood up hastily and tried to smile placatingly. At eight years old, her smile was largely formed of spaces, with growing teeth like half-drawn blinds in some of the gaps. She obviously had no idea what anyone had been saying, or why they were all looking at her like that, but they sho' was scarin' her plenty!

'I think perhaps we should rein in our imaginations for the moment, don't you?' Aunt Missy said sarcastically.

'Is there any point in going on with this?' Ruth asked with a catch in her voice, putting down the half-made posy in her hand. 'The ball will be cancelled for sure.'

'I think we should just carry on as usual until we know something definite,' Mary said. 'We must all keep calm, for the servants' sake.'

'Don't presume to give orders in this house,' Aunt Belle snapped.

'Hush, Belle!' Aunt Missy warned. 'Mary's right. Let's go on with what we were doing.'

Charles and Fenwick were the next arrivals. Fenwick was in gleeful mood. 'The Assyrian crept down like a wolf on the fold!' he cried. 'Unfortunately for the Assyrian, the sheep turned out to be wolves in sheep's clothing!'

'Oh, don't talk nonsense at a time like this,' Aunt Belle rebuked him. 'Charles, what is happening?'

'Beauregard and Governor Pickens are having a council of war,' Charles said. 'Unless Anderson can be induced to surrender, I don't doubt they will decide to reduce Sumter by fire. Then I suppose the men-o'-war will fire on our fortifications, and we will fire back on them.'

Aunt Belle waved away all this irrelevant information. 'I mean, is our ball to be cancelled?'

Charles raised both eyebrows. 'Good God, no! The negotiations will take hours. Nothing will happen today.'

Fenwick said, 'Everyone will be in a fine mood for a party tonight. I've never seen so many excited young men.'

Charles gave a cynical smile. 'And everyone knows that, on the eve of war, men propose marriage more readily than at any other time. We shall be the object of gratitude to every Charlestonian family with an unwed daughter of dancing age.'

Fenwick laughed and said to Mary, 'The Duchess of Richmond's ball all over again!'

Mary smiled dutifully, but she hoped he had not said something prophetic. Most of the young men who danced and proposed at the Duchess of Richmond's ball before Waterloo did not live to fulfil their engagements.

All day visitors came and went, interrupting the preparations. Some came to tell news, others to ask it; all speculated on what the future held. There were letters and messengers asking if the ball was to be cancelled, and at every enquiry Aunt Belle's reply grew firmer, until by mid-afternoon she was snapping, 'Of course not! Why ever should it be?' almost before the question was out.

The streets of the city were unusually alive, with soldiers everywhere, Charleston Zouaves marching smartly, scratch companies straggling along, singing and grinning and waving to passers-by. Carts of ammunition rattled horribly over the cobbles, cannon dashed by drawn by teams of horses, with artillery cadets clutching their caps as they bounced on the carriage-tail. Young men in civilian clothes, hastily transformed by a sash and sword, clattered by on horseback with messages from headquarters. The harbour was thick with boats, some transporting volunteers to the various batteries, others full of sightseers, pointing and waving their hats. Mr Lawrence, dropping in briefly, summed up the male view when he said, 'I'm sick of all this talk. Why don't we just open fire on Sumter? Let the war begin!'

Later in the afternoon Martial came in, just as Mary was about to go upstairs. 'Have you seen my father?' she asked him. 'He hasn't been here all day.'

'That's partly why I came. The Boomerang's been towed over to Sullivan's Island. There's been a lot of talk that it might capsize under the recoil of the guns, so they've decided to ground it. Your father sends his regrets, but he wants to stay and see the work finished. He doubts he'll be able to return before the ball begins.'

'I see,' she said. 'Martial, do you know what's happening?'

'Out there? Yes. Colonel Chesnut and I went over to Sumter this afternoon, with a message from Beauregard.'

'A request for surrender?'

'Of course. The terms were generous, but Anderson's unpersuadable. "His honour and his obligations prevented compliance," he said.' Martial sighed. 'Stubborn fool! He looked ill – any age – drawn and fatigued. I'm afraid this business will be the finish of him, poor devil.'

'Stubborn fool or poor devil, which?'

'Both. They're in a poor way in Sumter, you know. Since we stopped sending in fresh food back in January, they've had nothing to eat but salt pork and biscuit. They're short of firewood, too, which means they have to eat the pork barely warmed – and salt pork in the barrel is all but inedible unless it's boiled good and long.'

'But still Anderson won't surrender?'

'All he asked was to be warned before we opened fire. But then, just as we were leaving, he said, "I shall await the first shot, gentlemen, and if you do not batter us to pieces, we shall be starved out in a few days."'

She frowned. 'Surely if he were starved out, that would not impugn his honour?'

'Yes, precisely,' he said, appreciating her quickness. 'So now Beauregard's sent me back to Sumter to ask when that's likely to happen. But I fear it's just another delaying tactic – and, frankly, Peter is getting frisky. The old warhorse is impatient to be smelling gunpowder again. However, back I must go; so I came to tell you that I may be a late arrival at your ball.'

'I didn't think you would be able to come at all.'

'Oh, I shall come by hook or crook, even if I can't stay long,' he promised. 'I wouldn't miss Ruth's début for a "passel of damn Yankees".'

CHAPTER SEVENTEEN

Mary and Patty dressed Ruth between them, beginning from scratch. Chemise first – good plain cotton, with just a little scrap of eyelet lace about the neck – and drawers, and then Patty knelt down to roll on the white woollen stockings and fasten them with garters.

'Miz Ruthie, she got legs lahk a hoss – straight up and straight down agin,' Patty complained. 'She got no bumps to hol' she's stockin's up.'

'Tie the garters tighter,' Ruth instructed tersely.

'Ef Ah ties 'em tighter'n dis, yo' feet gwine go tuh sleep,' Patty warned. 'Huccome you got no bumps, when you bin runnin' aroun' an' climbin' trees all yo' lahf?'

Next came the corset, and Patty didn't need any urging to lace that up tight: she knew what was demanded of a young lady's waist. Then came the under-petticoat, and then Mary and Patty together, one on either side, lifted the enormously wide hoop-skirt over Ruth's head. Another petticoat went on top, to keep the lines of the hoop from showing through; then at last the gown itself. They lifted it on over the hoops and Patty hooked up the back while Mary smoothed the wrinkles out, settled the skirt and tweaked the bertha into place.

Frank had been pottering about all this while, more of a nuisance than a help, since she dropped anything she was asked to hold, and was usually found to have mislaid or even sat on whatever Mary or Patty were urgently seeking. But when Ruth finally stood before the long glass to see the result of their labours, Frank came into her own. She clasped her hands beneath her chin in genuine rapture and cried in a voice of absolute sincerity, 'Oh, Miz Ruthie, you is jus' the handsomes' creetur in the worl'!'

Mary met Ruth's eyes in the glass. 'Don't look so scared,' she said. 'You're going to have a wonderful ball.'

'I'd sooner be at Twelvetrees, going out night fishing with Knox Fairfax and Johnny Lawrence,' Ruth said.

But Mary shook her head, smiling. 'Your romping days are over, love.' And she saw that Ruth knew it too.

By the time the ball began, everyone in Charleston had heard about Anderson's refusal to surrender, and everyone believed that tomorrow the war would begin at last. Even for those who dreaded it, there was a sense of relief that the waiting was over; but for most there was an exhilaration and anticipation that raised their spirits better than wine. The men were wild with excitement: their enjoyment of everything was intense, their conversation audacious, their wit lively. There was an unspoken feeling that this would be the last party of peacetime, and the Morlands were credited, in a woolly-minded way, with having hit on the very thing everyone in Charleston wanted, a chance to reaffirm their identity by doing what Southerners did best: enjoy themselves. The champagne was hardly needed: everyone was drunk on patriotism and war fever. All the young men wanted to dance – even plain girls would not sit down much tonight.

Mary was glad to see Ruth so much approved. The general opinion seemed to be that the youngest Morland girl had turned out surprisingly well. Mary thought Ruth looked a little dazed, which did her no discredit. No-one could accuse her of being wild tonight, or bold, or hoydenish. She smiled gently, danced gracefully, and received the attentions of the over-excited boys with modesty.

Charles, standing beside Mary for a moment, said, 'She looks better than I ever thought she would. Phoebe Canfield has done wonders with her.' Ruth danced by in the arms of Beau Raven, and Charles watched them with cool, calculating eyes, as if assessing the worth of Beau's inheritance against Ruth's new beauty.

'She looks happy,' Mary ventured.

Charles looked at her and raised an eyebrow, as if she had said something irrational, and walked off.

Martial appeared beside her. 'Will you dance, Mrs Morland?'

'I'm a chaperone,' she said. 'I don't think your uncle would approve.'

'Didn't you see how I waited for him to go? He's in the card-room, so we're safe for the next rubber at least.' She still hesitated, and he said with a mocking smile, 'The condemned man is always granted one last request.'

Under the smile he looked tired. His hair was damp and there was a smell of salt about him. 'You saw Anderson? What did he say?' she asked.

'He said he would be forced to evacuate the fort on the fifteenth, but then he spoiled it by adding "unless he received other orders, or fresh supplies". So Beauregard decided it was just delaying tactics. He's sent Chesnut back with a final ultimatum. When I came in just now, there were blue lights hoisted over Sumter – Anderson communicating with the Federal fleet, no doubt. I don't suppose they will tell him to surrender. Lincoln wants us to fire the first shot.'

'And will we?'

He looked down at her. 'No more war talk. I have come to fulfil my promise that I wouldn't miss Ruthie's ball, and my tired soul demands the succour of a dance with you. You can't refuse me, you know. Tonight all men are heroes, and heroes must be indulged.'

'One dance,' she said, placing her hand in his. 'I don't suppose anyone will object.'

'No, why would they?' he said, and led her onto the crowded floor. A little way off Ruth was dancing with Pick Manning; the two men looked at each other across their partners' shoulders and exchanged a silent message.

Manning had stolen an extra dance with Ruth: the partner on her dance-card had not appeared to claim her and he had given the absentee no more than a second's grace before whisking her away onto the crowded floor.

'Any man who could keep you waiting doesn't deserve to dance with you at all,' he said. 'What was the creature's name?'

'Tradd Ogles,' said Ruth. 'But I haven't seen him for hours, and I don't care if I never see him again,' she added with some of her old vehemence. 'I've danced with him once tonight, and he breathes through his mouth and blows my hair about.'

'I think I saw him go out with Jack Preston and Willie Alston.'

'Out?'

'To volunteer for the batteries. Shocking behaviour at a ball, but they were pretty drunk by the look of it. And I fear tonight is not a night that will be distinguished by conventional behaviour.'

'I think you're right,' Ruth said. 'There seem to be far more people here than we invited.'

He smiled. 'The Morland ball has rather become public property.'

Ruth remembered all the flushed, laughing, braggart young men who had held her disagreeably tightly and regaled her with unlikely tales of what they were going to do to the Yankees, plainly more interested in themselves than her. Only Beaufain Raven had talked nicely to her, but Beau was a real gentleman. 'I don't think it's what my father intended,' she said.

Manning looked down at her, thinking how beautiful she was in her lovely creamy-yellow gown, with her burnished hair and pale skin and her long neck like a flower stem. 'Would it offend you if I were to tell you how lovely you look?' he asked.

She looked up in surprise. 'Why should it offend me?'

'Don't you remember when we were skating together on the ponds, you told me you had always wanted to be a boy?'

She blushed. 'You shouldn't recall everything a person says.'

'Most ungentlemanly of me to pay attention when you speak to me, I agree,' he said gravely. 'I apologise. But in the interests of truth I have to say that it would have been a great loss to the world if you had been a boy.'

'Oh,' she said, confused by the warmth in his voice. Then, shyly, 'Do you really think I look nice?'

'Nice? What a word!' he exclaimed. 'You look as I always imagined the Queen of the Iceni would look.'

Ruth had no idea who that was, but it was evidently a compliment. 'You do talk like Martial sometimes,' she said.

'I'll take that for approval,' he said. He said nothing more, and they revolved in happy silence, with Ruth thinking how pleasant it was sometimes to be with someone who didn't have to talk all the time.

After midnight, the dancing grew wilder. The musicians sawed away like men possessed, slapping their feet against the podium to drive themselves on, and the young men swung their partners round at dizzy speed. Not all were dancing: there was a little ferment of youths always hanging around the door, individuals slipping out to see if there was any more news, and coming back with another snippet about troop movements or signals or mysterious lights on the islands.

Then during a pause in the music young Robert Withers, hot-foot from the Battery, brought the news that the final ultimatum to Anderson had been delivered, and that if he did not surrender by half-past four, the bombardment of Fort Sumter would begin.

'That's less than an hour from now!' somebody discovered; and that was the end of the ball. There could be no more thought of dancing with such a prospect of action, and would-be heroes afraid they would miss their chance of glory could not be persuaded to stay for hot soup. There were hasty farewells, with perhaps more kissing than was usually allowed on these occasions, and then the young element was gone, rushing out into the night to find someone to volunteer to. Of the men of middling age, the men of authority, most had gone long before to their posts of duty; the rest now walked hastily off, leaving only the old men and the women, who hurried to find shawls or cloaks and to get up onto the leads to see the fun.

The Morland House had a space all the way round the roof behind the balustrade which was as broad and flat as a promenade. In the darkness, with that stout stone barrier before her, Mary had no sensation of being three storeys high. The air was cold, but not penetrating, and the night was anything but still. Carts rumbled past down on the cobbles, with a noise like distant thunder, mingling with shouts and the tramp of feet. Mary looked out towards the invisible water of the harbour and thought that all her menfolk were out there somewhere. Up here were just women and slaves, and one or two old fellows who had simply walked in off the street and come up for a better view. It was a night when no-one would wait for an invitation.

The church clock she had been listening to subconsciously began gathering itself to strike the half, but while it was still clearing its throat a cannon roared out, so suddenly that several people shrieked, and Mary jumped violently and bit her tongue. Then there was a lesser boom, and a bright flash in the sky which seemed to throw out fat sparks with long tails in all directions. It was a shell bursting.

'Too high,' said an old man's voice in the darkness near her.

Another voice answered, 'That's just the signal. You wait.'

And immediately another cannon boomed, and another, and soon there was the continuous sound of firing from all around the bay. Mary found Frank beside her, quivering with fear or excitement. She shrieked at every boom, but never took her eyes off the scene, unlike other slaves who were huddled on the ground with their arms over their heads. The noise of the bombardment made it difficult to think, and when Mary noticed in a bemused sort of way that Frank was wearing the embroidered cashmere shawl she herself had given to Ruth as a birthday present, she was unable to make any sense of the fact.

Fort Sumter was being fired on from all directions. The cannons' roar was intolerable; the sound seemed to drive the air from your lungs and the blood from your head; it made the house shake. How did the men bear it out there? Shells shrieked across the dark bay and exploded, sometimes revealing a glimpse of something, the edge of a building or a gleam of water, in the brief glare of their explosion. The smell of the smoke began to drift back to them and soon all that was illuminated was the edge of a cloud. Every cloud has a gold-red lining, Mary thought to herself, as though it meant something. The violence of the scene made her tremble. Noise, destruction, death: who was dying out there, blown to shreds by those screaming black demons? She thought of her father on the Boomerang; Fenwick out at Cummings Point; Eugene manning a gun, she didn't know where; all the gay dancers from the Duchess of Richmond's ball. She thought of Martial rowing about somewhere in a frail little boat, exposed and vulnerable in all the shot and shell.

'They're wasting ammunition,' said the old man who had spoken before. 'Why don't they wait until daylight?'

'You see Anderson ain't firing back,' the other agreed. 'Got more sense'n to waste his shells in the dark.'

Ruth was suddenly beside Mary, surprisingly calm. 'It's almost like fireworks,' she said. 'But the noise is terrible.'

'Aren't you afraid?' Mary asked.

'No. Are you?' She looked at Mary, her white face just distinguishable. 'They're not firing at *us*.' A little later she said, 'What an ending to my birthday ball! No-one will ever forget it.'

Let them live not to forget it, Mary thought. Oh God, keep them all safe! But not all her men were out there. Here was Lennox, coming up behind her, between her and Ruthie.

'It's getting light,' he said.

Yes, it was, Mary realised. The edge of the balustrade was visible, and the orange flashes were ringed with black fragments of exploding shells. Gradually the scene faded into visibility. The sky grew pale and the buildings solid, and now Mary could see that every rooftop was crowded with little grey figures, wide-skirted women and tall-hatted men, all looking out across the bay towards Sumter. It was a still morning, and the water was like pewter-coloured silk, with one faint streak of yellow, the reflection of the approaching dawn.

'It isn't so bad when you can see what's going on,' Ruth said.

Mary shivered, and Lennox, standing between them, put his arm round her shoulders; then, hesitantly, round Ruth's as well. A little black puff appeared above the fort, a sudden exclamation mark in the sky, followed a breath later by a flat smack of an explosion.

'Anderson's firing back,' Lennox said.

Mary was called to the Ausland House in King Street in the early hours of Saturday. She had been dozing fitfully when Patty came to wake her with the message. After a whole day of continuous bombardment, Sumter had ceased firing at nightfall on Friday. The Confederacy had also reduced fire for the hours of darkness, but still it was hard to sleep for the noise. Indeed, in some ways the intermittent fire was worse than the continuous: in the brief periods of quiet, nerves were a-jump wondering when the next shattering crash would come.

The air was cool when Mary stepped out onto the sidewalk,

with Patty dithering along beside her carrying the basket; cool, but smelling faintly of smoke, which made Mary think for a moment of autumns at home, in England. An instant of painful homesickness came and went. Patty shivered, but Mary understood that it was not with cold, but apprehension. She disliked the dark, disliked being out of doors in it, and was not eager to have to help with 'birthin' Miz May'. All in all, she was as jumpy as a sprat in a frying-pan, Mary thought, and she was not surprised when a moment later Patty grabbed her arm with a painful grip and a gasp of terror.

'Whut dat, Miz Mary? Whut dat comin'? Lawd, it de Yankees!'

A muffled figure was coming towards them, billowing in the darkness, seeming to reel like a drunkard. But as it came closer, Mary saw that it was just a man in a cloak who was skewing his head round as he walked to look for the flash of the latest cannon shot. And she knew that hat.

'It's Eugene,' she said, unclamping Patty's hand. 'Gene! What are you doing here?'

He stopped before her, not seeming surprised to see her. 'There was a boat coming back with messages for Old Borey.' This was what the men called Beauregard. 'So I took the chance to slip home while it's quiet. I can be back before daybreak. I need a bath and a change of coat,' he said. 'Look here!' He flung back his cloak with a laugh, to reveal his coat torn and singed all down the front and the left sleeve.

'Good God, are you hurt?' Mary said in alarm.

'Not a bit!' he said cheerfully, fingering the damage with some pride. 'A shell fragment whizzed past me but my coat took it all. A damn' shame – it's one I was fond of. It's been hot work over at Moultrie, I can tell you!'

'Is that where you've been? I didn't know.'

He stepped closer, and said confidentially, 'Yes, and d'you know, I wasn't a bit afraid! Of course, I was sure I shouldn't mind it really, but it's a thing you can't know beforehand, how you'll be under fire. But we were all as cool as could be! Some of the fellows were even making jokes about it. We have cotton-bag bomb-proofs, you know, and when a shot knocked them about right under Beau Raven's nose, he shouted out, "Cotton's falling, lads!" which made us all laugh. And then another shot knocked down the kitchen chimney and loaves of bread flew out, and Clay Fairfax shouted, "Yes, and wheat is rising!"' He chuckled. 'They are grand fellows! I don't know when I've had better fun.'

Mary was astonished at the change in him. Gone was the sneering, world-weary, conscious reprobate: he sounded like a normal, happy, high-spirited young man. Just for a moment, she almost liked him.

Eugene suddenly recollected where he was, and peering into her face, said, 'Where are you off to at this hour of the night? Is something up?'

'I'm going to the Ausland House. I had a message that May was in labour and asking for me.'

'Oh,' he said, his interest failing. Babies could not compete with cannonades and the newly discovered delights of comradeship under arms with a bunch of 'grand fellows'. 'Well, you'd better cut along, then.' He nodded dismissal, and went past her towards the house; then he thought of something else, and chuckled again in the darkness. 'I say, old Conrad will curse himself for going away when he realises he's missed all the fun!'

'Gone away? Where has he gone?' Mary asked, but Eugene didn't answer, had already been consumed by the shadows.

When they reached King Street, there were lights behind shutters in several windows of the Ausland House, and a lantern swinging gently in the front porch. Mary was met in the hall and escorted upstairs by the Auslands' mammy, a vast, shapeless woman more than a yard wide, who boosted herself up by the handrail, trying to spare her tortured feet, victims of a lifetime of obesity and tight shoes. They were now so misshapen that they had to be housed in list-slippers of brown felt, and resembled bags of potatoes flapping below her swollen ankles.

She gasped out the news between breaths as she heaved herself higher up the house, the human spirit defying the force of gravity.

'Miz Maybelle, she done go into labour fo', five hours ago, but de baby, hit don't mean to come yet awhile. Doctuh Trevylan he say dat baby hain gwine come fo' daylight, but Miz Maybelle bellering pow'ful hard fo' Miz Mary, an' Missus say she cayn stan' de noise no mo', de guns is bad 'nuff widout dat, so she up an' sen' for you ter quiet her.'

'Is Miss Margaret with Miss Maybelle?'

'No, ma'am.' Mammy Ausland paused on the half-landing to catch her breath and explained with the air of one enjoying a crisis. 'Miz Margaret done go back ter Cam'lot wid de chillun yes'day. It wuz 'tween her an' Missus ter take 'em, but dem chillun all gits sick in a cah'age, an' Missus say she sooner face Marse Anderson's guns dan sit 'n watch 'em th'oin' up.'

Mary frowned. 'And I understand Mr Conrad isn't at home?'

'No, ma'am, he done gone to Columbia a week since.'

'When is he expected back?'

'Hit don' do no good ter speck him, not when he go off on a

spree,' she said crossly. 'When he git the bug in he's head, he jist lights out and don' come back till that bug good an' gone.'

Mary heard the 'bellering' when she reached the next turn of the stairs, and it grew as Mammy Ausland led her down the corridor to May's room. May had her face in her pillows, sobbing hysterically. Her hair was a tangled briar-bush, the bedclothes rumpled with her thrashing about, and she was unattended save by her own servant, who was backed into a corner looking frightened, and the midwife, a free black called Aunt Matty, who was sitting with her hands in her lap, beaming a toothless smile at no-one in particular.

'Shouldn't you be doing something?' Mary asked her sharply.

Aunt Matty did not cease to smile. 'Ain' nuthin' to do, 'less you kin stop lil missus bellerin'. Hit ain' doin' her no good, but Ah cayn' stop her.'

May lifted her head at the sound of voices, and then held out pathetic arms to Mary. 'I knew you'd come! Oh, help me, help me!'

Mary took her in her arms and soothed her. Her wet face against Mary's neck felt very hot. 'Now, May, this isn't doing you any good. You've got to stop crying and be calm.'

'I can't! You don't know what I've been suffering! Oh, the pain, the pain!' And she began sobbing again.

Over her head, Mary addressed the midwife. 'Where's Mrs Judge? Where's Trevelyan?'

'Doctuh say to sen' fo' him when de baby really comin', an' Missus gone back to bed,' Aunt Matty said comfortably.

'Back to bed?'

'She say hif de doctuh done go home, dere no reason fo' her ter stay.'

'I'm going to die!' May wailed. 'That's why everyone's left me!'

'Nonsense! Of course you're not going to die,' Mary said. 'You must stop all this sobbing and thrashing about. Let me tidy you up and make you comfortable, and then you'll see, the baby will be here before you know it.'

She bathed May's face, brushed her hair and, with Patty's help, tidied the bedclothes. Mary thought May looked pathetic with her great swollen belly under her white nightgown, like a child dressed up with a pillow; her face was flushed, too, and her brow felt feverish – though that might have been the result of all the crying, she supposed.

'There now, does that feel better?'

May whimpered, 'Yes, a little, only I wish Con was here.'

'Birthing is women's business,' Mary said hastily.

'I just wish he was in the house, so I could know it. I miss him so.'

Mary patted her hand, and reflected wonderingly that May really did love him, no matter how he neglected her. It proved more about May's nature, she thought, than Conrad's worth.

It was Saturday evening when Mary and Patty emerged into King Street again. Mary was swaying with tiredness, and almost fell when someone running down the street brushed against her. 'Sorry, ma'am!' he cried over his shoulder, already yards away. He shouted something else she could not decipher. She shook her head, pulling her shawl closer round her shoulders. The city felt restless around her. There were lights shining at unshuttered windows, people moving across them; voices in the streets, and doors banging, and running footsteps; further up King Street a group of people on the steps of ex-Governor Manning's house were talking and waving their arms.

There was something else, too, she realised at last: the gunfire had ceased. They must have stopped for the night, she supposed vaguely, to give the city some rest. Along the Battery there seemed to be quite a crowd of men talking excitedly; she even heard some laughter. She thought they might be drunk, and kept well to the other side, hurrying with her head down, longing to be home, for a bath and her bed. She had not eaten all day, but she was not hungry. She wanted only to be alone, and to sleep.

The front door of the Morland House was open, and there were so many lights blazing it was as if they were having a party. Matthew was not in the hall; there was the same agitated air about the house as there had been about the city, but no-one came to greet her. She slipped off her shawl and bonnet and gave them to Patty, and told her to take herself off to bed. The morning-room door was open, and Mary went towards it. Charles, Heck and Fenwick were standing by the fireplace talking in low, urgent voices. Fenwick saw her first, and came across the room to take her hands, beaming.

'There you are, love! Isn't it wonderful news? And all without the loss of a single life, too – that's the best of it!'

She shook her head, her thoughts tumbling. 'I don't understand you,' she said numbly.

Fenwick laughed aloud. 'Good God, where have you been? I'm talking about Fort Sumter, of course! We've taken Fort Sumter! You must be the only person in Charleston who hasn't heard!'

Fenwick plunged into the story. He was too excited really to be interested in where she had been. 'It began this afternoon, about half-past one: some of our hot shot set fire to the roof of the officers' quarters in the fort, and they couldn't put it out. And then the flagpole came down, and Wigfall, who was on Morris Island, thought they had struck, so he had himself rowed over with a white flag. He parleyed a bit under the walls, and then we saw him go in through a porthole – the sally port was too close to the flames, it seems. Well, apparently Anderson said that he hadn't struck, the flagpole had been shot away by accident, and he was in process of erecting a new one. But Wigfall pointed out what a desperate state he was in, and eventually Anderson agreed to surrender.'

'Chesnut and Manning went over afterwards with Martial,' Uncle Heck took up the story. 'They've been negotiating all afternoon, and Martial just sent his boy Ratty to tell us that Anderson's accepted the terms.'

'He's to evacuate the fort tomorrow, and take his men out to the Federal ships for transport to New York,' Fenwick said. 'So the first battle of the war is ours! We took Fort Sumter! And in all that bombardment there hasn't been a single life lost, which will please you ladies no end.'

He stopped and looked at her, aware at last that she was not responding. 'But where have you been, not to have heard about it?'

Mary moved wearily. 'I've been at the Ausland House since before dawn.'

'The Ausland House?'

Her eyes instinctively turned to Charles. 'Your grandson has been born.'

Charles's face was expressionless, reading in hers that it was not good news. But Fenwick's euphoria waited for no more details. 'Grandson? She's had a boy?' he cried. 'Clever May to have a son right off! Pinckney Jefferson Ausland, eh – isn't that what they're calling him? Conrad will be delighted. The Judge, too!'

'Fen!' Heck said warningly.

Charles was still looking at Mary in silence, and to him she completed the news. 'The baby was born dead. And now, if you please, I am going to my bed. I am very tired.'

She turned away. Martha, one of the slaves, had appeared in the doorway with a tray of tea – no-one had sat down to a proper meal since the bombardment began, and tea had been everyone's mainstay. She heard Mary's words, and the cups rattled in the saucers. Martha's lips were quivering, and large tears like fat raindrops were rolling down her cheeks. The sight of them brought Mary's tears surging up, and she fought with them, not wanting to cry here, now, in front of these men. Not, above all, in front of Charles.

'Poor May, poor May,' Fenwick was saying, shaking his head. 'What a sad thing for her.' He gathered himself together. 'Well, but these things happen, I suppose. And she can have others. She's very young. How did the Auslands take it? I suppose Mrs Judge was very upset?'

'She took to her bed,' Mary said. Mrs Judge had not come near the confinement room. When she heard that the baby was still-born, she retired to her room to weep the justified tears of a cheated grandmother.

'Did you see Conrad?'

'He wasn't there. He's in Columbia.'

'In Columbia?'

Charles now took charge. He said in a cold, commanding voice, 'Martha, put the tray down and go away. Mary, you may go to bed.'

Fenwick was still puzzled over Columbia. 'What did he go there for? He'll have a thin time of it, if he went for company – everyone in Columbia came here as soon as the guns started firing. Poor Con, he's missed all the fun! How he'll kick himself when he hears!' His mind had slewed off again onto the preferred path of war. Babies were born and babies died every day: that was woman's business. But fortresses were not taken every day, and he had been in the thick of it: that was far more riveting stuff.

'What are you doing here?' Mary asked as she crossed the landing a few days later and found Ruth crouching behind the banisters looking down into the hall.

Ruth jumped up, blushing. 'Oh, you startled me! I didn't hear you.'

'Evidently.' She waited pointedly for an explanation.

'I'm keeping an eye on Pa's study, watching who comes to see him. I figured it was bound to be today – now all that Fort Sumter business is over.'

Mary followed with difficulty. 'Oh, you mean offers of marriage for you? But, love, do you really think it will happen so soon?'

'Pa wouldn't have paid out all that money for a ball without testing the water first. He'll have spoken to all the possibles before the invitations were sent out, and made sure they know what he expects.'

Mary was curious about her apparent equanimity. 'You don't mind?'

'I'd just as soon be married now,' Ruth said judiciously. 'As long as it's the right person.'

'And who is the right person?'

Ruth displayed two sets of crossed fingers. 'I can't say – it would be bad luck. But I can tell you – sshh! Wait! Here's someone!' She crouched down again to peer down through the banisters. 'It's Mr Raven and Beau,' she whispered. In a moment she straightened up and turned a transparent look on Mary. 'D'you know, Beau looked straight up here as he went down the hall, just as if he knew I was watching! Don't you think he's the *handsomest* man in Charleston?'

'He is very nice looking indeed,' Mary said. 'Now, do come away, Ruthie. Come and make yourself useful – there's an awful lot of sewing to be done. If one of the slaves sees you it will get about. You wouldn't want someone to tell Beau Raven that you were so eager for him, would you?'

Ruth saw the point. Her spell with Phoebe Canfield had aroused her natural vanity. She knew herself to be pretty, and wanted to be pursued, as pretty girls are, not hang about looking lovesick and foolish, as poor May had for Conrad. And look where that had got May: her first baby lost, and Conrad far away, not caring a jot. Her sister was an awful object lesson to her.

Ruth spent the rest of the day unimpeachably, sewing, making herb-bags for the closets, and taking a very docile walk along White Point Gardens with Aunt Belle – dull work, but better than going with Mary to visit May. She didn't like sick people, and had a superstitious feeling that May's matrimonial ill luck might rub off on her at this vulnerable point in her life.

But for all her mental preparation, when the summons to her father's study came, it took her off guard. The ladies were sitting in the parlour, working – Ruth was mending a fan – when Matthew came in and delivered it with due solemnity. 'Yo' pa wants you in his room, Miz Ruthie, right away, so scurry on, now. He's lookin' mighty seh'ious 'bout sompin.'

All eyes turned to Ruth. Her heart quickened, and her fingers trembled so that the scrap of glued paper she was trying to apply to the rent in the fan fluttered like a trapped moth and she had to put it down. 'Is anyone with Pa, Matthew?'

'No, Miz Ruth, Ah hain showed no-one in.'

Well, she'd know soon enough, she told herself. She smoothed her hair, balled her handkerchief in her damp palms, walked out past Mary's quick, reassuring smile, and went and knocked on that forbidding door.

Her father was sitting at his desk. He did not look up when she came in, and left her waiting for some minutes while he finished reading something in the paper in front of him. Ruth made herself stand still, knowing that to fidget would be to draw a sharp rebuke on herself, watching the shiny front of his bent head and trying to distract her mind by thinking how odd it was that some men went bald and not others.

Finally he looked up, and subjected her to a lengthy examination from top to toe, and back again. Ruth felt herself wither as his eye travelled over her. When she dressed that morning she had felt she looked extremely well, but now she became convinced that everything was wrong about her attire, and that she herself was the wrongest of all.

But at last he said, 'I have had several offers of marriage for you.'

She swallowed. The good thing about her father was that when he came to the point, he came to it. 'Yes, Pa?'

'The choice, however, was not hard to make. One suitor seemed very much more eligible than the others.'

Ruth's heart lifted. He must mean Beau Raven! The handsomest, charmingest man in South Carolina – and now all that handsomeness and charm would belong to her. Mrs Beaufain Raven: it sounded well. How the other girls would envy her!

Charles continued, 'He is of course well known to you – Mr Patrick Manning. In view of the situation, he does not wish a long engagement, and I agree with him. It will be announced tomorrow, and you will be married in June. That is all.'

Ruth did not move, trying to take it in, feeling there must be something more to be said at such a moment, when her whole future had been decided at a stroke and all her wonderings and speculations resolved into hard reality. She needed time to assimilate the news.

'But, sir,' she began, trying to sort out what she most wanted to say. Too late she realised she should not have begun with 'but'.

Charles frowned. 'What is it? Manning is a gentleman of means, and well known to our family, which must be more comfortable to you than marrying a comparative stranger. He has made an irreproachable offer, and, moreover, spoken of you in warm and generous terms. If I expected anything from you, it was gratitude and obedience. I certainly do not expect my decision to be disputed.'

Ruth was trembling with the effort not to burst into tears and run away, which was always how her father's disapproval affected her. Somehow she stood her ground and said, or rather blurted, 'But, sir, he's so old!'

Now her father seemed genuinely surprised. 'Old? What nonsense!' He studied her for a moment and then said, 'You have perhaps formed some fancy for another person, but I assure you that at your age it is nothing but a fancy and will quickly fade. A husband is something different. In choosing as I have, I have provided you with a man you may lean on and cleave to for your whole life, and if you do not yet perceive his worth, you soon will.' He had spoken more kindly to her than she could have expected, but now his face set hard again. 'You will receive him tomorrow morning, when he will make his addresses to you. And now you may go.'

She did not dare disobey that expression or that tone. She bowed her head meekly and left, shutting the door quietly behind her. As she turned from the door she found Mammy so close to her it made her jump. Mammy's face was a ludicrous study of gaping curiosity mingled with commiseration-at-the-ready. 'Who is it?' she hissed. 'Tell me, lamb, who gits to mahy ma baby? Tell your ol' mammy.'

Ruth hurried away from the door. 'Were you listening?' she asked sternly. 'Shame on you, you wicked old eavesdropper!'

Mammy skipped after her, managing to look indignant. 'Huccome you so col' to me, Miz Ruthie, whut nussed you at ma buzzum, an' took care o' you, even when Ah wuz po'ly – which Ah ullers wuz, nighly all the time.'

'What you "ullers wuz" was a listener at doors, so you've no need to sound so high-nose about it!'

Mammy sniffed. 'Ah din' need to lissen at no do'. Everbody know whut yo' Pa want you fo'. He been fixin' t' mahy you off jus' as soon as he could, an' whut fo' else did he sen' fo' you, 'cept t' tell you who he done fixed on? But hif you don' want t' tell me, Miz Ruthie, Ah is sho' Ah don' want t' know.'

'You old story-teller, you're nearly busting with curiosity,' Ruth said. 'But I don't mind telling you. It will be all over everywhere tomorrow, anyway. It's Mr Patrick Manning.'

It took a moment to sink in, and then Mammy looked pleased. 'Mist' Manning? Why, he almos' fambly awready! An' he a nice gemmun, always so civil an' 'greeable to ever'body – an' mighty rich besides! Yo'll be a fine lady, honey, an' have a nice house right heah in Charleston.'

'I expect I will,' Ruth said absently, trying to shake Mammy off. She wanted to be alone, and find out what she really felt about it.

Mammy stuck to her like a burr. 'A mah'd lady ullers gits homesick jus' at first. So when yo' Pa fixes to give you a weddin' present, lamb, you gwine ask fo' a nigger of yo' own, someone you knows real well. You gwine ask fo' ol' Mammy, ain't you, chile?' she concluded beguilingly.

So that was it! Ruth suddenly saw her marriage from another

point of view, as a matter of advantage to others than herself. How many more approaches like this would she receive in the weeks ahead? 'Why, Mammy,' she said, 'you wouldn't want to leave Aunt Belle. And what about Miss Mary's babies?'

'Dem is hof English babies,' Mammy said, 'an' Miz Belle hain good to dis ol' nigger, always crampin' an' complainin'. Hain' no pleasin' her. Ah'd sooner come wid you, honey!'

'We'll see,' Ruth said, finding for the first time the value of that irritating phrase. 'Now leave me alone, I want to be on my own for a while.'

And Mammy contorted her face into an expression of sympathy, elevated herself onto her tiptoes as though in a house of sickness, and waddled away, a mountain of tact, an elephant of understanding.

Ruth awaited the interview the next morning with extreme nervousness. When she had imagined, in the moments before falling asleep, receiving Beau Raven in these circumstances – or Clay Fairfax or Manny Miles or any of the other beaux – nervousness had never featured in the scene. They had been the supplicants while she had dispensed her favours in a queenly manner. Why did Patrick Manning fill her with this fluttering trepidation? Pick Manning was sensible as shoes, as plain as roast beef: there was nothing of the flirt in him, no dash or flourishing manners – in fact, nothing Beau Raven about him at all. Yet as she sat in the morning-room waiting, she was trembling all over like a tapped drum at the thought of having to face him.

There, the doorbell had jangled! Straining her ears, she caught Matthew's slip-slop feet across the hall and then his sing-song greeting as he opened the door; then the familiar deep tones of Pick Manning's voice. Her face went hot, and a strange panic possessed her – she wanted to run and hide under the dining-table as she did when she was six. Footsteps outside now, the click of a man's booted heels. The door handle turned, she shot to her feet with her heart hammering, and there he was.

He came in, closed the door behind him, and stood just within, looking at her quizzically. Ruth stared, unable to help herself. She stared as if she had never seen him before, and in a way she hadn't, because he had always before been Martial's friend, never a suitor. Now, as she realised with a deep and disturbing pang which seemed to go to the very centre of her stomach, she was looking at the man she was to spend the rest of her life with. She would live in the same house with him, look at him across the dinner-table every day, and – oh, trembling thought – sleep in the same bed with

him for ever and ever. With him! With Pick Manning! It was –
unnerving.

'They did tell you I was coming?' he said.

'Yes, of course,' Ruth said awkwardly.

'Because you're looking at me so strangely,' he went on.

'I – I feel strange,' she said.

'You're not afraid of me?'

'Afraid? No,' she said doubtfully. She sat down at the small table,
and he pulled out a chair and sat, his hat on his knee. His face was
so ordinary that she had never bothered to memorise it; but its very
ordinariness made it seem somehow more *personal*. Beau's face,
being handsome, belonged to an official body of handsomeness,
rather than to him individually. Beau's face could be the face of
any handsome man; Pick's face could only be his own.

'Well,' he said at last, 'I don't know whether to be flattered
or frightened by this long scrutiny of yours, but I must say I
rather like it. You never looked at me like that in Washington or
Alexandria.'

She frowned. 'But when I saw you there you weren't—' She
stopped, unable to think of a polite way to finish the sentence.

'You hadn't thought of me as a possible husband,' he helped her
out. 'Probably you never would have! No, it's all right, I have no
false vanity. It would be natural, if you thought of marriage, to
think of one of your own circle. Did you have a special fancy?' The
question startled her. She doubted whether it would be proper to
answer it, and remained silent. 'I see that you did,' he said. 'Shall
I guess? Was it Lennox Mynott?'

Now the answer was surprised out of her. 'Lennox? No! I'm very
fond of him, but – he's more like a brother.'

'I'm glad,' Manning said. 'That would have been a difficult barb
to cut out. So, then, who have I to replace in your heart?'

'If you must know, when Pa sent for me last night I thought he
was going to say it was Beau Raven.' She was sorry when she said
it, not wanting to hurt Pick's feelings, as surely they must be hurt
by comparison with so complete a rival, a man with looks, charm,
dash – and youth besides.

But Pick didn't seem hurt. He said kindly, 'Are you in love
with him?'

She felt suddenly impatient at all this talk. 'I thought you came
to propose to *me*. You know I have to accept, so why don't you just
do it? What does it matter about Beau?'

'It matters to me,' he said stubbornly.

'Well, then, the answer's yes!' she said irritably. 'Now what are
you going to do about it?'

He smiled, a full, wide smile that was as warming as the sun breaking through white morning fog. 'You're not in love with him. That's good. It gives us a better start.' He regarded her scowl with affection. 'I can't tell you what a relief it is to see that look on your face. Now I know I'm talking to the real Ruth.' Composing his face to gravity, he knelt before her in the time-honoured fashion. 'Miss Morland, will you do me the honour of accepting my hand and fortune in marriage?' She didn't say anything, and he prompted her, 'This is where you answer.'

'Can I ask you a question first?' she said.

'Yes, of course.'

She asked gravely, 'Why do you want to marry me?'

He paused a long moment. Their faces were on a level, and very close, and she discovered that she wasn't nervous of him any more, and that the ordinariness of his face had in some way over the last few minutes become something that appertained to her: if he went away now and never came back, she would mind, she would miss him. Now, wasn't *that* odd?

At last he answered. 'Because I'm in love with you.'

It was not what she had expected. It almost shocked her. 'Oh!' she said in a small voice.

He took up her hand in his, and she looked at it, small and white in his big brown one. 'I know you don't love me,' he said gently, 'but I hope that you will one day. And I would certainly think the worse of myself if you should ever wish you had married Mr Raven instead of me.'

'I don't care about Beau Raven,' she heard herself say.

'Good,' he said, smiling. And then he took her face between his hands and turned it upwards and kissed her. She was shocked and thrilled and excited and frightened all at the same time. It went on for a long time, and the feeling of it seemed to ripple through her like pins-and-needles from her lips to the crown of her head and down to her toes. When he finally stopped, she was dizzy and breathless, and he looked into her eyes with satisfaction and smiled. '*He* never kissed you like that.' She shook her head. 'It's the advantage, you will find, of marrying an older man. Boys don't know how to kiss.' And he did it again. When he paused the second time, she had discovered how to breathe but had forgotten how to think. She opened her eyes with a drowned look. 'What was the name of that paltry fellow you wanted to marry?' he asked tenderly.

'No-one,' she said. 'You. I want to marry you.'

'I'm so glad,' he murmured, and kissed her again.

CHAPTER EIGHTEEN

The fall of Fort Sumter was all the excuse President Lincoln needed: rebel forces had opened fire on a Federal fort for no reason, and now had taken control of it. He called for 75,000 militia to restore order in the Southern states. He did not speak of war, for to do so would be to acknowledge the separate nationhood of the South. This was a civil disturbance, a matter of policing, nothing more.

The immediate consequence of Lincoln's call to arms was that Virginia, which had been hoping still to heal the rift without bloodshed, was forced to choose one side or the other. Sadly, but with no hesitation, the Old Dominion declared for the Confederation; and when she left the Union, North Carolina, Tennessee and Arkansas followed. President Davis at once began to make arrangements to move the Confederate Government from Montgomery, Alabama, to Richmond, Virginia.

'That means,' said Benedict, poring with interest over a map, 'that the capital of the North, Washington, will be only a hundred miles away from the capital of the South, Richmond. In a country the size of this one, I find that remarkable! Your President Davis will certainly be in the thick of things.'

'That's where Jeff Davis likes to be,' Martial commented, lounging at his ease with the striped cat on his lap. He was with Lennox, Mary and Benedict on the verandah after breakfast. Everyone else had gone about their business. 'I think there's a touch of bravado in it,' he added. 'It will certainly give Lincoln no doubt where to attack when the moment comes.'

'Do you think it will be soon?' Benedict asked.

'I think it must be,' Martial said, stroking the cat firmly from ears to tail, making it clench its paws with pleasure. 'Half the Federal army is made up of ninety-day militia: the North has to attack before they finish their service and go home again.'

'You don't seem alarmed,' Benedict said. 'Surely all the advantages are with the North? They have a far larger population, to begin with – and half of *your* population is slave. They have all the factories, all the iron and coal, most of the turnpikes and railroads. And what does the South have?'

'What we have,' Martial said, 'is cotton. By selling that, we can buy all the arms we need. And, besides, we have the moral advantage. We already have what we want – independence. To get what *it* wants, the North has to be the aggressor. It must actually invade us.'

Mary lifted her head from the stocking she was knitting. 'Which puts it in a weaker position.'

'Like Napoleon invading Russia,' Lennox added, appreciating the point.

'Just like that! An invading army must set up supply lines, and when you are dealing with a vast country like America – yes, or Russia – the lines become dangerously long. The number of troops needed just to guard and maintain them is a heavy drain.'

'A good point,' said Benedict.

'Also the advantage in morale must lie with the people defending their homes from an invader,' Martial said. 'I think Lincoln will find it hard to persuade people to fight for something as intangible as "the Union", once the first excitement of war wears off.'

'All good points,' Benedict said, 'But I'm still worried. I have a stake in this country – three Southern grandsons.'

'Yes,' said Martial. 'I don't blame you for delaying your departure. I believe you were originally intending to stay for six months?'

Benedict had told Sibella three, and now it was twelve. He looked guilty. 'I couldn't leave until I knew how things were going to come out.'

Mary said, 'You've always been one for adventures, haven't you, Papa? Running away from home to be a railway engineer; then there was the Great Exhibition and then the Crimean War. I can see how the life of a private country gentleman must seem dull to you.'

'Not dull,' he protested, but without great conviction.

They were interrupted at that moment by the arrival of Patrick Manning, who walked out onto the verandah unannounced, in the privileged manner of the accepted suitor. 'So early, old friend?' Martial greeted him. 'It's touching to see how hard a man can fall when he falls late in life.'

Manning took it equably. 'Naturally I called in the hope of seeing the loveliest girl in Charleston – who wouldn't? – but I also came to bring you some news. I thought you'd like it hot from the telegraph.'

Mary said, 'Won't you sit down, Mr Manning? Is it news about the war?'

'What else, these days? It came in just this morning: Lincoln has proclaimed a blockade of all Southern ports.'

There was a brief silence as they assimilated this.

'A *blockade*?' Martial queried.

Manning nodded. 'That was his word.'

'A tactical error on Lincoln's part!' Martial said with satisfaction. 'I'm glad to know the man can make mistakes.'

'Why is it a mistake?' Lennox asked.

'Because you only "blockade" the ports of a foreign power,' Martial said. 'If you have trouble in your own ports, you merely close them.'

'You mean, by calling it a blockade he acknowledges that the South is a separate country?' Lennox said.

'But what difference does it make?' Mary said. 'We know it's a war, and so do they. What does it matter what it's called?'

'It may matter very much,' Martial said. 'Other countries – England in particular – wouldn't get involved with a country putting down an internal rebellion, even for the sake of protecting the cotton supply. But if the North acknowledges that the Confederacy is an independent nation, and then attacks us, England can legitimately come to our aid.'

'I should think you will need all the aid you can get,' Benedict said. 'You haven't got a navy, have you?'

'The Federal navy is not such a wonderful thing,' Manning said. 'No more than a hundred capital ships, mostly old sailing-vessels, and half of them laid up in ordinary. Not enough to mount a complete blockade on thousands of miles of coastline.'

'But what ships they have you can be sure they'll send to Charleston,' Martial said, looking at Benedict.

He took the point. 'It seems the moment has come for me to depart. I mustn't risk being trapped here. I have a duty to my family.'

Just then Ruth came out onto the verandah, her face far too eager for the studied nonchalance of her words. 'Oh, I didn't know we had a visitor. Good morning, Mr Manning. I didn't hear you arrive.'

Martial grinned at her and said, 'I shouldn't like to see the spots on your soul right this minute. Don't you know it's a sin to tell a lie?'

'Don't tease her, Martial,' Mary said. 'Ruthie, dear, I wonder if you'd make up a new posy for the vase on the hall table? You have such a talent with flowers. Take my basket and scissors and see what there is in the garden – and perhaps Mr Manning would go with you, to carry the basket.'

Martial watched them walk off. 'That is a very satisfactory arrangement.'

Mary nodded. 'I've never seen Ruth look so happy. And before the ball, I would have said if she fancied anyone, it was Beau Raven. Your friend must be very adept at making love, to have won her round so quickly.'

'It's a thing they teach you at West Point,' Martial said airily. 'Pick was an able student – he came second in the class.'

'Only second?'

'He was in the same class as me.'

Mary shook her head. 'I should have known better than to give you the cue.' She stood up. 'I must get ready to visit May. Papa, what will you do?'

'I had better make enquiries about a ship,' he said rather dolefully.

'Why not let me do that, sir?' Martial said. 'I'm better placed to get answers quickly.'

'Thank you, you're very good,' Benedict said gratefully. 'Do you think I can still get out?'

'If we move quickly,' Martial said. 'But you'll need to be ready to go very soon – in the next couple of days.'

Mary looked stricken. 'This is all happening so suddenly. I don't want to part with you, Papa. I shall miss you so.'

'I shall miss you, too,' Benedict said. 'But we've had longer together than I expected.'

'I think that only makes it worse,' Mary said with a shaky smile.

Benedict caught Lennox's eye fixed on him with a look that was both enquiring and apprehensive. Benedict cleared his throat uncomfortably. He didn't want to do it, and had put it off and put it off; but now there was no more time, and in fairness to both of them – 'If I am to go, Mary, there's something I need to tell you – explain to you.'

Martial looked quickly at him, and then at Lennox. 'Yes,' he said, 'I think you ought to.'

Benedict stared. 'You know?'

'I have guessed. I don't know the details, of course, but I think you're right that it should be told. I'll take my leave and give you privacy.'

Mary looked around them, bewildered. 'What is it? You all seem to know something I don't. Martial, don't go.'

He touched her hand briefly. 'You had better not have me here just now. But I shan't be far away.'

He walked into the house, and Lennox said awkwardly, 'Had I better go too, sir?'

Benedict looked surprised. 'Why? You know what I'm going to say.' He turned to Mary. 'My love, I have to tell you something painful. It's what I came to America to say, but I haven't found the courage to do it until now.'

'Don't tell me, if it's bad,' Mary said, alarmed.

But he went on as if she hadn't spoken. 'Your mother wasn't sent away to Scarborough for a cure. She had—' It was hard to say it aloud. 'She had a lover. She was with child by him. That's why I sent her away. She died giving birth. I suppose you can guess the rest? That child was Lennox.'

Mary's eyes were wide and she seemed to hear him with disbelief. But then she turned to Lennox and saw the truth in his face. 'You knew?' she said. He nodded. 'You're not my cousin? I wondered why I'd never heard that my mother had a sister.' She turned back to her father. 'But why didn't you tell me from the beginning?'

'I wanted to tell you face to face,' he said. 'It's hard for me to have to admit to you that your mother was a bad person, and it must be hard for you to hear it.'

But she shook her head. 'I can't think about that aspect of it yet. The rest is too strange. And I don't remember my mother very well. *You've* always been the most important person to me.' She shook her head as if trying to clear it. 'Then Lennox is my brother? You're my brother?'

Lennox cleared his throat to speak, but Benedict cut in quickly. 'It would be better if you kept this a secret between you. For everyone else, let him remain your cousin. Your mother's sins are not for everyone's knowing.' He saw she did not understand. 'It might reflect on him – and on you. Your father-in-law, for instance—'

She gave a painful smile. 'I don't think Charles could like me any less than he does.'

'Oh, I think he could, love.'

Mary shook her head again. 'I can't take this in all at once. I've had another half-brother all these years and didn't know it. I'm glad you told me, Papa. I love Lennox already, but this will make him even more special to me.'

'Not a half-brother,' Benedict said. There, the words were out, the deed was done, it could not be taken back. Like jumping into icy water, the moment of impact was the worst. A great silence seemed to hang over the verandah, in which the three of them were suspended, in sight of each other, but out of touch.

'What—' Mary said at last, 'what are you saying?'

It was all downhill now. Benedict spoke fluently. 'I brought Lennox to you because he had no-one in the world but you, and also because I wanted you to have someone of your own over here. And to explain something which I know gave you pain, and which may trouble you still. It troubles me, too, but if you understand and forgive me, I may be able to make my peace with myself. I wanted to make you heir to Morland Place, Mary love. No-one could have been a fitter guardian, and to keep you near me was the dearest wish of my heart. But I couldn't leave the estate to someone who is not a Morland.' Lennox had bowed his head; only Mary's blue eyes burned into him through the personal fog which seemed to have shrouded everything in the scene but their near-identical faces.

'Not—?' was all Mary managed to say.

'Your mother was untrue to me always,' Benedict said gently, 'from the beginning, with Lennox's father. I tried to keep it from you, to make a safe haven for you where you would not know what she was, where it wouldn't harm you. And I always loved you just the same. It never made any difference—'

'Yes, it did!' she cried suddenly. 'You sent me away, just as you're sending Lennox away. To be rid of us.'

'Mary—'

But she turned and ran, not indoors, but into the garden, clumsily with her hands to her face. Benedict started after her, but Lennox put a hand out to stop him and shook his head. 'Not yet,' he said. 'Let her cry a little; then I'll go.'

But in the event it was Martial who found her first. He had taken himself for a walk along the Battery, and came back in through the garden, to find Mary sitting on the swing under the yew tree; not swinging, just sitting with her hands in her lap. It was the darkest part of the garden, and he thought he might get by without disturbing her, but she looked up, and so he paused. Her face was quite blank, but he saw she had not been crying. Well, that was a good sign, wasn't it?

'Was it very bad?' he asked.

She seemed to consider. 'How much do you know?'

'I don't *know*,' he said, coming closer, since she seemed to want to talk. 'I guessed that he was not your cousin. You are very alike, and – the story seemed too strange.'

'Yes, it puzzled me,' Mary said. She seemed to make up her mind, and took a deep breath that quivered a little on its way out. 'He's my brother. My mother died giving birth to him.' He waited, seeing that this was not all, not what really troubled her. She searched his face for understanding. 'He's not my *half*-brother, Mart. The father who brought him up, that he talks about so warmly – was also my father.'

Ah, now he understood! What a devil of a mess, he thought. To most people it wouldn't matter very much, but Mary thought too much and too deeply on every subject. He came and sat on the tree-stump nearby, and she twisted the swing round to face him. 'Tell me then,' he said. 'Which part hurts the most?'

'I never knew him,' she said. 'I've been racking my brain and I think I do remember that he used to come to the house sometimes, but I can't remember what he looked like or if I liked him or anything. I suppose I couldn't have. He must have been a very wicked man.'

'Lennox doesn't think so.'

'No, and it's odd, isn't it, that he sent Lennox to Papa, who must have been his worst enemy. I don't understand it, any of it.'

'What about your mother?' Martial asked. 'Do you hate her?'

'I don't really remember her very well. She must have been very wicked, too. But why did she marry Papa if she loved this other man? And she must have loved him if she went on – doing what she did. Why didn't she go away with him after I was born?'

'These are things you must surely ask your father,' Martial said. The blue gaze flashed.

'But he's not my father!'

That was where the real pain lay, he saw. They had come to it.

'I've loved him all my life, he was the most dear person in all the world to me, I trusted him and depended on him. And all the time he was lying to me, living a pretence. He's not my father at all!'

Martial got up and crouched before her and took her hands – cold as stones – and shook them a little to make her attend him. 'Listen to me, love. What is a father if it's not the man who brings you up and cares for you and worries about you? He hid this from you to protect you, and that's not perfidy, it's another proof of his care.'

Her lips trembled. 'But we are not of the same blood,' she said in a small voice.

'Oh, I think this blood business is overrated, don't you?' he said lightly. 'People are what they are, not what label happens to hang round their necks. Your Papa is a splendid person and he loves you more than anything in the world.'

'Do you think so?'

Martial smiled. 'Take it from one who knows.'

She didn't quite understand what he meant by that, but she was comforted. 'I wish he'd told me sooner. Now he'll be going away, and there's so much to talk about, and so little time.'

Martial stood up. 'Then you'd better not waste any more of it sitting here, had you?'

⋆　　⋆　　⋆

The morning came only two days later for Benedict's departure. He had said goodbye to everyone the night before, since he would be away before dawn, but Mary insisted on coming down to the quay with him. She was ready, neatly dressed as always, when Martial arrived to escort him, bringing two dockyard men with a barrow to take his traps to the lugger that was to carry him out to the *Nottoway*, waiting beyond the bar. She was loaded with timber and cotton from Savannah and bound for Liverpool, if she was not intercepted. Martial was sanguine. No word had come yet of a blockading ship appearing from the north: it would take time to commission them and get them into position, as he had known. And the *Nottoway* was fast, faster than any ship in the Federal fleet. Once away from the coastal waters she ought to be able to avoid or outrun anything flying the Stars and Stripes.

When the barrow had rattled off over the cobbles, the three of them walked in silence, their footsteps echoing in the empty streets. It was a misty morning, and the darkness smelled of salt fog; up on a roof somewhere a gull was nattering its strange far-ocean cry, and another, invisible out over the bay, keened in reply. The quay was quiet except for the sound of slapping water, the creak of mooring-ropes fretting against the bollards, and the shiver of rigging against masts. The darkness was easing into grey, and they could see the shape of the two negroes loading the trunks down onto the lugger, moving like shadow-play back and forth across the crocus of light showing in the lugger's little deck-cabin.

'Sea's calm,' said Martial. The lugger's dipping mast prescribed only a small circle against the sky. He called down to the captain, 'Will you manage to get out of the harbour? There's no wind to speak of.'

'She'll pick up,' the captain called back. 'The sun's coming up. It'll suck up the mist and then we'll get the breeze all right. Tell your man to come aboard.'

Martial turned to them. 'It's time,' he said. He shook Benedict's hand. 'Good luck, sir,' he said, and walked away, to leave them alone.

Benedict put his arms round Mary, and she leaned against him, too moved to speak.

'You know you are very dear to me?' he said at last. His voice was unsteady.

She nodded. 'Oh, Papa, I shall miss you so!'

He closed his eyes for a moment, trying to keep control. 'I've brought you Lennox,' he said, as if that were an answer. 'Take care of him, and he'll take care of you.'

'Yes,' she said.

'Do you forgive me, Mary?' The words broke from him: he hadn't meant to ask that now, not now when there was no time left. In the two days they had had of talking, they had not said everything, but perhaps they had said everything that needed to be said.

But she looked up at him searchingly. 'I do love you,' she said. 'You're still . . . You're still Papa to me.'

It was enough. He sighed and hugged her tightly.

'Sir,' the lugger captain said warningly.

Benedict kissed Mary's forehead and put her gently back from him. 'God bless you, my darling,' he said, and turned quickly away.

He jumped down into the boat, the dock-hands cast her off, and her crew shoved her away from the quay wall and ran up the lugsail. For a moment she drifted, and then the sail filled and tautened, and she turned her forefoot into the first low running wave and flipped up a smack of water. Martial returned to Mary's side. Dawn had come, and the mist was a pearl illuminated from within; and then it was dispersing with astonishing speed, and the lugger was a dark solid shape on grey water ribbed with molten gold. Benedict stood at the rail, looking backwards. He did not wave, and neither did Mary, but they watched each other as long as they were in sight.

The sun lifted over Hog Island, and the sky became pale and uninteresting; the town stirred into life. A little cold finger of breeze touched Mary's neck, and she shivered, feeling tired and empty as if she had been up all night.

'What you need is a good solid breakfast,' Martial said comfortingly. 'Let's go home.'

She turned with him and began to walk back. It was good to have him there, she thought, someone always to be relied on. She shivered again, and felt him put his arm round her – which was odd, because he was not touching her at all.

No matter what Mr Lincoln called it, war fever swept the land. There seemed to be no-one who was not glad it had come at last, after so much agonised waiting; and it was the same in the North, according to Phoebe Canfield, who wrote to congratulate Ruth and passed on snippets she gleaned from friends still in Washington. The older men wanted it over with, so that they could get on with their business; the young men were in a ferment to get to the fighting, their biggest fear that the war would be over before they'd had a chance to see any action.

There was quite a spate of betrothals following Ruth's. Adeline Raven's to Chesney Ausland was announced the day afterwards. Then there was Baba Fairfax to Dolph Ratliffe, Sarah Trent to

Manningtree Miles, Cousin Cecilia Fenwick to John Green, Lizzie Cotesworth to Manningtree's brother Antipas. 'War weddings' people called them: part of the excitement of the times. Young men bent on going out and killing Yankees were so full of the manly juices they could hardly be restrained from proposing, and the girls caught the fever from them.

Mary was glad when the Morlands went back to Twelvetrees; glad too that the Auslands were going to Camelot. She felt the country air and quiet would do May good. She was recovering from the birth, though still very unhappy over the loss of the baby, but Mary was worried about her general health. She was still suffering from an intermittent low fever, accompanied by pains in the joints and sometimes devastating headaches. But she swore to Mary that Dr Trevelyan visited her regularly and was not worried about her, and Mammy Ausland averred that 'Doctuh Trevylan' said May was coming on nicely. Conrad was still absent, May didn't seem to know where, but she missed him and fretted about him.

Ruth was less eager to go to Twelvetrees, not wanting to be separated from her betrothed; but he promised to come out and see her every week, and reminded her that they would be married in June anyway, which was little enough time for her to prepare herself as it was, without the distraction of having him hanging on her sleeve. Ruth was to be married from Twelvetrees, as May had been. The wedding would be smaller, as Pick had no family apart from his uncle the ex-governor, but Ruth was determined it would make up in style what it lacked in size. Cousin Phoebe and Mr Canfield were to come down from Virginia, and she wanted to show them that the Morlands were as sophisticated as anyone from Alexandria. She worried over every detail and drew up elaborate plans calculated to drive Mary to distraction.

Even with the house full of wedding talk, it was not possible to forget the war. Everyone was doing something. Fenwick was in a private regiment of Hussars; Uncle Heck was organising a group of older men into a local guard in case of invasion; Charles was breaking in young horses to stand gunfire, so that they could be sold as cavalry mounts. Judge Ausland was winning the war single-handed by discussing strategy with his cronies, writing letters to the newspapers, sending detailed campaign plans to President Davis, and visiting the militia companies to tell them what they were doing wrong. He was the busiest of all except for the women who, in addition to their normal tasks, were making uniforms, havelocks, stockings, kit-bags, flags and blankets for the army. But they did not mind any effort. They were as urgent for their menfolk to go off and fight as the men themselves, proud of any son or brother who volunteered, and even dressed their little boys who were too young to fight in uniforms which were the exact replicas of their fathers'.

It worried Mary, who had read a great deal, that in their blind, exulting, flag-waving joy, no-one seemed to be able to comprehend that war and death had anything to do with each other. Somehow this war was to be bloodless: a thing of fine uniforms, marching, songs, battle cheers, flags and good fellowship. There would be roaring cannon, heroic stands and neck-or-nothing charges, yes; but it was to be utterly without casualties. At the end of it the Yankees would slink away with their tails between their legs and the Southern men would march triumphantly home without a scratch on them.

She was not so surprised, really, about the women, for they were completely uneducated, and most of them had never read a book in their lives. But even Fenwick, who had read the classics and histories of the French wars, did not seem to understand. 'Oh, of course there'll be casualties,' he would say if she mentioned the subject. 'You can't have a war without casualties.' But she could see they did not impinge on his mind. Casualties were merely detached figures: 'The French lost forty thousand at the battle of Waterloo.' They were not forty thousand *anythings*, just forty thousand, a number, a four and four noughts. He could not make the imaginative leap from the words on the page to the reality of bleeding and shattered men, of pain and death.

But he was happy in anticipation of the excitement, and kind to her in his happiness, more attentive, now he had so little leisure, than he had been for years.

They had not long been back when Martial and Pick Manning arrived from Charleston with the news that they were leaving for Richmond. Troops were pouring in there from all directions, but they were mostly raw recruits and hot-head volunteers, so every military man in the country was going to be needed to train them.

Eugene was scornful. 'What's the point of that? They don't need training. A soldier is just a civilian in arms. And what is there for a soldier to do, but kill the enemy? Just point any Southerner at a Yankee, and let him do the rest!'

Martial didn't argue with him. 'Peter Beauregard is in overall command,' he went on, 'and he wants people he knows for staff officers; so, whether as instructors or gallopers, Pick and I are summoned to Richmond.'

Manning had taken Ruth off by herself to tell her the news. 'When do you have to go?' Ruth asked.

'Almost at once,' Manning said.

'So – then – you'll come back in June for the wedding?'

'That's what I want to talk to you about,' he said, and her face sharpened with dismay.

'You're not coming back for the wedding,' she said wretchedly. 'That's what you're trying to say, isn't it?'

'I may not be able to,' he said. 'I don't know when the fighting is going to happen, but Martial is sure it won't be long, and there are signs of movement from the North. But in any case, we aren't likely to get furlough for a long time. So I want to ask you to make a great sacrifice for me.'

'I won't wait until the war is over!' she cried. 'It's not fair!'

'I don't want to wait either,' he assured her hastily. 'That's not the sacrifice I meant. What I want is to marry you at once and take you with me to Richmond.' Ruth's eyes opened wide and she was wordless. 'Your cousins the Canfields are taking a house there, and they'd be happy to have us live with them until I have to move up to camp. I don't know when that will be, but even so, if you are in Richmond I'll be able to get back to see you quite often, whereas if you were here it would be out of the question. Richmond's a nice town and I know you like Phoebe Canfield, and although it's not like having your own home, if it's a choice between that and having to wait—' He stopped, doubting himself since she was still silent and staring. 'I know it's a great deal to ask you to give up your grand wedding plans,' he said hopelessly.

She found her voice at last. 'No!' she cried. 'It isn't a lot to ask, not at all!' She flung herself into his arms, her face one blissful smile. 'To marry you right away and go to Richmond? How could you think I wouldn't like it? Everyone's going to be there! To be at the war, and live with Phoebe again, and see all the action – and be married as well! Let's do it right away!'

Manning held her, smiling with relief. 'We'll have to ask your father's permission.'

'Oh, Pa won't care. It'll save him money! Let's go and ask him now. How soon can we marry? Is Richmond like Alexandria? I can't wait to see the army camps! Oh, this is so exciting – much better than planning a wedding!'

So it was two days later that Ruth was married to Patrick Manning in a simple ceremony in the drawing-room at Twelvetrees. Charles made no objection. Having decided to marry Ruth to Manning, it mattered not to him when the ceremony took place, and it made sense to make sure of the bridegroom before he went off to the hazards of war.

There was no time to make a wedding-gown: Ruth was to wear her ball-gown, with the addition of her mother's lace, sent over by May. Hill, Lennox and Uncle Heck constructed a bower in the drawing-room, and Mary and Julie contrived to make a cake. Only the family was to be there, with the addition of Judge and Mrs Ausland, and May and Conrad. Aunt Belle, telegraphed with the news, sulkily said she could not possibly make the journey to Twelvetrees on such short notice, in her state of health. If Charles was so careless of appearances as to marry Ruth off in unseemly haste, she implied, she would have nothing to do with it.

Ruth's wedding day was the first time any of them had seen Conrad since his return. It was also May's first outing since her confinement, and when the Ausland barouche pulled up, Mary thought that of the two of them May looked in better health. Her joy at having her husband back suffused her face and gave her a glow which counteracted her drawn cheeks and shadowed eyes. Conrad, on the other hand, sat sullen and glowering, showed no pleasure in being there, did not wish Ruth happy, and evinced no interest in the plans of Martial and Pick Manning. Mary thought he was a bad colour, and he seemed to have lost weight; he also had several nasty boils on his face and neck which did nothing for his looks. May evidently still regarded him as her romantic hero, but he snapped at her, was barely polite to anyone else, and seemed overall in an unaccountably bad temper.

The ceremony, for all its simplicity, was moving. Mary thought Ruth had never looked lovelier, and Pick's plain face did not seem so plain when he held his bride's hands and claimed her with such triumph. And when Ruth made her vows, gazing up with trust in her clear, open face, all the house-slaves, May and Mrs Judge were in floods, Mary's throat was tight with tears, and even Fenwick sniffed and had to clear his throat. He put his arm round Mary's shoulders and squeezed her briefly as Ruth and Pick were pronounced man and wife. Mary caught Martial's eye at that moment and he raised one eyebrow and gave her a strange, equivocal smile. Only Conrad seemed unmoved, standing with his arms folded and his chin sunk on his chest, scowling at the floor as if his mind were very far from his present surroundings.

Afterwards there was champagne and cake, and Charles proposed the toast. Tammas, the Twelvetrees butler, filling glasses, asked if he could 'tek de liverty o' wishin' Miss Ruthie blessed and happy for evah, f'om all of us house-niggers', and she was so touched she almost kissed him.

Mary found Martial beside her. 'It will answer very well,' he said. 'He really does love her, and she needs an older man to keep her in check. She'd never have been happy with Beau Raven, you know.'

She was too accustomed to his reading her mind to question it. 'I know. I didn't like the idea at first of her marrying so young, but I think now that she's ready for it, and he will be a kind teacher.'

'That's very philosophical of you, considering you'll be the greatest loser.'

'I'm not so selfish as to weigh that in the balance.'

'I know. But you can't view with equanimity the loss of your only female companion – especially when you were so fond of her.'

'I hadn't expected her to be leaving the neighbourhood,' Mary admitted. 'I wish Mr Manning didn't have to go to Richmond.'

'Mr Manning? And what about Mr Flint? You don't care if he is pitched into the mouth of hell, I suppose?'

'Oh, hush! You're vain enough, I'm not going to flatter you. Do look at May and tell me how you think she looks.'

'Not well.'

'I thought she was looking better.'

'I haven't seen her since before the baby was born,' he reminded her. 'But I don't like the way she gazes adoringly at Conrad.'

'He's her husband,' Mary said, puzzled.

'Precisely,' Martial said grimly. 'It's bad enough that he has the power of life or death over her, without her worshipping him for it.'

'I don't understand you,' Mary said.

'I'm afraid you may come to,' Martial said. 'May I get you some more champagne?'

Eugene was trying to rekindle his old friendship with Conrad, and failing lamentably. 'Did you have a good time in Columbia? I'm surprised you stayed so long.'

'I wasn't in Columbia all the time,' Conrad said impatiently.

'Oh?' He waited, and when it was plain Conrad was not going to enlighten him further, Eugene added, 'But you missed all the fun here, the bombardment and everything.' Conrad only grunted. 'You never saw such a sight as the shells bursting all over the bay!' Eugene went on, trying to warm his companion to enthusiasm. 'I was over in Moultrie with Beau Raven and some of the other fellows. I served a gun myself – pulled the lanyard, you know – such a noise when it went off! It was the best fun I've ever had!'

Conrad moved impatiently. 'You're turning into an unbearable rattle-mouth. Worse than a woman. Must you talk such stuff?'

Eugene was more puzzled than hurt. 'It isn't stuff! You must be interested in the war?'

'Oh, must I?'

Eugene tried again. 'You know, with Mart and Pick Manning going to Richmond – well, that's where all the fun's going to be. Everyone's volunteering. They say if you want to kill Yankees, you've got to get in quick, while it lasts.'

'Oh, what are you rattling about now?' Conrad asked impatiently.

'About volunteering,' Eugene said. 'Con, why don't we both go? We could get the train to Richmond and join one of the crack companies with a really smart uniform, and be in on it from the start! They say the thing to do now is to go as a private soldier. There aren't enough commissions for all the gentlemen – and anyway it's more patriotic because you get to kill more Yankees.' He looked hopefully at his mentor's stony face. 'Do say let's go! Think of the fun we could have – the camp and the other fellows, singing round the fire and such-like.' No response. He tried another tack. 'They say Richmond is like a frontier town – bars, billiard-rooms, and more girls than you ever saw in your life—'

Now at last Conrad was roused to answer. 'Oh, damn your eyes, why don't you stop piping and leave me alone? You're like a kid with a toy drum, bang-bang-bang, driving me mad! Go and play at soldiers if that's what you want, but don't keep bothering me!'

'But don't you want to go and fight?' Eugene cried in hurt astonishment. 'Don't you want to win the war?'

Conrad balled his fists and his face grew red. 'I don't give a blistering damn about the war! And what's more, I don't give a damn about you! Now shut up and go away, you drivelling little penny whistle! I'm sick of the sight of you!'

Eugene backed away, alarmed and upset in almost equal quantities. 'All right, all right – I'm going.' He eyed Conrad doubtfully, wondering if he'd been drinking before he arrived, and thought it best to leave him alone. It wasn't like Con to turn down the suggestion of a little fun; but perhaps he'd overdone it in Columbia, or wherever he'd been, and got himself a touch of liver. Eugene decided he'd ride over to Camelot in a day or two and ask him again, when he might feel better. But whether or not Con went, Eugene was determined he would go. The thought of the delights of Richmond alone would have tempted him, even without the prospect of a battle, and in Richmond he'd be too far away for his exploits to reach Pa's ears. Ruth would be there, of course, but Ruth was no tattle. In any case, judging by the moony eyes she was making at old Pick Manning, she'd have other things on her mind.

BOOK THREE

The Cause

Say not the struggle nought availeth,
The labour and the wounds are vain,
The enemy faints not, nor faileth,
And as things have been they remain.

If hopes were dupes, fears may be liars;
It may be, in yon smoke conceal'd,
Your comrades chase e'en now the fliers,
And, but for you, possess the field.

Arthur Hugh Clough:
Say not the Struggle Nought Availeth

CHAPTER NINETEEN

Eugene sat in the shade of a bank topped by straggly thorn-bushes, and felt in his breast pocket for his segar-case. 'Smoke?' he said to Beau, who was sprawled beside him with his hands under his head. Beau grunted thanks and sat up, took a segar, and then said, 'Let me see that old case again.' Eugene gave it to him while he felt for a match, and Beau turned it over admiringly in his hands. 'It's really nifty! I wish I'd bought one like it.'

Eugene took it back. 'There isn't one like it, so you couldn't have.' He had bought it in Richmond in a billiard bar during their first days there, from a whiskery old man in threadbare uniform, who had told him it was made out of the metal of a captured gun from the Revolutionary War. 'It's m'lucky case,' the old man had warbled through the gaps in his teeth. 'Saved m'life a dozen times. See them scritches? Them's an ole mount'n lion's claws. Jumped on me while I was asleep, tried to clawer me to death, but he scairt hisself so bad on m'lucky case, he run off ahollerin' jist like a baby. See that 'ere dint? Turned a knife-point, aimed right at m'heart. Mexican War. Picked up a whore in Ticamajuma, 'til her brother took exception and tried to cut out m'collops. See this nick?' And so it went on. Eugene listened, fascinated. He'd have bought the thing after the mountain lion story, but he sensed that the rigmarole was part of its worth, and when the old man came to the price, he was glad he'd heard him out. He paid up like a lamb, however, and wouldn't now have parted with it for twice the price, though Martial had laughed at him and told him he had been taken for a sucker, and that such 'souvenirs' were on sale by the thousand in every bar and hardware shop in town. The thing Eugene had really liked best about the whiskery old boy was that his ancient uniform was embellished with bran-new insignia, which made him a major by his sleeves and a colonel by his shoulder-straps.

With their segars alight, the two young men leaned back against the bank and stretched out their legs, enjoying the shade and the pleasant breeze after a hot walk that morning.

'It's pretty country round here,' Beau said after a while, and Eugene grunted assent. The softly rolling hills were rounded and gentle as a woman's breasts; fertile, smiling meadows were broken up by little copses of birch, hazel, ash and chestnut, and deep green paths edged with thorn-banks. A few larger stands of pine reared up dark and silent; there were little meandering cricks everywhere, and far away against the sky a cool blue smudge of distant mountains.

'A bit like home,' Eugene said after another pause. 'Only softer.' And Beau nodded, squinting into the distance through the lifting veil of his smoke. They didn't need to talk much, after the weeks they'd spent together. At first they had chatted pretty much as they did at home, but they had soon learned that a soldier's life involved long periods of doing nothing, interspersed with episodes of strenuous and largely unexplained activity. You would stand around for a couple of hours, then be marched at double time across rough terrain, stop for a couple more hours, then as likely as not be marched back again. But Eugene was glad they had decided to do what they had done. When the four of them had arrived in Richmond – Beaufain Raven, Fontaine Lawrence, Clayton Fairfax and him – they had been sworn together in an indissoluble brotherhood sealed by a long and fitful railroad journey in a train containing twice as many bodies as seats.

Eugene had more or less been provoked into it. When he visited Camelot a few days after Ruth's departure from Twelvetrees, Conrad's attitude was so far from welcoming that it had produced a breach between them. Eugene couldn't understand his old friend's bad temper. Conrad didn't look well, but that was no excuse for snapping a fellow's head off and calling him a naïve fool and a spoilt child and – well, a lot of other things less complimentary. Eugene had ridden away feeling sore, rejected and defiant. He had done his share for friendship, come more than halfway to meet Con, and if Con wanted to be so damned rude and unpleasant, he could just stick it out alone. Eugene didn't need him! He'd show him who was naïve!

So he rode straight over to Pinelees, where he found not only both the elder Lawrence boys but Clay Fairfax and Beau Raven as well. Eugene did not tell them about his abortive visit to Camelot – less out of loyalty to Conrad than fear that he may have come out of it looking silly – but expounded his plan before this new audience as though for the first time. Quincey Lawrence did not say much, but to Clay and Fon, who were much younger than him, Eugene was a dashing figure, and Beau had served beside him during the bombardment and was ready to give him all possible credit. The three were flattered that someone so much their senior was willing to seek them out on equal terms, and when he proposed going off to Richmond right away to volunteer as rank-and-file, they thrilled to the twin calls of patriotism and adventure.

'What about it, Quin?' Fontaine asked his elder brother eagerly. 'Will you come too? Do, it'll be the greatest fun in the world!'

'You forget,' Quin said, 'I'm already in the county militia. We'll be called for when the time comes.'

'But it may all be over before then,' Eugene said impatiently. He didn't like being reminded that Quin had been invited to be an officer in the local militia company while he hadn't even been asked to join it.

'Our company's one of the best,' Quin said. 'They'll send for us when the time's right to secure the victory.'

So it was decided that the four of them would go. The neighbourhood took them to its heart as heroes. Many was the visit to Twelvetrees during the week of preparation to congratulate Charles on his son's patriotic behaviour, to wish Eugene luck, to shyly offer him presents of things the donor thought he might find useful on campaign, or to ask whether young Jimmy, who was fairly busting to get his hands on a rifle, could go along too. The whole neighbourhood turned out with flags to accompany them to the depot, and there was even a band which played stirring songs like 'Cheer, Boys, Cheer!' and 'The Bonnie Blue Flag' – sometimes, owing to a mix-up with the music, simultaneously. The euphoria of the send-off lasted through the train journey, helped on by a flask which Eugene had thoughtfully stowed in his coat pocket, and the first sight of Richmond sent their spirits shooting up again like rockets.

What Richmond had been like before Eugene had no idea, but it was now crammed and seething with people, so that the streets seemed to jump and jig with them like a cur-dog with fleas. The roads were jammed from side to side with wheeled traffic of every sort, dogs ran about getting under foot, and the hot air was heavy with the smell of manure, cooking food and new timber. The sidewalks were hazardous with extempore stalls set up to dispense food, lemonade, souvenirs, secondhand clothes and leather goods, and providers of various services from shoe-shining and hair-cutting to card-tricks and snake-charming. Every second shop seemed to be a bar or a billiard-room, every hotel had its doors open and music gushing forth, and there were so many pretty women walking about the streets and hanging out of upstairs windows that Eugene thought he must have died and gone to heaven. It was all the four of them could do to keep from staring about them like hayseeds as they inched their way through the packed streets.

It was all enough to distract the most pious patriot, and it had been a few days before they had calmed down enough to remember what they had come for. With sobriety came second thoughts. Clay Fairfax had been the first to rat, saying that he didn't fancy walking everywhere for three months, and going off to join an elite cavalry unit. Then Fon Lawrence had bumped into a second cousin, a colonel of a fancy militia company, who had told him in shocked tones that with his background he would be wasted as an infantryman. Fon had already begun to have grave doubts about living in a tent, and so allowed himself to be persuaded – with a show of deep reluctance – to accept a commission in his cousin's outfit.

And then there were two. The defection of Clay and Fon had hardened their resolve to do the thing properly, and Eugene and Beau had enlisted in the infantry. Anyone who enlisted for twelve months was supposed to be supplied with uniform and full equipment by the Government, but there was not nearly enough of everything to go round, so it was unofficial policy only to issue uniforms to the poorest recruits. But tailors, like every other kind of artisan, were as common as blackberries in Richmond. 'I'd sooner get something that fitted me properly in any case,' Beau had said to Eugene. 'Just because we're going to be infantrymen doesn't mean that we have to look like farmers.'

So they went to a very expensive tailor and had their frocks and trousers made of the best available material. The uniform was grey, with pale blue infantry facings, together with a small, stiff cap with a narrow brim. The official-issue rifle was a Richmond .58, but they were in short supply. However, there were quite a few Enfields for sale in Richmond, which could take the same-sized cartridge; many recruits brought their own firearms from home, which was well enough until they ran out of ammunition. In addition Eugene and Beau bought themselves bowie-knives and revolvers, and when hung about with those, plus the bayonet, cartridge-box, canteen, blanket-roll and haversack, they looked so warlike that they found it difficult to pass any reflective surface without pausing to admire themselves.

They hadn't long to strut. Almost at once they were moved up to camp at Manassas, well to the north of Richmond and only about thirty miles from Washington, and shop windows were a thing of the past. Camp was a shock for both young men. The training was difficult enough – stumbling about in the hot sun badgered by bugle calls and incomprehensible orders – but living in a tent with only a tiny fraction of their belongings and no servant was even tougher: Eugene had never had to take off his own boots in his life.

And, oh, the walking! No South Carolina gentleman ever went anywhere on his own two feet when he could use his horse's four, and Beau and Eugene had been riding since before they gained full mastery of their own legs. They soon found their boots would not do. They had naturally bought the best: long boots of fine leather with a stacked heel and tapering toe, boots a foot was proud to be seen in. But they were riding-boots: their weight made walking exhausting, and when the leather got wet it grew even heavier. On rough ground – and the ground was always rough – they were turning their ankles every other step, and pulling the boots on or off in a hurry was impossible. Under advice from a veteran they sadly discarded them and bought strong country brogans with a broad sole and a big, flat heel. Beau could hardly bear to look at his feet in them, but at least now they could walk without active pain.

And once they were brigaded and came into contact with some of the fancy irregular units, they were able to feel themselves wonderfully superior, real soldiers in plain, serviceable garb, not prancing jackanapes in Zouave pants, carnival-coloured jackets and elaborate feathered kepis. Eugene never really felt comfortable without someone to despise, and along with all the other enlistees he was able to despise the 'nursery soldiers' lavishly. The transition had been hard, but it had been worth it.

Eugene was impressed with the way Beau had stayed the course. He had always thought Beau effete and dandyish, and in any case his training in the school of Con Ausland made him mistrust any man who got on well with women. But Beau proved himself hardy and uncomplaining, and learned quickly. Eugene had to strive to keep up with him, began reluctantly to admire him, and finally came to establish with him the first friendship he had ever had in his life. He found, first with embarrassment and then with an awkward, shy pleasure, that he liked Beau, and that, even more strangely, Beau liked him.

So now here they were, in a field on a hill overlooking a river somewhere in Virginia, sitting in companionable silence, waiting for the Yankees to come. It seemed a long time since they had taken that train to Richmond; but they were soldiers now, and they'd got a lot better at waiting.

'D'you think we'll really see any action?' Eugene asked at last, tapping the ash off his segar.

'Dunno,' Beau said, drowsy with the heat. A fly circled his face, looking for a landing-spot, and he flapped it away. 'Bound to, I should think. I mean, when the Yankees come, they'll have to head for Richmond, won't they? And then – well, here we are.'

Eugene nodded. The Confederate army at Manassas was squarely across the Orange-to-Alexandria Railroad, the line of which was the obvious route from Washington to Richmond.

After a bit, Beau said, 'Gene, are you scared?'

'Scared of the Yankees? No, of course not,' Eugene said promptly.

'No, not of them, I don't mean that. But of getting into battle. Do you ever think about it? *Really* think about it, what it'll be like and all?'

Eugene didn't understand him, but he did his best. 'We stood up to the bombardment of Sumter all right, didn't we?'

'But then we didn't actually *see* the enemy. Just imagine them coming running up that hill—'

Eugene hadn't an imagination at his service. 'We'll shoot 'em, I guess. Like rabbits, when they go popping about all over the bank at home.' He put an imaginary rifle to his shoulder and picked off a few at leisure. 'Anyway,' he said, 'I don't suppose we'll have long to get our shots in. Once we open fire, they'll turn tail and flee like the cowards they are. We'll have to be quick if we're going to bag some before we go home.'

Beau grunted, accepting that this was the best answer he would get from his friend. It could be frustrating, this lack of imagination, but it could be comforting too: Eugene was never apprehensive about anything.

A movement along the bank caught his eye, and he turned his head to see that the company was getting to its feet. A corporal was coming along with the order, but the movement was contagious and running ahead of him. 'Oh, we're on the move again,' he said to Eugene, pinching out his segar as he got to his feet. Eugene did the same, and took out his lucky case to put the unsmoked halves away. It was a thing neither of them would have dreamed of doing before they enlisted, but now it had a sort of austere pleasure about it, an agreeable friction that proved they were real soldiers, better than Fon Lawrence in his fancy militia outfit, and heaps better than Quin Lawrence, still at home sleeping in a downy bed.

Phoebe and George Canfield were fortunate in coming to Richmond early, for they were able to rent a good-sized house: later comers found it hard even to find a bed. The Canfields had not left Alexandria as refugees, but anticipating that it would not be long before the North occupied their home town, they had brought a substantial part of their belongings with them. It was sad to think what might be happening to their pretty house and to wonder if they would ever see it again, but at least they could be comfortable.

The Canfields were delighted to receive Ruth and her new

husband, and Phoebe could see at once that Ruth was happy. In fact she wore a look of dazed rapture which Phoebe found touching, though it made her feel a little jealous. She and George were well suited and she was very fond of him, but she had never risen from the marriage bed so misty-eyed, or lifted her face for her husband's goodbye kiss with such a look of fulfilled passion. Phoebe regarded plain old Pick with puzzlement bordering on irritation. What did he *do* that could turn smart little Ruthie into this melting, sighing thing? To Phoebe, the lovemaking that went on between the Mannings seemed to set up vibrations that made the whole house quiver; but dear sensible George didn't notice a thing. When she once commented to him that 'Ruth and Pick seemed very much in love', he merely looked up a moment from his newspaper and said, 'Are they? Well, he's a clever fellow. Plays an excellent game of whist.'

Manning was appointed to the staff of General Beauregard, who was in overall command of the army at Richmond, and since staff officers were in short supply, he was kept very busy. But there was plenty for Ruth to do in Richmond, and once the drowned and besotted look wore off sufficiently after Pick's departure in the morning, she was ready and eager to accompany Phoebe and enjoy the liveliness of the town. Just to step out of doors was an adventure. Every street was thronged with men on foot or on horseback, every second one in a uniform of some sort, and with women whose freedom and lack of chaperonage thrilled Ruth to the core. Every hotel and teashop bulged, every promenade was packed with the smart and the lively. And every evening seemed to be a party: the Canfields were popular hosts and, with their Government connections, were a sort of clearing-house for news. Indeed, with old friends popping in, or asking for a bed as they passed through Richmond, it sometimes seemed that they ran not only a clearing-house but a lodging-house.

But it was not long before Manning had to move up to camp. 'I'm sorry, I'm not usually such a waterspout,' Ruth said to him in their bedroom on the morning of his departure.

He mopped her face tenderly with his handkerchief. 'If I weren't a man, I'd be doing the same. I don't want to leave you,' he said, provoking a fresh burst of tears. 'But I'll have to come in to Richmond quite often with messages, especially once the President gets here.'

'But most likely you'll have to dash in and dash out again, and I'll never even know you've been here.'

'Well, perhaps.' Pick was always honest. 'But I'm sure sometimes I'll have to stay for a few hours – perhaps even overnight – and then I'll send a message to let you know. I'll get to see you somehow.'

'Oh, Patrick, I love you so,' she said, lifting her lips to meet his. She had begun to call him Patrick on their wedding night, feeling 'Pick' was too insignificant a sound for such a magnificent creature. She was still in the stages of feeling slightly surprised to see what he looked like in the daytime, up and dressed and familiar from her childhood; she sometimes felt as if it was a kind of lordly joke on his part, that the emperor of her bed should don this plain and mild disguise to go out into the world of ordinary mortals. It was a delicious secret, that only she knew what he was really like inside. It made his power over her absolute. Just a sidelong look, or the briefest touch on her shoulder as he passed her chair, would spark off an explosion of memories that would leave her weakly longing for night so that she could be alone with him again.

The breakfast bell rang and they had to break reluctantly apart. 'We must go,' he said. She looked up at him earnestly for a moment, memorising his face, and then suddenly smiled. 'What is it?' he asked.

'I was thinking how wonderful it is that we're going to have our whole lives together! I'm only fifteen, so if I live to be three-score-and-ten like the Bible says, that's fifty-five years!'

'I'm older than you,' he pointed out.

'But men live longer than women, so it works out the same,' she said equably.

Martial stayed with the Canfields when he was in Richmond. He was also on Beauregard's staff, but with special responsibility for the intelligence service. The network was wide and used varied means to get information, from regular spies in Washington to a body of scouts Martial had recruited. These were beginning to be referred to as Flint's Irregulars because they were such independent operators, not amenable to discipline. The intelligence-gathering was excellent, and Martial was pretty sure they knew what the North was up to as soon as President Lincoln. He suspected the reverse was true as well; but it could hardly be otherwise in the curious situation of this particular civil war.

One day in early July Ruth was in her room taking off her bonnet, having just come in from a shopping expedition. Frank was at the window, leaning on her hands on the windowsill and looking out into the street, swinging her hips from side to side in time to a tune she was humming under her breath. Sometimes Ruth almost wished that her father had given her Mammy instead of Frank as a wedding-present, but she still had a perverse affection for her, 'wofless' as she was. The humming, however, was annoying, and Ruth was just about to tell her to come and help with the bonnet-strings, when Frank stiffened and said,

'Lawdy, Miz Ruth, heah come Mist' Pick, jist walkin' up de road!'

Ruth ran to the window, but Frank was slow to yield her place, and by the time Ruth had shoved her out of the way she could only catch a glimpse of an officer's kepi disappearing under the porch. 'Are you sure it was him?'

'Course Ah's sho',' Frank said in wounded tones. 'Ah knows Mist' Pick's unifohm by now. Mebbe he got furlough,' she called hopefully to Ruth's back. Frank sighed sentimentally. 'She sho' is in lurve,' she said to herself, and went to pick up the bonnet Ruth had dropped – not from any impulse of tidiness but so that she could try it on herself before the big cheval-glass.

Ruth, running breathlessly downstairs, saw a tall figure in the hall in the blue trousers and grey frock with buff facings of a staff officer. Her joy lasted one second longer, before she saw it was Martial. 'Oh,' she said, stopping dead.

'Yes, it's only me,' Martial said sorrowfully. 'Shall I go away again?'

'Oh, don't be silly,' Ruth said briskly, going up on tiptoe to kiss him. She wrinkled her nose. 'Whiskers!' she said. 'And you smell sweaty.'

'Thank you, child. I've been travelling all day. I hope you don't greet your hero husband in the same frank way?'

'Have you seen him?' she asked eagerly. 'Is he coming?'

'Yes, and no,' Martial said. 'I'm sorry, love, he's glued to Peter's side, and I don't think he'll be coming back to Richmond for a while. There's news, you see—'

Phoebe came into the hall. 'Oh, I thought I heard voices! Martial, how good to see you. Is Pick with you?'

'Why does everyone ask me that? No, I'm alone. Am I still welcome?'

'Don't be silly,' Phoebe said.

'That's what I said,' Ruth told her. 'But he has news.'

'Come and be comfortable and tell us. Are you hungry?'

'When did you know a soldier who wasn't?' Martial said. 'I've already sent Ratty to the kitchen. I thought I might take the liberty with you.'

'So you might,' Phoebe agreed. 'Well, come into the parlour, then, and I'll pour you a glass of wine.'

Sipping George Canfield's excellent sherry, Martial said, 'We've had word from Washington that General McDowell's been ordered to launch a thrust on our army at Manassas.'

'We've known for a long time it must come,' Phoebe said. 'The New York *Tribune* has been trumpeting "Forward to Richmond!" for weeks now. What force has McDowell got?'

'About thirty thousand men in camp around Washington. There's another fifteen thousand up the Potomac somewhere near Harper's Ferry, but they're busy pinning down our army in the Shenandoah Valley – Joe Johnston's command – so I don't think we need worry about them.'

'And what's our strength at Manassas now?' Phoebe asked.

'Twenty-two thousand,' Martial said.

They contemplated this imbalance in silence. 'But a Southerner is worth ten Yankees,' Ruth said.

'In the sense that most of our men are used to the outdoor life and know how to handle a gun, that's true,' Martial said. 'Many of the Northerners will be town-dwellers: shopkeepers and bank clerks. And of course we're in the better position. With untrained men it's always easier to defend than attack.'

'Is it?' Ruth said doubtfully.

'Oh yes,' Martial said. 'For an attack to succeed, the men need to act together as one unit, and that's the hardest thing for civilians to learn. But you don't need to be told how to defend. You see a man running at you and you shoot him. It's obvious.'

Phoebe's face grew grave. 'You know, we hide the reality from ourselves by calling them Yankees, but until a few months ago we were all Americans. They are our own people. We probably know some of them.'

'It's a truth better not spoken,' Martial said. 'There's no way out of it now.'

Ruth thought of the young men she had danced with in Washington, who were now the enemy, who must be killed if possible. 'If they attack you, you have to defend yourself, don't you?' she said at last.

'Yes, you do,' Martial said. 'They've invaded our country and are marching on our capital city with every intention of killing us if we get in their way. *That's* the reality to focus on.'

Ruth looked at him nakedly. 'Staff officers don't get hurt, do they?'

'Never,' Martial said promptly. 'But they are kept very busy, and we've all too few of them.'

'When's this attack going to come?' Fanny asked.

'It'll take McDowell time to get his unwieldy army on the move, so it gives us leeway to try to drum up some more men – which is why I've come to Richmond.'

'How long?' Phoebe pursued.

'My best guess would be a week or ten days before we see the whites of their eyes,' Martial said.

Phoebe wrinkled her nose. 'No, I meant how long will you be here?'

'Oh! A day or two at least.'

'Good, then you'll stay to dinner tonight,' said Phoebe the hostess.

Mary came back from Camelot feeling tired and depressed. Her visits to May always left her weary, but she felt it was her duty to keep going, for it was clear that no-one else was looking out for her. Aunt Margaret ran the house in Mrs Judge's absence as she ran it when she was there, leaving May nothing to do all day but sit and sew, usually alone. Most worrying to Mary was Conrad's growing irritability. He seemed to lose his temper at a moment's notice and for no reason, only barely restraining himself in Mary's presence. He had not been there today, for which Mary was thankful, but May had seemed nervous and upset, and had received Mary in the small back parlour with the shades drawn. After sitting in the gloom for a while, Mary said, 'May, dear, must we sit in the dark? Are you having the headaches again?'

'Oh – no – I just prefer the shades down,' May said lamely.

Mary stared at her a moment. 'Well, I don't,' she said, and went swiftly to the window and let up the blind.

'No, don't!' May cried. The light poured in, illuminating the bruise on the side of May's face, the darkening around the eye-socket, and the marks on her forearms below her three-quarter sleeves. May lifted pathetic eyes to her sister-in-law. 'I fell down the stairs,' she said. 'So stupid and clumsy of me. But I'm all right, really. There's nothing broken, and Dr Trevelyan said the bruises will go away in a day or two. I didn't want to worry you, that's why I kept the shades drawn.' Mary listened to all this in silence. May said hopefully, 'You won't tell anyone, will you?'

'What really happened?' Mary asked quietly.

May's eyes filled with tears and her lip trembled. 'I told you, I fell down the stairs,' she said. A tear spilled over. 'Don't ask me any more, *please*, Mary? It was all my own fault, so let's not talk about it any more. Tell me, how are the children?'

Mary let herself be sidetracked, but she continued to watch May anxiously and ponder on the problem. It was possible of course that May had fallen down the stairs, but in that case, why was she so averse to talking about it? Was it possible that Conrad's temper had led him to hit her? Of course it was possible; but even if she could get May to admit it, what then? No-one could interfere between a man and wife. A fond father or brother might remonstrate, but it was doubtful whether that would do more harm than good, if the man's temper were as uncertain as Conrad's had become. Mary thought, fearfully, that he was becoming a little mad.

At last the talk ran out, and the two women sat looking at each other unhappily. 'May, isn't there anything I can do for you?' Mary asked.

May's head drooped and she shook it slightly; but then she looked up and said, 'Maybe – there is one thing—?'

'Yes?' Mary prompted. 'Whatever it is, if I can help you I will.'

May seemed to have difficulty phrasing it. 'You know – when I married – Pa gave me Becka as part of my dowry?' Mary nodded. Becka was the slave assigned to May in the cradle, who became her waiting-woman when she married and left home. Mary had not thought May particularly attached to Becka – though that may have been because of Mammy, who looked on Maybelle as her own property and did not like anyone to interfere between them. But in any case, Becka was a strange girl, reserved, holding herself aloof from the other negroes, watching everything with sharp, noticing eyes – 'sly', Julie called her. Nobody liked her much. 'Well, I wonder,' May went on now, awkwardly, 'd'you think you could ask Pa if he'd take her back and maybe let me have someone else instead?' Mary looked her surprise, and May went on, blushing, 'You see, she misses Twelvetrees, and she's not happy here. If Pa would swap her for someone – Hebba would do – it would make everyone happy.'

'Your father would take more notice of you than me,' Mary said.

'Oh, I couldn't ask him. I *couldn't!*'

'In any case, May, you'd have to get Conrad's permission, or the Judge's, wouldn't you?'

Now an extraordinary defiance came over May's features. 'Becka's my own, not Con's. Please, Mary, just ask for me, won't you? I'm sure Pa would do it.'

So Mary had come home, primed with this strange request, and deeply puzzled about what was going on at Camelot. She was sure that Charles would refuse the request, and moreover would be angry with her for presuming to pass it on, so she thought she might as well get it over with as soon as possible and, finding Tammas in the hall, asked him where the master was. 'He in the lahbry. Miz Mary, where Mist' Fenwick gone? Ah has looked mos' everywhere, and deah a message jus' come fo' him, f'om Do'chester dreckshun. Look mighty seh'ious. De haws nigh on founderin'.'

'How could I know where Mr Fenwick is when I've just come

in? He's most probably at the stables. Why don't you send a boy to look?'

Tammas shook his head as if he had been given something too difficult to understand, and shuffled off. He was one of the stupidest of the slaves, but honest, a quality in a butler which outweighed any other consideration. Mary walked briskly to the library door, knocked and went in.

Charles looked up over his half-glasses, and at once Mary felt weak, foolish, nervous and silly. It was the effect he had. 'I've just been to see May,' she said. He did not speak, and looked at her utterly without interest. 'She asked me to relay a request to you, and I promised her I would do it,' Mary went on, and hastily repeated the plea about Becka. When she stopped speaking he stayed a moment in silent thought, and then said, 'Very well,' and looked down at his book again.

Mary felt as if she had pushed against an open door. 'You mean – you agree? You'll do it?'

He looked up again. 'Yes,' he said. 'Tell Hebba to pack. I'll give her a note to take with her. She can walk over in the morning.'

He went back to his reading, and Mary backed out, more bewildered than ever, but glad to have got away without being shouted at.

In the hall she found Tammas hovering while Fenwick read a note. He got to the end just as she reached him, and looked up with his future in his face. 'It's come, Mary!' he cried rapturously. 'We've been called! The Hussars are to go to Richmond! The Yankees are on the move, and everyone's wanted. We leave tomorrow!'

The rest of the afternoon was spent by Mary in frantic packing, while Fenwick and his father prepared the horses. She was in Fenwick's dressing-room when Lennox appeared at the door, his face a mixture of wistfulness and excitement.

'Have you come to help?' Mary asked. 'You might look in that closet and see if you think I've left anything a gentleman couldn't do without.'

He came further in, but didn't go to the closet. 'Mary, can I ask you something?' She looked up. 'What would you say to my going to Richmond too?'

She frowned. 'What do you want to go to Richmond for?'

He blushed a little. 'For the same thing as Fenwick, of course.'

'You want to go and fight?'

'Don't sound so surprised. It's my country now, isn't it? If I'm to stay here the rest of my life, I ought to do that for it.' She was silent with dismay. 'Well, why not? I see you don't like it, but I wish you'd say yes.'

'You're only sixteen,' was the first thing she could think of to say.

'Tradd Ogles has gone, and he's only seventeen. Boys *younger* than me go to war. And I'm grown-up for my age, you know I am.'

'But, Lennox, you know from your reading what war is like. It isn't just splendid uniforms and bands and flags – it's death and misery. People get killed in wars.'

'It doesn't make any difference. I think it's a thing women can't understand. I'm a man, and I want to go and fight for my country.'

She said helplessly, 'I don't know why you're asking me. It's not for me to say. You should ask Charles or Fenwick.'

'You're the one who matters,' he said firmly. 'I'm grateful to them for all they've done for me, but they couldn't stop me going. I'll ask them, because it's polite, but if they said no, I'd still go. It's your blessing I want.'

'Oh, Lennox!'

'I promise I won't get killed. I'll go to Martial. He said before he left for Richmond that if ever I wanted to come, he'd like to have me as a staff officer, and you know staff officers don't get killed. Please say yes.'

She put out a hand and brushed a feather of fine golden hair off his forehead, where it had descended in his agitation. His eyes were bright with distant visions, and she knew that he would go anyway, whatever she said, so it was better that she let him fly free than have him feel the drag of jesses. And it was a comfort, at least, to think he would be with Martial. Martial would take care of him, if it were at all possible. 'If it's what you really want,' she said.

'Thank you! I knew you'd be a trump! And you'll see, I'll make you proud of me. I'll come back a hero, and then no-one will ever wonder about my background again. You'll be able to tell everyone I'm your brother without being afraid. You know,' he went on, soaring now, 'I can't help wondering if it was my *purpose* for coming here. Don't you feel there has to be a reason why things happen as they do?'

Dinner was a strange affair, the men all in high spirits – even Charles – celebrating what Mary could not see in that light at all. She did her best for them, smiling and drinking the toasts in champagne, knowing that, all over the South, women were seeing their men off to war genuinely feeling what she only pretended. It was the proudest boast of the Southern lady that her men had volunteered; the greatest shame to have a man doing nothing for the Cause.

Charles and Fenwick were pleased with Lennox's desire to go to Richmond, and applauded his idea of joining Martial on the staff. Charles even said, 'You'll need some money in your pocket when you get there, for your uniform and such-like. Come and see me in the morning before you go.'

After dinner Fenwick invited Mary to come out for a walk. 'It's very warm, and the grass is quite dry. You will only need a shawl.'

Fenwick's pointer Mag ran ahead of them, nose down to the grass, snapping playfully at the pale night-moths that fluttered up before her. It was almost bat-time: the sky was luminous, and the air was vibrant with the smell of honeysuckle and the piercing fragrance of the lime blossoms.

'I wonder if we'll ever have another evening like this,' Mary said after a while. Mag ran back, circling their knees enquiringly with a silent lift of her yellow lamp-eyes, and then was away again.

'Of course we will. Many more, a lifetime of them,' Fenwick said. He looked at her sideways. 'Why do you doubt it? The war won't last long, you know. One good battle to beat them, and then perhaps a little clearing-up to do, and then we'll all come home and take up where we left off. There's nothing to be afraid of.'

'Isn't there?'

They reached the end of the lime avenue, and she stopped, looking at the trees sharply etched against the dark luminous sky. 'I love this place,' she said. 'When I talked to Papa, I always called England "home". But this is home to me now. I love the great wide skies and the dark pines and the rolling hills. I love the way the light comes purple off the birches on a winter morning, and the deer that come down, stepping on tiptoe like dancers. I love the whiteness of the tracks on a summer evening when the grass looks almost black beside them. I love the sound of the crickets, and the mocking-birds in the orchard, and the spring rain drumming on the furrows. I love the way the cotton-fields turn suddenly green when the first shoots come through, and how when the cotton's ripe to be picked, the field looks like a snowfall.' She stopped, suddenly aware of her own voice.

Fenwick was touched. She had put into words much of what he felt without expression. 'All that will stay the same,' he said.

'*We* will change. The war will change us. The land will be here, but we will be different, and we won't see it any more.' He started to protest, and she said, 'No, don't you see? Being able to love all this depends on our whole way of life. And that's going. Don't you know it? I can feel it all slipping away from me, like the ground going from under my feet.'

'But Mary, we're fighting to *preserve* our way of life. That's what it's all for.' She said nothing, staring away into the dusk, and he put his hands to her shoulders and turned her gently to him. 'I never knew you cared for it all so much. I'm glad you do, and I promise you, it won't change. I will fight – we'll all fight – to keep it from the Yankees. They shan't touch a single blade of grass or a single leaf of a tree.'

She stared up at him, having no words to span the gulf between them, a gulf he did not even know existed. And then Mag ran up and jabbed her cold nose into Mary's hand, making her jump. Fenwick thought she had shivered, and said, 'You're cold. We'd better go in. It's almost dark now, anyway.'

He put his arm round her shoulders and turned her back towards the house. There was a lamp on the verandah, and it made the dusk suddenly darker.

CHAPTER TWENTY

'I have a plan, my friend,' said General Pierre Gustav Toutant Beauregard, filling Martial's glass carefully from the heavy decanter.

'Thank you, sir,' Martial said – for the wine, not the plan. There was a glittery look to Beauregard's eye that he felt boded no good.

The General sat opposite him, an elegant figure with a handsome, high-cheekboned face, his hair elaborately curled at the sides and drawn in a careful veil over the dome of his head where the native growth had failed. He regarded Martial with interest and steepled his fingertips. 'You like the wine?'

Martial tasted. 'Excellent, sir.'

Beauregard nodded. 'It is one reason to finish this war quickly. If the blockade is a success, there will be no more wine. That is why we must attack the Northern army – strike it – crush it – *pah!*' He suddenly struck his fist into his cupped palm and made an explosive noise with his lips.

'Attack it, sir?' Martial questioned gently. 'But the defensive position we've been taking up—?' A little to the north of Manassas there was a river called Bull Run, a tributary of the Potomac. The Confederate army had taken up position along it, keeping it between them and the advancing Union troops.

'Just so, just so. We seem to be on the defensive, and the Union commanders will be expecting no attack. We have the surprise on our side. We make a rapier-swift movement – the North is taken all aback – and *pah!*' Another thump.

Martial thought of the troops at their disposal. Few of them were yet soldiers. You couldn't even get them to march properly, let alone make a rapier-swift movement. But he could not say this to Beauregard. He sipped the wine again in silence and waited for more.

Beauregard eyed him kindly. 'You see, my dear Flint, this is our opportunity to strike a great blow and finish things. Their army is

313

even more unready than ours, but their civilians do not know it. You have seen their newspapers – they crow like dunghill cocks, believing victory is certain! If we defeat the army now, decisively, it will destroy the morale of the whole Union. But it must be a crushing blow. Their army must be smashed and scattered.'

Martial nodded and cleared his throat. 'And this plan, sir?'

A proud smile decorated Beauregard's lips under his large curved moustaches. 'It is based on the battle plan of Napoleon at Austerlitz!'

Martial groaned inwardly. During his time at West Point he had come to the opinion that all professional soldiers were obsessed with Napoleon. Since then, he had never met a senior officer who did not think that the French army was the model for every army in the world, and Napoleon the greatest strategist ever to have lived. He had made himself unpopular with his instructors by pointing out that the French army had been largely made up of foreign mercenaries and that Napoleon had in fact *lost* the French Wars, but it didn't make any difference to their opinion. And he certainly could not say such things to a Creole from New Orleans.

Beauregard's plan was to spread the army along eight miles of Bull Run, covering the crossings, the bridges and fords, but to keep the larger part of his force on the right wing, whence, at his command, they would swing across the river and attack the unsuspecting Yankees in their left flank. The flank would cave in, allowing the Confederates to encircle them, trap them against the river and slaughter them wholesale.

Old Borey's moustaches bristled and his eyes glistened at the prospect. Martial felt compelled at least to point out that the staff deficiency was such that even routine orders often went astray and, when they were delivered, they were rarely understood. Moreover, the troops were so untrained that the simplest manoeuvres took hours to perform, and so undisciplined that they obeyed orders only if they felt like it. His protest had no effect at all on Beauregard – in fact Martial doubted whether he even heard it: his eyes were far away as he dreamed of military glory. In his mind tiny soldiers marched and wheeled in mechanical precision over a map-like terrain; in his mind the enemy died in swathes, the few survivors ran away in abject panic, and his own dusty men marched past him back to camp, cheering the victory while he saluted them with tears in his eyes.

Suddenly he came back to the present. 'What is the latest news of the enemy?'

An hour earlier Martial had received a report from one of his scouts, Buckman. Buckman was as different from Beauregard as it was possible to be, but typical of the 'Irregulars': a lanky, laconical Tennessee hillman, dressed in brown homespun, leather leggings, a shabby jacket and a comfortable, shapeless hat drawn down over his eyes. His hair and beard were straggly, his skin brown as walnut juice, both from the weather and from the fact that he had never known what it was to wash since his mother first put him into trousers. He sat his brown gelding as if they had been welded together by some accident of nature, and the two of them could cross any terrain, and disappear against any background, so that if they stood still, you'd have to know they were there to see them.

Buckman had told Martial that the Yankees had left Washington on the 16th of July, but that they would be a long time on the road.

'You've seen them?' Martial asked.

Buckman grinned. 'Sure I seen 'em.' In his amusement, he waxed loquacious. 'You never saw sich a sight! Look like a circus parade, 'cep there's mile on mile of 'em – and that's not countin' the baggage. You could stand a week watching them baggage trains go by an' not git to th'end of 'em. Must a' packed their whole houses! Dressed like clowns, too. Uniforms ever' colour of the rainbow – turbans – feathers – ever' damn thing. Even saw some in them Scotch skirts, what d'e call 'em?'

'Kilts?'

'That's it.' He chuckled. 'Can't call it marching. Your lot are bad enough, but the Yankees is like crabs with corns, creepin' along. Don't even stick together. They jist amble where they please, sit down when they fancy it, wander off into the fields to pick blackberries, stop at houses to axe for a drink o' water and then set down on the stoop like they was visiting. They ain't soldiers, that's for sure.'

Martial did not relay the detail of this to his general, thinking it was probably better that he did not have any more reason for over-confidence. 'They're very spread out, sir. They only covered five miles the first day.'

'Good, good, that gives us more time. Well, well, let's have Manning and Penrose in, and my secretary, and – what's that new fellow's name? Mynott? – we'll start making out the orders.'

The Canfields were at dinner when one of the maids came in and went quietly up to whisper to Ruth. She turned so white that Phoebe thought she was going to be sick.

'Excuse me,' she said, drew back her chair, and went out, the talk dipping for a moment and then surging back up as the door closed behind her. In the hall there was only one lamp burning and the shadows were thick, but Ruth did not need light to recognise the bareheaded figure in the great-coat. Without a word she ran into his arms. His great-coat was beaded with rain and cold against the bare skin of her arms. He closed his arms round her and kissed her, half-lifting her off her feet. She pressed her lips to his neck, his ear, his cheek, anything she could reach. His unshaved bristles were harsh against her cheek; his skin smelled cold and grimy from his travelling, but she caught the real scent of him underneath.

'I've only a few moments,' he said when he put her down again. Instinctively he kept his voice down: he didn't want anyone to come and be polite and waste his little time. 'I've got to get back to Manassas. The Yankees have reached Centreville.'

She hardly heard him. Her hands were plucking at his sleeves. 'Come upstairs,' she urged. She found his big, hard hand and tugged him towards the stairs.

'Love, I can't. There are more of them than we thought. Thirty-five thousand, the scouts say. Centreville's only five miles from the river. Beauregard wants reinforcements.'

She thought he sounded a little dazed. 'Is that what you were sent for?'

'Yes, to ask the Government to order General Johnston's troops down from the Shenandoah Valley, ten thousand of them. They're not far from the railhead, and the railway runs right into Manassas, so they could be here in hours, if they can give the Yankees the slip.'

The cloth of his great-coat was damp. 'Is it raining?' she asked.

'A little. Ruth, I've got to get back, but I had to see you, just for a moment.'

She lifted her arms to him again. 'Oh, my darling love, it's been so long!'

He kissed her, but his lips were hard. She knew he was restraining himself and for a moment she wanted to do everything in her power to break down that restraint, to steal him back from the army and the world of men, to *make* him go upstairs with her and make love to her. But if she made him – and she believed she could – he would be unhappy afterwards. A maturity came to her, to do what was right for him, rather than what she wanted. She gently withdrew her lips from his.

He looked down at her. 'I wish I didn't have to rush away. But you understand, don't you?'

'Yes,' she said. 'And I wouldn't try to stop you. Every man in the country must want to be there.'

'It will all be over soon. One great glorious victory will settle it, and the Yankees will leave us alone. Then you and I can set up house together.'

'In Charleston?'

'Wherever you like. The world shall be our oyster,' he smiled.

'I'd like to go to England.'

'So would I, with you. You can use the time until I come back again to decide our itinerary.' He kissed her once more, briefly, and let her go, already striding to the door.

'I love you, Patrick,' she said. 'Absolutely and for ever.'

He grinned over his shoulder. 'See you remember that. There's all too many men around in Richmond!' And then he was gone. She ran after him into the porch, and was just in time to see him step into the pool of light from the lamp at the corner of the street. 'My soldier hero!' she called softly. He turned and gave her a mock salute and she kissed her hand to him, laughing; then he turned and walked on, and disappeared into the darkness.

Martial was riding up the road to the junction, going against the flow past new troops just arriving by train from Richmond. He took his horse off the path to let a company of cavalry come clattering by. The uniform looked vaguely familiar, and then a slow smile spread over his face as he recognised the serious face under the fur of a captain's cap.

'Fenwick! Fen, old man!'

The head swivelled round, and then the horse was swung out of line, and Fenwick reined up beside him to clasp his hand with a painful enthusiasm.

'Dear old Mart! It's good to see you: a friendly face in all this crowd!'

'Lennox said you were here somewhere. I was hoping I'd see you. So you made it before the fun starts?' Martial said with a grin. 'You cut it fine, though. There's already been a skirmish or two down at Blackburn's Ford.'

'The fighting's started?'

'Don't look so tragic! The Yankees were just probing our defences. We gave them something to think about and they scuttled off again. They're not massing for the great attack yet.'

'Oh, good! The way they hurried us through Richmond, I thought it must have started. I didn't even get time to see Ruth. How is she?'

'She's very well. She and Pick are as happy as turtles.'

'I'm glad. He's a very decent sort of fellow,' Fenwick said.

'And how are things at home? Did you leave them all well?'

'Yes, very well,' Fenwick said. He was studying his cousin keenly.

'I say, Mart, you look very grey and grim. Not a bit like a soldier. I mean,' he added hastily, 'when you look at all these fellows,' he waved a hand to indicate the newly arrived volunteers, 'there's nothing very splendid about you.'

'We staff officers aren't supposed to look splendid,' Martial said gravely. 'We don't have to frighten the Yankees like you fighting men. We're supposed to be inconspicuous.'

'But you don't look as if you were enjoying it much.' Fenwick sounded puzzled at the idea.

'I haven't had much sleep in the last few days. But don't worry. I shall be as excited as the next man when the big battle starts.'

Fenwick was satisfied with that. 'I'm glad to have got here in time, anyway. I didn't like being outdone by my little brother. Have you seen anything of Eugene?'

'I saw him yesterday, though not to talk to. He's right over on the left wing, in Evans' Division. I dare say you'll bump into him sooner or later. You'll find a lot of friends here. I keep seeing people I know from back home.'

'Ah, that's us Carolinians all over,' Fenwick smiled. 'Charleston breeds a particularly fine sort of hero. Oh, my troop's disappearing! I'd better go and catch them up. Where will we meet again?'

'We'll crack a bottle together in Richmond when the battle's won.'

'Yes, we'll do that!' Fenwick said enthusiastically. He raised a hand in farewell and turned his horse to trot down the road in pursuit of his troop.

The road from Centreville to Gainesville, called the Warrenton Pike, crossed Bull Run on an old three-arch stone bridge. This was the last river crossing that Beauregard had ordered to be guarded, the furthest upstream, and marked the extreme left of the Confederate front. Most of the force was gathered behind Mitchell's Ford, where the road from Centreville to Manassas Junction crossed the river, to the centre-right of the line. That was the direct route for the Union troops to take, and where they were expected to make their big push.

'It's just our luck,' Eugene grumbled to Beau as they waited at the Stone Bridge on the night of the 20th of July. 'All the fighting's going to be on the other wing. We'll be lucky if we even see a Yankee here.'

Beau was equally disconsolate. 'I'll bet old Shanks is mad about it too,' he said. Shanks was the nickname for their commander, Colonel Nathan Evans, given for his skinny bow-legs. It was an affectionate nickname, for he was liked by his men, a gruff, hard-bitten, hard-drinking West Pointer, an experienced soldier and a South Carolinian to boot. His bow-legs came from a lifetime on horseback, a most worthy deformity.

The colonel was at his headquarters at the Van Pelt house, just up from the river on a ridge from which, in daylight, the Warrenton Pike could be clearly seen. Any Union troops advancing along it would be spotted from quite a distance. It was dark now, however, and Eugene and Beau were on guard duty, squatted down under a tree just beside the road. The bridge gleamed a little paler than the surrounding darkness, and they could hear the quiet sound of the water against its piers and the whispering of the trees that overhung the river. Occasionally they heard an owl cry or a fox bark; occasionally the heavier rustling of some night animal in the undergrowth.

'I'm hungry,' Eugene complained after a while. 'It seems so long since supper.'

'We'll get breakfast when we're relieved at dawn,' Beau said.

'If the wagons have got here,' Eugene grumbled. 'You need a good, hot meal when you've been on duty all night, not just hard tack and cold pork.'

'I've still got some coffee in my pack,' Beau said. 'We can share that.'

'Thanks,' Eugene grunted. It was a generous offer. Coffee was precious out here far from the commissariat. 'I'll bet they're doing all right up in the Van Pelt house. Old Shanks will have had fried chicken for supper, and plenty to drink. He won't—'

'Sshh!' Beau nudged him sharply and scrambled to his feet. Someone was coming up the path. It was the guard corporal checking on them.

He stopped in front of them, eyeing them suspiciously; a skinny veteran, tough as dried beef and up to all the tricks. 'All quiet?' he asked at last.

'All quiet,' Beau agreed. 'Not a sound anywhere.'

'The Yankees won't come this way,' Eugene grumbled. 'How long has the regiment got to stay here? We'll miss all the fun.'

'We stay till we're told to move,' the corporal said, turning towards the bridge and standing with his hands in his pockets and his shoulders hunched comfortably. His face caught the little starlight from the clear sky over the river, and floated whitely between the darkness of his cap and his coat. 'Starting to get light,' he said. 'You'll be relieved soon. Meanwhile, keep your eyes and ears open. I thought I saw something out there.'

'Is it the Yankees?' Beau whispered. 'D'you think they're coming this way, after all?'

The corporal turned back to them, and his face disappeared into the general darkness. 'No, I don't know that it was anything. Just an instinct. It's too damn quiet out there. There hasn't been a bird or a beast moving for half an hour. So keep awake.'

He went away, leaving Eugene and Beau feeling jittery. They stood facing the bridge, fingering their guns. The breeze had dropped and the leaves hung motionless, so that the only sound was the water under the bridge; to their stretched nerves it sometimes sounded like human voices, sometimes like footsteps, just under the level of real hearing.

Suddenly Beau grabbed Eugene's arm, his fingers digging deep. 'What's that?'

Something was coming from their left, a heavy body moving through the thin scrub under the trees along the river. Man or animal? Too big for a fox or rabbit. 'It's the Yankees!' Eugene whispered. He cocked his rifle, making a click that sounded disproportionately loud in the still morning, and lifted it to his shoulder.

At once a voice said quietly from close by, 'Don't shoot, you damned fools! I'm on your side.'

Beau found his voice. 'Come out,' he squeaked. 'Come out and show yourself.'

A piece of shadow detached itself from the rest and suddenly there was a man there beside them, shockingly close; a man in shabby, shapeless clothes and a felt hat with a battered brim. He eyed them curiously.

Beau kept his rifle pointed at the man's chest. 'Who are you?' he demanded. 'Why are you sneaking about like that, trying to creep up on us?'

'I'm a scout, of course,' the man said laconically. 'And, believe me, boys, if I'd wanted to creep up on you, you wouldn't have heard me. I made a noise on purpose – didn't trust those itchy fingers of your'n. Who's your commanding officer?'

Beau lowered his rifle. 'It's Colonel Evans,' he said. 'He's up at the house. What's up?'

The scout jerked a thumb back over his shoulder towards the bridge. 'Yankees. Massin' to attack at dawn.'

Eugene was dumb with excitement; only Beau had the presence of mind to say, 'Go on up, follow the road and there's a path off to the right that leads straight up to the house.'

The scout shook his head. 'You better 'scort me, son. I don't want m'damn head blown off by another one o' you anxious greenhorns.'

Left alone, Eugene stared through the murk towards the bridge till his eyes ached. He had never felt so alone in his life, but on the other hand he had never felt so alive, his blood tingling and his nerves on the stretch, and his heart bounding with pride that he and he alone was standing like Horatius holding the bridge against the whole Union army. He couldn't believe that only a little while before he had been feeling cold, sleepy and hungry. Now he felt as if he could have jumped over a barn.

But he was not required to hold the bridge alone. Evans moved quickly when the scout brought his report and, by the time it was fully light, had his two regiments well disposed. Now from the ridge he could see the Union soldiers moving down the road towards the Stone Bridge. Down at the bridge they saw nothing until the huge roar of a thirty-pounder Parrot shattered the morning quiet, and the shot sang through the cool air and smashed into a tree on the far side of the river.

'Jumpin' Jesus!' the man next to Eugene exclaimed, and further down the line someone's rifle went off as a finger involuntarily tightened. The shot had made Eugene jump, but now he felt absolutely calm. He turned his head and grinned at Beau as more guns roared out. 'We've done this before!' he said over the noise.

'Just like old times!' Beau grinned back. Then another shot blew a tree right out of its roots and it fell sideways, taking a swath of scrubby little saplings with it, and suddenly the road on the other side was clearly visible and there was the enemy, a solid mass of humanity advancing along the road, and a glimpse of the hated Stars and Stripes waving above their heads. Here at last were real, indisputable Yankees! And it was going to be like shooting rabbits! Eugene settled his Enfield more comfortably into his shoulder and almost licked his lips.

First blood, however, seemed hard to draw. He didn't know how long he had been firing; the sun had risen, shining into their eyes, but still the Yankees didn't rush the bridge, seeming content just to fire on them from a safe distance. 'Why don't they come on?' Eugene said to Beau beside him.

An officer came up behind them. Glancing round, Eugene saw it was Captain Cronart, another South Carolina man and an old colleague of Shanks's. 'What d'you think, Webb?' he said to the corporal. 'Something queer about it, wouldn't you say? If they were going to rush us at dawn, why did they fire off the guns and give us warning?'

'Untrained troops, maybe,' Webb said. 'Can't do much with 'em.'

'I don't like it,' Cronart said uneasily. 'The old man's not happy with it either, I can tell you.'

Another scout, mounted this time, came crashing through the

copse to the left, and pulled up his sweaty horse in a swirl of dust beside the captain. The animal waltzed on the spot, flinging its head and spattering foam over a wide area. 'Cap'n! Sir!' He flung his words out jerkily as his head whipped round, trying to keep the officer in view while his horse circled under him crazily. 'It's a feint! They're pinning us down here while they outflank us! Where's the colonel? I've got to get a message back to headquarters.'

The captain grabbed the horse's bit-rings to keep it still. 'You've seen the Yankees? Where away?'

'Keep firing, you bloody fools!' the corporal growled at the men.

The scout flung out an arm. 'To the north. Coming down the unfinished railroad. They're heading for Sudley Ford.'

'How many of 'em?'

The scout paused a second, screwing up his eyes. 'Hell of a lot. I seen four brigades, mebbe five.'

'It's the real push,' Cronart concluded. 'I knew there was something wrong with this set-out. Corporal, keep those men firing! You, come with me. I'll take you to the colonel.'

They were away in a swirl of movement. 'Four brigades?' Beau said to Eugene.

'And we're the only troops near,' Eugene said. 'Now what?'

When Evans heard the scout's story he saw the whole picture instantly. If the huge Union force to the north outflanked them, they would have a clear path along the Sudley Road to get between the Confederate army and Richmond. Evans sent a galloper off hell-for-leather to find Beauregard, eight miles away on the other wing and, leaving only a small force to hold the bridge, formed up the rest of his brigade and marched them off.

There was no time to be lost; they would have to go the shortest way across country if they were to intercept the Union force. There was no road, only a rough farm-track following the contours of the gently hilly countryside. The track was not wide enough to accommodate a column. Eugene and Beau soon found themselves stumbling through the tussocky grass, hampered by their packs and rifles, sweating in their uniforms under the strengthening July sun. Clouds of dust rose from under the feet of the hurrying men, coated their sweating faces and filled their gasping mouths, as they strained every sinew to get across this heartbreaking terrain and fling themselves in the Northerners' path.

There was no need for the officers to urge the men along: the knowledge of what had happened had filtered through the ranks, and they all knew now that everything depended on them. They had seen the grim face of their tough little commander. The

Yankees were coming at the back door, and no-one knew about it but Shanks and his two regiments.

'They've got – better marching – than us – damn them!' Beau gasped as they stumbled along. Silently he thanked God and the advice of the veteran that they had changed their high-heeled boots for flat brogans.

Eugene pushed his rifle back as it slipped round again and knocked his cap askew. Four brigades – half the Union army. Fifteen thousand Yankees, maybe – and Shanks's brigade was merely two regiments – fifteen hundred men. Fifteen hundred to fifteen thousand? Arithmetic was not his forte, but he could work that one out. Ten Yankees each! The glory was going to be all theirs: not just first blood, but saving the entire Confederation with a heroic stand against fearful odds! And he'd been complaining about being stuck on the left wing! Now he understood what God had had planned for him!

Over on the right wing, Martial and Pick were having an equally hot time, though they at least had horses between them and the tussocks. The Austerlitz plan had been a failure. Despite frantic activity on the part of the few staff officers who knew their business, the Confederate troops had not crossed the river. Repeated instructions and increasingly impatient urgings had produced no more than a few ineffectual twitches on the part of a few brigades.

'It's hopeless,' Pick said, meeting Martial outside headquarters. 'I just can't get them to understand. Those New Orleans Zouaves don't even speak English – and that's the least of my troubles!'

Martial shook his head. 'Without experienced staff officers, it could never work. Most of our boys don't understand what Peter's trying to do, so how can they explain it to the brigade officers?'

'In any case, if they're going to push, they've all got to move together. I actually got the Third Brigade to start, but they stopped again when nobody else went with them.' Pick took off his cap to wipe the sweat from his brow with the back of his arm. 'God, this is hot work! You've got to tell Peter to call it off, Mart.'

Martial opened his eyes wide. 'Me, tell a general he's wrong? What do you take me for?'

Pick frowned. 'I wish Lee were here. He'd tell him.'

'Don't worry, Peter's not stupid. He'll see it's not on. And don't forget Joe Johnston outranks him. Once he arrives, he'll be in overall command.'

Canny General Johnston had managed to give the Union army the slip in the Shenandoah Valley and got his men to the railhead. They had been arriving in batches by train at Manassas since yesterday, and two divisions, Bee's and Bartow's, were already formed up to the rear of Beauregard's main force. Barnard Bee was an experienced West Pointer with a reputation for courage and initiative, and Bartow, though self-taught, was an energetic and intelligent commander.

'I was impressed with how well disciplined Johnston's men are, compared with ours,' Pick said.

'They've had more experience,' Martial said. 'They've already seen some fighting, not like our nursery boys. Hullo! What's this?'

It was the galloper from Evans' Brigade. He skidded to a halt on his trembling, heaving horse and looked round wildly for someone to tell his news to. Martial hurried over to him, and the lieutenant, seeing his staff facings, almost clutched him with relief.

'Get your breath,' Martial said firmly. 'What's the trouble?'

Gulping like a fish for air, the messenger told his story in a few brutal words. Martial did not need more. He slapped his fist into his palm. 'Foxed us, by God! All right, come with me, lad. I'll take you to the general.' Pick fell in beside them, knowing he'd be wanted. 'You know what this means, don't you?' Martial said to him over the messenger's head.

Pick nodded grimly. 'It means Evans has thrown his two regiments in the way of half the Union army. They won't hold them long.'

'No, it means McDowell and Beauregard have both read the same books,' Martial corrected. 'Don't you see, they've both been trying the Austerlitz plan on each other. If our attempt had worked, we'd have made a huge circle and never caught each other up.'

The lieutenant stared at him with his mouth open, and Pick said reproachfully, 'How can you joke at a time like this?'

'I don't know a better time,' Martial said, 'than when you're in the gravest of peril.'

For Eugene and Beau there was no time to be afraid. There was no time even to remember that they had been on guard duty all night, and had had no breakfast. Something else had taken over their bodies, a ferocious determination that kept their legs and lungs working desperately to get them across the ground.

And at the end of the frantic march, here were the Yankees, a multicoloured mass coming down the Sudley Road and spreading out across the hillside – Matthews Hill, they were told by one of the men, Fidler, who was locally born. That was the Matthews farmhouse up there, a squatty little place with a white picket fence around its tiny patch of garden. That was the way it was round these parts: all little farms, forty acres or so; a man and his wife and a couple of slaves, cornfields and peach trees, a few cattle and a pumpkin-patch. A quiet, peaceful life without luxury or much hardship. No-count people who never bothered anyone.

Now these rolling fields were being torn by the sound of shot, a rippling, crackling noise, continuous as brush-fire, interspersed with the heavier boom of artillery. The Yankees had field guns which they had hastily galloped into place, but they couldn't make much use of them because the suddenness of the Confederates' arrival had forced them to throw their men into rank to meet them. So now the two armies were facing each other across a sloping field, firing at each other. Somehow it wasn't what Eugene had expected. It felt so exposed. Behind them was a belt of trees, which was vaguely comforting. Above them the hazy July sky was milky blue and decorated with clouds that sometimes ran shadows over the land like a great hand stroking the fields. Above the Yankees hung strangely round clouds of smoke – smoke-rings blown by cannon. He supposed there must be the same over their heads, but he hadn't time to look. He had to load and fire his gun as fast as possible. It seemed so strange to stand here and be fired at by the Yankees. A bit of him kept wanting to run away, but his legs were too tired to listen. He was glad, because he wanted to be brave.

First blood, he kept thinking to himself. But he hadn't meant, when he had proclaimed it and wanted it, actual blood, the real red stuff inside a man. His mouth was sour and slimy from biting cartridges, his eyes prickly from the gunpowder smoke. He fired again, and reached for another cartridge. 'Aim low, you bastards!' the sergeant was bellowing further up the line. 'You're wasting shots.'

'I'm so thirsty,' Eugene said. Beau said, 'Me, too.' Eugene turned to look at him, and saw his face black and his eyes red, and his teeth white as he grinned. 'Hot work!' Beau said, and then flinched and ducked towards him. A sudden whining noise ended in a wet smack of a sound, and the man next to Beau dropped his rifle and flung his hands to his throat, his eyes bulging and his mouth opening to scream, though no sound came out. Blood spurted and sheeted shockingly scarlet through his fingers and down his grey front, and he reeled backwards. Eugene felt his stomach turn over, and a sour belch of bile came up his throat, but he had nothing to be sick with. It was too long since dinner.

'First blood,' he said. His voice sounded most peculiar.

'Eyes front there. Keep firing,' the sergeant growled.

There was another sound, Eugene now realised, a counterpoint to the brattle of rifle fire, which he had been shutting out from his mind. It was men screaming as the hot, red stuff escaped them. He didn't want to know about it, but now he had become aware, he found it all around him. A man three along went down, shrieking high and horribly as a bullet ploughed into his belly, another cursed wildly as he collapsed with a shot through his knee. The whine of an artillery shell made Eugene duck, and a whole swath of men went down, six or seven together, and there was a moment of shocked silence followed by a low, desperate sobbing from the one man still left alive.

It was not what he had expected. Somehow in his visions of glory there had been fighting but no blood, dead Yankees but no screaming wounded, no mutilation, no horrible, unspeakable smashing of bone and flesh. And yet he kept on firing. He didn't run. And all along the line there were men, most of whom had never been in a battle before, who didn't run. They were soldiers now. His mind was a numb litany: *bite, load, cock, fire; I'm so thirsty; aim and fire; wish they'd stop that man screaming; cock, aim, fire; sweet Jesus that was close!* And below the litany was a deeper voice, adding a triumphant bourdon: *First blood! We're doing it! First blood!*

There were shouts and cheers coming from behind now, behind and to the right. Captain Cronart came cantering along behind them. 'We've got reinforcements, boys! Two more divisions just arrived! Now we'll show those Yankees a thing or two! Keep it up, boys.'

The word came down the line that the newcomers were Bee's and Bartow's divisions, part of General Johnston's army from the Shenandoah. 'But we were here first,' Beau said, grinning at Eugene. His teeth were black now, nearly as black as his face. 'First blood to us!'

First blood, first blood. It was so hot! He was so thirsty! How long had they been at it now? He tried to gauge by the height of the sun, but could not remember where it had been when they started. It must be an hour or more. There seemed to be so many Yankees, more all the time, and fewer of their own men. The man next to Eugene sat down suddenly with a grunt of surprise. He clutched Eugene's leg, and Eugene bent to help him. 'Wha?' the man grunted, looking up at Eugene with puzzled eyes. 'Huh? Wha?' A spreading stain soaked outwards across his chest. 'You're shot,' Eugene said, pulling the man's hands away from his leg. 'Go on back, go to the rear. They'll help you.' The man tried to smile, and then frowned, looking down, folding his hands over his tunic, and collapsed gently sideways. Eugene straightened up, and a bullet whined past him so close it was like a hornet circling his head. He felt a searing hot pain, clapped his hand to his ear and it came away sheeted with blood. The bullet must have just clipped the top of his ear; it bled copiously, as ears do. First blood, he said to himself, a little hysterically, and felt sick, and very, very tired.

The sun was high, and the situation was desperate. Even Eugene, with no knowledge of military strategy, could see that the Yankees were outflanking them on the left; then the word came down the line that the Union division they had been holding up at the Stone Bridge, a thousand years ago that morning, had crossed at the Farm Ford, a few yards further up from the Stone Bridge, and were marching up the same path they themselves had followed that morning. The Confederates were going to be surrounded.

'We must fall back,' Captain Cronart said behind him to Lieutenant Bragg.

'Retreat, sir?'

'There's no shame in it. We've done well to hold them up so long. It's eleven o'clock, Bragg.'

A bullet sang over Eugene's head. The Yankees were uphill of them, so their shots often went high.

'Sir! Sir!' Bragg's voice was high with shock. Eugene looked back, in time to see Cronart slip heavily from the saddle. But he saw something else, too – the backs of Confederate soldiers running for the woods.

'We're falling back,' Eugene said in a dazed voice.

Beau also turned to look, and the movement and the words ran through the grimy, beleaguered remnant of Evans' Division. *Fall back, fall back!* The officers and the sergeants and corporals tried to stem the flow, to make it an orderly retreat, and at first it worked. The front line stopped to fire, and then ran through the rear rank, reloading as they ran. But then the Yankees started to advance after them, and a panic at the thought of being left behind slithered through the men like a gulp of cold custard, and they began to hurry, and then to run. They scrambled down to the Warrenton Pike, across it, and up the slope opposite. There was a wooden farmhouse surrounded by a peach orchard, and they engulfed and passed it. Some of them, including Eugene, broke through the scraggy hedge and dodged between the peach trees. He glanced up and saw the little green globes of half-ripe fruit hanging amongst the dark leaves, and a lust for them seized him. He paused, reaching up his hand; but Beau was there, grabbing him roughly by the arm, shouting, 'Come on! Don't stop!'

'I'm thirsty!'

'They're not ripe. Come on! The Yankees are right behind us!'

He dragged Eugene away from the tree, and Eugene, trying to

catch his balance, looked back and saw a Union soldier in a blue coat appear in the gap in the hedge. His face was a white oval between cap and coat. He saw them and dropped to his knee, raising his rifle.

'Run!' Eugene said. Still clutching each other, he and Beau staggered forward, and a shot sang out past them. 'Goddam!' Eugene yelled. As soon as he got the other side of these damned trees he was going to turn round and shoot that bastard! He heard the explosion of another shot, and Beau jerked hard at his sleeve, as if trying to attract his attention. Eugene glanced at him and saw his eyes stretch wide in an expression of shock, and then Beau let go and fell face forward.

'Beau!' he yelled. His momentum and that of the men around him carried him forward, even though his head was twisted back trying to see his friend. He caught a glimpse of him unmoving on the ground, and then they were through the orchard and out on the open hillside again. Corporal Webb beside him turned and dropped to his knee to aim his rifle. 'Shoot the bastards!' he shouted, and Eugene and one or two others obeyed, turning back in time to fire at the Yankees as they poked themselves temptingly through the gaps on the further hedge. Eugene didn't know if any of them were hit, but they popped back like rabbits into their holes.

Webb was on his feet again. 'Come on!' he yelled, urging them on again, to take advantage of the moment they'd gained.

'I've got to go back!' Eugene cried. 'Beau – my friend—!'

'He's had it,' Webb said roughly. 'Come on, you fool!'

They went scrambling out onto the flat top of the hillside, Eugene with them, his legs obeying the corporal while his mind ululated with shocked grief for Beau. The officers were trying to get the men to turn and make a stand now. General Bee appeared, his chestnut horse fretting on a tight rein, his beard jutting with determination. 'Steady, men!' he shouted. 'Reinforcements are here.' Up ahead of them was a newly arrived brigade in Virginian blue, just marched up from the junction: more of Johnston's army from the Shenandoah Valley. They had formed up across the hill, and in front of them their general sat, an upright, burly, bearded figure, so still and unshakeable in the saddle amid the noise and confusion that he looked like a statue of himself; his little roan stood foursquare, swishing its tail calmly as if it were on a parade ground.

Bee waved his sword and gestured it towards the monumental figure. 'There stands General Jackson like a stone wall, men! Rally behind the Virginians!'

A cheer went up at the words; Eugene found himself cheering with them, and the Virginians answered with a heartening yell of welcome. The battered remnants of the morning's fight scrabbled through the lines, clapped on the back by grinning men with clean faces. Eugene grabbed hold of one of them and clawed at his canteen like a madman. Grinning, the man pulled it off and shoved it into Eugene's hands. There was a sudden crackle of rifles as the Virginians began firing on the pursuing Union troops, and the owner of the canteen turned hurriedly away. Eugene drank and swallowed and felt sick, drank again, then lowered the bottle, wiping the back of his arm across his sticky face. He looked around him. The firing was continuous now, and the men were biting and loading and ramming and cocking and aiming and firing with frantic haste. He felt as though he had fallen into a continuous dream. 'First blood,' he said, and abruptly, and not quite voluntarily, sat down on the grass.

CHAPTER TWENTY-ONE

When General Beauregard arrived at the field at about noon, the situation had stabilised. The Union army had halted its advance in order to reorganise; the Confederates were holding steady in position. The two armies were facing each other across the flattish top of Henry Hill, with the Union front on a line with the little farmhouse – the Henry House, occupied only by the old woman, Mrs Judith Henry, who owned the land.

Lennox, riding along behind the line looking for one of Martial's scouts, found Eugene sitting on a tree-stump, his clothes dusty, his face grimy and the left side of his head, neck and collar crusted with dried blood.

'Eugene! No, over here! It's me, Lennox.' Eugene looked up blankly. 'I say, are you wounded?'

Eugene rose slowly to his feet. 'Lennox? What're you doing here?' And without waiting for an answer, 'They've killed Beau,' he said.

'Beau Raven?'

'He got hit as we were coming across the orchard. By that house. They shot him in the back.'

'I'm so sorry. How dreadful! But are *you* all right? There's blood on your face.'

'Oh, I'm all right,' Eugene said vaguely. 'It's just a nick. But I got separated and now I can't find Shanks or any of the fellows.'

'I just passed Evans's – what's left of them – out on the right wing, over that way,' Lennox said, pointing. 'They're behind the line, actually – pretty battered, and not up to much more fighting. You bore the brunt of it this morning, didn't you?'

Eugene nodded seriously. 'We stood up to everything, and we weren't scared a bit. What's happening?'

'General Beauregard's here, and Johnston's on his way. And there are more reinforcements being sent up from Manassas. The Fifth Brigade, Cocke's, will be here very soon. Oh, and the cavalry under

Stuart is coming up the Sudley Road. Fenwick's with them – I saw him yesterday.'

Eugene nodded vaguely. 'They killed Beau, did I tell you?'

'Yes, old fellow, you did.' Lennox looked at him with concern. 'You ought to have someone look at your wound. Why don't you go and find your division? They're resting in the farm lane back there. I wish I could go with you.'

Eugene waved a hand. 'I'm all right. Go on.'

Lennox hesitated only an instant longer, and rode on.

The fighting resumed, each side trying to push the other off Henry Hill. It was evenly balanced until the Union army managed to bring up a field artillery unit of about twenty guns, which began to pound the heart out of the Confederate left and centre, General Jackson's Virginians.

Pick Manning, riding up with a message for General Jackson, saw a lone grey coat amid the Virginian blues, firing away as though his life depended on it. In curiosity he stopped a captain of the 33rd and asked who it was.

The captain almost shrugged. 'I don't know his name, sir. He's one of the survivors of Evans' Brigade, and all he wants to do is kill Yankees. When my sergeant tried to send him away, he got very abusive, so Colonel Cummings said to leave him alone. He's good for stiffening our men,' the captain added. 'Doesn't seem to have any fear – doesn't even flinch when a shell goes over his head.'

'Those Yankee guns are a damned nuisance, aren't they?' Manning said.

The captain nodded. 'Colonel Cummings wants to try charging them. They're much too far up, and they haven't proper support. Cummings thinks we could take them if we struck hard and fast. But General Jackson won't agree.'

'I should think not,' Pick said. 'You'd be slaughtered. Well, I must get on. Look after your mascot!' He nodded towards the lone grey figure, and rode away.

Eugene was happy. As long as he could stand in rank with the other men and fire at the enemy, he could forget how he had felt the bullet hit Beau; forget that he had left him behind in the orchard of the Henry House among the Yankees. Shot and shell howled round him, but he paid it no attention. The Virginians told him he was 'a mad bastard', but they seemed to like him. They thought he was lucky for them, for no-one in his immediate vicinity had been hit.

When they had been firing about an hour, an incident happened to confirm their faith in him. Eugene had just lowered his rifle to reload, when he heard a shrill whine like an angry hornet, and felt something slam into his chest with a force like the kick of a horse. The breath was knocked out of him, and at the same time a sharp pain lanced through him. *I'm shot*, he thought. His hands let go of his rifle. He saw it tumble and wanted to catch it, but couldn't; and then his legs started to buckle, and he couldn't control them either. He was numb, he had no feeling in any part of his body; he was falling in a terrible white silence. *That's it – I'm dead*, he thought; and instead of fear he felt a terrible scalding pity, quite detached, as though he were someone else that he was feeling sorry for. And then he was on the grass, in a sitting position, and taking his first long ragged breath, hearing the clamour from the men around him. Not dead, after all. He tried to move his hands and they lifted, trembling, his arms feeling like lead, to touch his breast where he had felt the pain. There was a rent in his uniform, but no blood. He bent his head, dropping his jaw to his chest, to look, and slow realisation seeped through his mind.

The man who had been standing next to him was kneeling beside him, his hands fluttering about in anxiety, looking for the wound.

'Where is it, friend? Where you hurt? Is it bad?'

Eugene pushed his hands away, shaking his head. He still couldn't speak, but he could manage to undo his button and put his hand into his breast pocket and pull out his segar-case. In the middle of the lid was a new and violent dent, so deep it had almost penetrated the metal.

He held it up, and found his voice at last. 'It's m'lucky case!' he quoted the old man's words. 'Saved m'life a score o' times!'

His companions heaved him to his feet, shook his hand, slapped him on the back, did everything but kiss him in their delight that he was still their lucky mascot – luckier than ever now.

Colonel Cummings rode over. 'What's going on here? Why are you men out of line?'

Eugene was shoved forward while the men clamoured out the story, grinning and waving their guns to emphasise the wonder of it. Cummings listened with a frown, and then began to smile. 'By God,' he said, slapping his thigh, 'that does it! It's a sign, lads! The general may disapprove, but you can't ignore an omen like that. We're going to charge the guns!'

A cheer answered his words. Someone shoved Eugene's rifle back into his hands and his cap back on his head, and he stumbled with them back into line. His chest was aching from the blow, but his blood was running hot again. They were going to charge the Yankee artillery! They were going to take the guns! The Charge of the Light Brigade was nothing to it!

Pick was taking General Jackson's reply back to Beauregard when the 33rd Virginians charged the Union artillery. Because the Union troops were still moving in down the Sudley Road, the Confederate line had shifted gradually left to counter it, and the 33rd Virginians were now therefore past the aim of the guns and were attacking them from the side. Even so, it was a crazy, dangerous move, for the artillerymen and the battalion of infantry who were protecting them were armed.

But as Pick watched, expecting the 33rd to be cut down by a hail of shot, he realised that the Yankees weren't defending themselves. It was extraordinary. 'What the heck is going on?' he muttered to himself, and then realised that Martial had ridden up beside him.

'They're not running away, they're just not firing,' Martial said, using his field-glass. He sounded equally puzzled. And then he gave a great shout. 'They think they're Yankees! Yes, yes, that's it! Look, now they're aiming their guns, but it's too late.' He lowered the glass. 'Virginia blue uniforms look like Union uniforms,' he said to Pick. 'And our "Stars and Bars" looks like the "Stars and Stripes" at a glance. Well, I'll be damned!'

'Their lucky mascot must have done the trick,' Pick said with a grin.

'How's that?'

'They've got a survivor from Evans' Brigade fighting with them – says all he wants to do is kill Yankees – shows absolutely no fear. They think he's lucky for them.'

Martial's grin widened. 'I wonder if it's Eugene?' he joked.

With the Warrenton Pike and the Sudley Road at its command, the Union army was able to move men up quickly onto the right wing, and if they could outflank the Confederates there, the road lay open to Manassas and thence to Richmond. But as the afternoon wore on, fresh Confederate troops arrived all the time, and were deployed by Beauregard on the left wing. First Cocke's Fifth Brigade, then Kirby Smith's Fourth Brigade from the Shenandoah strengthened the Confederate left. The battle lines spread across the Sudley Road onto Bald Hill and Chinn Ridge. Then around four o'clock Early's Sixth Brigade arrived and outflanked the Union army on Chinn Ridge, and with Kirby Smith launched a crashing attack that drove the Union forces back.

Beauregard sent Martial and Pick galloping to Generals Jackson and Cocke, telling them to drive home the attack on the Union left on Henry Hill, though they hardly needed telling. The two friends met behind the Virginian lines and watched in almost painful anticipation. Then, at last, 'They're falling back!' Pick cried.

Martial had his glass to his eye. 'Go, Virginians, go! Yes, McDowell's called off his hounds! There they go, streaming back down the road! He's a cool hand, though. He's using the regulars to cover the ninety-day-boys' retreat. He doesn't mean to let it turn into a rout.'

'We've beaten them, and that's good enough for me,' Pick said. 'Come on, we'd better get back to Beauregard.'

Beauregard had more orders, and the two friends had to turn their horses round and gallop straight out again, Martial to Jackson and Pick to Kirby Smith, to instruct them to follow up the fleeing Yankees and harry them as much as possible.

As the Confederates had found out already, the drill involved in falling back was complicated and the Union troops had not had time to master it either. Retreat turned into rout. Panic was contagious, and soon the Union soldiers were running for their lives, dropping their arms and their packs and scrambling back over Bull Run, some of them up the Sudley Road to the ford, and others turning off the way they had come, down the farm-track and back to the Stone Bridge. It would have been a great opportunity for the Confederates to mop them up, but they were just as tired as the Yankees, and would have become just as disorganised if their commanders had not kept them together and resisted the temptation of the fleeing Yankee backs.

Martial rode back to Henry Hill and found that President Davis had arrived with General Lee, and was conferring with Beauregard and Johnston as to whether to pursue or not. Martial delivered his report, and turned away. He would not be wanted for half an hour, and thought he'd try and find a bite to eat somewhere. Then he saw Lennox coming towards him.

'Sir, have you seen Eugene?'

'Should I have?' Martial asked.

'He was fighting with the 33rd Virginians, and when I went past them just now, he wasn't there. So I went to his own division, and they hadn't seen him either. The thing is, he'd had a bang on the head and I was afraid he might have wandered off somewhere.'

Martial listened with growing gravity. 'Good God, so he *was* the "lucky mascot"! I joked when Pick told me that it must be Eugene.' He put a hand on Lennox's shoulder. 'I'm afraid the 33rd took pretty heavy casualties.'

Lennox nodded, biting his lip. 'I was afraid—' He couldn't finish the sentence.

'Look here,' Martial said, 'why don't we go and check at the dressing-station? They might have him there. Oh, damnit, what now?' He was being beckoned by the generals. 'I'll have to go,' he said. 'Try the Henry House,' he added over his shoulder. 'That's the nearest.'

The Henry House had been in Yankee possession for most of the day, but now that they'd gone, it was being used for the wounded, despite a huge hole in the wall where it had been struck by a stray artillery shell. Inside, it was like a scene from hell. Lennox felt his stomach roll, and he swallowed hard and often. Soft .58 bullets made a terrible mess of a body.

An assistant surgeon, with a green medical sash and a gold 'MS' embroidered on his cap, was bandaging and splinting as fast as he could, trying to prepare the victims to be carried back to the field hospital at Manassas, and thence to the Chimborazo Hospital in Richmond. The infirmary detail – who were in fact the regimental band – were not helping much. They seemed to be paralysed by the appalling sights and sounds around them.

Lennox was about to leave when he saw a man with infantry flashes whose face looked familiar. He had a bandage round his own head, but was calmly winding one round the naked upper body of a sobbing young soldier whose downy face was smeared with red where he had knuckled the tears from his eyes with bloody hands. The soldier finished and stood up, and on an impulse Lennox accosted him.

'You're not infirmary detail, are you? You're an infantryman.'

'That's right,' he said. 'Fidler's my name, of Evans's.'

'I thought I'd seen your face before. What are you doing here?'

Fidler jerked a head eloquently at the Dantesque scene behind him. 'Someone's got t'do it. I'm a farmer by rights, but I've tended sick sheep and cows. Ain't much difference, 'cep' the hollerin'.'

Lennox accepted the point. 'I won't keep you from your good work, but I'm looking for Eugene Morland. You're in the same regiment, aren't you? Do you know where he is?'

Fidler nodded. 'Show you,' he said, and took Lennox out into the blessed sunshine and comparative peace. He walked slowly, and Lennox could see he was in a trance of tiredness, which probably helped him to stay calm. 'Didja hear about the old woman?' Fidler asked him suddenly.

'Which old woman?'

He jerked his head at the house. 'Her that lived here. Mrs Henry. It's a damned shame. Widder-woman. Lived here all her life, on'y she can't farm the land no more, 'count of she's too old – eighty-six come harvest.'

'I didn't know.'

'*I* knowed her,' Fidler said. 'Lived around here all m'life. Stubborn as a mule she was, and warn't scared o' no-one, so when the Yankees came she wouldn't leave the house. Then that ole shell came and knocked a hole in it and kilt her.'

Lennox said nothing, for there was nothing to say, but it seemed to him a perfect illustration of the stupidity of war. Fidler was leading him across the peach orchard – the trees splintered and broken, and the ground littered with their leaves and unripe fruit – and now he was stopping before two tumbled figures. 'There y'are,' he said.

Lennox saw that the one lying face up was Beau Raven, and despite all he had seen that day, it was a dreadful shock to see someone he knew lying there so still, with his eyes wide open and staring in death. Beau's cap was missing, and his dark hair was ruffled and white with dust. The other figure was sprawled face down beside him, one arm flung over him as if trying to protect him; his ear and the side of his head were crusted in blood. Lennox hunkered down to look at him. Eugene's face rested against the grass, his eyes were closed, and he looked peaceful – the only peaceful face Lennox had seen that day. He stood up, sadness weighting his chest.

'Do you know how he died?' he asked Fidler.

Fidler, who had been contemplating the two bodies, looked up at him, frowning in thought. At last he said, 'Y'mean Morland? He ain't dead. He's sleeping. Don't reckon you could wake him now if you blew a trumpet in his ear. He was on guard duty last night. Ain't stopped since.'

'Good God,' said Lennox blankly.

Scouts' reports came in of a great turmoil beyond the river. Thousands of sightseers had driven and ridden out from Washington to watch the battle from a distance, bringing rugs, folding chairs, picnic hampers, parasols, servants and plenty to drink. When the Northern army began to fall back, they decided it was time they packed up and went home, and got into their carriages and buggies and chaises and took to the road, just as the Union wagon trains, ambulances and reserve artillery arrived, heading the same way. The roads were soon jammed solid with locked wheels, braying mules, rearing horses and cursing, whip-cracking drivers; and when the fleeing militia came up behind the struggling mass of humanity and traffic, a general panic began. Ugly scenes ensued as fear turned to hysteria, wagons were abandoned, arms thrown away, and it was every man for himself. The Union army ceased to be, as the soldiers took to the fields and ran for home in what came to be known as 'The Great Skedaddle'.

Martial meanwhile had hovered on the edge of an interminable debate between the generals as to whether to pursue or not. Lee was for it, Johnston against, and President Davis turned his narrow, ascetic face from one to the other and seemed to favour each course alternately. But though Lee was his military adviser, Johnston was commander of the field, and finally the President came down on his side. 'I think our men are too tired, and if a pursuit turned into a disorganised scramble, it might do morale more harm than good,' he said.

Jackson, standing behind Martial with his arms folded squarely and his massive beard jutting, said, 'With five thousand men I could mop up the whole Yankee army – what's left of it.' He meant it to be heard, and the President flickered a distracted look in his direction.

'Well, perhaps we might send the cavalry out to harry them. And some working parties to collect up any discarded arms. Your scouts said the Union soldiers were throwing them away, Flint?'

'Yes, sir, and much else besides,' Martial said.

'Well, well, I think we'll leave it like that, then, shall we, gentlemen?' the President looked from face to face, and settled on Johnston. 'Organise some working parties, and get the rest of the men into camp.'

The group broke up, with Davis and Johnston walking away in private conversation. General Lee came towards Martial and, meeting his eyes for a moment, raised an expressive eyebrow and gave a tiny shake of his head. Martial translated it easily enough. To be a military adviser when one itched for a field command was bad enough, but to be an adviser whose advice was not taken was trying in the extreme.

Martial said, to comfort him, 'It *is* getting dark, sir.'

And Lee said, 'Tactful to the end. You should go far.' He looked at Jackson, bringing him into the conversation. 'Never mind, maybe next time, Tom. What have you done to your hand, by the way?'

Jackson glanced down carelessly. 'Broken finger. Bullet wound. Smarts a bit.'

'Evidently you got that *before* acquiring your lucky mascot!'

Martial laughed. 'You heard about him, did you, sir? It turns out to be my cousin, Eugene Morland. I never would have thought he was such a dangerous character – especially as he chose the law over West Point at seventeen!'

Jackson's rather round, blue eyes – veined with red now – turned slowly on Martial. 'Oh, he's your cousin, is he? Why isn't he an officer?'

'He thought he'd get to kill more Yankees as an enlisted man,' Martial said with a grin.

'Bloodthirsty fellow,' Jackson said. 'Wonder if I can poach him from Evans? Don't want to skew my luck at this stage.'

'Tempt him with a commission,' Lee suggested, smiling. 'If he's used to plantation life, he'll be very tired of sleeping in a tent by now.' Jackson laughed at that, and the three of them walked off together. 'How's that pretty young cousin of yours, by the way, Martial?' Lee asked. 'My wife took a great fancy to her.'

It was a long and complicated job to get the tired and excited soldiers together, to take roll-calls, to get them off the field and march them back to camp, to attend to the wounded and count the dead. The staff were the busiest men on the field, and it was only when Martial took five minutes off the back of his weary horse to eat some cold beef and stale bread – first food he'd had all day – that he realised he hadn't seen Pick since he went off with the message for Kirby Smith to pursue the fleeing Yankees. Kirby Smith's Fourth Brigade had gone off hot on the heels of Howard's, who had run for Washington the long way round, up the road to the Sudley Ford and along the line of the unfinished railroad.

He finished his food and went on a tour of the most likely places Pick might be, but could find no word of him. He found a major of the Fourth Brigade having an arm wound dressed and asked him, but the major had no recollection of the message or the messenger. 'But that's not to say he didn't exist. You know how it is on a battlefield. The Angel Gabriel could materialise a yard from you, and you'd never know it.'

It was some time later that a scrawny young bandsman with blood all over his uniform – other people's, presumably, since he was on infirmary detail – came up to Martial and asked if he was Major Flint. 'There's a fellow asking for you, sir, name of Buckman,' the boy said shyly. 'He looks a ruffian, but he said you knew him.'

'Yes, certainly. Where is he?'

'Just down there, sir, at the dressing station.'

'All right, I'll come,' Martial said. He wondered why Buckman had sent for him, rather than coming to him. 'Is he wounded?'

'I don't know,' the boy said, and abruptly his chin began to quiver, making him look younger even than his true age. 'I only came to play the cornet. I didn't know it was going to be like this. It's awful in there!'

Martial didn't see Buckman standing in the shadow of a hedge beside a shattered tree until he called in a low voice, 'Mister Flint!' Buckman acknowledged no military rank, nor any title of any sort, other than 'mister', which he bestowed on those he respected. Martial turned aside from the path and approached, seeing Buckman's horse, Pepper, standing quietly behind him, its head lowered wearily, some kind of bundle over the saddle.

'What is it?' Martial asked. 'Are you hurt, man?'

'Nope,' Buckman said. He pushed his hat backwards, removing its shadow from his face, and looked Martial squarely in the eyes, something so unusual that it gave Martial a frisson of apprehension. 'Brought you something. Wisht I didn't have to.'

And with one more firm look, he turned and took hold of the bundle on Pepper's saddle and half-lifted, half-dragged it off, tumbling it softly, heavily into the grass at Martial's feet.

Martial knew what it was. Nothing else had that falling shape and sound. He knelt abruptly, and Pepper gave a little grunt and stepped back a pace. Buckman hunkered at a small distance, his forearms on his knees, his hands clasped quietly.

'How did it happen?' Martial heard himself ask. He turned back the coat collar, which had got pulled up, and smoothed it down. Pick lay with his cheek to the grass, his hair disarrayed. His eyes were closed, and the lashes looked unexpectedly long and dark against the pallor of his skin. Martial had read so much in literature about Death being Sleep's older brother and so forth, but he discarded it all now, because death looked nothing like sleep. He would have known Pick was not sleeping, however he had come upon him. In fact, what he had here was not Pick at all, was so obviously an empty container, that he felt almost affronted that it should look like his friend. It was a fake, a cheat, a cruel sham.

'How did it happen?'

'Just down past the Stone House, over the turnpike. Your friend wuz with Kirby Smith's, and they wuz following the Yankees up the Sudley Road. Then another bunch of Yankees comes from the right, fixin' to join the skedaddle, see? Skeered and mad they wuz, firing off their guns in a panic, 'case anyone tried to stop 'em. Your friend here took one in the chest.' He paused a moment, and then went on, 'Six or seven got hurt. I come across 'em later when I wuz comin' back up from the ford. They wuz patching each other up, but he wuz dead. Died instant, they said.'

Took one in the chest, Martial thought. How impersonal, unemotional, objective. But it was Pick they were talking about, his friend since earliest childhood, whose life had now stopped, whose inanimate outer case now lay here under his fingers as limp as a dead hare, limp and useless. Pick's face, his ordinary, nice face; the crinkled eyelids, the slightly crooked nose, the tiny scar on the upper lip, and the golden stubble on the chin that had grown just that day, since this morning's hasty shave: Pick's face, waiting for Pick to come back and get into it. But he would never come back, never rise again from this dew-chilled grass, never walk, whistle, laugh. My friend! Martial's mind cried. He felt a desperate desire to weep without restraint, like a bereft child. My friend! I want him *back*!

His hand trembled stupidly as he reached out and laid the back of a finger against the cold cheek and stroked it.

'You okay, mister?' Buckman said at last.

Martial nodded, and cleared his throat. 'Thanks for bringing him back.'

Buckman wiped his nose on the back of his hand. Behind him, Pepper sighed the sigh of a tired horse and shifted his weight from one side to the other. 'Guess you won't want him on the cart with the rest of the bodies. Want I should take him back for you?' Martial met him with an utterly lost look. 'Guess I'll do that,' Buckman said, saving him the answer. 'Old Pepper'll go another mile or two.'

The news of the battle was received with huge rejoicing in South Carolina. They'd always said they could whup the Yankees, and they had! A magnificent victory: the Yankees put to flight, scrambling away in utter panic and confusion, throwing down their guns as they tried to save their cowardly hides! The Union army in such disarray it would be Christmas before it could be put back together – if it ever was!

But that was before the casualty figures were announced. Then a stunned and disbelieving silence fell over the rejoicing population. The Yankees had lost three thousand, the Confederates two thousand – dead, wounded and missing. The figures took a while to mean anything: they were ludicrous, they were absurdities to a people who had not expected anything from war but glory, gay flags and lilting tunes. And when at last it sank in, and the realisation came of what war really meant, a grim determination seeped down into their souls that these casualties should not be wasted. They were not going to play at war any more: this was the real thing, and the South was going to win it, by God she was!

Then the lists of names started to come in, and families ran trembling fingers down the lines, looking for their sons and brothers and fathers. Even when the family name was not there, the huge gladness was only temporary, for there was always someone they knew, some neighbouring family whose cries were not of relief but of pain. And if the name you dreaded wasn't on this list, it might be on the next. It took time to gather in and identify all the dead. The agony of anticipation was drawn out until assurance finally came from the living.

Mary went to visit the Ravens before even knowing the fate of her own menfolk. They were inconsolable. Beau was their only son, and there would never be another now. They looked bowed with age, holding on to each other, lost, as Adeline, grave as a nun, attended them, her lips white with her refusal to cry. No son now to inherit Wild Acre; no Raven grandsons to warm their old age. Mary cried for them as much as for Beau, that nice, handsome, cheerful boy Ruth had hoped to marry. As she left, she pressed Adeline's hand and said, 'It will be a big responsibility for you, taking care of them now. If I can help in any way, you've only to ask.'

'Thank you,' Adeline said rigidly. She seemed to have jumped in a day from sixteen to twenty-six.

'You'll have a husband soon to support you,' Mary said, groping for some comfort for her.

Adeline fixed her with a clear gaze. 'Oh no, that's all washed up now. I'm not going to marry Chesney.'

Mary was shocked. 'Oh, my dear, I'm so sorry. I didn't know.'

'Nobody knows yet. I haven't told him, even. I've only just decided: I'm going to Richmond to become a nurse.'

'But – Addy—' Mary was too bewildered to be coherent. 'What about your parents?' she managed at last. 'You're all they've got now.'

She made a small, impatient movement of her hand. 'I can't help that. I have to do what I'm called to. Beau went for a soldier; I'm not a man, so I must go and nurse.'

When Mary got home from that sad house, heavy of heart for Wild Acre, whose youth and beauty seemed all to have deserted it in a single day, there was a scribbled note for her from Lennox, and some relief. He was unhurt, Fenwick and Eugene were safe. Martial was safe. Eugene was a hero – imagine that! He mentioned Beau Raven, who had been killed right beside Eugene. And Pick Manning was dead. 'Ah,' Mary cried as she read it, and it was a cry of terrible pity.

It fell to Lennox to tell Ruth. Martial wanted to go, but the general wouldn't spare him, and he didn't want it announced in a telegraph or letter, so he made a reason for Lennox to go back to Richmond.

Lennox arrived at the Canfields' house quite early the next morning, but found everyone astir already. News of the victory had come in the night before, and everyone was up early to be ready for more news. Lennox was standing in the hall with his hat twisting in his hands when Phoebe came to meet him, and she knew from his face that he had brought them death. She drew a long, wavering breath. 'Which one of them is it?'

Before Lennox could answer there was a clattering of hurried feet on the stairs and Ruth ran down, holding up her skirt with one hand and with the other shoving the last pin into her hair. 'Is it news?' she was calling before she had come down enough stairs to see who was there. Now she appeared, jumped the last two steps, and smiled a wide greeting. 'Lennox! Oh, I am glad to see you! You're not hurt?'

'No,' he said.

'I'm glad! We heard there were a terrible lot of casualties. Phoebe and I are going down to the hospital to see if we can help.'

'Ruth,' Phoebe said, trying to stop her, warn her, but she had come forward to kiss Lennox, her face happy and unsuspecting, too full of her own thoughts to read his.

'How are the others? Are they in Richmond? Is P—?' She got as far as the first letter of Pick's name, and stopped dead, almost touching Lennox now and catching at last the atmosphere that hung about him.

'Ruth,' he said, 'I have something I have to tell you.'

'No,' she said. 'I don't want to hear.'

'Ruth, dear, come into the parlour,' Phoebe said.

Ruth moved away so that Phoebe shouldn't touch her, looking from face to face, as a cornered deer might look at the hunters raising their guns. She whitened, and seemed to reel, putting out her hands in a strange, fending-off motion. 'No. Oh, no! No, Lennox, please, no?' Lennox caught her hands as they passed, and she gripped him hard. 'You can't tell me he's dead. You can't.'

'I wish I could tell you anything else,' he said. 'I wish I could die instead so that it didn't have to be him.'

'No, I couldn't lose you,' she said. 'Patrick can't be dead. He has to come back – I *know* he has to come back.' She swayed on the spot, moaning, 'You've made a mistake, that's all. It was someone else who only looked like him.'

'I saw him myself,' Lennox said, and the great weight of sadness in his voice made her stop still. 'I saw him,' he went on quietly. 'It must have been very quick, Ruthie. He wouldn't have known anything about it. He didn't suffer.'

She seemed to accept it, standing quietly, looking at him with wide, pain-filled eyes. And then she shook her head, and went on shaking it. 'No. It wasn't him. I know he's coming back, you see,' she went on almost conversationally, 'because I'm going to have a baby. Patrick has to come back, now I'm having a baby.'

A long time later, she and Lennox sat together on the sofa in the parlour, his arm round her shoulders, his other hand locked between hers.

'Isn't it strange,' she said after a long silence, 'that I wanted to marry Beau Raven instead of Patrick. And it wouldn't have mattered which I married, because I'd still be a widow. What a strange word, widow. I can't think of it as anything to do with me. But I must have been born to be one, mustn't I?'

'Of course it mattered,' Lennox said firmly. 'You had that time with Patrick.' It seemed better to use that name to her, the name she used herself.

'Eleven weeks and four days. Only that.'

'But whatever it was, you had what you had, and no-one can take that away from you.'

'I love him so,' she said, and her voice wavered. She hadn't cried yet, and Lennox wished she would. He felt somehow that the transaction was incomplete otherwise, and that he would never be free of his hateful role as messenger.

'I know,' he said.

'I love you, too,' she said unexpectedly. 'I'm glad you're here. I'm so glad it was you came to tell me. It would have been much, much worse without you.'

'I don't see how,' he said unhappily.

'No, I don't either. I suppose I'm just saying things. But I *am* glad of you. You won't go away? You won't leave me? Not for a bit?'

'Of course not,' he said. And then, 'I'd do anything for you. Anything in the world.'

'I know. But I don't want anything. Only Patrick back.' She was silent a moment, and then said, 'At my wedding, Tammas wished me blessed and happy for ever. For ever, Lennox.'

And they sat on in silence, waiting. Not waiting *for* anything, just waiting.

CHAPTER TWENTY-TWO

The emotional turmoil of his last days in America, and a long and difficult journey, added to Benedict's gladness to be home. He sent a telegraph message from Cork, where the *Nottoway* first touched land after her crossing, and when she finally docked at Liverpool, Sibella was there to meet him. Benedict's mind was reeling with tiredness and a confusion of images, half his heart still in South Carolina, and the dark wharves, the grey sea and grey sky, the accents of the dockside workers, the very cries of the seagulls seemed strange to him, as coming from a different and alien world. The ground of England heaved under his feet when he first set foot on it, and he had a painful and absurd moment of not being able to remember where he lived. But then he came out of the customs shed and saw Sibella waiting for him, and everything dropped away from him but a simple gladness.

Half a dozen steps, and he had her in his arms. They hugged, paused to look at each other, and hugged again, between laughter and tears. How thin she had grown! And there was grey in her hair. He suddenly realised what a burden she had taken up when he went away, while at the same time he realised how much he had missed her, and the quiet comfort of knowing she was near.

'I shall never go away again!' he said.

Sibella said, 'Don't promise what you can't keep. I'm just glad to have you back.' She laughed shakily. 'I don't know why I'm crying. Oh dear, what a sight I must look!'

'You look very beautiful to me. There's not a woman in all America to touch you.'

'Except Mary,' Sibella said, and then wished she hadn't.

Benedict looked grave for a moment. 'Don't tease me, Sib. It was hard to leave her.'

'Did you tell her?' Sibella asked carefully, afraid to jog a wound.

'I told her everything.'

'And?'

'She said I was still her Papa.'

Sibella slipped her arm through his and turned him to walk towards the gates. 'I'm glad,' she said. 'Everything's come out all right. Now we can put all that behind us.'

Although Benedict made a sound of agreement, Sibella thought there was some reservation in it, but his next words reassured her. 'I'm longing to be home,' he said cheerfully. 'Your letters, delightful though they were, didn't give half enough detail. The first thing we must do is ride all round the estate so that I can see what's changed. How's my dear old Monarch?'

'Very well. Henrietta rides him now. She comes with me when I go out on Ebony, and manages him beautifully.'

'But he's much too big for her!' Benedict protested.

'You forget,' Sibella said, 'she's almost eight now, and she's grown quite tall this last year. And he's very quiet with her. He seems to know she's only a child.'

Almost eight! Grown tall! There would be so much to catch up on. 'I've been a fool to stay away so long,' he said, and Sibella did not contradict him.

'Did you accomplish everything you went there to do?' Sibella asked him the next day, when they were discussing – as they would discuss for weeks yet – his trip. 'Did you renovate the mill and reorganise the factory?'

Benedict smiled ruefully. 'You can't imagine how difficult it is to get anything done over there! I think there is something in the air that slows your mind and body to a sort of languid dawdle. I arrived full of busy intentions, but by the end I was spending half my days in the clubs smoking segars and the other half sitting on a verandah drinking tea.'

'You?' Sibella laughed. 'I can't imagine it!'

'I was as indolent as any planter,' he assured her. 'I left Lennox to complete the work at the mill – if the war doesn't interfere too much. As to the factory, Charles Morland has the same problem any Southerner would have: he depends on poor whites for manpower, and there aren't enough of them. And he hasn't anyone who understands the business to manage it for him.'

'I'd have thought they'd use slaves,' Sibella said.

'It's impossible to get slaves to work at the rhythm of the machines, and they either hurt themselves or damage the machinery. He did experiment at one time with using slave children, who are more lively and teachable, meaning to keep them in the factory until they were old enough to be field-hands, and then replace them with new picaninnies. But he soon discovered that factory work does not breed strong and healthy field-hands, and was forced to give it up. No sensible man damages his own property.'

Sibella looked uneasy. 'I don't like to hear you talk about human souls being property!'

'I don't like to do it,' he said, and then asked, 'What do people over here think about the war?'

'Well, of course, everybody hates slavery,' she said thoughtfully, 'but as President Lincoln said from the beginning that he would not interfere with it, people feel there's nothing to choose between the two sides on that score. And since the North imposed the blockade on the South, there seems to be a feeling that this is typical American arrogance and bullying, and that the South ought to be allowed to go its own way if it wants. We always like to side with the under-dog, don't we? And what right has the North to say the South can't be a separate country?'

'But what does the Government say about it?'

Sibella raised an eyebrow. 'Really, Mr Morland, you will have to ask the Government that. What time do you think I've had to follow politics, with the house and the estate to run, besides bringing up five children?'

Benedict firmly meant not to leave home again – at least not for many months – but once the immediate business at Morland Place had been settled, he felt obliged to take a trip to Manchester to check on the state of affairs there. Four-fifths of the textile industry's cotton – and almost all of that used in Manchester – came from America.

He found matters better than he had feared. The blockade was proving surprisingly effective, at least as far as raw cotton was concerned, and virtually none was coming in, though Benedict knew he had left South Carolina with warehouses full of the stuff. But the cotton harvests of 1859 and 1860 had been extremely heavy, so there was still plenty of raw cotton in store in Lancashire. What would happen when those stores ran out was another matter. Benedict visited various fellow mill-masters and tried to interest them in the problem, but without success. They had already started to raise their prices in anticipation of a shortage, and expected to raise them still further when output dropped. Since their profits were actually rising, they were not prepared to be alarmed. Benedict was maddened by their lack of foresight, but he could not shake them. Something would turn up: it always had and it always would. God would take care of the mill-masters, who were His special favourites.

The Government's stance, Benedict discovered, had been careful. It had responded to the proclamation of the blockade with a statement of neutrality, forbidding British subjects to enlist on either side in the war or to build or equip ships of war in British ports, and acknowledged the South's right to belligerency but without mentioning any right to independence. Lord Russell's stated intention was to 'keep out of it'.

News came of the battle at Manassas, of a Southern victory with heavy casualties on both sides. Benedict was anxious about the people he knew, for naturally nothing was reported about the fate of individuals; Sibella did her best to worry alongside him, and managed to hope sincerely that Fenwick had not been harmed. But she couldn't help resenting that after so long away from her, her husband's mind could still be claimed by the Carolinians; and besides, she suspected she was pregnant again, which was a worry, for she had passed her fortieth birthday, and the last eighteen months had tired her.

And then in October a letter arrived from Martial, brought out by a blockade-runner to Nassau, and thence on a British mail-ship. It contained a few more details of the battle, and news of the family. Fenwick and Eugene were unharmed, he learnt. Lennox had been in it too – had joined the staff under Martial, and was much valued for his quickness in learning and his initiative. Benedict was sorry to learn that Beau Raven had died, and that some other young men he knew had been wounded – Berry Ogles slightly, but Dolph Ratliffe was still gravely ill and Manningtree Miles had lost a leg. And poor little Ruthie, so newly married, was a widow: that pleasant, agreeable, fellow Pick Manning was dead.

The letter brought it all so vividly before Benedict's imagination that Richmond and Charleston seemed just then far more real to him than Morland Place and the Vale of York. But the family news was only a small part of Martial's letter. What was contained in the rest sent Benedict scurrying for paper and pen; and soon Sibella was resignedly waving him off in the carriage to the railway station to catch a train to London.

Charlotte had spent the summers of 1860 and 1861 at Shawes, and the repairs and refurbishment of the house were complete. Her times there had been a refreshment to her. With Benedict away and Sibella doubly busy, there had been no need to be sociable. She had sent a courteous note on first arrival mentioning her desire for utter seclusion, and Sibella had sent one back equally courteous expressing perfect understanding and compliance. There was no-one else in the neighbourhood whose feelings she needed to consider and, by engaging a taciturn housekeeper and a perfectly ferocious gateman, she was able to keep the socially ambitious and the casually curious at bay. Besides, the building work going on made superfluous any other excuse for not entertaining. She was able to walk in the overgrown gardens in peace, or ride out on the moors, accompanied only by Wildey, and in the evenings she read, pored over plans of the house and its renovation, and went to bed early.

She often thought about the boy she had met here, Lennox Mynott, and wondered how he had got on. She learned that Benedict had taken him to America, and thought that on the whole it would be the best place for him. But she was grateful to him for concentrating her mind and crystallising her understanding of herself and her situation. She was, if not exactly happy, much more content now. In London she went less often to the hospital, saw Sir Frederick less and never alone, and occupied herself with a variety of schemes. Her hurt and sadness over the loss of Oliver's love and company did not diminish, but she was no longer resentful and angry, and that made everything easier to bear. She was a sinner, too, and was paying the price, quietly and patiently, and hoping that one day her sentence would be completed and she would be received again into the world.

The outbreak of the war in America had engaged her attention, if for no other reason than because she had distant relatives there, and because Benedict, she understood, was still over there. She had been heavily pregnant when Fenwick was in London, so had not met him, but her grandmother had spoken of him in glowing terms, so she felt an interest. When Lord Palmerston dropped in, as he still liked to do, she asked him whether it would not be possible for the British Government to act as a mediator between the two sides.

'We thought of it,' he said. 'In fact, we've had a plan before the Cabinet on more than one occasion. But I doubt anything could be done at present. In the nature of things – in human nature, m'dear – the sharp edge must be taken off the hunger for armed conflict first. Until they've had a chance to come to blows and found out how much it hurts, they won't feel enough desire for peace to secure it by making concessions.'

Charlotte nodded sadly. 'I know that's true of my own boys when they quarrel. Until they have a bloody nose apiece, they won't listen to reason. But it seems hard on the Americans – and especially the women – to make them learn by experience.'

'I'd like to ease your mind, Duchess,' Palmerston said, eyeing her with sympathy, 'but I suspect the Americans would regard any offer of mediation as an impertinence on our part. You know how they dislike what they call "interference" by the old world.'

'You haven't recognised the Southern states yet?'

'That would put the cat among the pigeons! This American business isn't something to get into a war over. No, no, we must rest on our oars and not give Washington any excuse to quarrel with us. I dare say we may have to recognise the South some of these days. At all events, we'll accept a *fait accompli* if we see the North is *not* going to beat 'em.'

'That,' said Charlotte severely, 'does not sound very principled.'

He raised a languid eyebrow. 'Saving English blood from being spilled not principled? And when it was you who wanted me to save the Americans from killing each other?'

She smiled. 'I can't argue with you! You always win.'

'I should hope I do,' he said. 'After a lifetime of practice in Parliament I ought to be able to outwit a chit of a girl like you!'

'I shall be thirty-nine in a few months!'

'My dear child,' he chuckled, 'when you get to my vast age, any female under fifty is a girl.

When Benedict sent a note asking if he could call on a matter of business, Charlotte assumed it was something to do with Fanny's Portion. She took only a distant interest in the running of the mills, happy to allow Benedict to oversee her half as well as his.

'I hope things have gone smoothly during your absence?' she said when she received him in her sitting-room the next day. 'You don't come to tell me the agent has run off with all the money while you were abroad?'

'Oh, no!' he said. 'Business is thriving, and the books are being properly kept. In fact, profits are up this year on last. Fanny's inheritance is safe for the moment.'

'For the moment?'

'Until the cotton runs out.'

'Ah,' she said. 'What will happen then?'

'The mills will have to shut down. Hardly anything is getting through the blockade, and won't do unless we do something to help the South.'

'I understand *your* eagerness to help them,' Charlotte said doubtfully.

'If the mills shut down, the hands will be laid off. Half a million people work in the cotton-mills in Lancashire. No work – no wages.'

This was something she would rather not imagine. 'I see your point,' she said, 'but what can we do?'

'I have a letter here from Fenwick and Mary's cousin Martial. Before the war started he bought up large quantities of cotton and shipped it over to England, where it lies in a secure warehouse. He wants me to sell it, and use the money to commission the building of a ship.'

'With cotton in short supply, he ought to get a good price. The man has foresight,' Charlotte said.

'I wish more Southerners had,' Benedict said. 'Their warehouses are full of cotton they can't get out, and cotton deteriorates in store.'

'What does he want this ship for? To bring the cotton out?'

'Yes, and to take arms and supplies in,' Benedict said. 'She'll need to be fast, and she'll need to be armed for her protection.'

'But that's against the law,' Charlotte pointed out.

'Only if she's armed in a British port. If she's built here and armed elsewhere, nothing can be done about it.'

'Well, perhaps you're right,' Charlotte said. 'I'm not sure where the law stands in that regard.'

'At all events, it's a risk I'm prepared to take.'

'But what has all this to do with me?'

Benedict hesitated, and then plunged in. 'I want you to help. If you and I both put money into it, we can order two ships instead of just one, which will bring down the cost of each, as well as double the help to the South. I will put up everything I can, though my resources don't pretend to match yours; and if you'll countenance it, we might put in some money on Fanny's behalf, from her inheritance, and do even better. As joint trustees, we both have to agree to it.'

'Fanny's money?' Charlotte said. 'How could we justify that?'

'As a sound investment on Fanny's behalf,' Benedict said promptly. 'A blockade-runner would command such prices that two or three cargoes would recoup the capital outlay – after that, she'd make a profit. The only risk would be if the ship were captured or sunk by the Yankees.'

'The *only* risk? I don't know about that. You don't consider my position. The Government is maintaining a neutral position on the war. If I were to do anything to jeopardise that – with Oliver being who he is—'

'Yes, of course, and I had thought of that. Naturally you would have to ask his permission, and ways could be found to keep your part in it secret,' Benedict said, but then added eagerly, 'though, of course, if it were known that you were helping in this way, it would encourage others to join in. It would be of the greatest benefit to the South to have your name on its list of supporters.'

'You're going much too fast,' Charlotte said, desperate to stem the flow.

'I'm sorry, I don't mean to badger you, but we need to move

fast. Ships take time to build, and every month makes the threat more real. We *must* do something to help – not only for the South, but to save the mill-hands from starvation.'

Charlotte thought she knew where his loyalties really lay, but it didn't negate the point about the mill-hands. She knew from experience how close to disaster the lower orders lived their lives. While there was work and money coming in, they could survive, but they had no safety-margin, no savings, no resources. If work failed, they starved and died, and while she saw this every day on an individual basis, the idea of half a million all at once in the same place did not bear thinking about.

'Very well,' she said. 'I will give it my closest consideration. You must give me a day or two to think about it.' And she added as he seemed about to protest, 'In reason, you must see I can't decide on the instant.'

'Yes, of course, I'm sorry. And you will want to consult the duke, too.'

Charlotte said thoughtfully, 'I think perhaps it would be better not to let him know anything about it at this stage. If it were to prove illegal, any complicity on his part could be dangerous. Even if he condemned it, there would always be those to say he planned it himself.'

Benedict went away hopefully, and his hopes were not unfounded. Towards the end of October 1861, he was able to place an order with a shipyard on the Mersey for two ships. He used the duchess's money, but not the duchess's name.

A month later Oliver came into Charlotte's dressing-room and sent Norton away. Charlotte's heart sank, remembering another occasion, assuming this was the precursor to a quarrel. When they were alone, he began abruptly, 'What are your feelings about this American business? Do you think the Government is right to maintain a neutral stance?'

His face was thoughtful rather than angry, but it was such an odd subject to bring up without preamble that she believed she must have been found out. But while there was a chance, she would not give away her position. 'Palmerston says there's no hope of mediation until both sides really want it,' she said neutrally.

'Hmph,' he grunted, evidently deep in thought. 'There was an incident today. It will be in the papers by this evening, and then I dare say the Furies will be let loose. I fancy we may have to change our minds about keeping out of it.'

'What's happened?' Charlotte asked nervously.

'President Davis sent two envoys, Mason and Sidell, to represent

Confederate views to Europe. Mason was coming here, Sidell to France. They got out of Charleston on a blockade-runner, went via Nassau to Havana, and boarded one of our mail-steamers, the *Trent*. But an American warship intercepted the *Trent* in the Bahama Channel, fired a shot across her bows, and took off the envoys by force. They are now languishing in a Boston military prison.'

'But – but they can't do that!'

'They have done it.'

'To take civilian passengers off a British ship on the high seas? It's outrageous! It's almost piracy!'

'The offending captain, I understand, had a novel way of justifying himself. International law says a country at war has the right to stop and search a neutral merchant ship suspected of carrying enemy despatches. He reasoned that Mason and Sidell were themselves despatches of a sort, and confiscated them. All this, you understand, without ever once admitting that the Confederacy exists for the Union to be at war with!'

'What will the Government do?' Charlotte asked.

Oliver hesitated. 'I'm not sure. There is bound to be a huge public outcry, and demands for war with the United States. But Palmerston and Russell still don't want to get involved, and the Queen is dead set against it – or the Prince is, which comes to the same thing. I think there'll be a demand for release of the envoys and an apology to us; what happens after that will depend on how President Lincoln reacts.'

They talked over it a little more, and then Charlotte said, 'Thank you for bringing me the news – but why did you? Had you some special reason?'

He walked over to the window and fiddled with the curtain cords, his face hidden from her. 'I have heard that your cousin from Morland Place is rather more actively involved in the war than the law might countenance. Of course it's understandable, given that his daughter is married to a planter, and that he has Confederate grandchildren, but he may be sailing close to the wind all the same. I have heard that he has placed contracts for ships with a Mersey yard on behalf of the Confederate government, and that he has sunk some of his own money into the project.'

'How – how did you hear that?'

'Oh, these things can't be kept secret, you know,' he said lightly, still not looking at her. 'The Northern states' envoy, Charles Adams, is furious about it, but he hasn't any proof that the ships are intended for use as belligerents, so there are no grounds for interference. My relationship, through you, with Benedict Morland seemed to him to make me guilty by association. He was quite impertinent on the subject,' he added thoughtfully.

Charlotte swallowed. 'Oliver,' she said. He turned and surveyed her with bright, steady eyes, and she could not begin to fathom what he was thinking. But in fairness, she thought, she must tell him. 'It is not only Benedict's money that's been sunk in the scheme to buy ships. There is some of Fanny's, too, and – and some of mine. In fact, quite a lot of mine.'

She expected the storm to break then, but instead, when she dared to look at his face, she saw he was *smiling*.

'I know,' he said.

'You know?'

'As I said, these things can't be kept secret. I know all about your involvement, but I wanted to see if you would tell me.'

She stared at him in astonishment and some indignation. 'You were testing me?'

'You passed with flying colours,' he pointed out. 'But why didn't you tell me before?'

'Because I thought if there were an outcry, it would be better for you to be able to say you knew nothing about it.'

He continued to look at her steadily with that unfathomable expression. 'You're a very honest person, really, aren't you?'

'I try to be. I didn't keep this from you to deceive you, but to protect you.'

'Yes, I know. And why *did* you put up the money?'

'Because if we don't help the South, there will be no cotton for the mills, and if the mills close, the workers will starve.'

'Ah, as simple as that?'

'Yes. And because I feel—' She was more hesitant about this, because it was more nebulous. 'The Southern states have every right to make themselves into a separate nation, and the Northern states have no right to try to stop them.'

Oliver nodded. 'As it happens, I agree with you. I had not cared enough about it before to want to do anything myself, but now that Mr Adams has seen fit to abuse me in my own country, and now the Union has taken to boarding our ships and forcibly removing legitimate passengers, I think the time has come to declare myself.'

'What do you mean?'

'I mean, my dear ma'am, that not only do I approve of your actions, I shall emulate them. Is there room for another investor in your scheme? Perhaps I may contribute towards the wheel or the anchor, or buy a spar or two.'

'You want to invest in ships for the Confederacy?' Charlotte said in astonishment. 'But – but suppose they do find some way of proving it illegal?'

'I shall talk my way out of it, I dare say. Or, if not, perhaps you and I can share adjacent cells in gaol?' He laughed. 'Don't look so blue, Duchess! It won't come to that, really.'

'I wasn't worried about gaol. I was thinking of your career.'

His expression grew softer. 'Were you? Yes, I really believe you were. How generous of you.'

'Don't tease me,' she said quietly.

'I meant it. You are generous.' He paused a moment, looking at her thoughtfully. 'You have so many good qualities that I miss. I miss *you*, in fact,' he said. 'We were such good friends once. Could we be friends again, do you think?'

'Friends?' she said. He was looking at her so kindly that she thought perhaps she would never have a better chance than this. She screwed up her courage and said, 'I want more than to be friends. I want to be your wife again. I love you.'

He was silent so long her heart sank. But at last he said, 'I love you, too,' as if it were painful for him to admit it.

'Then can't we be as we were? I can't bear this distance between us.' She didn't mean to say it, but the words broke from her: 'I'm so lonely.'

It seemed to surprise him. He surveyed her face as if trying to understand something; and at last he said, 'Would you be prepared to accept Mrs Galbraith, then? The fact of her existence, I mean – I should never force her on your attention, of course.'

The hope which had risen up in Charlotte withered again. 'I can't,' she said miserably. She saw his lips tighten and said desperately, 'I wish you would try to understand. I don't want to deny you pleasure or comfort, but I can't accept what is simply *wrong*.'

'Is that what it is that you object to?' he said. 'That it's wrong?'

'I know Society accepts it, at least for men of your order, but it's against God's law. I can't help it, Oliver. We made vows to each other before God, and nothing, *nothing* can release us from those.'

'So you wouldn't divorce me, no matter what I did? Even if this new law made it possible?'

'What are you talking about?' she said in surprise and hurt. 'I am your wife. Only death can change that.'

He came closer. Now he was looking down into her face with an intense expression. 'You didn't take Sir Frederick Friedman as your lover,' he said at the end of this strange scrutiny. 'You didn't break your marriage vows, did you?'

She didn't answer. At the last moment she realised that it was not a question; and that, in any case, the answer had always had to come from him, not from her. It didn't matter what she said, it mattered what he believed.

He caught her hand, imprisoned the fingers, brought them to his lips. 'I wonder if you will ever be able to forgive me?'

'Forgiveness doesn't come into it.' She was trembling at his touch, at his nearness after so many weary years.

'All the same, I need to be forgiven. I don't deserve you—'

'Don't say that! Don't elevate me into something – oh, *outside* you!'

'No, you're right. We must be equal partners, or nothing,' he said thoughtfully.

Hope revived again – foolish, unquenchable hope that would not learn from experience. He was silent a long moment, and she had no idea what he was thinking, though she could see he was struggling with something. She waited in silence for his conclusion.

'Well then, let us be equal and honest,' he said at last. 'No more Mrs Galbraith. Shall we try, Charlotte? Shall we try to get back to where we were?'

'Yes,' she said. 'Yes, please.'

He nodded, and bent his head to seal the new covenant with a light touch of his lips on hers that did nothing to stop the trembling. 'I think I've been a fool,' he said seriously. 'I somehow lost sight of what was important. These last few years have been a sort of madness.'

'We've all been a little mad, since Balaclava,' she said, remembering Friedman's words.

'No, I can't blame it on that,' he said. 'Mine was a particular and very common sort – ambition. But career and worldly influence are nothing if they can't be used for what's lasting, and if they take you away from what you really love. It took you to show me that.'

For a fortnight the country trembled on the brink of war with the United States. When the news of the *Trent* incident broke, the country was frantic with rage. The newspapers thundered, the lower house fulminated, arguments over the interpretation of international law occupied every club and dinner-party. Despite the report that the American captain had acted on his own initiative, without orders, the rumour somehow grew that the whole thing had been planned by Washington to provoke war with Britain, so that France could be brought in on the United States' side with the promise of giving them Canada.

Palmerston and Russell could not but be affected by the mood of the country, and a note was written by Russell to the Union government demanding the release and restoration of the two prisoners, plus a full and humble apology to Britain for the incident. The letter was written in such cold and imperious language that it was more likely to provoke war than elicit an apology. There were eight thousand British soldiers in Canada, ready to invade the United States, and even as it demanded apology from the United States, the Government was ordering fifteen thousand reinforcements for the Canada garrisons.

At the last moment Prince Albert, who had been sent a copy of the note, rewrote it, toning down the language and inserting a hint that the captain had acted without orders and that there had been no intention on the part of Washington to insult Great Britain, thus giving the young nation an opportunity to make reparation while still saving face. Before the deadline expired the two envoys had been released, and though the apology that came with them was far from satisfactory, the Cabinet had by then had time for cooler second thoughts, and the whole thing blew over. The Confederacy would have to get along without England after all.

Only a week later, on the 14th of December 1861, Prince Albert died at Windsor – it was said, of typhoid – and the Court and all those connected with it were plunged into deepest mourning. Charlotte put on her blacks and cancelled or modified various planned entertainments. She sincerely pitied the Queen, who was beside herself with grief; but though she adopted a suitably grave public face, inwardly and in private Charlotte could feel only a great and growing contentment. She was a wife again. A little creakingly at first, from lack of practice, and with an unexpected shyness, she and Oliver were finding their way back to each other. It would have taken a tragedy of no uncommon order to outweigh the joy of that.

It was the hospital that got Ruth through the first weeks of her bereavement. The gravely wounded from the battle at Manassas were brought to the Chimborazo Hospital in Richmond; but though the battle had long been expected, preparations had been inadequate. Most of the surgeons had gone with the regiments to the battlefield, and as the carts and litters and even wheelbarrows began to arrive at the hospital, there were not enough present to receive them.

On the day after the battle, a note came for Phoebe from a friend who was a nursing superintendent at the hospital, asking her in the most urgent tones to go there and help, and to bring with her as many ladies as she could persuade to come. Phoebe went to the parlour, where Ruth was sitting dully with her hands in her lap, her eyes heavy with sleeplessness.

'Ruth, my dear,' Phoebe said, and explained the situation. 'I hate to leave you here all alone at such a time, but the need is so immediate and so desperate, I hardly know how to refuse. You do see, don't you?'

'Of course you must go,' Ruth said. 'And I'll come with you.' Phoebe immediately protested, and Ruth said, 'Yes, I must. I will. It is as much my duty to help as yours.'

'But, my love,' Phoebe said gently, but urgently, it's not necessary. No-one would expect it of you, given your circumstances.'

Ruth stood up, and turned her drawn face to Phoebe. 'I know what you are trying to say, Phoebe, and I promise you nothing I could witness at the hospital could make my pain worse. Everything here reminds me of him. I want to help – so let me help?'

So reluctantly Phoebe had agreed, and the two women put on their bonnets, gathered some items they thought might be useful, and went to the Chimborazo. The streets surrounding it were so full of traffic that they left their carriage and walked the last part. A stream of vehicles of every sort was bringing in wounded men. The hospital was already crowded with those who had straggled in during the night and there were no beds available, but Phoebe's friend, Mrs Pember, was organising the removal of less wounded men onto blankets or palliasses on the floor, to make beds available for the grievously hurt, while the duty surgeon and such assistants as he could muster were trying to register and dispose them.

When Phoebe and Ruth reached the entrance hall it was crowded with wounded men sitting on the floor, lying on stretchers or leaning against the walls, waiting with astonishing patience to be 'ticketed'. The very first moment, to Ruth, was the worst. She had never seen, never imagined, sights like these. 'Our brave boys', as every paper called them, were now wrecks of humanity, torn and broken, blood-soaked, with shattered limbs and missing limbs and ripped faces. The smell of blood, which overlaid another, deep-rooted, smell she was to come to know as 'hospital stink', made her want to retch; the low bourdon of sound, a composite of terse conversation and the moans of the desperate, was like the buzzing of some unimaginable insect-hive. Her steps faltered and her heart failed; duty seemed a distant concept and she wanted deeply and cravenly to be safely back at Phoebe's house – or, better still, far away at home at Twelvetrees.

But Twelvetrees was not home now: she was Mrs Manning, and Patrick's death came home to her with piercing reality as she saw what a wounded man looked like. Phoebe had wanted to save her that, but it was better that she knew. She thrust down her fear and her nausea and prepared to help, in his name and memory.

A new influx of litters drove Ruth and Phoebe apart, and immediately afterwards Ruth was accosted by a tough-looking little woman in a plain brown dress and purple apron, her sleeves rolled to the elbow and her hair dragged into a tight little button behind. 'Are you here to help, or to gawp?' she demanded.

'To help,' Ruth replied in kind.

'Good, then take these—' she thrust into Ruth's hands a basin, sponge, and block of brown soap, and hung two towels over the top, 'and come with me. You can start washing the men.'

She bustled off and Ruth hopped after her. 'Wash the men?' she asked anxiously.

'Certainly,' said the little woman with a touch of irritability. She flicked a glance at Ruth over her shoulder. 'You're married, ain't you?'

'Yes,' Ruth said unthinkingly.

'Very well, then. They're all the same in their skins. Start here, and work down the row that way.' Then she was gone, leaving Ruth with her basin facing a man old enough to be her father, whose expression was grimly scandalised under the roughly wound bandage on his head.

'I ain't never been washed by a lady,' he said.

'There's a first time for everything,' Ruth said, and, hearing her voice come out so strong and calm, she was comforted, and knelt down to start work. She pretended to herself that she was a mammy washing her children on a Saturday night: that was the way to get through it. And indeed some of the weary wounded rested their heads against her like sleepy children as she soaped and rinsed them. Skin was skin, she thought, and where it was whole it filled her with a tenderness than enabled her to forget that these were male strangers and she a gently-born planter's daughter.

Their wounds were horrible, their patience and courage immense, their gratitude for any attention touching. One man, when she came to wash him, forestalled her and said, 'I'm wounded in the stomach, ma'am, no point in washing me. But I'd appreciate a drink of water, if you ain't too busy.' Ruth hurried off to look for drinking-water, but it took her some time to find the pails, and then to find a tin cup, for she hadn't thought to ask the solider for his own. When she got back he seemed to be sleeping, but when she crouched down to him again there was something in his tired white face that warned her otherwise, and when she touched him his skin felt quite different, not like human skin at all.

The thought of Patrick leapt up again in her mind (had his skin felt like that?) and she turned hastily to the next man before her tears overcame her. It was a very young soldier in Virginia blue – what was left of it – with curly brown hair and the sort of face that made you know he had sisters who adored him. His left leg was gone, and his left arm was so mangled that even Ruth in her ignorance could guess that he would lose that, too; but seeing the tears standing in her eyes he managed a shaky smile, and said, 'Don't you fret about me, ma'am, I'm doing finely. This is a treat after being jolted about in that ambulance; and now a washing to come, with a lady on t'other end of it.'

Ruth began her work, and desperate to think of something to say, could only come up with, 'I'm sorry you have lost your leg.'

'It's a common complaint,' he said, and then, 'What a scramble there'll be for arms and legs come Judgement Day, when we all come out of our graves! I wonder if we'll get our own back?' He went on talking all the time she was stripping and washing him, and knowing that he was trying to cheer her up, when his own case was so grievous, made her want to cry even more.

Other women were taking round trays of bread, meat, soup and coffee to those who had already been cleaned up, and the surgeons were coming after to deal with the wounds. The tough little superintendent appeared again and said to Ruth, 'You're doing very well. We could use more of your quality – only tomorrow leave off some of your petticoats – you take up too much room.' Ruth could only stare, pleasure at the compliment mingled with astonishment that a lady should say the word 'petticoat' in the hearing of so many men. The little woman went on, 'Now then, you've served your 'prenticeship, so go and help Dr Hooker – that's him over there with the grey beard. Scurry on, now,' she added as Ruth hesitated, and gave her a shove in the right direction, simultaneously removing any possibility of refusal by disappearing in the opposite direction.

The doctor didn't seem in the least surprised to see her. 'Done any nursing?' he asked tersely.

'No, sir.'

He looked her over keenly. 'Likely to swoon?'

'I don't think so, sir,' Ruth said doubtfully.

He nodded. 'If you feel queer, look the other way; but try to keep a cheerful face, so the men don't lose heart.'

Ruth saw the point and, taking the basin of instruments he handed her, followed him, determined to think about the men and not herself, and not to look if she could help it. But there was a ghastly fascination in watching him work, and she found that, little as she liked it, her eyes were drawn back again and again. Dr Hooker was brisk and cheerful, and probed and cut and stitched away at the bodies before him as matter-of-factly as if he had been a tailor and they were dilapidated uniforms. He chatted all the time, told the men what he thought of their wounds and what he meant to do, asked them their histories, and in between told Ruth his own. He was an Englishman, and had served as a medical officer in the Crimea; he told the soldiers how much worse it had been there, and how their chances were so much better that they might consider themselves as good as recovered.

The day wore on. The superintendent, whose name was Mrs Ogilvy, moved her from time to time to a different job, now carrying trays of food, now spoon-feeding the soldiers who could not help themselves, now stripping and making beds, now back to her old duty of washing the new arrivals. Ruth guessed this was to keep her from becoming too fatigued or despairing. She did not see Phoebe, although her friend Mrs Pember stopped by at one point and asked if she had had any dinner, and when she said no, sent her off to a tiny room next to the kitchen to get some. Ruth ate some bread and drank some coffee, but she could not fancy anything heartier. Her stays were cutting into her, and her whole upper body felt as though it were bathed in sweat.

She was returning from her 'dinner' when a soldier called to her from a litter, and she saw from his condition that he was newly brought in.

'Can you give me a moment?' he said.

'What can I do for you?' Ruth asked. 'They will be by in a moment to wash you.'

He grunted, his steady blue eyes holding her gaze. 'Won't you get me some strong liquor to revive me, so that I shan't die before the surgeon can see me?'

Ruth looked at the soaked stuff of his uniform coat: it was sodden from the breast to the knees. 'I will see what I can do, but I must ask the doctor if it will harm you.'

She scurried off and found Dr Hooker, who listened to her brief exposition. 'I know the one. Shot right through, half his intestines gone. There's no hope for him. Give him anything he wants. Mrs Pember has the brandy.'

When she got back, the soldier was lying with his head turned to one side, drops of sweat standing out on his forehead like glass beads. She lifted his head and helped him sip the brandy, and when it was gone she laid the cup aside and was about to get up when he grasped her wrist in a big, hard hand, blood-caked where he had been holding his wound. 'It's the end, isn't it?' he asked her hoarsely.

Ruth swallowed. 'There's always hope,' she said, searching help-lessly for words to comfort him. 'If we trust in God—'

'No,' he said, still holding her wrist. 'I see it in your face.' Tears began to seep out of his eyes, and it horrified her, for it was the first man she had seen crying. 'I don't want to die. My mother's a widow, and I'm her only son. Who'll look after her?' The tears rolled faster and he panted with sorrow and pain. 'Her name's in my pocket-book in here.' He gestured to his breast pocket. 'Oh, won't you write to her? Please tell her that I died in what I consider the defence of civil rights and liberties. I may be wrong. God alone knows.' Ruth nodded, unable to speak. 'Tell her how kindly I was nursed, and that I had all I needed. Tell her—' He stopped, grimaced with pain, and drew in a sharp breath. Ruth heard it slowly let out; the exhalation seemed to go on and on. The brown-crusted fingers uncurled from her wrist, and the blue eyes were now opaque glass, from behind which the soldier had gone for ever.

That evening Mr Canfield sent the carriage with Amos, the coachman, to the hospital, to demand on his behalf that 'the misses come on home right now an' git a Christian supper, or 'fore God he wiz comin' hisself ter fitch 'em'.

Ruth and Phoebe met in the foyer and smiled wearily at each other. Tomorrow the surgeons would start the amputations, and another long day was in view. But Ruth had hardly thought of Patrick all day, and now, as she did, she knew that helping the men had helped her. The agony of losing him was the same, but she was stronger, and more able to bear it.

'Will you go back tomorrow?' Phoebe asked in the carriage.

'Tomorrow, and every day I'm needed,' Ruth said.

CHAPTER TWENTY-THREE

After the battle at Manassas, both sides went into camp to lick their wounds, and to think again about the meaning of war. It was now plain to everybody that it was not going to be over by Christmas, that it was not going to be a delightful picnic ride with musical accompaniment. Many of the militia and more colourful volunteers went home. Mary thought that Fenwick and Eugene would return to Twelvetrees, having done their duty. But Fenwick wrote to say that his Hussars were being reorganised and brigaded under General 'Jeb' Stuart, and that steadier officers like himself were in short supply. He could not be spared yet for furlough, but she was to assure herself that when leave was finally granted, he would come back to her without a scratch.

Fenwick also wrote about Eugene, for Eugene would never have thought of doing it himself. In the autumn of 1861, General Jackson – Old Jack to his men – was given command of all Confederate forces in the Shenandoah Valley. This fertile valley in West Virginia, a hundred and sixty-five miles long, was known as The Breadbasket, and provided food for a large part of the Southern army. As Jackson said, 'If the Valley is lost, the South is lost.' He did not forget the lone Greycoat who had fought with his Virginians at Manassas, and when his command was confirmed he sought Eugene out and asked if he would like to join him. 'You've done enough walking for this war,' he said. 'I need good men on my staff. How would you like to become one of my aides?'

So Mary packed a trunk and sent it with Eugene's slave, Bo; Charles sent two horses by railroad to Richmond; and thus resurrected as a gentleman Eugene went with Old Jack to Winchester. Through the autumn he spent long hours in the saddle, riding with the general to consolidate the small and scattered forces into an army, and institute discipline and seriousness of purpose. Then, in the bitter snows of January 1862, the Valley Campaign began.

Jackson had eight thousand men; against him the Union had thirty-five thousand in two main forces. What it lacked in numbers,

Jackson's army had to make up for in mobility. Eugene came to be very glad of his horses, as in a dazzling campaign Jackson's 'Foot Cavalry' covered the ground with astonishing speed, quick-marching through the valley, attacking first one Union army and then the other, doubling, circling, disappearing and reappearing, so that the Union commanders never had any idea where 'Stonewall' would be next. So successful was the plan that Washington believed he had twice the men he actually had, and at one time was convinced that a full-scale invasion of the North was beginning. Fifty thousand Union soldiers were kept occupied panting after and retreating before Old Jack's little army.

The plan of the Valley Campaign had been worked out by General Jackson in consultation with General Lee, whose original idea it was. When Jackson went to Shenandoah, Lee had gone to Charleston, to inspect and strengthen the coastal defences. Charleston was bound to be a prime target to the North, as both the cradle of secession and an important trading port; and in November the Union fleet had captured Port Royal, only fifty miles from Charleston.

The general was fêted in the town, and Aunt Belle was the first to give a grand dinner for him, to which Charles was summoned to act as host. More reluctantly, Aunt Belle asked Mary to come to town for the occasion – not because she wanted her, but because the general had asked after her and evidently thought that she would be there, and Aunt Belle was not quick-witted enough to think of a reason why she shouldn't be.

Mary enjoyed meeting General Lee who, she found to her surprise, knew a great deal about her: both Martial and Ruth had spoken of her to him. He was full of praise for Lennox, whose quick intelligence and quiet good sense was making him invaluable. 'It's wonderful what that boy's read! I think he knows the details of every military campaign that's been written about.' Lee spoke with regret of Pick Manning's death, and of Ruth with respect for the way she was overcoming her grief with hard work. Ruth was nursing regularly at the Chimborazo, and meant to continue as long as she could. Her baby was due in March, and she intended to go back to the hospital once she had recovered from the birth.

General Lee's popularity amongst the planters did not last. After inspecting the fortifications along the coastal islands, he pronounced them inadequate, and ordered them abandoned. Instead, a new chain of defensive works was to be constructed several miles up the rivers on the mainland; the drawback was that it meant a great deal of coastal land had to be given up, and the owners had to refugee inland. Some of them were wealthy and influential planters, and their wails of protest went all the way to Richmond. Uncle

Hemp's eldest daughter Louisa was married to a coastal planter, John McLeod, and they had to leave their plantation and come with bags, baggage, children and servants to Charleston to stay with Hemp and Missy, while their field-hands were sent to the Fenwick family estate.

'It isn't that we don't have room,' Aunt Missy said to Mary on a visit to Twelvetrees. 'What with Troy and Tom away at school and Hamilton on the city defences, the house seems quite empty; but as Louisa's John points out, all that coastal land won't be cultivated, and what will we do without the rice it grows? And, of course, with land like that you can't take your eye off it for a minute. If this war lasts any length of time, Louisa's John says he'll go back to find nothing there but the ocean.'

In December Charleston was devastated by a terrible fire. In a city of wooden buildings, fire had always been the most feared hazard, and Charleston had ten engines, ten volunteer white companies and ten slave companies. But despite their efforts, the fire swept like a storm through the most crowded section of the city, only stopping when it reached the Ashley River. Five hundred and forty acres of buildings were laid waste, and the city, already crowded with coastal refugees, now had to find room for those whose houses had been destroyed. It was never discovered how the fire started, though naturally rumours abounded that it was a Unionist plot or the forerunner of a slave insurrection.

In January Mary's household was reduced by the departure of Uncle Heck. The war was not only being waged in Virginia: there was a grim struggle going on in the west. The border state of Kentucky, with a population evenly divided in its sympathies, had been neutral, but occupation by the armies of the North now forced it to declare for the Union. From Kentucky the North mounted a campaign to take control of the Tennessee and Mississippi Rivers. The Confederate Army of Tennessee was commanded by General Albert Sidney Johnston, an experienced professional soldier, but he had a wide territory and inadequate manpower. Anyone with experience in the terrain would be invaluable for scouting and reconnaissance work, and soon the call came for Hector Fenwick to prove his worth.

Hill, of course, went with him. Mary was in the kitchen supervising the packing of a food parcel for the two men for the journey when the door darkened and Cookie shrieked with alarm, and Mary looked up to see Heck's villainous-looking 'friend' leaning against the door-jamb.

'Did you want something?' Mary asked politely. 'Be quiet, Cookie! And look what you're doing,' she added sharply as Cookie backed into her in her retreat from Hill's shadow. Many of the negroes believed he had supernatural powers, a rumour Hill did nothing to contradict. 'Is there anything I can do for you? Anything you want for the journey?' She had never forgotten Hill's taking care of her little boy at May's wedding. It had never been mentioned between them, but she fancied he knew she knew, and accepted her silent thanks.

Hill jerked his head in the direction of the outside world, and Mary wiped her hands on her apron and followed the lanky figure as he lounged out into the yard. Yaller Dawg, who had been sitting a little way off, got up politely, swinging his tail, but did not approach.

Hill turned and faced her. 'Goin' to be leavin' you without menfolk,' he said.

'There's still my father-in-law,' Mary mentioned.

Hill gave a graphic shrug, which suggested he didn't count Charles for much. 'Reckon you'll have to take care of yourself and them pretty boys. Well, y've larnt how to shoot—'

'How on earth do you know that?' Mary said in astonishment.

Hill gave a grim quirk of the lips that the charitable might have described as a smile. 'Y'ain't invisible,' he said. 'I've hid a rifle and some boxes o' bullets for you, in case o' need. In the apple barn, under Ruthie's swing, brush away the earth and there's a plank. Lift the plank and there's a store under the floor.' His eyes bored into hers. 'Don't tell no-one – especially don't tell none o' the niggers. They ain't to be trusted, and y' don't want y'r damn head blown off.'

Mary nodded acquiescence.

He looked at her hard. 'Whether it's Yankees or niggers, when the time comes, don't waste time talkin' or pleadin' or worryin' about sin. Shoot while you got the chanst.'

He swung on his heel and was gone, Yaller Dawg at his heels like his shadow. Mary watched him go, unhappily aware that he had said 'when' the time came, and not 'if'.

In the early months of 1862 the engagement was announced of Kitten Ausland to Hemp and Missy's eldest son Hamilton. Hamilton had been Kitten's suitor for as long as anyone remembered, and she had returned to him from time to time when no more exciting beaux had been on her horizon, but no-one had ever really expected her to marry him. It was known that Judge Ausland was indulgent to a fault towards Kitten, his favourite, and that she would be permitted to choose her own husband, provided he came from a list of suitable candidates. Hamilton was suitable, but Kitten thought him dull.

However, the war had changed her perceptions. So many of her friends had married, so many of her suitors had gone off to war or had even been killed or wounded, that she began to be nervous. The worst fate of all would be to be left on the shelf. Hamilton in the uniform of the elite Palmetto Guard began to look much more attractive, and when he offered for the umpteenth time, almost routinely, without really expecting her to accept, she surprised him into a stammering wreck by saying yes.

Aunt Missy was not best pleased. Kitten was from one of Charleston's First Families and she would have a large dowry; but there was something a little shabby-seeming, even outré, about a marriage arranged by the bride rather than her father. The Judge wrote to Uncle Hemp with his hearty consent, but he was having too much fun in Richmond to come back just yet. He delegated the arrangements to Conrad; but nobody saw anything of Conrad these days, and there were rumours that he was becoming a little odd. He had driven away Aunt Margaret, who had gone back to stay in Charleston – the house in King Street had escaped the fire – and Maybelle didn't seem capable of running Camelot properly, let alone organising a wedding. In the end, Kitten's older sister Connie Fairfax and Aunt Margaret between them decided to hold the wedding in Charleston. The Judge agreed to it, and promised to return to give the bride away.

Mary had been too busy to visit Camelot much in the last nine months. Since Fenwick went away, she had had to take over his management of the estate, for Charles would not interest himself in anything but the horses. Hazelteen now came to her for orders. It was time-consuming, and she made mistakes, and often wished the overseer would take more decisions himself; but his stupidity was the price of his honesty and loyalty, and gradually she was learning, and coming to enjoy it, too. Now, however, the talk of Kitten's wedding reminded Mary that she hadn't seen May for some time, so she ordered the carriage and went visiting.

Camelot presented the image of a place going to seed. Mary tried to analyse the impression. The lawn was a little ragged, perhaps – though it had never rivalled Moses' velvet sward – and there were dead leaves in a corner of the verandah, not swept up since the last fall. In the parlour into which she was shown there was dust on the polished surfaces and a dead spider on the windowsill. But, more than that, it was the silence of the house that made her uneasy. At Twelvetrees there was never silence: always there was a background noise of living, of footsteps and voices and doors and the faint rustling flip-flap of fans.

May came in at last with a social smile stitched to her lips. She looked neat and tidy, but her face was tired and puffy and her eyes were circled. She asked eagerly for news of the family, and Mary answered her willingly, putting in as much detail as she could remember, suspecting poor May was starved of company. 'Where is everybody?' Mary asked at last. 'Are you all alone here today?'

'Clara's in Charleston with Kitten and Connie, and Sneed and Juve have gone riding over to Fairoaks. Chesney's with his regiment, of course.'

'And Conrad?'

May seemed to hesitate. 'Oh, he's somewhere about. Probably in the library. You know what men are,' she added vaguely.

Mary found it hard work to talk to May. She seemed distracted, as though listening or waiting for something. She did not offer Mary refreshments, and Mary concluded that she was not entirely welcome, or at least that she was adding to May's burdens rather than reducing them, so after a while she gave up the struggle and got up to leave. May did not try to delay her, going with her to the parlour door almost eagerly. As they reached it, Mary thought she heard a heavy crash, like glass or china, from somewhere in the house, and turned to May with an enquiring look, but she avoided her eyes and said quickly, 'It really was kind of you to call. I ought to have called on you before now, but time does fly away, doesn't it?'

Mary looked at her doubtfully. 'Are you really all right, May dear? Is there anything I can do for you, or get for you?'

'Thank you, but I've a house full of servants to do anything that needs doing,' May said brightly, with an unnatural smile.

'But you really don't look very well to me,' Mary persisted.

'I'm quite all right, there's nothing to worry about.' She seemed to have an inspiration. 'But I'm expecting a visit from Dr Trevelyan at any moment, as it happens, so you must forgive me if I hurry you away. I need to prepare for him.'

'You should have told me, love. I hope I haven't stayed too long,' Mary said, and took her leave. The phaeton was standing ready, with Cedar at the horses' heads fanning them with his hat and looking cross. As they drove off, Cedar said, 'Miss Mary, Ah don't t'ink you should call at dat place any more. Dey is ignorant people. Dey lef' me and my hosses standin' dere, instead of offerin' to put de outfit away and stable de hosses. Not so much as a drink o' water did dey offer us.'

Not to put the horses away suggested the servants thought the visit would be a short one. Had they been told visitors were not welcome? All visitors, or only Mary? And why?

Cedar proceeded to add to her worries. 'Dey somepin' queer

goin' on, mark my words,' he said darkly, turning the horses onto the road. 'Just 'fore you come out, Ah hears a crashin' noise from inside, like someone tho'in de china about. An' just after, Mister Conrad come out o' the stableyard and ride off hell for leather, beatin' his hoss like he runnin' from a bush-fire! He scroch past so fast he never even see me.'

Mary would not encourage speculation from a servant, and in the face of her refusal to comment, Cedar shrugged and fell silent. He drove her home at a slow walk to register his annoyance with her and her Camelot relatives; and they had not reached Twelvetrees when there was a sound of galloping hooves somewhere nearby, the sound increasing in volume until suddenly a horse appeared, leaping over the hedge into the road just ahead of them, making the carriage horses shy violently. Cedar struggled with reins and whip as the ridden horse stumbled, regained its balance, and began to plunge on the spot, foam flying from its lips. Its eyes were white and sweat and dust caked its neck and flanks. In the saddle, controlling it with hard hands and vicious jabs of the spurs, was Conrad.

To Mary's frightened eyes he looked at first glance quite mad. Indeed, she recognised him more by the horse and his coat and hat than by his face, which was white and haggard, the eyes red-rimmed, furious but oddly unfocused. *Possessed* was the word that came to her mind, and she felt a frisson of superstitious fear. You couldn't live as closely with negroes as she did without absorbing some of their belief in evil spirits.

Cedar had the horses under control again, and shouted, 'Whut in de worl' you doin', Mister Conrad, jumpin' out on us like dat? You could ha' killt us.'

'Don't you dare speak to me, nigger!' Conrad shouted furiously, making his horse plunge again. His speech was slurred, as if he were drunk, but the left side of his mouth hung slack, and a thread of drool swung from it.

'Ah's a free black,' Cedar cried angrily.

'Hush, Cedar, be still,' Mary murmured urgently. Conrad looked mad enough to come to blows, and if Cedar struck him back, which *he* was angry enough to do, he'd be hanged, free black or not. 'Conrad, what are you doing? Have you been to Twelvetrees?' she called, trying for a normal tone.

Conrad glared at her. 'Oh yes, I've been there – much good it did me! *He*'s in it with you, that's plain enough! But I'll trouble you, madam, not to go poking your nose into my affairs again! A fine thing to make trouble between a man and his wife – but you won't get a second chance! Mark me, if you come anywhere near Camelot ever again, I'll have you thrown out by your neck and heels!'

Cedar goggled with outraged fury. 'Don't you talk to Miss Mary like that!' he began, but Mary laid a restraining hand on his trembling arm.

'I don't know what you're talking about, Con,' she said calmly.

Conrad dug in his spurs, making the horse lunge at her, and leaned over to thrust out his face almost into hers as it passed. 'Liar!' he shouted. She felt his spittle on her face and her bonnet almost knocked off by the wind of movement; he swayed so violently that for a delirious instant she thought he was going to fall into the carriage on top of her. Then he was gone down the road, the horse galloping madly and Conrad beating it wildly.

'You all right, Miss Mary?' Cedar cried.

'Yes, I'm all right.'

'Hit true what people been sayin'. He is mad as a dawg.'

'Drive on,' Mary said, 'and don't repeat rubbish like that to me.' It had been a horrible and frightening experience, and she was very much shaken. She didn't doubt Cedar was right. How could it have gone so far without anything being done? But of course the Judge and Chesney were away. What was she to do? She thought of pale, anxious May; Charles must do something, before Conrad hurt her. May must be got away from him, or Conrad must be locked up for his own good. It would be a delicate business, but Charles had the right to interfere to protect his own daughter.

She jumped down as soon as the carriage stopped and hurried into the house, and went straight to the library. Charles looked up as she burst in. 'Yes, I've seen him,' he said harshly, before she could speak. 'Close the door.' She obeyed, and he went on, 'Conrad has been here, shouting abuse, blaming you for interfering and me for allowing you to.'

Mary hardly listened. 'Sir, you must do something,' she said urgently. 'I passed him going back to Camelot. He was violently angry, and I'm afraid he may do something to harm May. You must go there at once and bring her away!'

Charles raised his eyebrows at the 'must', but he seemed quite calm. 'She is in no danger. Did I not tell you his anger was directed towards you, and me?'

Mary looked distracted. 'He shouted something at me – I couldn't understand it. I took it to be raving.'

'It was not raving. He objected to the exchange I made at your request last year, of Hebba for Becka.' Mary could only stare. 'He was angry that you had dared interfere in his household, and with me for having helped you. I told him that Becka was May's own to do what she liked with, and that if she wanted to exchange her, I had no objection. Conrad said that *he* objected very strongly, that he was master of Camelot, and that he would have Becka returned.'

'But, sir,' Mary said, 'that *is* raving. If he objected to the exchange, why did he not say something before?'

'I suppose he has only just noticed Becka's absence,' Charles said with a shrug. 'From what I understand, he shuts himself up in his room most of the time, and he is often in drink.'

Mary was shocked that he said it so calmly, but she said only, 'Then why should he mind which woman May has?'

'I suspect it's not May's having he minds,' Charles said. Mary didn't understand this, but Charles went on, 'I told him I would not reverse the exchange, and he ranted until I was obliged to call Tammas and have him shown out, and there is an end of it.'

'An end of it? But how can you say so? You say he is mad and a drunkard and he is married to your daughter—'

'Don't presume to tell me my duty, madam!' Charles snapped. 'I've told you he will not harm May. It is not for anyone to interfere in a domestic matter between a man and his wife, and I wish you will remember that in future. And now leave me. I have been disturbed enough today.'

Mary tried to tell herself that Charles would know better about whether Conrad was likely to hurt May than she, and that if he had really feared anything, he *would* have acted. She wondered why he had insisted on keeping Becka. Surely the best way to calm the situation would have been to hand her over and take Hebba back? But, perhaps, she told herself afterwards, Charles's pride would not allow him to yield to a demand so arrogantly made by a man his junior in age and status. She continued to worry about May, even though no dire reports came from Camelot through the usual route of the servants. She did not dare to call, for fear of provoking Conrad, and she felt guilty about deserting her, but she didn't know what else to do.

In that spring of 1862, General Lee was recalled to Richmond, and Fenwick came back to Twelvetrees for a brief furlough. Charles, unusually, showed distinct pleasure in seeing him, and wanted at once to bear him off to the library to talk about the strategic situation. Fenwick, however, for once in his life, opposed his father, saying that he wanted to see Mary and the children, take a very deep bath, and then sit on the verandah with a julep while he waited for dinner. Mary took the hint and whispered to Tammas to tell Julie to get Cookie to hurry dinner along.

Mary felt strangely shy of her husband. He seemed to have been away much longer than nine months, and for a long time her world had been almost exclusively female. She hardly knew what to say to him, but it didn't matter, because he was quite ready to talk himself, leaving her free to study him. He had changed physically. The most obvious difference was that he had grown a full beard and moustache which, being wiry like his hair, had a massive and jutting appearance. It was sandy-fair, but with sparks of quite dark red, like the colour of Ruth's. His hair, which he had grown quite long before the war, was cropped close to his skull; his skin was very much tanned, and his face, indeed his whole body, looked leaner and harder. There was a firmness in his voice and expression which she supposed was the result of taking command and living on his wits.

He spoke of having missed her and said frequently how wonderful it was to be with her again, but it was plain he did not really see her. He was still in Virginia, and his mental landscape was more real to him than the once familiar scenes of home. He was restless, looking around him all the time, getting up and walking from room to room, picking things up and putting them down. He asked questions about home, but did not listen to the answers; if Mary began to speak, he would interrupt after a few words to talk about the war again. The war was all that mattered: the campaign, the forays, the night rides, the near escapes; the hardships and the jokes shared; the love of men and horses.

Charles got on better with him, for he wanted to hear everything Fenwick said and had nothing to tell him; but Charles wanted more than Fenwick could give. He wanted an overview, a plan, a philosophy, where Fenwick could only offer the minute detail of one small area of campaign. He soon got bored with Fenwick, and retreated into his shell of hardness again.

Fenwick slept like the dead the first night. The second day he got into his old civilian clothes and took a horse and rode out on the estate, returning at the end of the morning to say that everything looked very good. 'You're managing very well without me,' he said to Mary, with a mixture of surprise and dismay. 'Who would have thought a female could cope without a man to guide her?' But then he comforted himself, 'But, of course, Pa is still here. I was forgetting.'

In the afternoon he rode off again to visit neighbours, and finding Quin Lawrence also on furlough at Pinelees, remained there for dinner, sending a note back to Twelvetrees that he would not be back until very late. The slaves were upset, having put a lot of effort into a special dinner, with 'Mist' Fenwick's mos' favourite dishes', and Mary dined alone with Charles, who noticed the difference in the food only halfway through, and then chided her for extravagance.

Mary went early to bed, before Fenwick had returned, but could not sleep. Her mind revolved in crooked, overlapping circles over the war, her tasks for tomorrow, Fenwick, the clearance of the outlying fields that ought to be started soon, what to do with the left-overs from dinner, the war, Fenwick. She must have dozed a little, because she became aware with violent suddenness that there was someone in the room. She heard the door-latch click, and sat up in bed, wrapping her arms round her as women do in fear. A light was shining against the bed-curtains; the yellow, swaying light of a candle.

'Who is it?' she said.

The answer was a chuckle, and then the curtain was pulled back, and Fenwick said, 'Now that's a silly question. Who but your loving husband would come into your room at this time of night?' He was in his dressing-gown. His hair was ruffled and the edges of it spiked with dampness, as though he had hastily washed his face. His breath was sharp with brandy, and a smell of segars hung about him. He put down the candle on the night stand, making the shadows flow wildly up his face and fling themselves like fleeing bats at the ceiling. Then he stooped blackly across the little light to blow it out.

'Don't,' she said quickly. 'Don't put out the light.' She didn't want to be left alone in the dark with him. It was so long since he had come to her room, her body had been her own private space for so long, that she was almost afraid of him. And he was drunk, too – not reeling, just what Eugene used to call 'lit up'. Perhaps with the light burning she could keep him talking until he fell asleep.

But he misunderstood her request. If he had not been in drink, the implication he read into her words would have shocked him; bosky as he was, it delighted him. 'Well,' he said, 'why not? We are man and wife, after all. And no-one will ever know.'

Abruptly he pulled off his dressing-gown and tossed it on the floor. Underneath, he was naked. She turned her eyes away in shock: she had never seen his naked body before, and in the instant before she averted her gaze she had seen that which she had never wanted to see. He bent over her and undid her little buttons, his rough breath disturbing the ribbons on the bodice and making them flutter. Then with slow, deliberate movements he pulled the cloth of her nightgown up, hitch by hitch from under the covers, until it was free enough for him to pull it off over her head. She remained still, neither helping nor hindering, her mind frozen, but then, when her nightgown was gone, he took hold of the bedclothes and pulled them away. Now she was naked except for her hair in its long, thick night-plait and he was looking at her! Shame flooded her. Helplessly exposed, with nowhere to hide from him, she thought if he touched her she would die; but he pressed her back into the pillows and his mouth smothered hers, his body slithered over hers, heavy and stupid, crushing her, and she did not die.

How had she ever endured it before, this alien, hateful possession of her body? She struggled feebly under his great weight, but she could make no difference to him; probably he did not even feel the movement. She moaned a protest, and he pulled back his head and laid a hand over her mouth, and nuzzled into her ear, murmuring, 'I know, I know! But don't make a noise, someone might hear.'

Now there was nowhere else for humiliation to go. *He thought she was enjoying it.* Her feelings could take no more. She lay under him, dumb and dead to all sensation, until it was over, and he was kissing her ear and hair and murmuring endearments of gratitude. After a while the words stopped, and his breathing slowed and he grew heavier, and she realised he had fallen asleep. The candle burned down. When it guttered out he woke abruptly, as if he had heard it. He rolled off her without a word, pulled up the bedclothes and settled on his side with his back to her.

She lay for a long time thinking that what had been endurable in the dark and in silence became a ghastly violation when sight and sound were added to sensation. He had been gone a long time, and her body had forgotten him, but, more than that, during these months she had reclaimed her heart, her soul, her self. She could not give them back to him; she could not love him. Soon he would go away to the war again, but when it was over, what then? What would she do? She could not, *could not* live with him like this again. She felt, in the aftermath of shock and the lack of proportion that midnight engenders, that she would kill herself rather than live with him. Kill herself – or him.

Then she slept, too exhausted even to dream. She woke early in the morning to hear him noisily using the chamber-pot, and then from the rustling sounds guessed he was pulling on his dressing-gown. She kept her eyes closed, even when she felt him lean over and look closely into her face, felt his breath on her cheek. She kept still and breathed slowly and steadily, and after a while he left her, and she heard the door-latch click. Then she slept again.

He was very cheerful when she met him at breakfast – cheerful and kind – and remained so the rest of the day, the last day of his furlough. He spent it on the verandah, talking with Charles about horses, playing with the children, receiving the smiling attentions of the house-slaves, while Mary sat nearby and sewed, and tried not to take too many decisions in his presence. In the afternoon he grew quieter, a little sad: he had to catch the train at four o'clock, and too soon Abel brought down his bag stuffed with fresh linen, Cookie flapped out of the kitchen with a food-basket, and it was time to say goodbye. The children were excited at the movement, saw no sadness in it: Preston clamoured to be sent back a piece of a Yankee shell, because Moultrie Fairfax had one. Charles shook his hand and asked for more and longer letters, with details of the campaign. Finally he came to Mary, took her hands, looked down into her face with an odd, intent look, more awake, more *here*, than he had been all the three days.

'Don't come to the depot with me,' he said. 'I want to remember you standing here at home, smiling like this.' She was not smiling, but perhaps in his mind she was. He bent his head to kiss her. 'Think about me a lot,' he whispered. 'Don't go giving your heart to anyone else.'

Ruth's baby was born on the 20th of March. Lennox was in Richmond, and came hurrying to the house as soon as Phoebe's note came to let him know she was in labour. He walked up and down the parlour as nervously as any prospective father, twisting his hands behind his back, chewing at the handsome white-blond moustache he had grown to give his face more maturity and dignity. Phoebe came downstairs from time to time to say, 'Nothing yet,' and, 'It will be ages yet. You don't need to stay – I'll send word as soon as it's born.'

But Lennox shook his head. He was as superstitious as an actress now, and felt that, if he left, something terrible would happen. It went on so long that, always short of sleep, he dozed off in the fireside chair. He was aroused by the clock striking, and, from upstairs, the indisputable wail of a baby. He struggled up. A quarter to midnight. Still Thursday. He waited, straining his ears for distant sounds, until the door opened and the midwife came in, all smiles, with a white bundle in her arms.

'A fine baby boy!' she said, placing the bundle into his astonished arms. He took it in exquisite trembling, looked down into the tiny red face with the quivering eyelids and the unexpected switch of ginger hair on the otherwise bald head, and wanted to cry. A passionate desire came over him to rush about leaping over furniture and uttering Confederate war-cries, and simultaneously to creep off somewhere secret and safe with this tiny nurseling and hold it close to his breast for ever. But mostly, he wanted to cry.

The midwife was a stranger to the Canfields and not fully aware of the circumstances of the house. She observed Lennox's expression with a high cackle of delight and said, 'Ah kin see he yo' fust chile, you so dumbfounded! But you gwine feel just the same ever' time.

Ain't no shame in bawlin', honey. Ain't nothin' so like to trim a man than lookin' in the face of his own new-bohn chile!'

She was so pleased with the baby, and so happy for him, that he couldn't bring himself to tell her she had just driven a knife into his heart. 'Can I see the mother?' he asked instead.

'Sho' can,' she said. 'Ah'll sen' fo' you dreckly.' And she took the baby out of Lennox's arms and went away.

Half an hour later he was called upstairs. The bedchamber was stuffy from burning lamps, and had a strange smell about it, but he noticed that for no more than an instant, for there was Ruth, sitting up in bed with a lacy jacket over her night-gown, her hair in a long, burnished plait over one shoulder, the baby in her arms, and tears flowing down her cheeks.

'Isn't he beautiful?' she said to Lennox as he hurried to her side. She smiled smearily at him. 'I don't know why I keep crying. I can't seem to stop.'

'I cried, too,' Lennox said.

'Did you? But he is beautiful, isn't he?'

'Most beautiful,' Lennox confirmed. 'I never saw anything so perfect. But are you all right, Ruthie?' he asked, a little shyly, because Ruth-the-mother was a new entity to him.

'Yes. Just tired.' She looked at him with a shy smile. 'It was kind of you to stay all the time. Phoebe said you've been waiting downstairs for hours.' He didn't know what to say. 'I was glad. It was comforting to know you were there, since Patrick – since Patrick couldn't be.'

He nodded, his throat tight. 'I suppose you'll call him Patrick?'

'Yes. I hope he grows up to look like him. I'm afraid he looks more like me at the moment.'

They both gazed at the baby for a while in silence. Then Ruth said diffidently, 'Lennox, would you – would you be his godfather? And a sort of honorary uncle? You know, not to take Patrick's place, exactly, but to see after him, and tell him things, like a father would, and take care of him if anything happens to me.'

'Nothing's going to happen to you,' he said quickly. 'But, yes, I'd be glad to be godfather – and uncle, and anything else you want. I'm honoured that you should ask me.' He put a finger to the baby's palm, and the tiny fingers closed round it, blindly trusting. Lennox looked up and met Ruth's eyes, and they both smiled. He felt such deep content and joy, it was hard to make himself remember this was not his family.

The Union changed its plan, abandoned the direct route, and instead landed troops at Hampton and tried to advance on Richmond up the Virginia peninsula. All that spring the Confederate General Magruder fought a cunning delaying action, while General Lee recruited reinforcements and threw a ring of defences around Richmond. It was not until the end of May that the Union troops actually came within sight of their objective. Then on the last day of the month the Confederates attacked them at Seven Pines, only nine miles from the city. A desperate and bloody struggle failed to dislodge the Union army, and the South's commander-in-chief, General Joe Johnston, was gravely wounded. Lennox was an onlooker all day, sitting his horse behind President Davis and General Lee. As the party rode away from the battlefield at dusk, through the jam of ambulances and the litter of debris, he saw the President turn his lean, grave face to Lee and say, '*You* will be the new leader of the Confederate army. You shall take over from Joe Johnston – will you?'

Two days later, Lennox was back in Richmond, calling at the Canfield house. Ruth was preparing to go to the hospital. She was recovered from the birth and had no milk for little Patrick anyway, and the need was desperate: the two days' battle at Seven Pines, though the result was inconclusive, had produced a huge casualty list.

'I can't stay,' she said as Lennox appeared. 'I must go on duty.'

'I know: I can't stay long either. I just came to tell you that I'm leaving the President's staff.' She stopped fastening her apron-strings and looked at him with raised eyebrows. 'General Lee has asked for me to be transferred to his staff,' Lennox said, his face pink with pleasure. 'It's a tremendous compliment.'

'Yes, I imagine so,' Ruth said.

'He is such a wonderful man – so clever, full of ideas – one trusts him instinctively. Now we shall really see something! The war's as good as won, now General Lee is in charge.'

'I hope you're right.'

He was hurt by her reception. 'Aren't you pleased for me?'

'Of course – but what does it mean for me? Now you'll be going away on campaign, and I shall hardly ever see you.'

His heart leapt at this evidence that she would mind, that she would miss him. 'I may not be here so often, but whenever I can, I shall come and see you, and Patrick. You may depend on that.'

She was looking at him with a faintly quizzical expression. 'I depend on *you*,' she said, as though it had just that moment occurred to her.

CHAPTER TWENTY-FOUR

It was Mrs Raven who brought Mary the news. She called from time to time, lonely at Wild Acre now Beau was dead, Adeline nursing in Richmond, and Mr Raven sunk into sadness and old age by the loss of his only son. When the isolation grew too much, she had her buggy sent round and went calling in the old, pre-war fashion. Mary felt so sorry for her that she concealed how inconvenient it was to stop work and be sociable.

'Have you heard about Conrad Ausland?' she asked on this occasion, after rambling for some time about her own affairs. 'Quite shocking! I had it from Mrs Lawrence, and she had it from her boy John, who had it from Sneed and Juve when they rode over to play with him. Those boys are just as wild as rabbits,' she diverged severely, 'but I suppose it's no wonder really, with their father's eye off them for such a long time. The Judge should have sent them to school when he went to Richmond, or taken them with him. Well, I suppose he'll have to now – one or the other – unless Chesney gives up his regiment and comes home. But I don't suppose he'll want to do that until the war's over.'

'What has happened to Conrad?' Mary asked when she could get a word in. 'Has he had an accident?'

'Haven't you heard? My dear, I was sure you would have, May being your sister – poor thing! When I think what a pretty bride she made – such a time ago it all seems, I declare! My poor Beau dancing with all the girls at May's wedding—' It was some sentences before Mary could repeat the urgent question, and Mrs Raven delivered herself, with a certain relish, of the news. 'It seems Conrad had some kind of a fit – well, according to Dr Trevelyan that's what must have happened, because I'm sorry to say no-one was with him at the time. He had a habit lately of shutting himself up in his room for hours on end and wouldn't be disturbed, and it was one of the slaves found him there on the floor in the morning when she went to dust the room, so I suppose he was lying there all night. Anyway, he's quite paralysed, can't move hand or foot, can't even speak, and Dr Trevelyan doesn't think there's much hope he'll come out of it. Of course, it's poor May one feels most sorry for—'

With tact and determination Mary got rid of Mrs Raven, sent for the carriage, and had herself driven over to Camelot. She remembered the last time she had seen Conrad. Presumably he had been sitting alone drinking day after day and night after night, and this was the consequence. Poor May! My God, what she had suffered through marrying Conrad! But she supposed Charles could not have foreseen this – and indeed, had it not been for the war, probably the Judge would have kept his son in some kind of order.

The doctor's rig was standing outside the house when she arrived, and Mary hurried in. The air of neglect was intensified, dust everywhere, no servants to receive her. It was only when she called out that Hebba came down the stairs, her anxious face lightening a little at the sight of Mary.

'Oh, Miz Mary, t'ank God you's come! Dis place is teh'ble. Ah wants t' go home tuh Twelvetrees. Ah cayn stay heah no more!'

'Where is everybody?'

'De house niggers all locked deyselves up in de kitchen-side. Dey say Mist' Conrad possessed by de debil. Dere on'y me t' look efter Miz May.'

'Where is she?'

'She in her room, lyin' down wid de 'sterics, but Doctuh Trevylan he wid Mist' Conrad and he keep callin' for someone to he'p him.'

'Very well,' Mary said, trying not to feel the hammering of her heart. 'You go back to Miss May and tell her I'll be there in just a minute. I'll go and see the doctor. Which room is it?'

She felt diffident about entering a strange man's bedchamber, but the door was ajar, which made things easier. Inside the room was frowsty-smelling and wildly untidy, with clothes strewn about as if no-one had been in it for days. There was the doctor with his back to her, bending over the bed. Mary's eyes leapt to the figure on the bed without her volition. Someone had put Conrad into his nightshirt, but he was lying on top of the bedclothes, as if they hadn't been able to put him properly to bed. His white face was gaunt and looked slippery, like sweating cheese, under his matted, unkempt hair. It seemed to have warped like green wood, one side pulled sideways and up, making his mouth hang to the left. His eyes were open, but fixed and staring, the right at the ceiling, the left, which seemed all pupil and horribly black, like a pistol-mouth, at the wardrobe. His legs below the hem of his nightshirt were bare, and there was a string of ulcers down the right shin like volcanoes on a map, and another at the corner of his mouth the size of a half-crown. He lay motionless, and she would have thought him dead except that she could see his chest flutter with his breathing.

The doctor's head snapped round as he heard her rustling approach. He seemed relieved rather than surprised to see her.

'Mrs Morland! Thank heaven for someone sensible. The slaves have locked themselves in the kitchen and Maybelle's having hysterics, and there's no-one to help me. Have you anyone with you?'

'Only my groom.'

'He'll do. I need someone to go with a message to my assistant. But first you must help me to get him into bed. The slaves just dropped him here and ran.'

Mary looked at Conrad with horror. 'I – I can't—'

Trevelyan was impatient. 'Oh, don't be missish with me! There's no time for that. You'll see worse things before this war is over. Come here, on the other side of the bed.'

Mary pulled herself together, though her flesh crawled at the thought of touching him. She helped lift his legs and pull the bedclothes down from under him, shift him further up the bed, and – with relief – cover him up.

'Now,' said the doctor, 'I shall need my assistant to find a suitable nurse to send out here – no use expecting the slaves to look after him – until we can arrange for him to be removed to the hospital. The family will have to be told, of course, and they'll have to decide what to do about May, poor child.' He shook his head. 'It's a bad business.'

Mary could only stare at him in bewilderment. 'Is there no hope for Conrad?' she managed to ask.

Trevelyan gave the merest glance at the bed. 'None, I'm afraid. The disease is too far advanced. This paralysis happens when the disease gets into the nerves, and they never recover. The only thing to do is to put him in a place where they're used to this kind of nursing – there's one in Columbia that I'd recommend. Very discreet. It won't be for long; two or three months at the most.'

'But what did you mean about May?' Mary asked, dazed with shock at his words. 'About deciding what's to be done about her?'

Trevelyan raised his eyebrows. 'She ought to go for the cure, if I can persuade the family to send her. There is a slight chance for her, but of course the longer they delay, the slighter that becomes.'

'The cure?' Mary whispered. Terrible thoughts were coming to her – whispered and half-understood things converging from the four corners of her memory. May's fever and rash soon after she was married; the headaches; the miscarriage; Conrad's long absence in Columbia and his ill appearance when he returned; his increasing irrationality. 'Columbia?' she queried. What was it she had heard about Columbia?

Trevelyan nodded. 'Yes, that's the best place, though it didn't save Conrad, of course. But May hasn't had it so long. I tried to persuade her to go, but she wouldn't talk about it, or even let me mention the word, and the rest of the family is as bad, or worse. Pig-headed fools! Pretending a thing isn't so won't make it go away. Well, they'll have to face up to it now. And God knows who else has been infected, because no-one would admit the truth.'

Syphilis. Mary remembered the word now, and she blushed with shame that she knew it, and knew what it was, and that she was here discussing it with Dr Trevelyan. But it was horrible, horrible! Conrad dying – and poor, poor May infected too with only 'a slight chance' of being cured. Why hadn't she realised before? She wondered how she could have been so blind, except that her upbringing had not prepared her for such things. But here in the South, where miscegenation was an accepted fact, even if it was not talked about, the women must know as well as the men. The Judge and Mrs Judge knew, but had pretended nothing was wrong, rather than admit the shame of it.

Mary did not return to Twelvetrees that day, nor the next. There was a great deal to do and no-one but her to do it, before she could leave Camelot – a mis-named place if ever there was one. It was her fury that sustained her through the ordeal, her fury that May had been abandoned by all her new family. First she had to winkle out the slaves from their hiding-place and persuade and bully them into resuming their duties. She packed bags for Sneed and Juvenal and sent them with their boys, their ponies and a covering note to Fairoaks, where kindly Mrs Fairfax would take them in.

Meanwhile a carefully worded telegraph was sent to the Judge; Trevelyan's assistant sent a nurse to take care of Conrad; and Aunt Margaret, summoned by Trevelyan in terms that brooked no denial, arrived to take care of May and the house. She was white-faced and tight-lipped and Mary read in her hostile expression that she had known, or at least long suspected, the truth. As soon as she had sent her bag up to her room and put on her apron, she dismissed Mary without thanks. 'I can manage now,' she said. 'Don't come here again.' The bitterness in her voice said that Mary did the family more harm by knowing the truth than she had done good by coping with the emergency.

When she reached home, she went in search of Charles. The note she had sent the first day had said only that May could not be left and that she would stay until help came. Now she walked into the library and cornered him. After his initial protest at being disturbed, he listened to her in silence, his face grey and immobile, but a red spark of anger growing in his eyes. When she paused at last he said, 'How dare you say these things to me? Have you no natural modesty? How dare you even know such words, let alone speak them aloud?'

Her own anger flared in response. 'How dare *you* talk about natural modesty at such a time? Where was Conrad's natural modesty? If he had had any, he would not be dying now. He brought this on himself. But what did May do to deserve it? And you married her to him, knowing what he was!'

'You are impertinent!' he snapped. 'Yes, and that doesn't surprise me. It's all of a piece with your character – a penniless nobody without the vestige of proper feeling or feminine delicacy! You deceived my son into thinking you were an heiress – don't bother to deny it! Do you think I'd have allowed the marriage if I'd known the true state of affairs? Then you come here so full of your own conceit that you refuse to learn anything or be guided by your betters. You set up your own opinions in opposition to mine, you dispute and contradict, and use language that would make a darkie blush. And now you dare to speak to me of subjects no decent woman would know about, let alone air in that disgusting, bold-faced way!'

Mary was trembling with rage and pain, but she controlled herself, knowing that if she let her temper off the leash she would lose all coherence and all hope of making any impression on him. His attitude and assumptions were so different from hers, it was worse than trying to speak a foreign language, it was like trying to communicate across the barrier of species. In a low, impassioned voice she said, 'I wish with all my heart I did *not* know these things, or have to speak to you about them. But your daughter is ill, perhaps dying, and you may be able to persuade the Auslands to do the right thing by her.'

He glared. 'Don't presume to tell me my duty with regard to my own daughter!'

'Very well,' she said with furious calm, 'but there is another matter. If you don't care for her, you may care for your own property. You must know the reason why May wanted to be rid of Becka, and why Conrad wanted her back. And I have seen enough of your journeys across the yard to the quarters to guess why you refused to give her back—'

She got no further. Charles stepped forward and hit her across the face with his open palm. The blow made a loud smack which seemed to echo in the sudden silence, but Mary was already so angry it startled more than hurt her. She stared at him steadily, and saw his focus move from her eyes to her crimsoning cheek, and saw what she had never expected to see, a hint of shame in his expression.

'I have nothing more to say,' she said, and left him.

Tight-lipped Southern propriety took over and dealt with the matter in its own way. Judge and Mrs Judge came back to Camelot, and Charles rode over there to speak with them – Mary learned that from Cedar, for certainly Charles did not tell her. There was just the one visit: when he returned from it, he never mentioned May or the Auslands again. The next day Becka departed with her bundle to walk to Camelot; the rest Mary learned piece by piece from other sources.

Conrad was taken off in an ambulance to the depot and then to Columbia; May followed the next day, with Becka to wait on her, and Aunt Margaret to escort her. Kitten broke off her engagement to Cousin Hamilton, and departed for Savannah to live with an elderly cousin of her mother's who wanted a companion. Sneed, who was now fifteen, went to join Chesney's regiment. Clara was taken out of school and she and Juvenal went with Aunt Margaret to live in Atlanta, where the Judge had property interests. The house in King Street was shut up, and the house-slaves brought out to Camelot, where the Judge and Mrs Judge lived in complete seclusion, not visiting anyone or being visited. The person, apart from May, that Mary felt most sorry for was Trevelyan, who was blamed for the fact that the Auslands' shame had become public knowledge. In luckier times the whole thing would have been kept a close secret within the family: Conrad and May could have been spirited away, Kitten would have got to marry her beau, and no-one would have been any the wiser. As it was, Trevelyan found his customers slipping away, changing to other physicians, and people crossing the road to avoid speaking to him. After a few months he left what little remained of his practice and went to Richmond, where there was always a need for doctors, more than could ever be fulfilled.

As 1862 progressed, the cotton ran out, and more and more hands were laid off. Poverty came to Lancashire. A quarter of a million were out of work, and as many more on short-time working. The parishes could not cope with the numbers, and private charity had to be encouraged into action.

Benedict found himself once again taken away from home: in conscience he could not ignore the demands of his own workers, though he was loath to leave Sibella. She had had a son in April, whom they had called Manfred – she had read the name in a novel and taken a fancy to it. But Sibella herself said, 'You must go. This is a superior claim to mine.'

Some mill-masters had closed their factory gates, the doors of their fine houses, and their minds all at the same time. Cotton had always come from America: one day it would again. In the meantime it was none of their business how their laid-off hands survived. Such people had their ways, no doubt. Lord Palmerston said to Charlotte that these mill-masters were like men holding out bowls and waiting for it to rain plum-pudding.

But far more of them gave what they could and threw themselves into the organisation of relief, setting up soup kitchens, and handing out the relief parcels which were being sent by the charitable from all over the country. Local traders gave long credit to the sufferers, and many, especially butchers, drove themselves out of business and sank into the same poverty as their former customers.

The hardest burden had already been suffered, during the winter months, because of the application of the Labour Test. Parish relief was linked to the willingness to work, and such work as there was was usually hard labour such as stone-breaking. For indoor workers, poorly clothed and close to starvation, such work was cruel, and in many cases proved fatal. By the summer of 1862 a special commissioner had been appointed to Lancashire and new regulations drawn up concerning relief, which helped matters considerably.

But still Benedict found such terrible poverty and suffering, usually so bravely borne, that he began to regret having put so much money into the building of the two ships, which could otherwise have provided relief in Manchester. But perhaps helping the South to win the war would help more people in the long run. The first of the ships had been launched in March and was already operating with great success. The second, launched in May, was held up at the demand of the Union representative, Charles Adams, who was furious that the first ship had got away and wanted strenuous action taken. The papers were sent to the Foreign Office, who sent them to the customs commissioners in Liverpool, who shrugged and sent them back to Lord Russell saying they saw no grounds for detaining the ship. Adams sought legal opinion, and the matter was referred to the Queen's advocate, who passed the papers to the attorney-general and solicitor-general, and in the midst of this amiable paperchase the ship went out on a trial voyage to test her engines and somehow forgot to return.

'Nevertheless,' Russell told Charlotte and Oliver in his blunt way, 'there's to be no more of this. Adams says I should have ordered the ship stopped until the law officers had given their opinion, and of course he's right; now he says that if she does any damage to Northern shipping, he'll demand compensation from Her Majesty's Government.'

'You won't give it, of course?' Oliver said, raising his eyebrows.

Russell gave a grimace. 'Of course not. I'll talk him to a standstill and hold him off one way and another: but I won't protect you again, Southport, so mark me! It's a sword that cuts with both edges, you know: they have armed privateers which could interfere with our shipping. And it's a dangerous precedent to set. Suppose we go to war again, and the United States takes it into its head to fit out ships for our enemy? So no more of this, d'ye understand? Or I'll have to come down heavily on you both.'

Oliver accepted the reprimand, Charlotte thought, with surprising meekness: she herself had never liked Russell's manner, and could not get on with him as she did with Lord Palmerston. But Oliver told her that what Russell had said was true, and that the business had become too public. 'Adams is a damned nuisance. If he hadn't gone ferreting out the details, we could have got away with it, but he'll have his eye on all the shipyards now. We don't want to provoke war with the United States.'

'Don't we?' Charlotte said rebelliously. 'Leaving aside any philosophical question, don't we want American cotton?'

Oliver made an equivocal grimace. 'Naturally, my love – but we need American wheat even more, and the wheat is grown in the North.'

So Charlotte gave her mind and energies for the rest of the summer to trying to raise funds and organise relief work in Manchester. The machine of pity was hard to get started and moved agonisingly slowly, and the problems of administration were heartbreaking when the suffering was so vast and so widespread. Overall, two million pounds were raised in private donations – the largest amount ever given to such a fund – and Oliver cajoled and bullied the Cabinet into agreeing another one and a half million of public works, such as paving streets, laying drains and creating public parks, to provide work for the workless. And by the beginning of 1863 some cotton was beginning to come in from India and Egypt to ease the situation. But there was still desperate and widespread suffering, and so there would be until the war in America was won and the regular supply of cotton was restored; but that still looked to be a long way into the future.

In the summer of 1862 fortune swung the Confederate way. When General Lee had taken over in spring, the South was on the retreat

384

in both theatres of war, and the Union Army of the Potomac under General McClellan was camped almost on Richmond's doorstep. By the end of August, he had beaten that army, beaten the army that was sent to relieve it, and virtually cleared Virginia of Union troops, driving them right back to Washington.

It had been a brilliant campaign, but not without price. On the 29th and 30th of August the enemies met again on the old battleground at Manassas, and the South inflicted a decisive and bloody defeat on the North. The Union lost nearly fifteen thousand men; but the South lost nearly ten thousand. Yet though the Confederate army was mauled and depleted in numbers, its morale was strong, and Lee decided to keep up the momentum and press ahead into Maryland. There were many good reasons for this, not least that Virginia was war-ravaged, and there was little left there to feed the army: Maryland was untouched and promised good eating. There was good political reason, too: the North's tail was down, and actual invasion of its territory by the South could be the thing to crystallise popular discontent and force Lincoln to sue for peace.

And there were strong hints that the British Government was poised to recognise the South: there was no doubt, the British papers were saying, that Jefferson Davis and his colleagues had created a nation, which had a successful army and was building itself a navy. One resounding defeat of the Union on its own territory might be enough, Lee reasoned, to bring Britain in to mediate and put pressure on the Union to let the South go in peace.

So Lee marched into Maryland, passing well to the north-west of Washington, aiming for Pennsylvania. Feeling it would be as well to secure his lines of communication, he detached Jackson's division to take Harper's Ferry, where the North had a garrison of twelve thousand soldiers, and where, years before, the fanatic John Brown had tried to start a slave insurrection. The rest of the army was divided into two sections, one to cover the gaps in the South Mountains, to stop McClellan breaking through, the other pushing ahead to Hagerstown, near the Pennsylvania border. Then sheer, stupid chance took a hand. A Confederate officer lost his copy of the orders, which was found by two Union soldiers, who took it to General McClellan's headquarters.

The Confederates' speed was what saved them, enabling Jackson to take Harper's Ferry and still get back to join the other two divisions at a dusty little town called Sharpsburg on the Antietam Creek. By the time slow-moving McClellan reached the scene, Lee had most of his army in place and deployed in defensive positions. The Union army attacked at dawn the next day, September the 17th, and went on attacking savagely all day, forcing the Confederates to give ground, but never managing to dislodge them. It was the bloodiest single day's fighting yet, both sides losing close to twelve thousand men: the dead lay in heaps like a strange, grim harvest; the tall corn was trampled flat and the dust was laid with blood. The next day McClellan did not renew the failed attack, but the Confederate army was too exhausted and depleted in numbers to continue the invasion. During the night of September the 18th General Lee slipped away with his army and marched it back to Virginia.

It was at that point that President Lincoln changed the nature of the game. The people of the South had never doubted what they were fighting for: they were defending their homeland from an invading enemy. But the people of the North were sick of a war which demanded their sons' blood for a cause as nebulous as 'the Union', and the newspapers constantly asked whether the South was worth the keeping. Morale was flagging and recruitment had all but dried up. So on September the 22nd Mr Lincoln gave the North a new cause. His Emancipation Proclamation decreed that from January the 1st 1863, all slaves held in a state that was in rebellion would be 'thenceforward and forever free'.

In itself the proclamation was an absurdity: it abolished slavery in those states where the North had no authority, and preserved it in the states under its control. But the mass of people didn't care about logic: the emotional appeal was everything. The Washington government hoped that the people would now feel that they had a clear war-aim, to rid the world of the curse of slavery. The North, it hoped, would be able to believe God was on its side, an advantage which had always before rested with the South. And President Lincoln hoped that, by making slavery an issue, he had forestalled any British intervention.

On the same day a letter arrived at Twelvetrees for Mary from General Stuart. She knew what it was without opening it, and held it for a long time, staring at the stained and dog-eared envelope unseeingly, afraid of what she might feel, or worse, not feel, when she read the words.

'Dear Madam, it is with the most profound regret that I have to inform you . . .'

Fenwick had been mortally wounded by artillery fire during a skirmish on the edge of the West Woods. He had been carried back behind the lines into Sharpsburg, but had died a few hours later. Without comment, Mary handed the letter to the white-faced Charles, who knew as well as she did what it meant. As he read it, his face seemed to drag into lines of age, as though years were flowing into him now his defences were down. May's fate had not touched him, but this – this was different. The hand that held the page shook violently, and he had to catch it with the other to hold it steady enough to read.

'Sharpsburg,' he said at last. 'Maryland. He will be buried in a foreign land.' His voice sounded most unlike his own – Mary wouldn't have recognised it.

'It is the fate of the soldier throughout history,' she said.

Charles flared. 'Damn you, is that all you can say? Aren't you even woman enough to weep for him?' And with a weak, terrible gesture he threw the letter at her, and then fumbled in his pocket for his handkerchief, taking off his spectacles with the other hand, his eyes looking frightened and vulnerable without them. 'Damn you!' he gasped. 'Damn you for marrying him! Here's an end to it all now. Here's an end to my son.' He couldn't find his handkerchief and his tears were running over. Mary held out her own to him, her throat tight with pity at the sight of his sorrow, but he knocked it from her hand and turned away, and almost blundered out.

Mary stood where she was, bowing her head to ease the pain of her throat. Fenwick was dead, buried in a foreign land. He would be below ground by now. Odd that that made a difference to Charles – or perhaps that was the only part he could speak about. She tried to find her own sorrow, but she had been without him for so long that she couldn't make him real in her mind – not the Fenwick she had last seen, the lean bearded soldier on furlough. He seemed to have no connection with her.

Yet she felt an enormous sense of loss: a sense of being exposed and vulnerable, as if her sheltering tree had been cut down, and she had been left naked to the elements and the bitter wind. She thought of her boys – but they had their grandfather, and if they grew up without a father's influence, they would have his legend, and the knowledge of the Cause, and the whole of the South for which he had died. Their lives would never lack meaning; would perhaps even gain, hard though it was to think it, because they were young enough to have been brought up mostly among women and slaves and had known their father more as a fact than a presence.

But she – what was she? She was now only a widow in a land increasingly rich in widows. Her father-in-law hated her, though since the departure of May and Conrad they had rubbed along together with stiff politeness, because they had to. The South, though she had come to love it, did not accept her in that way that one's homeland did, like the curve of a nest to the curve of a bird's breast. It came to her that what Fenwick had given her all these years was a reason to be here. While he lived, she had not had to think much about herself or her future. He had been the full-stop beyond which nothing was written or read. But now the story had been reopened, and what was she to do with it? How was she to end it?

A few days later Fenwick's servant Abel came home, riding Fenwick's second horse, with Fenwick's possessions slung from the saddle. He brought more details of his master's act of courage, riding his troop to the aid of a beleaguered infantry company, and of his end, in a Yankee woman's house in Sharpsburg.

'She wuz good to him,' Abel said, to comfort Mary. 'He didn't never have no chance, but she look after him real kin', bathin' he's head and hol'in' he's han' to the end. And she said to tell you, Miss Mary, that she wouldn't let him go to no common grabe. She said she get her neighbour to buh'y him in the family buh'yin plot, so one day when the war was over you could come an' see it.'

Abel sounded astonished with what he had to tell, but Mary listened without surprise. The war was men's business: it was not for women to hate, and she thought she would have done the same for a dying Yankee soldier. It would comfort Charles a little, she thought, to know that Fenwick was not in some unmarked pit; but she could not imagine she would ever go visiting his grave. What for? He would not be there, and to look at an oblong of turf would not help or comfort her.

Abel went on in a puzzled voice, 'Miss Mary, Ah cayn understand them Yankee folks. This Yankee woman was as kahnd as could be to Mister Fenwick, but at fust she wouldn't even let me come in de house, lahk Ah was somepin dirty – me, that wash Mister Fenwick an' shaved him ever' day of he's lahf, an' wash he's close too in th' army! She look at me lahk Ah was some coorious kind o' bug, y'know? Kind of wierd an' hawble at the same time.' He shook his head. 'When he was dyin', she say to me she cayn understan' why a gemmun lahk him would fight so's to keep black folks as slabes. But she didn't lahk me, Miss Mary. Them Yankees don't lahk us black folks. Huccome they want to free us? And when Ah tellt her Ah wuz no slabe but a free black, she didn't believe me.'

It was a puzzle beyond Mary to explain to him. She sent him off to the kitchen to get something to eat. Later, when she went there herself, she found him recounting the same story to the kitchen slaves. She asked him what he would do now. 'You can go anywhere, you know: Columbia, Charleston – New York, even.'

He took the last suggestion seriously. 'Ah don' want to go to the North. Ah don' want to go no place they think Ah'm dirty. Mebbe I could go to Charleston. But Ah don't know whut Ah kin do there.'

'You could work in a barber's shop, shaving gentlemen and

cutting their hair: you know how to do that. Or a tailor's shop – you've made and mended Mr Fenwick's clothes long enough. Things are getting harder in Charleston because of the war, but there will always be gentlemen who need services like that.'

Abel still hesitated, and looked sidelong at Mary. 'Ah spose,' he said at last, 'Ah couldn't stay heah? This kahnd o' lahk home to me now. But dere on'y Marse Morland lef', and he got Prince to take care o' him.'

Mary smiled inwardly. 'Well, there is something you could do,' she said. 'My boys are getting to the age when they need a man to keep an eye on them. Rosa can't keep up with them, and their body-slaves are too young. Would you like to take on that job?'

Abel's face lit. 'Tek care o' Pres an' Ash an' Corton? Why, Miss Mary, there ain't nothin' Ah'd lahk better in the worl'! Ah love them lil boys!'

'I know you do – and there's no-one I'd sooner trust them to,' Mary said. 'So it's settled, then. I'm sure it's what Mr Fenwick would have wanted.'

She didn't think Charles would have any objection. It would be the best way to keep Fenwick's memory green in his sons' hearts, to have his servant tell them the story of his heroism – and if she knew anything about negroes, the tale would gain with every telling.

There was one more action before the winter weather closed down the Virginia theatre – a Confederate victory at Fredericksburg, halfway between Richmond and Washington. General McClellan had been replaced after Sharpsburg by General Burnside, but after Fredericksburg, where the Union lost twelve thousand men and Lee's veterans were never close to being moved from their position, Burnside too was dismissed. The armies separated into their winter camps, and some men were allowed home for Christmas on short furloughs.

Eugene was offered furlough, because of his brother's death, but refused it with a touch of surprise. There was nothing he wanted to go home for. His whole life was now the army, and his whole love was General Jackson. If Old Jack did not go home for Christmas, why should Eugene?

Lennox accepted the offer of three days eagerly, and went to Richmond, to spend it with the Canfields and Ruth. His little godson was growing apace, was walking, if a little unsteadily, and talking, though his words were as yet more onomatopoeia than conversation. 'I feel as if I've been away for years,' Lennox complained. 'How can a baby change so much in such a short time?'

'That's what babies do,' Ruth said calmly, removing Patrick's hand from the coal-bucket and wiping it on her skirt. 'Do you think he looks like his father yet?'

Lennox studied the boy but felt he could not tell a lie. 'He looks like you. Don't be disappointed, Ruthie! You're a good thing to look like.'

'He's supposed to keep his father's memory alive,' Ruth said sternly.

'That's a large burden to place on such little shoulders,' Lennox said lightly, but meaning it. 'Can't he just be himself? That's hard enough in this uncertain life, without trying to be someone else as well.'

But Ruth turned to him, her eyes suddenly revealing. 'I'm forgetting him,' she said starkly. 'When I got to bed at night I always think about him before I go to sleep, and sometimes – sometimes lately I can't remember what he looked like.'

Lennox stepped closer. 'It's all right,' he said. 'That's just life. It moves on.'

'I don't want it to move on!'

'But it will, whether you want it or not. It won't be denied. And don't you think Patrick would have wanted you to move on? He wouldn't have wanted your life to stop because his had.'

She turned her head away from his words. 'I don't want to lose him again. I've lost so much already.' She looked into the fire, absently holding the baby's hands and jigging them a little. 'When I'm at the hospital, that's real enough. The war, the men's wounded bodies, the smells, the tiredness – they're all bright and hard as glass, something to be grasped and dealt with. Everything else is just a dream. Twelvetrees, my childhood—' She paused, looking back. Everything about it had a quality like mist, soft and lovely but insubstantial: the ghostly smell of apples in the barn, and the swooping shadows as she pushed herself on her swing, the milky fog that lay over the cricks at dawn, the white dust that coated the green cotton-stalks at the track-sides, the scent of bean-flower in the morning, the scent of lime-flower at dusk. She remembered the pale-haired youth she had shown all her treasures to when she had been a pampered little girl, who stood before her now a lean, campaign-hardened man, with the faint odour of carbolic soap about him, and the coat fraying into shabbiness with hard wear. And she was no longer a velvet-palmed planter's daughter, but a woman with eyes that had seen too much pain. She knew there was a hungry look to her that no beau would think feminine and attractive. She had calloused hands, too, and chapped wrists from being in water all day, and straight hair there was never time to curl. She was so thin she didn't need lacing, and there were black bands for her brother on her sleeves, and no hoops under her skirts. She didn't suppose there would ever be hoops again. They were something that belonged in that dream-place 'before the war', not this inhospitable world.

And between the two places there had been Patrick, for those few rapturous weeks when she had been a child still, but sailing on grown-up waters in a magic boat shaped like a swan, with silken sails and a prince for a boatman. The only way back to her childhood world was through Patrick; if she lost him, she felt she would have lost herself, too, and everything that made this war worth fighting – the things Patrick had died for.

Lennox watched her face and tried to fathom what she was thinking, what was best to tell her. In the end he said, 'Memories are good, but that's not all there is to life, Ruthie. When the war's over we'll make a new life, and start creating new memories. Little Patrick's going to grow up in that world; let's not make him feel it's second-best, that he's missed a golden time he never had the chance to know.'

Ruth smiled at him rather pallidly. 'I know you're right,' she said, 'but just now I don't feel it. Don't let's talk like this any more now. Tell me about the campaign instead, and General Lee and the fellows.'

But Lennox shook his head. 'There's nothing to tell about the war. It's just war, and always the same. But we've got them on the run now: next year when the campaigning season starts again we'll take the fight to them and lick them good and hard, and they'll be suing for peace by the summer's end. So let's forget all about it for now, and concentrate on having a good Christmas.'

Ruth did her best, and succeeded so well that the whole house was merry, and she and Lennox were as wild as children, romping and singing and playing foolish games until George Canfield said little Patrick seemed the oldest and most sensible of the three. They had all hoped Martial would be able to join them, at least for Christmas Day, but it was more than ever vital to find out what the North's dispositions were, and he was far away with his scouts in the fields and woods between Fredericksburg and Washington.

On the last day of the year there was a fierce, desperate and inconclusive battle fought in the desolate, frozen country around Murfreesboro in Tennessee. When darkness fell the two sides disengaged but neither left the field, so nothing had been decided. But when the dreary dawn of the 1st of January 1863 dawned, neither side was willing to resume the pointless slaughter. For two days they remained within sight of each other, with no contact but sporadic firing along the picket-lines, and a few half-hearted advances; and then during the darkness of the night of the 3rd of January, both armies withdrew, the Northern to Murfreesboro and the Southern back towards Tullahoma on the Nashville and Chattanooga railroad. Both sides were too badly mauled to continue the campaign for some time; the losses in this action had been terrible, thirteen thousand Union soldiers and ten thousand Confederates, and nothing had been gained or lost.

Mary pondered on the news, and on the meaningless figures. Twenty-three thousand Americans killed or wounded by each other: blood and agony, human bodies lying stiffening in the frozen mud, eyes blank for ever and a family somewhere with a piece torn out of it; but how quickly it had become numbers. You scanned the casualty lists with flinching eyes, and if your own menfolk were not there, the rest became cyphers.

It was not until a week afterwards that a telegraph came saying starkly, 'Regret Major Hector Fenwick missing. Letter follows.'

The letter came from General Braxton Bragg himself, commander-in-chief of the Army of Tennessee, who had been a personal friend of Uncle Heck's, and the fact that Heck's name had not been on the casualty list was soon explained.

'Because of the detached nature of his duties, he did not belong to any particular corps, and on this occasion, during the retreat from the field, Polk thought he was with Hardee, and Hardee that he was with Polk. When the melancholy truth was known, we hastened to enquire throughout the army if anyone had seen him, but it seems that he disappeared during the hours of darkness on the night of January 2nd – January 3rd.

'The field and all surrounding areas are now in the hands of the Federal army, as you will be aware. If Major Fenwick is wounded, I am confident he will be taken care of; and if captured, treated with humanity and respect. In either case, word will eventually reach you. As to that other melancholy possibility, I can only refer you to God's will and recommend the comfort of prayer.'

Charles received the news impassively, and passed the letter to Mary to read. Looking up at the end of it, she said, 'It doesn't mention Hill.'

'No, why should it? He was not a soldier. He was Heck's servant.'

'Do you think they've been captured?'

He turned away impatiently. 'What use is speculation? If they have, we'll hear from them. It's customary.'

He left her alone with her thoughts. Though she didn't believe all the tales of atrocity, it was not pleasant to think of Uncle Heck as languishing in a Yankee prison, but it was better than believing him dead. She didn't want to think she would never see him again. Oddly, she could not imagine Hill as dead: she simply didn't believe he would let a Yankee kill him. But one thing was sure – dead or alive, wherever Uncle Heck was, Hill was too.

CHAPTER TWENTY-FIVE

On Saturday the 10th of January 1863, the Metropolitan Railway was officially opened with a ceremonial journey from Paddington to Farringdon Street. The occasion was graced with the presence of the Duke and Duchess of Southport. The duke made a short speech praising the ingenuity and skill of the British engineers and workmen who had brought this marvel of the modern world so swiftly to pass; and the duchess commented for the benefit of several reporters that she had found the journey underground a thrilling experience, and that she was sure there would be many more such railways in the future, enabling honest working men and industrious citizens to reach their places of employment quickly and easily.

Afterwards the directors of the railway company entertained their honoured guests to what *The Times* was pleased to describe as 'a splendid luncheon'.

And afterwards again, the duke and duchess shared a modest and private celebration at the home of Mr Thomas Weston, MP, in Upper Grosvenor Street.

'I was pleasantly surprised that we were so little incommoded by the smoke,' Charlotte said, accepting a cup of tea.

'I don't know why you should be surprised,' Benedict said. 'We dealt with that fear when we built the Kilsby Tunnel. Everyone said that travellers would be suffocated, and we built those huge ventilation shafts, but I always said that the passage of the trains would do the trick. You only have to think of the action of a bellows—'

'I never do think of the action of a bellows,' Charlotte said firmly. 'But I must say I think your stations very handsome – quite as nice as anything above ground.'

'And the carriages were very comfortable,' Emily added.

'My only regret was that I couldn't be both in the train and on the platform to photograph it coming in,' Tom said.

'But you took a dozen plates last week,' Benedict objected, 'when I took you and Tommy through.'

'It was very kind of you to arrange that special journey for us,' Emily said. 'Tommy hasn't stopped talking about it since. What a pity,' she added to Charlotte, 'that your boys couldn't have come too. They're just the age to have enjoyed it.'

'I can always arrange it for you, any time you like,' Benedict said quickly. 'You have only to say the word.'

'I shouldn't dream of disrupting the working of the railway for that,' Charlotte said. 'They'll have plenty of opportunities to ride on an underground train. And, I have to tell you, neither of them has the slightest interest in anything that doesn't move on four legs. I'm sorry to have such unnatural children, but they don't care a fig about engines.'

Benedict shook his head at this terrible state of affairs and said, 'At least Tommy does you credit, Tom. I think he's one of the nicest youngsters I know.'

'Of course, he'll never be really handsome,' Emily began, and paused for the statement to be refuted, but her audience disappointed her.

'Perhaps not,' Benedict said, 'but he is a perfect pleasure to be with – so polite and friendly – and he always asks intelligent questions. That's more than can be said for most adults.'

'I'm glad you find him so personable,' Tom said, 'because I was hoping that one day you will take him round one of your mills and explain all the machinery to him. I think he rather wants to be an engineer when he grows up.'

'With great pleasure,' Benedict said, 'but he won't see many engines working in the mills at the moment.'

'Are things very bad up there?' Emily asked.

'Very bad,' Benedict said. 'No raw cotton coming in, the machines idle, and the hands out of work. We do what we can to help, but the scale of the problem is immense. And yet they are so cheerful and polite, and so grateful for anything one does,' he frowned. 'I think they must be the best people in the world. I'm sure the lower orders in other countries aren't so stout-hearted.'

It was this conversation that drove Charlotte the following day to cancel her engagements and tell Norton to get out one of her plain gowns and her stoutest boots. 'No hoops. And dress my hair as plainly as possible.'

Norton was dismayed. 'You're going slum-visiting?'

'You needn't come if you don't want.'

Norton ignored that. 'There's no need. And it's not your place.'

'It's usually the housemaid who's told to remember her place,' Charlotte said, faintly amused.

'Housemaid or duchess, we all have our sphere appointed by

395

God. That's what keeps the world turning,' Norton said severely.

'Well, I believe my sphere is helping the unfortunate. And it's all too easy to forget people when you're busy doing them good. I thought of that yesterday. I haven't been out in the streets for a long time, and I'm afraid my soul might be hardening. I need to see them for myself again.'

'The unfortunate aren't there for the good of your soul,' Norton said stiffly.

Charlotte was wounded. 'How could you say such a thing? You know I don't go to stare, like those country missions up for the day for a trip to the slums and tea at the Station Hotel.'

Norton softened, and her real fear burst out. 'Oh, miss, you don't know what a target you make! Everyone knows who you are, and all poor people aren't angels, you know!'

Charlotte laughed. 'Oh, I know that all right! That's why I want you to dress me at my plainest. And if there are villains about, I'm sure we will have many more friends to take our part. If Lord Shaftesbury can walk about the rookeries without harm, I'm sure I can. So don't argue any more, there's a dear, but fetch out the basket, and let's see what we need to take with us.'

She came home at dusk tired and sobered, feeling she was right to have gone. The intensity of individual suffering was hard to keep before one's mind when dealing with large numbers; and giving money was all too easy when you had it to give. To meet one suffering person face to face and to give them relief seemed to her more valuable and also more Christian than donating cash to a fund; and she reasoned that if every comfortable person in the city helped one unfortunate person in that way, perhaps there would be no more unfortunates. Wasn't that what was meant by 'loving one's neighbour as oneself'? Norton held her tongue when that question was directed towards her, and merely hastened to get her lady into the bath to wash off the smell of poverty before dinner.

Charlotte went again the next day. It was a beast of a day, bitterly cold and sleety, with the sort of damp chill that nothing seemed to keep out. Even in her thick dress and good boots, Charlotte could feel it creeping into her limbs and stiffening her blood. How much worse would they feel it, who had poor, thin clothing and nothing between their feet and the earth but a bit of cardboard?

She went to help at a soup-kitchen she had discovered the day before, where good intentions were being hampered by a lack of organisation. A fair and flustered young woman from a Christian mission had been in charge; the kitchen itself was an old coach-house in one of the poor streets off Drury Lane, converted by the simple means of a large copper and a number of trestles and benches. The young woman, Miss Tyler, knew little of how to make soup, and her assistants knew less; and all were too nervous to impose any discipline on the 'customers', with the result that some of the ingredients had been stolen before ever finding their way into the soup, and those most in need had been pushed aside by the bold-faced and strong.

Miss Tyler was evidently relieved when Charlotte arrived early with Norton, and was only too glad to hand over the operation to her. Soon the soup was brewing in the copper, the trestles were laid out in such a way as to keep the human traffic flowing, and the kitchen was ready to open its doors. It was such a day as would make anyone want to seek shelter, and though there was no fireplace in the room, the heat from the copper and from all the bodies kept the chill off. Charlotte had to be firm about moving people on when they had finished their soup, so that others could take their place, but she had a row of benches placed along one wall where the most vulnerable were allowed to remain out of the weather for an hour or two.

Trade was brisk, and when all the places at table were taken up, many more ate their soup leaning against the wall. Most were simply grateful for the shelter and food, but still Charlotte had to place one of the women on guard at the door to make sure all the empty bowls and spoons were given up. It was strange how so many managed to find their way into people's coats and pockets and attempted to escape the premises.

Miss Tyler, mindful of her mission, was worried that no attempt was being made to distinguish the deserving from the undeserving, and that the recipients of the soup were not being made to say a prayer as she had been told they must. Charlotte had dealt with this objection before, and had the words ready to soothe her. 'Doesn't it say in the Good Book that God more regardeth the thoughts of the heart than the words of the mouth? Then I'm sure He hears the gratitude of these poor people. They are praying as they eat.'

Miss Tyler didn't think her superintendent would agree with that, but she felt it would be impolite to argue with a duchess.

In the middle of the day the sleet came on more heavily, and there was a surge as a great many people tried to come in off the street all at once. Charlotte saw a thin, poor-looking woman with a small child by the hand appear hesitantly at the door. She was barged aside by the ingress of a group of cheerful prostitutes, who presumably had just got up and were looking for something tasty by way of breakfast. They were chattering too hard to notice the woman, but Charlotte thought she did not look forceful enough to get herself into such a hearty queue.

So Charlotte called to the prostitutes, 'Now, ladies, fair dealing! I dare say you ate last night, but the woman there with a little girl probably didn't. Let her through and don't crush her. She doesn't look as if she'll eat much, so there'll still be plenty for you when she's done.'

The prostitutes, tickled perhaps at being called ladies, looked round, saw the woman, and good-naturedly hauled her and the child out of the corner and passed her hand to hand up the line. The woman looked famished, and so weak she had no resistance to the manhandling. Then about halfway to the serving-table she lifted her head in a lack-lustre way, looked at Miss Tyler and then at Charlotte, and her eyes widened in shock. She tried to turn back, and struggled feebly against the kindly crowd. 'Let me go!' she gasped weakly, and the child, seeing her fear, grew afraid too and began to cry.

To Charlotte, recognition came a moment later. She went cold all over with shock, and for a moment could not speak or act, so dumbfounded was she to have discovered accidentally what she had sought so long.

'Fanny!' she cried. The woman turned her head just slightly, her eyes swivelling back in fear, and then she struggled more wildly to get out. 'Fanny, don't go! Don't let her go!' Charlotte called, but there was hardly any need. Fanny was too weak to force her way through the press of bodies, and when the crowd realised that Charlotte wanted her, they renewed their efforts to get her to the head of the queue. In a moment Charlotte and Norton were half-pulling, half-lifting her through the gap between the serving-table and the wall.

Fanny looked white and shocked, and the little girl was crying noisily, 'Don't hurt my mama! Don't hurt my mama!'

'Hush, little one, I won't hurt her. I'm her friend,' Charlotte said. 'Come into the back room where it's quiet, and you shall have hot soup. Miss Tyler, can you manage without me for a while? Norton, stay and help her.'

The back room was furnished with two wooden chairs and a narrow table, and otherwise contained only sacks of potatoes, carrots and cabbage for renewing the soup, and the umbrellas and mantles of the charitable ladies. Charlotte helped Fanny, half-fainting, to one of the chairs, and the little girl crept just inside the door and stood with her back pressed against the wall, looking ready to run.

A tear ran out from under Fanny's closed eyelids. 'Let me go,' she moaned weakly. 'I'm ashamed. I don't want you to see me like this.'

With a great effort Charlotte controlled her emotions, which were threatening to reduce her to tears, so as to be able to say in a matter-of-fact voice, 'Don't be silly, Fanny. I've been looking for you for years; I'm not going to let you go now I've found you at last. Besides, you're not fit to go anywhere.' She turned to the little girl. 'What's your name, dear?'

The child, staring with wide, frightened eyes, whispered, 'Emma.'

'Well, Emma, if you look back through the door you'll see a nice lady in a grey dress. She'll give you a bowl of soup to bring to your poor mama. And when you've done that, she'll give you another for yourself, which you can come and eat at this table.'

It reassured the child to have something to do. Meanwhile, Charlotte chafed Fanny's hands to try to bring some blood to them. It was no wonder, she thought, that she had not immediately recognised Fanny. She was so thin! Her cheap gown was a summer cotton, so it was not cut high at the neck, and Charlotte could see her ribs quite plainly below the jutting hollows of her collar-bones. Her face was thin too, and the lines from her nostrils to her mouth corners were cut so deeply they looked like scars. Her hair was dirty and unkempt, and she wore a small rusty bonnet tied under her chin with kitchen string. Her dress was soaked through from the sleet, as was the thin shawl round her shoulders, and Charlotte dreaded to think what the state of her boots would be. The little girl, who was coming back in now with the soup-bowl, frowning in anguished concentration, afraid she might spill a drop, seemed slightly better clad. Her frock was no better, but she did at least have a coat on, though no gloves or bonnet, and her boots had no obvious holes in them. But she too looked much too thin, and she was very dirty.

'Thank you, Emma,' Charlotte said, making herself smile as she took the bowl from the child. 'Now fetch some for yourself, and come and eat. You must be hungry.'

The child only looked at her for a moment, but she did as she was told. Charlotte put the bowl down before Fanny and said, 'Now, Fanny, eat this soup. It's the quickest way to warm you. And then I'm going to take you home.'

Fanny shook her head feebly. 'No – no! I can't go with you. Don't make me.'

'Oh, don't be a fool,' Charlotte said, amiably. 'Eat the soup. You can't want to die – what would happen to Emma if you did?' Fanny opened her eyes at that. 'Eat the soup anyway,' Charlotte said, as though compromising. 'After all, that's what you came here for, isn't it?'

'I couldn't help it, I smelled it in the street and I was so hungry.' Fanny tried, but couldn't grip the spoon. 'I can't feel my hands,' she said through chattering teeth.

'I'll feed you, then. Come, foolish, don't you think I've done this before? Here you are. It's not too hot to swallow.' Fanny took a few mouthfuls, and then seemed disposed to speak again. 'No, hush, be still. Finish the soup first. It will give you more strength for arguing with me.'

When the bowl was empty, Charlotte went back to the door and said softly to Norton, 'Send someone to fetch a hackney, and be ready to come back with me. I may need help.'

When she returned to Fanny, her eyes were opened and though she was still shivering, there was just a hint of colour in her lips, and of defiance on her eyes. 'I heard you. I can't come back with you,' she said. 'You know I can't go into your house.'

Charlotte was putting her own mantle round Fanny's shoulders. 'This is no time for pride.'

'It's all I have,' Fanny said starkly. 'I'm ashamed you should see me here, and I won't shame you by going into your house.'

'There, I told you the soup would do you good,' Charlotte said, trying to make her smile. But Fanny had not smiled for a long time. 'Fanny, I promise no-one shall see you,' Charlotte went on. 'We'll be in a common hackney, not in my coach, and when we get home Norton shall smuggle you in through the side door.'

She talked a little more, seeing how the warm soup was making Fanny sleepy. Weak from famine and utterly weary, she would soon be asleep, Charlotte thought, and beyond resistance.

They put her into the little bedroom next to the sewing-room, where Charlotte put sick servants if they needed to be isolated or kept quiet. It was spare but comfortable, and given Fanny's state of mind, Charlotte thought it would agitate her less than putting her in a chamber on the family's side.

They stripped off Fanny's wet clothing and chafed her with towels, put her in a clean night-dress and got her to bed. Norton did not think she would be able to stand bathing yet. Fanny's shivering seemed to get worse the more they dried and warmed her. Charlotte sent the housemaid who was helping them running to the kitchen for hot bottles, and Norton heaped more coal in the small fireplace. A message had been sent to Dr Reynolds at the hospital: Charlotte thought he would seem less daunting to Fanny than Sir Frederick Friedman, who, while kindness itself, could never be mistaken for anything but a five-guinea-minimum sort of physician.

Charlotte was longing to know Fanny's story, but it was plain that she would have to wait some time for it. She did, however, ask little Emma one thing that couldn't wait. 'Where is your papa, my dear?'

'Papa's gone to be with the angels,' she said, looking towards her mother's bed, her lip trembling ominously. 'Mama won't go away too, will she?'

'I hope not,' Charlotte said. 'We shall do everything we can to make her stay, and you and I shall say a special prayer when you go to bed.' She eyed the dirty child and her clogged hair and asked tentatively, 'When did you last have a bath?' Emma looked blank; Charlotte remembered the time they had tried to bathe the sweep's boy, and her heart sank a little. 'I'm sure your mama used to bathe you before, didn't she?'

'Oh yes,' Emma said, to Charlotte's relief. 'But when papa went to the angels we had to leave the place where we lived and since then there hasn't been any baths.'

'Well, my dear, you shall have one now. Will you go along with Sally? She will bathe you and wash your hair and put you in a nice clean night-gown. And then you shall come straight back here and have some supper.' Emma went with the housemaid, though with reluctant backward looks at her mother, afraid of being parted. Charlotte was filled with pity for them. What hardships must they have borne together? Now all they had was each other.

Reynolds came while Emma was being bathed. He examined Fanny and diagnosed a severe chill and long-term starvation. 'You must watch her carefully and pray it doesn't turn into pneumonia, for I doubt her constitution would stand it. Keep her warm and feed her frequent small amounts of warm milk, gruel and beef-tea. No solid food at present.'

When Emma was brought back, he examined her. She was evidently very frightened of him, though he spoke so gently to her. In the world she and her mother inhabited, men represented authority, and authority was never kind. Reynolds pronounced her well enough, though underweight for her age. 'I suppose the mother must have starved herself to feed the child. One sees it all the time.'

When he was gone and Sally was giving Emma her bread and milk and chatting to her quietly by the fire, Fanny, who had been dozing fitfully since they left the soup-kitchen, woke with a start and looked round in fear. 'Emma?' she cried weakly.

'She's here. She's quite all right,' Charlotte said, coming close and leaning over her. Fanny stared at her, seeming rather dazed. 'Well,' Charlotte said at last, 'who am I?'

'Charlotte? Where am I?'

'In my house. In the servants' sick-room. You wanted to be kept a secret, or you could have had your old room again.'

She grew agitated. 'I can't stay here. I must move on. Let me go.' She tried to struggle to one elbow, and couldn't. 'What's wrong with me?' she said, bewildered.

'You have a chill, and you're very weak. But the doctor says you'll be well by and by. For now, you must rest and let me feed you up and make you strong again. You mustn't be afraid. You're quite safe here, and so is Emma.'

Fanny let her head fall back on the pillow, and looked too tired even to cry. Norton brought her some hot milk and she drank half of it, and then fell into an uneasy doze.

By the next evening, Fanny was very ill. 'Pneumonia,' Reynolds said, removing his stethoscope and pulling the covers over her again. 'I was afraid of this. She'll need careful nursing, and complete quiet. Even then—' He shook his head over her starved body. 'Well, she is in the best place.'

'It's a good thing you found her and took her in when you did,' Oliver said when Charlotte told him. 'She would have been dead by now otherwise.'

'You don't mind, then?' Charlotte said anxiously.

'Mind?' He shook his head. 'My love, we have disagreed many times in the past, and it was usually my fault – yes, it was, don't argue with me! – but if you think back, you will remember that I never wanted Fanny to be roaming the streets rather than safely here under my roof. She shall not leave again by my will.'

'Thank you,' Charlotte said feelingly. 'Oliver – I may be rather occupied for the next few days—'

'Do what you must, and don't think about me. Shall I cancel our engagements?'

'Oh please! But Fanny wants her presence to remain a secret.'

'Very well, then, I'll say you're unwell.'

Fanny was soon too ill to notice when Reynolds brought Sir Frederick in for a second opinion. Sir Frederick agreed with the diagnosis and the treatment. 'Good, old-fashioned nursing, that's all. None of these new fads does any good. Hot poultices to the back to warm the lungs, and plenty of champagne: you must keep the heart going until the crisis comes. After that, it will be a matter of long recuperation.'

They sat with her round the clock, Charlotte, Norton, and a nurse sent from the hospital to help, while Sally took care of Emma, played with her and distracted her. But Charlotte felt they were losing the battle. There was so little of Fanny left, not enough to put up a decent fight. When Charlotte sat beside her and held her frail, bird-like hand, she thought that if Fanny died, it would really be her fault. If Charlotte had supported her decision in the very beginning, when she first ran away from Anthony, she would not be here now in this desperate strait. But she had told Fanny she must go back to her husband, and so Fanny had run away into the streets.

'Don't die, Fanny,' she whispered to that unconscious, uneasy face. 'Don't leave me to my remorse.'

But the fever was burning her up, and day by day she seemed to shrink a little under the bedclothes, as though the meagre fabric of her body were being consumed by the fire.

On the eighth day she raved, muttering confused sentences which Charlotte could not decipher; occasionally crying out in a toneless voice. Only once did she seem to know where she was, when she suddenly gripped Charlotte's hand, opened her eyes, and said in a hoarse whisper, 'Emma. Take care of Emma.'

'I will, I promise,' Charlotte said. She didn't know whether Fanny had heard or understood her, but the grip slackened, her eyes closed, and she did not speak again.

'I thought we'd lost you,' Charlotte said many weeks later, when she was sitting with Fanny in the yellow sitting-room, a pleasant, light room at the back of the house. Fanny was on the chaise-longue, placed so that she could look out of the window. Her hair was curled and dressed and she was wearing a gown of blue merino and a paisley shawl, with another spread over her legs, and apart from the thinness of her face and the fact that the gown hung on her, she looked like a lady. But the experiences she had suffered were in her face, and Charlotte often thought when she looked at her of the lively, merry young woman Fanny had been when they first met.

Charlotte liked to come and sit with her whenever she had time to spare, and she brought her work with her, and always gave Fanny a piece to do, for Fanny said it worried her to be idle. But there were rarely many stitches set. Often they would just sit in silence together, Fanny looking out of the window, Charlotte looking at Fanny, each absorbed in her own thoughts. At other times they would talk and talk with all the thirst of long abstinence. Charlotte had known she missed her friend, but she hadn't realised until now how much.

'I never really had a friend except you, you know,' she said. 'I was quite alone all through my childhood: meeting you when I came to London was such a revelation. I didn't know what it was to chat until then. And these last years, since you disappeared—'

'You had Oliver,' Fanny said.

'Yes,' Charlotte said. She hadn't told Fanny of her difficulties with Oliver: that was private between them. 'But he didn't replace you, any more than you could have replaced him. I searched for you, Fanny – you can't think how hard. And I thought of you, I believe, every single day. Then when I found you, you were so ill that Reynolds despaired of you. And there came that terrible day when you suddenly fell so quiet that I thought you'd gone. I couldn't hear you breathing. I tried to tell myself it was God's will and that you were at peace at last—'

She stopped, remembering her despair. Fanny's profile was against the window and the gentle, grey rain of early spring. 'Peace,' Fanny said. 'Is there any such thing?'

Over the course of their long days together, Fanny had told her story: not all together in one narrative, but in episodes as the strength came to her and the memories occurred. It was for Charlotte to piece together the whole fabric, and to calculate for herself the depth of suffering it must have been to a creature as gently-born and helpless as Fanny. It was, perhaps, her inability to believe that the kind of life she was living could endure, that had sustained Fanny for so long; and the realisation in the end that it could which almost destroyed her.

She told Charlotte about her desperate wandering when she first left Southport House, and how she had expected and almost longed to die; how she had come to the Wellands' house, her years there, and her growing love for Peter.

'It seems like a dream now,' she said, watching the fire leap and spit, where the servant had just refreshed it and stirred it up. 'And in a way it was rather like a dream even at the time. I think I was always waiting for real life to begin again; and yet I could have gone on like that for ever, and not have been unhappy. I had work to do to keep me busy, and Peter to love me, and a child to care for. That's real life for most people, isn't it?'

'For the lucky ones,' Charlotte said.

'Yes, I *was* lucky, and I wish I had known it, really known it, while it was happening. But I wasn't brought up to work, you see, so I couldn't believe that was the way it would always be. It was like a play. I kept waiting for someone to come and say, that's enough, you're rich again now, you can let the servants do that.'

'Poor Fanny,' Charlotte said gently.

She looked at her. 'Poor Fanny for not knowing when I was lucky – not for anything else. When I was rich I was such a doll, being dressed and shown off, taken here and there, played with and put back in my box. I never did anything for myself. I never did anything for anyone else, either.'

'You came with me to the slums. That was brave of you.'

'It was just play, though. And I have to tell you I hated it – the smells and the dirt and the hopelessness.'

'Dearest, everyone hates it. I hate it. That's why I go. If the slums were a sweet garden full of plenty, they wouldn't need me.'

'But you do good,' Fanny objected, restlessly.

'So did you – more than you knew. Just to look at you and see you smile helped people. Beauty is a positive good as well, you know. The ugliness of poverty kills the spirit, just as hunger and disease kill the body.' She caught herself up. 'Ah, but you must know that better than me,' she added quietly. 'I'm sorry.'

Painfully, Fanny told of the disasters that had struck them, of the typhoid, the deaths of Mrs Welland and Boy, the lodgers going, the debts mounting, the bailiffs coming in. 'We had to leave, just with what we could carry. We sold the few bits of furniture we had left. I suppose the man rooked us, knowing we were in a hurry,' she said with a shrug. 'The worst thing was separating. Harriet got a living-in job at an inn, you see, but we couldn't do that of course, with Emma, and another on the way. Harriet made us take most of the money – not that it was much – because we needed it more. Why are the poorest people the most generous?' she added wonderingly.

'It's more frightening to fall from a great height,' Charlotte said.

Fanny looked at her curiously. 'You never condemn people, do you? You always have some good word to say for everyone.'

'Not quite everyone,' Charlotte shook her head. 'But if there's one thing I've learned from my experiences – pallid as they are compared with yours – it's that you can't judge from the outside what people suffer inwardly. Most of us are good, and we try to do our best, according to our lights.'

After they had left Lamb's Conduit Street, Fanny's and Peter's lives had started on the downward spiral so familiar to Charlotte from the stories she heard in the mean streets. A shabby but decent lodging to begin with, a job as a clerk for Peter, Fanny trying to keep the rooms clean, wash their clothes, buy and cook their food, look after Emma and prepare for the new baby – all things she had never been taught how to do. And always their income trotted along a little behind their outgoings, like a small child running after its older brother. When the baby came, the big brother got further ahead, and the small child's legs began to grow tired. Fanny was not a good manager. The tradespeople knew she did not understand her business, and some of them took advantage of her, overcharged her, cheated her in the change, gave her the goods no-one else would take.

'Peter used to get so angry; and I can't blame him, now I look back, for he worked so hard for that little bit of money, and I was such a fool with it. When he came home on a Thursday night to find no fire and nothing to eat and the baby crying and me without a penny in my purse, and no wages until Saturday – well, it must have driven him to despair.'

'Poor Fanny!'

'Poor Peter. And I used to get into rages with him and accuse him of not working hard enough and not giving me enough money and being unreasonable and cruel – oh, to remember how unkind I was! But I was so ashamed, Charley, that was the thing. I could never forget that I was a ruined woman, and however much I loved Peter, it was always there, underneath, spoiling things. If only I could have married him, I would have borne it all much better, I think.'

Then the baby came, and there was more expense, and Fanny was quite ill, and Peter had to do her work as well, and hardly got any sleep, and pretty soon he lost the clerking job. They had to borrow money, and the interest was another expense, and the little brother income got left far behind. They moved to a cheaper lodging, Peter got a less-well-paid job, and so began a process that seemed irreversible, moving steadily down ever deeper into poverty.

'Then Peter got sick. I don't know what it was – we couldn't afford the doctor. Fever and pains in the stomach and the side, and terrible headaches, and a sore throat. I nursed him as best I could. He got better in the end, but he was never really strong again. Our clothes were worn thin, and he sold his great-coat when the baby died. Little Henry.' She was silent a moment, her head drooping in thought. 'I'm glad he died, really. What sort of life would he have had? But Peter insisted he had to have a proper burial, and he sold his great-coat to pay for it. And after that he was never really well. He had a cough that never went away. Such a cough! I used to think it would shake him to pieces.'

He took to his bed at last and died slowly over a number of weeks, while Fanny sold their possessions and their clothes to buy food for them. As soon as he was dead, the landlord threw Fanny and Emma out for unpaid rent. Since then, they had just wandered. Fanny got a little work from time to time – a day here and a day there – just enough to keep them alive. She could not bring herself to beg – 'I almost did, once, when I was standing in a doorway to keep out of the rain and a lady passing by stopped and looked at me. She looked so kind, I'm sure she'd have given me something if I'd asked. And as soon as I thought that, I was so horrified I grabbed Emma's hand and ran away.' She once accepted a mess of sandwich-crusts and cheese trimmings at the kitchen door of a public house. 'I felt bad afterwards, but when you've done one bad thing, the next gets easier. Coming to that soup-house was another step down. I think I must have come to begging next.'

'You did what you had to, as we all do,' Charlotte said soothingly.

Fanny's thin hands stirred in her lap, where they had been lying idle over the piece of work she had not been sewing. 'No, it isn't as easy as that,' she said. 'You can't excuse everything like that.'

'*I* have no right to judge you,' Charlotte said.

'But I have – and I must. I've brought nothing but trouble and sorrow to everyone I've known. And now there's Emma.'

'She's perfectly happy,' Charlotte said. 'She's doing her lessons and playing in the garden – when the rain lets up – and going through every cupboard in the nursery. Sally loves looking after her, and the governess who comes in dotes on her and is glad of the work besides. She's not strong enough to take a full-time job, but coming in for a few hours each day to teach Emma is perfect for her. So you mustn't worry.'

Fanny turned to look at her with a stern and weary look. 'I can't stay here. You must know that. I can't live on your charity.'

'I didn't ask you to,' Charlotte said lightly.

'Well, I don't know what else you'd call it,' Fanny said, a little angrily. 'And sooner or later it would get about, who I was – and what I was. I am a shamed woman, Charley, and there's no escaping from that. I must live with my shame, but I won't impose it on you, and besmirch your life, too. I can never be accepted again, and I won't be pitied. So I must go back to the gutters, where I belong.'

'You can't afford that sort of pride,' Charlotte said.

'I can't afford not to have it,' Fanny retorted. 'It's what keeps me alive.' Charlotte was going to speak, but she saw Fanny hesitate on the brink of something more, and waited. At last Fanny said, 'I'm so afraid for Emma. Given what her mother is, I'm so afraid she will turn out the same way. Is it a taint, Charley? Does it pass in the blood? I don't know how to keep her true and straight. I watch her all the time, and worry about her. Suppose she grows up to become—' She couldn't say the word.

Charlotte remembered suddenly, as she had not remembered for a long time, her aunt Barbarina who had brought her up. All through her childhood, Aunt had told Charlotte that she must be extra-scrupulous, because of what her mother was; that she was more susceptible to sin, because her mother had been a sinner.

'I don't think it works that way,' Charlotte said. She felt it was time to change the subject. 'At all events, there's to be no more talk of returning to the gutter. If you don't care about yourself, think of poor Emma. Doesn't she deserve a decent home? And think of me. Must I go through more years of torture wondering where you are and how you are? I can't lose my friend again, Fanny. Pity me.'

Fanny's eyes filled with tears. 'I can't live here, Charley. I can't go into Society with a duchess. What do you think Society would say?'

'That's not what I propose. I haven't told you before because I wanted you to get well and strong first, but the time has come now.' And she told her about the trust fund and the mills. 'Times are hard in Manchester at the moment, but the fund was so solid before that it has withstood the slump very well. You are a comfortably wealthy woman, which is what Papa wanted.'

'Dear Uncle Jes,' Fanny said wonderingly. 'To think he loved me so much! Oh, I wish I could tell him how much I always loved him – but it's too late now!'

'He knew, Fanny, don't torment yourself. And that's not all – he also bought Hobsbawn House for you. It's yours – your childhood home. You can go home if you want.'

It was too much for Fanny's weakened state, and she put her face into her hands and cried. Charlotte let her alone, seeing she needed the release. When at last she was able to speak, Fanny lifted her tear-stained face and said, 'But it's no good – you know it isn't! If I went home, Philip would be sure to hear about it. He'd take everything. He couldn't bear to see me in possession of my own fortune again.'

'No, love, you don't understand. There's been a change in the law since you ran away. All this belongs to you alone, and he can't touch it.' Charlotte told her about the Divorce Act, and added, 'That's why Papa Jes worked so hard to get it through, so that when we found you – as he always believed we would – you would be able to have what was yours again.'

There was a great deal for Fanny to think about, a great deal to talk over with Charlotte. And there was time to do it, for whatever she had intended, she was physically too weak to leave the shelter of Southport House yet. But now she knew that she could if she wanted, the urgency seemed to go out of it. Provided she remained hidden from Society, and no-one came to disturb her, she was content just to lie on the sofa day by day and watch the year broadening outside the window, and drift through her long tangle of memories. The rooms she occupied were out of the way in the old part of the house, not on the servants' side, but not part of the grand ducal apartments, an ambiguity that pleased her. The yellow sitting-room was a place out of the world, and for an outcast, as Fanny must now always be, that was a good place to be. Fanny liked to talk of Hobsbawn House as 'home', but it became apparent that she was in no great hurry to go there. Charlotte, who did not want to lose her friend again, began to hope that Fanny might simply stay – or, not to put it so definitely, might simply never get round to going away.

CHAPTER TWENTY-SIX

In the autumn of 1862, General Beauregard, who had been serving in the western theatre, was sent back to Charleston to take command of the defences there. It had always been known that the Yankees would make Charleston a target, and since the taking of Port Royal they had a secure base from which to mount attacks. An attack on Fort Sumter in the June of 1862 had been beaten off, but plainly the Yankees would not leave it at that, so 'Peter' was sent back to take up where he had left off in 1861.

In March 1863, Charles announced one day at breakfast without preamble that he was going to Charleston to serve on the city defences.

Mary was surprised and dismayed at the thought of being left quite alone here. 'But, sir, you don't have to go,' she said. The Confederate government had just passed the Conscription Act, giving them the power to call on all male citizens over the age of eighteen, but slave-owners or overseers controlling more than twenty slaves were exempt.

'General Beauregard needs every man he can get,' Charles said, 'particularly mature men able to take command. He has asked for my help, and I must go and do my duty.' He paused over his fried ham and said reflectively, 'This year we will make our big push, in Virginia and in the west. The younger men must be released for the front line, so we older men must take their place on the defences.'

He had taken the trouble to explain to her, and so she dared to say, 'But how shall I manage here alone?'

'Hazelteen knows what to do,' he said. 'And Adam can be trusted with the horses. You have only to give orders, as you are accustomed to. If you run into difficulties you may write to me.' She opened her mouth to protest, and he said impatiently, 'Everyone has a duty to do. Why should you be different? Many women are taking care of plantations while their men are at war.'

Afterwards Mary reflected that before the war, women were

supposed to be silly, helpless creatures incapable of anything but simpering and needlework; now that it suited the men, women were supposed to be strong enough to do their own jobs and the men's too. But there was no point in remarking on it to Charles; it would only put him into a temper.

He departed with his trunk, horses, and body-slave Prince for Charleston at the end of March. A week later news came that a huge Union fleet had assembled outside Charleston harbour, and a direct attack had been made on Fort Sumter by a flotilla of ironclads. The attack failed and the ironclads withdrew, but the fleet did not disperse, and from that time the blockade on Charleston was almost total. What had been a minor annoyance now became a serious problem; and it could only be a matter of time before another attempt was made to take the city. Charles had gone at the right time.

Mary did not find his absence made much difference in her life at first. The work of the estate went on, with Hazelteen coming for his orders from her as he had done for some time, and, as Charles had said, Adam, the head horseman, knew his business, and only needed a little 'telling' from time to time. Without the master to be particular, meals did not need to be so formal, which eased the household duties a little. But Mary did find, to her surprise, that she missed him. Though he had not been much company, he had been *some*; now she was entirely alone with the slaves and the children, and no adult to talk to at all. She buried herself in the work of the plantation to smother her loneliness, making plans for cultivation and improvement, drawing out rotations and schedules late into the night when she couldn't sleep.

There was one positive benefit to Charles's departure: she could now use the library whenever she wanted. He might object when he heard about it, but she thought she could weather objections made from as far away as Charleston. And if a woman was equal to taking care of a whole plantation single-handed, she could surely be trusted with a collection of books.

She didn't remain entirely alone for long. At the end of April a telegraph came from Aunt Nora demanding to be met at the railroad depot. Mary sent the buggy, and it came back with the old lady sitting high and stiff beside the driver, with her holdall on her lap and her battered trunk slithering about in the back.

'I've come to stay. Charleston ain't what it used to be,' she said tersely to Mary. 'Rubbish in the streets, guns going off in the night, all sorts of riff-raff walking about the Battery.'

'I'm glad to see you, Aunty,' Mary said truthfully.

'Hmph!' Aunt Nora said sceptically, and stumped off up to her usual room. But when she sat down with Mary to dinner that night, at the small table in the morning-room – Mary had shut up the drawing-room and dining-room when Charles left – Nora said abruptly, 'Truth is, I couldn't stand hearing those two. Charles and Belle: you'd think no man ever volunteered and no woman ever kept house before! Congratulating each other day and night, the pair of babies! I'd had enough.'

'Oh, Aunty, don't be so harsh. Charles was needed. General Beauregard asked for him.'

'Asked for him, huh! Charles volunteered. You should see him strut! He just wanted to be in uniform.'

'But he really does care about the Cause. And he feels he must do his part, now Fenwick is gone.'

'He didn't like Fenwick,' Nora asserted with a snort. 'Never cared for anyone or anything in his whole life, except that simpleton he married – and then his little girl that died, because she looked like her. He's spent the rest of his life making everyone else miserable.' Aunt Nora's expression softened a fraction. 'It's you I'm sorry for, child. You don't look well in black. How are you getting by?'

Mary shook her head ruefully. 'Don't be kind to me, Aunty, I'm not used to it, I might cry. I get by well enough.'

Aunt Nora cocked her head like a knowing old parrot. 'I won't coddle you, don't worry. You're one of life's fighters. But I'll say this just once: Fenwick wasn't half good enough for you, and you done Twelvetrees more favour by coming here than it done you by taking you in, so don't let anyone tell you different. Now I'm done on the subject. What's for dinner? And why're we eating in here? Don't you think I'm good enough for the dining-room?'

Mary summoned her cunning. 'On the contrary. The dining-room's all right for men, who don't know anything about good food and comfort, but now we're alone we can dine where the dishes reach us hot and we don't have to be stared at by all those gloomy paintings by bad artists.'

Aunt Nora gave a shout of laughter. 'You're a wicked piece! I think I'll stay here for ever. Well—' she corrected herself, 'until the war's over and Charles comes back, anyway.'

Winter and spring had been wet in Virginia, so wet it was impossible for the armies to move. But in April the rain stopped and the wind dried the tracks, and the campaign re-opened. General Hooker had reorganised the Union troops and restored much of their morale over the winter; large bounties had improved recruitment, and Hooker's army outnumbered the Army of Northern Virginia two to one. He had been openly boasting that it was not a question of 'if' he would take Richmond, but 'when', and at the end of April he opened his offensive. He established a large force before the Confederate position at Fredericksburg to keep them busy, and then marched the rest in a wide loop round to the north-west to position them, unseen, on the Confederate left and rear. His plan was then to send his cavalry to attack the lines of communication near Richmond, forcing the Confederates to retreat from Fredericksburg, when Hooker would fall on them.

Hooker had a plan, and a huge advantage in manpower. But the Confederates had Lee and Jackson. They also had eyes and ears: 'Jeb' Stuart's cavalry, and Martial's invisible scouts. Hooker, by despatching his cavalry, had left himself blind, without any way of knowing where the Confederates were or what they were up to. He had chosen a strange piece of ground to be blindfold on: a parcel of land ten miles or so to the west of Fredericksburg, called by the local people The Wilderness. It was a waste land of bog, heather and bramble, copses of stunted pines and scrawny saplings crowding together over heavy underbrush. No birds lived there, giving it an eerie, brooding silence, and the ragged white stumps of dead birches stood out in the tree-shadowed gloom like ghosts.

It was poor fighting country, too: there was only one large open space, centred on the intersection of two wagon-roads. A large, strange-looking red-brick mansion called the Chancellor House was built at this crossroads, which was therefore known locally as Chancellorsville.

On April the 30th Martial's scouts reported that General Hooker had around seventy thousand men established in The Wilderness, as well as the forty thousand standing before Fredericksburg under General Sedgwick. Between the two, on the south side of Fredericksburg, was General Lee's army, numbering forty-six thousand.

On the night of May the 1st, Lennox, Martial and Eugene all met together for the first time in two years, at a council of war in a clearing in the woods of The Wilderness, no more than half a mile from the Union front line. A couple of small fires had been lit, making welcome small pools of comfort in this inhospitable place, and coffee was on the brew. The cousins exchanged news and asked after family; but home seemed far away and unreal, compared with this strange place, with its white dead trees, and bog-smells of moss and stagnant water. They stood around one fire, waiting for the water to boil, and listened to the brooding silence of the place, which lay under the small domestic sounds of the group of men and horses, the crack and spit of burning wood, the scratch of a match on a boot-sole.

Eugene was fussing about the horses. 'Little Sorrel seems to be holding up all right, but my poor old boy wasn't bred for campaigning. Look how thin he's got,' he said, passing a hand over Robin's flanks. Little Sorrel, General Jackson's horse, nudged in to see if the caress meant food, and Eugene stroked his nose consolingly, having nothing for him. 'And this bog-grass is good for nothing,' Eugene went on, digging a heel into the spongy ground. 'They'll get no goodness from it.'

'I think they're all too tired to graze anyway,' Lennox said. 'What they need is corn and hay and rest.'

'Wait till we've beaten the Yankees, boys,' Martial said with a touch of irony. 'This life is hell on horses. But it's not much good for us, either. I suppose that stuff over the fire is acorn coffee? No chance of the real thing?'

'No chance,' Lennox agreed with a smile. 'Where d'you think we are – Paris?'

'Sometimes I find myself thinking I'd give the whole Confederacy for a decent cup of coffee,' Martial said.

Eugene was shocked. 'You shouldn't say such things! Not even in jest. Anyway, we'll have the Yankees on the run soon.'

'You have special information?' Martial asked ironically.

'I don't need it,' Eugene said. 'With Old Jack leading us, we're bound to win, that's all.' Having found someone to idolise, Eugene had given himself unstintingly: General Jackson was his pole star, second in rank only to God, and not such a poor second, either. Martial reflected that it was as well Eugene had decided to love so wisely this time. Another Conrad Ausland would have been a disaster.

'Well, they've got their heads together all right,' Lennox said, nodding to where the generals were sitting on upturned boxes by the fire, their arms resting on their knees: burly Jackson in his battered forage cap, his leather raincoat hanging open; gentle, fine-boned Lee bareheaded, his hair and beard quite white now, but stained yellow by the lapping firelight. 'Deciding our fate. What's to do, Martial? You're more in the know than anyone, I guess.'

Martial took off his hat and scratched his head long and luxuriously. What wouldn't I give for a bath? he thought inconsequentially. 'Well, my brothers, there's one good thing about our position,' he said. 'We're so heavily outnumbered, there's nothing we can do to make our situation worse. The maddest gamble looks sensible from where we stand now.'

'Oh, Mart, can't you be serious?' Eugene said.

Lennox interrupted. 'Here's General Stuart come to join them.' They turned to look. Stuart, the cavalry commander, with his huge red beard and flashing blue eyes, his hat decorated with black cocks' feathers and his fancy, gold-frogged uniform, was a welcome touch of flamboyance in the increasingly frayed and shabby Confederate army.

'The map's out,' Eugene commented. Jackson stood up to get a better overview, and traced a line on the map with the end of a long stick. Then Lee looked round, and seeing the three men together, beckoned them all over. 'This is it,' Eugene muttered.

'You had better know what we're planning,' said Lee, making room for them. 'It's something of a gamble.'

'Desperate times call for desperate measures,' Stuart said, but with a grin, as though he relished it.

'Hardly desperate,' Jackson objected. 'It's a good plan.'

'It is,' Lee agreed. 'To outflank the outflankers – a nice irony there, don't you think, Mr Flint?'

'But will General Hooker appreciate the irony, sir?' Martial asked with a smile.

'We shall do our best to make him see the point,' said Lee, and explained the plan. It was bold, it was simple – it was risky: to divide the small army still smaller, to leave one force to engage the enemy's attention on the south-east, and send the other off on a long, looping march across country to come round on the enemy unseen and attack from the north-west.

To succeed, the march had to be swift and undetected, and the holding force had to be able to hold out for long enough. 'How long do you estimate the march will take?' Lee asked of General Stuart. He and Martial conferred, tracing the roads on the map, exchanging what they knew of the terrain.

'Thirteen miles, I make it,' Martial said. 'And nothing but mud-tracks.'

'Not less than eight hours,' Stuart said at last.

'You'll be marching the whole day. There won't be much daylight left for attacking once you get into position,' Martial pointed out.

'All the better,' said Jackson. 'After a day doing nothing they won't expect an attack in the late afternoon. We'll have 'em off guard.'

'How many men do you want to take?' Lee asked.

'My entire corps,' Jackson said with hesitation. The two generals looked into each other's eyes, exchanging thoughts in that uncanny way they had. Martial did a quick calculation. Jackson wanted to take twenty-eight thousand men, leaving Lee with only eighteen thousand to hold the entire Union army at bay for a whole day. He wanted to laugh. He had said the maddest gamble would look sensible, and here it was! It was so crazy it had to work.

Lee was silent, thinking it through. Then he nodded slightly and said in his unemphatic way, 'Very well. Go ahead.'

The rest of the night was spent in making out the detailed orders. Martial was busy with his scouts. Lennox and Eugene discussed the plan together. 'You'll have to move quickly,' Lennox said.

'That's what we're good at,' Eugene said. 'Why do you suppose we're called the Foot Cavalry?'

'I don't believe it could be done with any corps other than yours; but after what you've done in the Valley and at Harper's Ferry—'

'We'll do it, don't you worry. You just see that you keep old Hooker facing your way until we come up behind him.'

Lennox grinned. 'They call Hooker "Fighting Joe", did you know that? But he's no match for our old fox. Brains will beat brawn any day of the week.'

Jackson's corps moved out at daybreak, marching four abreast and in absolute silence. They knew by now the value of the swift, silent movement of troops in this war. A little later General Jackson mounted Little Sorrel and beckoned to his staff, and Eugene clasped Lennox's hand in a swift farewell, mounted his own bay Robin and followed. 'See you in Fredericksburg tomorrow!' Lennox called after him softly, and Eugene lifted a hand in acknowledgement, trotting Robin to catch up with the general.

Most of Saturday was taken up with skirmishing, as Lee moved men about the field, made little testing sallies, and altogether created a splendid charade of a confident general preparing to mount a full frontal attack with a large force. There was no movement from the enemy except a settling into position, and Martial once again blessed the foolishness which had sent off the Union cavalry and prevented Hooker from knowing how many men he really faced.

Meanwhile Jackson's corps performed its extraordinary march along wagon-trails, through open country at first, then through the outer edges of the woodland, and then swinging round to come down through the Wilderness from the north-west. It was hard going, but the men were very different now from the eager boys who had started this war. If it had not been exactly true in the beginning that one Confederate was worth ten Yankees, it might be so now, at least of these lean, hard, steady-eyed veterans.

In the late afternoon they halted and under murmured orders spread out into line of battle. The little disturbance of movement died away, and now in the Wilderness silence they could hear the unsuspecting enemy ahead of them. An army band was playing a cheerful tune – 'The Girl I Left Behind Me', Eugene recognised – and there were conversational voices and little clinking sounds of cooking. A hint of woodsmoke lightened the brooding air, and a fragrance of something savoury, which could only serve to make the Confederate soldiers more determined: it was well known that the Northern soldiers ate better than they.

Then the order was given. The Confederates burst out from the trees, howling the 'rebel yell' and firing their muskets, upon a scene of perfect unreadiness. Some of the Union soldiers had stacked their arms, some were lying down snoozing with their hats over their eyes. None was ready for this wild attack out of nowhere, out of silence and stillness and the darkness of the trees. A few brave souls tried to make a stand, but it was hopeless. They were swept forward and overrun by a Confederate line a mile long; snatched up and flung helplessly like debris by a tidal wave. Many of them were new intake and had not been in battle before, and fear and confusion quelled any desire to resist. When darkness fell, the Union right had fallen back on its centre: the Yankees were being driven through the woods like rabbits back towards Chancellorsville.

Eugene was still at Old Jack's side, as a good staff officer should be, though it was hard work to keep up with the fast-moving general. Nightfall did not halt him: the rout was not enough for him, he wanted to drive on and finish it. At about half-past nine, in the full dark, Jackson took Eugene and a couple of other aides and a scout and set off through the woods to find out the North's present position. Fighting in woodland had that disadvantage, that once you lost sight of the enemy, it was hard to know exactly where he was.

If they have a position, Eugene thought to himself. Probably they were in such confusion it would be possible to ride right up to General Hooker's campfire and take a cup of coffee from his can. Probably had real coffee, too, he thought wistfully. The blockade had inflicted no worse hardship on the Confederate officers than that.

Suddenly the hand of the scout ahead of him went up, and they all stopped. General Jackson threw Sorrel's rein to Eugene and slipped down, walking forward with lithe silence to where the scout was waiting. There was a sound of voices ahead, and a crack of a stepped-on twig, and a smell of tobacco smoke. The Yankees had set up a picket-line of sorts, which pinpointed the Union position.

After exploring along the line for a distance, the general signalled for them to go back; mounted Little Sorrel and swung round, heading for the Confederate line. Eugene pressed up alongside him, wanting to know what the plan was. The general's brow was drawn down in a frown, and he was evidently far away in thought, too far for Eugene to interrupt him.

They were trotting through the trees as fast as the darkness and terrain would allow, and a sudden horrid thought came to Eugene: their own side would have picket-lines out by now, and Old Jack had not told anyone where he was going, apart from those he took with him. Supposing—

His thought was never completed. There was a yell just ahead of them, and the darkness exploded in a dazzle of fireballs, followed by the noise, like ripping cloth, of a volley of musket-fire. The night was rent with lethal, singing shot. The horses reared and screamed, men shouted, men fell; Eugene, fighting to control his horse, was shouting, 'No! No!' over and over. Collins fell backwards from his horse, clutching his throat. Hammond screamed, 'Don't shoot! Don't shoot!' A horse was down, kicking. Eugene felt his hat whipped off and his hair parted by something that stung like a hornet. And he saw General Jackson hit.

The general's arms fell to his sides like useless lengths of stove-wood, his eyes widened with shock; Little Sorrel was plunging in fear, and Jackson slipped awkwardly from the saddle to the ground. 'No!' Eugene howled in anguish, flinging himself from his horse; and at the same time felt something strike him hard in the back, as though he had been thumped below the shoulder-blade with a mallet. There was no pain; but when he hit the ground, he found he could not move. Old Jack was a few feet from him, on his knees, trying to get up, his face contorted with agony; without the use of his arms he couldn't rise. Eugene had to get to him! The firing had stopped now, and a different babble of voices was rising, a horrified wailing of realisation that they had shot their own men. Eugene tried again to crawl towards his hero, but though his head knew what it wanted to do, his body didn't seem to be listening. And then he felt something give, a gruesome, horrid little feeling, like a snap, followed by a sensation of wetness as if a vial of liquid had broken inside him. And then everything stopped.

'When is a victory not a victory?' Lennox asked Ruth as she unwound the clumsy and dirty bandage from his arm.

'It's only a flesh-wound,' she said, inspecting it. 'I'll clean it up and bandage it again. But you must try and rest it, or you'll keep opening it up.'

The fighting had gone on around Chancellorsville and Fredericks-burg for several days after that first attack, but the Union army had never recovered from the first shock. In the morning Stuart took over command of Jackson's force and attacked again from the north-west while Lee attacked from the south-east, driving Hooker's corps in on itself and forcing it to fall back. Then General

Sedgwick's corps, unaware of what was happening, attacked the thin line left to hold Fredericksburg, only to have Lee's force double back and attack them from another direction. The quick marching and the ferocity of the attacks won the day; the Union army lost heart and on the 6th of May retreated and marched off through the rain towards Washington.

It was a resounding victory: the Confederates had beaten an army of more than twice their size, and Hooker had lost more than seventeen thousand men. But the Confederate loss of thirteen thousand was almost a quarter of its strength; and Jackson was dead. The deep understanding and effective partnership of Lee and Jackson was broken. Grieving General Lee said, 'I have lost my right arm.'

Lee and his staff had come to Richmond for the state funeral, and to consult with President Davis on what the next move in the war should be; Lennox had taken the opportunity to come and see Ruth and his godson. Little Patrick had grown enormously and was walking and talking and getting into endless scrapes while his mother was busy at the hospital. Martial had brought him a puppy, which he had found as a stray hanging around the wagon-trains, and the two of them, Patrick and Tompy, tumbled about like brothers, as if they'd come out of the same litter. Ruth had unexpectedly found a use for Frank at last: she had taken an inexplicable fancy to Patrick, and after watching her cautiously for some time, Ruth had made her his nursemaid.

Ruth, dressing Lennox's arm, took his question to be rhetorical; in any case she hardly ever thought about the war in its larger sense. Her life had a narrow focus, and when she came back from the hospital at night she was so tired she could hardly think at all. The wounded, her work, and the increasing unavailability of things: that was the war to her. And the soaring, ridiculous prices, of course. She didn't understand why the war meant prices went up, but Martial assured her it was always so. It was only during his infrequent visits that she ever thought about the war in a strategic or universal sense. She thought perhaps women weren't built that way. The shortage of bandages, the mysterious absence of string from the shops: those were the waymarks of the war for womankind – until someone died.

That evening Phoebe and George were out, dining with the President, so Ruth and Lennox were alone together. After dinner they retired to the parlour and sat by the fire, necessary on this chill, wet evening. Tompy was fast asleep, flat out on the hearthrug, and Patrick was asleep in Lennox's lap with his thumb firmly plugged in his mouth. Ruth made a movement to get up and put him to bed, but Lennox said, 'No, leave me hold him for a bit. I don't get much chance; I must enjoy it while I can.' She subsided, and took up the knitting which was always near to hand these days to every woman in the South.

'I suppose,' Lennox said after a while, 'that this is who we're fighting the war for – Patrick and his generation.'

'Are we?' Ruth asked peacefully.

'To keep the South for our children,' he said. 'But not the old South. When the war is over, we'll build a new and better land for them, without the stain of slavery. We'll free the slaves, and teach them to work properly and stand on their own feet.'

'Free the slaves?' She sounded doubtful, but it was only because she was trying to turn the heel and she'd never been very good at knitting.

'For our own sake as well as theirs,' Lennox said. 'We'll need free labour if we're going to open factories, and we'll need factories if we're to be an independent nation, and not dependent on the North. Mills and ironworks and shipyards – new roads and railways! Cotton will provide the capital – the price is bound to leap up after the war – but we won't make the mistake again of relying solely on cotton. And we'll make friends with the North again. It'll take a little time for everyone to forget, perhaps, but we can't afford to be on bad terms with such a close neighbour. After all, when we've beaten them in a fair fight, there'll be no cause for resentment on either side.'

Ruth looked up and smiled. 'What a golden future you see.'

'Don't you?'

'I never think about it. All I see at the moment is men without arms and men without legs and men without eyes and noses. There seem so many of them, I sometimes think there won't be a whole man in the country by the time the war's over. I think I need a little of your vision to keep me from despair.'

'Poor Ruth,' he said tenderly. 'It's been a hard war for you. A husband and two brothers gone. What a price you've paid!'

'Papa has, too. There's only me left now, of all of us,' she said. 'Thank heaven Mary and Fen had the three boys – at least there's someone to carry on at Twelvetrees. You should say "poor Mary" – I notice you never go and visit her. You're not much of a brother to her, Lennox Mynott,' she added sternly.

'My free time is never enough to get there and back,' he protested. 'And Mary understands, anyway.'

'Understands what?'

'That I have a stronger claim here. That you and Patrick will always come first with me.'

Ruth was suddenly nervous. 'You mustn't say that.'

'Why not? It's true.' He decided to take the plunge. There might never be a better opportunity. 'You must know by now how I feel about you, Ruthie. In fact, I think I've been in love with you since I first saw you at Twelvetrees.'

'Oh, don't. Don't,' she said softly.

The baby stirred at her voice, and Lennox rocked him closer. 'Please let me. I know how you loved Patrick, and perhaps it's too soon yet, but one day, when it's further in the past and you don't miss him so badly, one day, don't you think perhaps you might come to love me? Not the same, of course, and probably not as much, but enough for us to be happy together? I shall never love anyone but you, and if you find you can't ever love me, well, then, I'll just go on being your brother. But we could have a good life together, you know.'

She looked at him mutely for a long time. Then she sighed and said, 'I can't say how I may feel one day. But I am very fond of you, and if it's any consolation, I can't imagine life without you.'

He grinned suddenly. 'Well, I suppose that must do for now, but I warn you, I mean to try for a great deal more, as soon as we both have the time.'

She smiled too. 'I give you leave to try. But, Lennox,' she grew serious, 'what about little Patrick? Could you really accept him? Can any man really care for another man's child?'

He shook his head at her. 'How can you ask me that, seeing the only reason Mary and I are here at all is that someone cared for another man's children?'

'I hadn't thought of that,' Ruth said. Lennox relapsed into thought, staring into the fire, and she looked unobserved at his strong, handsome face, and lean, broad-shouldered body; and she thought with a little inward shiver that, yes, she might easily come to love him in that way. Indeed, the time might not be so far in the future as he supposed, and how was that possible? She tried to imagine Patrick's face and Patrick's voice, but just then she couldn't find them. But for once she didn't feel the customary sharp pang of loss: she thought that his spirit somewhere was glad for her, as if he was telling her that love was not a closed circle, but a treasure that increased, paradoxically, the more you spent it.

Lennox came back from his thoughts and was looking at her, and she said, suddenly nervous, 'Let's just stay as we are, until the war's over. I don't want to care for anyone too much, in case I may lose them.'

Lennox nodded. 'Whatever you say.' And then he smiled and added, 'But I shall take that as a good sign.'

*   *   *

Mr Lawrence of Pinelees was the local requisitioning officer. He came to Twelvetrees in May for more horses, and it was he who told Mary that the Army of Northern Virginia was preparing to march once again on Pennsylvania.

'General Lee whipped the Yankees so badly at Chancellorsville, we only need one decisive victory on Union soil to clinch it. The war's unpopular in the North, and Lincoln will never be able to stand another defeat. But we need every man and horse we can get for the big push. I'm afraid I'm going to have to see what stock you have.'

Mary shrugged. 'Take what you must. I know Mr Morland would do anything for the Cause.'

The stables were sadly depleted already, but the core stock of fleet, beautiful racehorses remained. Adam wept like a child when Mr Lawrence gave an order to take them all, bar some brood mares in foal, a couple who were too old, and the remaining stallion. Campaign life was hell on horses, and if they weren't wounded in the fighting, they just lay down and died from the long marching and poor food. Adam caressed their faces and wept into their manes, and they nudged him like children, not understanding what was happening, unafraid, who had never known anything but gentleness from men. Lawrence took Mary's saddle-horse Oriole too, but left the children's ponies, and two harness horses to pull the carriage. The field-work was done by mules, and he took only four of those, having taken so many horses: other plantations could do their share and make up the numbers, he said.

But he requisitioned wagonloads of corn and hay for the campaign. Mary reflected as she watched it being driven off that, without the horses to feed, they could manage on less anyway. And it was for the Cause. Nothing could be resented or held back, when it was for the Cause. In its name the prudent Charles, who had succeeded in life largely because he had hard cash when most Southern planters had only credit notes, had given up all his gold in return for Confederate Bonds. Mary had thought that it was the greatest sacrifice Charles could make; until, that was, Mr Lawrence came for the horses. There was no more racing in Charleston now, of course, and the Planters' Cup gathered dust on the library chimney-piece, until the war should be over and normality restored. But it would be a long time before magnificent Twelvetrees 'scuds' floated round the track to glory again, and came home decked in ribbons to take their rest in the green paddocks under the beech trees.

On the day after the horses went, Mary was standing by the

paddock rails, inwardly mourning their emptiness, and outwardly trying to console Adam and tell him what to do with his time from now on, when the head horseman broke off and looked into the distance across her shoulder, and said, 'Who dat comin', Miz Mary? Look lahk a wagabone, or a beggarman. Whut he doin' heah? Hit a long way f'om anyweah a beggar want to be.'

Mary turned and looked. A tallish, rake-thin man in shabby, no-coloured clothes was limping up the track which wound round various parts of the plantation and eventually connected with the old road to Walterboro and Augusta. His trouser-ends were ragged, and she could see from here that he had a wad of dirty bandages wound round his left leg, and that he wore no shoes. He had a small leather sack slung by its draw-cords on his right shoulder, and as he drew nearer she saw he was followed by a thin and mud-crusted dog.

It was the dog that gave it away. 'Yaller Dawg,' she breathed in astonishment; and then began to run. Adam worked it out a few seconds behind her. 'Yaller Dawg? Why – hit mus' be dat ole willain, Mister Hill!'

Mary reached him and stopped dead, appalled by the state of him. Yaller Dawg stopped when he stopped, automatically, not looking up to see why, as if simply glad not to have to go on moving. 'Hill,' she said. 'Hill. Where have you come from? How did you get here?'

He was swaying with weariness, and it took him a moment or two to assemble the spittle to answer. Then he reached up a slow hand and took off his hat. It was the first time Mary had ever seen him without it, and she was surprised to see he had a quantity of hair, which was quite white. It made him look older.

'He's dead,' Hill said.

She made a gesture as if to touch him, but did not. 'I didn't know. We heard he was missing, that's all. We thought – hoped – he might be a prisoner.'

Hill went on speaking without acknowledging her words, as if he had long planned what to say, and would say it. 'We wuz out reconnoitring that night, an' we tripped a picket-line. There was shootin'. We got separated. They wuz beatin' the brush lookin' for us, like we wuz game-birds. I crawled back an' found him, dyin'. That's when I got captured.'

'The Yankees took you prisoner?' It seemed incredible to Mary that he could have been taken, that untameable spirit.

He shrugged. 'I didn't care at fust,' he said economically. She imagined the depth of his despair and understood. 'Then they say they goin' to send us to jails up north, so I 'scaped.' His eyes met hers for the first time, and the lonely blackness of them made her shiver. 'Didn't know where else to go, so I came here. Thought you might use a man about the place.'

'You did quite right,' she said warmly. 'This is your home, and I'm very glad to see you. You must be starved. Come on into the house and I'll fix you some food. You've hurt your leg?' she asked as he lurched into motion beside her.

'Yankees shot me. How d'ye think they caught me?' he grunted. 'Won't heal.'

'We'll see about that. You may need to rest it.' She looked down at his bare, filthy feet. 'Did they take your boots, too?'

'Wore out,' he said. 'S'a long way from Murfreesboro.'

She asked no more, feeling it would be unfair to quiz him in his present condition. She could not begin to calculate the distance, or the endurance it must have taken to complete the journey, barefoot and with a wounded leg, or how he had lived on the way. She imagined he must have been dazed with grief to begin with; and afterwards, perhaps, dazed with weariness. But he could have gone back to his native mountains and his old, pre-Heck life. It touched her unbearably that he had come here, to her, as the only place with a claim on what served him for a heart.

Their progress towards the house was slow, and the dog plodded behind, almost walking with its eyes shut. She had to know one more thing, despite her resolve not to tease him with questions. 'How did you find Yaller Dawg again? Or did the Yankees take him prisoner too?'

Hill shook his head, just once each way, to save effort. 'When I 'scaped, I went back t' the woods where Heck wuz killed. He was waitin' for me.'

They walked on towards the house in silence, Mary vowing that as soon as she had attended to Hill's immediate wants, the hound should have the best dinner a dog ever dreamed of.

Hill had never been a talkative man, and his experiences in Tennessee were not likely to change that. But now and then he would vouchsafe a snippet of information to Mary, or let slip a fragment of a word-picture, which in their way were as graphic as long speeches from other men. Long afterwards she found images in her memory that must have come from him, though she didn't remember the telling of them: of the campaign, the battle, the terrain. She had a picture, for instance, of the Union general Ulysses Grant: a firm-featured face, grave, level eyes, a close-clipped beard, a uniform coat as plain as Lee's; a shy, dogged man, dangerous precisely because he was not dashing.

'He'll never give up. He'll just keep on coming.' Those must have been Hill's words.

She had a picture, too, of the negroes the Yankees freed from every farm and plantation in the west they had rolled over. Some were kept as labourers by the armies, some sent north, many thousands put into refugee camps – where conditions were said to be so appalling that half of them died. Some were formed into regiments under white officers and sent out on foraging duties. The most frightening were those who simply followed the Union armies in a rabble, pillaging in the army's wake, knowing no-one would lift a hand to prevent them, and that the houses they would sack held mostly undefended women.

'If they get this far, if they come here, remember what I told you,' Hill said. 'Don't bandy words, just shoot 'em.'

'But they won't get this far,' Mary said. She didn't remember Hill telling her in so many words, but she somehow acquired the idea that the Confederacy was losing in the west and falling back, that the Union armies were creeping inexorably closer, and that the only thing that would stop them was victory in the North, and a negotiated peace. It was a race which Lee must win, before the South was shrunk to four states, and then three, and two. He must win a resounding victory in Pennsylvania, before the quiet enemy, Grant, ate up the South and made victory academic.

If she knew it, Lee certainly did. In June he marched north again with every man he could scrape together. His army was followed by General Hooker's Army of the Potomac, which had been ordered to keep itself between the Confederates and Washington. And at the beginning of July, word began to filter south that the two forces had met in battle at a town called Gettysburg.

CHAPTER TWENTY-SEVEN

Mary and Aunt Nora were sitting on the verandah late one August evening, rocking and sewing. Fenwick's pointer, Mag, lay at Mary's feet, only half sleeping, keeping one eye on Yaller Dawg, who lay at the extreme edge of the verandah. Hill was somewhere about – he would never sit with them – but since his long walk home, Yaller Dawg no longer kept behind his master like a shadow. He would never be far away, but he preferred to lie down than to walk, and would get up only if Hill moved too far off. Best of all, the hound liked to be where he could be near both Mary and Hill at the same time. Mag had been fiercely jealous at first, snarling horribly and driving Yaller Dawg away from Mary, but she had settled down now, and only kept a wary eye on the intruder, who smelled too much of the wild to Mag to be trusted near people.

Suddenly both dogs' heads went up, listening, and Mag gave a little warning growl. There were sounds from the front of the house. Aunt Nora looked up too. 'Someone's arriving.'

'At this time of night?' Mary said. Her heart sank. Unseasonable visitors could only mean bad news. Neighbours never called sociably any more – everyone was too busy. They came only to inform, when a telegraph arrived, as when Connie Fairfax called to say that her brother Chesney Ausland had been killed at Champion's Hill; or when Mr Lawrence came to say his young son John was being sent home after the fall of Vicksburg, under parole to the Yankees not to fight again – a matter of deep relief to his mother, and of deep pain to the Lawrence menfolk.

There were footsteps now, Tammas's shuffle, and a dragging booted step. Mag's head was up, her nose working, her look puzzled. Tammas appeared in the door, his face a battleground of emotions. 'Miz Mary, we got a vis'tor,' he said tremblingly.

He didn't get any further, for Mary was on her feet with an inarticulate cry, beating Mag to it, and in two steps she had her arms round Martial and was being hugged so tightly by him she could not have spoken had she wanted to.

426

Mag worked it out at last, and frisked about them like a puppy, barking. Yaller Dawg stood up, his tail swinging uncertainly, looking from face to face for clues. Hill appeared in the pool of light at the bottom of the verandah steps, his unlit segar clenched warily in his teeth. Tammas was explaining to Aunt Nora the minutiae of the arrival and his surprise and happiness about it. Julie and Martha and Patty and Rosa and Cookie were crowding their faces in at the parlour door and chattering excitedly. But Mary and Martial only stood with their arms round each other and their eyes closed as though the commotion did not exist.

Aunt Nora finally broke the tableau. 'Well, now, Martial Flint, y' might give a greeting to your elders and betters! Besides, I c'n smell you from here. You ain't in a fit state to be huggin' ladies.'

They released each other slowly, and Mary stepped back a pace to examine him. He looked older – thinner, of course – very dirty. The hair at his temples had thinned and greyed, and the lines in his face spoke of experiences he would never forget and perhaps never be able to share. His great-coat was much stained and worn at the seams, but at least it was whole; his uniform was all patches and there was a hole in one knee of the trousers. Mary felt compassion, fear, and a strange sense of loss: the dashing, amusing, witty rake, the sportsman, the wealthy Charlestonian man of leisure and means, was gone. But then she met his eyes and thought that perhaps that man had never been more than an illusion. The real Martial was still here, inside this grim soldier.

'Well?' he said at last, raising a quizzical eyebrow.

Mary responded with a slow smile. 'Aunt Nora's right – you do smell!'

'Ah, now I know I'm home,' he said with satisfaction. He turned to Nora. 'How are you, Aunty?'

'Better than you, by the look of you,' Nora grunted. Martial nodded to Hill, who returned the courtesy, and then drifted back a step out of the light, but stayed watching.

Mary asked the urgent question. 'How long have you got?'

'A week,' he said, 'unless I get an urgent summons. But Jeff Davis knows I haven't had any furlough since the war began. It was he who told me to go.'

Mary remembered the dragging step. 'You're wounded?'

'It's not too bad,' he said. 'Ratty can dress it fresh for me later, if you've got some clean rags. But first I'd like some food, and then a bath.'

'Yes, of course,' Mary said. She was going to speak to the servants, but Nora forestalled her.

'I'll see to the fixin',' she said. 'You sit an' talk.' And she went through the parlour and drove the servants before her towards the kitchen, telling them when they protested that they could get the whole story from Ratty there, for he would need feeding, too.

On the verandah Martial sat in a collapsing kind of way, easing his wounded leg straight before him, and Mag came fussing up to shove her face in his lap and her nose under his hand. Hill had disappeared, and Yaller Dawg with him: giving her privacy, Mary thought – without questioning why he might think she needed privacy. But she was aware in the background of her mind of a vibration of something, like a faint, far-off singing almost too high for hearing, which was something to do with the pleasure of seeing Martial again.

He looked around him with an air of content. 'It's so good to see a place in good order again – no trampled crops, no shell-damage. I seem to have been looking on ruins for half my life. Everything's so beautiful here. And the smells – the roses and jasmine – the dew coming off the grass. And a hint of autumn in the air. Do you smell it? The leaves are beginning to die. I don't know when I last smelled trees dying naturally.'

She didn't know what to say. 'It must have been terrible.'

'It still is,' he said with a grimace. 'Thank God it's far away from here. But don't let's talk about that now. Not now. Tell me how your boys are doing.'

'Much better, now Hill's back. They were getting quite out of hand, even though Abel was looking after them. Hill's got them eating out of his hand – I don't know how. Charles would have a fit, but I'd trust him with their lives.'

'I wondered when I saw him what he was doing here. Is it a story that'll last until supper comes?'

'I'll try to make it so,' Mary said, smiling. 'And if not, you can tell me how Ruth and Lennox are, and anyone else I know whom you've seen recently.'

After supper and his bath, Martial went straight to bed, desperately needing sleep. Ratty removed all his clothes and Julie took them downstairs to clean, but they turned out to need boiling, and then the seams pressing with a hot iron to kill the 'visitors', so they were not ready for him the next morning. He had no others, and Fenwick's and Eugene's clothes and boots had already been requisitioned by Mr Lawrence, but there were some of Charles's things still in his room. Mary wouldn't have thought Martial could get into them, Charles being a much smaller man, but though they were too short for him in the arms and legs, he was so thin that they went round him all right.

In this rather harlequin garb he appeared for a late and enormous breakfast, and then the boys wanted his attention, so it wasn't until the afternoon that he and Mary found themselves out on the verandah again with time to talk. Hill had taken the boys away, out riding so that they wouldn't be a bother; Mary and Nora took up their work, and, slowly and ramblingly, Martial told them about Gettysburg.

The Army of Northern Virginia that marched into Union territory in June had numbered some seventy-six thousand of the toughest and most disciplined soldiers who had ever walked American soil. They were held together by a deep understanding and common purpose that enabled them to move in unison with a deadly speed and purpose. A newly recruited Texan had given Martial his opinion, that 'no army on earth can whip these men. They may be cut to pieces and killed, but routed and whipped – never!'

The weakness was in the officers. So many had been killed at Chancellorsville that there had been promotions all through the officer ranks, and too many now were new to command, especially at the highest level. And Lee himself was unwell, having suffered a heart attack in May, and being pulled down, as many of them were, by dysentery, the universal plague of armies. The new corps commanders did not know each other's minds, so did not pull together, and there were misunderstandings and petty resentments.

The choice of Gettysburg as a battlefield was accidental. It was a pleasant little town on the crossroads of many routes, but it also happened to have, so one of Martial's scouts reported, a warehouse full of shoes.

'Half our boys were barefoot,' Martial said. 'It's a sore trial to a soldier to march and fight in his bare feet. How could we pass up the opportunity?'

The scout reported a detachment of Union cavalry there, so a division was ordered to march in, deal with the cavalry, and take the shoes. What the scout had not realised was that the cavalry he had seen was the tip of an iceberg: two full brigades of horse, the advance guard of the approaching Army of the Potomac.

So on the 1st of July the fierce fighting had begun. 'It was like the Farewell Symphony in reverse,' Martial said, 'with reinforcements joining the battle on both sides, section by section as they arrived.'

The fighting on the first day swirled around a hill to the west of the town. 'Lee saw it was an important strategic position,' Martial said. 'If Jackson had been alive, things might have gone differently. Lee sent the order to Ewell to take it "if practicable", which was the way he'd have put it to Old Jack – and Old Jack would have stormed in without hesitation and taken it. But Ewell took his time wondering if it *was* practicable, and asking everyone's opinion, and before he'd come to a conclusion, the Union troops had taken it instead.'

At the end of the first day, the Confederacy had given good account of itself, and hopes were high that the next day would finish it. But a bloody second day led to a third day of such violence and loss that both sides were rocked and appalled by it. Confederate soldiers in heroic charges against the Union artillery were cut down like corn by the sickle; orchards and wheatfields were soaked in blood where combatants reeled hand to hand in desperate struggle. But, at the end of it all, the Union still had not been dislodged from its superior position, and the Southern army was so damaged that there was no possibility of going on. Survivors stumbled back to the woods in shock, and began the miserable retreat towards Virginia. So fierce had been the fighting, however, that the Union army was too badly mauled to pursue. It had lost twenty-three thousand men.

The journey back was a nightmare. Through heavy rain a hospital train seven miles long lurched slowly over rutted roads, unsprung wagons jolting desperately wounded men against the bare wooden floors until the bravest cried out in agony. A third of Lee's army had been killed, wounded or captured, including a vast number of officers – seventeen of Lee's generals were gone. The Army of Northern Virginia was not beaten, but the invasion had failed. There was no victory on Union soil; there would be no suing for peace by humiliated Yankees.

'What will happen now?' Mary asked in the silence that followed the story.

'We can't fight again, not this year. Fortunately, the Army of the Potomac is in no better shape. We'll all go into camp for the winter.'

'And next year? Another invasion?'

Martial shook his head heavily. 'I don't think it can be done. I don't think at heart Jeff Davis believed it could be done this year, but we hoped for a miracle; had Old Jack been there we might just have pulled it off. But there was nothing else we could do, you see. We couldn't just stay put in Virginia and let the Union throw wave after wave of troops at us until we drowned in them.'

'Martial, you're talking like a defeatist,' Nora said sternly.

'I don't think we can win,' he said. The two women looked at him silently. He spread his hands. 'Every man they lose they replace with ease. For every captured rifle, every breeched gun, their armouries make two more. The factories in New England turn out new uniforms and shirts, tents and blankets by the thousand. The farmlands of the North send bread and beef by the trainload to their soldiers. But our men can't be replaced. Our resources are finite. We can't grow enough food for our men in Virginia, and we can't ship it in from further south because we haven't the railroads and we don't command the seas. We can't make enough ammunition to keep our men supplied, and if we didn't capture Yankee rifles, we wouldn't even be able to give them an empty firearm to hold. Our men are in rags and half starved, our horses are dying, and in the west the Union pushes us back all the time. The Confederacy is shrinking, and every battle, won or lost, costs us more than we can afford. We're bleeding to death, don't you understand?'

He was sorry when he stopped that he had spoken so forcefully. What use was it to worry them? But he had served throughout this war with the fear, almost amounting to conviction, that it couldn't be won, and the strain of keeping silent was telling on him.

Mary spoke at last. 'But what can we do?' she asked falteringly.

He shrugged. 'Just what we're doing. Hold on, give ground as slowly as we can. Fight it out to the bitter end.'

She looked a little relieved. 'I thought you might say, give in.'

'Not that. Not until the last of us drops in his tracks. We can't give in to them, because we are right and they are wrong. And perhaps there might still be a miracle.'

'That wicked man, Lincoln!' Mary suddenly burst out. 'It's all his fault! Why wouldn't he let us go? All this blood is on his hands!'

'Maybe he'll lose the election,' Nora said over her sewing. 'Or maybe he'll catch a chill and die.'

'It's too late for that to help now,' Martial said. 'There's an impetus to war, and it doesn't really matter any more why the North is fighting, or even why they *think* they're fighting. They'll go on doing what they have to do, and we'll do what we have to do, and sense and logic and humanity and love will have to bide their time, because no-one will consult them until this is all over.'

Later, Mary took Martial for a walk. 'I wish we still had some horses so that we could ride out, and I could show you what I've been doing,' she said. 'I hate to see the paddocks empty. We're breeding with the mares we have left, but it'll be a long, slow business.'

Martial smiled. 'Do you remember how scandalised Aunt Belle used to get when you used the words "mare" or "bitch"?'

'That world seems a thousand years away, and mostly I'm not sorry it's gone. Now I'm not obliged to pretend to be a fool. I give the orders here, and decide what happens to the land, and it's a good feeling.' She thought of Morland Place, and how she had hoped so much when she was younger that it would one day be hers. Well, she had her estate now: it belonged to her by virtue of caring for it.

'And you manage it all on your own?' Martial marvelled.

'Hazelteen works the slaves, of course, and Hill's a great help. I sometimes used to feel a little nervous, not having a man on the place. There was a time—'

She told him how a group of field-hands had come up to the house one day asking to speak with her, and when she appeared, their leader – Habbuk – had asked if they were free or not.

'Of course you're not free,' Mary had said, though her heart beat faster, and she had to fold her hands tightly together to hide their shaking.

Habbuk had rubbed the sole of one foot on the top of the other and scratched his head a bit, and said, 'Ma'am, we heerd Mist' Lincum done freed us. Dis nigger f'om ober Cam'lot, he stop on de way to Do'chester and he tell us dat Mist' Lincum say we all free now.'

Mary had looked ostentatiously one way and another. 'Where is Mr Lincoln, then?' she asked. 'Is he here?'

Habbuk looked around too, puzzled and uneasy. 'No, ma'am, Ah don' tink so. Ah hain seen 'm no place.'

'No, you haven't seen him. None of you has seen him, have you?' she asked the rest of the group. They shuffled and shook their heads and looked bewildered. 'Very well, then,' she said, 'when Mr Lincoln comes here, you bring him straight to me, you hear? Then him and me will talk about it. Until then, you belong to Mr Morland, and you do what Mr Hazelteen tells you, and what I tell you. You understand?'

They had gone away without fuss, to Mary's relief; and afterwards, quietly, she had taken Hazelteen to task for letting them bring the question up to the house as though it *were* a question.

'But I must admit I was scared,' she told Martial. 'I wondered what would happen if they decided they were free after all and just took what they wanted. But they're so scared of Hill, they're as good as gold now. He scares them, and I pet them. It's a good system.'

'You seem cheerful, in spite of everything,' he said as they walked on.

'I think I am, most of the time. Aunt Nora runs the house for me, which leaves me free to concentrate on the plantation, and that's work I enjoy. I haven't planted any cotton – I suppose you noticed that. There didn't seem any point, if we can't get it out. I've put down every acre I can to growing food. I'm growing a lot more wheat and corn, and oats, too, on the outlying fields. Lots more vegetables – vast quantities of beans, tomatoes, potatoes – and of course a lot of hay and feed crops, because I'm increasing the beef production. The surplus goes into Charleston for the army. I wish my father were here – I would really welcome his advice. I try to remember what I saw and heard at Morland Place, but it was so long ago, and I wasn't really paying attention when I was a child. Failing my father, I wish Lennox were here. He's had practical experience of running an estate. When the war's over—'

She stopped abruptly, remembering that when the war was over, Charles would return and Twelvetrees would no longer be hers. 'Well,' she said, with a flat gesture of her hand, 'I shall enjoy it while I may.'

Dinner was a more lively affair than might have been expected, for word had got out that Martial was home, and one or two neighbours called and were asked to stay for dinner. John Lawrence was at home now on parole, and came over from Pinelees with his sister Annabella, who was fifteen, to talk war with good old Mart Flint. Knox Fairfax was also at home at Fairoaks, recovering from a wound got in his first battle, and when he proposed going to pay his respects to Martial, Connie made him take Millie and Effie, because at nineteen and seventeen they ought to be married, and men were in short supply now. Martial Flint was still unmarried, and everyone knew soldiers on leave were sentimental and thus easy targets.

So Aunt Nora had the dining-room hastily opened and dusted, and repaired to the kitchen to see that dinner would not disgrace the Twelvetrees tradition. The food would be simpler than pre-war, but thanks to Mary's stewardship it was plentiful, and if there was no wine to be put out, at least there was cider and peach cordial.

Martial was glad to see the young visitors. The men were flatteringly respectful of his reputation, and the girls even more flatteringly interested in his glamour, but he'd had enough of the war for now, and steered the conversation into more lively channels. So the well-spread dinner-table was surrounded by smiling, talking faces, and there was laughter such as Mary never remembered in that dining-room before. Charles at the head of the table had not been the sort of host to inspire mirth.

After dinner they went into the drawing-room where, to forestall questions about Gettysburg and the campaign, Martial suggested music. 'That's one thing we soldiers don't get enough of – do we?' he said, generously including Knox and Johnny in the category.

'No pianos in the front line, no lovely young ladies to charm us with their sweet voices. Come, who will be first? Miss Millicent, don't I remember you had a reputation as a song-bird?'

He didn't remember any such thing about a girl who, last time he saw her, at a Fairoaks barbecue, had been fourteen and indistinguishable from all the other schoolgirls; but it was a fair bet that any planter's daughter would have been taught to play and sing. Millie, mindful of sister-in-law's injunctions, was eager to comply, and hastened to the instrument; and the others were not behindhand in wanting their turns.

Eventually the moment came when Martial said, 'Now Mary must sing for us. Yes, I insist! And I know what I want to hear.' He came and fetched her from her seat, escorted her to the piano, found the music and placed it in front of her, and then retired across the room where he could watch her face. Mary played the introduction without really knowing what it was, and then found herself singing:

> So we'll go no more a-roving
> So late into the night,
> Though the heart be still as loving,
> And the moon be still as bright.

Everyone was listening. The little eddies of movement and talk about the room died down, and a profound silence settled over them. They were listening with more than their ears, they were listening with their hearts and spirits. The haunting words and the sad, lilting tune had nothing to do with the war, but seemed all the same to bring home to each of them what they had lost, not just as individuals, but as a nation.

Mary's voice was sweet and true, and she knew the piece too well to need to look at the music or the keyboard. She sang, but her mind was elsewhere. The room seemed to be nothing but a bright blur, the people in it moving cloud shadows amid the rough radiance of fire and candles. Only Martial stood out clearly, etched on the shadowy background with the sharp-edged clarity one sometimes saw before a rainstorm, when distant things seem suddenly near. She began the last verse.

> Though the night was made for loving
> And the dawn returns too soon,
> Still we'll go no more a-roving
> By the light of the moon.

It was over. After a moment of silence, everyone began to clap. Mary heard their compliments and comments like the background murmur of water. She was crying. She knew she was crying, she was awash with it, a great outpouring flood of tears carrying her helplessly away like a straw on a river; yet oddly no-one seemed to notice, and when she put her hand to her face it was quite dry, and her mouth seemed to be fixed in a polite smile.

'Another,' said Knox Fairfax eagerly.

'Oh yes, please, Mrs Morland!'

'But let's have one we can all sing,' Aunt Nora said firmly, lifting her eyes from her work to look warningly at two people in the room.

Mary hardly heard them, did not know what had caught Aunt Nora's attention. She was aware of nothing but Martial's dark, insistent gaze, his presence which tugged her across the room, whether she looked at him or not, like the invisible north pole tugging ineluctably at a frail little compass-needle. She felt suddenly that wherever he was in the world, even if he were on the other side of it from her, some part of her would turn that way, blindly but surely, feeling him across the stream of space; in the dark of night or the heat of noonday, in her sleep, at her work, in her leisure, turning always, dumbly but obediently like a thing with no sense, turning to where he was.

She had to carry on behaving normally, be the hostess for the rest of the evening; eventually say goodnight to everyone, give the last orders to the servants, walk up the stairs to her room and endure Patty undressing her and brushing out her hair, chattering all the while about God-knew-what. But then at last she was alone, lying in her bed, her hands resting on her aching body, alone with her thoughts.

As the whirl stilled, as the scattered words and images settled like leaves drifting down when the breeze stops, as the silence seeped back in through the darkness, she looked into herself, and found there at the core the thing she had known for some time and not been able to face.

She was in love with Martial. She loved him.

How long had it been going on? Dear God! She had loved him for so long, from the time when she was a married woman and it was forbidden by every canon of decency, every law human or divine, by the tenets of society, by her own self-respect. What would he think of her if he knew that? What would he think of her even now, her husband dead less than a year? He would be shocked; he would despise her. She had no reason to think he cared for her other than as a cousin: her feelings for him must be unrequited, even if they were not in the circumstances horribly improper.

And yet, even as her mind was saying these things, she was feeling something else. The love, sealed so long under the stone she had just moved aside, came surging up, strong and clear as water, with all the power of the earth behind it. It came springing and gushing out of that dark place with a kind of primeval joy, so glad to be in the light at last that it sprang high like a fountain, dancing and frothing, and filled the whole room with rapture. For a moment she let it have its way with her, let it take her and fling her high over the world, scattering her in tiny bright droplets like stars over the immensity of the night. She loved him! Every spinning, sparkling fragment of her laughed with joy at the knowledge of him, that he was in the world, that he existed! His face was before her, the face she knew every plane and indentation of; it was before her and in her and of her, and she knew then how poor an imitation her feeling for Fenwick had been. A spoilt child's desire for a toy, shallow and fleeting, that was all, bearing so slight a resemblance to love that, now she knew what it really was, she could not understand how she could have been deceived for an instant.

The power ebbed, the fountain of joy failed and fell back to earth, and she with it, tumbling down from dazzling rapture to reality. In a few days he would be going away, back to the war, and she who had already lost a husband and a brother knew the chances that she would lose him, too. Lose him? she pulled herself up. He was not hers to lose. If he survived the war unscathed, what would he do? He had always been a wanderer, and he might go anywhere in the world; at the very least, he would probably live in Charleston. She would remain here at Twelvetrees with her father-in-law and her three sons, and see him, if she were lucky, once or twice a year.

All she had was this one week. Well, if it's all there is, she told herself, it has to be enough.

She was gay the next day, in a way she had hardly ever been at Twelvetrees. It enchanted the children, and though Aunt Nora might regard her with suspicion, her mood carried everyone along with her. She sent slaves scurrying to the neighbours with messages inviting them to a picnic in honour of Martial's visit, and organised everything with such pre-war flair that the day was bound to be a success. Everyone remembered Ruthie's ball on the eve of the war, and retrospectively credited her with that, now that she had hit on the very thing needed to cheer everybody up. Martial watched her, laughing his silent laugh, and once, as she passed him, touched her arm and said, 'If this is for my benefit, you might have saved yourself the effort, you know. I couldn't be more impressed with you than I already am.'

'Oh, everyone needs a holiday,' was all she said, hurrying on, his fingertip imprinted on her arm like a scorch.

Even Hill went along with it, helping with the wagons, recommending a good picnic place, and even – greatest tribute to Mary of all – bringing out Uncle Heck's mouthorgan and playing for them while they sat digesting. Then Mary organised games for the children, and had them almost sick with laughter; and everyone rode or drove home as the sun sank down the sky with a feeling that life was still worth living, in spite of everything.

There was no need for dinner that evening, after the large luncheon. They had a light supper, and then Aunt Nora said she was going early to bed. 'You'll do the same, if you've any sense,' she said as she stumped off.

Martial looked at Mary and raised his brows. 'What do you suppose she meant by that? And which of us was she speaking to?'

'I don't know,' Mary said, and felt suddenly self-conscious. Now she was alone with him for the first time that day, she realised she had been trying to avoid that very thing. Was that why she had organised the picnic? She felt that he must read her guilty secret in her face, or that, left at his mercy, under the powerful influence of his presence, she might blurt the whole thing out and humiliate herself. Oh, but to be with him! She couldn't stop the joy, though she thrust it down as hard as she could.

He was looking at her with that familiar, quizzical look, and she felt she must break the silence. She sought for the saddest, least romantic subject she could find, to damp down her rapture.

'Conrad Ausland died, did you know? About six weeks ago. Mrs Lawrence told me – she had it from Connie Fairfax. The Judge and Mrs Judge don't talk to anyone about him, and Connie isn't supposed to either, but she does. And now they've lost Chesney, too, poor creatures. They've had such troubles. One can't help feeling sorry for them, all alone at Camelot.'

'Did you hear anything about May?' he asked.

'Only that she's still in the asylum in Columbia. Connie says it's a very nice place, quiet and withdrawn from the world, almost like a convent. They have lovely gardens, and it seems May likes to help tend them. They've given her a flower patch of her own and Connie says she's quite happy. They don't tell them anything about the war, so it must be very peaceful.'

'Poor little May,' Martial said. 'Do you remember at her wedding, how you told me she'd be no worse off with Conrad than with any other man?'

'Yes, I was wrong there. I hadn't fully realised what his character and actions could lead to.'

'No, how could you? But her father might have guessed.'

'I think Charles did feel badly about it in the end. But the war changed everything. If Fen had been at home, he might have done something – brought her home, perhaps. But maybe she's better off where she is.'

'Poor Fenwick. Poor Mary, too,' Martial said softly. Mary lowered her eyes, not wanting him to read hers at that point. There was a moment's silence, and then he said, 'But, as you say, war changes everything. I remember that wedding for another reason.' She was silent, remembering too much. 'Don't you want to know what? Really, that is a most *interesting* reticence, Mrs Morland!' She was goaded into looking up, and found his eyes much too bright, his expression knowingly amused. He understood her all too well – she could not hide from him. She blushed. 'That's better,' he said. 'I thought that's what you were thinking, but I didn't want to assume too much.' He grew serious a moment. 'Fen was my cousin and I loved him. But life has its duties, too, and its call is a great deal more urgent. I have so little time, Mary, and the future is so uncertain. Let me at least be sure of one thing.'

'What – what thing?' she asked in the ghost of a voice.

'Oh, I think you know what.' His voice was warm, with all the power of life in it, a voice you wanted to creep under for comfort and shelter. 'Do you remember I told you that I had once said I would never fall in love?'

She nodded. 'And you said that "never" was a word that liked to fall on you like a boulder. I didn't understand what you meant.'

'Didn't you?' He stood up. 'Come here, and I'll explain it to you.'

She didn't mean to, but somehow her body just wanted to obey him. She stood up and walked the two steps to where he stood, tall and thin in Charles's clothes, burning like a beacon in an empty night, calling her insistently. 'It's been a long wait,' he said. 'So many times I've wanted to tell you, but it could not be done. I ought to wait longer yet, for propriety's sake, but what place has propriety in a war? So be it: everything on one throw, like Old Jack! Come into my arms, Mary love. They long for you so, I can hardly bear it.'

She lifted to him such a perfect expression of bewildered happiness, joy and submission that he would have laughed aloud if he had not been so afraid. And then she stepped into his embrace, and he closed his arms round her and kissed her. He could feel her trembling at the touch of his lips; at the touch of hers, his passion took flame. Her bare arms and shoulders were so smooth to his touch, her body was so supple, her neck smelled of rose-water: she was everything exotic and feminine to senses which had been fed for months only with the roughness and hardness of men and horses. He wanted her more wildly than he had ever wanted anyone or anything in his life, so much that the considerations of etiquette or propriety or even military duty had no more chance than a scrap of paper in a bonfire. If she had restrained him, he would somehow have dragged himself back to hand, though he felt it would have killed him; but the response of her body said she wanted him just as much, and his joy burned up brightly.

'I love you,' he whispered, burying his face in her hair, finding the rim of her ear with his lips. 'I've always loved you, I always will, from the world's beginning until time's end. I don't care about custom or convention! You belong to me, Mary, Mary.'

She couldn't speak, only turned her face like a flower turning to the sun, seeking his mouth again. There were no words in her mind, only a triumphant singing, a background to that wild uprushing of joy she had known the night before. Under its force she had no power of discretion, no ability to think or fear. She only knew that she wanted to be closer to him, to be part of him; that she must have him and make sure of him, before he was taken from her again.

It was he who had to think for them. 'Go to your room. Send Patty away. I'll come to you as soon as she goes.'

In her room, alone, second thoughts tried to sober her, but she turned away from them, fixed her mind's eye on his face, his eyes, his voice saying that he loved her. Then the door opened almost soundlessly, he slipped in and closed it behind him with a soft click. He didn't speak, just crossed the room quickly and gathered her up again with a sigh of pleasure and relief. She felt the same: the few minutes out of his arms had seemed cold and lonely. They kissed for a long time, and then he drew back from her enough to see her face, and said, 'I have to be sure. Is it what you want, too?'

So she had to find words for him. 'I love you,' she said, and since that did not seem to be all, 'I want to be in bed with you.'

He laughed his soundless laugh and carried her there.

The birds woke her with their before-dawn clamour. She woke with that sense of excitement she had had as a child at Christmas, that something wonderful had happened that for a moment she had forgotten. She was lying on her side, facing the window. The hard muscle of Martial's arm was under her neck, and his other arm was round her waist, his whole body pressed against hers from behind, naked flesh to naked flesh. Martial! She didn't move, only lay smiling, feeling the warmth and security of his body close to hers, letting the rapture have its way with her.

How strange it was that she should feel so safe! Every moment in bed with Fenwick had seemed alien and embarrassing, tolerable only in dark and silence, and because it had been infrequent and of short duration. Yet with Martial she felt as natural and easy as a bird in its nest or a puppy in a basket. Even nakedness seemed only natural and delightful, not shameful at all. They had looked at each other, they had talked, exchanging murmured words and caresses far into the night, and it had all been so good. The act of love which she had always thought horrid and small and fumbling was with Martial something great and splendid and winged, like glorious music, like a wild leaping bonfire – and at the same time soft and close and intimate.

She smiled again at the memory, and he must have felt her smile, for he closed his arms on her and she gave a little grunt of contentment. She felt his lips on the back of her neck, and he murmured, 'What is it, love?'

'Yes, I think it is love,' she answered teasingly.

'What were you thinking?'

'That now I am one of those shameless women one used to hear whispered about – one of those who *like it*.'

'Shameless indeed! I am horrified.'

'But only with you.'

'So I should hope! You had better not plan to do it with anyone else as long as I live.'

She turned over within his arms and was now breast to breast with him, looking seriously into his loved face. 'Never! No-one but you. How could I?'

'Didn't I tell you not to say never?' he said tenderly, stroking her cheek with one forefinger.

'That's one never I can say with confidence. I didn't know anything about love before. You've shown me something different from anything I could have imagined. Now everything's changed.'

He had to ask – his vanity demanded it. 'It wasn't like this with Fenwick, then?'

'Oh no!' she said with such emphasis that he laughed. 'How could you think it?'

'Dear little love! You are so very beautiful, my Mary, I can't believe you're mine. You are mine, aren't you?'

'Every particle of me, every hair of my head, every breath of my soul.'

He put the finger on her lips. 'Hush, or God may get jealous.'

She caught the finger and kissed it. 'No, for God gave me you

440

– how could this be other than from God? I love you, Martial Flint.'

They made love again, as dawn broke outside the window, and then fell into a deep and dreamless sleep, utterly at peace with each other. They were woken by Patty's little shriek of surprise as she came to call her mistress and found a hairy masculine arm lying along the bedclothes.

'Oh, Miss Mary! Ah's sorry. Ah'll go right away!'

'It's all right, Patty.' Mary struggled to wakefulness and found she couldn't even manage to feel guilty, especially as Patty was now convulsed with giggles at the situation, rather than wide-eyed with disapproval.

'Ah's sorry Ah woke you hup, but when Ah see dat arm, Ah t'ink you done change in de night!' Patty giggled.

Martial stirred himself and lifted a head from the bedclothes. 'Changed into what? Be careful what you say, Patty my girl. I've a mighty savage temper in the morning!'

Patty only giggled harder. 'Mist' Mart, you is awful! Miss Mary, you don' need to worry – Ah won't say nuttin' to nobody.'

Probably she didn't – or at least, not at first – but Mary didn't care, and Martial found it hard to. They drifted through the day wrapped in a dream of love; and though they behaved circumspectly at all times, it would have taken a less noticing person than Aunt Nora not to feel the waves of happiness coming off them, not to see the aura of contentment around them that was practically visible, like a fog-halo round a street lamp. But Nora was a realist, and she only said Hmph! to herself once or twice, and for the rest contrived to leave them alone together as much as possible, while she got on with altering Charles's clothes for him.

'I'll tell you who time gallops withal,' Martial said to Mary at the end of the week. 'The man who has just found his life's love at the age of thirty-one and has to go back to a war he never believed in from the beginning.'

They were walking under the lime trees, hands linked, with Mag running before them, nose coursing the ground.

'But now we've found each other, it will be all right, won't it?' Mary said anxiously. 'Nothing can go wrong now. I mean, you won't get—'

'Killed, or anything?' he filled in for her with an ironic smile. 'Thank you for raising the possibility, which had not, of course, occurred to me.'

'Oh, Martial!' she protested.

'Oh, Mary!' He gave her a comical look. 'Listen, love, there's nothing we can do about anything, except just go on loving each other. Everything else is in God's hands.'

They walked in silence for a while, and then he said, 'I don't know when I'll be able to come again. Maybe not for a long time. Maybe not until the war's over. You won't lose faith?'

She thought of the image she had had before, of the compass-needle turning to the invisible north. 'I'll wait for you, however long it is.'

'I'll come back, Mary.' He turned and took her face in his hands, staring to try and memorise it. 'I'll come back. God knows what sort of a world we'll face, but whatever it is, we'll be together.'

She put her hands over his. 'You'll take care?' she whispered out of the depths of a great cold foreboding.

'If you will,' he said. He kissed her, and then gently wiped the tears from her cheeks with the side of his thumb. They walked on, the low sun throwing the shadows of trees like bars across the avenue, so that they walked alternately in sunlight and shadow.

CHAPTER TWENTY-EIGHT

The Union advance seemed inexorable, but it was slow. In November 1863 the Union army pushed the Confederates back into Georgia, but not until September 1864 could it take Atlanta. That autumn Ulysses Grant, the quiet soldier, was appointed Northern commander-in-chief, and took over the Virginia theatre, leaving the western theatre to General Sherman. The naval blockade was strangling the South – Mobile was lost in August 1864; Charleston had been under bombardment since August 1863 – and the constant attrition of war was bleeding her to death, but she did not yield. Sherman might have Atlanta, but Grant could not take Richmond, and the newspapers of the North published horrifying casualty lists for what seemed like no advantage. Yet in November President Lincoln was re-elected, and that was taken as a vote of confidence in the war. It must be waged now to the bitter end.

The end was to be very bitter indeed. In November 1864 General Sherman put Atlanta to the torch and marched his army of sixty thousand south towards Savannah, living off the rich Georgia harvest and destroying what it could not eat or carry away. The march was leisurely, the army spread out on a front sixty miles wide, made wider by the wings it carried with it of stragglers – deserters, miscreants and men absent-without-leave – and followed by a second army of freed and runaway slaves, who didn't know what else to do with themselves but to follow the men in blue.

The triple army marched unopposed, leaving a trail of devastation behind it. Confederate forces were small and scattered, defending individual towns, unable to leave them or to confront the huge force that was laying Georgia waste. In December Sherman occupied Savannah, displacing the small force of Confederate soldiers who had been holding it, and settled down for a brief winter camp. Then on the 1st of February 1865, General Sherman started north into South Carolina. The Palmetto State was the hated cradle of secession, deserving of the most condign punishment. Orders from Washington were to devastate it.

At Twelvetrees the numbers had been swollen by the addition of refugees from Charleston. Its defences had held, and the Union had not been able to take any of the fortresses, even though Sumter's superstructure had been reduced to rubble and the defending soldiers were living underground like moles. So the Union had built batteries in the coastal swamps and in August 1863 began the bombardment of the town. The action caused unprecedented out-rage: to bomb unarmed civilians, mostly women and children, was an act of barbarism, not war, and it engendered in Charlestonians a fierce determination never to surrender. Every able-bodied man in Charleston – and even some not so able – served on the defences. The lower end of the town was reduced almost to rubble. The occupants either refugeed to Columbia, went to relatives in the country, or moved in with friends north of Calhoun Street, leaving the south end a ghost town, burned and broken, with grass growing in the streets.

Aunt Belle went to some Fenwick cousins in Columbia; Aunt Missy, Louisa and her three youngest children went to Twelvetrees, leaving their men behind to fight on. Twelvetrees could feed them, despite the removal by the requisition officer of twenty field-hands, to be sent to Richmond to dig defences. Mary was glad of the company, and Missy and Louisa meant more hands to knit and sew and amuse the children. Mary ran the plantation and tried not to think about the war news. She had heard from Martial only once since he left that August day sixteen months ago: a stained and scribbled note, most of which, frustratingly, she could not read. But he was alive, she was sure. When she lay down at night, her mind reeling with tiredness, she would unlatch her thoughts from the troubles of the day and let it loose over the dark waters of the night, like the dove from the ark. She believed she always found him, and the belief kept her going. She thought that was what he meant when he had said: Don't lose faith. She believed she would know if he died: she would *feel* it.

One grey February afternoon in 1865 they were all gathered in the morning-room having a little party in honour of Corton's seventh birthday. Mary tried to keep up some semblance of normal life for the children. They had all made little presents for him. Aunt Nora had knitted him gloves. Aunt Missy and Louisa between them had made him a coat of grey homespun cut like a soldier's, onto which Missy had sewn the buttons she had saved from her husband's Mexican War uniform. Corton was wearing it with great pride:

all the boys longed to be soldiers. Mary had painted him a picture on glass of his father on horseback, doing the horse from memory, and copying Fen's face from a photograph of him taken shortly after their marriage. She had painted Fenwick in civilian clothes, which rather disappointed Corton. He thanked her politely, but she could see he liked Aunt Missy's present better.

But his favourite thing was undoubtedly the wooden sword Hill had carved for him out of hickory wood. It was a beautiful piece of work, the hilt elaborately decorated and the balance perfect, and he would not be parted from it, even sitting down to tea with it across his knees.

They were just starting the meal when there was a sound of horses out at the front of the house, and everyone stopped speaking to listen. 'Now who can that be?' Nora muttered. But it was not just one set of hooves, or even several. The sound gathered and increased – dozens of hooves; and then there was a bang and a shout, one of the slaves screamed, there was a splurge of voices, and then Tammas came running through the house, his coat-tails flying, crying hoarsely the words they had all feared for so long: 'Miz Mary, Miz Mary, de Yankees coming! De Yankees is hyah!'

Every woman went pale; Louisa gave a little shriek, instantly stifled; the children looked up into their faces to see what was wrong. 'Mama, is it Sherman?' Preston asked quietly, trying to be the man of the house, though his voice shook. Mary noticed how much like Lennox he looked, with his straight pale forelock of hair. 'I don't know, darling. We shall see.' She thought of the pistol concealed under the mattress in her bedroom and the rifle Hill had told her about, and wondered if she could run and get one or the other. Then Aunt Nora said stoutly, 'Well, we can't stand here like a bunch of ninnies. Might's well go and face 'em!'

'I couldn't!' Missy said, trembling, clutching Ashley to her. Louisa put her hands over her mouth and shook her head.

'I'll go,' Mary said. Better to walk out and face it, she thought, whatever it was, than be hunted and dragged out helpless like a rabbit. 'You stay here, Aunty. Keep the children quiet.' Mary walked firmly out into the hall, seeing through the open front door that it was a large troop of men – forty or fifty, she supposed – in Yankee blue: the enemy. She felt sick with fear: until now, none of them had ever seen a Yankee. But they were soldiers, and surely soldiers did not hurt unarmed women? The leaders were just coming up the steps and through the door; from the kitchen she could hear screams and crashes; others must have gone round to the side door.

Mary stepped out before the leaders. 'Who are you?' She tried to inject cold authority into her voice. 'What do you want?'

'Git out the way, lady, an' you won't git hurt,' said one.

'Any men in the house?' said another. 'Any wounded soldiers? Any arms?'

'None of those things. Where is your officer? This is a private residence.' More men were pouring in, thrusting past them, scattering about the house. There was a crash and laughter as one of them knocked the small table over, breaking the vase that stood on it. Mary accosted a man carrying a riding-whip, who was standing watching the others with something of detachment. 'Are you the officer? Will you control your men?'

He grinned. 'I'll do that fer you, lady!' he said, and then, raising his voice to a ludicrous falsetto, cried, 'Oh, you naughty men, don't you touch anything now!'

A couple of them laughed, but mostly they ignored him, intent on booty. Mary was shoved unceremoniously out of the way. They were pouring into the different rooms now, opening the sideboard in the dining-room and dragging out the cutlery and silver, taking Charles's segars and upending the decanters of sherry and whisky into their mouths; rifling the drawing-room of ornaments; breaking open cupboards and drawers in the morning-room and throwing their contents out. Others had gone upstairs, and there were ominous sounds from above. From the kitchen came a perfect frenzy of crashes, and Julie came running out, her clothes awry, crying, 'Miss Mary, stop 'em! They takin' all the food! They busted down the pantry door!'

But before Mary could say anything, a rough hand grasped her arm and pulled her round. 'Whisky! C'mon, where is it? You got some somewheres!'

Julie was horrified, 'Don't you touch Miss Mary! Don't you touch her!'

The soldier pulled out a wicked-looking knife, still holding Mary's arm. 'I'll do more'n touch her, ef she don't git me the whisky. Why're you tekkin' up for her anyways, nigger? You're free now. Why'n'cha git?'

'Ah ain't goin' nowhere!' Julie retorted. Mary put out a hand to quiet her, keeping her eye on the knife. 'In the cellar,' she said. 'The whisky's in the cellar, but it's locked.'

'Gimme the keys.'

'I haven't got them,' Mary said. Julie screamed as the knife approached Mary's throat. 'You can threaten me all you like,' Mary gasped, 'but it won't change the facts. I haven't got the keys. The master has them, and he's in Charleston.'

'I'll break it down, then, damn you!' The soldier threw her from him in disgust, and she went staggering back and hit the wall hard.

Julie ran to her. She felt the imprint of the man's fingers on her arm, and fought a terrible desire to hide her face and weep. The men were swarming everywhere, and now they were going out of the front door with sacks of things, loot bundled up in rugs and carpets, stuffed in their pockets and down the breast of their coats. Mary whispered to Julie, 'We can't stop them. There's too many. We'd better get back to the children.'

They hurried back towards the morning-room. It was down a short side-passage and Mary hoped it might have been missed, but a chorus of shrieks ended that hope. They ran, and reached the door to see Louisa and Missy and some of the servants huddled in a corner with the children, Aunt Nora sprawled on the carpet, and a burly soldier brandishing a pistol in the air as he felt around in the sewing-box on the table with the other hand.

Mary's heart was knocking hard with fear, but her anger counterbalanced it. Aunt Nora looked as frail as a bundle of twigs, next to the well-fed Yankee. 'What have you done? Did you hit her, you coward?'

He looked round, startled, and then seeing it was only more women, relaxed. 'I didn't hit her. She come at me like a wild-cat, an' I jist pushed her a li'l bit,' he said. 'Y'got any whisky in here?'

'Of course not. Please go away, you're frightening the children.'

He ignored her, abandoned the sewing-box and went over to the fireplace, and took down the miniatures from the chimney wall and threw them into his knapsack, followed by the ornaments from the mantelpiece. Julie slipped past him and helped Aunt Nora up. She seemed shaken and looked about her in a dazed way. Mary signalled to the others to be silent. Best to let this man take what he wanted and go, she thought. He turned from the fireplace and saw the table set for tea, and hurried over to it, treading on Corton's birthday picture of Fenwick, which someone must have dropped in the panic. The soldier didn't notice the crunch underfoot, gorging as if he hadn't eaten for a week, stuffing biscuits and rolls into his pockets with the other hand.

It was too much for Corton, who suddenly broke from the restraining arms and ran at the soldier, brandishing his wooden sword, and crying, 'It's my birthday! Leave that alone, you dirty Yankee! It's my birthday!'

Before the horrified eyes of the women, he hit the soldier on the leg with his sword. The man swivelled, his eyes bulging above his bulging mouth. Corton tried to hit him again, his face scarlet, his eyes full of tears. 'You trod on my *father*!'

The man snatched the sword from Corton's hand and flung it aside, and at the same time jammed his pistol in the boy's chest. Three of the women screamed, and Mary cried out in anguish, '*No!*' It was their fear that made Corton freeze, his eyes going wide.

'Drop it, you little rat,' the soldier bellowed, spraying cake-crumbs and saliva. 'Your birthday, is it? Do that again and it'll be your last.'

'Leave him alone! He's only a child!' Mary cried.

The mean eyes swivelled her way. 'You the mother? Suppose the father's a Johnny-Reb! Oughtta kill the little rat now, so's he don't grow up to be like his pa.'

For a moment they were locked in a frozen tableau, Mary and the soldier staring at each other, Corton wild-eyed and white with the pistol against his narrow childish chest. And then Mary said in a cold, shaking voice, 'His father was killed at Sharpsburg.'

The soldier's eyes shifted and dropped. He spat on the carpet, and said, 'Wouldn't waste a bullet on the little rat, anyways.' He stuffed his pistol back in his belt, hitched the bag over his shoulder, overturned the tea-table with a crash, kicked the chairs over, and went out of the door onto the verandah. Corton ran to Mary and she folded him tightly against her, listening to the sounds of destruction all around the house.

They ransacked every room, taking what they fancied, and destroy-ing much they did not, breaking furniture, slashing pictures and curtains, smashing china. They dragged the books out from the shelves in the library and ripped and slashed at them until they got bored. But more seriously, they took all the food, putting it into sacks and loading it onto their horses. They took the farm wagons, hitched up the mules, and loaded sacks of grain, potatoes and apples from the barn and barrels of molasses and salt from the dry-store. They took all the chickens they could round up, and drove off the pigs and cattle. Mary ran out to appeal to them. 'Don't take everything! What will we live on? We have six little children here. We shall all starve!'

Mostly they ignored her, but one of them said, 'We want you to starve. We got orders to take everything.'

'This can't be right!' she cried. 'Where is your officer?'

Someone laughed. 'We're all officers now, lady. We can do as we like.'

They rounded up the male house-servants, all but Moses and Tammas, who they said were too old. They wanted them to drive the carts and animals and carry the plunder.

'Why are you taking my young men away?' Mary asked, trying to interpose herself between the guard and the servants.

'They ain't your young men any more. We just freed 'em,' said a Yankee.

'Well, if they are free, you can't make them go,' she said.

'Oh, they don't have to go if they don't want to,' he said, grinning.

Mary turned to the servants. 'Boys, do you want to go, or to stay?' They were huddled together like sheep before butchers, looking wildly round them in terror. 'We want to stay,' said one, and the others murmured agreement. 'Stay – stay – stay.' Mary looked at the Yankees. 'You hear them?'

The guard switched the stick he was chewing from one side of his mouth to the other. 'Well, don't that jest show how you twisted their mines?' He grinned at his colleague, and they both laughed, and hustled the boys away. The soldiers were starting to leave now, mounting their horses, settling their bags of loot around them. A bluecoat came out from the house dragging Abel by the arm, shaking him to keep him on his feet. Abel was crying, 'You can't make me go! I'm not a slave, I'm a free black. You can't make me!'

The man only shook him harder and said, 'Shaddap, nigger. I'm sick o' your bawlin'!'

Abel saw Mary and called to her. 'Miss Mary, make him let me go! Tell him I'm a free black! Tell him!'

'Why, boy, you're all free now,' the man said in assumed surprise. 'That's why you're comin' with us.'

Mary did her best, but they wouldn't listen to her. Abel was hustled along with the others, and the train moved out in the dusk, leaving behind at last a stinging silence, a scattered mess of debris and, rising gradually in volume, the frightened sobbing of the women.

At first they were too shocked and miserable to begin to clear up. All they could do was to huddle together, rocking the children. Mary sat with Corton in her lap; he sucked his thumb, something he hadn't done in years, and pressed his head to her breast. Missy comforted Aunt Nora, who seemed badly shaken by her fall. Louisa, tending her own children, said over and again, 'To treat helpless women so! They aren't soldiers, they're beasts!'

There was a footstep outside in the darkness, and the women stiffened in fear; Corton wriggled his head as if he would burrow into his mother; Mag, who had only just crept out from her hiding-place under the sofa, growled a shivery warning. Mary felt her heart contract with fear; but in a moment Hazelteen appeared at the door, and said, 'You awl right, ma'am?'

'Oh! You frightened us. We thought they were coming back.'

He removed his hat and scratched his head, and said, 'You didn't ought to leave the doors open like this, ma'am. Might be stragglers aroun'.'

'You're right,' Mary said wearily, dragging herself to her feet, and passing Corton to Rosa. 'I'll shut them.'

'They's hundreds and thousands of 'em, crawlin' round the country like flies,' Hazelteen said. He gave her an anxious, urgent look. 'If they do come, you just let 'em have what they want, Mrs Morland, don't you face 'em none.'

She nodded, acknowledging his advice, and said, 'Did they take anything from you?'

'Took ever'thing,' he said sadly. 'Said they'd a min' to kill me, 'cause I was a slaver. Called me a heap o' names. Took the quilt Mrs Hazelteen's been makin' for ten years. She's cryin' like a baby.'

'I'm so sorry,' Mary said. She knew about the quilt – it was a legend on the plantation.

'They went through the darkies' huts, too,' Hazelteen said. 'Took their stuff, close an' bits and pieces an' all.'

'They robbed the slaves?' Mary cried indignantly. 'How could they do such a thing?'

Hazelteen shook his head. 'Mos' of our boys went with 'em anyways. But some of 'em took up for the fambly, and the Yankees cussed 'em for it. Told Big Isa if they fed anyone up at the house, or did anything for you ladies, they'd come back and slit their throats.'

'Oh, good God!'

'S'fact,' Hazelteen said.

When he had gone, Mary roused herself to take stock. The kitchen was a mess of broken crockery, smashed eggs and spilled flour. Mary couldn't find Cookie, but she roused out Martha and Leah and chivvied and jollied them into sweeping up, while she looked to see what food was left. She was going to shut the door onto the yard when a shadow appeared in it, making her jump, but it was only Hill. Yaller Dawg stood beside him, looking round the kitchen with his ears at a puzzled angle.

'Where were you all this while?' Mary demanded bitterly. 'The only man on the place, while we were being ransacked and insulted by the Yankees, and you were in hiding! I thought you might have come to our protection, after all your fine words about shooting Yankees.'

Hill surveyed her coolly. 'Don't be a damned fool,' he said. 'There was fifty or sixty of 'em. How many d'you think I'd've got before they got me?'

'So what were you doing?'

'Guardin' the food I hid. Else you'd have nothing to eat when them locusts left.'

Mary's heart lightened a little. 'You've hidden some food?'

'Bin doin' it fer weeks. Somebody had to.'

'Where?'

He shook his head. 'If you don't know, they can't make you tell.'

'Yes, that's sensible,' Mary said. 'Thank you, Hill.'

He merely shrugged. 'I'll go round and check the doors and windows.'

The next morning in the first grey light of dawn a commotion in the yard woke Mary. There were half a dozen Union soldiers trying to round up some stray chickens that had escaped yesterday's rapine. It was the keynote to the day. Squads of Yankees came and went all day, so that there was never a moment's rest or peace. The servants were in a constant state of fear, and ran in and hid themselves at the first sight of a blue coat. The smokehouse was broken into, and all the hams taken, and the jar of honey used to dress them. Another squad went through the quarters again, taking the slaves' food, and insulting the women. The cornstore was broken into and the remaining corn taken. Another group, finding nothing immediately to hand, stole the well-bucket and dropped the chain down the well, so that they should not be able to get up any more water.

Then in the afternoon a quieter squad of about twenty in the charge of an officer came up. He looked a decent sort of man, so Mary went out to meet him, and asked him not to let his men come in the house.

'We've been ransacked so many times already, there's nothing left to take. We have little children here. I ask you as a gentleman not to let your men frighten them for nothing.'

He looked sympathetic, but said, 'I'm sorry, ma'am, but I'm under orders to search the house for men and for weapons.'

'There are neither in the house,' Mary said.

'I'm sorry, I must still search. But if you and your children will stay in one room, I will see you are not disturbed.'

She gathered her household into the morning-room and they waited while footsteps and voices, thumps and rattles sounded all round the house. Eventually the men left, carrying more sacks of plunder: one of them carried an alabaster bust of Shakespeare from the drawing-room, another staggered with the huge dining-room mantel-clock. When the women emerged, they found that the pot of potatoes and the boiled bacon that Cookie had been preparing for their dinner were gone also.

On the third day Abel came back, having escaped from the Yankees in the darkness, to bring the news that old Judge Ausland was dead. He had refused to let the Yankees in, and one of them had knocked him down. 'He's heart couldn't take it, Miz Mary, dat's what Ah hear. He took a fit an' died – so dat makes it murder all right. An' then they made Missus Auslan' and de slabes git out, and they set fire to the house.' He shook his head in awe. 'Hit all burned down, an' Missus Auslan', ma'am, she refugee all de way to Fairoaks on her own feet.'

Mary was appalled at the news. It seemed God was intent on destroying the Auslands root and branch. 'I'm glad you've come back,' she told Abel.

'Dis ma home,' he said simply.

Not all the slaves were loyal. Julie came to report that Mammy and Cookie had disappeared, taking with them some of Mary's clothes, the meal and meat Hill had brought up the night before for today's breakfast, and the silver spoons from the kitchen drawer, which had miraculously survived repeated raids.

'Where have they gone?' Mary asked.

'To follow de Yankees, Miz Mary. Ah heah Mammy say to Cookie dat de Yankees'll put 'em on a train to Washin'ton, an' Mist' Lincum'll give 'em a house and servants of dey own.'

The poor fools, Mary thought. She hoped that they would be all right. They were too old and fat to be of any interest to the bluecoats; but, by the same token, they'd be unlikely to be supported by them. She thought they'd be forced to come back eventually, but she never saw them again.

There were more visits from Yankee squads during the day. Hill kept himself out of sight, and it was well that he did so, for one of the squads took Hazelteen away. Big Isa came up to the house with the news, nervous and ill-at-ease at speaking face to face with the mistress, and even more uneasy as to what might happen next.

'Dey done tuk 'm away wid he's hans tahd,' he confided when he saw Mary was not angry with him. 'Huccome dey do dat, Miz Mary?'

Mary shook her head wearily. 'I suppose because he's a white man, and they think he might be a soldier,' she said. 'But you did right to come and tell me. Thank you, Big Isa.'

'Miz Mary, whut we do now? Mos' all de fiel' hans up and follow de Yankees. Dey on'y jus' a few of us lef' now, an' how we gwine work widout Mist' Hazelteen t' tell us?'

'I don't think you'd better go out to work while the Yankees are here,' Mary said. 'You best stay in the quarters and mind your women and children and what things you have left. When the Yankees are gone, we'll see what to do.'

Big Isa sighed and shuffled off, uneasy about a holiday granted for such a purpose. Mary sent Patty over to fetch Mrs Hazelteen to the house. She came trembling and sobbing, and it was more than Mary could do to convince her that her husband would not be murdered by the Yankees, but only put in prison with their brave boys taken in battle. 'They'll all be released when the war's over,' she said, and hoped it was true. There was nothing in the world she could do to get Hazelteen back.

There was a lull then, for a few hours, and as dusk fell Mary locked the doors and they all gathered in the parlour around the fire and a single lamp. They tried to work, but their nerves were stretched, and every crack of the fire and creak of the house made them jump. But when the interruption came, there was no doubt about it: a thunderous hammering on the door, accompanied by shouts and oaths. Mary got up and went into the hall, where Tammas was standing trembling helplessly, unable to move or speak. 'I'll go, Tammas,' she said. She had been afraid so often her fear was growing blunted.

'Open the damn door, d'ye hear, or we'll break it down!'

Mary opened it, and found six bluecoats outside. The nearest one, his face contorted with rage, shoved his pistol against her breast and bellowed, 'How dare you keep your house closed? You hidin' rebels in here? You'll be sorry if you are!'

'There is no-one here but women and children. That's why we keep the door locked,' Mary said. She could smell the drink on the man's breath, and her fear wound up again like a slow spring tightening.

'We're coming in,' he said, 'damned if we ain't. You got drink in here somewheres. Some of the men got drink here yesterday, and we'll have some, or you'll be sorry.'

'There's nothing in the house,' she said. 'Your friends had it all.'

'Damn rebel women all lie like dogs,' one of the men growled. 'She's got drink all right.'

'She's got rebels hid, too,' said another. 'Lyin' rebel bitch!'

Mary felt her rage rising higher than her fear. 'There's no drink and no men, and if you *brave* men can't take the word of a defenceless woman, you had better look for yourselves, for it's certain I can't stop you.'

She thought it might shame them, but it didn't. 'Damn right

you can't!' said the ringleader, shoving her backwards and coming into the hall, looking round suspiciously. Tammas whimpered and backed into the shadows. 'You boys look for drink,' the man said, grabbing Mary's arm. 'I'll look for rebels, and I'll take *her* with me, 'case they shoot at me.'

He shoved her towards the stairs as the others crowded in. Mary's heart was thudding so fast she could hear it, and despite the chill of the evening away from the fire, there was sweat running down her back. Keeping her in front of him, the soldier looked into one room, and then another. Coming to a third – it happened to be her own – he pushed her inside. 'Let's look in the wardyrobes,' he said. 'Mebbe there's rebs hidin' there.'

The wardrobes were almost empty, the Yankees having taken everything Mammy had not. The soldier found her hampering to his search and pushed her down to sit on the edge of the bed while he opened drawers and poked in cupboards. Mary watched him warily. Finally, finding nothing, he turned and considered her.

'You wasn't lyin',' he said. 'Pity for you. I'd'a' been feelin' more kindly ef I'd found anythin' worth havin'. But still,' he added in a voice that chilled her, 'you ain't bad-lookin'. I ain't never had me a high-nose rebel bitch before. Mebbe I'll just have a piece o' this one.'

He crossed the room towards her. 'Get away from me!' she cried.

'Shet y'r mouth, lean-meat!' he said, ripped open the bodice of her dress and pushed his hand in. She was so appalled she could make no sound, only struggle in desperate silence. He was strong, well-fed and hard with campaigning; she had no chance against him. She saw his face looming closer, dirty, unshaven, with missing teeth; heard the panting of his foul breath, felt his greasy hands on her flesh. Her terror surged up. He shoved her back on the bed, bringing one knee up to hold her down. She flung her hand out, reaching under her pillow: between the mattress and the headboard was the pistol Martial had left her. She stretched and strained, her mind screaming with revulsion, while he tore at her gown, breaking the stitching, exposing more of her to his filthy view; and then her fingers closed on the ivory butt.

She dragged it out and pressed the muzzle to his head, and had the momentary relief of seeing his eyes widen with surprise. But then he smiled slowly and said, 'You wouldn't do it, rebel bitch!'

She didn't know she had done it – she was never sure afterwards that she had really meant to do it – but there was an explosion which deafened her at such close quarters, and the bluecoat seemed to jump sideways. Something warm and wet hit her left shoulder and arm, and she smelled gunsmoke and blood. He collapsed half across her, and then slid down on to the floor, and she scrambled up, gasping with terror and disgust, the pistol still in her hand, and the soldier's blood and brains on her skin, while he lay tumbled like a heap of dirty coats on the carpet.

A noise at the door made her jump round, and there was another Yankee, his pistol in his hand. She was frozen with shock; he crossed the room in two strides and snatched the little gun from her. 'You murderin' bitch!' he shouted, and hit her across the side of the face, knocking her down. She saw her death in his face; and at that moment another shot rang out. The man flung his hands out and his head back as though he were about to sing, and then tumbled slowly down in a heap like a collapsing wall.

Mary was still stunned, hardly understood what was happening, even as Hill crossed the room and picked up Martial's pistol from the floor and stuffed it into his pocket. Then he seized her chin in his hand and shook it, forcing her eyes to his. 'Listen to me! I'll take the blame. The food's hid where I hid the rifle – understand? *Where I hid the rifle.*'

And then there was no more time. The other four Yankees came crowding into the room, guns at the ready. They grabbed Hill and disarmed him. They were shouting, frightened and angry, and Hill's calm scared them more.

'Y'r pals was rapin' the lady. I warn't about to stan' aroun' an' let it happen.' They wouldn't believe him. 'See f'r y'self,' he said indifferently. 'How d'ye think she got her close all torn? Them dirty dogs was rapin' her.'

It sobered them a little, and they looked at Mary and at each other, unsure what to do. Then one said, 'We'll have to take him prisoner, anyways.'

'Yeah. Take 'im back. Let the captain decide.'

They forced Hill's hands behind his back, and he stood and let them tie him, his eyes never leaving Mary's face. Then two of them took him, the other two heaved their companions' bodies over their shoulders, and they started away down the stairs. It took Mary two attempts to get to her feet, her legs were shaking so badly, and then she ran after them. Through the hall filled with shocked and frightened faces the strange procession passed. As they went out into the darkness she found her voice at last. 'He saved my life. Your friends were going to kill me. He had to act to save my life!'

'The captain can decide,' they said again as they plodded away.

Yaller Dawg ran up, puzzled, afraid, flattened his ears and growled at the strangers, and then tried to run after Hill. Hill turned his head and fixed the dog with a look. 'No. Stay,' he said. '*Stay!*'

Yaller Dawg folded his tail and sat on it, and watched, whining softly with unease, as his master was dragged away.

For almost a year a stalemate had existed in Virginia. Grant was trying to capture the vital railroad junction of Petersburg, south of Richmond, to cut off the rail links to the capital. Lee's small army was dug in behind zig-zagging breastworks, defending a long line that grew longer as Grant tried to outflank him and cut the railroad. Somehow the gaunt veterans held out; Grant was no nearer Richmond than McDowell had ever got. There was constant skirmishing, with losses on both sides. In the warm weather, Virginia stank like a charnel-house; when the bitter winter came on, the Confederates, shivering in their rags, starved.

It was Lee who held them together; Lee who had come to represent all they loved and fought for, cause, country and all. Lennox kept close to him for comfort, but worried about him too. The general was exhausted and ill: he complained once that the surgeons 'tapped him all over like a steam boiler before condemning it'. He hated to be forced into a static and defensive position, when his instincts were always to attack and to keep moving. But more than that, as Lennox and Martial were aware, the general knew, and he had always known, that this was a siege that could not be won. Ill-fed, exhausted and hopelessly outnumbered, the Confederates could not replace what they spent in lives or materials; the Union had close to a million men under arms, and supplies without limit coming up the James River.

So on March the 25th Lee tried to break out with a surprise attack on the Union line at Fort Stedman, to the east of Petersburg. The speed and ferocity of the attack carried the fort, but when the Union forces recovered and regrouped, they mounted a counter-attack which was too strong to resist, and the Confederates had to withdraw behind their defences again. The end came on April the 2nd, with an all-out attack by Grant on Petersburg; by evening all but the innermost defences had been taken, and after dark the order went out to Petersburg and Richmond to evacuate.

Lennox was desperately worried about Ruth and the child. 'I should be there with them. How will they manage?'

'Phoebe and George will look to them,' Martial told him. 'They'll all go with the President's suite. They'll be quite safe.'

'I wish she would go to Twelvetrees. She'd be safe there until I could get to her. Do you think if I asked the general he'd let me send her word?'

Martial shook his head. 'The telegraph lines will be too busy with official messages, you know that.'

Another thought struck Lennox. 'I suppose she *will* go? She won't insist on staying with the wounded?'

Martial laid a hand on his shoulder. 'Even if she does, the Yankees won't harm her. They wouldn't harm a lady, and a nurse.'

Lennox was hardly comforted, but there was nothing he could do except fret. He could not leave his general at such a desperate moment.

The plan was to try to march south-westwards and join up with the remains of the Army of Tennessee under General Joe Johnston in the hills of North Carolina, and then turn and face Grant again. But even as he explained it to Martial, Lee's eyes betrayed his hopelessness. After a short silence he said, 'The end is near, I believe.'

'We do what we can, sir,' Martial said.

They went westwards, meaning to turn south at Amelia Court House, thirty-five miles away; but the exhausted and starving men could not march in tight formation, and the lines straggled. Many of them were not armed, and were in no condition to fight. They followed 'Marse Robert' in blind faith, as the only light in the gathering darkness. Grant's forces were in hot pursuit, pressing on their flanks as well as from the rear, preventing the turn southwards, driving them ever further west. At Sayler's Creek the Union attacked, and the Confederates fought with staggering desperation, unarmed men rolling with their enemies on the ground, trying to bite out their throats. Eight thousand were lost or taken prisoner; the rest staggered on. But the Confederate supply train was captured, and when they reached Appomatox Court House, the Union cavalry got across the line of march and they were surrounded. On the morning of April the 9th there was fighting on all sides, but there was nowhere left to go. Lee had no more than thirty thousand men, only half of them armed, no food, and little ammunition left.

'We must surrender, sir,' Martial urged. Behind the general, Lennox lifted a face of anguished denial and shook his head, but Lee, though he was white and haggard, said calmly, 'Yes, you are right. There is nothing left for me to do but to go and see General Grant.' He stood up. 'If it must be done, it had better be done now, before any more give their lives. Martial, my boy, have you a handkerchief or a scarf? Will you do this for me?'

Martial bent his head for a moment, afraid he might cry; then he said, 'I will do it, sir.' He borrowed Lennox's handkerchief and tied it together with his own. He looked once more at the general.

'We were never defeated, sir. They have not defeated us now.' Lee nodded, and Martial turned and limped away to find his horse.

The Union cavalry and infantry were massing for another attack when Martial rode out from the lines with the handkerchiefs fluttering from a staff. He might have been shot – the handkerchiefs were not very large – and part of him almost wished he would be, so that he should not have to face this heartbreak; but then a stunned silence fell over the field, and slowly weapons were lowered and the two armies stared at each other, unable to believe that the fighting was over.

The generals and their aides met in the parlour of Wilmer McLean's house inside the little town. Grant seemed as stunned and dazed as Lee at this outcome: it hardly seemed possible that it was all over, that four years of bitterness and blood had come to this. And then Grant said quietly, 'It was an honourable fight, sir. We were brothers before the fighting began, let us be brothers again now it has ended.'

'What terms do you want of me?' Lee asked wearily.

'If your men will lay down their arms and give their oath not to fight again, there will be no further action taken against them. They can go home.'

Lee looked his surprise. 'You are generous, sir.'

Grant spread his hand in a little open gesture. 'What we must make here, General, is a peace, not a surrender. We fought this war to prove that we are one nation, and one nation we must become again, or it was all in vain.'

Late in the afternoon, Lee rode his grey stallion Traveller back to the Confederate lines. Behind him, Lennox was in tears; Martial's jaw was set, his heart aching worse even than his leg. As the men saw Lee coming, they raised a huge cheer and rushed towards him, forming a corridor down which he passed. Faces were turned up to him, love and grief struggling for supremacy; the cheering turned to an ululation. Grim bearded men sat down on the ground and wept, tears making clean tracks down campaign-grimed cheeks; others reached out to touch Lee as he passed, to touch Traveller; the grey bent his head and mouthed his bit, his ears moving nervously, feeling the great current of emotion. Martial saw the men, ragged, thin, many of them wounded, through a haze that went back to the hazy rim of trees on the horizon. Through the mist he seemed to see more men than he knew there could be: grey figures, insubstantial as the haze themselves, raised their hats and cheered, but silently, fading before him, thousand upon thousand, the ghosts of all those fallen men who had fought with such steadfast courage for their country, and who lay now under her earth. God forgive us all, Martial whispered in his mind, but we didn't know what else we could do.

It was not until the middle of May that Martial reached Twelvetrees. He had to walk from the depot, but at least he had no luggage to carry. When he came to the edge of the property, he took a short cut, climbed through the hedge and made his way across the paddocks instead of going round by the road. The paddocks were all empty, and he thought for a moment of the glorious horses that had once grazed and run here, silken, bright-eyed beauties, fleet of foot and gentle of mouth. Then he shook the thought away. He had made a rule for himself not to think of what had been or what might have been, and he kept to it pretty well. It was the first time of seeing anything or anyone again that was so difficult.

The land went uphill from the road, a trial to his aching leg, and it meant he did not see the house until he topped the rise. He paused to rest and feast his eyes, only to find, with a sense of shock that made him dizzy and brought a strange coppery taste to his mouth, that he was looking at a ruin. The magnificent stables had burned to the ground. The great frontage of the house with its massive portico and columns was gone, collapsed inwards into a heap of blackened rubbish, from which jagged charred beams protruded.

He hurried down to the house as fast as his leg would carry him, despair gnawing at his heart. They had heard, at the end, of Sherman's depredations, but he had thought Twelvetrees would have escaped, not being in the direct line of march either to Columbia or to Charleston, both of which had been taken and destroyed on the same day. He cursed himself now for a fool for not realising how widely the army had spread out across the country.

He reached the ruins, and walked around the side, past the collapsed verandah, to the far end. The apple-barn had lost its roof, though the rest of the farmyard buildings seemed intact; the negro cabins were burned to the ground. Only the overseer's house, the laundress's house and the cookhouse had survived. Then he saw there was smoke rising from the latter, and hope revived.

He was about to call out when a woman emerged with a basket, heading away from him towards the overseer's house, with a scrawny yellow hound at her heels. The woman was thin, shabbily dressed, and with a rag tied round her hair like a servant; but anywhere, in any disguise, he would have known her. He tried to call, 'Mary!' but his voice failed him. He could only stand and stare helplessly. But Yaller Dawg heard him, stopped and turned warily, and whined a warning. She turned too, and saw him, and for a long moment only looked at him, as he looked at her, unable to move.

Then she said, 'You're lame.'

'It's the old wound. It never really healed.'

He saw her sigh, a sigh that seemed to fetch up from the soles of her feet. Then she put the basket down and came to him. They embraced in absolute silence, holding each other so tightly each could feel the other's bones through their thin clothing. Yaller Dawg came sniffing anxiously round them, and then sat at a little distance, watching. At last Martial found his tongue to ask, 'What happened to the house?'

'The Yankees burned it,' she said, without emotion. 'A squad came one day and found nothing left to take, we'd been looted so often. They made us all go outside and held us there under guard. We thought it was so that they could search again, but after they left we found they'd laid slow-match everywhere. We managed to get some of it out, but we couldn't find it all in time. They burned the quarters, too. I don't know why.' Now she removed her face from his chest for the first time and looked up at him. 'We're living in the overseer's house, and the slaves that are left are in the laundress's. It's awfully crowded.'

He couldn't take it in. He looked around at the devastation, and then back at her. 'Is Uncle Charles here?'

She pushed herself away from him gently and passed a forearm across her brow. It was an habitual gesture of tiredness, he could see. 'He died,' she said in that same unemotional voice. 'He was sick when he came back, after Charleston fell. There was a terrible lot of sickness on the defences. He brought the fever with him. I think it was typhoid. There was nothing I could do for him.'

He read her face. 'Who else?'

'Aunt Nora. She never really got over the Yankees coming. And Moses.' She swallowed. 'And Corton.'

'Oh, Mary!'

The tears rose suddenly and welled over from her eyes, but she stood straight like a soldier, facing him, her hands down by her sides. 'I thought you weren't coming back. All the time I never doubted – until the end. But the sickness – and then the surrender – I didn't know we would feel it so much. And then, when you didn't come—'

He took her in his arms again, aching for her. Over her shoulder he saw more people coming out to see what was happening. There was Julie, and Tammas and Patty. There was Ruth, thin as a rail, with little Patrick on her hip, and a barefooted, tow-headed boy he supposed was Pres or Ashley – he didn't know which. There was Lennox, in his shirt with the sleeves rolled up, an axe in his hand and sweat on his brow, coming round the side of the house, his face lighting in joy as he saw who it was. But none of them – none of this – seemed real to Martial, and it was a hard thing to bear. He held Mary in his arms at last, but he could feel nothing but weariness and bewilderment.

Many days later, he and Mary went for a walk together at dusk, taking the rifle with them – the one Hill had hidden, their only gun now – in case they should see a rabbit. Thanks to Hill they had meal and rice and beans, but no meat, since the Yankees had taken all their animals. They had never heard from Hill again. Mary thought the Yankees had probably killed him. If he were not dead, he'd surely have escaped by now.

They walked out towards the birch wood, talking, as they had talked for days, in desultory bursts.

'Do you know,' Mary said, 'when I first heard that Lincoln had been murdered, I was almost glad. It was no more than he deserved, seeing it was he who made the war that cost us all so much. The first thing I thought was that he was at the theatre when he was shot. We were living amongst ruins with nothing but bean soup to eat and rags to wear, and Lincoln, who was to blame for everything, was spending the evening *at the theatre!*' She sighed. 'But I see now that madman Booth has doomed us. The North was inclined to be merciful after the surrender. Now they will persecute us to death.'

'I'm afraid you're right,' Martial said. 'Lincoln was our best hope in Washington for a decent settlement.'

'How can we go on, Martial? What's to become of us? We can't live for ever on bean soup and bread. We can grow a little food this summer, but we've no pigs or hens or cattle. The children need milk and meat. And what will happen next winter? We've no money – the Confederate Bonds Charles bought are worthless – and without the field-hands, we can't grow a cash crop to sell. Most of the slaves are gone, and the ones that are left I can't afford to feed; but I can't turn them out to starve when they've been loyal.'

Martial limped on, his face grim. He had no answers for her, and she knew it. All through the war men had talked about *when it was over* and *going back*, but you didn't go back after a war. You went on to something different; for the South, the something different was this nightmare of poverty and hopelessness.

After a while she said, 'Ruth and Lennox mean to go to England, did you know?'

'Yes, Lennox told me. I think he's quite right. They'll have a better chance of a life there.'

Mary sighed. 'I shall miss her so much. And Lennox – to have found him, and then to lose him again so soon, is hard. But I'm glad they have each other.'

He stopped, and she turned to look at him enquiringly. 'Do you want to go to England, too?' he asked.

He saw that she had been ready for this question, and that even though she took her time to answer, there was no doubt in her mind. 'No,' she said. 'This is Preston's inheritance, and Ashley's home. Their father died for it; I can't take them away from it. I don't know what sort of a South it will be that they grow up to, but it's their country. Mine, too, now.'

'I thought that's what you'd say.' He reached out and took her hand and drew it through his arm. 'We'll stay here together, then, and try to keep them safe.'

When they reached the top of the rise, she said, 'The other day, Julie said to me that though the war had been terrible, she was glad at least that she had got her freedom. I said to her, "But you're still here, doing the same work for no reward. In fact, you're worse off, because I can't even feed you properly." And she said, "I like to be here, and I like to work for you. You were always good to us; but no-one can bear to be a slave."'

They stopped and looked across the gently folded fields, past the edge of the woods in their soft early summer foliage to the distant blue hills. The silence of the land came up to them like tranquil thought, and over it lay a whisper of breeze, and the birdsong, and from far down in the birch woods the chatter of the crick over its stones.

'The land endures,' Martial said. 'Away from the ruined towns and the ruined houses, all this is still fresh and new and good. This is where we must come, when we grow downhearted. This is where hope is.'

She leaned against him lightly, the breeze stirring the fair wisps at her brow; the long light of evening turned the birch leaves rosy, and gave her pale cheeks colour.

'I thought of you so often,' he said. 'At the darkest moments, I thought of that time we'd spent together, listening to each other's heartbeats. It was just you and I then, and nothing could touch that or make it not to be. And I thought, if death came for me, that was where I'd be – not in the place where death was, but in the place where you and I were together, and would always be.'

She looked up into his tired, lined face and felt the deep quiet of love, like the silence of the land, which lay under everything, too powerful to be expressed. She said only, 'We are together now. Don't think about death.' There had been so much of it that they were no longer children to believe themselves immortal. But they had learned what was important. It would come for them one day; but not yet, not for many, many heartbeats, and for every one of those, they would be together.